EARLY SHORT STORIES
1883-1888

ANTON CHEKHOV

EARLY SHORT STORIES

1883-1888

EDITED BY SHELBY FOOTE

TRANSLATED BY CONSTANCE GARNETT

THE MODERN LIBRARY

NEW YORK

1999 Modern Library Edition

LIBRARY OF CONGRESS CATALOGING-IN-PUBLICATION DATA
Chekhov, Anton Pavlovich, 1860–1904.
[Short stories. English. Selections]
Anton Chekhov: early short stories, 1883–1888/edited by Shelby Foote.
p. cm.
ISBN 0-679-60317-4
1. Chekhov, Anton Pavlovich, 1860–1904—Translations into English.
I. Foote, Shelby.   II. Title.
PG3456.A15F66   1998b
891.73′3—dc21   98-20049

Modern Library website address: www.modernlibrary.com

Printed in the United States of America on acid-free paper

4   6   8   9   7   5

ANTON CHEKHOV

Anton Pavlovich Chekhov was born on January 17, 1860, in Taganrog, a small provincial port in southern Russia located on the Sea of Azov. His grandfather had been a serf who for 3,500 rubles had purchased the family's freedom. Chekhov's domineering father was a lower-middle-class bigot: a petty merchant who kept a grocery store, bullied his wife, and beat his six children. Although Anton Pavlovich's early life was monotonous and oppressive ("In my childhood there was no childhood," the writer recalled), he found his own strange way of compensating for the dismal atmosphere. Possessing a natural gift for clowning and mimicry, the boy delighted schoolmates with hilarious imitations of virtually everyone in the village. (Much as in his later stories, things for him were funny and sad at the same time, but you would not see their sadness if you did not see their fun, because both were linked up.)

Chekhov was sixteen when the family business failed and his father escaped debtors' prison by fleeing to Moscow. The young man's mother and siblings soon followed, but Anton Pavlovich remained behind to complete his education at the Taganrog Secondary School; three years later, in 1879, he joined them in Moscow and entered the medical faculty of Moscow University. During his university years Chekhov became the family's chief breadwinner: He supported them by writing stories, sketches, and parodies for humor magazines. All his early works were signed with pseudonyms, most frequently "Antosha Chekhonte." He completed medical school in 1884 and practiced medicine intermittently for several years while continuing to write. "Medicine is my lawful wife," Chekhov wrote to a friend, "and literature is my mistress. When I get fed up with one, I spend the night with the other. Though it is irregular, it is less boring this way, and besides, neither of them loses anything through my infidelity."

All the while, Chekhov's fiction continued to grow in depth and range. He published his first volume of stories, *Motley Stories,* in 1886; a year later he brought out his second collection, *In the Twilight,* for which he was awarded the Pushkin Prize for distinguished literary achievement by the Russian Academy. Fellow countryman Vladimir Nabokov perfectly explained Chekhov's appeal: "What really attracted the Russian reader was that in Chekhov's heroes he recognized the Russian idealist . . . a man who combined the deepest human decency of which man is capable with an almost ridiculous inability to put his ideals and principles into action; a man devoted to moral beauty, the welfare of his people, the welfare of the universe, but unable in his private life to do anything useful; frittering away his provincial existence in a haze of utopian dreams; knowing exactly what is good, what is worth while living for, but at the same time sinking lower and lower in the mud of a humdrum existence, unhappy in love, hopelessly inefficient in everything—a good man who cannot make good. This is the character that passes—in the guise of a doctor, a student, a village teacher, many other professional people—all through Chekhov's stories."

Despite the success of his literary career, Chekhov felt guilty about neglecting medicine. Moreover, he still owed a dissertation to obtain a full M.D. Partly to discharge this debt, partly for the sake of adventure, Chekhov in 1890 undertook an exhausting—and at times dangerous— six-thousand-mile journey (prerailroad) across Siberia to Sakhalin Island. There he made a thorough study of social, economic, and medical conditions, both of the Russian settlers (mostly convicts) and of native populations. Upon his return (by sea, via the Suez Canal) from this "descent into hell," circumstances quickly forced him back into medicine and public health service—first the terrible famine of 1891 and then the cholera epidemic that followed. In 1892 Chekhov bought a six-hundred-acre country estate near the village of Melihovo, where for the next five years he served as doctor to the local peasants and even helped build schools, while his literary output continued unabated.

The turn of the century witnessed a dramatic new phase in Chekhov's career. Between 1896 and 1903 he wrote the plays that established his reputation as one of the great dramatists of modern times: *The Sea Gull* (1896), *Uncle Vanya* (1897), *Three Sisters* (1901), and *The Cherry Orchard* (1904). However, in 1897 a massive pulmonary hemorrhage forced him finally to acknowledge that he was stricken with tuberculosis, an illness he had long concealed. For the remainder of his life, Chekhov was virtually a semi-invalid; he lived mostly in a villa at Yalta, his "warm Siberia" where he met Tolstoy and Gorky. In 1901 Chekhov married Olga Knipper, an actress with the Moscow Art Theater who had played the role of Irina in *The Sea Gull.*

Chekhov's last public appearance took place at the Moscow premiere of *The Cherry Orchard* on January 17, 1904, the playwright's forty-fourth birthday. Shaken with coughing, he was hardly able to stand and acknowledge a thunderous ovation. In June Chekhov was rushed to a health resort at Badenweiler in the Black Forest, where he died of consumption on July 2. His body was transported back to Moscow in a refrigerating car used for the transportation of oysters— a quirk of fate that no doubt he would have been amused to jot down in his notebook.

Contents

Contents

Introduction
by Shelby Foote

Anton Chekhov had a writing life of just under twenty-five years—from 1880, when he turned twenty as a medical student in Moscow, to 1904, when he died of tuberculosis in a Black Forest sanitorium. Within this span, in addition to four plays admired worldwide as modern classics, he wrote perhaps five hundred "stories," long and short—ranging from newspaper squibs and fillers to near-*Gatsby*-length novellas—which set the pattern for the short story in the century whose beginning was all he saw before his forty-four years were up.

On its eve, in 1899, under pressure from his publisher and the unrelenting need for money to sustain his generosity, he began selecting from his so-far six books of stories—together with a clutch of fugitive pieces that had appeared in various periodicals all the way back to his youth—a *Collected Works* whose ten volumes were released in the course of the next two years. They contained 240 stories in all, and another 196 were added in ten supplementary volumes after his death. Of these 436 stories, Constance Garnett[*] translated 188, and I have

[*] I agree with V. S. Pritchett, who called her work "remarkable." Although he noted that "inaccuracies have been pounced on," he preferred her translations mainly, as he said, because "her voice is close to Chekhov's period." Moreover, it was she who passed his work on to Virginia Woolf, E. M. Forster, D. H. Lawrence, and H. E. Bates, as well as to practically every American short-story writer who, at one time or another, sat at his and her feet during the past eight decades.

chosen 123 for inclusion in these three Modern Library volumes: volume I, seventy "early" stories, from 1883 to 1888, his breakthrough year when he received the Pushkin Prize; volume II, forty-two "later" stories, 1888 to 1903, containing most of his best-known work; and finally volume III, eleven "Longer Stories of the Last Decade," which I believe calls attention to a broader and deeper talent than has generally been recognized, either by critics or the reading public, down the years. Aside from his one full-length novel, an early experimental detective story of limited literary worth, nearly all the omitted stories are quite brief ones out of his journalistic youth. By way of summation, then, these three volumes include barely one fourth of his fiction titles, but they do contain, by page count, about three fourths of his output in that category—including all fifty-five of the great stories of his final fifteen years. All are printed here in the order in which they were written.

Few major writers have had fewer detractors regarding either their person or their work. A rare detractive exception is Ernest Hemingway, who enjoyed turning bumptious in his spare time; and in one such, in his middle twenties, referred to Chekhov as "an amateur writer" who "wrote about six good stories." Six is rather a large figure in the category of goodness, but I would put the number closer to one hundred, and so would many grateful practitioners of the art of the short story. Raymond Carver, for example: "Chekhov's stories are as wonderful (and necessary) now as when they first appeared. They present, in an extraordinarily precise manner, an unparalleled account of human activity and behavior in his time; and so they are valid for all time. Anyone who reads literature, anyone who believes, as one must, in the transcendent power of art, sooner or later has to read Chekhov." Or Elizabeth Hardwick: "The short stories of Chekhov are an inexhaustible treasury of humanity and wisdom. The naturalness of their form and the luminous simplicity of their turning away from the forced conclusion defined a large part of the modern tradition in short fiction." Or Cynthia Ozick: "Each story, no matter how allusive or broken-off, is nevertheless exhaustive—like the curve of a shard that implies not simply the form of the pitcher entire, but also the thirsts of its shattered civilization." Or John Barth: "Dr. Chekhov is a superb anatomist of the human heart and an utter master of his literary means. The details of scene and behavior, the emotions registered—seldom bravura, typically muted and complex, often as surprising to the characters themselves as to the reader, but always right—move, astonish, and delight us, line after line, story after story, volume after volume." Or William Maxwell: "It seems to be part of the human condition that a wall of glass separates one life from another. For Chekhov it did not exist. . . . The greatest of his stories are, no matter how many times reread, always an experience that strikes deep into the soul and produces an alteration there."

Little or none of this was the case at the start. "Oh, with what trash I began; my God, with what trash!" Chekhov declared later, looking back with amused dismay. Parodies, jokes, boutades, all limited to a thousand words by close-fisted editors, earned him the roubles needed to pay for his education and that of his two younger brothers and his sister, along with the support of two older brothers and his mother and bankrupt father. After half a dozen years of this, having received his license to practice medicine, he confessed to an established older novelist, who urged him to take his work seriously, that he had never spent more than a day on a story, and moreover had written them "the way reporters write notices of fires: mechanically, half-consciously, without caring a pin either about the reader or myself." Coincidentally, around this time, he combined a baleful definition with a hopeful prophecy: "The word newspaper-writer means, at the very least, a scoundrel. I am one of them; I work with them; I shake hands with them; I'm even told that I've begun to look like one. But I shan't die as one."

He didn't, of course, though in the process of transition that followed close on the heels of his confession, he underrated what he had gained from those half-dozen years of comic-writer apprenticeship. For one thing, the elderly novelist had noted his "feeling for the plastic," and, for another, the stipulated compression had encouraged him to develop what William Trevor later called "the art of the glimpse," a start-to-finish major component of his style. Moreover, there were, among those various humoristic bits and pieces, such things as "A Daughter of Albion," "The Fish," and "The Huntsman," which had drawn the elderly novelist's attention and admiration. And now there followed, with the help of Maupassant's Norman and Parisian tales and Turgenev's *Sportsman's Sketches,* such things as "Anyuta," "Agafya," "The Chorus Girl," and "Vanka." Those came out in 1886. By then he had moved on to the so-called "thick journals," which paid better and, above all, gave him room to stretch his talent. The following year he produced a solid fifty stories, and "The Steppe"—at forty thousand words, the longest of his stories, called by Pritchett "a superb and sustained prose poem"—appeared in early 1888, followed by "Lights," which also broke new ground. By way of an upshot, he won the Pushkin Prize that year, along with the admiration of his fellow Russian writers, who two years before had mostly seen him, as he himself did, as a bits-and-pieces hack. He was clearly on his way.

That "way" has been marveled and wondered at by critics ever since, perhaps most successfully by his compatriot Vladimir Nabokov, who contrived to lift him to the skies by bringing him down to earth: "Chekhov managed to convey an impression of artistic beauty far surpassing that of writers who thought they knew what rich, beautiful prose was. He did it by keeping all his words in the same dim light of the same exact tint of gray, a tint between the color of an old fence and that of a low cloud. The variety of his moods, the flicker of his charming wit, the deeply artistic economy of characterization, the vivid detail, and the fade-out of human life—all peculiar Chekhovian features—are enhanced by being suffused and surrounded by a faintly iridescent verbal haziness." In simpler words Nabokov also defined a specific many Chekhov readers felt the force of down the years: "Things for him were funny and sad at the same time, but you would not see their sadness if you did not see their fun, because both were linked up." Chekhov himself pointed out something along this line, carried over from his early days, in advice to a fellow writer: "When you want to touch a reader's heart, try to be colder. It gives their grief, as it were, a background against which it stands out in greater relief." In much the same vein, he declared at another time: "Patients in a fever do not want food, but they do want something, and that vague craving they express as 'longing for something sour.' I want something sour."

For the most part, though, he kept his opinions and judgments to himself—especially in his fiction, where, as he said, he aimed not at solutions to problems but rather at their correct presentation. Walker Percy, a fellow physician-writer, called him a diagnostician, and in his choice of subjects for delineation he was guided by what Susan Sontag defined as "perfect moral pitch." As a result, there were those who, in the absence of didactic comments and summations in his work, accused him of having no philosophy of life. His friend Maxim Gorky found the charge absurd and such readers deaf and blind. "Often our ears can catch in his stories the melancholy but severe and deserved reproach that men do not know how to live. But at the same time, his sympathy with all men glows even brighter." Chekhov himself met the charge head-on, along with others by critics who fine-tooth-combed his work in search of "convictions," whether political or religious: "I am afraid of those who look for a tendency between the lines and insist on seeing me as necessarily a liberal or a conservative. I am not a liberal, not a conservative, not a gradualist, not a monk, not an indifferentist. I should like to be a free artist and nothing more, and I regret that God has not given me the power to be one. . . . I regard trademarks and labels as prejudicial. My holy of holies is the human body, health, intelligence, talent, inspiration, love, and absolute freedom—freedom from force and falsehood."

His overriding subject was the Russia of his time and the failure of men of goodwill to find contentment, or even peace, from having exercised that goodwill all their lives. "We Russians of the educated class have a partiality for questions that remain unanswered," he observed. He later added: "To an educated Russian his past is always beautiful, his present a state of calamity." He seemed always to have to ponder things, turning them over and over in his mind, as if in search not of an answer but of a new phrasing of the question. Once while abroad he was asked to write "an international story" set in the region, and he replied that he couldn't do it until he got back home, if at all. "I can write only from memory," he explained; "I never write directly from life. The subject must pass through the sieve of my memory, so that only what is important or typical remains, as on a filter."

He had a habit of expressing himself obliquely, as when he said of his portrait by an artist whose work he did not admire, "It smells of horseradish." And though he could be insightful—forty-odd years before the Holocaust, in the wake of the Dreyfus affair, he wrote to a friend a definition of anti-Semitism as "a fuel that reeks of the slaughterhouse"—he still could not abide the strained delivery of a "message" in a story or a novel. After reading *Uncle Tom's Cabin,* for example, he experienced "an unpleasant sensation which mortals feel after eating too many raisins or currants." He liked to be precise in a general way, as when he described "the genial expression of a man who has just said goodbye to his relatives and has had a good drink at parting." It is important in this depiction that the people are relatives and that the drink was a good one.

Similarly in a late story, "In the Ravine," a young woman loses her infant son to a sudden and painful death by scalding, and is comforted at the funeral dinner by a priest who, "lifting his fork on which there was a salted mushroom, said to her: 'Grieve not for the babe, for of such is the Kingdom of Heaven.'" The forked mushroom is very Chekhovian, and even more so are the words spoken earlier, in a quite different tone, by an old man who gave her a lift in his wagon while she was returning from the hospital, walking along the road at night with her dead baby wrapped in a quilt in her arms. "Never mind," he told her. "Yours is not the worst of sorrows. Life is long, there will be good and bad to come, there will be everything. Great is Mother Russia." Chekhov dealt in powerful iotas, such as a sidelong glance in his last story, "Betrothed," in which a young man "took off his hat, and his hair floated in the wind."

Consequential or inconsequential, such wonderments abound in the nearly two thousand pages of these three volumes. Moreover, like most good writers, his work is even better on rereading, since then you can better appreciate how he goes about getting where he's going. Often, after a stretch of such rereading, I wax enthusiastic beyond all bounds. (Like Hemingway, I sometimes play the fool, but in the opposite direction.) Walker Percy and I shared this reaction, and once, in the course of a discussion, I asked him if he had read "In the Ravine." He said he hadn't, and I said: "I'd rather have written 'In the Ravine' than *Moby Dick.*" His eyebrows rose at this, as well they might, but he went home and read that great last long story—in which all the author's talents seem to be gathered together as naturally as a hand closing into a fist—and wound up in a state of exaltation similar to my own. Echoing Nabokov on Chekhov's near-miraculous combination of the funny and the sad, he shook his head in wonder. "I don't know how it can be so pitiful and funny," he wrote me later. "I have to laugh out loud."

We saw clearly enough what this Russian master had done, but *how* he did it we could never really figure out—until finally we happened on the answer provided by Buffon in his mid-eighteenth-century *Discourse on Style,* which pronounces that "style is the man himself." We settled for that: Chekhov did it by being Chekhov. That was as close as we could come to a solution.

EARLY SHORT STORIES
1883-1888

Joy

It was twelve o'clock at night.

Mitya Kuldarov, with excited face and ruffled hair, flew into his parents' flat, and hurriedly ran through all the rooms. His parents had already gone to bed. His sister was in bed, finishing the last page of a novel. His schoolboy brothers were asleep.

"Where have you come from?" cried his parents in amazement. "What is the matter with you?"

"Oh, don't ask! I never expected it; no, I never expected it! It's ... it's positively ... incredible!"

Mitya laughed and sank into an armchair, so overcome by happiness that he could not stand on his legs.

"It's incredible! You can't imagine! Look!"

His sister jumped out of bed and, throwing a quilt round her, went in to her brother. The schoolboys woke up.

"What's the matter? You don't look like yourself!"

"It's because I am so delighted, Mamma! Do you know, now all Russia knows of me! All Russia! Till now only you knew that there was a registration clerk called Dmitry Kuldarov, and now all Russia knows it! Mamma! Oh, Lord!"

Mitya jumped up, ran up and down all the rooms, and then sat down again.

"Why, what has happened? Tell us sensibly!"

"You live like wild beasts, you don't read the newspapers and take no notice of what's published, and there's so much that is interesting in the papers. If anything happens it's all known at once, nothing is hidden! How happy I am! Oh, Lord! You know it's only celebrated people whose names are published in the papers, and now they have gone and published mine!"

"What do you mean? Where?"

The papa turned pale. The mamma glanced at the holy image and crossed herself. The schoolboys jumped out of bed and, just as they were, in short nightshirts, went up to their brother.

"Yes! My name has been published! Now all Russia knows of me! Keep the paper, mamma, in memory of it! We will read it sometimes! Look!"

Mitya pulled out of his pocket a copy of the paper, gave it to his father, and pointed with his finger to a passage marked with blue pencil.

"Read it!"

The father put on his spectacles.

"Do read it!"

The mamma glanced at the holy image and crossed herself. The papa cleared his throat and began to read: "At eleven o'clock on the evening of the 29th of December, a registration clerk of the name of Dmitry Kuldarov . . ."

"You see, you see! Go on!"

". . . a registration clerk of the name of Dmitry Kuldarov, coming from the beershop in Kozihin's buildings in Little Bronnaia in an intoxicated condition . . ."

"That's me and Semyon Petrovitch. . . . It's all described exactly! Go on! Listen!"

". . . intoxicated condition, slipped and fell under a horse belonging to a sledge-driver, a peasant of the village of Durikino in the Yuhnovsky district, called Ivan Drotov. The frightened horse, stepping over Kuldarov and drawing the sledge over him, together with a Moscow merchant of the second guild called Stepan Lukov, who was in it, dashed along the street and was caught by some house-porters. Kuldarov, at first in an unconscious condition, was taken to the police station and there examined by the doctor. The blow he had received on the back of his head . . ."

"It was from the shaft, papa. Go on! Read the rest!"

". . . he had received on the back of his head turned out not to be serious. The incident was duly reported. Medical aid was given to the injured man. . . ."

"They told me to foment the back of my head with cold water. You have read it now? Ah! So you see. Now it's all over Russia! Give it here!"

Mitya seized the paper, folded it up and put it into his pocket.

"I'll run round to the Makarovs and show it to them. . . . I must show it to the Ivanitskys too, Natasya Ivanovna, and Anisim Vassilyitch. . . . I'll run! Good-bye!"

Mitya put on his cap with its cockade and, joyful and triumphant, ran into the street.

The Death of a Government Clerk

One fine evening, a no less fine government clerk called Ivan Dmitritch Tchervyakov was sitting in the second row of the stalls, gazing through an opera glass at the *Cloches de Corneville*. He gazed and felt at the acme of bliss. But suddenly.... In stories one so often meets with this "But suddenly." The authors are right: life is so full of surprises! But suddenly his face puckered up, his eyes disappeared, his breathing was arrested ... he took the opera glass from his eyes, bent over and ... "Aptchee!!!" he sneezed as you perceive. It is not reprehensible for anyone to sneeze anywhere. Peasants sneeze and so do police superintendents, and sometimes even privy councillors. All men sneeze. Tchervyakov was not in the least confused, he wiped his face with with his handkerchief, and like a polite man, looked round to see whether he had disturbed any one by his sneezing. But then he was overcome with confusion. He saw that an old gentleman sitting in front of him in the first row of the stalls was carefully wiping his bald head and his neck with his glove and muttering something to himself. In the old gentleman, Tchervyakov recognized Brizzhalov, a civilian general serving in the Department of Transport.

"I have spattered him," thought Tchervyakov, "he is not the head of my department, but still it is awkward. I must apologise."

Tchervyakov gave a cough, bent his whole person forward, and whispered in the general's ear.

"Pardon, your Excellency, I spattered you . . . accidentally. . . ."

"Never mind, never mind."

"For goodness sake excuse me, I . . . I did not mean to."

"Oh, please, sit down! let me listen!"

Tchervyakov was embarrassed, he smiled stupidly and fell to gazing at the stage. He gazed at it but was no longer feeling bliss. He began to be troubled by uneasiness. In the interval, he went up to Brizzhalov, walked beside him, and overcoming his shyness, muttered:

"I spattered you, your Excellency, forgive me . . . you see . . . I didn't do it to. . . ."

"Oh, that's enough . . . I'd forgotten it, and you keep on about it!" said the general, moving his lower lip impatiently.

"He has forgotten, but there is a fiendish light in his eye," thought Tchervyakov, looking suspiciously at the general. "And he doesn't want to talk. I ought to explain to him . . . that I really didn't intend . . . that it is the law of nature or else he will think I meant to spit on him. He doesn't think so now, but he will think so later!"

On getting home, Tchervyakov told his wife of his breach of good manners. It struck him that his wife took too frivolous a view of the incident; she was a little frightened, but when she learned that Brizzhalov was in a different department, she was reassured.

"Still, you had better go and apologise," she said, "or he will think you don't know how to behave in public."

"That's just it! I did apologise, but he took it somehow queerly . . . he didn't say a word of sense. There wasn't time to talk properly."

Next day Tchervyakov put on a new uniform, had his hair cut and went to Brizzhalov's to explain; going into the general's reception room he saw there a number of petitioners, and among them the general himself, who was beginning to interview them. After questioning several petitioners the general raised his eyes and looked at Tchervyakov.

"Yesterday at the *Arcadia,* if you recollect, your Excellency," the latter began, "I sneezed and . . . accidentally spattered . . . Exc. . . ."

"What nonsense. . . . It's beyond anything! What can I do for you," said the general addressing the next petitioner.

"He won't speak," thought Tchervyakov, turning pale; "that means that he is angry.... No, it can't be left like this.... I will explain to him."

When the general had finished his conversation with the last of the petitioners and was turning towards his inner apartments, Tchervyakov took a step towards him and muttered:

"Your Excellency! If I venture to trouble your Excellency, it is simply from a feeling I may say of regret! ... It was not intentional if you will graciously believe me."

The general made a lachrymose face, and waved his hand.

"Why, you are simply making fun of me, sir," he said as he closed the door behind him.

"Where's the making fun in it?" thought Tchervyakov, "there is nothing of the sort! He is a general, but he can't understand. If that is how it is I am not going to apologise to that *fanfaron* any more! The devil take him. I'll write a letter to him, but I won't go. By Jove, I won't."

So thought Tchervyakov as he walked home; he did not write a letter to the general, he pondered and pondered, and could not make up that letter. He had to go next day to explain in person.

"I ventured to disturb your Excellency yesterday," he muttered, when the general lifted enquiring eyes upon him, "not to make fun as you were pleased to say. I was apologising for having spattered you in sneezing.... And I did not dream of making fun of you. Should I dare to make fun of you, if we should take to making fun, then there would be no respect for persons, there would be...."

"Be off!" yelled the general, turning suddenly purple, and shaking all over.

"What?" asked Tchervyakov, in a whisper turning numb with horror.

"Be off!" repeated the general, stamping.

Something seemed to give way in Tchervyakov's stomach. Seeing nothing and hearing nothing he reeled to the door, went out into the street, and went staggering along. . . . Reaching home mechanically, without taking off his uniform, he lay down on the sofa and died.

A Daughter of Albion

A fine carriage with rubber tyres, a fat coachman, and velvet on the seats, rolled up to the house of a landowner called Gryabov. Fyodor Andreitch Otsov, the district Marshal of Nobility, jumped out of the carriage. A drowsy footman met him in the hall.

"Are the family at home?" asked the Marshal.

"No, sir. The mistress and the children are gone out paying visits, while the master and mademoiselle are catching fish. Fishing all the morning, sir."

Otsov stood a little, thought a little, and then went to the river to look for Gryabov. Going down to the river he found him a mile and a half from the house. Looking down from the steep bank and catching sight of Gryabov, Otsov gushed with laughter.... Gryabov a large stout man, with a very big head, was sitting on the sand, angling, with his legs tucked under him like a Turk. His hat was on the back of his head and his cravat had slipped on one side. Beside him stood a tall thin Englishwoman, with prominent eyes like a crab's, and a big bird-like nose more like a hook than a nose. She was dressed in a white muslin gown through which her scraggy yellow shoulders were very distinctly apparent. On her gold belt hung a little gold watch. She too was angling. The stillness of the grave reigned about them both. Both were motionless, as the river upon which their floats were swimming.

"A desperate passion, but deadly dull!" laughed Otsov. "Good-day, Ivan Kuzmitch."

"Ah . . . is that you?" asked Gryabov, not taking his eyes off the water. "Have you come?"

"As you see . . . And you are still taken up with your crazy nonsense! Not given it up yet?"

"The devil's in it. . . . I begin in the morning and fish all day. . . . The fishing is not up to much to-day. I've caught nothing and this dummy hasn't either. We sit on and on and not a devil of a fish! I could scream!"

"Well, chuck it up then. Let's go and have some vodka!"

"Wait a little, maybe we shall catch something. Towards evening the fish bite better . . . I've been sitting here, my boy, ever since the morning! I can't tell you how fearfully boring it is. It was the devil drove me to take to this fishing! I know that it is rotten idiocy for me to sit here. I sit here like some scoundrel, like a convict, and I stare at the water like a fool. I ought to go to the haymaking, but here I sit catching fish. Yesterday His Holiness held a service at Haponyevo, but I didn't go. I spent the day here with this . . . with this she-devil."

"But . . . have you taken leave of your senses?" asked Otsov, glancing in embarrassment at the Englishwoman. "Using such language before a lady and she . . ."

"Oh, confound her, it doesn't matter, she doesn't understand a syllable of Russian, whether you praise her or blame her, it is all the same to her! Just look at her nose! Her nose alone is enough to make one faint. We sit here for whole days together and not a single word! She stands like a stuffed image and rolls the whites of her eyes at the water."

The Englishwoman gave a yawn, put a new worm on, and dropped the hook into the water.

"I wonder at her not a little," Gryabov went on, "the great stupid has been living in Russia for ten years and not a word of Russian! . . . Any little aristocrat among us goes to them and learns to babble away in their lingo, while they . . . there's no making them out. Just look at her nose, do look at her nose!"

"Come, drop it . . . it's uncomfortable. Why attack a woman?"

"She's not a woman, but a maiden lady. . . . I bet she's dreaming of suitors. The ugly doll. And she smells of something decaying . . . I've got a loathing for her, my boy! I can't look at her with indifference. When she turns her ugly eyes on me it sends a twinge all through me as though I had knocked my elbow on the parapet. She likes fishing too. Watch her: she fishes as though it were a holy rite! She looks upon everything with disdain . . . She stands there, the wretch, and is conscious that she is a human being, and that therefore she is the monarch of nature. And do you know what her name is? Wilka Charlesovna Fyce! Tfoo! There is no getting it out!"

The Englishwoman, hearing her name, deliberately turned her nose in Gryabov's direction and scanned him with a disdainful glance; she raised her eyes from Gryabov to Otsov and steeped him in disdain. And all this in silence, with dignity and deliberation.

"Did you see?" said Gryabov chuckling. "As though to say 'take that.' Ah, you monster! It's only for the children's sake that I keep that triton. If it weren't for the children, I wouldn't let her come within ten miles of my estate. . . . She has got a nose like a hawk's . . . and her figure! That doll makes me think of a long nail, so I could take her, and knock her into the ground, you know. Stay, I believe I have got a bite. . . ."

Gryabov jumped up and raised his rod. The line drew taut. . . . Gryabov tugged again, but could not pull out the hook.

"It has caught," he said, frowning, "on a stone I expect . . . damnation take it . . ."

There was a look of distress on Gryabov's face. Sighing, moving uneasily, and muttering oaths, he began tugging at the line.

"What a pity, I shall have to go into the water."

"Oh, chuck it!"

"I can't. . . . There's always good fishing in the evening. . . . What a nuisance. Lord, forgive us, I shall have to wade into the water, I must! And if only you knew, I have no inclination to undress, I shall have to get rid of the Englishwoman. . . . It's awkward to undress before her. After all, she is a lady, you know!"

Gryabov flung off his hat, and his cravat.

"Meess . . . er, er . . ." he said, addressing the Englishwoman, "Meess

Fyce, je voo pree . . . ? Well, what am I to say to her? How am I to tell you so that you can understand? I say . . . over there! Go away over there! Do you hear?"

Miss Fyce enveloped Gryabov in disdain, and uttered a nasal sound.

"What? Don't you understand? Go away from here, I tell you! I must undress, you devil's doll! Go over there! Over there!"

Gryabov pulled the lady by her sleeve, pointed her towards the bushes, and made as though he would sit down, as much as to say: Go behind the bushes and hide yourself there. . . . The Englishwoman, moving her eyebrows vigorously, uttered rapidly a long sentence in English. The gentlemen gushed with laughter.

"It's the first time in my life I've heard her voice. . . . There's no denying, it is a voice! She does not understand! Well, what am I to do with her?"

"Chuck it, let's go and have a drink of vodka!"

"I can't. Now's the time to fish, the evening. . . . It's evening . . . Come, what would you have me do? It is a nuisance! I shall have to undress before her. . . ."

Gryabov flung off his coat and his waistcoat and sat on the sand to take off his boots.

"I say, Ivan Kuzmitch," said the marshal, chuckling behind his hand. "It's really outrageous, an insult."

"Nobody asks her not to understand! It's a lesson for these foreigners!"

Gryabov took off his boots and his trousers, flung off his undergarments and remained in the costume of Adam. Otsov held his sides, he turned crimson both from laughter and embarrassment. The Englishwoman twitched her brows and blinked . . . A haughty disdainful smile passed over her yellow face.

"I must cool off," said Gryabov, slapping himself on the ribs. "Tell me if you please, Fyodor Andreitch, why I have a rash on my chest every summer."

"Oh, do get into the water quickly or cover yourself with something, you beast."

"And if only she were confused, the nasty thing," said Gryabov, crossing himself as he waded into the water. "Brrr . . . the water's cold. . . . Look how she moves her eyebrows! She doesn't go away . . . she is far above the crowd he, he, he . . . and she doesn't reckon us as human beings."

Wading knee deep in the water and drawing his huge figure up to its full height, he gave a wink and said:

"This isn't England, you see!"

Miss Fyce coolly put on another worm, gave a yawn, and dropped the hook in. Otsov turned away, Gryabov released his hook, ducked into the water and, spluttering, waded out. Two minutes later he was sitting on the sand and angling as before.

Fat and Thin

Two friends—one a fat man and the other a thin man—met at the Nikolaevsky station. The fat man had just dined in the station and his greasy lips shone like ripe cherries. He smelt of sherry and *fleur d'orange*. The thin man had just slipped out of the train and was laden with portmanteaus, bundles, and bandboxes. He smelt of ham and coffee grounds. A thin woman with a long chin, his wife, and a tall schoolboy with one eye screwed up came into view behind his back.

"Porfiry," cried the fat man on seeing the thin man. "Is it you? My dear fellow! How many summers, how many winters!"

"Holy saints!" cried the thin man in amazement. "Misha! The friend of my childhood! Where have you dropped from?"

The friends kissed each other three times, and gazed at each other with eyes full of tears. Both were agreeably astounded.

"My dear boy!" began the thin man after the kissing. "This is unexpected! This is a surprise! Come have a good look at me! Just as handsome as I used to be! Just as great a darling and a dandy! Good gracious me! Well, and how are you? Made your fortune? Married? I am married as you see. . . . This is my wife Luise, her maiden name was Vantsenbach . . . of the Lutheran persuasion. . . . And this is my son

Nafanail, a schoolboy in the third class. This is the friend of my childhood, Nafanya. We were boys at school together!"

Nafanail thought a little and took off his cap.

"We were boys at school together," the thin man went on. "Do you remember how they used to tease you? You were nicknamed Herostratus because you burned a hole in a schoolbook with a cigarette, and I was nicknamed Ephialtes because I was fond of telling tales. Ho-ho!... we were children!... Don't be shy, Nafanya. Go nearer to him.... And this is my wife, her maiden name was Vantsenbach, of the Lutheran persuasion...."

Nafanail thought a little and took refuge behind his father's back.

"Well, how are you doing my friend?" the fat man asked, looking enthusiastically at his friend. "Are you in the service? What grade have you reached?"

"I am, dear boy! I have been a collegiate assessor for the last two years and I have the Stanislav. The salary is poor, but that's no great matter! The wife gives music lessons, and I go in for carving wooden cigarette cases in a private way. Capital cigarette cases! I sell them for a rouble each. If any one takes ten or more I make a reduction of course. We get along somehow. I served as a clerk, you know, and now I have been transferred here as a head clerk in the same department. I am going to serve here. And what about you? I bet you are a civil councillor by now? Eh?"

"No dear boy, go higher than that," said the fat man. "I have risen to privy councillor already . . . I have two stars."

The thin man turned pale and rigid all at once, but soon his face twisted in all directions in the broadest smile; it seemed as though sparks were flashing from his face and eyes. He squirmed, he doubled together, crumpled up. . . . His portmanteaus, bundles and cardboard boxes seemed to shrink and crumple up too. . . . His wife's long chin grew longer still; Nafanail drew himself up to attention and fastened all the buttons of his uniform.

"Your Excellency, I . . . delighted! The friend, one may say, of childhood and to have turned into such a great man! He-he!"

"Come, come!" the fat man frowned. "What's this tone for? You and

I were friends as boys, and there is no need of this official obsequious-
ness!"

"Merciful heavens, your Excellency! What are you saying . . . ?"
sniggered the thin man, wriggling more than ever. "Your Excellency's
gracious attention is like refreshing manna. . . . This, your Excellency,
is my son Nafanail, . . . my wife Luise, a Lutheran in a certain sense."

The fat man was about to make some protest, but the face of the
thin man wore an expression of such reverence, sugariness, and mawkish respectfulness that the privy councillor was sickened. He turned
away from the thin man, giving him his hand at parting.

The thin man pressed three fingers, bowed his whole body and sniggered like a Chinaman: "He-he-he!" His wife smiled. Nafanail scraped
with his foot and dropped his cap. All three were agreeably overwhelmed.

The Bird Market

There is a small square near the monastery of the Holy Birth which is called Trubnoy, or simply Truboy; there is a market there on Sundays. Hundreds of sheepskins, wadded coats, fur caps, and chimneypot hats swarm there, like crabs in a sieve. There is the sound of the twitter of birds in all sorts of keys, recalling the spring. If the sun is shining, and there are no clouds in the sky, the singing of the birds and the smell of hay make a more vivid impression, and this reminder of spring sets one thinking and carries one's fancy far, far away. Along one side of the square there stands a string of waggons. The waggons are loaded, not with hay, not with cabbages, nor with beans, but with goldfinches, siskins, larks, blackbirds and thrushes, bluetits, bullfinches. All of them are hopping about in rough, home-made cages, twittering and looking with envy at the free sparrows. The goldfinches cost five kopecks, the siskins are rather more expensive, while the value of the other birds is quite indeterminate.

"How much is a lark?"

The seller himself does not know the value of a lark. He scratches his head and asks whatever comes into it, a rouble, or three kopecks, according to the purchaser. There are expensive birds too. A faded old blackbird, with most of its feathers plucked out of its tail, sits on a dirty perch. He is dignified, grave, and motionless as a retired general. He has waved his claw in resignation to his captivity long ago, and looks at the blue sky with indifference. Probably, owing to this indifference, he is considered a sagacious bird. He is not to be bought for less than forty kopecks. Schoolboys, workmen, young men in stylish greatcoats, and bird-fanciers in incredibly shabby caps, in ragged trousers that are turned up at the ankles, and look as though they had been gnawed by mice, crowd round the birds, splashing through the mud. The young people and the workmen are sold hens for cocks, young birds for old ones. . . . They know very little about birds. But there is no deceiving the bird-fancier. He sees and understands his bird from a distance.

"There is no relying on that bird," a fancier will say, looking into a siskin's beak, and counting the feathers on its tail. "He sings now, it's true, but what of that? I sing in company too. No, my boy, shout, sing to me without company; sing in solitude, if you can. . . . You give me that one yonder that sits and holds its tongue! Give me the quiet one! That one says nothing, so he thinks the more. . . ."

Among the waggons of birds there are some full of other live creatures. Here you see hares, rabbits, hedgehogs, guinea-pigs, polecats. A hare sits sorrowfully nibbling the straw. The guinea-pigs shiver with cold, while the hedgehogs look out with curiosity from under their prickles at the public.

"I have read somewhere," says a post-office official in a faded overcoat, looking lovingly at the hare, and addressing no one in particular, "I have read that some learned man had a cat and a mouse and a falcon and a sparrow, who all ate out of one bowl."

"That's very possible, sir. The cat must have been beaten, and the falcon, I dare say, had all its tail pulled out. There's no great cleverness in that, sir. A friend of mine had a cat who, saving your presence, used to eat his cucumbers. He thrashed her with a big whip for a fortnight, till he taught her not to. A hare can learn to light matches if you beat it. Does that surprise you? It's very simple! It takes the match in its mouth and strikes it. An animal is like a man. A man's made wiser by beating, and it's the same with a beast."

Men in long, full-skirted coats move backwards and forwards in the crowd with cocks and ducks under their arms. The fowls are all lean and hungry. Chickens poke their ugly, mangy-looking heads out of their cages and peck at something in the mud. Boys with pigeons stare into your face and try to detect in you a pigeon-fancier.

"Yes, indeed! It's no use talking to you," someone shouts angrily. "You should look before you speak! Do you call this a pigeon? It is an eagle, not a pigeon!"

A tall thin man, with a shaven upper lip and side whiskers, who looks like a sick and drunken footman, is selling a snow-white lap-dog. The old lap-dog whines.

"She told me to sell the nasty thing," says the footman, with a contemptuous snigger. "She is bankrupt in her old age, has nothing to eat, and here now is selling her dogs and cats. She cries, and kisses them on their filthy snouts. And then she is so hard up that she sells them. 'Pon my soul, it is a fact! Buy it, gentlemen! The money is wanted for coffee."

But no one laughs. A boy who is standing by screws up one eye and looks at him gravely with compassion.

The most interesting of all is the fish section. Some dozen peasants are sitting in a row. Before each of them is a pail, and in each pail there is a veritable little hell. There, in the thick, greenish water are swarms of little carp, eels, small fry, water-snails, frogs, and newts. Big water-beetles with broken legs scurry over the small surface, clambering on the carp, and jumping over the frogs. The creatures have a strong hold on life. The frogs climb on the beetles, the newts on the frogs. The dark green tench, as more expensive fish, enjoy an exceptional position; they are kept in a special jar where they can't swim, but still they are not so cramped. . . .

"The carp is a grand fish! The carp's the fish to keep, your honour, plague take him! You can keep him for a year in a pail and he'll live! It's a week since I caught these very fish. I caught them, sir, in Pererva, and have come from there on foot. The carp are two kopecks each, the eels are three, and the minnows are ten kopecks the dozen, plague take them! Five kopecks' worth of minnows, sir? Won't you take some worms?"

The seller thrusts his coarse rough fingers into the pail and pulls out of it a soft minnow, or a little carp, the size of a nail. Fishing lines, hooks, and tackle are laid out near the pails, and pond-worms glow with a crimson light in the sun.

An old fancier in a fur cap, iron-rimmed spectacles, and goloshes that look like two dread-noughts, walks about by the waggons of birds and pails of fish. He is, as they call him here, "a type." He hasn't a far-thing to bless himself with, but in spite of that he haggles, gets excited, and pesters purchasers with advice. He has thoroughly examined all the hares, pigeons, and fish; examined them in every detail, fixed the kind, the age, and the price of each one of them a good hour ago. He is as interested as a child in the goldfinches, the carp, and the minnows. Talk to him, for instance, about thrushes, and the queer old fellow will tell you things you could not find in any book. He will tell you them with enthusiasm, with passion, and will scold you too for your igno-rance. Of goldfinches and bullfinches he is ready to talk endlessly, opening his eyes wide and gesticulating violently with his hands. He is only to be met here at the market in the cold weather; in the summer he is somewhere in the country, catching quails with a bird-call and angling for fish.

And here is another "type," a very tall, very thin, close-shaven gen-tleman in dark spectacles, wearing a cap with a cockade, and looking like a scrivener of by-gone days. He is a fancier; he is a man of decent position, a teacher in a high school, and that is well known to the *habitués* of the market, and they treat him with respect, greet him with bows, and have even invented for him a special title: "Your Scholar-ship." At Suharev market he rummages among the books, and at Trub-noy looks out for good pigeons.

"Please, sir!" the pigeon-sellers shout to him, "Mr. Schoolmaster, your Scholarship, take notice of my tumblers! your Scholarship!"

"Your Scholarship!" is shouted at him from every side.

"Your Scholarship!" an urchin repeats somewhere on the boulevard.

And his "Scholarship," apparently quite accustomed to his title, grave and severe, takes a pigeon in both hands, and lifting it above his head, begins examining it, and as he does so frowns and looks graver than ever, like a conspirator.

And Trubnoy Square, that little bit of Moscow where animals are so tenderly loved, and where they are so tortured, lives its little life, grows noisy and excited, and the business-like or pious people who pass by along the boulevard cannot make out what has brought this crowd of people, this medley of caps, fur hats, and chimneypots together; what they are talking about there, what they are buying and selling.

Choristers

The Justice of the Peace, who had received a letter from Petersburg, had set the news going that the owner of Yefremovo, Count Vladimir Ivanovitch, would soon be arriving. When he would arrive—there was no saying.

"Like a thief in the night," said Father Kuzma, a grey-headed little priest in a lilac cassock. "And when he does come the place will be crowded with the nobility and other high gentry. All the neighbours will flock here. Mind now, do your best, Alexey Alexeitch.... I beg you most earnestly."

"You need not trouble about me," said Alexey Alexeitch, frowning. "I know my business. If only my enemy intones the litany in the right key. He may ... out of sheer spite...."

"There, there.... I'll persuade the deacon ... I'll persuade him."

Alexey Alexeitch was the sacristan of the Yefremovo church. He also taught the schoolboys church and secular singing, for which he received sixty roubles a year from the revenues of the Count's estate. The schoolboys were bound to sing in church in return for their teaching. Alexey Alexeitch was a tall, thick-set man of dignified deportment, with a fat, clean-shaven face that reminded one of a cow's udder.

His imposing figure and double chin made him look like a man occupying an important position in the secular hierarchy rather than a sacristan. It was strange to see him, so dignified and imposing, flop to the ground before the bishop and, on one occasion, after too loud a squabble with the deacon Yevlampy Avdiessov, remain on his knees for two hours by order of the head priest of the district. Grandeur was more in keeping with his figure than humiliation.

On account of the rumours of the Count's approaching visit he had a choir practice every day, morning and evening. The choir practice was held at the school. It did not interfere much with the school work. During the practice the schoolmaster, Sergey Makaritch, set the children writing copies while he joined the tenors as an amateur.

This is how the choir practice was conducted. Alexey Alexeitch would come into the school-room, slamming the door and blowing his nose. The trebles and altos extricated themselves noisily from the school-tables. The tenors and basses, who had been waiting for some time in the yard, came in, tramping like horses. They all took their places. Alexey Alexeitch drew himself up, made a sign to enforce silence, and struck a note with the tuning fork.

"To-to-li-to-tom . . . Do-mi-sol-do!"

"A-a-a-men."

"Adagio, adagio. . . . Once more."

After the "Amen" there followed "Lord have mercy upon us" from the Great Litany. All this had been learned long ago, sung a thousand times and thoroughly digested, and it was gone through simply as a formality. It was sung indolently, unconsciously. Alexey Alexeitch waved his arms calmly and chimed in now in a tenor, now in a bass voice. It was all slow, there was nothing interesting. . . . But before the "Cherubim" hymn the whole choir suddenly began blowing their noses, coughing and zealously turning the pages of their music. The sacristan turned his back on the choir and with a mysterious expression on his face began tuning his violin. The preparations lasted a couple of minutes.

"Take your places. Look at your music carefully. . . . Basses, don't overdo it . . . rather softly."

Bortnyansky's "Cherubim" hymn, No. 7, was selected. At a given signal silence prevailed. All eyes were fastened on the music, the trebles opened their mouths. Alexey Alexeitch softly lowered his arm.

"Piano ... piano.... You see 'piano' is written there.... More lightly, more lightly."

When they had to sing "piano" an expression of benevolence and amiability overspread Alexey Alexeitch's face, as though he was dreaming of a dainty morsel.

"Forte ... forte! Hold it!"

And when they had to sing "forte" the sacristan's fat face expressed alarm and even horror.

The "Cherubim" hymn was sung well, so well that the schoolchildren abandoned their copies and fell to watching the movements of Alexey Alexeitch. People stood under the windows. The schoolwatchman, Vassily, came in wearing an apron and carrying a dinner-knife in his hand and stood listening. Father Kuzma, with an anxious face appeared suddenly as though he had sprung from out of the earth. ... After 'Let us lay aside all earthly cares' Alexey Alexeitch wiped the sweat off his brow and went up to Father Kuzma in excitement.

"It puzzles me, Father Kuzma," he said, shrugging his shoulders, "why is it that the Russian people have no understanding? It puzzles me, may the Lord chastise me! Such an uncultured people that you really cannot tell whether they have a windpipe in their throats or some other sort of internal arrangement. Were you choking, or what?" he asked, addressing the bass Gennady Semitchov, the innkeeper's brother.

"Why?"

"What is your voice like? It rattles like a saucepan. I bet you were boozing yesterday! That's what it is! Your breath smells like a tavern. ... E-ech! You are a clodhopper, brother! You are a lout! How can you be a chorister if you keep company with peasants in the tavern? Ech, you are an ass, brother!"

"It's a sin, it's a sin, brother," muttered Father Kuzma. "God sees everything ... through and through...."

"That's why you have no idea of singing—because you care more for vodka than for godliness, you fool."

"Don't work yourself up," said Father Kuzma. "Don't be cross. . . . I will persuade him."

Father Kuzma went up to Gennady Semitchov and began "persuading" him: "What do you do it for? Try and put your mind to it. A man who sings ought to restrain himself, because his throat is . . . er . . . tender."

Gennady scratched his neck and looked sideways towards the window as though the words did not apply to him.

After the "Cherubim" hymn they sang the Creed, then "It is meet and right"; they sang smoothly and with feeling, and so right on to "Our Father."

"To my mind, Father Kuzma," said the sacristan, "the old 'Our Father' is better than the modern. That's what we ought to sing before the Count."

"No, no. . . . Sing the modern one. For the Count hears nothing but modern music when he goes to Mass in Petersburg or Moscow. . . . In the churches there, I imagine . . . there's very different sort of music there, brother!"

After "Our Father" there was again a great blowing of noses, coughing and turning over of pages. The most difficult part of the performance came next: the "concert." Alexey Alexeitch was practising two pieces, "Who is the God of glory" and "Universal Praise." Whichever the choir learned best would be sung before the Count. During the "concert" the sacristan rose to a pitch of enthusiasm. The expression of benevolence was continually alternating with one of alarm.

"Forte!" he muttered. "Andante! let yourselves go! Sing, you image! Tenors, you don't bring it off! To-to-ti-to-tom. . . . Sol . . . si . . . sol, I tell you, you blockhead! Glory! Basses, glo . . . o . . . ry."

His bow travelled over the heads and shoulders of the erring trebles and altos. His left hand was continually pulling the ears of the young singers. On one occasion, carried away by his feelings he flipped the bass Gennady under the chin with his bent thumb. But the choristers were not moved to tears or to anger at his blows: they realised the full gravity of their task.

After the "concert" came a minute of silence. Alexey Alexeitch, red, perspiring and exhausted, sat down on the window-sill, and turned upon the company lustreless, wearied, but triumphant eyes. In the listening crowd he observed to his immense annoyance the deacon Avdiessov. The deacon, a tall thick-set man with a red pock-marked face, and straw in his hair, stood leaning against the stove and grinning contemptuously.

"That's right, sing away! Perform your music!" he muttered in a deep bass. "Much the Count will care for your singing! He doesn't care whether you sing with music or without. . . . For he is an atheist."

Father Kuzma looked round in a scared way and twiddled his fingers.

"Come, come," he muttered. "Hush, deacon, I beg."

After the "concert" they sang "May our lips be filled with praise," and the choir practice was over. The choir broke up to reassemble in the evening for another practice. And so it went on every day.

One month passed and then a second. . . . The steward, too, had by then received a notice that the Count would soon be coming. At last the dusty sunblinds were taken off the windows of the big house, and Yefremovo heard the strains of the broken-down, out-of-tune piano. Father Kuzma was pining, though he could not himself have said why, or whether it was from delight or alarm. . . . The deacon went about grinning.

The following Saturday evening Father Kuzma went to the sacristan's lodgings. His face was pale, his shoulders drooped, the lilac of his cassock looked faded.

"I have just been at his Excellency's," he said to the sacristan, stammering. "He is a cultivated gentleman with refined ideas. But . . . er . . . it's mortifying, brother. . . . 'At what o'clock, your Excellency, do you desire us to ring for Mass to-morrow?' And he said: 'As you think best . . . Only, couldn't it be as short and quick as possible . . . without a choir.' Without a choir! Er . . . do you understand, without, without a choir. . . ."

Alexey Alexeitch turned crimson. He would rather have spent two hours on his knees again than have heard those words! He did not sleep all night. He was not so much mortified at the waste of his labours as at the fact that the deacon would give him no peace now with his jeers. The deacon was delighted at his discomfiture. Next day all through the service he was casting disdainful glances towards the choir where Alexey Alexeitch was booming responses in solitude. When he passed by the choir with the censer he muttered:

"Perform your music! Do your utmost! The Count will give a ten-rouble note to the choir!"

After the service the sacristan went home, crushed and ill with mortification. At the gate he was overtaken by the red-faced deacon.

"Stop a minute, Alyosha!" said the deacon. "Stop a minute, silly, don't be cross! You are not the only one, I am in for it too! Immediately after the Mass Father Kuzma went up to the Count and asked: 'And what did you think of the deacon's voice, your Excellency. He has a deep bass, hasn't he?' And the Count—do you know what he answered by way of compliment? 'Anyone can bawl,' he said. 'A man's voice is not as important as his brains.' A learned gentleman from Petersburg! An atheist is an atheist, and that's all about it! Come, brother in misfortune, let us go and have a drop to drown our troubles!"

And the enemies went out of the gate arm-in-arm.

Minds in Ferment

(from the annals of a town)

The earth was like an oven. The afternoon sun blazed with such energy that even the thermometer hanging in the excise officer's room lost its head: it ran up to 112.5 and stopped there, irresolute. The inhabitants streamed with perspiration like overdriven horses, and were too lazy to mop their faces.

Two of the inhabitants were walking along the market-place in front of the closely shuttered houses. One was Potcheshihin, the local treasury clerk, and the other was Optimov, the agent, for many years a correspondent of the *Son of the Fatherland* newspaper. They walked in silence, speechless from the heat. Optimov felt tempted to find fault with the local authorities for the dust and disorder of the market-place, but, aware of the peace-loving disposition and moderate views of his companion, he said nothing.

In the middle of the market-place Potcheshihin suddenly halted and began gazing into the sky.

"What are you looking at?"

"Those starlings that flew up. I wonder where they have settled. Clouds and clouds of them. . . . If one were to go and take a shot at them, and if one were to pick them up . . . and if . . . They have settled in the Father Prebendary's garden!"

"Oh no! They are not in the Father Prebendary's, they are in the Father Deacon's. If you did have a shot at them from here you wouldn't kill anything. Fine shot won't carry so far; it loses its force. And why should you kill them, anyway? They're birds destructive of the fruit, that's true; still, they're fowls of the air, works of the Lord. The starling sings, you know. . . . And what does it sing, pray? A song of praise. . . . 'All ye fowls of the air, praise ye the Lord.' No. I do believe they have settled in the Father Prebendary's garden."

Three old pilgrim women, wearing bark shoes and carrying wallets, passed noiselessly by the speakers. Looking enquiringly at the gentlemen who were for some unknown reason staring at the Father Prebendary's house, they slackened their pace, and when they were a few yards off stopped, glanced at the friends once more, and then fell to gazing at the house themselves.

"Yes, you were right; they have settled in the Father Prebendary's," said Optimov. "His cherries are ripe now, so they have gone there to peck them."

From the garden gate emerged the Father Prebendary himself, accompanied by the sexton. Seeing the attention directed upon his abode and wondering what people were staring at, he stopped, and he, too, as well as the sexton, began looking upwards to find out.

"The father is going to a service somewhere, I suppose," said Potcheshihin. "The Lord be his succour!"

Some workmen from Purov's factory, who had been bathing in the river, passed between the friends and the priest. Seeing the latter absorbed in contemplation of the heavens and the pilgrim women, too, standing motionless with their eyes turned upwards, they stood still and stared in the same direction.

A small boy leading a blind beggar and a peasant, carrying a tub of stinking fish to throw into the market-place, did the same.

"There must be something the matter, I should think," said Potcheshihin, "a fire or something. But there's no sign of smoke anywhere. Hey! Kuzma!" he shouted to the peasant, "what's the matter?"

The peasant made some reply, but Potcheshihin and Optimov did not catch it. Sleepy-looking shopmen made their appearance at the doors of all the shops. Some plasterers at work on a warehouse near left their ladders and joined the workmen.

The fireman, who was describing circles with his bare feet, on the watch-tower, halted, and, after looking steadily at them for a few minutes, came down. The watch-tower was left deserted. This seemed suspicious.

"There must be a fire somewhere. Don't shove me! You damned swine!"

"Where do you see the fire? What fire? Pass on, gentlemen! I ask you civilly!"

"It must be a fire indoors!"

"Asks us civilly and keeps poking with his elbows. Keep your hands to yourself! Though you are a head constable, you have no sort of right to make free with your fists!"

"He's trodden on my corn! Ah! I'll crush you!"

"Crushed? Who's crushed? Lads! a man's been crushed!"

"What's the meaning of this crowd? What do you want?"

"A man's been crushed, please your honour!"

"Where? Pass on! I ask you civilly! I ask you civilly, you blockheads!"

"You may shove a peasant, but you daren't touch a gentleman! Hands off!"

"Did you ever know such people? There's no doing anything with them by fair words, the devils! Sidorov, run for Akim Danilitch! Look sharp! It'll be the worse for you, gentlemen! Akim Danilitch is coming, and he'll give it to you! You here, Parfen? A blind man, and at his age too! Can't see, but he must be like other people and won't do what he's told. Smirnov, put his name down!"

"Yes, sir! And shall I write down the men from Purov's? That man there with the swollen cheek, he's from Purov's works."

"Don't put down the men from Purov's. It's Purov's birthday tomorrow."

The starlings rose in a black cloud from the Father Prebendary's garden, but Potcheshihin and Optimov did not notice them. They stood staring into the air, wondering what could have attracted such a crowd, and what it was looking at.

Akim Danilitch appeared. Still munching and wiping his lips, he cut his way into the crowd, bellowing:

"Firemen, be ready! Disperse! Mr. Optimov, disperse, or it'll be the worse for you! Instead of writing all kinds of things about decent people in the papers, you had better try to behave yourself more conformably! No good ever comes of reading the papers!"

"Kindly refrain from reflections upon literature!" cried Optimov hotly. "I am a literary man, and I will allow no one to make reflections upon literature! though, as is the duty of a citizen, I respect you as a father and benefactor!"

"Firemen, turn the hose on them!"

"There's no water, please your honour!"

"Don't answer me! Go and get some! Look sharp!"

"We've nothing to get it in, your honour. The major has taken the fire-brigade horses to drive his aunt to the station."

"Disperse! Stand back, damnation take you! . . . Is that to your taste? Put him down, the devil!"

"I've lost my pencil, please your honour!"

The crowd grew larger and larger. There is no telling what proportions it might have reached if the new organ just arrived from Moscow had not fortunately begun playing in the tavern close by. Hearing their favourite tune, the crowd gasped and rushed off to the tavern. So nobody ever knew why the crowd had assembled, and Potcheshihin and Optimov had by now forgotten the existence of the starlings who were innocently responsible for the proceedings.

An hour later the town was still and silent again, and only a solitary figure was to be seen—the fireman pacing round and round on the watch-tower.

The same evening Akim Danilitch sat in the grocer's shop drinking *limonade gaseuse* and brandy, and writing:

"In addition to the official report, I venture, your Excellency, to append a few supplementary observations of my own. Father and benefactor! In very truth, but for the prayers of your virtuous spouse in her salubrious villa near our town, there's no knowing what might not have come to pass. What I have been through to-day I can find no words to express. The efficiency of Krushensky and of the major of the fire brigade are beyond all praise! I am proud of such devoted servants of our country! As for me, I did all that a weak man could do, whose only desire is the welfare of his neighbour; and sitting now in the bosom of my family, with tears in my eyes I thank Him Who spared us bloodshed! In absence of evidence, the guilty parties remain in custody, but I propose to release them in a week or so. It was their ignorance that led them astray!"

A Chameleon

The police superintendent Otchumyelov is walking across the market square wearing a new overcoat and carrying a parcel under his arm. A red-haired policeman strides after him with a sieve full of confiscated gooseberries in his hands. There is silence all around. Not a soul in the square. . . . The open doors of the shops and taverns look out upon God's world disconsolately, like hungry mouths; there is not even a beggar near them.

"So you bite, you damned brute?" Otchumyelov hears suddenly. "Lads, don't let him go! Biting is prohibited nowadays! Hold him! ah . . . ah!"

There is the sound of a dog yelping. Otchumyelov looks in the direction of the sound and sees a dog, hopping on three legs and looking about her, run out of Pitchugin's timber-yard. A man in a starched cotton shirt, with his waistcoat unbuttoned, is chasing her. He runs after her, and throwing his body forward falls down and seizes the dog by her hind legs. Once more there is a yelping and a shout of "Don't let go!" Sleepy countenances are protruded from the shops, and soon a crowd, which seems to have sprung out of the earth, is gathered round the timber-yard.

"It looks like a row, your honour . . ." says the policeman.

Otchumyelov makes a half turn to the left and strides towards the crowd.

He sees the aforementioned man in the unbuttoned waistcoat standing close by the gate of the timber-yard, holding his right hand in the air and displaying a bleeding finger to the crowd. On his half-drunken face there is plainly written: "I'll pay you out, you rogue!" and indeed the very finger has the look of a flag of victory. In this man Otchumyelov recognises Hryukin, the goldsmith. The culprit who has caused the sensation, a white borzoy puppy with a sharp muzzle and a yellow patch on her back, is sitting on the ground with her fore-paws outstretched in the middle of the crowd, trembling all over. There is an expression of misery and terror in her tearful eyes.

"What's it all about?" Otchumyelov inquires, pushing his way through the crowd. "What are you here for? Why are you waving your finger . . . ? Who was it shouted?"

"I was walking along here, not interfering with anyone, your honour," Hryukin begins, coughing into his fist. "I was talking about fire-wood to Mitry Mitritch, when this low brute for no rhyme or reason bit my finger. . . . You must excuse me, I am a working man. . . . Mine is fine work. I must have damages, for I shan't be able to use this finger for a week, may be. . . . It's not even the law, your honour, that one should put up with it from a beast. . . . If everyone is going to be bitten, life won't be worth living. . . ."

"H'm. Very good," says Otchumyelov sternly, coughing and raising his eyebrows. "Very good. Whose dog is it? I won't let this pass! I'll teach them to let their dogs run all over the place! It's time these gentry were looked after, if they won't obey the regulations! When he's fined, the blackguard, I'll teach him what it means to keep dogs and such stray cattle! I'll give him a lesson! . . . Yeldyrin," cries the superintendent, addressing the policeman, "find out whose dog this is and draw up a report! And the dog must be strangled. Without delay! It's sure to be mad. . . . Whose dog is it, I ask?"

"I fancy it's General Zhigalov's," says someone in the crowd.

"General Zhigalov's, h'm. . . . Help me off with my coat, Yeldyrin . . . it's frightfully hot! It must be a sign of rain. . . . There's one thing I can't make out, how it came to bite you?" Otchumyelov turns to Hryukin.

"Surely it couldn't reach your finger. It's a little dog, and you are a great hulking fellow! You must have scratched your finger with a nail, and then the idea struck you to get damages for it. We all know . . . your sort! I know you devils!"

"He put a cigarette in her face, your honour, for a joke, and she had the sense to snap at him. . . . He is a nonsensical fellow, your honour!"

"That's a lie, Squinteye! You didn't see, so why tell lies about it? His honour is a wise gentleman, and will see who is telling lies and who is telling the truth, as in God's sight. . . . And if I am lying let the court decide. It's written in the law. . . . We are all equal nowadays. My own brother is in the gendarmes . . . let me tell you. . . ."

"Don't argue!"

"No, that's not the General's dog," says the policeman, with profound conviction, "the General hasn't got one like that. His are mostly setters."

"Do you know that for a fact?"

"Yes, your honour."

"I know it, too. The General has valuable dogs, thoroughbred, and this is goodness knows what! No coat, no shape. . . . A low creature. . . . And to keep a dog like that! . . . where's the sense of it. If a dog like that were to turn up in Petersburg or Moscow, do you know what would happen? They would not worry about the law, they would strangle it in a twinkling! You've been injured, Hryukin, and we can't let the matter drop. . . . We must give them a lesson! It is high time . . . . !"

"Yet maybe it is the General's," says the policeman, thinking aloud. "It's not written on its face. . . . I saw one like it the other day in his yard."

"It is the General's, that's certain!" says a voice in the crowd.

"H'm, help me on with my overcoat, Yeldyrin, my lad . . . the wind's getting up. . . . I am cold. . . . You take it to the General's, and inquire there. Say I found it and sent it. And tell them not to let it out into the street. . . . It may be a valuable dog, and if every swine goes sticking a cigar in its mouth, it will soon be ruined. A dog is a delicate animal. . . . And you put your hand down, you blockhead. It's no use your displaying your fool of a finger. It's your own fault. . . ."

"Here comes the General's cook, ask him. . . . Hi, Prohor! Come here, my dear man! Look at this dog. . . . Is it one of yours?"

"What an idea! We have never had one like that!"

"There's no need to waste time asking," says Otchumyelov. "It's a stray dog! There's no need to waste time talking about it. . . . Since he says it's a stray dog, a stray dog it is. . . . It must be destroyed, that's all about it."

"It is not our dog," Prohor goes on. "It belongs to the General's brother, who arrived the other day. Our master does not care for hounds. But his honour is fond of them. . . ."

"You don't say his Excellency's brother is here? Vladimir Ivanitch?" inquires Otchumuyelov, and his whole face beams with an ecstatic smile. "Well, I never! And I didn't know! Has he come on a visit?"

"Yes."

"Well, I never. . . . He couldn't stay away from his brother. . . . And there I didn't know! So this is his honour's dog? Delighted to hear it. . . . Take it. It's not a bad pup. . . . A lively creature. . . . Snapped at this fellow's finger! Ha-ha-ha. . . . Come, why are you shivering? Rrr . . . Rrrr. . . . The rogue's angry . . . a nice little pup."

Prohor calls the dog, and walks away from the timber-yard with her. The crowd laughs at Hryukin.

"I'll make you smart yet!" Otchumyelov threatens him, and wrapping himself in his greatcoat, goes on his way across the square.

In the Graveyard

"The wind has got up, friends, and it is beginning to get dark. Hadn't we better take ourselves off before it gets worse?"

The wind was frolicking among the yellow leaves of the old birch trees, and a shower of thick drops fell upon us from the leaves. One of our party slipped on the clayey soil, and clutched at a big grey cross to save himself from falling.

"Yegor Gryaznorukov, titular councillor and cavalier . . ." he read. "I knew that gentleman. He was fond of his wife, he wore the Stanislav ribbon, and read nothing. . . . His digestion worked well. . . . His life was all right, wasn't it? One would have thought he had no reason to die, but alas! fate had its eye on him. . . . The poor fellow fell a victim to his habits of observation. On one occasion, when he was listening at a keyhole, he got such a bang on the head from the door that he sustained concussion of the brain (he had a brain), and died. And here, under this tombstone, lies a man who from his cradle detested verses and epigrams. . . . As though to mock him his whole tombstone is adorned with verses. . . . There is someone coming!"

A man in a shabby overcoat, with a shaven, bluish-crimson countenance, overtook us. He had a bottle under his arm and a parcel of sausage was sticking out of his pocket.

"Where is the grave of Mushkin, the actor?" he asked us in a husky voice.

We conducted him towards the grave of Mushkin, the actor, who had died two years before.

"You are a government clerk, I suppose?" we asked him.

"No, an actor. Nowadays it is difficult to distinguish actors from clerks of the Consistory. No doubt you have noticed that. . . . That's typical, but it's not very flattering for the government clerk."

It was with difficulty that we found the actor's grave. It had sunken, was overgrown with weeds, and had lost all appearance of a grave. A cheap, little cross that had begun to rot, and was covered with green moss blackened by the frost, had an air of aged dejection and looked, as it were, ailing.

". . . forgotten friend Mushkin . . ." we read.

Time had erased the *never,* and corrected the falsehood of man.

"A subscription for a monument to him was got up among actors and journalists, but they drank up the money, the dear fellows . . ." sighed the actor, bowing down to the ground and touching the wet earth with his knees and his cap.

"How do you mean, drank it?"

"That's very simple. They collected the money, published a paragraph about it in the newspaper, and spent it on drink. . . . I don't say it to blame them. . . . I hope it did them good, dear things! Good health to them, and eternal memory to him."

"Drinking means bad health, and eternal memory nothing but sadness. God give us remembrance for a time, but eternal memory—what next!"

"You are right there. Mushkin was a well-known man, you see; there were a dozen wreaths on the coffin, and he is already forgotten. Those to whom he was dear have forgotten him, but those to whom he did harm remember him. I, for instance, shall never, never forget him, for I got nothing but harm from him. I have no love for the deceased."

"What harm did he do you?"

"Great harm," sighed the actor, and an expression of bitter resentment overspread his face. "To me he was a villain and a scoundrel—the Kingdom of Heaven be his! It was through looking at him and listening to him that I became an actor. By his art he lured me from the parental home, he enticed me with the excitements of an actor's life, promised me all sorts of things—and brought tears and sorrow. . . . An actor's lot is a bitter one! I have lost youth, sobriety, and the divine semblance. . . . I haven't a half-penny to bless myself with, my shoes are down at heel, my breeches are frayed and patched, and my face looks as if it had been gnawed by dogs. . . . My head's full of freethinking and nonsense. . . . He robbed me of my faith—my evil genius! It would have been something if I had had talent, but as it is, I am ruined for nothing. . . . It's cold, honoured friends. . . . Won't you have some? There is enough for all. . . . B-r-r-r. . . . Let us drink to the rest of his soul! Though I don't like him and though he's dead, he was the only one I had in the world, the only one. It's the last time I shall visit him. . . . The doctors say I shall soon die of drink, so here I have come to say good-bye. One must forgive one's enemies."

We left the actor to converse with the dead Mushkin and went on. It began drizzling a fine cold rain.

At the turning into the principal avenue strewn with gravel, we met a funeral procession. Four bearers, wearing white calico sashes and muddy high boots with leaves sticking on them, carried the brown coffin. It was getting dark and they hastened, stumbling and shaking their burden. . . .

"We've only been walking here for a couple of hours and that is the third brought in already. . . . Shall we go home, friends?"

Oysters

I need no great effort of memory to recall, in every detail, the rainy autumn evening when I stood with my father in one of the more frequented streets of Moscow, and felt that I was gradually being overcome by a strange illness. I had no pain at all, but my legs were giving way under me, the words stuck in my throat, my head slipped weakly on one side ... It seemed as though, in a moment, I must fall down and lose consciousness.

If I had been taken into a hospital at that minute, the doctors would have had to write over my bed: *Fames,* a disease which is not in the manuals of medicine.

Beside me on the pavement stood my father in a shabby summer overcoat and a serge cap, from which a bit of white wadding was sticking out. On his feet he had big heavy goloshes. Afraid, vain man, that people would see that his feet were bare under his goloshes, he had drawn the tops of some old boots up round the calves of his legs.

This poor, foolish, queer creature, whom I loved the more warmly the more ragged and dirty his smart summer overcoat became, had come to Moscow, five months before, to look for a job as copying-clerk. For those five months he had been trudging about Moscow looking for work, and it was only on that day that he had brought himself to go into the street to beg for alms.

Before us was a big house of three storeys, adorned with a blue signboard with the word "Restaurant" on it. My head was drooping feebly backwards and on one side, and I could not help looking upwards at the lighted windows of the restaurant. Human figures were flitting about at the windows. I could see the right side of the orchestrion, two oleographs, hanging lamps ... Staring into one window, I saw a patch of white. The patch was motionless, and its rectangular outlines stood out sharply against the dark, brown background. I looked intently and made out of the patch a white placard on the wall. Something was written on it, but what it was, I could not see ...

For half an hour I kept my eyes on the placard. Its white attracted my eyes, and, as it were, hypnotised my brain. I tried to read it, but my efforts were in vain.

At last the strange disease got the upper hand.

The rumble of the carriages began to seem like thunder, in the stench of the street I distinguished a thousand smells. The restaurant lights and the lamps dazzled my eyes like lightning. My five senses were overstrained and sensitive beyond the normal. I began to see what I had not seen before.

"Oysters ..." I made out on the placard.

A strange word! I had lived in the world eight years and three months, but had never come across that word. What did it mean? Surely it was not the name of the restaurant-keeper? But signboards with names on them always hang outside, not on the walls indoors!

"Papa, what does 'oysters' mean?" I asked in a husky voice, making an effort to turn my face towards my father.

My father did not hear. He was keeping a watch on the movements of the crowd, and following every passer-by with his eyes.... From his eyes I saw that he wanted to say something to the passers-by, but the fatal word hung like a heavy weight on his trembling lips and could not be flung off. He even took a step after one passer-by and touched him on the sleeve, but when he turned round, he said, "I beg your pardon," was overcome with confusion, and staggered back.

"Papa, what does 'oysters' mean?" I repeated.

"It is an animal . . . that lives in the sea. . . ."

I instantly pictured to myself this unknown marine animal. . . . I thought it must be something midway between a fish and a crab. As it was from the sea they made of it, of course, a very nice hot fish soup with savoury pepper and laurel leaves, or broth with vinegar and fricassee of fish and cabbage, or crayfish sauce, or served it cold with horse-radish. . . . I vividly imagined it being brought from the market, quickly cleaned, quickly put in the pot, quickly, quickly, for everyone was hungry . . . awfully hungry! From the kitchen rose the smell of hot fish and crayfish soup.

I felt that this smell was tickling my palate and nostrils, that it was gradually taking possession of my whole body. . . . The restaurant, my father, the white placard, my sleeves were all smelling of it, smelling so strongly that I began to chew. I moved my jaws and swallowed as though I really had a piece of this marine animal in my mouth . . .

My legs gave way from the blissful sensation I was feeling, and I clutched at my father's arm to keep myself from falling, and leant against his wet summer overcoat. My father was trembling and shivering. He was cold . . .

"Papa, are oysters a Lenten dish?" I asked.

"They are eaten alive . . ." said my father. "They are in shells like tortoises, but . . . in two halves."

The delicious smell instantly left off affecting me, and the illusion vanished. . . . Now I understood it all!

"How nasty," I whispered, "how nasty!"

So that's what "oysters" meant! I imagined to myself a creature like a frog. A frog sitting in a shell, peeping out from it with big, glittering eyes, and moving its revolting jaws. I imagined this creature in a shell with claws, glittering eyes, and a slimy skin, being brought from the market. . . . The children would all hide while the cook, frowning with an air of disgust, would take the creature by its claw, put it on a plate, and carry it into the dining-room. The grown-ups would take it and eat it, eat it alive with its eyes, its teeth, its legs! While it squeaked and tried to bite their lips. . . .

I frowned, but . . . but why did my teeth move as though I were munching? The creature was loathsome, disgusting, terrible, but I ate it, ate it greedily, afraid of distinguishing its taste or smell. As soon as I had eaten one, I saw the glittering eyes of a second, a third . . . I ate them too. . . . At last I ate the table-napkin, the plate, my father's goloshes, the white placard . . . I ate everything that caught my eye, because I felt that nothing but eating would take away my illness. The oysters had a terrible look in their eyes and were loathsome. I shuddered at the thought of them, but I wanted to eat! To eat!

"Oysters! Give me some oysters!" was the cry that broke from me and I stretched out my hand.

"Help us, gentlemen!" I heard at that moment my father say, in a hollow and shaking voice. "I am ashamed to ask but—my God!—I can bear no more!"

"Oysters!" I cried, pulling my father by the skirts of his coat.

"Do you mean to say you eat oysters? A little chap like you!" I heard laughter close to me.

Two gentlemen in top hats were standing before us, looking into my face and laughing.

"Do you really eat oysters, youngster? That's interesting! How do you eat them?"

I remember that a strong hand dragged me into the lighted restaurant. A minute later there was a crowd round me, watching me with curiosity and amusement. I sat at a table and ate something slimy, salt with a flavour of dampness and mouldiness. I ate greedily without chewing, without looking and trying to discover what I was eating. I fancied that if I opened my eyes I should see glittering eyes, claws, and sharp teeth.

All at once I began biting something hard, there was a sound of a scrunching.

"Ha, ha! He is eating the shells," laughed the crowd. "Little silly, do you suppose you can eat that?"

After that I remember a terrible thirst. I was lying in my bed, and could not sleep for heartburn and the strange taste in my parched mouth. My father was walking up and down, gesticulating with his hands.

"I believe I have caught cold," he was muttering. "I've a feeling in my head as though someone were sitting on it.... Perhaps it is because I have not ... er ... eaten anything to-day.... I really am a queer, stupid creature.... I saw those gentlemen pay ten roubles for the oysters. Why didn't I go up to them and ask them ... to lend me something? They would have given something."

Towards morning, I fell asleep and dreamt of a frog sitting in a shell, moving its eyes. At midday I was awakened by thirst, and looked for my father: he was still walking up and down and gesticulating.

The Marshal's Widow

On the first of February every year, St. Trifon's day, there is an extraordinary commotion on the estate of Madame Zavzyatov, the widow of Trifon Lvovitch, the late marshal of the district. On that day, the nameday of the deceased marshal, the widow Lyubov Petrovna has a requiem service celebrated in his memory, and after the requiem a thanksgiving to the Lord. The whole district assembles for the service. There you will see Hrumov, the present marshal, Marfutkin, the president of the Zemstvo, Potrashkov, the permanent member of the Rural Board, the two justices of the peace of the district, the police captain, Krinolinov, two police-superintendents, the district doctor, Dvornyagin, smelling of iodoform, all the landowners, great and small, and so on. There are about fifty people assembled in all.

Precisely at twelve o'clock, the visitors, with long faces, make their way from all the rooms to the big hall. There are carpets on the floor and their steps are noiseless, but the solemnity of the occasion makes them instinctively walk on tip-toe, holding out their hands to balance themselves. In the hall everything is already prepared. Father Yevmeny, a little old man in a high faded cap, puts on his black vestments. Konkordiev, the deacon, already in his vestments, and as red as a crab, is noiselessly turning over the leaves of his missal and putting slips of paper in it. At the door leading to the vestibule, Luka, the sacristan, puffing out his cheeks and making round eyes, blows up the censer. The hall is gradually filled with bluish transparent smoke and the smell of incense.

Gelikonsky, the elementary schoolmaster, a young man with big pimples on his frightened face, wearing a new greatcoat like a sack, carries round wax candles on a silver-plated tray. The hostess, Lyubov Petrovna, stands in the front by a little table with a dish of funeral rice on it, and holds her handkerchief in readiness to her face. There is a profound stillness, broken from time to time by sighs. Everybody has a long, solemn face. . . .

The requiem service begins. The blue smoke curls up from the censer and plays in the slanting sunbeams, the lighted candles faintly splutter. The singing, at first harsh and deafening, soon becomes quiet and musical as the choir gradually adapt themselves to the acoustic conditions of the rooms. . . . The tunes are all mournful and sad. . . . The guests are gradually brought to a melancholy mood and grow pensive. Thoughts of the brevity of human life, of mutability, of worldly vanity stray through their brains. . . . They recall the deceased Zavzyatov, a thick-set, red-cheeked man who used to drink off a bottle of champagne at one gulp and smash looking-glasses with his forehead. And when they sing "With Thy Saints, O Lord," and the sobs of their hostess are audible, the guests shift uneasily from one foot to the other. The more emotional begin to feel a tickling in their throat and about their eyelids. Marfutkin, the president of the Zemstvo, to stifle the unpleasant feeling, bends down to the police captain's ear and whispers:

"I was at Ivan Fyodoritch's yesterday. . . . Pyotr Petrovitch and I took all the tricks, playing no trumps. . . . Yes, indeed. . . . Olga Andreyevna was so exasperated that her false tooth fell out of her mouth."

But at last the "Eternal Memory" is sung. Gelikonsky respectfully takes away the candles, and the memorial service is over. Thereupon there follows a momentary commotion; there is a changing of vestments and a thanksgiving service. After the thanksgiving, while Father Yevmeny is disrobing, the visitors rub their hands and cough, while their hostess tells some anecdote of the good-heartedness of the deceased Trifon Lvovitch.

"Pray come to lunch, friends," she says, concluding her story with a sigh.

The visitors, trying not to push or tread on each other's feet, hasten into the dining-room. . . . There the luncheon is awaiting them. The repast is so magnificent that the deacon Konkordiev thinks it his duty every year to fling up his hands as he looks at it and, shaking his head in amazement, say:

"Supernatural! It's not so much like human fare, Father Yevmeny, as offerings to the gods."

The lunch is certainly exceptional. Everything that the flora and fauna of the country can furnish is on the table, but the only thing supernatural about it, perhaps, is that on the table there is everything except . . . alcoholic beverages. Lyubov Petrovna has taken a vow never to have in her house cards or spirituous liquors—the two sources of her husband's ruin. And the only bottles contain oil and vinegar, as though in mockery and chastisement of the guests who are to a man desperately fond of the bottle, and given to tippling.

"Please help yourselves, gentlemen!" the marshal's widow presses them. "Only you must excuse me, I have no vodka. . . . I have none in the house. . . ."

The guests approach the table and hesitatingly attack the pie. But the progress with eating is slow. In the plying of forks, in the cutting up and munching, there is a certain sloth and apathy. . . . Evidently something is wanting.

"I feel as though I had lost something," one of the justices of the peace whispers to the other. "I feel as I did when my wife ran away with the engineer. . . . I can't eat."

Marfutkin, before beginning to eat, fumbles for a long time in his pocket and looks for his handkerchief.

"Oh, my handkerchief must be in my greatcoat," he recalls in a loud voice, "and here I am looking for it," and he goes into the vestibule where the fur coats are hanging up.

He returns from the vestibule with glistening eyes, and at once attacks the pie with relish.

"I say, it's horrid munching away with a dry mouth, isn't it?" he whispers to Father Yevmeny. "Go into the vestibule, Father. There's a bottle there in my fur coat. . . . Only mind you are careful; don't make a clatter with the bottle."

Father Yevmeny recollects that he has some direction to give to Luka, and trips off to the vestibule.

"Father, a couple of words in confidence," says Dvornyagin, overtaking him.

"You should see the fur coat I've bought myself, gentlemen," Hrumov boasts. "It's worth a thousand, and I gave . . . you won't believe it . . . two hundred and fifty! Not a farthing more."

At any other time the guests would have greeted this information with indifference, but now they display surprise and incredulity. In the end they all troop out into the vestibule to look at the fur coat, and go on looking at it till the doctor's man Mikeshka carries five empty bottles out on the sly. When the steamed sturgeon is served, Marfutkin remembers that he has left his cigar case in his sledge and goes to the stable. That he may not be lonely on this expedition, he takes with him the deacon, who appropriately feels it necessary to have a look at his horse. . . .

On the evening of the same day, Lyubov Petrovna is sitting in her study, writing a letter to an old friend in Petersburg:

"To-day, as in past years," she writes among other things, "I had a memorial service for my dear husband. All my neighbours came to the service. They are a simple, rough set, but what hearts! I gave them a splendid lunch, but of course, as in previous years, without a drop of alcoholic liquor. Ever since he died from excessive drinking I have vowed to establish temperance in this district and thereby to expiate his sins. I have begun the campaign for temperance at my own house. Father Yevmeny is delighted with my efforts, and helps me both in word and deed. Oh, *ma chère,* if you knew how fond my bears are of me! The president of the Zemstvo, Marfutkin, kissed my hand after lunch, held it a long while to his lips, and, wagging his head in an absurd way, burst into tears: so much feeling but no words! Father Yevmeny, that delightful little old man, sat down by me, and looking tearfully at me kept babbling something like a child. I did not understand what he said, but I know how to understand true feeling. The police captain, the handsome man of whom I wrote to you, went down on his knees to me, tried to read me some verses of his own composition (he is a poet), but . . . his feelings were too much for him, he lurched and fell over . . . that huge giant went into hysterics, you can imagine my delight! The day did not pass without a hitch, however. Poor Alalykin, the president of the judges' assembly, a stout and apoplectic man, was overcome by illness and lay on the sofa in a state of unconsciousness for two hours. We had to pour water on him. . . . I am thankful to Doctor Dvornyagin: he had brought a bottle of brandy from his dispensary and he moistened the patient's temples, which quickly revived him, and he was able to be moved. . . ."

The Fish

A summer morning. The air is still; there is no sound but the churring of a grasshopper on the river bank, and somewhere the timid cooing of a turtle-dove. Feathery clouds stand motionless in the sky, looking like snow scattered about. . . . Gerassim, the carpenter, a tall gaunt peasant, with a curly red head and a face overgrown with hair, is floundering about in the water under the green willow branches near an unfinished bathing shed. . . . He puffs and pants and, blinking furiously, is trying to get hold of something under the roots of the willows. His face is covered with perspiration. A couple of yards from him, Lubim, the carpenter, a young hunchback with a triangular face and narrow Chinese-looking eyes, is standing up to his neck in water. Both Gerassim and Lubim are in shirts and linen breeches. Both are blue with cold, for they have been more than an hour already in the water.

"But why do you keep poking with your hand?" cries the hunchback Lubim, shivering as though in a fever. "You blockhead! Hold him, hold him, or else he'll get away, the anathema! Hold him, I tell you!"

"He won't get away. . . . Where can he get to? He's under a root," says Gerassim in a hoarse, hollow bass, which seems to come not from his throat, but from the depths of his stomach. "He's slippery, the beggar, and there's nothing to catch hold of."

"Get him by the gills, by the gills!"

"There's no seeing his gills. . . . Stay, I've got hold of something. . . . I've got him by the lip. . . . He's biting, the brute!"

"Don't pull him out by the lip, don't—or you'll let him go! Take him by the gills, take him by the gills. . . . You've begun poking with your hand again! You are a senseless man, the Queen of Heaven forgive me! Catch hold!"

"Catch hold!" Gerassim mimics him. "You're a fine one to give orders. . . . You'd better come and catch hold of him yourself, you hunchback devil. . . . What are you standing there for?"

"I would catch hold of him if it were possible. But can I stand by the bank, and me as short as I am? It's deep there."

"It doesn't matter if it is deep. . . . You must swim."

The hunchback waves his arms, swims up to Gerassim, and catches hold of the twigs. At the first attempt to stand up, he goes into the water over his head and begins blowing up bubbles.

"I told you it was deep," he says, rolling his eyes angrily. "Am I to sit on your neck or what?"

"Stand on a root . . . there are a lot of roots like a ladder." The hunchback gropes for a root with his heel, and tightly gripping several twigs, stands on it. . . . Having got his balance, and established himself in his new position, he bends down, and trying not to get the water into his mouth, begins fumbling with his right hand among the roots. Getting entangled among the weeds and slipping on the mossy roots he finds his hand in contact with the sharp pincers of a crayfish.

"As though we wanted to see you, you demon!" says Lubim, and he angrily flings the crayfish on the bank.

At last his hand feels Gerassim's arm, and groping its way along it comes to something cold and slimy.

"Here he is!" says Lubim with a grin. "A fine fellow! Move your fingers, I'll get him directly . . . by the gills. Stop, don't prod me with your elbow. . . . I'll have him in a minute, in a minute, only let me get hold of him. . . . The beggar has got a long way under the roots, there is nothing to get hold of.... One can't get to the head ... one can only feel its belly.... Kill that gnat on my neck—it's stinging! I'll get him by the gills, directly.... Come to one side and give him a push! Poke him with your finger!"

The hunchback puffs out his cheeks, holds his breath, opens his eyes wide, and apparently has already got his fingers in the gills, but at that moment the twigs to which he is holding on with his left hand break, and losing his balance he plops into the water! Eddies race away from the bank as though frightened, and little bubbles come up from the spot where he has fallen in. The hunchback swims out and, snorting, clutches at the twigs.

"You'll be drowned next, you stupid, and I shall have to answer for you," wheezes Gerassim. "Clamber out, the devil take you! I'll get him out myself."

High words follow.... The sun is baking hot. The shadows begin to grow shorter and to draw in on themselves, like the horns of a snail.... The high grass warmed by the sun begins to give out a strong, heavy smell of honey. It will soon be midday, and Gerassim and Lubim are still floundering under the willow tree. The husky bass and the shrill, frozen tenor persistently disturb the stillness of the summer day.

"Pull him out by the gills, pull him out! Stay, I'll push him out! Where are you shoving your great ugly fist? Poke him with your finger—you pig's face! Get round by the side! get to the left, to the left, there's a big hole on the right! You'll be a supper for the water-devil! Pull it by the lip!"

There is the sound of the flick of a whip.... A herd of cattle, driven by Yefim, the shepherd, saunter lazily down the sloping bank to drink. The shepherd, a decrepit old man, with one eye and a crooked mouth, walks with his head bowed, looking at his feet. The first to reach the water are the sheep, then come the horses, and last of all the cows.

"Push him from below!" he hears Lubim's voice. "Stick your finger in! Are you deaf, fellow, or what? Tfoo!"

"What are you after, lads?" shouts Yefim.

"An eel-pout! We can't get him out! He's hidden under the roots. Get round to the side! To the side!"

For a minute Yefim screws up his eye at the fishermen, then he takes off his bark shoes, throws his sack off his shoulders, and takes off his shirt. He has not the patience to take off his breeches, but, making the sign of the cross, he steps into the water, holding out his thin dark arms to balance himself. . . . For fifty paces he walks along the slimy bottom, then he takes to swimming.

"Wait a minute, lads!" he shouts. "Wait! Don't be in a hurry to pull him out, you'll lose him. You must do it properly!"

Yefim joins the carpenters and all three, shoving each other with their knees and their elbows, puffing and swearing at one another, bustle about the same spot. Lubim, the hunchback, gets a mouthful of water, and the air rings with his hard spasmodic coughing.

"Where's the shepherd?" comes a shout from the bank. "Yefim! Shepherd! Where are you? The cattle are in the garden! Drive them out, drive them out of the garden! Where is he, the old brigand?"

First men's voices are heard, then a woman's. The master himself, Andrey Andreitch, wearing a dressing-gown made of a Persian shawl and carrying a newspaper in his hand, appears from behind the garden fence. He looks inquiringly towards the shouts which come from the river, and then trips rapidly towards the bathing shed.

"What's this? Who's shouting?" he asks sternly, seeing through the branches of the willow the three wet heads of the fishermen. "What are you so busy about there?"

"Catching a fish," mutters Yefim, without raising his head.

"I'll give it to you! The beasts are in the garden and he is fishing! . . . When will that bathing shed be done, you devils? You've been at work two days, and what is there to show for it?"

"It . . . will soon be done," grunts Gerassim; "summer is long, you'll have plenty of time to wash, your honour. . . . Pfrrr! . . . We can't manage this eel-pout here anyhow. . . . He's got under a root and sits there as if he were in a hole and won't budge one way or another. . . ."

"An eel-pout?" says the master, and his eyes begin to glisten. "Get him out quickly then."

"You'll give us half a rouble for it presently . . . if we oblige you. . . . A huge eel-pout, as fat as a merchant's wife. . . . It's worth half a rouble, your honour, for the trouble. . . . Don't squeeze him, Lubim, don't squeeze him, you'll spoil him! Push him up from below! Pull the root upwards, my good man . . . what's your name? Upwards, not down-wards, you brute! Don't swing your legs!"

Five minutes pass, ten. . . . The master loses all patience.

"Vassily!" he shouts, turning towards the garden. "Vaska! Call Vass-ily to me!"

The coachman Vassily runs up. He is chewing something and breathing hard.

"Go into the water," the master orders him. "Help them to pull out that eel-pout. They can't get him out."

Vassily rapidly undresses and gets into the water.

"In a minute. . . . I'll get him in a minute," he mutters. "Where's the eel-pout? We'll have him out in a trice! You'd better go, Yefim. An old man like you ought to be minding his own business instead of being here. Where's that eel-pout? I'll have him in a minute. . . . Here he is! Let go."

"What's the good of saying that? We know all about that! You get it out!"

"But there is no getting it out like this! One must get hold of it by the head."

"And the head is under the root! We know that, you fool!"

"Now then, don't talk or you'll catch it! You dirty cur!"

"Before the master to use such language," mutters Yefim. "You won't get him out, lads! He's fixed himself much too cleverly!"

"Wait a minute, I'll come directly," says the master, and he begins hurriedly undressing. "Four fools, and can't get an eel-pout!"

When he is undressed, Audrey Andreitch gives himself time to cool and gets into the water. But even his interference leads to nothing.

"We must chop the root off," Lubim decides at last. "Gerassim, go and get an axe! Give me an axe!"

"Don't chop your fingers off," says the master, when the blows of the axe on the root under water are heard. "Yefim, get out of this! Stay, I'll get the eel-pout. . . . You'll never do it."

The root is hacked a little. They partly break it off, and Andrey An-dreitch, to his immense satisfaction, feels his fingers under the gills of the fish.

"I'm pulling him out, lads! Don't crowd round . . . stand still. . . . I am pulling him out!"

The head of a big eel-pout, and behind it its long black body, nearly a yard long, appears on the surface of the water. The fish flaps its tail heavily and tries to tear itself away.

"None of your nonsense, my boy! Fiddlesticks! I've got you! Aha!"

A honied smile overspreads all the faces. A minute passes in silent contemplation.

"A famous eel-pout," mutters Yefim, scratching under his shoulder-blades. "I'll be bound it weighs ten pounds."

"Mm! . . . Yes," the master assents. "The liver is fairly swollen! It seems to stand out! A-ach!"

The fish makes a sudden, unexpected upward movement with its tail and the fishermen hear a loud splash . . . they all put out their hands, but it is too late; they have seen the last of the eel-pout.

The Huntsman

A sultry, stifling midday. Not a cloudlet in the sky.... The sun-baked grass had a disconsolate, hopeless look: even if there were rain it could never be green again.... The forest stood silent, motionless, as though it were looking at something with its tree-tops or expecting something.

At the edge of the clearing a tall, narrow-shouldered man of forty in a red shirt, in patched trousers that had been a gentleman's, and in high boots, was slouching along with a lazy, shambling step. He was sauntering along the road. On the right was the green of the clearing, on the left a golden sea of ripe rye stretched to the very horizon. He was red and perspiring, a white cap with a straight jockey peak, evidently a gift from some open-handed young gentleman, perched jauntily on his handsome flaxen head. Across his shoulder hung a game-bag with a blackcock lying in it. The man held a double-barrelled gun cocked in his hand, and screwed up his eyes in the direction of his lean old dog who was running on ahead sniffing the bushes. There was stillness all round, not a sound... everything living was hiding away from the heat.

"Yegor Vlassitch!" the huntsman suddenly heard a soft voice.

He started and, looking round, scowled. Beside him, as though she had sprung out of the earth, stood a pale-faced woman of thirty with a sickle in her hand. She was trying to look into his face, and was smiling diffidently.

"Oh, it is you, Pelagea!" said the huntsman, stopping and deliberately uncocking the gun. "H'm! . . . How have you come here?"

"The women from our village are working here, so I have come with them. . . . As a labourer, Yegor Vlassitch."

"Oh . . ." growled Yegor Vlassitch, and slowly walked on.

Pelagea followed him. They walked in silence for twenty paces.

"I have not seen you for a long time, Yegor Vlassitch . . ." said Pelagea looking tenderly at the huntsman's moving shoulders. "I have not seen you since you came into our hut at Easter for a drink of water . . . you came in at Easter for a minute and then God knows how . . . drunk . . . you scolded and beat me and went away . . . I have been waiting and waiting . . . I've tired my eyes out looking for you. Ah, Yegor Vlassitch, Yegor Vlassitch! you might look in just once!"

"What is there for me to do there?"

"Of course there is nothing for you to do . . . though to be sure . . . there is the place to look after. . . . To see how things are going. . . . You are the master. . . . I say, you have shot a blackcock, Yegor Vlassitch! You ought to sit down and rest!"

As she said all this Pelagea laughed like a silly girl and looked up at Yegor's face. Her face was simply radiant with happiness.

"Sit down? If you like . . ." said Yegor in a tone of indifference, and he chose a spot between two fir-trees. "Why are you standing? You sit down too."

Pelagea sat a little way off in the sun and, ashamed of her joy, put her hand over her smiling mouth. Two minutes passed in silence.

"You might come for once," said Pelagea.

"What for?" sighed Yegor, taking off his cap and wiping his red forehead with his hand. "There is no object in my coming. To go for an hour or two is only waste of time, it's simply upsetting you, and to live continually in the village my soul could not endure. . . . You know yourself I am a pampered man. . . . I want a bed to sleep in, good tea to drink, and refined conversation. . . . I want all the niceties, while you live in poverty and dirt in the village. . . . I couldn't stand it for a day.

Suppose there were an edict that I must live with you, I should either set fire to the hut or lay hands on myself. From a boy I've had this love for ease; there is no help for it."

"Where are you living now?"

"With the gentleman here, Dmitry Ivanitch, as a huntsman. I furnish his table with game, but he keeps me . . . more for his pleasure than anything."

"That's not proper work you're doing, Yegor Vlassitch. . . . For other people it's a pastime, but with you it's like a trade . . . like real work."

"You don't understand, you silly," said Yegor, gazing gloomily at the sky. "You have never understood, and as long as you live you will never understand what sort of man I am. . . . You think of me as a foolish man, gone to the bad, but to anyone who understands I am the best shot there is in the whole district. The gentry feel that, and they have even printed things about me in a magazine. There isn't a man to be compared with me as a sportsman. . . . And it is not because I am pampered and proud that I look down upon your village work. From my childhood, you know, I have never had any calling apart from guns and dogs. If they took away my gun, I used to go out with the fishing-hook, if they took the hook I caught things with my hands. And I went in for horse-dealing too, I used to go to the fairs when I had the money, and you know that if a peasant goes in for being a sportsman, or a horse-dealer, it's good-bye to the plough. Once the spirit of freedom has taken a man you will never root it out of him. In the same way, if a gentleman goes in for being an actor or for any other art, he will never make an official or a landowner. You are a woman, and you do not understand, but one must understand that."

"I understand, Yegor Vlassitch."

"You don't understand if you are going to cry. . . ."

"I . . . I'm not crying," said Pelagea, turning away. "It's a sin, Yegor Vlassitch! You might stay a day with luckless me, anyway. It's twelve years since I was married to you, and . . . and . . . there has never once been love between us! . . . I . . . I am not crying."

"Love . . ." muttered Yegor, scratching his hand. "There can't be any love. It's only in name we are husband and wife; we aren't really. In your eyes I am a wild man, and in mine you are a simple peasant woman with no understanding. Are we well matched? I am a free, pampered, profligate man, while you are a working woman, going in bark shoes and never straightening your back. The way I think of myself is that I am the foremost man in every kind of sport, and you look at me with pity. . . . Is that being well matched?"

"But we are married, you know, Yegor Vlassitch," sobbed Pelagea.

"Not married of our free will. . . . Have you forgotten? You have to thank Count Sergey Pavlovitch and yourself. Out of envy, because I shot better than he did, the Count kept giving me wine for a whole month, and when a man's drunk you could make him change his religion, let alone getting married. To pay me out he married me to you when I was drunk. . . . A huntsman to a herd-girl! You saw I was drunk, why did you marry me? You were not a serf, you know; you could have resisted. Of course it was a bit of luck for a herd-girl to marry a huntsman, but you ought to have thought about it. Well, now be miserable, cry. It's a joke for the Count, but a crying matter for you. . . . Beat yourself against the wall."

A silence followed. Three wild ducks flew over the clearing. Yegor followed them with his eyes till, transformed into three scarcely visible dots, they sank down far beyond the forest.

"How do you live?" he asked, moving his eyes from the ducks to Pelagea.

"Now I am going out to work, and in the winter I take a child from the Foundling Hospital and bring it up on the bottle. They give me a rouble and a half a month."

"Oh. . . ."

Again a silence. From the strip that had been reaped floated a soft song which broke off at the very beginning. It was too hot to sing.

"They say you have put up a new hut for Akulina," said Pelagea.

Yegor did not speak.

"So she is dear to you. . . ."

"It's your luck, it's fate!" said the huntsman, stretching. "You must put up with it, poor thing. But good-bye, I've been chattering long enough. . . . I must be at Boltovo by the evening."

Yegor rose, stretched himself, and slung his gun over his shoulder; Pelagea got up.

"And when are you coming to the village?" she asked softly.

"I have no reason to, I shall never come sober, and you have little to gain from me drunk; I am spiteful when I am drunk. Good-bye!"

"Good-bye, Yegor Vlassitch."

Yegor put his cap on the back of his head and, clicking to his dog, went on his way. Pelagea stood still looking after him. . . . She saw his moving shoulder-blades, his jaunty cap, his lazy, careless step, and her eyes were full of sadness and tender affection. . . . Her gaze flitted over her husband's tall, lean figure and caressed and fondled it. . . . He, as though he felt that gaze, stopped and looked round. . . . He did not speak, but from his face, from his shrugged shoulders, Pelagea could see that he wanted to say something to her. She went up to him timidly and looked at him with imploring eyes.

"Take it," he said, turning round.

He gave her a crumpled rouble note and walked quickly away.

"Good-bye, Yegor Vlassitch," she said, mechanically taking the rouble.

He walked by a long road, straight as a taut strap. She, pale and motionless as a statue, stood, her eyes seizing every step he took. But the red of his shirt melted into the dark colour of his trousers, his step could not be seen, and the dog could not be distinguished from the boots. Nothing could be seen but the cap, and . . . suddenly Yegor turned off sharply into the clearing and the cap vanished in the greenness.

"Good-bye, Yegor Vlassitch," whispered Pelagea, and she stood on tiptoe to see the white cap once more.

A Malefactor

An exceedingly lean little peasant, in a striped hempen shirt and patched drawers, stands facing the investigating magistrate. His face overgrown with hair and pitted with smallpox, and his eyes scarcely visible under thick, overhanging eyebrows have an expression of sullen moroseness. On his head there is a perfect mop of tangled, unkempt hair, which gives him an even more spider-like air of moroseness. He is barefooted.

"Denis Grigoryev!" the magistrate begins. "Come nearer, and answer my questions. On the seventh of this July the railway watchman, Ivan Semyonovitch Akinfov, going along the line in the morning, found you at the hundred-and-forty-first mile engaged in unscrewing a nut by which the rails are made fast to the sleepers. Here it is, the nut! . . . With the aforesaid nut he detained you. Was that so?"

"Wha-at?"

"Was this all as Akinfov states?"

"To be sure, it was."

"Very good; well, what were you unscrewing the nut for?"

"Wha-at?"

"Drop that 'wha-at' and answer the question; what were you unscrewing the nut for?"

"If I hadn't wanted it I shouldn't have unscrewed it," croaks Denis, looking at the ceiling.

"What did you want that nut for?"

"The nut? We make weights out of those nuts for our lines."

"Who is 'we'?"

"We, people.... The Klimovo peasants, that is."

"Listen, my man; don't play the idiot to me, but speak sensibly. It's no use telling lies here about weights!"

"I've never been a liar from a child, and now I'm telling lies..." mutters Denis, blinking. "But can you do without a weight, your honour? If you put live bait or maggots on a hook, would it go to the bottom without a weight?... I am telling lies," grins Denis.... "What the devil is the use of the worm if it swims on the surface! The perch and the pike and the eel-pout always go to the bottom, and a bait on the surface is only taken by a shillisper, not very often then, and there are no shillispers in our river.... That fish likes plenty of room."

"Why are you telling me about shillispers?"

"Wha-at? Why, you asked me yourself! The gentry catch fish that way too in our parts. The silliest little boy would not try to catch a fish without a weight. Of course anyone who did not understand might go to fish without a weight. There is no rule for a fool."

"So you say you unscrewed this nut to make a weight for your fishing line out of it?"

"What else for? It wasn't to play knuckle-bones with!"

"But you might have taken lead, a bullet... a nail of some sort...."

"You don't pick up lead in the road, you have to buy it, and a nail's no good. You can't find anything better than a nut.... It's heavy, and there's a hole in it."

"He keeps pretending to be a fool! as though he'd been born yesterday or dropped from heaven! Don't you understand, you blockhead, what unscrewing these nuts leads to? If the watchman had not noticed it the train might have run off the rails, people would have been killed—you would have killed people."

"God forbid, your honour! What should I kill them for? Are we heathens or wicked people? Thank God, good gentlemen, we have lived all our lives without ever dreaming of such a thing. . . . Save, and have mercy on us, Queen of Heaven! . . . What are you saying?"

"And what do you suppose railway accidents do come from? Unscrew two or three nuts and you have an accident."

Denis grins, and screws up his eye at the magistrate incredulously.

"Why! how many years have we all in the village been unscrewing nuts, and the Lord has been merciful; and you talk of accidents, killing people. If I had carried away a rail or put a log across the line, say, then maybe it might have upset the train, but . . . pouf! a nut!"

"But you must understand that the nut holds the rail fast to the sleepers!"

"We understand that. . . . We don't unscrew them all . . . we leave some. . . . We don't do it thoughtlessly . . . we understand. . . ."

Denis yawns and makes the sign of the cross over his mouth.

"Last year the train went off the rails here," says the magistrate. "Now I see why!"

"What do you say, your honour?"

"I am telling you that now I see why the train went off the rails last year. . . . I understand!"

"That's what you are educated people for, to understand, you kind gentlemen. The Lord knows to whom to give understanding. . . . Here you have reasoned how and what, but the watchman, a peasant like ourselves, with no understanding at all, catches one by the collar and hauls one along. . . . You should reason first and then haul me off. It's a saying that a peasant has a peasant's wit. . . . Write down, too, your honour, that he hit me twice—in the jaw and in the chest."

"When your hut was searched they found another nut. . . . At what spot did you unscrew that, and when?"

"You mean the nut which lay under the red box?"

"I don't know where it was lying, only it was found. When did you unscrew it?"

"I didn't unscrew it; Ignashka, the son of one-eyed Semyon, gave it me. I mean the one which was under the box, but the one which was in the sledge in the yard Mitrofan and I unscrewed together."

"What Mitrofan?"

"Mitrofan Petrov.... Haven't you heard of him? He makes nets in our village and sells them to the gentry. He needs a lot of those nuts. Reckon a matter of ten for each net."

"Listen. Article 1081 of the Penal Code lays down that every wilful damage of the railway line committed when it can expose the traffic on that line to danger, and the guilty party knows that an accident must be caused by it . . . (Do you understand? Knows! And you could not help knowing what this unscrewing would lead to . . .) is liable to penal servitude."

"Of course, you know best.... We are ignorant people.... What do we understand?"

"You understand all about it! You are lying, shamming!"

"What should I lie for? Ask in the village if you don't believe me. Only a bleak is caught without a weight, and there is no fish worse than a gudgeon, yet even that won't bite without a weight."

"You'd better tell me about the shillisper next," said the magistrate, smiling.

"There are no shillispers in our parts.... We cast our line without a weight on the top of the water with a butterfly; a mullet may be caught that way, though that is not often."

"Come, hold your tongue."

A silence follows. Denis shifts from one foot to the other, looks at the table with the green cloth on it, and blinks his eyes violently as though what was before him was not the cloth but the sun. The magistrate writes rapidly.

"Can I go?" asks Denis after a long silence.

"No. I must take you under guard and send you to prison."

Denis leaves off blinking and, raising his thick eyebrows, looks inquiringly at the magistrate.

"How do you mean, to prison? Your honour! I have no time to spare, I must go to the fair; I must get three roubles from Yegor for some tallow! . . ."

"Hold your tongue; don't interrupt."

"To prison.... If there was something to go for, I'd go; but just to go for nothing! What for? I haven't stolen anything, I believe, and I've not been fighting.... If you are in doubt about the arrears, your honour, don't believe the elder.... You ask the agent ... he's a regular heathen, the elder, you know."

"Hold your tongue."

"I am holding my tongue, as it is," mutters Denis; "but that the elder has lied over the account, I'll take my oath for it.... There are three of us brothers: Kuzma Grigoryev, then Yegor Grigoryev, and me, Denis Grigoryev."

"You are hindering me.... Hey, Semyon," cries the magistrate, "take him away!"

"There are three of us brothers," mutters Denis, as two stalwart soldiers take him and lead him out of the room. "A brother is not responsible for a brother. Kuzma does not pay, so you, Denis, must answer for it.... Judges indeed! Our master the general is dead—the Kingdom of Heaven be his—or he would have shown you judges.... You ought to judge sensibly, not at random.... Flog if you like, but flog someone who deserves it, flog with conscience."

The Head of the Family

It is, as a rule, after losing heavily at cards or after a drinking-bout when an attack of dyspepsia is setting in that Stepan Stepanitch Zhilin wakes up in an exceptionally gloomy frame of mind. He looks sour, rumpled, and dishevelled; there is an expression of displeasure on his grey face, as though he were offended or disgusted by something. He dresses slowly, sips his Vichy water deliberately, and begins walking about the rooms.

"I should like to know what b-b-beast comes in here and does not shut the door!" he grumbles angrily, wrapping his dressing-gown about him and spitting loudly. "Take away that paper! Why is it lying about here? We keep twenty servants, and the place is more untidy than a pot-house. Who was that ringing? Who the devil is that?"

"That's Anfissa, the midwife who brought our Fedya into the world," answers his wife.

"Always hanging about . . . these cadging toadies!"

"There's no making you out, Stepan Stepanitch. You asked her yourself, and now you scold."

"I am not scolding; I am speaking. You might find something to do, my dear, instead of sitting with your hands in your lap trying to pick a quarrel. Upon my word, women are beyond my comprehension! Beyond my comprehension! How can they waste whole days doing nothing? A man works like an ox, like a b-beast, while his wife, the partner of his life, sits like a pretty doll, sits and does nothing but watch for an opportunity to quarrel with her husband by way of diversion. It's time to drop these schoolgirlish ways, my dear. You are not a schoolgirl, not a young lady; you are a wife and mother! You turn away? Aha! It's not agreeable to listen to the bitter truth!"

"It's strange that you only speak the bitter truth when your liver is out of order."

"That's right; get up a scene."

"Have you been out late? Or playing cards?"

"What if I have? Is that anybody's business? Am I obliged to give an account of my doings to any one? It's my own money I lose, I suppose? What I spend as well as what is spent in this house belongs to me—me. Do you hear? To me!"

And so on, all in the same style. But at no other time is Stepan Stepanitch so reasonable, virtuous, stern or just as at dinner, when all his household are sitting about him. It usually begins with the soup. After swallowing the first spoonful Zhilin suddenly frowns and puts down his spoon.

"Damn it all!" he mutters; "I shall have to dine at a restaurant, I suppose."

"What's wrong?" asks his wife anxiously. "Isn't the soup good?"

"One must have the taste of a pig to eat hogwash like that! There's too much salt in it; it smells of dirty rags . . . more like bugs than onions. . . . It's simply revolting, Anfissa Ivanovna," he says, addressing the midwife. "Every day I give no end of money for housekeeping. . . . I deny myself everything, and this is what they provide for my dinner! I suppose they want me to give up the office and go into the kitchen to do the cooking myself."

"The soup is very good to-day," the governess ventures timidly.

"Oh, you think so?" says Zhilin, looking at her angrily from under his eyelids. "Every one to his taste, of course. It must be confessed our tastes are very different, Varvara Vassilyevna. You, for instance, are satisfied with the behaviour of this boy" (Zhilin with a tragic gesture points to his son Fedya); "you are delighted with him, while I . . . I am disgusted. Yes!"

Fedya, a boy of seven with a pale, sickly face, leaves off eating and drops his eyes. His face grows paler still.

"Yes, you are delighted, and I am disgusted. Which of us is right, I cannot say, but I venture to think as his father, I know my own son better than you do. Look how he is sitting! Is that the way decently brought up children sit? Sit properly."

Fedya tilts his chin up, cranes his neck, and fancies that he is holding himself better. Tears come into his eyes.

"Eat your dinner! Hold your spoon properly! You wait. I'll show you, you horrid boy! Don't dare to whimper! Look straight at me!"

Fedya tries to look straight at him, but his face is quivering and his eyes fill with tears.

"A-ah! . . . you cry? You are naughty and then you cry? Go and stand in the corner, you beast!"

"But . . . let him have his dinner first," his wife intervenes.

"No dinner for him! Such bla . . . such rascals don't deserve dinner!"

Fedya, wincing and quivering all over, creeps down from his chair and goes into the corner.

"You won't get off with that!" his parent persists. "If nobody else cares to look after your bringing up, so be it; I must begin. . . . I won't let you be naughty and cry at dinner, my lad! Idiot! You must do your duty! Do you understand? Do your duty! Your father works and you must work, too! No one must eat the bread of idleness! You must be a man! A m-man!"

"For God's sake, leave off," says his wife in French. "Don't nag at us before outsiders, at least. . . . The old woman is all ears; and now, thanks to her, all the town will hear of it."

"I am not afraid of outsiders," answers Zhilin in Russian. "Anfissa Ivanovna sees that I am speaking the truth. Why, do you think I ought to be pleased with the boy? Do you know what he costs me? Do you know, you nasty boy, what you cost me? Or do you imagine that I coin money, that I get it for nothing? Don't howl! Hold your tongue!

Do you hear what I say? Do you want me to whip you, you young ruffian?"

Fedya wails aloud and begins to sob.

"This is insufferable," says his mother, getting up from the table and flinging down her dinner-napkin. "You never let us have dinner in peace! Your bread sticks in my throat."

And putting her handkerchief to her eyes, she walks out of the dining-room.

"Now she is offended," grumbles Zhilin, with a forced smile. "She's been spoilt. . . . That's how it is, Anfissa Ivanovna; no one likes to hear the truth nowadays. . . . It's all my fault, it seems."

Several minutes of silence follow. Zhilin looks round at the plates, and noticing that no one has yet touched their soup, heaves a deep sigh, and stares at the flushed and uneasy face of the governess.

"Why don't you eat, Varvara Vassilyevna?" he asks. "Offended, I suppose? I see. . . . You don't like to be told the truth. You must forgive me, it's my nature; I can't be a hypocrite. . . . I always blurt out the plain truth" (a sigh). "But I notice that my presence is unwelcome. No one can eat or talk while I am here. . . . Well, you should have told me, and I would have gone away. . . . I will go."

Zhilin gets up and walks with dignity to the door. As he passes the weeping Fedya he stops.

"After all that has passed here, you are free," he says to Fedya, throwing back his head with dignity. "I won't meddle in your bringing up again. I wash my hands of it! I humbly apologise that as a father, from a sincere desire for your welfare, I have disturbed you and your mentors. At the same time, once for all I disclaim all responsibility for your future. . . ."

Fedya wails and sobs more loudly than ever. Zhilin turns with dignity to the door and departs to his bedroom.

When he wakes from his after-dinner nap he begins to feel the stings of conscience. He is ashamed to face his wife, his son, Anfissa Ivanovna, and even feels very wretched when he recalls the scene at dinner, but his amour-propre is too much for him; he has not the manliness to be frank, and he goes on sulking and grumbling.

Waking up next morning, he feels in excellent spirits, and whistles gaily as he washes. Going into the dining-room to breakfast, he finds there Fedya, who, at the sight of his father, gets up and looks at him helplessly.

"Well, young man?" Zhilin greets him good-humouredly, sitting down to the table. "What have you got to tell me, young man? Are you all right? Well, come, chubby; give your father a kiss."

With a pale, grave face Fedya goes up to his father and touches his cheek with his quivering lips, then walks away and sits down in his place without a word.

A Dead Body

A still August night. A mist is rising slowly from the fields and casting an opaque veil over everything within eyesight. Lighted up by the moon, the mist gives the impression at one moment of a calm, boundless sea, at the next of an immense white wall. The air is damp and chilly. Morning is still far off. A step from the bye-road which runs along the edge of the forest a little fire is gleaming. A dead body, covered from head to foot with new white linen, is lying under a young oak-tree. A wooden ikon is lying on its breast. Beside the corpse almost on the road sits the "watch"—two peasants performing one of the most disagreeable and uninviting of peasants' duties. One, a tall young fellow with a scarcely perceptible moustache and thick black eyebrows, in a tattered sheepskin and bark shoes, is sitting on the wet grass, his feet stuck out straight in front of him, and is trying to while away the time with work. He bends his long neck, and breathing loudly through his nose, makes a spoon out of a big crooked bit of wood; the other—a little scraggy, pock-marked peasant with an aged face, a scanty moustache, and a little goat's beard—sits with his hands dangling loose on his knees, and without moving gazes listlessly at the light. A small camp-fire is lazily burning down between them, throwing a red glow on their faces. There is perfect stillness. The only sounds are the scrape of the knife on the wood and the crackling of damp sticks in the fire.

"Don't you go to sleep, Syoma . . ." says the young man.

"I . . . I am not asleep . . ." stammers the goat-beard.

"That's all right. . . . It would be dreadful to sit here alone, one would be frightened. You might tell me something, Syoma."

"I . . . I can't. . . ."

"You are a queer fellow, Syomushka! Other people will laugh and tell a story and sing a song, but you—there is no making you out. You sit like a scarecrow in the garden and roll your eyes at the fire. You can't say anything properly . . . when you speak you seem frightened. I dare say you are fifty, but you have less sense than a child. . . . Aren't you sorry that you are a simpleton?"

"I am sorry," the goat-beard answers gloomily.

"And we are sorry to see your foolishness, you may be sure. You are a good-natured, sober peasant, and the only trouble is that you have no sense in your head. You should have picked up some sense for yourself if the Lord has afflicted you and given you no understanding. You must make an effort, Syoma. . . . You should listen hard when anything good's being said, note it well, and keep thinking and thinking. . . . If there is any word you don't understand, you should make an effort and think over in your head in what meaning the word is used. Do you see? Make an effort! If you don't gain some sense for yourself you'll be a simpleton and of no account at all to your dying day."

All at once a long drawn-out, moaning sound is heard in the forest. Something rustles in the leaves as though torn from the very top of the tree and falls to the ground. All this is faintly repeated by the echo. The young man shudders and looks enquiringly at his companion.

"It's an owl at the little birds," says Syoma, gloomily.

"Why, Syoma, it's time for the birds to fly to the warm countries!"

"To be sure, it is time."

"It is chilly at dawn now. It is co-old. The crane is a chilly creature, it is tender. Such cold is death to it. I am not a crane, but I am frozen. . . . Put some more wood on!"

Syoma gets up and disappears in the dark undergrowth. While he is busy among the bushes, breaking dry twigs, his companion puts his hand over his eyes and starts at every sound. Syoma brings an armful of wood and lays it on the fire. The flame irresolutely licks the black twigs with its little tongues, then suddenly, as though at the word of command, catches them and throws a crimson light on the faces, the road, the white linen with its prominences where the hands and feet of the corpse raise it, the ikon. The "watch" is silent. The young man bends his neck still lower and sets to work with still more nervous haste. The goat-beard sits motionless as before and keeps his eyes fixed on the fire....

"Ye that love not Zion . . . shall be put to shame by the Lord." A falsetto voice is suddenly heard singing in the stillness of the night, then slow footsteps are audible, and the dark figure of a man in a short monkish cassock and a broad-brimmed hat, with a wallet on his shoulders, comes into sight on the road in the crimson firelight.

"Thy will be done, O Lord! Holy Mother!" the figure says in a husky falsetto. "I saw the fire in the outer darkness and my soul leapt for joy. . . . At first I thought it was men grazing a drove of horses, then I thought it can't be that, since no horses were to be seen. 'Aren't they thieves,' I wondered, 'aren't they robbers lying in wait for a rich Lazarus? Aren't they the gypsy people offering sacrifices to idols? And my soul leapt for joy. 'Go, Feodosy, servant of God,' I said to myself, 'and win a martyr's crown!' And I flew to the fire like a light-winged moth. Now I stand before you, and from your outer aspect I judge of your souls: you are not thieves and you are not heathens. Peace be to you!"

"Good-evening."

"Good orthodox people, do you know how to reach the Makuhinsky Brickyards from here?"

"It's close here. You go straight along the road; when you have gone a mile and a half there will be Ananova, our village. From the village, father, you turn to the right by the river-bank, and so you will get to the brickyards. It's two miles from Ananova."

"God give you health. And why are you sitting here?"

"We are sitting here watching. You see, there is a dead body...."

"What? what body? Holy Mother!"

The pilgrim sees the white linen with the ikon on it, and starts so violently that his legs give a little skip. This unexpected sight has an overpowering effect upon him. He huddles together and stands as though rooted to the spot, with wide-open mouth and staring eyes. For three minutes he is silent as though he could not believe his eyes, then begins muttering:

"O Lord! Holy Mother! I was going along not meddling with anyone, and all at once such an affliction."

"What may you be?" enquires the young man. "Of the clergy?"

"No ... no.... I go from one monastery to another.... Do you know Mi ... Mihail Polikarpitch, the foreman of the brickyard? Well, I am his nephew.... Thy will be done, O Lord! Why are you here?"

"We are watching ... we are told to."

"Yes, yes ..." mutters the man in the cassock, passing his hand over his eyes. "And where did the deceased come from?"

"He was a stranger."

"Such is life! But I'll ... er ... be getting on, brothers.... I feel flustered. I am more afraid of the dead than of anything, my dear souls! And only fancy! while this man was alive he wasn't noticed, while now when he is dead and given over to corruption we tremble before him as before some famous general or a bishop.... Such is life; was he murdered, or what?"

"The Lord knows! Maybe he was murdered, or maybe he died of himself."

"Yes, yes.... Who knows, brothers? Maybe his soul is now tasting the joys of Paradise."

"His soul is still hovering here, near his body," says the young man. "It does not depart from the body for three days."

"H'm, yes!... How chilly the nights are now! It sets one's teeth chattering.... So then I am to go straight on and on? ..."

"Till you get to the village, and then you turn to the right by the river-bank."

"By the river-bank.... To be sure.... Why am I standing still? I must go on. Farewell, brothers."

The man in the cassock takes five steps along the road and stops.

"I've forgotten to put a kopeck for the burying," he says. "Good orthodox friends, can I give the money?"

"You ought to know best, you go the round of the monasteries. If he died a natural death it would go for the good of his soul; if it's a suicide it's a sin."

"That's true. . . . And maybe it really was a suicide! So I had better keep my money. Oh, sins, sins! Give me a thousand roubles and I would not consent to sit here. . . . Farewell, brothers."

The cassock slowly moves away and stops again.

"I can't make up my mind what I am to do," he mutters. "To stay here by the fire and wait till daybreak. . . . I am frightened; to go on is dreadful, too. The dead man will haunt me all the way in the darkness. . . . The Lord has chastised me indeed! Over three hundred miles I have come on foot and nothing happened, and now I am near home and there's trouble. I can't go on. . . ."

"It is dreadful, that is true."

"I am not afraid of wolves, of thieves, or of darkness, but I am afraid of the dead. I am afraid of them, and that is all about it. Good orthodox brothers, I entreat you on my knees, see me to the village."

"We've been told not to go away from the body."

"No one will see, brothers. Upon my soul, no one will see! The Lord will reward you a hundred-fold! Old man, come with me, I beg! Old man! Why are you silent?"

"He is a bit simple," says the young man.

"You come with me, friend; I will give you five kopecks."

"For five kopecks I might," says the young man, scratching his head, "but I was told not to. If Syoma here, our simpleton, will stay alone, I will take you. Syoma, will you stay here alone?"

"I'll stay," the simpleton consents.

"Well, that's all right, then. Come along!"

The young man gets up, and goes with the cassock. A minute later the sound of their steps and their talk dies away. Syoma shuts his eyes and gently dozes. The fire begins to grow dim, and a big black shadow falls on the dead body.

The Cook's Wedding

Grisha, a fat, solemn little person of seven, was standing by the kitchen door listening and peeping through the keyhole. In the kitchen something extraordinary, and in his opinion never seen before, was taking place. A big, thick-set, red-haired peasant, with a beard, and a drop of perspiration on his nose, wearing a cabman's full coat, was sitting at the kitchen table on which they chopped the meat and sliced the onions. He was balancing a saucer on the five fingers of his right hand and drinking tea out of it, and crunching sugar so loudly that it sent a shiver down Grisha's back. Aksinya Stepanovna, the old nurse, was sitting on the dirty stool facing him, and she, too, was drinking tea. Her face was grave, though at the same time it beamed with a kind of triumph. Pelageya, the cook, was busy at the stove, and was apparently trying to hide her face. And on her face Grisha saw a regular illumination: it was burning and shifting through every shade of colour, beginning with a crimson purple and ending with a deathly white. She was continually catching hold of knives, forks, bits of wood, and rags with trembling hands, moving, grumbling to herself, making a clatter, but in reality doing nothing. She did not once glance at the table at which they were drinking tea, and to the questions put to her by the nurse she gave jerky, sullen answers without turning her face.

"Help yourself, Danilo Semyonitch," the nurse urged him hospitably. "Why do you keep on with tea and nothing but tea? You should have a drop of vodka!"

And nurse put before the visitor a bottle of vodka and a wine-glass, while her face wore a very wily expression.

"I never touch it. . . . No . . ." said the cabman, declining. "Don't press me, Aksinya Stepanovna."

"What a man! . . . A cabman and not drink! . . . A bachelor can't get on without drinking. Help yourself!"

The cabman looked askance at the bottle, then at nurse's wily face, and his own face assumed an expression no less cunning, as much as to say, "You won't catch me, you old witch!"

"I don't drink; please excuse me. Such a weakness does not do in our calling. A man who works at a trade may drink, for he sits at home, but we cabmen are always in view of the public. Aren't we? If one goes into a pothouse one finds one's horse gone; if one takes a drop too much it is worse still; before you know where you are you will fall asleep or slip off the box. That's where it is."

"And how much do you make a day, Danilo Semyonitch?"

"That's according. One day you will have a fare for three roubles, and another day you will come back to the yard without a farthing. The days are very different. Nowadays our business is no good. There are lots and lots of cabmen as you know, hay is dear, and folks are paltry nowadays and always contriving to go by tram. And yet, thank God, I have nothing to complain of. I have plenty to eat and good clothes to wear, and . . . we could even provide well for another . . ." (the cabman stole a glance at Pelageya) "if it were to their liking. . . ."

Grisha did not hear what was said further. His mamma came to the door and sent him to the nursery to learn his lessons.

"Go and learn your lesson. It's not your business to listen here!"

When Grisha reached the nursery, he put "My Own Book" in front of him, but he did not get on with his reading. All that he had just seen and heard aroused a multitude of questions in his mind.

"The cook's going to be married," he thought. "Strange—I don't understand what people get married for. Mamma was married to papa, Cousin Verotchka to Pavel Andreyitch. But one might be married to papa and Pavel Andreyitch after all: they have gold watch-chains and nice suits, their boots are always polished; but to marry that dreadful cabman with a red nose and felt boots. . . . Fi! And why is it nurse wants poor Pelageya to be married?"

When the visitor had gone out of the kitchen, Pelageya appeared and began clearing away. Her agitation still persisted. Her face was red and looked scared. She scarcely touched the floor with the broom, and swept every corner five times over. She lingered for a long time in the room where mamma was sitting. She was evidently oppressed by her isolation, and she was longing to express herself, to share her impressions with some one, to open her heart.

"He's gone," she muttered, seeing that mamma would not begin the conversation.

"One can see he is a good man," said mamma, not taking her eyes off her sewing. "Sober and steady."

"I declare I won't marry him, mistress!" Pelageya cried suddenly, flushing crimson. "I declare I won't!"

"Don't be silly; you are not a child. It's a serious step; you must think it over thoroughly, it's no use talking nonsense. Do you like him?"

"What an idea, mistress!" cried Pelageya, abashed. "They say such things that . . . my goodness. . . ."

"She should say she doesn't like him!" thought Grisha.

"What an affected creature you are. . . . Do you like him?"

"But he is old, mistress!"

"Think of something else," nurse flew out at her from the next room. "He has not reached his fortieth year; and what do you want a young man for? Handsome is as handsome does. . . . Marry him and that's all about it!"

"I swear I won't," squealed Pelageya.

"You are talking nonsense. What sort of rascal do you want? Anyone else would have bowed down to his feet, and you declare you won't marry him. You want to be always winking at the postmen and tutors. That tutor that used to come to Grishenka, mistress . . . she was never tired of making eyes at him. O-o, the shameless hussy!"

"Have you seen this Danilo before?" mamma asked Pelageya.

"How could I have seen him? I set eyes on him to-day for the first time. Aksinya picked him up and brought him along . . . the accursed devil. . . . And where has he come from for my undoing!"

At dinner, when Pelageya was handing the dishes, everyone looked into her face and teased her about the cabman. She turned fearfully red, and went off into a forced giggle.

"It must be shameful to get married," thought Grisha. "Terribly shameful."

All the dishes were too salt, and blood oozed from the half-raw chickens, and, to cap it all, plates and knives kept dropping out of Pelageya's hands during dinner, as though from a shelf that had given way; but no one said a word of blame to her, as they all understood the state of her feelings. Only once papa flicked his table-napkin angrily and said to mamma:

"What do you want to be getting them all married for? What business is it of yours? Let them get married of themselves if they want to."

After dinner, neighbouring cooks and maid-servants kept flitting into the kitchen, and there was the sound of whispering till late evening. How they had scented out the matchmaking, God knows. When Grisha woke in the night he heard his nurse and the cook whispering together in the nursery. Nurse was talking persuasively, while the cook alternately sobbed and giggled. When he fell asleep after this, Grisha dreamed of Pelageya being carried off by Tchernomor and a witch.

Next day there was a calm. The life of the kitchen went on its accustomed way as though the cabman did not exist. Only from time to time nurse put on her new shawl, assumed a solemn and austere air, and went off somewhere for an hour or two, obviously to conduct negotiations. . . . Pelageya did not see the cabman, and when his name was mentioned she flushed up and cried:

"May he be thrice damned! As though I should be thinking of him! Tfoo!"

In the evening mamma went into the kitchen, while nurse and Pelageya were zealously mincing something, and said:

"You can marry him, of course—that's your business—but I must tell you, Pelageya, that he cannot live here. . . . You know I don't like to have anyone sitting in the kitchen. Mind now, remember. . . . And I can't let you sleep out."

"Goodness knows! What an idea, mistress!" shrieked the cook. "Why do you keep throwing him up at me? Plague take him! He's a regular curse, confound him!..."

Glancing one Sunday morning into the kitchen, Grisha was struck dumb with amazement. The kitchen was crammed full of people. Here were cooks from the whole courtyard, the porter, two policemen, a non-commissioned officer with good-conduct stripes, and the boy Filka.... This Filka was generally hanging about the laundry playing with the dogs; now he was combed and washed, and was holding an ikon in a tinfoil setting. Pelageya was standing in the middle of the kitchen in a new cotton dress, with a flower on her head. Beside her stood the cabman. The happy pair were red in the face and perspiring and blinking with embarrassment.

"Well...I fancy it is time," said the non-commissioned officer, after a prolonged silence.

Pelageya's face worked all over and she began blubbering....

The soldier took a big loaf from the table, stood beside nurse, and began blessing the couple. The cabman went up to the soldier, flopped down on his knees, and gave a smacking kiss on his hand. He did the same before nurse. Pelageya followed him mechanically, and she too bowed down to the ground. At last the outer door was opened, there was a whiff of white mist, and the whole party flocked noisily out of the kitchen into the yard.

"Poor thing, poor thing," thought Grisha, hearing the sobs of the cook. "Where have they taken her? Why don't papa and mamma protect her?"

After the wedding there was singing and concertina-playing in the laundry till late evening. Mamma was cross all the evening because nurse smelt of vodka, and owing to the wedding there was no one to heat the samovar. Pelageya had not come back by the time Grisha went to bed.

"The poor thing is crying somewhere in the dark!" he thought. "While the cabman is saying to her 'shut up!'"

Next morning the cook was in the kitchen again. The cabman came in for a minute. He thanked mamma, and glancing sternly at Pelageya, said:

"Will you look after her, madam? Be a father and a mother to her. And you, too, Aksinya Stepanovna, do not forsake her, see that everything is as it should be ... without any nonsense. ... And also, madam, if you would kindly advance me five roubles of her wages. I have got to buy a new horse-collar."

Again a problem for Grisha: Pelageya was living in freedom, doing as she liked, and not having to account to anyone for her actions, and all at once, for no sort of reason, a stranger turns up, who has somehow acquired rights over her conduct and her property! Grisha was distressed. He longed passionately, almost to tears, to comfort this victim, as he supposed, of man's injustice. Picking out the very biggest apple in the store-room he stole into the kitchen, slipped it into Pelageya's hand, and darted headlong away.

Overdoing It

Glyeb Gavrilovitch Smirnov, a land surveyor, arrived at the station of Gnilushki. He had another twenty or thirty miles to drive before he would reach the estate which he had been summoned to survey. (If the driver were not drunk and the horses were not bad, it would hardly be twenty miles, but if the driver had had a drop and his steeds were worn out it would mount up to a good forty.)

"Tell me, please, where can I get post-horses here?" the surveyor asked of the station gendarme.

"What? Post-horses? There's no finding a decent dog for seventy miles round, let alone post-horses. . . . But where do you want to go?"

"To Dyevkino, General Hohotov's estate."

"Well," yawned the gendarme, "go outside the station, there are sometimes peasants in the yard there, they will take passengers."

The surveyor heaved a sigh and made his way out of the station.

There, after prolonged enquiries, conversations, and hesitations, he found a very sturdy, sullen-looking pock-marked peasant, wearing a tattered grey smock and bark-shoes.

"You have got a queer sort of cart!" said the surveyor, frowning as he clambered into the cart. "There is no making out which is the back and which is the front."

"What is there to make out? Where the horse's tail is, there's the front, and where your honour's sitting, there's the back."

The little mare was young, but thin, with legs planted wide apart and frayed ears. When the driver stood up and lashed her with a whip made of cord, she merely shook her head; when he swore at her and lashed her once more, the cart squeaked and shivered as though in a fever. After the third lash the cart gave a lurch, after the fourth, it moved forward.

"Are we going to drive like this all the way?" asked the surveyor, violently jolted and marvelling at the capacity of Russian drivers for combining a slow tortoise-like pace with a jolting that turns the soul inside out.

"We shall ge-et there!" the peasant reassured him. "The mare is young and frisky.... Only let her get running and then there is no stopping her.... No-ow, cur-sed brute!"

It was dusk by the time the cart drove out of the station. On the surveyor's right hand stretched a dark frozen plain, endless and boundless.... If you drove over it you would certainly get to the other side of beyond. On the horizon, where it vanished and melted into the sky, there was the languid glow of a cold autumn sunset.... On the left of the road, mounds of some sort, that might be last year's stacks or might be a village, rose up in the gathering darkness. The surveyor could not see what was in front as his whole field of vision on that side was covered by the broad clumsy back of the driver. The air was still, but it was cold and frosty.

"What a wilderness it is here," thought the surveyor, trying to cover his hears with the collar of his overcoat. "Neither post nor paddock. If, by ill-luck, one were attacked and robbed no one would hear you, whatever uproar you made.... And the driver is not one you could depend on.... Ugh, what a huge back! A child of nature like that has only to move a finger and it would be all up with one! And his ugly face is suspicious and brutal-looking."

"Hey, my good man!" said the surveyor, "What is your name?"

"Mine? Klim."

"Well, Klim, what is it like in your parts here? Not dangerous? Any robbers on the road?"

"It is all right, the Lord has spared us. . . . Who should go robbing on the road?"

"It's a good thing there are no robbers. But to be ready for anything I have got three revolvers with me," said the surveyor untruthfully. "And it doesn't do to trifle with a revolver, you know. One can manage a dozen robbers. . . ."

It had become quite dark. The cart suddenly began creaking, squeaking, shaking, and, as though unwillingly, turned sharply to the left.

"Where is he taking me to?" the surveyor wondered. "He has been driving straight and now all at once to the left. I shouldn't wonder if he'll take me, the rascal, to some den of thieves . . . and. . . . Things like that do happen."

"I say," he said, addressing the driver, "so you tell me it's not dangerous here? That's a pity . . . I like a fight with robbers. . . . I am thin and sickly-looking, but I have the strength of a bull. . . . Once three robbers attacked me and what do you think? I gave one such a dressing that . . . that he gave up his soul to God, you understand, and the other two were sent to penal servitude in Siberia. And where I got the strength I can't say. . . . One grips a strapping fellow of your sort with one hand and . . . wipes him out."

Klim looked round at the surveyor, wrinkled up his whole face, and lashed his horse.

"Yes . . ." the surveyor went on. "God forbid anyone should tackle me. The robber would have his bones broken, and, what's more, he would have to answer for it in the police court too. . . . I know all the judges and the police captains, I am a man in the Government, a man of importance. Here I am travelling and the authorities know . . . they keep a regular watch over me to see no one does me a mischief. There are policemen and village constables stuck behind bushes all along the road. . . . Sto . . . sto . . . stop!" the surveyor bawled suddenly. "Where have you got to? Where are you taking me to?"

"Why, don't you see? It's a forest!"

"It certainly is a forest," thought the surveyor. "I was frightened! But it won't do to betray my feelings. . . . He has noticed already that I am in a funk. Why is it he has taken to looking round at me so often? He is plotting something for certain. . . . At first he drove like a snail and now how he is dashing along!"

"I say, Klim, why are you making the horse go like that?"

"I am not making her go. She is racing along of herself. . . . Once she gets into a run there is no means of stopping her. It's no pleasure to her that her legs are like that."

"You are lying, my man, I see that you are lying. Only I advise you not to drive so fast. Hold your horse in a bit. . . . Do you hear? Hold her in!"

"What for?"

"Why . . . why, because four comrades were to drive after me from the station. We must let them catch us up. . . . They promised to overtake us in this forest. It will be more cheerful in their company. . . . They are a strong, sturdy set of fellows. . . . And each of them has got a pistol. Why do you keep looking round and fidgeting as though you were sitting on thorns? eh? I, my good fellow, er . . . my good fellow . . . there is no need to look around at me . . . there is nothing interesting about me. . . . Except perhaps the revolvers. Well, if you like I will take them out and show you. . . ."

The surveyor made a pretence of feeling in his pockets and at that moment something happened which he could not have expected with all his cowardice. Klim suddenly rolled off the cart and ran as fast as he could go into the forest.

"Help!" he roared. "Help! Take the horse and the cart, you devil, only don't take my life. Help!"

There was the sound of footsteps hurriedly retreating, of twigs snapping—and all was still. . . . The surveyor had not expected such a *dénouement*. He first stopped the horse and then settled himself more comfortably in the cart and fell to thinking.

"He has run off . . . he was scared, the fool. . . . Well, what's to be done now? I can't go on alone because I don't know the way; besides they may think I have stolen his horse. . . . What's to be done?"

"Klim! Klim," he cried.

"Klim," answered the echo.

At the thought that he would have to sit through the whole night in the cold and dark forest and hear nothing but the wolves, the echo, and the snorting of the scraggy mare, the surveyor began to have twinges down his spine as though it were being rasped with a cold file.

"Klimushka," he shouted. "Dear fellow! Where are you, Klimushka?"

For two hours the surveyor shouted, and it was only after he was quite husky and had resigned himself to spending the night in the forest that a faint breeze wafted the sound of a moan to him.

"Klim, is it you, dear fellow? Let us go on."

"You'll mu-ur-der me!"

"But I was joking, my dear man! I swear to God I was joking! As though I had revolvers! I told a lie because I was frightened. For goodness sake let us go on, I am freezing!"

Klim, probably reflecting that a real robber would have vanished long ago with the horse and cart, came out of the forest and went hesitatingly up to his passenger.

"Well, what were you frightened of, stupid? I . . . I was joking and you were frightened. Get in!"

"God be with you, sir," Klim muttered as he clambered into the cart, "if I had known I wouldn't have taken you for a hundred roubles. I almost died of fright. . . ."

Klim lashed at the little mare. The cart swayed. Klim lashed once more and the cart gave a lurch. After the fourth stroke of the whip when the cart moved forward, the surveyor hid his ears in his collar and sank into thought.

The road and Klim no longer seemed dangerous to him.

Old Age

Uzelkov, an architect with the rank of civil councillor, arrived in his native town, to which he had been invited to restore the church in the cemetery. He had been born in the town, had been at school, had grown up and married in it. But when he got out of the train he scarcely recognized it. Everything was changed. . . . Eighteen years ago when he had moved to Petersburg the street-boys used to catch marmots, for instance, on the spot where now the station was standing; now when one drove into the chief street, a hotel of four storeys stood facing one; in old days there was an ugly grey fence just there; but nothing—neither fences nor houses—had changed as much as the people. From his enquiries of the hotel waiter Uzelkov learned that more than half of the people he remembered were dead, reduced to poverty, forgotten.

"And do you remember Uzelkov?" he asked the old waiter about himself. "Uzelkov the architect who divorced his wife? He used to have a house in Svirebeyevsky Street . . . you must remember."

"I don't remember, sir."

"How is it you don't remember? The case made a lot of noise, even the cabmen all knew about it. Think, now! Shapkin the attorney managed my divorce for me, the rascal . . . the notorious card-sharper, the fellow who got a thrashing at the club. . . .

"Ivan Nikolaitch?"

"Yes, yes. . . . Well, is he alive? Is he dead?"

"Alive, sir, thank God. He is a notary now and has an office. He is very well off. He has two houses in Kirpitchny Street. . . . His daughter was married the other day. . . ."

Uzelkov paced up and down the room, thought a bit, and in his boredom made up his mind to go and see Shapkin at his office. When he walked out of the hotel and sauntered slowly towards Kirpitchny Street it was midday. He found Shapkin at his office and scarcely recognized him. From the once well-made, adroit attorney with a mobile, insolent, and always drunken face Shapkin had changed into a modest, grey-headed, decrepit old man.

"You don't recognize me, you have forgotten me," began Uzelkov. "I am your old client, Uzelkov."

"Uzelkov, what Uzelkov? Ah!" Shapkin remembered, recognized, and was struck all of a heap. There followed a shower of exclamations, questions, recollections.

"This is a surprise! This is unexpected!" cackled Shapkin. "What can I offer you? Do you care for champagne? Perhaps you would like oysters? My dear fellow, I have had so much from you in my time that I can't offer you anything equal to the occasion. . . ."

"Please don't put yourself out . . ." said Uzelkov. "I have no time to spare. I must go at once to the cemetery and examine the church; I have undertaken the restoration of it."

"That's capital! We'll have a snack and a drink and drive together. I have capital horses. I'll take you there and introduce you to the church-warden; I will arrange it all. . . . But why is it, my angel, you seem to be afraid of me and hold me at arm's length? Sit a little nearer! There is no need for you to be afraid of me nowadays. He-he! . . . At one time, it is true, I was a cunning blade, a dog of a fellow . . . no one dared approach me; but now I am stiller than water and humbler than the grass. I have grown old, I am a family man, I have children. It's time I was dead."

The friends had lunch, had a drink, and with a pair of horses drove out of the town to the cemetery.

"Yes, those were times!" Shapkin recalled as he sat in the sledge. "When you remember them you simply can't believe in them. Do you remember how you divorced your wife? It's nearly twenty years ago, and I dare say you have forgotten it all; but I remember it as though I'd divorced you yesterday. Good Lord, what a lot of worry I had over it! I was a sharp fellow, tricky and cunning, a desperate character. . . . Sometimes I was burning to tackle some ticklish business, especially if the fee were a good one, as, for instance, in your case. What did you pay me then? Five or six thousand! That was worth taking trouble for, wasn't it? You went off to Petersburg and left the whole thing in my hands to do the best I could, and, though Sofya Mihailovna, your wife, came only of a merchant family, she was proud and dignified. To bribe her to take the guilt on herself was difficult, awfully difficult! I would go to negotiate with her, and as soon as she saw me she called to her maid: 'Masha, didn't I tell you not to admit that scoundrel?' Well, I tried one thing and another. . . . I wrote her letters and contrived to meet her accidentally—it was no use! I had to act through a third person. I had a lot of trouble with her for a long time, and she only gave in when you agreed to give her ten thousand. . . . She couldn't resist ten thousand, she couldn't hold out. . . . She cried, she spat in my face, but she consented, she took the guilt on herself!"

"I thought it was fifteen thousand she had from me, not ten," said Uzelkov.

"Yes, yes . . . fifteen—I made a mistake," said Shapkin in confusion. "It's all over and done with, though, it's no use concealing it. I gave her ten and the other five I collared for myself. I deceived you both. . . . It's all over and done with, it's no use to be ashamed. And indeed, judge for yourself, Boris Petrovitch, weren't you the very person for me to get money out of? . . . You were a wealthy man and had everything you wanted. . . . Your marriage was an idle whim, and so was your divorce. You were making a lot of money. . . . I remember you made a scoop of twenty thousand over one contract. Whom should I have fleeced if not you? And I must own I envied you. If you grabbed anything they took off their caps to you, while they would thrash me for a rouble and slap me in the face at the club. . . . But there, why recall it? It is high time to forget it."

"Tell me, please, how did Sofya Mihailovna get on afterwards?"

"With her ten thousand? Very badly. God knows what it was—she lost her head, perhaps, or maybe her pride and her conscience tormented her at having sold her honour, or perhaps she loved you; but, do you know, she took to drink. . . . As soon as she got her money she was off driving about with officers. It was drunkenness, dissipation, debauchery. . . . When she went to a restaurant with officers she was not content with port or anything light, she must have strong brandy, fiery stuff to stupefy her."

"Yes, she was eccentric. . . . I had a lot to put up with from her . . . sometimes she would take offence at something and begin being hysterical. . . . And what happened afterwards?"

"One week passed and then another. . . . I was sitting at home, writing something. All at once the door opened and she walked in . . . drunk. 'Take back your cursed money,' she said, and flung a roll of notes in my face. . . . So she could not keep it up. I picked up the notes and counted them. It was five hundred short of the ten thousand, so she had only managed to get through five hundred."

"Where did you put the money?"

"It's all ancient history . . . there's no reason to conceal it now. . . . In my pocket, of course. Why do you look at me like that? Wait a bit for what will come later. . . . It's a regular novel, a pathological study. A couple of months later I was going home one night in a nasty drunken condition. . . . I lighted a candle, and lo and behold! Sofya Mihailovna was sitting on my sofa, and she was drunk, too, and in a frantic state— as wild as though she had run out of Bedlam. 'Give me back my money,' she said, 'I have changed my mind; if I must go to ruin I won't do it by halves, I'll have my fling! Be quick, you scoundrel, give me my money!' A disgraceful scene!"

"And you . . . gave it her?"

"I gave her, I remember, ten roubles."

"Oh! How could you?" cried Uzelkov, frowning. "If you couldn't or wouldn't have given it her, you might have written to me. . . . And I didn't know! I didn't know!"

"My dear fellow, what use would it have been for me to write, considering that she wrote to you herself when she was lying in the hospital afterwards?"

"Yes, but I was so taken up then with my second marriage. I was in such a whirl that I had no thoughts to spare for letters. . . . But you were an outsider, you had no antipathy for Sofya . . . why didn't you give her a helping hand? . . ."

"You can't judge by the standards of to-day, Boris Petrovitch; that's how we look at it now, but at the time we thought very differently. . . . Now maybe I'd give her a thousand roubles, but then even that ten-rouble note I did not give her for nothing. It was a bad business! . . . We must forget it. . . . But here we are. . . ."

The sledge stopped at the cemetery gates. Uzelkov and Shapkin got out of the sledge, went in at the gate, and walked up a long, broad avenue. The bare cherry-trees and acacias, the grey crosses and tombstones, were silvered with hoar-frost, every little grain of snow reflected the bright, sunny day. There was the smell there always is in cemeteries, the smell of incense and freshly dug earth. . . .

"Our cemetery is a pretty one," said Uzelkov, "quite a garden!"

"Yes, but it is a pity thieves steal the tombstones. . . . And over there, beyond that iron monument on the right, Sofya Mihailovna is buried. Would you like to see?"

The friends turned to the right and walked through the deep snow to the iron monument.

"Here it is," said Shapkin, pointing to a little slab of white marble. "A lieutenant put the stone on her grave."

Uzelkov slowly took off his cap and exposed his bald head to the sun. Shapkin, looking at him, took off his cap too, and another bald patch gleamed in the sunlight. There was the stillness of the tomb all around as though the air, too, were dead. The friends looked at the grave, pondered, and said nothing.

"She sleeps in peace," said Shapkin, breaking the silence. "It's nothing to her now that she took the blame on herself and drank brandy. You must own, Boris Petrovitch . . ."

"Own what?" Uzelkov asked gloomily.

"Why. . . . However hateful the past, it was better than this."

And Shapkin pointed to his grey head.

"I used not to think of the hour of death. . . . I fancied I could have given death points and won the game if we had had an encounter; but now. . . . But what's the good of talking!"

Uzelkov was overcome with melancholy. He suddenly had a passionate longing to weep, as once he had longed for love, and he felt those tears would have tasted sweet and refreshing. A moisture came into his eyes and there was a lump in his throat, but . . . Shapkin was standing beside him and Uzelkov was ashamed to show weakness before a witness. He turned back abruptly and went into the church.

Only two hours later, after talking to the church-warden and looking over the church, he seized a moment when Shapkin was in conversation with the priest and hastened away to weep. . . . He stole up to the grave secretly, furtively, looking round him every minute. The little white slab looked at him pensively, mournfully, and innocently as though a little girl lay under it instead of a dissolute, divorced wife.

"To weep, to weep!" thought Uzelkov.

But the moment for tears had been missed; though the old man blinked his eyes, though he worked up his feelings, the tears did not flow nor the lump come in his throat. After standing for ten minutes, with a gesture of despair, Uzelkov went to look for Shapkin.

Sorrow

The turner, Grigory Petrov, who had been known for years past as a splendid craftsman, and at the same time as the most senseless peasant in the Galtchinskoy district, was taking his old woman to the hospital. He had to drive over twenty miles, and it was an awful road. A government post driver could hardly have coped with it, much less an incompetent sluggard like Grigory. A cutting cold wind was blowing straight in his face. Clouds of snowflakes were whirling round and round in all directions, so that one could not tell whether the snow was falling from the sky or rising from the earth. The fields, the telegraph posts, and the forest could not be seen for the fog of snow. And when a particularly violent gust of wind swooped down on Grigory, even the yoke above the horse's head could not be seen. The wretched, feeble little nag crawled slowly along. It took all its strength to drag its legs out of the snow and to tug with its head. The turner was in a hurry. He kept restlessly hopping up and down on the front seat and lashing the horse's back.

"Don't cry, Matryona, . . ." he muttered. "Have a little patience. Please God we shall reach the hospital, and in a trice it will be the right thing for you. . . . Pavel Ivanitch will give you some little drops, or tell them to bleed you; or maybe his honor will be pleased to rub you with some sort of spirit—it'll... draw it out of your side. Pavel Ivanitch will do his best. He will shout and stamp about, but he will do his best.... He is a nice gentleman, affable, God give him health! As soon as we get there he will dart out of his room and will begin calling me names. 'How? Why so?' he will cry. 'Why did you not come at the right time? I am not a dog to be hanging about waiting on you devils all day. Why did you not come in the morning? Go away! Get out of my sight. Come again to-morrow.' And I shall say: 'Mr. Doctor! Pavel Ivanitch! Your honor!' Get on, do! plague take you, you devil! Get on!"

The turner lashed his nag, and without looking at the old woman went on muttering to himself:

" 'Your honor! It's true as before God.... Here's the Cross for you, I set off almost before it was light. How could I be here in time if the Lord.... The Mother of God ... is wroth, and has sent such a snowstorm? Kindly look for yourself.... Even a first-rate horse could not do it, while mine—you can see for yourself—is not a horse but a disgrace.' And Pavel Ivanitch will frown and shout: 'We know you! You always find some excuse! Especially you, Grishka; I know you of old! I'll be bound you have stopped at half a dozen taverns!' And I shall say: 'Your honor! am I a criminal or a heathen? My old woman is giving up her soul to God, she is dying, and am I going to run from tavern to tavern! What an idea, upon my word! Plague take them, the taverns!' Then Pavel Ivanitch will order you to be taken into the hospital, and I shall fall at his feet.... 'Pavel Ivanitch! Your honor, we thank you most humbly! Forgive us fools and anathemas, don't be hard on us peasants! We deserve a good kicking, while you graciously put yourself out and mess your feet in the snow!' And Pavel Ivanitch will give me a look as though he would like to hit me, and will say: 'You'd much better not be swilling vodka, you fool, but taking pity on your old woman instead of falling at my feet. You want a thrashing!' 'You are right there—a thrashing, Pavel Ivanitch, strike me God! But how can we help bowing down at your feet if you are our benefactor, and a real father to us? Your honor! I give you my word, ... here as before God, ... you may spit in my face if I deceive you: as soon as my Matryona, this same here, is well again and restored to her natural condition, I'll make anything for your honor that you would like to order! A cigarette-case, if you like, of the best birchwood, . . . balls for croquet, skittles of the most foreign pattern I can turn. . . . I will make anything for you! I won't take a farthing from you. In Moscow they would charge you four roubles for such a cigarette-case, but I won't take a farthing.' The doctor will laugh and say: 'Oh, all right, all right. . . . I see! But it's a pity you are a drunkard. . . .' I know how to manage the gentry, old girl. There isn't a gentleman I couldn't talk to. Only God grant we don't get off the road. Oh, how it is blowing! One's eyes are full of snow."

And the turner went on muttering endlessly. He prattled on mechanically to get a little relief from his depressing feelings. He had plenty of words on his tongue, but the thoughts and questions in his brain were even more numerous. Sorrow had come upon the turner unawares, unlooked-for, and unexpected, and now he could not get over it, could not recover himself. He had lived hitherto in unruffled calm, as though in drunken half-consciousness, knowing neither grief nor joy, and now he was suddenly aware of a dreadful pain in his heart. The careless idler and drunkard found himself quite suddenly in the position of a busy man, weighed down by anxieties and haste, and even struggling with nature.

The turner remembered that his trouble had begun the evening before. When he had come home yesterday evening, a little drunk as usual, and from long-established habit had begun swearing and shaking his fists, his old woman had looked at her rowdy spouse as she had never looked at him before. Usually, the expression in her aged eyes was that of a martyr, meek like that of a dog frequently beaten and badly fed; this time she had looked at him sternly and immovably, as saints in the holy pictures or dying people look. From that strange, evil look in her eyes the trouble had begun. The turner, stupefied with amazement, borrowed a horse from a neighbor, and now was taking his old woman to the hospital in the hope that, by means of powders and ointments, Pavel Ivanitch would bring back his old woman's habitual expression.

"I say, Matryona, . . ." the turner muttered, "if Pavel Ivanitch asks you whether I beat you, say, 'Never!' and I never will beat you again. I swear it. And did I ever beat you out of spite? I just beat you without thinking. I am sorry for you. Some men wouldn't trouble, but here I am taking you. . . . I am doing my best. And the way it snows, the way it snows! Thy Will be done, O Lord! God grant we don't get off the road. . . . Does your side ache, Matryona, that you don't speak? I ask you, does your side ache?"

It struck him as strange that the snow on his old woman's face was not melting; it was queer that the face itself looked somehow drawn, and had turned a pale gray, dingy waxen hue and had grown grave and solemn.

"You are a fool!" muttered the turner. . . . "I tell you on my conscience, before God, . . . and you go and . . . Well, you are a fool! I have a good mind not to take you to Pavel Ivanitch!"

The turner let the reins go and began thinking. He could not bring himself to look round at his old woman: he was frightened. He was afraid, too, of asking her a question and not getting an answer. At last, to make an end of uncertainty, without looking round he felt his old woman's cold hand. The lifted hand fell like a log.

"She is dead, then! What a business!"

And the turner cried. He was not so much sorry as annoyed. He thought how quickly everything passes in this world! His trouble had hardly begun when the final catastrophe had happened. He had not had time to live with his old woman, to show her he was sorry for her before she died. He had lived with her for forty years, but those forty years had passed by as it were in a fog. What with drunkenness, quarreling, and poverty, there had been no feeling of life. And, as though to spite him, his old woman died at the very time when he felt he was sorry for her, that he could not live without her, and that he had behaved dreadfully badly to her.

"Why, she used to go the round of the village," he remembered. "I sent her out myself to beg for bread. What a business! She ought to have lived another ten years, the silly thing; as it is I'll be bound she thinks I really was that sort of man. . . . Holy Mother! but where the devil am I driving? There's no need for a doctor now, but a burial. Turn back!"

Grigory turned back and lashed the horse with all his might. The road grew worse and worse every hour. Now he could not see the yoke at all. Now and then the sledge ran into a young fir tree, a dark object scratched the turner's hands and flashed before his eyes, and the field of vision was white and whirling again.

"To live over again," thought the turner.

He remembered that forty years ago Matryona had been young, handsome, merry, that she had come of a well-to-do family. They had married her to him because they had been attracted by his handicraft. All the essentials for a happy life had been there, but the trouble was that, just as he had got drunk after the wedding and lay sprawling on the stove, so he had gone on without waking up till now. His wedding he remembered, but of what happened after the wedding—for the life of him he could remember nothing, except perhaps that he had drunk, lain on the stove, and quarreled. Forty years had been wasted like that.

The white clouds of snow were beginning little by little to turn gray. It was getting dusk.

"Where am I going?" the turner suddenly bethought him with a start. "I ought to be thinking of the burial, and I am on the way to the hospital. . . . It as is though I had gone crazy."

Grigory turned round again, and again lashed his horse. The little nag strained its utmost and, with a snort, fell into a little trot. The turner lashed it on the back time after time. . . . A knocking was audible behind him, and though he did not look round, he knew it was the dead woman's head knocking against the sledge. And the snow kept turning darker and darker, the wind grew colder and more cutting. . . .

"To live over again!" thought the turner. "I should get a new lathe, take orders, . . . give the money to my old woman. . . ."

And then he dropped the reins. He looked for them, tried to pick them up, but could not—his hands would not work. . . .

"It does not matter," he thought, "the horse will go of itself, it knows the way. I might have a little sleep now. . . . Before the funeral or the requiem it would be as well to get a little rest. . . ."

The turner closed his eyes and dozed. A little later he heard the horse stop; he opened his eyes and saw before him something dark like a hut or a haystack. . . .

He would have got out of the sledge and found out what it was, but he felt overcome by such inertia that it seemed better to freeze than move, and he sank into a peaceful sleep.

He woke up in a big room with painted walls. Bright sunlight was streaming in at the windows. The turner saw people facing him, and his first feeling was a desire to show himself a respectable man who knew how things should be done.

"A requiem, brothers, for my old woman," he said. "The priest should be told...."

"Oh, all right, all right; lie down," a voice cut him short.

"Pavel Ivanitch!" the turner cried in surprise, seeing the doctor before him. "Your honor, benefactor!"

He wanted to leap up and fall on his knees before the doctor, but felt that his arms and legs would not obey him.

"Your honor, where are my legs, where are my arms!"

"Say good-by to your arms and legs.... They've been frozen off. Come, come!... What are you crying for? You've lived your life, and thank God for it! I suppose you have had sixty years of it—that's enough for you!..."

"I am grieving.... Graciously forgive me! If I could have another five or six years!..."

"What for?"

"The horse isn't mine, I must give it back.... I must bury my old woman.... How quickly it is all ended in this world! Your honor, Pavel Ivanitch! A cigarette-case of birchwood of the best! I'll turn you croquet balls...."

The doctor went out of the ward with a wave of his hand. It was all over with the turner.

Mari d'Elle

It was a free night. Natalya Andreyevna Bronin (her married name was Nikitin), the opera singer, is lying in her bedroom, her whole being abandoned to repose. She lies, deliciously drowsy, thinking of her little daughter who lives somewhere far away with her grandmother or aunt. . . . The child is more precious to her than the public, bouquets, notices in the papers, adorers . . . and she would be glad to think about her till morning. She is happy, at peace, and all she longs for is not to be prevented from lying undisturbed, dozing and dreaming of her little girl.

All at once the singer starts, and opens her eyes wide: there is a harsh abrupt ring in the entry. Before ten seconds have passed the bell tinkles a second time and a third time. The door is opened noisily and some one walks into the entry stamping his feet like a horse, snorting and puffing with the cold.

"Damn it all, nowhere to hang one's coat!" the singer hears a husky bass voice. "Celebrated singer, look at that! Makes five thousand a year, and can't get a decent hat-stand!"

"My husband!" thinks the singer, frowning. "And I believe he has brought one of his friends to stay the night too. . . . Hateful!"

No more peace. When the loud noise of some one blowing his nose and putting off his goloshes dies away, the singer hears cautious footsteps in her bedroom. . . . It is her husband, *mari d'elle,* Denis Petrovitch Nikitin. He brings a whiff of cold air and a smell of brandy. For a long while he walks about the bedroom, breathing heavily, and, stumbling against the chairs in the dark, seems to be looking for something. . . .

"What do you want?" his wife moans, when she is sick of his fussing about. "You have woken me."

"I am looking for the matches, my love. You . . . you are not asleep then? I have brought you a message. . . . Greetings from that . . . what's-his-name? . . . red-headed fellow who is always sending you bouquets. . . . Zagvozdkin. . . . I have just been to see him."

"What did you go to him for?"

"Oh, nothing particular. . . . We sat and talked and had a drink. Say what you like, Nathalie, I dislike that individual—I dislike him awfully! He is a rare blockhead. He is a wealthy man, a capitalist; he has six hundred thousand, and you would never guess it. Money is no more use to him than a radish to a dog. He does not eat it himself nor give it to others. Money ought to circulate, but he keeps tight hold of it, is afraid to part with it. . . . What's the good of capital lying idle? Capital lying idle is no better than grass."

Mari d'elle gropes his way to the edge of the bed and, puffing, sits down at his wife's feet.

"Capital lying idle is pernicious," he goes on. "Why has business gone downhill in Russia? Because there is so much capital lying idle among us; they are afraid to invest it. It's very different in England. . . . There are no such queer fish as Zagvozdkin in England, my girl. . . . There every farthing is in circulation. . . . Yes. . . . They don't keep it locked up in chests there. . . ."

"Well, that's all right. I am sleepy."

"Directly. . . . Whatever was it I was talking about? Yes. . . . In these hard times hanging is too good for Zagvozdkin. . . . He is a fool and a scoundrel. . . . No better than a fool. If I asked him for a loan without security—why, a child could see that he runs no risk whatever. He doesn't understand, the ass! For ten thousand he would have got a hundred. In a year he would have another hundred thousand. I asked, I talked . . . but he wouldn't give it me, the blockhead."

"I hope you did not ask him for a loan in my name."

"H'm.... A queer question...." *Mari d'elle* is offended. "Anyway he would sooner give me ten thousand than you. You are a woman, and I am a man anyway, a business-like person. And what a scheme I propose to him! Not a bubble, not some chimera, but a sound thing, substantial! If one could hit on a man who would understand, one might get twenty thousand for the idea alone! Even you would understand if I were to tell you about it. Only you ... don't chatter about it ... not a word ... but I fancy I have talked to you about it already. Have I talked to you about sausage-skins?"

"M'm ... by and by."

"I believe I have.... Do you see the point of it? Now the provision shops and the sausage-makers get their sausage-skins locally, and pay a high price for them. Well, but if one were to bring sausage-skins from the Caucasus where they are worth nothing, and where they are thrown away, then ... where do you suppose the sausage-makers would buy their skins, here in the slaughterhouses or from me? From me, of course! Why, I shall sell them ten times as cheap! Now let us look at it like this: every year in Petersburg and Moscow and in other centres these same skins would be bought to the ... to the sum of five hundred thousand, let us suppose. That's the minimum. Well, and if...."

"You can tell me to-morrow ... later on...."

"Yes, that's true. You are sleepy, *pardon,* I am just going ... say what you like, but with capital you can do good business everywhere, wherever you go.... With capital even out of cigarette ends one may make a million.... Take your theatrical business now. Why, for example, did Lentovsky come to grief? It's very simple. He did not go the right way to work from the very first. He had no capital and he went headlong to the dogs.... He ought first to have secured his capital, and then to have gone slowly and cautiously.... Nowadays, one can easily make money by a theatre, whether it is a private one or a people's one.... If one produces the right plays, charges a low price for admission, and hits the public fancy, one may put a hundred thousand in one's pocket the first year.... You don't understand, but I am talking sense.... You see you are fond of hoarding capital; you are no better than that fool Zagvozdkin, you heap it up and don't know what for.... You won't listen, you don't want to. . . . If you were to put it into circulation, you wouldn't have to be rushing all over the place. . . . You see for a private theatre, five thousand would be enough for a beginning. . . . Not like Lentovsky, of course, but on a modest scale . . . in a small way. I have got a manager already, I have looked at a suitable building. . . . It's only the money I haven't got. . . . If only you understood things you would have parted with your Five per cents . . . your Preference shares. . . ."

"No, *merci*. . . . You have fleeced me enough already. . . . Let me alone, I have been punished already. . . ."

"If you are going to argue like a woman, then of course . . ." sighs Nikitin, getting up. "Of course. . . ."

"Let me alone. . . . Come, go away and don't keep me awake. . . . I am sick of listening to your nonsense."

"H'm. . . . To be sure . . . of course! Fleeced . . . plundered. . . . What we give we remember, but we don't remember what we take."

"I have never taken anything from you."

"Is that so? But when we weren't a celebrated singer, at whose expense did we live then? And who, allow me to ask, lifted you out of beggary and secured your happiness? Don't you remember that?"

"Come, go to bed. Go along and sleep it off."

"Do you mean to say you think I am drunk? . . . if I am so low in the eyes of such a grand lady . . . I can go away altogether."

"Do. A good thing too."

"I will, too. I have humbled myself enough. And I will go."

"Oh, my God! Oh, do go, then! I shall be delighted!"

"Very well, we shall see."

Nikitin mutters something to himself, and, stumbling over the chairs, goes out of the bedroom. Then sounds reach her from the entry of whispering, the shuffling of goloshes and a door being shut. *Mari d'elle* has taken offence in earnest and gone out.

"Thank God, he has gone!" thinks the singer; "Now I can sleep."

And as she falls asleep she thinks of her *mari d'elle,* what sort of a man he is, and how this affliction has come upon her. At one time he used to live at Tchernigov, and had a situation there as a book-keeper. As an ordinary obscure individual and not the *mari d'elle,* he had been quite endurable: he used to go to his work and take his salary, and all his whims and projects went no further than a new guitar, fashionable trousers, and an amber cigarette-holder. Since he had become "the husband of a celebrity" he was completely transformed. The singer remembered that when first she told him she was going on the stage he had made a fuss, been indignant, complained to her parents, turned her out of the house. She had been obliged to go on the stage without his permission. Afterwards, when he learned from the papers and from various people that she was earning big sums, he had 'forgiven her,' abandoned book-keeping, and become her hanger-on. The singer was overcome with amazement when she looked at her hanger-on: when and where had he managed to pick up new tastes, polish, and air and graces? Where had he learned the taste of oysters and of different Burgundies? Who had taught him to dress and do his hair in the fashion and call her 'Nathalie' instead of Natasha?

"It's strange," thinks the singer. "In old days he used to get his salary and put it away, but now a hundred roubles a day is not enough for him. In old days he was afraid to talk before schoolboys for fear of saying something silly, and now he is overfamiliar even with princes . . . wretched, contemptible little creature!"

But then the singer starts again; again there is the clang of the bell in the entry. The housemaid, scolding and angrily flopping with her slippers, goes to open the door. Again some one comes in and stamps like a horse.

"He has come back!" thinks the singer. "When shall I be left in peace? It's revolting!" She is overcome by fury.

"Wait a bit. . . . I'll teach you to get up these farces! You shall go away. I'll make you go away!"

The singer leaps up and runs barefoot into the little drawing-room where her *mari* usually sleeps. She comes at the moment when he is undressing, and carefully folding his clothes on a chair.

"You went away!" she says, looking at him with bright eyes full of hatred. "What did you come back for?"

Nikitin remains silent, and merely sniffs.

"You went away! Kindly take yourself off this very minute! This very minute! Do you hear?"

Mari d'elle coughs and, without looking at his wife, takes off his braces.

"If you don't go away, you insolent creature, I shall go," the singer goes on, stamping her bare foot, and looking at him with flashing eyes. "I shall go! Do you hear, insolent . . . worthless wretch, flunkey, out you go!"

"You might have some shame before outsiders," mutters her husband. . . .

The singer looks round and only then sees an unfamiliar countenance that looks like an actor's. . . . The countenance, seeing the singer's uncovered shoulders and bare feet, shows signs of embarrassment, and looks ready to sink through the floor.

"Let me introduce . . ." mutters Nikitin, "Bezbozhnikov, a provincial manager."

The singer utters a shriek, and runs off into her bedroom.

"There, you see . . ." says *mari d'elle*, as he stretches himself on the sofa, "it was all honey just now . . . my love, my dear, my darling, kisses and embraces . . . but as soon as money is touched upon, then. . . . As you see . . . money is the great thing. . . . Good night!"

A minute later there is a snore.

The Looking-glass

New Year's Eve. Nellie, the daughter of a landowner and general, a young and pretty girl, dreaming day and night of being married, was sitting in her room, gazing with exhausted, half-closed eyes into the looking-glass. She was pale, tense, and as motionless as the looking-glass.

The non-existent but apparent vista of a long, narrow corridor with endless rows of candles, the reflection of her face, her hands, of the frame—all this was already clouded in mist and merged into a boundless grey sea. The sea was undulating, gleaming and now and then flaring crimson. . . .

Looking at Nellie's motionless eyes and parted lips, one could hardly say whether she was asleep or awake, but nevertheless she was seeing. At first she saw only the smile and soft, charming expression of someone's eyes, then against the shifting grey background there gradually appeared the outlines of a head, a face, eyebrows, beard. It was he, the destined one, the object of long dreams and hopes. The destined one was for Nellie everything, the significance of life, personal happiness, career, fate. Outside him, as on the grey background of the looking-glass, all was dark, empty, meaningless. And so it was not strange that, seeing before her a handsome, gently smiling face, she was conscious of bliss, of an unutterably sweet dream that could not be expressed in speech or on paper. Then she heard his voice, saw herself living under the same roof with him, her life merged into his. Months and years flew by against the grey background. And Nellie saw her future distinctly in all its details.

Picture followed picture against the grey background. Now Nellie saw herself one winter night knocking at the door of Stepan Lukitch, the district doctor. The old dog hoarsely and lazily barked behind the gate. The doctor's windows were in darkness. All was silence.

"For God's sake, for God's sake!" whispered Nellie.

But at last the garden gate creaked and Nellie saw the doctor's cook. "Is the doctor at home?"

"His honour's asleep," whispered the cook into her sleeve, as though afraid of waking her master. "He's only just got home from his fever patients, and gave orders he was not to be waked."

But Nellie scarcely heard the cook. Thrusting her aside, she rushed headlong into the doctor's house. Running through some dark and stuffy rooms, upsetting two or three chairs, she at last reached the doctor's bedroom. Stepan Lukitch was lying on his bed, dressed, but without his coat, and with pouting lips was breathing into his open hand. A little night-light glimmered faintly beside him. Without uttering a word Nellie sat down and began to cry. She wept bitterly, shaking all over.

"My husband is ill!" she sobbed out. Stepan Lukitch was silent. He slowly sat up, propped his head on his hand, and looked at his visitor with fixed, sleepy eyes. "My husband is ill!" Nellie continued, restraining her sobs. "For mercy's sake come quickly. Make haste. . . . Make haste!"

"Eh?" growled the doctor, blowing into his hand.

"Come! Come this very minute! Or . . . it's terrible to think! For mercy's sake!"

And pale, exhausted Nellie, gasping and swallowing her tears, began describing to the doctor her husband's illness, her unutterable terror. Her sufferings would have touched the heart of a stone, but the doctor looked at her, blew into his open hand, and—not a movement.

"I'll come to-morrow!" he muttered.

"That's impossible!" cried Nellie. "I know my husband has typhus! At once ... this very minute you are needed!"

"I ... er ... have only just come in," muttered the doctor. "For the last three days I've been away, seeing typhus patients, and I'm exhausted and ill myself.... I simply can't! Absolutely! I've caught it myself! There!"

And the doctor thrust before her eyes a clinical thermometer.

"My temperature is nearly forty.... I absolutely can't. I can scarcely sit up. Excuse me. I'll lie down...."

The doctor lay down.

"But I implore you, doctor," Nellie moaned in despair. "I beseech you! Help me, for mercy's sake! Make a great effort and come! I will repay you, doctor!"

"Oh, dear! ... Why, I have told you already. Ah!"

Nellie leapt up and walked nervously up and down the bedroom. She longed to explain to the doctor, to bring him to reason.... She thought if only he knew how dear her husband was to her and how unhappy she was, he would forget his exhaustion and his illness. But how could she be eloquent enough?

"Go to the Zemstvo doctor," she heard Stepan Lukitch's voice.

"That's impossible! He lives more than twenty miles from here, and time is precious. And the horses can't stand it. It is thirty miles from us to you, and as much from here to the Zemstvo doctor. No, it's impossible! Come along, Stepan Lukitch. I ask of you an heroic deed. Come, perform that heroic deed! Have pity on us!"

"It's beyond everything.... I'm in a fever ... my head's in a whirl ... and she won't understand! Leave me alone!"

"But you are in duty bound to come! You cannot refuse to come! It's egoism! A man is bound to sacrifice his life for his neighbour, and you ... you refuse to come! I will summon you before the Court."

Nellie felt that she was uttering a false and undeserved insult, but for her husband's sake she was capable of forgetting logic, tact, sympathy for others.... In reply to her threats, the doctor greedily gulped a glass of cold water. Nellie fell to entreating and imploring like the very lowest beggar.... At last the doctor gave way. He slowly got up, puffing and panting, looking for his coat.

"Here it is!" cried Nellie, helping him. "Let me put it on to you. Come along! I will repay you. . . . All my life I shall be grateful to you. . . ."

But what agony! After putting on his coat the doctor lay down again. Nellie got him up and dragged him to the hall. Then there was an agonizing to-do over his goloshes, his overcoat. . . . His cap was lost. . . . But at last Nellie was in the carriage with the doctor. Now they had only to drive thirty miles and her husband would have a doctor's help. The earth was wrapped in darkness. One could not see one's hand before one's face. . . . A cold winter wind was blowing. There were frozen lumps under their wheels. The coachman was continually stopping and wondering which road to take.

Nellie and the doctor sat silent all the way. It was fearfully jolting, but they felt neither the cold nor the jolts.

"Get on, get on!" Nellie implored the driver.

At five in the morning the exhausted horses drove into the yard. Nellie saw the familiar gates, the well with the crane, the long row of stables and barns. At last she was at home.

"Wait a moment, I will be back directly," she said to Stepan Lukitch, making him sit down on the sofa in the dining-room. "Sit still and wait a little, and I'll see how he is going on."

On her return from her husband, Nellie found the doctor lying down. He was lying on the sofa and muttering.

"Doctor, please! . . . doctor!"

"Eh? Ask Domna!" muttered Stepan Lukitch.

"What?"

"They said at the meeting . . . Vlassov said . . . Who? . . . what?"

And to her horror Nellie saw that the doctor was as delirious as her husband. What was to be done?

"I must go for the Zemstvo doctor," she decided.

Then again there followed darkness, a cutting cold wind, lumps of frozen earth. She was suffering in body and in soul, and delusive nature has no arts, no deceptions to compensate these sufferings. . . .

Then she saw against the grey background how her husband every spring was in straits for money to pay the interest for the mortgage to the bank. He could not sleep, she could not sleep, and both racked their brains till their heads ached, thinking how to avoid being visited by the clerk of the Court.

She saw her children: the everlasting apprehension of colds, scarlet fever, diphtheria, bad marks at school, separation. Out of a brood of five or six one was sure to die.

The grey background was not untouched by death. That might well be. A husband and wife cannot die simultaneously. Whatever happened one must bury the other. And Nellie saw her husband dying. This terrible event presented itself to her in every detail. She saw the coffin, the candles, the deacon, and even the footmarks in the hall made by the undertaker.

"Why is it, what is it for?" she asked, looking blankly at her husband's face.

And all the previous life with her husband seemed to her a stupid prelude to this.

Something fell from Nellie's hand and knocked on the floor. She started, jumped up, and opened her eyes wide. One looking-glass she saw lying at her feet. The other was standing as before on the table.

She looked into the looking-glass and saw a pale, tear-stained face. There was no grey background now.

"I must have fallen asleep," she thought with a sigh of relief.

Art

A gloomy winter morning.

On the smooth and glittering surface of the river Bystryanka, sprinkled here and there with snow, stand two peasants, scrubby little Seryozhka and the church beadle, Matvey. Seryozhka, a short-legged, ragged, mangy-looking fellow of thirty, stares angrily at the ice. Tufts of wool hang from his shaggy sheepskin like a mangy dog. In his hands he holds a compass made of two pointed sticks. Matvey, a fine-looking old man in a new sheepskin and high felt boots, looks with mild blue eyes upwards where on the high sloping bank a village nestles picturesquely. In his hands there is a heavy crowbar.

"Well, are we going to stand like this till evening with our arms folded?" says Seryozhka, breaking the silence and turning his angry eyes on Matvey. "Have you come here to stand about, old fool, or to work?"

"Well, you ... er ... show me ..." Matvey mutters, blinking mildly.

"Show you.... It's always me: me to show you, and me to do it. They have no sense of their own! Mark it out with the compasses, that's what's wanted! You can't break the ice without marking it out. Mark it! Take the compass."

Matvey takes the compasses from Seryozhka's hands, and, shuffling heavily on the same spot and jerking with his elbows in all directions, he begins awkwardly trying to describe a circle on the ice. Seryozhka screws up his eyes contemptuously and obviously enjoys his awkwardness and incompetence.

"Eh-eh-eh!" he mutters angrily. "Even that you can't do! The fact is you are a stupid peasant, a wooden-head! You ought to be grazing geese and not making a Jordan! Give the compasses here! Give them here, I say!"

Seryozhka snatches the compasses out of the hands of the perspiring Matvey, and in an instant, jauntily twirling round on one heel, he describes a circle on the ice. The outline of the new Jordan is ready now, all that is left to do is to break the ice . . .

But before proceeding to the work Seryozhka spends a long time in airs and graces, whims and reproaches . . .

"I am not obliged to work for you! You are employed in the church, you do it!"

He obviously enjoys the peculiar position in which he has been placed by the fate that has bestowed on him the rare talent of surprising the whole parish once a year by his art. Poor mild Matvey has to listen to many venomous and contemptuous words from him. Seryozhka sets to work with vexation, with anger. He is lazy. He has hardly described the circle when he is already itching to go up to the village to drink tea, lounge about, and babble . . .

"I'll be back directly," he says, lighting his cigarette, "and meanwhile you had better bring something to sit on and sweep up, instead of standing there counting the crows."

Matvey is left alone. The air is grey and harsh but still. The white church peeps out genially from behind the huts scattered on the river bank. Jackdaws are incessantly circling round its golden crosses. On one side of the village where the river bank breaks off and is steep a hobbled horse is standing at the very edge, motionless as a stone, probably asleep or deep in thought.

Matvey, too, stands motionless as a statue, waiting patiently. The dreamily brooding look of the river, the circling of the jackdaws, and the sight of the horse make him drowsy. One hour passes, a second, and still Seryozhka does not come. The river has long been swept and a box brought to sit on, but the drunken fellow does not appear. Matvey waits and merely yawns. The feeling of boredom is one of which he knows nothing. If he were told to stand on the river for a day, a month, or a year he would stand there.

At last Seryozhka comes into sight from behind the huts. He walks with a lurching gait, scarcely moving. He is too lazy to go the long way round, and he comes not by the road, but prefers a short cut in a straight line down the bank, and sticks in the snow, hangs on to the bushes, slides on his back as he comes—and all this slowly, with pauses.

"What are you about?" he cries, falling on Matvey at once. "Why are you standing there doing nothing! When are you going to break the ice?"

Matvey crosses himself, takes the crowbar in both hands, and begins breaking the ice, carefully keeping to the circle that has been drawn. Seryozhka sits down on the box and watches the heavy clumsy movements of his assistant.

"Easy at the edges! Easy there!" he commands. "If you can't do it properly, you shouldn't undertake it, once you have undertaken it you should do it. You!"

A crowd collects on the top of the bank. At the sight of the spectators Seryozhka becomes even more excited.

"I declare I am not going to do it . . ." he says, lighting a stinking cigarette and spitting on the ground. "I should like to see how you get on without me. Last year at Kostyukovo, Styopka Gulkov undertook to make a Jordan as I do. And what did it amount to—it was a laughingstock. The Kostyukovo folks came to ours—crowds and crowds of them! The people flocked from all the villages."

"Because except for ours there is nowhere a proper Jordan . . ."

"Work, there is no time for talking. . . . Yes, old man . . . you won't find another Jordan like it in the whole province. The soldiers say you would look in vain, they are not so good even in the towns. Easy, easy!"

Matvey puffs and groans. The work is not easy. The ice is firm and thick; and he has to break it and at once take the pieces away that the open space may not be blocked up.

But, hard as the work is and senseless as Seryozhka's commands are, by three o'clock there is a large circle of dark water in the Bystryanka.

"It was better last year," says Seryozhka angrily. "You can't do even that! Ah, dummy! To keep such fools in the temple of God! Go and bring a board to make the pegs! Bring the ring, you crow! And er . . . get some bread somewhere . . . and some cucumbers, or something."

Matvey goes off and soon afterwards comes back, carrying on his shoulders an immense wooden ring which had been painted in previous years in patterns of various colours. In the centre of the ring is a red cross, at the circumference holes for the pegs. Seryozhka takes the ring and covers the hole in the ice with it.

"Just right . . . it fits. . . . We have only to renew the paint and it will be first-rate. . . . Come, why are you standing still? Make the lectern. Or—er—go and get logs to make the cross . . ."

Matvey, who has not tasted food or drink all day, trudges up the hill again. Lazy as Seryozhka is, he makes the pegs with his own hands. He knows that those pegs have a miraculous power: whoever gets hold of a peg after the blessing of the water will be lucky for the whole year. Such work is really worth doing.

But the real work begins the following day. Then Seryozhka displays himself before the ignorant Matvey in all the greatness of his talent. There is no end to his babble, his fault-finding, his whims and fancies. If Matvey nails two big pieces of wood to make a cross, he is dissatisfied and tells him to do it again. If Matvey stands still, Seryozhka asks him angrily why he does not go; if he moves, Seryozhka shouts to him not to go away but to do his work. He is not satisfied with his tools, with the weather, or with his own talent; nothing pleases him.

Matvey saws out a great piece of ice for a lectern.

"Why have you broken off the corner?" cries Seryozhka, and glares at him furiously. "Why have you broken off the corner? I ask you."

"Forgive me, for Christ's sake."

"Do it over again!"

Matvey saws again . . . and there is no end to his sufferings. A lectern is to stand by the hole in the ice that is covered by the painted ring; on the lectern is to be carved the cross and the open gospel. But that is not all. Behind the lectern there is to be a high cross to be seen by all the crowd and to glitter in the sun as though sprinkled with diamonds and rubies. On the cross is to be a dove carved out of ice. The path from the church to the Jordan is to be strewn with branches of fir and juniper. All this is their task.

First of all Seryozhka sets to work on the lectern. He works with a file, a chisel, and an awl. He is perfectly successful in the cross on the lectern, the gospel, and the drapery that hangs down from the lectern. Then he begins on the dove. While he is trying to carve an expression of meekness and humility on the face of the dove, Matvey, lumbering about like a bear, is coating with ice the cross he has made of wood. He takes the cross and dips it in the hole. Waiting till the water has frozen on the cross he dips it in a second time, and so on till the cross is covered with a thick layer of ice. . . . It is a difficult job, calling for a great deal of strength and patience.

But now the delicate work is finished. Seryozhka races about the village like one possessed. He swears and vows he will go at once to the river and smash all his work. He is looking for suitable paints.

His pockets are full of ochre, dark blue, red lead, and verdigris; without paying a farthing he rushes headlong from one shop to another. The shop is next door to the tavern. Here he has a drink; with a wave of his hand he darts off without paying. At one hut he gets beetroot leaves, at another an onion skin, out of which he makes a yellow colour. He swears, shoves, threatens, and . . . not a soul murmurs! They all smile at him, they sympathise with him, call him Sergey Nikititch; they all feel that his art is not his personal affair but something that concerns them all, the whole people. One creates, the others help him. Seryozhka in himself is a nonentity, a sluggard, a drunkard, and a wastrel, but when he has his red lead or compasses in his hand he is at once something higher, a servant of God.

Epiphany morning comes. The precincts of the church and both banks of the river for a long distance are swarming with people. Everything that makes up the Jordan is scrupulously concealed under new mats. Seryozhka is meekly moving about near the mats, trying to control his emotion. He sees thousands of people. There are many here from other parishes; these people have come many a mile on foot through the frost and the snow merely to see his celebrated Jordan. Matvey, who had finished his coarse, rough work, is by now back in the church, there is no sight, no sound of him; he is already forgotten. . . . The weather is lovely. . . . There is not a cloud in the sky. The sunshine is dazzling.

The church bells ring out on the hill . . . Thousands of heads are bared, thousands of hands are moving, there are thousands of signs of the cross!

And Seryozhka does not know what to do with himself for impatience. But now they are ringing the bells for the Sacrament; then half an hour later a certain agitation is perceptible in the belfry and among the people. Banners are borne out of the church one after the other, while the bells peal in joyous haste. Seryozhka, trembling, pulls away the mat . . . and the people behold something extraordinary. The lectern, the wooden ring, the pegs, and the cross in the ice are iridescent with thousands of colors. The cross and the dove glitter so dazzlingly that it hurts the eyes to look at them. Merciful God, how fine it is! A murmur of wonder and delight runs through the crowd; the bells peal more loudly still, the day grows brighter; the banners oscillate and move over the crowd as over the waves. The procession, glittering with the settings of the ikons and the vestments of the clergy, comes slowly down the road and turns towards the Jordan. Hands are waved to the belfry for the ringing to cease, and the blessing of the water begins. The priests conduct the service slowly, deliberately, evidently trying to prolong the ceremony and the joy of praying all gathered together. There is perfect stillness.

But now they plunge the cross in, and the air echoes with an extraordinary din. Guns are fired, the bells peal furiously, loud exclamations of delight, shouts, and a rush to get the pegs. Seryozhka listens to this uproar, sees thousands of eyes fixed upon him, and the lazy fellow's soul is filled with a sense of glory and triumph.

A Blunder

Ilya Sergeitch Peplov and his wife Kleopatra Petrovna were standing at the door, listening greedily. On the other side in the little drawing-room a love scene was apparently taking place between two persons: their daughter Natashenka and a teacher of the district school, called Shchupkin.

"He's rising!" whispered Peplov, quivering with impatience and rubbing his hands. "Now, Kleopatra, mind; as soon as they begin talking of their feelings, take down the ikon from the wall and we'll go in and bless them.... We'll catch him.... A blessing with an ikon is sacred and binding.... He couldn't get out of it, if he brought it into court."

On the other side of the door this was the conversation:

"Don't go on like that!" said Shchupkin, striking a match against his checked trousers. "I never wrote you any letters!"

"I like that! As though I didn't know your writing!" giggled the girl with an affected shriek, continually peeping at herself in the glass. "I knew it at once! And what a queer man you are! You are a writing master, and you write like a spider! How can you teach writing if you write so badly yourself?"

"H'm!... That means nothing. The great thing in writing lessons is not the hand one writes, but keeping the boys in order. You hit one on the head with a ruler, make another kneel down. . . . Besides, there's nothing in handwriting! Nekrassov was an author, but his handwriting's a disgrace, there's a specimen of it in his collected works."

"You are not Nekrassov. . . ." (A sigh). "I should love to marry an author. He'd always be writing poems to me."

"I can write you a poem, too, if you like."

"What can you write about?"

"Love—passion—your eyes. You'll be crazy when you read it. It would draw a tear from a stone! And if I write you a real poem, will you let me kiss your hand?"

"That's nothing much! You can kiss it now if you like."

Shchupkin jumped up, and making sheepish eyes, bent over the fat little hand that smelt of egg soap.

"Take down the ikon," Peplov whispered in a fluster, pale with excitement, and buttoning his coat as he prodded his wife with his elbow. "Come along, now!"

And without a second's delay Peplov flung open the door.

"Children," he muttered, lifting up his arms and blinking tearfully, "the Lord bless you, my children. May you live—be fruitful—and multiply."

"And—and I bless you, too," the mamma brought out, crying with happiness. "May you be happy, my dear ones! Oh, you are taking from me my only treasure!" she said to Shchupkin. "Love my girl, be good to her. . . ."

Shchupkin's mouth fell open with amazement and alarm. The parents' attack was so bold and unexpected that he could not utter a single word.

"I'm in for it! I'm spliced!" he thought, going limp with horror. "It's all over with you now, my boy! There's no escape!"

And he bowed his head submissively, as though to say, "Take me, I'm vanquished."

"Ble-blessings on you," the papa went on, and he, too, shed tears. "Natashenka, my daughter, stand by his side. Kleopatra, give me the ikon."

But at this point the father suddenly left off weeping, and his face was contorted with anger.

"You ninny!" he said angrily to his wife. "You are an idiot! Is that the ikon?"

"Ach, saints alive!"

What had happened? The writing master raised himself and saw that he was saved; in her flutter the mamma had snatched from the wall the portrait of Lazhetchnikov, the author, in mistake for the ikon. Old Peplov and his wife stood disconcerted in the middle of the room, holding the portrait aloft, not knowing what to do or what to say. The writing master took advantage of the general confusion and slipped away.

Children

Papa and mamma and Aunt Nadya are not at home. They have gone to a christening party at the house of that old officer who rides on a little grey horse. While waiting for them to come home, Grisha, Anya, Alyosha, Sonya, and the cook's son, Andrey, are sitting at the table in the dining-room, playing at loto. To tell the truth, it is bedtime, but how can one go to sleep without hearing from mamma what the baby was like at the christening, and what they had for supper? The table, lighted by a hanging lamp, is dotted with numbers, nutshells, scraps of paper, and little bits of glass. Two cards lie in front of each player, and a heap of bits of glass for covering the numbers. In the middle of the table is a white saucer with five kopecks in it. Beside the saucer, a half-eaten apple, a pair of scissors, and a plate on which they have been told to put their nutshells. The children are playing for money. The stake is a kopeck. The rule is: if anyone cheats, he is turned out at once. There is no one in the dining-room but the players, and nurse, Agafya Ivanovna, is in the kitchen, showing the cook how to cut a pattern, while their elder brother, Vasya, a schoolboy in the fifth class, is lying on the sofa in the drawing-room, feeling bored.

They are playing with zest. The greatest excitement is expressed on the face of Grisha. He is a small boy of nine, with a head cropped so

that the bare skin shows through, chubby cheeks, and thick lips like a
negro's. He is already in the preparatory class, and so is regarded as
grown up, and the cleverest. He is playing entirely for the sake of the
money. If there had been no kopecks in the saucer, he would have been
asleep long ago. His brown eyes stray uneasily and jealously over the
other players' cards. The fear that he may not win, envy, and the financial combinations of which his cropped head is full, will not let
him sit still and concentrate his mind. He fidgets as though he were sitting on thorns. When he wins, he snatches up the money greedily, and
instantly puts it in his pocket. His sister, Anya, a girl of eight, with a
sharp chin and clever shining eyes, is also afraid that someone else may
win. She flushes and turns pale, and watches the players keenly. The
kopecks do not interest her. Success in the game is for her a question
of vanity. The other sister, Sonya, a child of six with a curly head, and
a complexion such as is seen only in very healthy children, expensive
dolls, and the faces on bonbon boxes, is playing loto for the process of
the game itself. There is bliss all over her face. Whoever wins, she
laughs and claps her hands. Alyosha, a chubby, spherical little figure,
gasps, breathes hard through his nose, and stares open-eyed at the
cards. He is moved neither by covetousness nor vanity. So long as he is
not driven out of the room, or sent to bed, he is thankful. He looks
phlegmatic, but at heart he is rather a little beast. He is not there so
much for the sake of the loto, as for the sake of the misunderstandings
which are inevitable in the game. He is greatly delighted if one hits
another, or calls him names. He ought to have run off somewhere long
ago, but he won't leave the table for a minute, for fear they should steal
his counters or his kopecks. As he can only count the units and numbers which end in nought, Anya covers his numbers for him. The fifth
player, the cook's son, Andrey, a dark-skinned and sickly looking boy
in a cotton shirt, with a copper cross on his breast, stands motionless,
looking dreamily at the numbers. He takes no interest in winning, or
in the success of the others, because he is entirely engrossed by the
arithmetic of the game, and its far from complex theory; "How many
numbers there are in the world," he is thinking, "and how is it they
don't get mixed up?"

They all shout out the numbers in turn, except Sonya and Alyosha.

To vary the monotony, they have invented in the course of time a number of synonyms and comic nicknames. Seven, for instance, is called the "ovenrake," eleven the "sticks," seventy-seven "Semyon Semyonitch," ninety "grandfather," and so on. The game is going merrily.

"Thirty-two," cries Grisha, drawing the little yellow cylinders out of his father's cap. "Seventeen! Ovenrake! Twenty-eight! Lay them straight. . . ."

Anya sees that Andrey has let twenty-eight slip. At any other time she would have pointed it out to him, but now when her vanity lies in the saucer with the kopecks, she is triumphant.

"Twenty-three!" Grisha goes on, "Semyon Semyonitch! Nine!"

"A beetle, a beetle," cries Sonya, pointing to a beetle running across the table. "Aie!"

"Don't kill it," says Alyosha, in his deep bass, "perhaps it's got children. . . ."

Sonya follows the black beetle with her eyes and wonders about its children: what tiny little beetles they must be!

"Forty-three! One!" Grisha goes on, unhappy at the thought that Anya has already made two fours. "Six!"

"Game! I have got the game!" cries Sonya, rolling her eyes coquettishly and giggling.

The players' countenances lengthen.

"Must make sure!" says Grisha, looking with hatred at Sonya.

Exercising his rights as a big boy, and the cleverest, Grisha takes upon himself to decide. What he wants, that they do. Sonya's reckoning is slowly and carefully verified, and to the great regret of her fellow players, it appears that she has not cheated. Another game is begun.

"I did see something yesterday!" says Anya, as though to herself. "Filipp Filippitch turned his eyelids inside out somehow and his eyes looked red and dreadful, like an evil spirit's."

"I saw it too," says Grisha. "Eight! And a boy at our school can move his ears. Twenty-seven!"

Andrey looks up at Grisha, meditates, and says:

"I can move my ears too. . . ."

"Well then, move them."

Andrey moves his eyes, his lips, and his fingers, and fancies that his ears are moving too. Everyone laughs.

"He is a horrid man, that Filipp Filippitch," sighs Sonya. "He came into our nursery yesterday, and I had nothing on but my chemise . . . And I felt so improper!"

"Game!" Grisha cries suddenly, snatching the money from the saucer. "I've got the game! You can look and see if you like."

The cook's son looks up and turns pale.

"Then I can't go on playing any more," he whispers.

"Why not?"

"Because . . . because I have got no more money."

"You can't play without money," says Grisha.

Andrey ransacks his pockets once more to make sure. Finding nothing in them but crumbs and a bitten pencil, he drops the corners of his mouth and begins blinking miserably. He is on the point of crying. . . .

"I'll put it down for you!" says Sonya, unable to endure his look of agony. "Only mind you must pay me back afterwards."

The money is brought and the game goes on.

"I believe they are ringing somewhere," says Anya, opening her eyes wide.

They all leave off playing and gaze open-mouthed at the dark window. The reflection of the lamp glimmers in the darkness.

"It was your fancy."

"At night they only ring in the cemetery," says Andrey. . . .

"And what do they ring there for?"

"To prevent robbers from breaking into the church. They are afraid of the bells."

"And what do robbers break into the church for?" asks Sonya.

"Everyone knows what for: to kill the watchmen."

A minute passes in silence. They all look at one another, shudder, and go on playing. This time Andrey wins.

"He has cheated," Alyosha booms out, apropos of nothing.

"What a lie, I haven't cheated."

Andrey turns pale, his mouth works, and he gives Alyosha a slap on the head! Alyosha glares angrily, jumps up, and with one knee on the table, slaps Andrey on the cheek! Each gives the other a second blow, and both howl. Sonya, feeling such horrors too much for her, begins crying too, and the dining-room resounds with lamentations on various notes. But do not imagine that that is the end of the game. Before five minutes are over, the children are laughing and talking peaceably again. Their faces are tear-stained, but that does not prevent them from smiling; Alyosha is positively blissful, there has been a squabble!

Vasya, the fifth form schoolboy, walks into the dining-room. He looks sleepy and disillusioned.

"This is revolting!" he thinks, seeing Grisha feel in his pockets in which the kopecks are jingling. "How can they give children money? And how can they let them play games of chance? A nice way to bring them up, I must say! It's revolting!"

But the children's play is so tempting that he feels an inclination to join them and to try his luck.

"Wait a minute and I'll sit down to a game," he says.

"Put down a kopeck!"

"In a minute," he says, fumbling in his pockets. "I haven't a kopeck, but here is a rouble. I'll stake a rouble."

"No, no, no. . . . You must put down a kopeck."

"You stupids. A rouble is worth more than a kopeck anyway," the schoolboy explains. "Whoever wins can give me change."

"No, please! Go away!"

The fifth form schoolboy shrugs his shoulders, and goes into the kitchen to get change from the servants. It appears there is not a single kopeck in the kitchen.

"In that case, you give me change," he urges Grisha, coming back from the kitchen. "I'll pay you for the change. Won't you? Come, give me ten kopecks for a rouble."

Grisha looks suspiciously at Vasya, wondering whether it isn't some trick, a swindle.

"I won't," he says, holding his pockets.

Vasya begins to get cross, and abuses them, calling them idiots and blockheads.

"I'll put down a stake for you, Vasya!" says Sonya. "Sit down." He sits down and lays two cards before him. Anya begins counting the numbers.

"I've dropped a kopeck!" Grisha announces suddenly, in an agitated voice. "Wait!"

He takes the lamp, and creeps under the table to look for the kopeck. They clutch at nutshells and all sorts of nastiness, knock their heads together, but do not find the kopeck. They begin looking again, and look till Vasya takes the lamp out of Grisha's hands and puts it in its place. Grisha goes on looking in the dark. But at last the kopeck is found. The players sit down at the table and mean to go on playing.

"Sonya is asleep!" Alyosha announces.

Sonya, with her curly head lying on her arms, is in a sweet, sound, tranquil sleep, as though she had been asleep for an hour. She has fallen asleep by accident, while the others were looking for the kopeck.

"Come along, lie on mamma's bed!" says Anya, leading her away from the table. "Come along!"

They all troop out with her, and five minutes later mamma's bed presents a curious spectacle. Sonya is asleep. Alyosha is snoring beside her. With their heads to the others' feet, sleep Grisha and Anya. The cook's son, Andrey too, has managed to snuggle in beside them. Near them lie the kopecks, that have lost their power till the next game. Good-night!

Misery

"To whom shall I tell my grief?"

The twilight of evening. Big flakes of wet snow are whirling lazily about the street lamps, which have just been lighted, and lying in a thin soft layer on roofs, horses' backs, shoulders, caps. Iona Potapov, the sledge-driver, is all white like a ghost. He sits on the box without stirring, bent as double as the living body can be bent. If a regular snow-drift fell on him it seems as though even then he would not think it necessary to shake it off.... His little mare is white and motionless too. Her stillness, the angularity of her lines, and the stick-like straightness of her legs make her look like a halfpenny gingerbread horse. She is probably lost in thought. Anyone who has been torn away from the plough, from the familiar gray landscapes, and cast into this slough, full of monstrous lights, of unceasing uproar and hurrying people, is bound to think.

It is a long time since Iona and his nag have budged. They came out of the yard before dinner-time and not a single fare yet. But now the shades of evening are falling on the town. The pale light of the street lamps changes to a vivid color, and the bustle of the street grows noiser.

"Sledge to Vyborgskaya!" Iona hears. "Sledge!"

Iona starts, and through his snow-plastered eyelashes sees an officer in a military overcoat with a hood over his head.

"To Vyborgskaya," repeats the officer. "Are you asleep? To Vyborgskaya!"

In token of assent Iona gives a tug at the reins which sends cakes of snow flying from the horse's back and shoulders. The officer gets into the sledge. The sledge-driver clicks to the horse, cranes his neck like a swan, rises in his seat, and more from habit than necessity brandishes his whip. The mare cranes her neck, too, crooks her stick-like legs, and hesitatingly sets off. . . .

"Where are you shoving, you devil?" Iona immediately hears shouts from the dark mass shifting to and fro before him. "Where the devil are you going? Keep to the r-right!"

"You don't know how to drive! Keep to the right," says the officer angrily.

A coachman driving a carriage swears at him; a pedestrian crossing the road and brushing the horse's nose with his shoulder looks at him angrily and shakes the snow off his sleeve. Iona fidgets on the box as though he were sitting on thorns, jerks his elbows, and turns his eyes about like one possessed, as though he did not know where he was or why he was there.

"What rascals they all are!" says the officer jocosely. "They are simply doing their best to run up against you or fall under the horse's feet. They must be doing it on purpose."

Iona looks as his fare and moves his lips. . . . Apparently he means to say something, but nothing comes but a sniff.

"What?" inquires the officer.

Iona gives a wry smile, and straining his throat, brings out huskily: "My son . . . er . . . my son died this week, sir."

"H'm! What did he die of?"

Iona turns his whole body round to his fare, and says:

"Who can tell! It must have been from fever. . . . He lay three days in the hospital and then he died. . . . God's will."

"Turn round, you devil!" comes out of the darkness. "Have you gone cracked, you old dog? Look where you are going!"

"Drive on! drive on!...." says the officer. "We shan't get there till to-morrow going on like this. Hurry up!"

The sledge-driver cranes his neck again, rises in his seat, and with heavy grace swings his whip. Several times he looks round at the officer, but the latter keeps his eyes shut and is apparently disinclined to listen. Putting his fare down at Vyborgskaya, Iona stops by a restaurant, and again sits huddled up on the box.... Again the wet snow paints him and his horse white. One hour passes, and then another....

Three young men, two tall and thin, one short and hunchbacked, come up, railing at each other and loudly stamping on the pavement with their goloshes.

"Cabby, to the Police Bridge!" the hunchback cries in a cracked voice. "The three of us,... twenty kopecks!"

Iona tugs at the reins and clicks to his horse. Twenty kopecks is not a fair price, but he has no thoughts for that. Whether it is a rouble or whether it is five kopecks does not matter to him now so long as he has a fare.... The three young men, shoving each other and using bad language, go up to the sledge, and all three try to sit down at once. The question remains to be settled: Which are to sit down and which one is to stand? After a long altercation, ill-temper, and abuse, they come to the conclusion that the hunchback must stand because he is the shortest.

"Well, drive on," says the hunchback in his cracked voice, settling himself and breathing down Iona's neck. "Cut along! What a cap you've got, my friend! You wouldn't find a worse one in all Petersburg...."

"He-he!... he-he!..." laughs Iona. "It's nothing to boast of!"

"Well, then, nothing to boast of, drive on! Are you going to drive like this all the way? Eh? Shall I give you one in the neck?"

"My head aches," says one of the tall ones. "At the Dukmasovs' yesterday Vaska and I drank four bottles of brandy between us."

"I can't make out why you talk such stuff," says the other tall one angrily. "You lie like a brute."

"Strike me dead, it's the truth!..."

"It's about as true as that a louse coughs."

"He-he!" grins Iona. "Me-er-ry gentlemen!"

"Tfoo! the devil take you!" cries the hunchback indignantly. "Will you get on, you old plague, or won't you? Is that the way to drive? Give her one with the whip. Hang it all, give it her well."

Iona feels behind his back the jolting person and quivering voice of the hunchback. He hears abuse addressed to him, he sees people, and the feeling of loneliness begins little by little to be less heavy on his heart. The hunchback swears at him, till he chokes over some elaborately whimsical string of epithets and is overpowered by his cough. His tall companions begin talking of a certain Nadyezhda Petrovna. Iona looks round at them. Waiting till there is a brief pause, he looks round once more and says:

"This week . . . er . . . my . . . er . . . son died!"

"We shall all die, . . ." says the hunchback with a sigh, wiping his lips after coughing. "Come, drive on! drive on! My friends, I simply cannot stand crawling like this! When will he get us there?"

"Well, you give him a little encouragement . . . one in the neck!"

"Do you hear, you old plague? I'll make you smart. If one stands on ceremony with fellows like you one may as well walk. Do you hear, you old dragon? Or don't you care a hang what we say?"

And Iona hears rather than feels a slap on the back of his neck.

"He-he! . . ." he laughs. "Merry gentlemen. . . . God give you health!"

"Cabman, are you married?" asks one of the tall ones.

"I? He-he! Me-er-ry gentlemen. The only wife for me now is the damp earth. . . . He-ho-ho! . . . The grave that is! . . . Here my son's dead and I am alive. . . . It's a strange thing, death has come in at the wrong door. . . . Instead of coming for me it went for my son. . . ."

And Iona turns round to tell them how his son died, but at that point the hunchback gives a faint sigh and announces that, thank God! they have arrived at last. After taking his twenty kopecks, Iona gazes for a long while after the revelers, who disappear into a dark entry. Again he is alone and again there is silence for him. . . . The misery which has been for a brief space eased comes back again and tears his heart more cruelly than ever. With a look of anxiety and suffering Iona's eyes stray restlessly among the crowds moving to and fro on both sides of the street: can he not find among those thousands someone who will listen to him? But the crowds flit by heedless of him and his misery. . . . His misery is immense, beyond all bounds. If Iona's heart were to burst and his misery to flow out, it would flood the whole world, it seems, but yet it is not seen. It has found a hiding-place in such an insignificant shell that one would not have found it with a candle by daylight. . . .

Iona sees a house-porter with a parcel and makes up his mind to address him.

"What time will it be, friend?" he asks.

"Going on for ten. . . . Why have you stopped here? Drive on!"

Iona drives a few paces away, bends himself double, and gives himself up to his misery. He feels it is no good to appeal to people. But before five minutes have passed he draws himself up, shakes his head as though he feels a sharp pain, and tugs at the reins. . . . He can bear it no longer.

"Back to the yard!" he thinks. "To the yard!"

And his little mare, as though she knew his thoughts, falls to trotting. An hour and a half later Iona is sitting by a big dirty stove. On the stove, on the floor, and on the benches are people snoring. The air is full of smells and stuffiness. Iona looks at the sleeping figures, scratches himself, and regrets that he has come home so early. . . .

"I have not earned enough to pay for the oats, even," he thinks. "That's why I am so miserable. A man who knows how to do his work, . . . who has had enough to eat, and whose horse has had enough to eat, is always at ease. . . ."

In one of the corners a young cabman gets up, clears his throat sleepily, and makes for the water-bucket.

"Want a drink?" Iona asks him.

"Seems so."

"May it do you good. . . . But my son is dead, mate. . . . Do you hear? This week in the hospital. . . . It's a queer business. . . ."

Iona looks to see the effect produced by his words, but he sees nothing. The young man has covered his head over and is already asleep. The old man sighs and scratches himself. . . . Just as the young man had been thirsty for water, he thirsts for speech. His son will soon have been dead a week, and he has not really talked to anybody yet. . . . He wants to talk of it properly, with deliberation. . . . He wants to tell how his son was taken ill, how he suffered, what he said before he died, how he died. . . . He wants to describe the funeral, and how he went to the hospital to get his son's clothes. He still has his daughter Anisya in the country. . . . And he wants to talk about her too. . . . Yes, he has plenty to talk about now. His listener ought to sigh and exclaim and lament. . . . It would be even better to talk to women. Though they are silly creatures, they blubber at the first word.

"Let's go out and have a look at the mare," Iona thinks. "There is always time for sleep. . . . You'll have sleep enough, no fear. . . ."

He puts on his coat and goes into the stables where his mare is standing. He thinks about oats, about hay, about the weather. . . . He cannot think about his son when he is alone. . . . To talk about him with someone is possible, but to think of him and picture him is insufferable anguish. . . .

"Are you munching?" Iona asks his mare, seeing her shining eyes. "There, munch away, munch away. . . . Since we have not earned enough for oats, we will eat hay. . . . Yes, . . . I have grown too old to drive. . . . My son ought to be driving, not I. . . . He was a real cabman. . . . He ought to have lived. . . ."

Iona is silent for a while, and then he goes on:

"That's how it is, old girl. . . . Kuzma Ionitch is gone. . . . He said good-by to me. . . . He went and died for no reason. . . . Now, suppose you had a little colt, and you were own mother to that little colt. . . . And all at once that same little colt went and died. . . . You'd be sorry, wouldn't you? . . ."

The little mare munches, listens, and breathes on her master's hands. Iona is carried away and tells her all about it.

An Upheaval

Mashenka Pavletsky, a young girl who had only just finished her studies at a boarding school, returning from a walk to the house of the Kushkins, with whom she was living as a governess, found the household in a terrible turmoil. Mihailo, the porter who opened the door to her, was excited and red as a crab.

Loud voices were heard from upstairs.

"Madame Kushkin is in a fit, most likely, or else she has quarrelled with her husband," thought Mashenka.

In the hall and in the corridor she met maid-servants. One of them was crying. Then Mashenka saw, running out of her room, the master of the house himself, Nikolay Sergeitch, a little man with a flabby face and a bald head, though he was not old. He was red in the face and twitching all over. He passed the governess without noticing her, and throwing up his arms, exclaimed:

"Oh, how horrible it is! How tactless! How stupid! How barbarous! Abominable!"

Mashenka went into her room, and then, for the first time in her life, it was her lot to experience in all its acuteness the feeling that is so familiar to persons in dependent positions, who eat the bread of the rich and powerful, and cannot speak their minds. There was a search going on in her room. The lady of the house, Fedosya Vassilyevna, a stout, broad-shouldered, uncouth woman with thick black eyebrows, a faintly perceptible moustache, and red hands, who was exactly like a plain, illiterate cook in face and manners, was standing, without her cap on, at the table, putting back into Mashenka's work-bag balls of wool, scraps of materials, and bits of paper. . . . Evidently the governess's arrival took her by surprise, since, on looking round and seeing the girl's pale and astonished face, she was a little taken aback, and muttered:

"*Pardon.* I . . . I upset it accidentally. . . . My sleeve caught in it. . . ."

And saying something more, Madame Kushkin rustled her long skirts and went out. Mashenka looked round her room with wondering eyes, and, unable to understand it, not knowing what to think, shrugged her shoulders, and turned cold with dismay. What had Fedosya Vassilyevna been looking for in her work-bag? If she really had, as she said, caught her sleeve in it and upset everything, why had Nikolay Sergeitch dashed out of her room so excited and red in the face? Why was one drawer of the table pulled out a little way? The money-box, in which the governess put away ten kopeck pieces and old stamps, was open. They had opened it, but did not know how to shut it, though they had scratched the lock all over. The whatnot with her books on it, the things on the table, the bed—all bore fresh traces of a search. Her linen-basket, too. The linen had been carefully folded, but it was not in the same order as Mashenka had left it when she went out. So the search had been thorough, most thorough. But what was it for? Why? What had happened? Mashenka remembered the excited porter, the general turmoil which was still going on, the weeping servant-girl; had it not all some connection with the search that had just been made in her room? Was not she mixed up in something dreadful? Mashenka turned pale, and feeling cold all over, sank on to her linen-basket.

A maid-servant came into the room.

"Liza, you don't know why they have been rummaging in my room?" the governess asked her.

"Mistress has lost a brooch worth two thousand," said Liza.

"Yes, but why have they been rummaging in my room?"

"They've been searching every one, miss. They've searched all my things, too. They stripped us all naked and searched us.... God knows, miss, I never went near her toilet-table, let alone touching the brooch. I shall say the same at the police-station."

"But . . . why have they been rummaging here?" the governess still wondered.

"A brooch has been stolen, I tell you. The mistress has been rummaging in everything with her own hands. She even searched Mihailo, the porter, herself. It's a perfect disgrace! Nikolay Sergeitch simply looks on and cackles like a hen. But you've no need to tremble like that, miss. They found nothing here. You've nothing to be afraid of if you didn't take the brooch."

"But, Liza, it's vile . . . it's insulting," said Mashenka, breathless with indignation. "It's so mean, so low! What right had she to suspect me and to rummage in my things?"

"You are living with strangers, miss," sighed Liza. "Though you are a young lady, still you are . . . as it were . . . a servant. . . . It's not like living with your papa and mamma."

Mashenka threw herself on the bed and sobbed bitterly. Never in her life had she been subjected to such an outrage, never had she been so deeply insulted. . . . She, well-educated, refined, the daughter of a teacher, was suspected of theft; she had been searched like a street-walker! She could not imagine a greater insult. And to this feeling of resentment was added an oppressive dread of what would come next. All sorts of absurd ideas came into her mind. If they could suspect her of theft, then they might arrest her, strip her naked, and search her, then lead her through the street with an escort of soldiers, cast her into a cold, dark cell with mice and woodlice, exactly like the dungeon in which Princess Tarakanov was imprisoned. Who would stand up for her? Her parents lived far away in the provinces; they had not the money to come to her. In the capital she was as solitary as in a desert, without friends or kindred. They could do what they liked with her.

"I will go to all the courts and all the lawyers," Mashenka thought, trembling. "I will explain to them, I will take an oath. . . . They will believe that I could not be a thief!"

Mashenka remembered that under the sheets in her basket she had some sweetmeats, which, following the habits of her schooldays, she had put in her pocket at dinner and carried off to her room. She felt hot all over, and was ashamed at the thought that her little secret was known to the lady of the house; and all this terror, shame, resentment, brought on an attack of palpitation of the heart, which set up a throbbing in her temples, in her heart, and deep down in her stomach.

"Dinner is ready," the servant summoned Mashenka.

"Shall I go, or not?"

Mashenka brushed her hair, wiped her face with a wet towel, and went into the dining-room. There they had already begun dinner. At one end of the table sat Fedosya Vassilyevna with a stupid, solemn, serious face; at the other end Nikolay Sergeitch. At the sides there were the visitors and the children. The dishes were handed by two footmen in swallowtails and white gloves. Every one knew that there was an upset in the house, that Madame Kushkin was in trouble, and every one was silent. Nothing was heard but the sound of munching and the rattle of spoons on the plates.

The lady of the house, herself, was the first to speak.

"What is the third course?" she asked the footman in a weary, injured voice.

"*Esturgeon à la russe,*" answered the footman.

"I ordered that, Fenya," Nikolay Sergeitch hastened to observe. "I wanted some fish. If you don't like it, *ma chère,* don't let them serve it. I just ordered it. . . ."

Fedosya Vassilyevna did not like dishes that she had not ordered herself, and now her eyes filled with tears.

"Come, don't let us agitate ourselves," Mamikov, her household doctor, observed in a honeyed voice, just touching her arm, with a smile as honeyed. "We are nervous enough as it is. Let us forget the brooch! Health is worth more than two thousand roubles!"

"It's not the two thousand I regret," answered the lady, and a big tear rolled down her cheek. "It's the fact itself that revolts me! I cannot put up with thieves in my house. I don't regret it—I regret nothing; but to steal from me is such ingratitude! That's how they repay me for my kindness. . . ."

They all looked into their plates, but Mashenka fancied after the lady's words that every one was looking at her. A lump rose in her throat; she began crying and put her handkerchief to her lips.

"*Pardon,*" she muttered. "I can't help it. My head aches. I'll go away."

And she got up from the table, scraping her chair awkwardly, and went out quickly, still more overcome with confusion.

"It's beyond everything!" said Nikolay Sergeitch, frowning. "What need was there to search her room? How out of place it was!"

"I don't say she took the brooch," said Fedosya Vassilyevna, "but can you answer for her? To tell the truth, I haven't much confidence in these learned paupers."

"It really was unsuitable, Fenya. . . . Excuse me, Fenya, but you've no kind of legal right to make a search."

"I know nothing about your laws. All I know is that I've lost my brooch. And I will find the brooch!" She brought her fork down on the plate with a clatter, and her eyes flashed angrily. "And you eat your dinner, and don't interfere in what doesn't concern you!"

Nikolay Sergeitch dropped his eyes mildly and sighed. Meanwhile Mashenka, reaching her room, flung herself on her bed. She felt now neither alarm nor shame, but she felt an intense longing to go and slap the cheeks of this hard, arrogant, dull-witted, prosperous woman.

Lying on her bed she breathed into her pillow and dreamed of how nice it would be to go and buy the most expensive brooch and fling it into the face of this bullying woman. If only it were God's will that Fedosya Vassilyevna should come to ruin and wander about begging, and should taste all the horrors of poverty and dependence, and that Mashenka, whom she had insulted, might give her alms! Oh, if only she could come in for a big fortune, could buy a carriage, and could drive noisily past the windows so as to be envied by that woman!

But all these were only dreams, in reality there was only one thing left to do—to get away as quickly as possible, not to stay another hour in this place. It was true it was terrible to lose her place, to go back to her parents, who had nothing; but what could she do? Mashenka could not bear the sight of the lady of the house nor of her little room; she felt stifled and wretched here. She was so disgusted with Fedosya Vassilyevna, who was so obsessed by her illnesses and her supposed aristocratic rank, that everything in the world seemed to have become coarse and unattractive because this woman was living in it. Mashenka jumped up from the bed and began packing.

"May I come in?" asked Nikolay Sergeitch at the door; he had come up noiselessly to the door, and spoke in a soft, subdued voice. "May I?"

"Come in."

He came in and stood still near the door. His eyes looked dim and his red little nose was shiny. After dinner he used to drink beer, and the fact was perceptible in his walk, in his feeble, flabby hands.

"What's this?" he asked, pointing to the basket.

"I am packing. Forgive me, Nikolay Sergeitch, but I cannot remain in your house. I feel deeply insulted by this search!"

"I understand. . . . Only you are wrong to go. . . . Why should you? They've searched your things, but you . . . what does it matter to you? You will be none the worse for it."

Mashenka was silent and went on packing. Nikolay Sergeitch pinched his moustache, as though wondering what he should say next, and went on in an ingratiating voice:

"I understand, of course, but you must make allowances. You know my wife is nervous, headstrong; you mustn't judge her too harshly."

Mashenka did not speak.

"If you are so offended," Nikolay Sergeitch went on, "well, if you like, I'm ready to apologise. I ask your pardon."

Mashenka made no answer, but only bent lower over her box. This exhausted, irresolute man was of absolutely no significance in the household. He stood in the pitiful position of a dependent and hanger-on, even with the servants, and his apology meant nothing either.

"H'm! . . . You say nothing! That's not enough for you. In that case, I will apologise for my wife. In my wife's name. . . . She behaved tactlessly, I admit it as a gentleman. . . ."

Nikolay Sergeitch walked about the room, heaved a sigh, and went on:

"Then you want me to have it rankling here, under my heart. . . . You want my conscience to torment me. . . ."

"I know it's not your fault, Nikolay Sergeitch," said Mashenka, looking him full in the face with her big tear-stained eyes. "Why should you worry yourself?"

"Of course, no. . . . But still, don't you . . . go away. I entreat you."

Mashenka shook her head. Nikolay Sergeitch stopped at the window and drummed on the pane with his finger-tips.

"Such misunderstandings are simply torture to me," he said. "Why, do you want me to go down on my knees to you, or what? Your pride is wounded, and here you've been crying and packing up to go; but I have pride, too, and you do not spare it! Or do you want me to tell you what I would not tell as Confession? Do you? Listen; you want me to tell you what I won't tell the priest on my death-bed?"

Mashenka made no answer.

"I took my wife's brooch," Nikolay Sergeitch said quickly. "Is that enough now? Are you satisfied? Yes, I . . . took it. . . . But, of course, I count on your discretion. . . . For God's sake, not a word, not half a hint to any one!"

Mashenka, amazed and frightened, went on packing; she snatched her things, crumpled them up, and thrust them anyhow into the box and the basket. Now, after this candid avowal on the part of Nikolay Sergeitch, she could not remain another minute, and could not understand how she could have gone on living in the house before.

"And it's nothing to wonder at," Nikolay Sergeitch went on after a pause. "It's an everyday story! I need money, and she . . . won't give it to me. It was my father's money that bought this house and everything, you know! It's all mine, and the brooch belonged to my mother, and . . . it's all mine! And she took it, took possession of everything. . . . I can't go to law with her, you'll admit. . . . I beg you most earnestly, overlook it . . . stay on. *Tout comprendre, tout pardonner*. Will you stay?"

"No!" said Mashenka resolutely, beginning to tremble. "Let me alone, I entreat you!"

"Well, God bless you!" sighed Nikolay Sergeitch, sitting down on the stool near the box. "I must own I like people who still can feel resentment, contempt, and so on. I could sit here forever and look at your indignant face. . . . So you won't stay, then? I understand. . . . It's bound to be so. . . . Yes, of course. . . . It's all right for you, but for me— wo-o-o-o! . . . I can't stir a step out of this cellar. I'd go off to one of our estates, but in every one of them there are some of my wife's rascals . . . stewards, experts, damn them all! They mortgage and remortgage. . . . You mustn't catch fish, must keep off the grass, mustn't break the trees."

"Nikolay Sergeitch!" his wife's voice called from the drawing-room. "Agnia, call your master!"

"Then you won't stay?" asked Nikolay Sergeitch, getting up quickly and going towards the door. "You might as well stay, really. In the evenings I could come and have a talk with you. Eh? Stay! If you go, there won't be a human face left in the house. It's awful!"

Nikolay Sergeitch's pale, exhausted face besought her, but Mashenka shook her head, and with a wave of his hand he went out.

Half an hour later she was on her way.

The Requiem

In the village church of Verhny Zaprudy mass was just over. The people had begun moving and were trooping out of church. The only one who did not move was Andrey Andreyitch, a shopkeeper and old inhabitant of Verhny Zaprudy. He stood waiting, with his elbows on the railing of the right choir. His fat and shaven face, covered with indentations left by pimples, expressed on this occasion two contradictory feelings: resignation in the face of inevitable destiny, and stupid, unbounded disdain for the smocks and striped kerchiefs passing by him. As it was Sunday, he was dressed like a dandy. He wore a long cloth overcoat with yellow bone buttons, blue trousers not thrust into his boots, and sturdy goloshes—the huge clumsy goloshes only seen on the feet of practical and prudent persons of firm religious convictions.

His torpid eyes, sunk in fat, were fixed upon the ikon stand. He saw the long familiar figures of the saints, the verger Matvey puffing out his cheeks and blowing out the candles, the darkened candle stands, the threadbare carpet, the sacristan Lopuhov running impulsively from the altar and carrying the holy bread to the churchwarden.... All these things he had seen for years, and seen over and over again like the five fingers of his hand.... There was only one thing, however, that was somewhat strange and unusual. Father Grigory, still in his vest-

ments, was standing at the north door, twitching his thick eyebrows angrily.

"Who is it he is winking at? God bless him!" thought the shopkeeper. "And he is beckoning with his finger! And he stamped his foot!
What next! What's the matter, Holy Queen and Mother! Whom does
he mean it for?"

Andrey Andreyitch looked round and saw the church completely
deserted. There were some ten people standing at the door, but they
had their backs to the altar.

"Do come when you are called! Why do you stand like a graven
image?" he heard Father Grigory's angry voice. "I am calling you."

The shopkeeper looked at Father Grigory's red and wrathful face,
and only then realized that the twitching eyebrows and beckoning finger might refer to him. He started, left the railing, and hesitatingly
walked towards the altar, tramping with his heavy goloshes.

"Andrey Andreyitch, was it you asked for prayers for the rest of
Mariya's soul?" asked the priest, his eyes angrily transfixing the shopkeeper's fat, perspiring face.

"Yes, Father."

"Then it was you wrote this? You?" And Father Grigory angrily
thrust before his eyes the little note.

And on this little note, handed in by Andrey Andreyitch before
mass, was written in big, as it were staggering, letters:

"For the rest of the soul of the servant of God, the harlot Mariya."

"Yes, certainly I wrote it, . . ." answered the shopkeeper.

"How dared you write it?" whispered the priest, and in his husky
whisper there was a note of wrath and alarm.

The shopkeeper looked at him in blank amazement; he was perplexed, and he, too, was alarmed. Father Grigory had never in his life
spoken in such a tone to a leading resident of Verhny Zaprudy. Both
were silent for a minute, staring into each other's face. The shopkeeper's amazement was so great that his fat face spread in all directions like split dough.

"How dared you?" repeated the priest.

"Wha . . . what?" asked Andrey Andreyitch in bewilderment.

"You don't understand?" whispered Father Grigory, stepping back in astonishment and clasping his hands. "What have you got on your shoulders, a head or some other object? You send a note up to the altar, and write a word in it which it would be unseemly even to utter in the street! Why are you rolling your eyes? Surely you know the meaning of the word?"

"Are you referring to the word harlot?" muttered the shopkeeper, flushing crimson and blinking. "But you know, the Lord in His mercy . . . forgave this very thing, . . . forgave a harlot. . . . He has prepared a place for her, and indeed from the life of the holy saint, Mariya of Egypt, one may see in what sense the word is used—excuse me . . ."

The shopkeeper wanted to bring forward some other argument in his justification, but took fright and wiped his lips with his sleeve.

"So that's what you make of it!" cried Father Grigory, clasping his hands. "But you see God has forgiven her—do you understand? He has forgiven, but you judge her, you slander her, call her by an unseemly name, and whom! Your own deceased daughter! Not only in Holy Scripture, but even in worldly literature you won't read of such a sin! I tell you again, Andrey, you mustn't be over-subtle! No, no, you mustn't be over-subtle, brother! If God has given you an inquiring mind, and if you cannot direct it, better not go into things. . . . Don't go into things, and hold your peace!"

"But you know, she, . . . excuse my mentioning it, was an actress!" articulated Andrey Andreyitch, overwhelmed.

"An actress! But whatever she was, you ought to forget it all now she is dead, instead of writing it on the note."

"Just so, . . ." the shopkeeper assented.

"You ought to do penance," boomed the deacon from the depths of the altar, looking contemptuously at Andrey Andreyitch's embarrassed face, "that would teach you to leave off being so clever! Your daughter was a well-known actress. There were even notices of her death in the newspapers. . . . Philosopher!"

"To be sure, . . . certainly," muttered the shopkeeper, "the word is not a seemly one; but I did not say it to judge her, Father Grigory, I only meant to speak spiritually, . . . that it might be clearer to you for whom you were praying. They write in the memorial notes the various callings, such as the infant John, the drowned woman Pelagea, the warrior Yegor, the murdered Pavel, and so on. . . . I meant to do the same."

"It was foolish, Andrey! God will forgive you, but beware another time. Above all, don't be subtle, but think like other people. Make ten bows and go your way."

"I obey," said the shopkeeper, relieved that the lecture was over, and allowing his face to resume its expression of importance and dignity. "Ten bows? Very good, I understand. But now, Father, allow me to ask you a favor. . . . Seeing that I am, anyway, her father, . . . you know yourself, whatever she was, she was still my daughter, so I was, . . . excuse me, meaning to ask you to sing the requiem to-day. And allow me to ask you, Father Deacon!"

"Well, that's good," said Father Grigory, taking off his vestments. "That I commend. I can approve of that! Well, go your way. We will come out immediately."

Andrey Andreyitch walked with dignity from the altar, and with a solemn, requiem-like expression on his red face took his stand in the middle of the church. The verger Matvey set before him a little table with the memorial food upon it, and a little later the requiem service began.

There was perfect stillness in the church. Nothing could be heard but the metallic click of the censer and slow singing. . . . Near Andrey Andreyitch stood the verger Matvey, the midwife Makaryevna, and her one-armed son Mitka. There was no one else. The sacristan sang badly in an unpleasant, hollow bass, but the tune and the words were so mournful that the shopkeeper little by little lost the expression of dignity and was plunged in sadness. He thought of his Mashutka, . . . he remembered she had been born when he was still a lackey in the service of the owner of Verhny Zaprudy. In his busy life as a lackey he had not noticed how his girl had grown up. That long period during which she was being shaped into a graceful creature, with a little flaxen head and dreamy eyes as big as kopeck-pieces, passed unnoticed by him. She had been brought up like all the children of favorite lackeys, in ease and comfort in the company of the young ladies. The gentry, to fill up their idle time, had taught her to read, to write, to dance; he had had no hand in her bringing up. Only from time to time casually meeting her at the gate or on the landing of the stairs, he would remember that she was his daughter, and would, so far as he had leisure for it, begin teaching her the prayers and the scripture. Oh, even then he had the reputation of an authority on the church rules and the holy scriptures! Forbidding and stolid as her father's face was, yet the girl listened readily. She repeated the prayers after him yawning, but on the other hand, when he, hesitating and trying to express himself elaborately, began telling her stories, she was all attention. Esau's pottage, the punishment of Sodom, and the troubles of the boy Joseph made her turn pale and open her blue eyes wide.

Afterwards when he gave up being a lackey, and with the money he had saved opened a shop in the village, Mashutka had gone away to Moscow with his master's family. . . .

Three years before her death she had come to see her father. He had scarcely recognized her. She was a graceful young woman with the manners of a young lady, and dressed like one. She talked cleverly, as though from a book, smoked, and slept till midday. When Andrey Andreyitch asked her what she was doing, she had announced, looking him boldly straight in the face: "I am an actress." Such frankness struck the former flunkey as the acme of cynicism. Mashutka had begun boasting of her successes and her stage life; but seeing that her father only turned crimson and threw up his hands, she ceased. And they spent a fortnight together without speaking or looking at one another till the day she went away. Before she went away she asked her father to come for a walk on the bank of the river. Painful as it was for him to walk in the light of day, in the sight of all honest people, with a daughter who was an actress, he yielded to her request.

"What a lovely place you live in!" she said enthusiastically. "What ravines and marshes! Good heavens, how lovely my native place is!"

And she had burst into tears.

"The place is simply taking up room, . . ." Andrey Andreyitch had thought, looking blankly at the ravines, not understanding his daughter's enthusiasm. "There is no more profit from them than milk from a billy-goat."

And she had cried and cried, drawing her breath greedily with her whole chest, as though she felt she had not a long time left to breathe.

Andrey Andreyitch shook his head like a horse that has been bitten, and to stifle painful memories began rapidly crossing himself. . . .

"Be mindful, O Lord," he muttered, "of Thy departed servant, the harlot Mariya, and forgive her sins, voluntary or involuntary. . . ."

The unseemly word dropped from his lips again, but he did not notice it: what is firmly imbedded in the consciousness cannot be driven out by Father Grigory's exhortations or even knocked out by a nail. Makaryevna sighed and whispered something, drawing in a deep breath, while one-armed Mitka was brooding over something. . . .

"Where there is no sickness, nor grief, nor sighing," droned the sacristan, covering his right cheek with his hand.

Bluish smoke coiled up from the censer and bathed in the broad, slanting patch of sunshine which cut across the gloomy, lifeless emptiness of the church. And it seemed as though the soul of the dead woman were soaring into the sunlight together with the smoke. The coils of smoke like a child's curls eddied round and round, floating upwards to the window and, as it were, holding aloof from the woes and tribulations of which that poor soul was full.

Anyuta

In the cheapest room of a big block of furnished apartments Stepan Klotchkov, a medical student in his third year, was walking to and fro, zealously conning his anatomy. His mouth was dry and his forehead perspiring from the unceasing effort to learn it by heart.

In the window, covered by patterns of frost, sat on a stool the girl who shared his room—Anyuta, a thin little brunette of five-and-twenty, very pale with mild grey eyes. Sitting with bent back she was busy embroidering with red thread the collar of a man's shirt. She was working against time.... The clock in the passage struck two drowsily, yet the little room had not been put to rights for the morning. Crumpled bed-clothes, pillows thrown about, books, clothes, a big filthy slop-pail filled with soap-suds in which cigarette ends were swimming, and the litter on the floor—all seemed as though purposely jumbled together in one confusion....

"The right lung consists of three parts . . ." Klotchkov repeated. "Boundaries! Upper part on anterior wall of thorax reaches the fourth or fifth rib, on the lateral surface, the fourth rib . . . behind to the *spina scapulæ* . . ."

Klotchkov raised his eyes to the ceiling, striving to visualise what he had just read. Unable to form a clear picture of it, he began feeling his upper ribs through his waistcoat.

"These ribs are like the keys of a piano," he said. "One must familiarise oneself with them somehow, if one is not to get muddled over them. One must study them in the skeleton and the living body. . . . I say, Anyuta, let me pick them out."

Anyuta put down her sewing, took off her blouse, and straightened herself up. Klotchkov sat down facing her, frowned, and began counting her ribs.

"H'm! . . . One can't feel the first rib; it's behind the shoulder-blade. . . . This must be the second rib. . . . Yes . . . this is the third . . . this is the fourth. . . . H'm! . . . yes. . . . Why are you wriggling?"

"Your fingers are cold!"

"Come, come . . . it won't kill you. Don't twist about. That must be the third rib, then . . . this is the fourth. . . . You look such a skinny thing, and yet one can hardly feel your ribs. That's the second . . . that's the third. . . . Oh, this is muddling, and one can't see it clearly. . . . I must draw it. . . . Where's my crayon?"

Klotchkov took his crayon and drew on Anyuta's chest several parallel lines corresponding with the ribs.

"First-rate. That's all straightforward. . . . Well, now I can sound you. Stand up!"

Anyuta stood up and raised her chin. Klotchkov began sounding her, and was so absorbed in this occupation that he did not notice how Anyuta's lips, nose, and fingers turned blue with cold. Anyuta shivered, and was afraid the student, noticing it, would leave off drawing and sounding her, and then, perhaps, might fail in his exam.

"Now it's all clear," said Klotchkov when he had finished. "You sit like that and don't rub off the crayon, and meanwhile I'll learn up a little more."

And the student again began walking to and fro, repeating to himself. Anyuta, with black stripes across her chest, looking as though she had been tattooed, sat thinking, huddled up and shivering with cold. She said very little as a rule; she was always silent, thinking and thinking. . . .

In the six or seven years of her wanderings from one furnished room to another, she had known five students like Klotchkov. Now they had all finished their studies, had gone out into the world, and, of course, like respectable people, had long ago forgotten her. One of them was living in Paris, two were doctors, the fourth was an artist, and the fifth was said to be already a professor. Klotchkov was the sixth. . . . Soon he, too, would finish his studies and go out into the world. There was a fine future before him, no doubt, and Klotchkov probably would become a great man, but the present was anything but bright; Klotchkov had no tobacco and no tea, and there were only four lumps of sugar left. She must make haste and finish her embroidery, take it to the woman who had ordered it, and with the quarter rouble she would get for it, buy tea and tobacco.

"Can I come in?" asked a voice at the door.

Anyuta quickly threw a woollen shawl over her shoulders. Fetisov, the artist, walked in.

"I have come to ask you a favour," he began, addressing Klotchkov, and glaring like a wild beast from under the long locks that hung over his brow. "Do me a favour; lend me your young lady just for a couple of hours! I'm painting a picture, you see, and I can't get on without a model."

"Oh, with pleasure," Klotchkov agreed. "Go along, Anyuta."

"The things I've had to put up with there," Anyuta murmured softly.

"Rubbish! The man's asking you for the sake of art, and not for any sort of nonsense. Why not help him if you can?"

Anyuta began dressing.

"And what are you painting?" asked Klotchkov.

"Psyche; it's a fine subject. But it won't go, somehow. I have to keep painting from different models. Yesterday I was painting one with blue legs. 'Why are your legs blue?' I asked her. 'It's my stockings stain them,' she said. And you're still grinding! Lucky fellow! You have patience."

"Medicine's a job one can't get on with without grinding."

"H'm! . . . Excuse me, Klotchkov, but you do live like a pig! It's awful the way you live!"

"How do you mean? I can't help it. . . . I only get twelve roubles a month from my father, and it's hard to live decently on that."

"Yes . . . yes . . ." said the artist, frowning with an air of disgust; "but, still, you might live better. . . . An educated man is in duty bound to have taste, isn't he? And goodness knows what it's like here! The bed not made, the slops, the dirt . . . yesterday's porridge in the plates. . . . Tfoo!"

"That's true," said the student in confusion; "but Anyuta has had no time to-day to tidy up; she's been busy all the while."

When Anyuta and the artist had gone out Klotchkov lay down on the sofa and began learning, lying down; then he accidentally dropped asleep, and waking up an hour later, propped his head on his fists and sank into gloomy reflection. He recalled the artist's words that an educated man was in duty bound to have taste, and his surroundings actually struck him now as loathsome and revolting. He saw, as it were in his mind's eye, his own future, when he would see his patients in his consulting-room, drink tea in a large dining-room in the company of his wife, a real lady. And now that slop-pail in which the cigarette ends were swimming looked incredibly disgusting. Anyuta, too, rose before his imagination—a plain, slovenly, pitiful figure . . . and he made up his mind to part with her at once, at all costs.

When, on coming back from the artist's, she took off her coat, he got up and said to her seriously:

"Look here, my good girl . . . sit down and listen. We must part! The fact is, I don't want to live with you any longer."

Anyuta had come back from the artist's worn out and exhausted. Standing so long as a model had made her face look thin and sunken, and her chin sharper than ever. She said nothing in answer to the student's words, only her lips began to tremble.

"You know we should have to part sooner or later, anyway," said the student. "You're a nice, good girl, and not a fool; you'll understand. . . ."

Anyuta put on her coat again, in silence wrapped up her embroidery in paper, gathered together her needles and thread: she found the screw of paper with the four lumps of sugar in the window, and laid it on the table by the books.

"That's . . . your sugar . . ." she said softly, and turned away to conceal her tears.

"Why are you crying?" asked Klotchkov.

He walked about the room in confusion, and said:

"You are a strange girl, really. . . . Why, you know we shall have to part. We can't stay together for ever."

She had gathered together all her belongings, and turned to say good-bye to him, and he felt sorry for her.

"Shall I let her stay on here another week?" he thought. "She really may as well stay, and I'll tell her to go in a week;" and vexed at his own weakness, he shouted to her roughly:

"Come, why are you standing there? If you are going, go; and if you don't want to, take off your coat and stay! You can stay!"

Anyuta took off her coat, silently, stealthily, then blew her nose also stealthily, sighed, and noiselessly returned to her invariable position on her stool by the window.

The student drew his textbook to him and began again pacing from corner to corner. "The right lung consists of three parts," he repeated; "the upper part, on anterior wall of thorax, reaches the fourth or fifth rib . . ."

In the passage some one shouted at the top of his voice: "Grigory! The samovar!"

The Witch

It was approaching nightfall. The sexton, Savély Gykin, was lying in his huge bed in the hut adjoining the church. He was not asleep, though it was his habit to go to sleep at the same time as the hens. His coarse red hair peeped from under one end of the greasy patchwork quilt, made up of coloured rags, while his big unwashed feet stuck out from the other. He was listening. His hut adjoined the wall that encircled the church and the solitary window in it looked out upon the open country. And out there a regular battle was going on. It was hard to say who was being wiped off the face of the earth, and for the sake of whose destruction nature was being churned up into such a ferment; but, judging from the unceasing malignant roar, someone was getting it very hot. A victorious force was in full chase over the fields, storming in the forest and on the church roof, battering spitefully with its fists upon the windows, raging and tearing, while something vanquished was howling and wailing. . . . A plaintive lament sobbed at the window, on the roof, or in the stove. It sounded not like a call for help, but like a cry of misery, a consciousness that it was too late, that there was no salvation. The snowdrifts were covered with a thin coating of ice; tears quivered on them and on the trees; a dark slush of mud and

melting snow flowed along the roads and paths. In short, it was thawing, but through the dark night the heavens failed to see it, and flung
flakes of fresh snow upon the melting earth at a terrific rate. And the
wind staggered like a drunkard. It would not let the snow settle on the
ground, and whirled it round in the darkness at random.

Savély listened to all this din and frowned. The fact was that he
knew, or at any rate suspected, what all this racket outside the window
was tending to and whose handiwork it was.

"I know!" he muttered, shaking his finger menacingly under the
bedclothes; "I know all about it."

On a stool by the window sat the sexton's wife, Raïssa Nilovna. A tin
lamp standing on another stool, as though timid and distrustful of its
powers, shed a dim and flickering light on her broad shoulders, on the
handsome, tempting-looking contours of her person, and on her thick
plait, which reached to the floor. She was making sacks out of coarse
hempen stuff. Her hands moved nimbly, while her whole body, her
eyes, her eyebrows, her full lips, her white neck were as still as though
they were asleep, absorbed in the monotonous, mechanical toil. Only
from time to time she raised her head to rest her weary neck, glanced
for a moment towards the window, beyond which the snowstorm was
raging, and bent again over her sacking. No desire, no joy, no grief,
nothing was expressed by her handsome face with its turned-up nose
and its dimples. So a beautiful fountain expresses nothing when it is
not playing.

But at last she had finished a sack. She flung it aside, and, stretching
luxuriously, rested her motionless, lack-lustre eyes on the window.
The panes were swimming with drops like tears, and white with short-
lived snowflakes which fell on the window, glanced at Raïssa, and
melted. . . .

"Come to bed!" growled the sexton. Raïssa remained mute. But suddenly her eyelashes flickered and there was a gleam of attention in her
eye. Savély, all the time watching her expression from under the quilt,
put out his head and asked:

"What is it?"

"Nothing. . . . I fancy someone's coming," she answered quietly.

The sexton flung the quilt off with his arms and legs, knelt up in bed, and looked blankly at his wife. The timid light of the lamp illuminated his hirsute, pock-marked countenance and glided over his rough matted hair.

"Do you hear?" asked his wife.

Through the monotonous roar of the storm he caught a scarcely audible thin and jingling monotone like the shrill note of a gnat when it wants to settle on one's cheek and is angry at being prevented.

"It's the post," muttered Savély, squatting on his heels.

Two miles from the church ran the posting road. In windy weather, when the wind was blowing from the road to the church, the inmates of the hut caught the sound of bells.

"Lord! fancy people wanting to drive about in such weather," sighed Raïssa.

"It's government work. You've to go whether you like or not."

The murmur hung in the air and died away.

"It has driven by," said Savély, getting into bed.

But before he had time to cover himself up with the bedclothes he heard a distinct sound of the bell. The sexton looked anxiously at his wife, leapt out of bed and walked, waddling, to and fro by the stove. The bell went on ringing for a little, then died away again as though it had ceased.

"I don't hear it," said the sexton, stopping and looking at his wife with his eyes screwed up.

But at that moment the wind rapped on the window and with it floated a shrill jingling note. Savély turned pale, cleared his throat, and flopped about the floor with his bare feet again.

"The postman is lost in the storm," he wheezed out glancing malignantly at his wife. "Do you hear? The postman has lost his way! . . . I . . . I know! Do you suppose I . . . don't understand?" he muttered. "I know all about it, curse you!"

"What do you know?" Raïssa asked quietly, keeping her eyes fixed on the window.

"I know that it's all your doing, you she-devil! Your doing, damn you! This snowstorm and the post going wrong, you've done it all—you!"

"You're mad, you silly," his wife answered calmly.

"I've been watching you for a long time past and I've seen it. From the first day I married you I noticed that you'd bitch's blood in you!"

"Tfoo!" said Raïssa, surprised, shrugging her shoulders and crossing herself. "Cross yourself, you fool!"

"A witch is a witch," Savély pronounced in a hollow, tearful voice, hurriedly blowing his nose on the hem of his shirt; "though you are my wife, though you are of a clerical family, I'd say what you are even at confession. . . . Why, God have mercy upon us! Last year on the Eve of the Prophet Daniel and the Three Young Men there was a snowstorm, and what happened then? The mechanic came in to warm himself. Then on St. Alexey's Day the ice broke on the river and the district policeman turned up, and he was chatting with you all night . . . the damned brute! And when he came out in the morning and I looked at him, he had rings under his eyes and his cheeks were hollow! Eh? During the August fast there were two storms and each time the huntsman turned up. I saw it all, damn him! Oh, she is redder than a crab now, aha!"

"You didn't see anything."

"Didn't I! And this winter before Christmas on the Day of the Ten Martyrs of Crete, when the storm lasted for a whole day and night—do you remember?—the marshal's clerk was lost, and turned up here, the hound. . . . Tfoo! To be tempted by the clerk! It was worth upsetting God's weather for him! A drivelling scribbler, not a foot from the ground, pimples all over his mug and his neck awry! If he were good-looking, anyway—but he, tfoo! he is as ugly as Satan!"

The sexton took breath, wiped his lips and listened. The bell was not to be heard, but the wind banged on the roof, and again there came a tinkle in the darkness.

"And it's the same thing now!" Savély went on. "It's not for nothing the postman is lost! Blast my eyes if the postman isn't looking for you! Oh, the devil is a good hand at his work; he is a fine one to help! He will turn him round and round and bring him here. I know, I see! You can't conceal it, you devil's bauble, you heathen wanton! As soon as the storm began I knew what you were up to."

"Here's a fool!" smiled his wife. "Why, do you suppose, you thickhead, that I make the storm?"

"H'm! . . . Grin away! Whether it's your doing or not, I only know that when your blood's on fire there's sure to be bad weather, and when there's bad weather there's bound to be some crazy fellow turning up here. It happens so every time! So it must be you!"

To be more impressive the sexton put his finger to his forehead, closed his left eye, and said in a sing-song voice:

"Oh, the madness! oh, the unclean Judas! If you really are a human being and not a witch, you ought to think what if he is not the mechanic, or the clerk, or the huntsman, but the devil in their form! Ah! You'd better think of that!"

"Why, you are stupid, Savély," said his wife, looking at him compassionately. "When father was alive and living here, all sorts of people used to come to him to be cured of the ague: from the village, and the hamlets, and the Armenian settlement. They came almost every day, and no one called them devils. But if anyone once a year comes in bad weather to warm himself, you wonder at it, you silly, and take all sorts of notions into your head at once."

His wife's logic touched Savély. He stood with his bare feet wide apart, bent his head, and pondered. He was not firmly convinced yet of the truth of his suspicions, and his wife's genuine and unconcerned tone quite disconcerted him. Yet after a moment's thought he wagged his head and said:

"It's not as though they were old men or bandy-legged cripples; it's always young men who want to come for the night. . . . Why is that? And if they only wanted to warm themselves—— But they are up to mischief. No, woman; there's no creature in this world as cunning as your female sort! Of real brains you've not an ounce, less than a starling, but for devilish slyness—oo-oo-oo! The Queen of Heaven protect us! There is the postman's bell! When the storm was only beginning I knew all that was in your mind. That's your witchery, you spider!"

"Why do you keep on at me, you heathen?" His wife lost her patience at last. "Why do you keep sticking to it like pitch?"

"I stick to it because if anything—God forbid—happens to-night . . . do you hear? . . . if anything happens to-night, I'll go straight off to-morrow morning to Father Nikodim and tell him all about it.

'Father Nikodim,' I shall say, 'graciously excuse me, but she is a witch.'
'Why so?' 'H'm! do you want to know why?' 'Certainly. . . .' And I shall
tell him. And woe to you, woman! Not only at the dread Seat of Judg-
ment, but in your earthly life you'll be punished, too! It's not for nothing there are prayers in the breviary against your kind!"

Suddenly there was a knock at the window, so loud and unusual that
Savély turned pale and almost dropped backwards with fright. His
wife jumped up, and she, too, turned pale.

"For God's sake, let us come in and get warm!" They heard in a trembling deep bass. "Who lives here? For mercy's sake! We've lost our way."

"Who are you?" asked Raïssa, afraid to look at the window.

"The post," answered a second voice.

"You've succeeded with your devil's tricks," said Savély with a wave
of his hand. "No mistake; I am right! Well, you'd better look out!"

The sexton jumped on to the bed in two skips, stretched himself on
the feather mattress, and sniffing angrily, turned with his face to the
wall. Soon he felt a draught of cold air on his back. The door creaked
and the tall figure of a man, plastered over with snow from head to
foot, appeared in the doorway. Behind him could be seen a second figure as white.

"Am I to bring in the bags?" asked the second in a hoarse bass voice.

"You can't leave them there." Saying this, the first figure began untying his hood, but gave it up, and pulling it off impatiently with his
cap, angrily flung it near the stove. Then taking off his greatcoat, he
threw that down beside it, and, without saying good-evening, began
pacing up and down the hut.

He was a fair-haired, young postman wearing a shabby uniform and
black rusty-looking high boots. After warming himself by walking to
and fro, he sat down at the table, stretched out his muddy feet towards
the sacks and leaned his chin on his fist. His pale face, reddened in
places by the cold, still bore vivid traces of the pain and terror he had
just been through. Though distorted by anger and bearing traces of recent suffering, physical and moral, it was handsome in spite of the
melting snow on the eyebrows, moustaches, and short beard.

"It's a dog's life!" muttered the postman, looking round the walls and seeming hardly able to believe that he was in the warmth. "We were nearly lost! If it had not been for your light, I don't know what would have happened. Goodness only knows when it will all be over! There's no end to this dog's life! Where have we come?" he asked, dropping his voice and raising his eyes to the sexton's wife.

"To the Gulyaevsky Hill on General Kalinovsky's estate," she answered, startled and blushing.

"Do you hear, Stepan?" The postman turned to the driver, who was wedged in the doorway with a huge mail-bag on his shoulders. "We've got to Gulyaevsky Hill."

"Yes . . . we're a long way out." Jerking out these words like a hoarse sigh, the driver went out and soon after returned with another bag, then went out once more and this time brought the postman's sword on a big belt, of the pattern of that long flat blade with which Judith is portrayed by the bedside of Holofernes in cheap woodcuts. Laying the bags along the wall, he went out into the outer room, sat down there and lighted his pipe.

"Perhaps you'd like some tea after your journey?" Raïssa inquired.

"How can we sit drinking tea?" said the postman, frowning. "We must make haste and get warm, and then set off, or we shall be late for the mail train. We'll stay ten minutes and then get on our way. Only be so good as to show us the way."

"What an infliction it is, this weather!" sighed Raïssa.

"H'm, yes. . . . Who may you be?"

"We? We live here, by the church. . . . We belong to the clergy. . . . There lies my husband. Savély, get up and say good-evening! This used to be a separate parish till eighteen months ago. Of course, when the gentry lived here there were more people, and it was worth while to have the services. But now the gentry have gone, and I need not tell you there's nothing for the clergy to live on. The nearest village is Markovka, and that's over three miles away. Savély is on the retired list now, and has got the watchman's job; he has to look after the church. . . ."

And the postman was immediately informed that if Savély were to go to the General's lady and ask her for a letter to the bishop, he would be given a good berth. "But he doesn't go to the General's lady because he is lazy and afraid of people. We belong to the clergy all the same ..." added Raïssa.

"What do you live on?" asked the postman.

"There's a kitchen garden and a meadow belonging to the church. Only we don't get much from that," sighed Raïssa. "The old skinflint, Father Nikodim, from the next village celebrates here on St. Nicolas' Day in the winter and on St. Nicolas' Day in the summer, and for that he takes almost all the crops for himself. There's no one to stick up for us!"

"You are lying," Savély growled hoarsely. "Father Nikodim is a saintly soul, a luminary of the Church; and if he does take it, it's the regulation!"

"You've a cross one!" said the postman, with a grin. "Have you been married long?"

"It was three years ago the last Sunday before Lent. My father was sexton here in the old days, and when the time came for him to die, he went to the Consistory and asked them to send some unmarried man to marry me that I might keep the place. So I married him."

"Aha, so you killed two birds with one stone!" said the postman, looking at Savély's back. "Got wife and job together."

Savély wriggled his leg impatiently and moved closer to the wall. The postman moved away from the table, stretched, and sat down on the mail-bag. After a moment's thought he squeezed the bags with his hands, shifted his sword to the other side, and lay down with one foot touching the floor.

"It's a dog's life," he muttered, putting his hands behind his head and closing his eyes. "I wouldn't wish a wild Tatar such a life."

Soon everything was still. Nothing was audible except the sniffing of Savély and the slow, even breathing of the sleeping postman, who uttered a deep prolonged "h-h-h" at every breath. From time to time there was a sound like a creaking wheel in his throat, and his twitching foot rustled against the bag.

Savély fidgeted under the quilt and looked round slowly. His wife was sitting on the stool, and with her hands pressed against her cheeks was gazing at the postman's face. Her face was immovable, like the face of some one frightened and astonished.

"Well, what are you gaping at?" Savély whispered angrily.

"What is it to you? Lie down!" answered his wife without taking her eyes off the flaxen head.

Savély angrily puffed all the air out of his chest and turned abruptly to the wall. Three minutes later he turned over restlessly again, knelt up on the bed, and with his hands on the pillow looked askance at his wife. She was still sitting motionless, staring at the visitor. Her cheeks were pale and her eyes were glowing with a strange fire. The sexton cleared his throat, crawled on his stomach off the bed, and going up to the postman, put a handkerchief over his face.

"What's that for?" asked his wife.

"To keep the light out of his eyes."

"Then put out the light!"

Savély looked distrustfully at his wife, put out his lips towards the lamp, but at once thought better of it and clasped his hands.

"Isn't that devilish cunning?" he exclaimed. "Ah! Is there any creature slyer than womenkind?"

"Ah, you long-skirted devil!" hissed his wife, frowning with vexation. "You wait a bit!"

And settling herself more comfortably, she stared at the postman again.

It did not matter to her that his face was covered. She was not so much interested in his face as in his whole appearance, in the novelty of this man. His chest was broad and powerful, his hands were slender and well formed, and his graceful, muscular legs were much comelier than Savély's stumps. There could be no comparison, in fact.

"Though I am a long-skirted devil," Savély said after a brief interval, "they've no business to sleep here. . . . It's government work; we shall have to answer for keeping them. If you carry the letters, carry them, you can't go to sleep. . . . Hey! you!" Savély shouted into the outer room. "You, driver. . . . What's your name? Shall I show you the way? Get up; postmen mustn't sleep!"

And Savély, thoroughly roused, ran up to the postman and tugged him by the sleeve.

"Hey, your honour, if you must go, go; and if you don't, it's not the thing. . . . Sleeping won't do."

The postman jumped up, sat down, looked with blank eyes round the hut, and lay down again.

"But when are you going?" Savély pattered away. "That's what the post is for—to get there in good time, do you hear? I'll take you."

The postman opened his eyes. Warmed and relaxed by his first sweet sleep, and not yet quite awake, he saw as through a mist the white neck and the immovable, alluring eyes of the sexton's wife. He closed his eyes and smiled as though he had been dreaming it all.

"Come, how can you go in such weather!" he heard a soft feminine voice; "you ought to have a sound sleep and it would do you good!"

"And what about the post?" said Savély anxiously. "Who's going to take the post? Are you going to take it, pray, you?"

The postman opened his eyes again, looked at the play of the dimples on Raïssa's face, remembered where he was, and understood Savély. The thought that he had to go out into the cold darkness sent a chill shudder all down him, and he winced.

"I might sleep another five minutes," he said, yawning. "I shall be late, anyway. . . ."

"We might be just in time," came a voice from the outer room. "All days are not alike; the train may be late for a bit of luck."

The postman got up, and stretching lazily began putting on his coat. Savély positively neighed with delight when he saw his visitors were getting ready to go.

"Give us a hand," the driver shouted to him as he lifted up a mail-bag.

The sexton ran out and helped him drag the post-bags into the yard. The postman began undoing the knot in his hood. The sexton's wife gazed into his eyes, and seemed trying to look right into his soul.

"You ought to have a cup of tea . . ." she said.

"I wouldn't say no . . . but, you see, they're getting ready," he assented. "We are late, anyway."

"Do stay," she whispered, dropping her eyes and touching him by the sleeve.

The postman got the knot undone at last and flung the hood over his elbow, hesitating. He felt it comfortable standing by Raïssa.

"What a . . . neck you've got! . . ." And he touched her neck with two fingers. Seeing that she did not resist, he stroked her neck and shoulders.

"I say, you are . . ."

"You'd better stay . . . have some tea."

"Where are you putting it?" The driver's voice could be heard outside. "Lay it crossways."

"You'd better stay. . . . Hark how the wind howls."

And the postman, not yet quite awake, not yet quite able to shake off the intoxicating sleep of youth and fatigue, was suddenly overwhelmed by a desire for the sake of which mail-bags, postal trains . . . and all things in the world, are forgotten. He glanced at the door in a frightened way, as though he wanted to escape or hide himself, seized Raïssa round the waist, and was just bending over the lamp to put out the light, when he heard the tramp of boots in the outer room, and the driver appeared in the doorway. Savély peeped in over his shoulder. The postman dropped his hands quickly and stood still as though irresolute.

"It's all ready," said the driver. The postman stood still for a moment, resolutely threw up his head as though waking up completely, and followed the driver out. Raïssa was left alone.

"Come, get in and show us the way!" she heard.

One bell sounded languidly, then another, and the jingling notes in a long delicate chain floated away from the hut.

When little by little they had died away, Raïssa got up and nervously paced to and fro. At first she was pale, then she flushed all over. Her face was contorted with hate, her breathing was tremulous, her eyes gleamed with wild, savage anger, and, pacing up and down as in a cage, she looked like a tigress menaced with red-hot iron. For a moment she stood still and looked at her abode. Almost half of the room was filled up by the bed, which stretched the length of the whole wall and consisted of a dirty feather-bed, coarse grey pillows, a quilt, and nameless rags of various sorts. The bed was a shapeless ugly mass which suggested the shock of hair that always stood up on Savély's head whenever it occurred to him to oil it. From the bed to the door that led into the cold outer room stretched the dark stove surrounded by pots and hanging clouts. Everything, including the absent Savély himself, was dirty, greasy, and smutty to the last degree, so that it was strange to see a woman's white neck and delicate skin in such surroundings.

Raïssa ran up to the bed, stretched out her hands as though she wanted to fling it all about, stamp it underfoot, and tear it to shreds. But then, as though frightened by contact with the dirt, she leapt back and began pacing up and down again.

When Savély returned two hours later, worn out and covered with snow, she was undressed and in bed. Her eyes were closed, but from the slight tremor that ran over her face he guessed that she was not asleep. On his way home he had vowed inwardly to wait till next day and not to touch her, but he could not resist a biting taunt at her.

"Your witchery was all in vain: he's gone off," he said, grinning with malignant joy.

His wife remained mute, but her chin quivered. Savély undressed slowly, clambered over his wife, and lay down next to the wall.

"To-morrow I'll let Father Nikodim know what sort of wife you are!" he muttered, curling himself up.

Raïssa turned her face to him and her eyes gleamed.

"The job's enough for you, and you can look for a wife in the forest, blast you!" she said. "I am no wife for you, a clumsy lout, a slug-a-bed, God forgive me!"

"Come, come . . . go to sleep!"

"How miserable I am!" sobbed his wife. "If it weren't for you, I might have married a merchant or some gentleman! If it weren't for you, I should love my husband now! And you haven't been buried in the snow, you haven't been frozen on the highroad, you Herod!"

Raïssa cried for a long time. At last she drew a deep sigh and was still. The storm still raged without. Something wailed in the stove, in the chimney, outside the walls, and it seemed to Savély that the wailing was within him, in his ears. This evening had completely confirmed him in his suspicions about his wife. He no longer doubted that his wife, with the aid of the Evil One, controlled the winds and the post sledges. But to add to his grief, this mysteriousness, this supernatural, weird power gave the woman beside him a peculiar, incomprehensible charm of which he had not been conscious before. The fact that in his stupidity he unconsciously threw a poetic glamour over her made her seem, as it were, whiter, sleeker, more unapproachable.

"Witch!" he muttered indignantly. "Tfoo, horrid creature!"

Yet, waiting till she was quiet and began breathing evenly, he touched her head with his finger . . . held her thick plait in his hand for a minute. She did not feel it. Then he grew bolder and stoked her neck.

"Leave off!" she shouted, and prodded him on the nose with her elbow with such violence that he saw stars before his eyes.

The pain in his nose was soon over, but the torture in his heart remained.

A Joke

It was a bright winter midday.... There was a sharp snapping frost and the curls on Nadenka's temples and the down on her upper lip were covered with silvery frost. She was holding my arm and we were standing on a high hill. From where we stood to the ground below there stretched a smooth sloping descent in which the sun was reflected as in a looking-glass. Beside us was a little sledge lined with bright red cloth.

"Let us go down, Nadyezhda Petrovna!" I besought her. "Only once! I assure you we shall be all right and not hurt."

But Nadenka was afraid. The slope from her little goloshes to the bottom of the ice hill seemed to her a terrible, immensely deep abyss. Her spirit failed her, and she held her breath as she looked down, when I merely suggested her getting into the sledge, but what would it be if she were to risk flying into the abyss! She would die, she would go out of her mind.

"I entreat you!" I said. "You mustn't be afraid! You know it's poor-spirited, it's cowardly!"

Nadenka gave way at last, and from her face I saw that she gave way in mortal dread. I sat her in the sledge, pale and trembling, put my arm round her and with her cast myself down the precipice.

The sledge flew like a bullet. The air cleft by our flight beat in our faces, roared, whistled in our ears, tore at us, nipped us cruelly in its anger, tried to tear our heads off our shoulders. We had hardly strength to breathe from the pressure of the wind. It seemed as though the devil himself had caught us in his claws and was dragging us with a roar to hell. Surrounding objects melted into one long furiously racing streak . . . another moment and it seemed we should perish.

"I love you, Nadya!" I said in a low voice.

The sledge began moving more and more slowly, the roar of the wind and the whirr of the runners was no longer so terrible, it was easier to breathe, and at last we were at the bottom. Nadenka was more dead than alive. She was pale and scarcely breathing. . . . I helped her to get up.

"Nothing would induce me to go again," she said, looking at me with wide eyes full of horror. "Nothing in the world! I almost died!"

A little later she recovered herself and looked enquiringly into my eyes, wondering had I really uttered those four words or had she fancied them in the roar of the hurricane. And I stood beside her smoking and looking attentively at my glove.

She took my arm and we spent a long while walking near the ice-hill. The riddle evidently would not let her rest. . . . Had those words been uttered or not? . . . Yes or no? Yes or no? It was the question of pride, or honour, of life—a very important question, the most important question in the world. Nadenka kept impatiently, sorrowfully looking into my face with a penetrating glance; she answered at random, waiting to see whether I would not speak. Oh, the play of feeling on that sweet face! I saw that she was struggling with herself, that she wanted to say something, to ask some question, but she could not find the words; she felt awkward and frightened and troubled by her joy. . . .

"Do you know what," she said without looking at me.

"Well?" I asked.

"Let us . . . slide down again."

We clambered up the ice-hill by the steps again. I sat Nadenka, pale and trembling, in the sledge; again we flew into the terrible abyss, again the wind roared and the runners whirred, and again when the flight of our sledge was at its swiftest and noisiest, I said in a low voice:

"I love you, Nadenka!"

When the sledge stopped, Nadenka flung a glance at the hill down which we had both slid, then bent a long look upon my face, listened to my voice which was unconcerned and passionless, and the whole of her little figure, every bit of it, even her muff and her hood expressed the utmost bewilderment, and on her face was written: "What does it mean? Who uttered *those* words? Did he, or did I only fancy it?"

The uncertainty worried her and drove her out of all patience. The poor girl did not answer my questions, frowned, and was on the point of tears.

"Hadn't we better go home?" I asked.

"Well, I . . . I like this tobogganning," she said, flushing. "Shall we go down once more?"

She "liked" the tobogganning, and yet as she got into the sledge she was, as both times before, pale, trembling, hardly able to breathe for terror.

We went down for the third time, and I saw she was looking at my face and watching my lips. But I put my handkerchief to my lips, coughed, and when we reached the middle of the hill I succeeded in bringing out:

"I love you, Nadya!"

And the mystery remained a mystery! Nadenka was silent, pondering on something. . . . I saw her home, she tried to walk slowly, slackened her pace and kept waiting to see whether I would not say those words to her, and I saw how her soul was suffering, what effort she was making not to say to herself:

"It cannot be that the wind said them! And I don't want it to be the wind that said them!"

Next morning I got a little note:

"If you are tobogganning to-day, come for me.—N."

And from that time I began going every day tobogganning with Nadenka, and as we flew down in the sledge, every time I pronounced in a low voice the same words: "I love you, Nadya!"

Soon Nadenka grew used to that phrase as to alcohol or morphia. She could not live without it. It is true that flying down the ice-hill terrified her as before, but now the terror and danger gave a peculiar fascination to words of love—words which as before were a mystery and tantalized the soul. The same two—the wind and I were still suspected.... Which of the two was making love to her she did not know, but apparently by now she did not care; from which goblet one drinks matters little if only the beverage is intoxicating.

It happened I went to the skating-ground alone at midday; mingling with the crowd I saw Nadenka go up to the ice-hill and look about for me ... then she timidly mounted the steps.... She was frightened of going alone—oh, how frightened! She was white as the snow, she was trembling, she went as though to the scaffold, but she went, she went without looking back, resolutely. She had evidently determined to put it to the test at last: would those sweet amazing words be heard when I was not there? I saw her, pale, her lips parted with horror, get into the sledge, shut her eyes and saying good-bye for ever to the earth, set off.... "Whrrr!" whirred the runners. Whether Nadenka heard those words I do not know. I only saw her getting up from the sledge looking faint and exhausted. And one could tell from her face that she could not tell herself whether she had heard anything or not. Her terror while she had been flying down had deprived of her all power of hearing, of discriminating sounds, of understanding....

But then the month of March arrived ... the spring sunshine was more kindly.... Our ice-hill turned dark, lost its brilliance and finally melted. We gave up tobogganning. There was nowhere now where poor Nadenka could hear those words, and indeed no one to utter them, since there was no wind and I was going to Petersburg—for long, perhaps for ever.

It happened two days before my departure I was sitting in the dusk in the little garden which was separated from the yard of Nadenka's house by a high fence with nails in it.... It was still pretty cold, there was still snow by the manure heap, the trees looked dead but there was already the scent of spring and the rooks were cawing loudly as they settled for their night's rest. I went up to the fence and stood for a long while peeping through a chink. I saw Nadenka come out into the porch and fix a mournful yearning gaze on the sky.... The spring wind was blowing straight into her pale dejected face.... It reminded her of the wind which roared at us on the ice-hill when she heard those four words, and her face became very, very sorrowful, a tear trickled down her cheek, and the poor child held out both arms as though begging the wind to bring her those words once more. And waiting for the wind I said in a low voice:

"I love you, Nadya!"

Mercy! The change that came over Nadenka! She uttered a cry, smiled all over her face and looking joyful, happy and beautiful, held out her arms to meet the wind.

And I went off to pack up. . . .

That was long ago. Now Nadenka is married; she married—whether of her own choice or not does not matter—a secretary of the Nobility Wardenship and now she has three children. That we once went tobogganning together, and that the wind brought her the words "I love you, Nadenka," is not forgotten; it is for her now the happiest, most touching, and beautiful memory in her life. . . .

But now that I am older I cannot understand why I uttered those words, what was my motive in that joke. . . .

Agafya

During my stay in the district of S. I often used to go to see the watchman Savva Stukatch, or simply Savka, in the kitchen gardens of Dubovo. These kitchen gardens were my favorite resort for so-called "mixed" fishing, when one goes out without knowing what day or hour one may return, taking with one every sort of fishing tackle as well as a store of provisions. To tell the truth, it was not so much the fishing that attracted me as the peaceful stroll, the meals at no set time, the talk with Savka, and being for so long face to face with the calm summer nights. Savka was a young man of five-and-twenty, well grown and handsome, and as strong as a flint. He had the reputation of being a sensible and reasonable fellow. He could read and write, and very rarely drank, but as a workman this strong and healthy young man was not worth a farthing. A sluggish, overpowering sloth was mingled with the strength in his muscles, which were strong as cords. Like everyone else in his village, he lived in his own hut, and had his share of land, but neither tilled it nor sowed it, and did not work at any sort of trade. His old mother begged alms at people's windows and he himself lived like a bird of the air; he did not know in the morning what he would eat at midday. It was not that he was lacking in will, or energy, or feeling for his mother; it was simply that he felt no inclination for work and did not recognize the advantage of it. His whole figure suggested unruffled serenity, an innate, almost artistic passion for living carelessly, never with his sleeves tucked up. When Savka's young, healthy body had a physical craving for muscular work, the young man abandoned himself completely for a brief interval to some free but nonsensical pursuit, such as sharpening skates not wanted for any special purpose, or racing about after the peasant women. His favorite attitude was one of concentrated immobility. He was capable of standing for hours at a stretch in the same place with his eyes fixed on the same spot without stirring. He never moved except on impulse, and then only when an occasion presented itself for some rapid and abrupt action: catching a running dog by the tail, pulling off a woman's kerchief, or jumping over a big hole. It need hardly be said that with such parsimony of movement Savka was as poor as a mouse and lived worse than any homeless outcast. As time went on, I suppose he accumulated arrears of taxes and, young and sturdy as he was, he was sent by the commune to do an old man's job—to be watchman and scarecrow in the kitchen gardens. However much they laughed at him for his premature senility he did not object to it. This position, quiet and convenient for motionless contemplation, exactly fitted his temperament.

It happened I was with this Savka one fine May evening. I remember I was lying on a torn and dirty sackcloth cover close to the shanty from which came a heavy, fragrant scent of hay. Clasping my hands under my head I looked before me. At my feet was lying a wooden fork. Behind it Savka's dog Kutka stood out like a black patch, and not a dozen feet from Kutka the ground ended abruptly in the steep bank of the little river. Lying down I could not see the river; I could only see the tops of the young willows growing thickly on the nearer bank, and the twisting, as it were gnawed away, edges of the opposite bank. At a distance beyond the bank on the dark hillside the huts of the village in which Savka lived lay huddling together like frightened young partridges. Beyond the hill the afterglow of sunset still lingered in the sky. One pale crimson streak was all that was left, and even that began to be covered by little clouds as a fire with ash.

A copse with alder-trees, softly whispering, and from time to time shuddering in the fitful breeze, lay, a dark blur, on the right of the kitchen gardens; on the left stretched the immense plain. In the distance, where the eye could not distinguish between the sky and the plain, there was a bright gleam of light. A little way off from me sat Savka. With his legs tucked under him like a Turk and his head hanging, he looked pensively at Kutka. Our hooks with live bait on them had long been in the river, and we had nothing left to do but to abandon ourselves to repose, which Savka, who was never exhausted and always rested, loved so much. The glow had not yet quite died away, but the summer night was already enfolding nature in its caressing, soothing embrace.

Everything was sinking into its first deep sleep except some night bird unfamiliar to me, which indolently uttered a long, protracted cry in several distinct notes like the phrase, "Have you seen Ni-ki-ta?" and immediately answered itself, "Seen him, seen him, seen him!"

"Why is it the nightingales aren't singing tonight?" I asked Savka.

He turned slowly towards me. His features were large, but his face was open, soft, and expressive as a woman's. Then he gazed with his mild, dreamy eyes at the copse, at the willows, slowly pulled a whistle out of his pocket, put it in his mouth and whistled the note of a hen-nightingale. And at once, as though in answer to his call, a landrail called on the opposite bank.

"There's a nightingale for you . . ." laughed Savka. "Drag-drag! drag-drag! just like pulling at a hook, and yet I bet he thinks he is singing, too."

"I like that bird," I said. "Do you know, when the birds are migrating the landrail does not fly, but runs along the ground? It only flies over the rivers and the sea, but all the rest it does on foot."

"Upon my word, the dog . . ." muttered Savka, looking with respect in the direction of the calling landrail.

Knowing how fond Savka was of listening, I told him all I had learned about the landrail from sportsman's books. From the landrail I passed imperceptibly to the migration of the birds. Savka listened attentively, looking at me without blinking, and smiling all the while with pleasure.

"And which country is most the bird's home? Ours or those foreign parts?" he asked.

"Ours, of course. The bird itself is hatched here, and it hatches out its little ones here in its native country, and they only fly off there to escape being frozen."

"It's interesting," said Savka. "Whatever one talks about it is always interesting. Take a bird now, or a man ... or take this little stone; there's something to learn about all of them. . . . Ah, sir, if I had known you were coming I wouldn't have told a woman to come here this evening. . . . She asked to come to-day."

"Oh, please don't let me be in your way," I said. "I can lie down in the wood. . . ."

"What next! She wouldn't have died if she hadn't come till to-morrow. . . . If only she would sit quiet and listen, but she always wants to be slobbering. . . . You can't have a good talk when she's here."

"Are you expecting Darya?" I asked, after a pause.

"No ... a new one has asked to come this evening ... Agafya, the signalman's wife."

Savka said this in his usual passionless, somewhat hollow voice, as though he were talking of tobacco or porridge, while I started with surprise. I knew Agafya. . . . She was quite a young peasant woman of nineteen or twenty, who had been married not more than a year before to a railway signalman, a fine young fellow. She lived in the village, and her husband came home there from the line every night.

"Your goings on with the women will lead to trouble, my boy," said I.

"Well, may be, . . ."

And after a moment's thought Savka added:

"I've said so to the women; they won't heed me. . . . They don't trouble about it, the silly things!"

Silence followed. . . . Meanwhile the darkness was growing thicker and thicker, and objects began to lose their contours. The streak behind the hill had completely died away, and the stars were growing brighter and more luminous. . . . The mournfully monotonous chirping of the grasshoppers, the call of the landrail, and the cry of the quail did not destroy the stillness of the night, but, on the contrary, gave it an added monotony. It seemed as though the soft sounds that enchanted the ear came, not from birds or insects, but from the stars looking down upon us from the sky. . . .

Savka was the first to break the silence. He slowly turned his eyes from black Kutka and said:

"I see you are dull, sir. Let's have supper."

And without waiting for my consent he crept on his stomach into the shanty, rummaged about there, making the whole edifice tremble like a leaf; then he crawled back and set before me my vodka and an earthenware bowl; in the bowl there were baked eggs, lard scones made of rye, pieces of black bread, and something else. . . . We had a drink from a little crooked glass that wouldn't stand, and then we fell upon the food. . . . Coarse grey salt, dirty, greasy cakes, eggs tough as india-rubber, but how nice it all was!

"You live all alone, but what lots of good things you have," I said, pointing to the bowl. "Where do you get them from?"

"The women bring them," mumbled Savka.

"What do they bring them to you for?"

"Oh . . . from pity."

Not only Savka's menu, but his clothing, too, bore traces of feminine "pity." Thus I noticed that he had on, that evening, a new woven belt and a crimson ribbon on which a copper cross hung round his dirty neck. I knew of the weakness of the fair sex for Savka, and I knew that he did not like talking about it, and so I did not carry my inquiries any further. Besides there was not time to talk. . . . Kutka, who had been fidgeting about near us and patiently waiting for scraps, suddenly pricked up his ears and growled. We heard in the distance repeated splashing of water.

"Someone is coming by the ford," said Savka.

Three minutes later Kutka growled again and made a sound like a cough.

"Shsh!" his master shouted at him.

In the darkness there was a muffled thud of timid footsteps, and the silhouette of a woman appeared out of the copse. I recognized her, although it was dark—it was Agafya. She came up to us diffidently and stopped, breathing hard. She was breathless, probably not so much from walking as from fear and the unpleasant sensation everyone experiences in wading across a river at night. Seeing near the shanty not one but two persons, she uttered a faint cry and fell back a step.

"Ah . . . that is you!" said Savka, stuffing a scone into his mouth.

"Ye-es . . . I," she muttered, dropping on the ground a bundle of some sort and looking sideways at me. "Yakov sent his greetings to you and told me to give you . . . something here. . . ."

"Come, why tell stories? Yakov!" laughed Savka. "There is no need for lying; the gentleman knows why you have come! Sit down; you shall have supper with us."

Agafya looked sideways at me and sat down irresolutely.

"I thought you weren't coming this evening," Savka said, after a prolonged silence. "Why sit like that? Eat! Or shall I give you a drop of vodka?"

"What an idea!" laughed Agafya; "do you think you have got hold of a drunkard? . . ."

"Oh, drink it up. . . . Your heart will feel warmer. . . . There!"

Savka gave Agafya the crooked glass. She slowly drank the vodka, ate nothing with it, but drew a deep breath when she had finished.

"You've brought something," said Savka, untying the bundle and throwing a condescending, jesting shade into his voice. "Women can never come without bringing something. Ah, pie and potatoes. . . . They live well," he sighed, turning to me. "They are the only ones in the whole village who have got potatoes left from the winter!"

In the darkness I did not see Agafya's face, but from the movement of her shoulders and head it seemed to me that she could not take her eyes off Savka's face. To avoid being the third person at this tryst, I decided to go for a walk and got up. But at that moment a nightingale in the wood suddenly uttered two low contralto notes. Half a minute later it gave a tiny high trill and then, having thus tried its voice, began singing. Savka jumped up and listened.

"It's the same one as yesterday," he said. "Wait a minute."

And, getting up, he went noiselessly to the wood.

"Why, what do you want with it?" I shouted out after him, "Stop!"

Savka shook his hand as much as to say, "Don't shout," and vanished into the darkness. Savka was an excellent sportsman and fisherman when he liked, but his talents in this direction were as completely thrown away as his strength. He was too slothful to do things in the routine way, and vented his passion for sport in useless tricks. For instance, he would catch nightingales only with his hands, would shoot pike with a fowling piece, he would spend whole hours by the river trying to catch little fish with a big hook.

Left alone with me, Agafya coughed and passed her hand several times over her forehead. . . . She began to feel a little drunk from the vodka.

"How are you getting on, Agasha?" I asked her, after a long silence, when it began to be awkward to remain mute any longer.

"Very well, thank God. . . . Don't tell anyone, sir, will you?" she added suddenly in a whisper.

"That's all right," I reassured her. "But how reckless you are, Agasha! . . . What if Yakov finds out?"

"He won't find out."

"But what if he does?"

"No . . . I shall be at home before he is. He is on the line now, and he will come back when the mail train brings him, and from here I can hear when the train's coming. . . ."

Agafya once more passed her hand over her forehead and looked away in the direction in which Savka had vanished. The nightingale was singing. Some night bird flew low down close to the ground and, noticing us, was startled, fluttered its wings and flew across to the other side of the river.

Soon the nightingale was silent, but Savka did not come back. Agafya got up, took a few steps uneasily, and sat down again.

"What is he doing?" she could not refrain from saying. "The train's not coming in to-morrow! I shall have to go away directly."

"Savka," I shouted. "Savka."

I was not answered even by an echo. Agafya moved uneasily and sat down again.

"It's time I was going," she said in an agitated voice. "The train will be here directly! I know when the trains come in."

The poor woman was not mistaken. Before a quarter of an hour had passed a sound was heard in the distance.

Agafya kept her eyes fixed on the copse for a long time and moved her hands impatiently.

"Why, where can he be?" she said, laughing nervously. "Where has the devil carried him? I am going! I really must be going."

Meanwhile the noise was growing more and more distinct. By now one could distinguish the rumble of the wheels from the heavy gasps of the engine. Then we heard the whistle, the train crossed the bridge with a hollow rumble . . . another minute and all was still.

"I'll wait one minute more," said Agafya, sitting down resolutely. "So be it, I'll wait."

At last Savka appeared in the darkness. He walked noiselessly on the crumbling earth of the kitchen gardens and hummed something softly to himself.

"Here's a bit of luck; what do you say to that now?" he said gaily. "As soon as I got up to the bush and began taking aim with my hand it left off singing! Ah, the bald dog! I waited and waited to see when it would begin again, but I had to give it up."

Savka flopped clumsily down to the ground beside Agafya and, to keep his balance, clutched at her waist with both hands.

"Why do you look cross, as though your aunt were your mother?" he asked.

With all his soft-heartedness and good-nature, Savka despised women. He behaved carelessly, condescendingly with them, and even stooped to scornful laughter of their feelings for himself. God knows, perhaps this careless, contemptuous manner was one of the causes of his irresistible attraction for the village Dulcineas. He was handsome and well-built; in his eyes there was always a soft friendliness, even when he was looking at the women he so despised, but the fascination was not to be explained by merely external qualities. Apart from his happy exterior and original manner, one must suppose that the touching position of Savka as an acknowledged failure and an unhappy exile from his own hut to the kitchen gardens also had an influence upon the women.

"Tell the gentleman what you have come here for!" Savka went on, still holding Agafya by the waist. "Come, tell him, you good married woman! Ho-ho! Shall we have another drop of vodka, friend Agasha?"

I got up and, threading my way between the plots, I walked the length of the kitchen garden. The dark beds looked like flattened-out graves. They smelt of dug earth and the tender dampness of plants beginning to be covered with dew. . . . A red light was still gleaming on the left. It winked genially and seemed to smile.

I heard a happy laugh. It was Agafya laughing.

"And the train?" I thought. "The train has come in long ago."

Waiting a little longer, I went back to the shanty. Savka was sitting motionless, his legs crossed like a Turk, and was softly, scarcely audibly humming a song consisting of words of one syllable something like: "Out on you, fie on you . . . I and you." Agafya, intoxicated by the vodka, by Savka's scornful caresses, and by the stifling warmth of the night, was lying on the earth beside him, pressing her face convulsively to his knees. She was so carried away by her feelings that she did not even notice my arrival.

"Agasha, the train has been in a long time," I said.

"It's time—it's time you were gone," Savka, tossing his head, took up my thought. "What are you sprawling here for? You shameless hussy!"

Agafya started, took her head from his knees, glanced at me, and sank down beside him again.

"You ought to have gone long ago," I said.

Agafya turned round and got up on one knee. . . . She was unhappy. . . . For half a minute her whole figure, as far as I could distinguish it through the darkness, expressed conflict and hesitation. There was an instant when, seeming to come to herself, she drew herself up to get upon her feet, but then some invincible and implacable force seemed to push her whole body, and she sank down beside Savka again.

"Bother him!" she said, with a wild, guttural laugh, and reckless determination, impotence, and pain could be heard in that laugh.

I strolled quietly away to the copse, and from there down to the river, where our fishing lines were set. The river slept. Some soft, fluffy-petalled flower on a tall stalk touched my cheek tenderly like a child who wants to let one know it's awake. To pass the time I felt for one of the lines and pulled at it. It yielded easily and hung limply—nothing had been caught. . . . The further bank and the village could not be seen. A light gleamed in one hut, but soon went out. I felt my way along the bank, found a hollow place which I had noticed in the daylight, and sat down in it as in an arm-chair. I sat there a long time. . . . I saw the stars begin to grow misty and lose their brightness; a cool breath passed over the earth like a faint sigh and touched the leaves of the slumbering osiers. . . .

"A-ga-fya!" a hollow voice called from the village. "Agafya!"

It was the husband, who had returned home, and in alarm was looking for his wife in the village. At that moment there came the sound of unrestrained laughter: the wife, forgetful of everything, sought in her intoxication to make up by a few hours of happiness for the misery awaiting her next day.

I dropped asleep.

When I woke up Savka was sitting beside me and lightly shaking my shoulder. The river, the copse, both banks, green and washed, trees and fields—all were bathed in bright morning light. Through the slim trunks of the trees the rays of the newly risen sun beat upon my back.

"So that's how you catch fish?" laughed Savka. "Get up!"

I got up, gave a luxurious stretch, and began greedily drinking in the damp and fragrant air.

"Has Agasha gone?" I asked.

"There she is," said Savka, pointing in the direction of the ford.

I glanced and saw Agafya. Dishevelled, with her kerchief dropping off her head, she was crossing the river, holding up her skirt. Her legs were scarcely moving. . . .

"The cat knows whose meat it has eaten," muttered Savka, screwing up his eyes as he looked at her. "She goes with her tail hanging down. . . . They are sly as cats, these women, and timid as hares. . . . She didn't go, silly thing, in the evening when we told her to! Now she will catch it, and they'll flog me again at the peasant court . . . all on account of the women. . . ."

Agafya stepped upon the bank and went across the fields to the village. At first she walked fairly boldly, but soon terror and excitement got the upper hand; she turned round fearfully, stopped and took breath.

"Yes, you are frightened!" Savka laughed mournfully, looking at the bright green streak left by Agafya in the dewy grass. "She doesn't want to go! Her husband's been standing waiting for her for a good hour.... Did you see him?"

Savka said the last words with a smile, but they sent a chill to my heart. In the village, near the furthest hut, Yakov was standing in the road, gazing fixedly at his returning wife. He stood without stirring, and was as motionless as a post. What was he thinking as he looked at her? What words was he preparing to greet her with? Agafya stood still a little while, looked round once more as though expecting help from us, and went on. I have never seen anyone, drunk or sober, move as she did. Agafya seemed to be shrivelled up by her husband's eyes. At one time she moved in zigzags, then she moved her feet up and down without going forward, bending her knees and stretching out her hands, then she staggered back. When she had gone another hundred paces she looked round once more and sat down.

"You ought at least to hide behind a bush ..." I said to Savka. "If the husband sees you ..."

"He knows, anyway, who it is Agafya has come from.... The women don't go to the kitchen garden at night for cabbages—we all know that."

I glanced at Savka's face. It was pale and puckered up with a look of fastidious pity such as one sees in the faces of people watching tortured animals.

"What's fun for the cat is tears for the mouse ..." he muttered.

Agafya suddenly jumped up, shook her head, and with a bold step went towards her husband. She had evidently plucked up her courage and made up her mind.

$\mathcal{A}$ Story
Without an End

Soon after two o'clock one night, long ago, the cook, pale and agitated, rushed unexpectedly into my study and informed me that Madame Mimotih, the old woman who owned the house next door, was sitting in her kitchen.

"She begs you to go in to her, sir . . ." said the cook, panting. "Something bad has happened about her lodger. . . . He has shot himself or hanged himself. . . ."

"What can I do?" said I. "Let her go for the doctor or for the police!"

"How is she to look for a doctor! She can hardly breathe, and she has huddled under the stove, she is so frightened. . . . You had better go round, sir."

I put on my coat and hat and went to Madame Mimotih's house. The gate towards which I directed my steps was open. After pausing beside it, uncertain what to do, I went into the yard without feeling for the porter's bell. In the dark and dilapidated porch the door was not locked. I opened it and walked into the entry. Here there was not a glimmer of light, it was pitch dark, and, moreover, there was a marked smell of incense. Groping my way out of the entry I knocked my elbow against something made of iron, and in the darkness stumbled against a board of some sort which almost fell to the floor. At last the door covered with torn baize was found, and I went into a little hall.

I am not at the moment writing a fairy tale, and am far from intending to alarm the reader, but the picture I saw from the passage was fantastic and could only have been drawn by death. Straight before me was a door leading to a little drawing-room. Three five-kopeck wax candles, standing in a row, threw a scanty light on the faded slate-coloured wallpaper. A coffin was standing on two tables in the middle of the little room. The two candles served only to light up a swarthy yellow face with a half-open mouth and sharp nose. Billows of muslin were mingled in disorder from the face to the tips of the two shoes, and from among the billows peeped out two pale motionless hands, holding a wax cross. The dark gloomy corners of the little drawing-room, the ikons behind the coffin, the coffin itself, everything except the softly glimmering lights, were still as death, as the tomb itself.

"How strange!" I thought, dumbfoundered by the unexpected panorama of death. "Why this haste? The lodger has hardly had time to hang himself, or shoot himself, and here is the coffin already!"

I looked round. On the left there was a door with a glass panel; on the right a lame hat-stand with a shabby fur coat on it. . . .

"Water. . . ." I heard a moan.

The moan came from the left, beyond the door with the glass panel. I opened the door and walked into a little dark room with a solitary window, through which there came a faint light from a street lamp outside.

"Is anyone here?" I asked.

And without waiting for an answer I struck a match. This is what I saw while it was burning. A man was sitting on the blood-stained floor at my very feet. If my step had been a longer one I should have trodden on him. With his legs thrust forward and his hands pressed on the floor, he was making an effort to raise his handsome face, which was deathly pale against his pitch-black beard. In the big eyes which he lifted upon me, I read unutterable terror, pain, and entreaty. A cold sweat trickled in big drops down his face. That sweat, the expression of his face, the trembling of the hands he leaned upon, his hard breathing and his clenched teeth, showed that he was suffering beyond endurance. Near his right hand in a pool of blood lay a revolver.

"Don't go away," I heard a faint voice when the match had gone out. "There's a candle on the table."

I lighted the candle and stood still in the middle of the room not knowing what to do next. I stood and looked at the man on the floor, and it seemed to me that I had seen him before.

"The pain is insufferable," he whispered, "and I haven't the strength to shoot myself again. Incomprehensible lack of will."

I flung off my overcoat and attended to the sick man. Lifting him from the floor like a baby, I laid him on the American-leather covered sofa and carefully undressed him. He was shivering and cold when I took off his clothes; the wound which I saw was not in keeping either with his shivering nor the expression on his face. It was a trifling one. The bullet had passed between the fifth and sixth ribs on the left side, only piercing the skin and the flesh. I found the bullet itself in the folds of the coat-lining near the back pocket. Stopping the bleeding as best I could and making a temporary bandage of a pillow-case, a towel, and two handkerchiefs, I gave the wounded man some water and covered him with a fur coat that was hanging in the passage. We neither of us said a word while the bandaging was being done. I did my work while he lay motionless looking at me with his eyes screwed up as though he were ashamed of his unsuccessful shot and the trouble he was giving me.

"Now I must trouble you to lie still," I said, when I had finished the bandaging, "while I run to the chemist and get something."

"No need!" he muttered, clutching me by the sleeve and opening his eyes wide.

I read terror in his eyes. He was afraid of my going away.

"No need! Stay another five minutes . . . ten. . . . If it doesn't disgust you, do stay, I entreat you."

As he begged me he was trembling and his teeth were chattering. I obeyed, and sat down on the edge of the sofa. Ten minutes passed in silence. I sat silent, looking about the room into which fate had brought me so unexpectedly. What poverty! This man who was the possessor of a handsome, effeminate face and a luxuriant well-tended beard, had surroundings which a humble working man would not have envied. A sofa with its American-leather torn and peeling, a humble greasy-looking chair, a table covered with a little of paper, and a wretched oleograph on the wall, that was all I saw. Damp, gloomy, and grey.

"What a wind!" said the sick man, without opening his eyes, "How it whistles!"

"Yes," I said. "I say, I fancy I know you. Didn't you take part in some private theatricals in General Luhatchev's villa last year?"

"What of it?" he asked, quickly opening his eyes.

A cloud seemed to pass over his face.

"I certainly saw you there. Isn't your name Vassilyev?"

"If it is, what of it? It makes it no better that you should know me."

"No, but I just asked you."

Vassilyev closed his eyes and, as though offended, turned his face to the back of the sofa.

"I don't understand your curiosity," he muttered. "You'll be asking me next what it was drove me to commit suicide!"

Before a minute had passed, he turned round towards me again, opened his eyes and said in a tearful voice:

"Excuse me for taking such a tone, but you'll admit I'm right! To ask a convict how he got into prison, or a suicide why he shot himself is not generous . . . and indelicate. To think of gratifying idle curiosity at the expense of another man's nerves!"

"There is no need to excite yourself. . . . It never occurred to me to question you about your motives."

"You would have asked. . . . It's what people always do. Though it would be no use to ask. If I told you, you would not believe or understand. . . . I must own I don't understand it myself. . . . There are phrases used in the police reports and newspapers such as: 'unrequited love,' and 'hopeless poverty,' but the reasons are not known. . . . They are not known to me, nor to you, nor to your newspaper offices, where they have the impudence to write 'The diary of a suicide.' God alone understands the state of a man's soul when he takes his own life; but men know nothing about it."

"That is all very nice," I said, "but you oughtn't to talk. . . ."

But my suicide could not be stopped, he leaned his head on his fist, and went on in the tone of some great professor:

"Man will never understand the psychological subtleties of suicide! How can one speak of reasons? To-day the reason makes one snatch up a revolver, while to-morrow the same reason seems not worth a rotten egg. It all depends most likely on the particular condition of the individual at the given moment.... Take me for instance. Half an hour ago, I had a passionate desire for death, now when the candle is lighted, and you are sitting by me, I don't even think of the hour of death. Explain that change if you can! Am I better off, or has my wife risen from the dead? Is it the influence of the light on me, or the presence of an outsider?"

"The light certainly has an influence ..." I muttered for the sake of saying something. "The influence of light on the organism...."

"The influence of light.... We admit it! But you know men do shoot themselves by candle-light! And it would be ignominious indeed for the heroes of your novels if such a trifling thing as a candle were to change the course of the drama so abruptly. All this nonsense can be explained perhaps, but not by us. It's useless to ask questions or give explanations of what one does not understand...."

"Forgive me," I said, "but ... judging by the expression of your face, it seems to me that at this moment you ... are posing."

"Yes," Vassilyev said, startled. "It's very possible! I am naturally vain and fatuous. Well, explain it, if you believe in your power of reading faces! Half an hour ago I shot myself, and just now I am posing.... Explain that if you can."

These last words Vassilyev pronounced in a faint, failing voice. He was exhausted, and sank into silence. A pause followed. I began scrutinising his face. It was as pale as a dead man's. It seemed as though life were almost extinct in him, and only the signs of the suffering that the "vain and fatuous" man was feeling betrayed that it was still alive. It was painful to look at that face, but what must it have been for Vassilyev himself who yet had the strength to argue and, if I were not mistaken, to pose?

"You here—are you here?" he asked suddenly, raising himself on his elbow. "My God, just listen!"

I began listening. The rain was pattering angrily on the dark window, never ceasing for a minute. The wind howled plaintively and lugubriously.

" 'And I shall be whiter than snow, and my ears will hear gladness and rejoicing.' " Madame Mimotih, who had returned, was reading in the drawing-room in a languid, weary voice, neither raising nor dropping the monotonous dreary key.

"It is cheerful, isn't it?" whispered Vassilyev, turning his frightened eyes towards me. "My God, the things a man has to see and hear! If only one could set this chaos to music! As Hamlet says, it would—

> Confound the ignorant, and amaze indeed,
> The very faculties of eyes and ears.

How well I should have understood that music then! How I should have felt it! What time is it?"

"Five minutes to three."

"Morning is still far off. And in the morning there's the funeral. A lovely prospect! One follows the coffin through the mud and rain. One walks along, seeing nothing but the cloudy sky and the wretched scenery. The muddy mutes, taverns, woodstacks. . . . One's trousers drenched to the knees. The never-ending streets. The time dragging out like eternity, the coarse people. And on the heart a stone, a stone!"

After a brief pause he suddenly asked:

"Is it long since you saw General Luhatchev?"

"I haven't seen him since last summer."

"He likes to be cock of the walk, but he is a nice little old chap. And are you still writing?"

"Yes, a little."

"Ah. . . . Do you remember how I pranced about like a needle, like an enthusiastic ass at those private theatricals when I was courting Zina? It was stupid, but it was good, it was fun. . . . The very memory of it brings back a whiff of spring. . . . And now! What a cruel change of scene! There is a subject for you! Only don't you go in for writing 'the diary of a suicide.' That's vulgar and conventional. You make something humorous of it."

"Again you are . . . posing," I said. "There's nothing humorous in your position."

"Nothing laughable? You say nothing laughable?" Vassilyev sat up, and tears glistened in his eyes. An expression of bitter distress came into his pale face. His chin quivered.

"You laugh at the deceit of cheating clerks and faithless wives," he said, "but no clerk, no faithless wife has cheated as my fate has cheated me! I have been deceived as no bank depositor, no duped husband has ever been deceived! Only realise what an absurd fool I have been made! Last year before your eyes I did not know what to do with myself for happiness. And now before your eyes. . . ."

Vassilyev's head sank on the pillow and he laughed.

"Nothing more absurd and stupid than such a change could possibly be imagined. Chapter one: spring, love, honeymoon . . . honey, in fact; chapter two: looking for a job, the pawnshop, pallor, the chemist's shop, and . . . to-morrow's splashing through the mud to the graveyard."

He laughed again. I felt acutely uncomfortable and made up my mind to go.

"I tell you what," I said, "you lie down, and I will go to the chemist's."

He made no answer. I put on my great-coat and went out of his room. As I crossed the passage I glanced at the coffin and Madame Mimotih reading over it. I strained my eyes in vain, I could not recognise in the swarthy, yellow face Zina, the lively, pretty *ingénue* of Luhatchev's company.

"*Sic transit*," I thought.

With that I went out, not forgetting to take the revolver, and made my way to the chemist's. But I ought not to have gone away. When I came back from the chemist's, Vassilyev lay on the sofa fainting. The bandages had been roughly torn off, and blood was flowing from the reopened wound. It was daylight before I succeeded in restoring him to consciousness. He was raving in delirium, shivering, and looking with unseeing eyes about the room till morning had come, and we heard the booming voice of the priest as he read the service over the dead.

When Vassilyev's rooms were crowded with old women and mutes, when the coffin had been moved and carried out of the yard, I advised him to remain at home. But he would not obey me, in spite of the pain and the grey, rainy morning. He walked bareheaded and in silence behind the coffin all the way to the cemetery, hardly able to move one leg after the other, and from time to time clutching convulsively at his wounded side. His face expressed complete apathy. Only once when I roused him from his lethargy by some insignificant question he shifted his eyes over the pavement and the grey fence, and for a moment there was a gleam of gloomy anger in them.

" 'Weelright,' " he read on a signboard. "Ignorant, illiterate people, devil take them!"

I led him home from the cemetery.

—

Only one year has passed since that night, and Vassilyev has hardly had time to wear out the boots in which he tramped through the mud behind his wife's coffin.

At the present time as I finish this story, he is sitting in my drawing-room and, playing on the piano, is showing the ladies how provincial misses sing sentimental songs. The ladies are laughing, and he is laughing too. He is enjoying himself.

I call him into my study. Evidently not pleased at my taking him from agreeable company, he comes to me and stands before me in the attitude of a man who has no time to spare. I give him this story, and ask him to read it. Always condescending about my authorship, he stifles a sigh, the sigh of a lazy reader, sits down in an armchair and begins upon it.

"Hang it all, what horrors," he mutters with a smile.

But the further he gets into the reading, the graver his face becomes. At last, under the stress of painful memories, he turns terribly pale, he gets up and goes on reading as he stands. When he has finished he begins pacing from corner to corner.

"How does it end?" I ask him.

"How does it end? H'm. . . ."

He looks at the room, at me, at himself. . . . He sees his new fashionable suit, hears the ladies laughing and . . . sinking on a chair, begins laughing as he laughed on that night.

"Wasn't I right when I told you it was all absurd? My God! I have had burdens to bear that would have broken an elephant's back; the devil knows what I have suffered—no one could have suffered more, I think, and where are the traces? It's astonishing. One would have thought the imprint made on a man by his agonies would have been everlasting, never to be effaced or eradicated. And yet that imprint wears out as easily as a pair of cheap boots. There is nothing left, not a scrap. It's as though I hadn't been suffering then, but had been dancing a mazurka. Everything in the world is transitory, and that transitoriness is absurd! A wide field for humorists! Tack on a humorous end, my friend!"

"Pyotr Nikolaevitch, are you coming soon?" The impatient ladies call my hero.

"This minute," answers the "vain and fatuous" man, setting his tie straight. "It's absurd and pitiful, my friend, pitiful and absurd, but what's to be done? *Homo sum.* . . . And I praise Mother Nature all the same for her transmutation of substances. If we retained an agonising memory of toothache and of all the terrors which every one of us has had to experience, if all that were everlasting, we poor mortals would have a bad time of it in this life."

I look at his smiling face and I remember the despair and the horror with which his eyes were filled a year ago when he looked at the dark window. I see him, entering into his habitual rôle of intellectual chatterer, prepare to show off his idle theories, such as the transmutation of substances before me, and at the same time I recall him sitting on the floor in a pool of blood with his sick imploring eyes.

"How will it end?" I ask myself aloud.

Vassilyev, whistling and straightening his tie, walks off into the drawing-room, and I look after him, and feel vexed. For some reason I regret his past sufferings, I regret all that I felt myself on that man's account on that terrible night. It is as though I had lost something. . . .

Grisha

Grisha, a chubby little boy, born two years and eight months ago, is walking on the boulevard with his nurse. He is wearing a long, wadded pelisse, a scarf, a big cap with a fluffy pom-pom, and warm over-boots. He feels hot and stifled, and now, too, the rollicking April sunshine is beating straight in his face, and making his eyelids tingle.

The whole of his clumsy, timidly and uncertainly stepping little figure expresses the utmost bewilderment.

Hitherto Grisha has known only a rectangular world, where in one corner stands his bed, in the other nurse's trunk, in the third a chair, while in the fourth there is a little lamp burning. If one looks under the bed, one sees a doll with a broken arm and a drum; and behind nurse's trunk, there are a great many things of all sorts: cotton reels, boxes without lids, and a broken Jack-a-dandy. In that world, besides nurse and Grisha, there are often mamma and the cat. Mamma is like a doll, and puss is like papa's fur-coat, only the coat hasn't got eyes and a tail. From the world which is called the nursery a door leads to a great expanse where they have dinner and tea. There stands Grisha's chair on high legs, and on the wall hangs a clock which exists to swing its pendulum and chime. From the dining-room, one can go into a room where there are red arm-chairs. Here, there is a dark patch on the carpet, concerning which fingers are still shaken at Grisha. Beyond that room is still another, to which one is not admitted, and where one sees glimpses of papa—an extremely enigmatical person! Nurse and mamma are comprehensible: they dress Grisha, feed him, and put him to bed, but what papa exists for is unknown. There is another enigmatical person, auntie, who presented Grisha with a drum. She appears and disappears. Where does she disappear to? Grisha has more than once looked under the bed, behind the trunk, and under the sofa, but she was not there....

In this new world, where the sun hurts one's eyes, there are so many papas and mammas and aunties, that there is no knowing to whom to run. But what is stranger and more absurd than anything is the horses. Grisha gazes at their moving legs, and can make nothing of it. He looks at his nurse for her to solve the mystery, but she does not speak.

All at once he hears a fearful tramping.... A crowd of soldiers, with red faces and bath brooms under their arms, move in step along the boulevard straight upon him. Grisha turns cold all over with terror, and looks inquiringly at nurse to know whether it is dangerous. But nurse neither weeps nor runs away, so there is no danger. Grisha looks after the soldiers, and begins to move his feet in step with them himself.

Two big cats with long faces run after each other across the boulevard, with their tongues out, and their tails in the air. Grisha thinks that he must run too, and runs after the cats.

"Stop!" cries nurse, seizing him roughly by the shoulder. "Where are you off to? Haven't you been told not to be naughty?"

Here there is a nurse sitting holding a tray of oranges. Grisha passes by her, and, without saying anything, takes an orange.

"What are you doing that for?" cries the companion of his travels, slapping his hand and snatching away the orange. "Silly!"

Now Grisha would have liked to pick up a bit of glass that was lying at his feet and gleaming like a lamp, but he is afraid that his hand will be slapped again.

"My respects to you!" Grisha hears suddenly, almost above his ear, a loud thick voice, and he sees a tall man with bright buttons.

To his great delight, this man gives nurse his hand, stops, and begins talking to her. The brightness of the sun, the noise of the carriages, the horses, the bright buttons are all so impressively new and not dreadful, that Grisha's soul is filled with a feeling of enjoyment and he begins to laugh.

"Come along! Come along!" he cries to the man with the bright buttons, tugging at his coattails.

"Come along where?" asks the man.

"Come along!" Grisha insists.

He wants to say that it would be just as well to take with them papa, mamma, and the cat, but his tongue does not say what he wants to.

A little later, nurse turns out of the boulevard, and leads Grisha into a big courtyard where there is still snow; and the man with the bright buttons comes with them too. They carefully avoid the lumps of snow and the puddles, then, by a dark and dirty staircase, they go into a room. Here there is a great deal of smoke, there is a smell of roast meat, and a woman is standing by the stove frying cutlets. The cook and the nurse kiss each other, and sit down on the bench together with the man, and begin talking in a low voice. Grisha, wrapped up as he is, feels insufferably hot and stifled.

"Why is this?" he wonders, looking about him.

He sees the dark ceiling, the oven fork with two horns, the stove which looks like a great black hole.

"Mam-ma," he drawls.

"Come, come, come!" cries the nurse. "Wait a bit!"

The cook puts a bottle on the table, two wine-glasses, and a pie. The two women and the man with the bright buttons clink glasses and empty them several times, and the man puts his arm round first the cook and then the nurse. And then all three begin singing in an undertone.

Grisha stretches out his hand towards the pie, and they give him a piece of it. He eats it and watches nurse drinking. . . . He wants to drink too.

"Give me some, nurse!" he begs.

The cook gives him a sip out of her glass. He rolls his eyes, blinks, coughs, and waves his hands for a long time afterwards, while the cook looks at him and laughs.

When he gets home Grisha begins to tell mamma, the walls, and the bed where he has been, and what he has seen. He talks not so much with his tongue, as with his face and his hands. He shows how the sun shines, how the horses run, how the terrible stove looks, and how the cook drinks. . . .

In the evening he cannot get to sleep. The soldiers with the brooms, the big cats, the horses, the bit of glass, the tray of oranges, the bright buttons, all gathered together, weigh on his brain. He tosses from side to side, babbles, and, at last, unable to endure his excitement, begins crying.

"You are feverish," says mamma, putting her open hand on his forehead. "What can have caused it?"

"Stove!" wails Grisha. "Go away, stove!"

"He must have eaten too much . . ." mamma decides.

And Grisha, shattered by the impressions of the new life he has just experienced, receives a spoonful of castor-oil from mamma.

Love

"Three o'clock in the morning. The soft April night is looking in at my windows and caressingly winking at me with its stars. I can't sleep, I am so happy!

"My whole being from head to heels is bursting with a strange, incomprehensible feeling. I can't analyse it just now—I haven't the time, I'm too lazy, and there—hang analysis! Why, is a man likely to interpret his sensations when he is flying head foremost from a belfry, or has just learned that he has won two hundred thousand? Is he in a state to do it?"

This was more or less how I began my love-letter to Sasha, a girl of nineteen with whom I had fallen in love. I began it five times, and as often tore up the sheets, scratched out whole pages, and copied it all over again. I spent as long over the letter as if it had been a novel I had to write to order. And it was not because I tried to make it longer, more elaborate, and more fervent, but because I wanted endlessly to prolong the process of this writing, when one sits in the stillness of one's study and communes with one's own day-dreams while the spring night looks in at one's window. Between the lines I saw a beloved image, and it seemed to me that there were, sitting at the same table writing with me, spirits as naïvely happy, as foolish, and as blissfully smiling as I. I wrote continually, looking at my hand, which still ached deliciously where hers had lately pressed it, and if I turned my eyes away I had a vision of the green trellis of the little gate. Through that trellis Sasha gazed at me after I had said good-bye to her. When I was saying good-bye to Sasha I was thinking of nothing and was simply admiring her figure as every decent man admires a pretty woman; when I saw through the trellis two big eyes, I suddenly, as though by inspiration, knew that I was in love, that it was all settled between us, and fully decided already, that I had nothing left to do but to carry out certain formalities.

It is a great delight also to seal up a love-letter, and, slowly putting on one's hat and coat, to go softly out of the house and to carry the treasure to the post. There are no stars in the sky now: in their place there is a long whitish streak in the east, broken here and there by clouds above the roofs of the dingy houses; from that streak the whole sky is flooded with pale light. The town is asleep, but already the water-carts have come out, and somewhere in a far-away factory a whistle sounds to wake up the workpeople. Beside the postbox, slightly moist with dew, you are sure to see the clumsy figure of a house porter, wearing a bell-shaped sheepskin and carrying a stick. He is in a condition akin to catalepsy: he is not asleep or awake, but something between.

If the boxes knew how often people resort to them for the decision of their fate, they would not have such a humble air. I, anyway, almost kissed my postbox, and as I gazed at it I reflected that the post is the greatest of blessings.

I beg anyone who has ever been in love to remember how one usually hurries home after dropping the letter in the box, rapidly gets into bed and pulls up the quilt in the full conviction that as soon as one wakes up in the morning one will be overwhelmed with memories of the previous day and look with rapture at the window, where the daylight will be eagerly making its way through the folds of the curtain.

Well, to facts. . . . Next morning at midday, Sasha's maid brought me the following answer: "I am delited be sure to come to us to day please I shall expect you. Your S."

Not a single comma. This lack of punctuation, and the misspelling of the word "delighted," the whole letter, and even the long, narrow envelope in which it was put filled my heart with tenderness. In the sprawling but diffident handwriting I recognised Sasha's walk, her way of raising her eyebrows when she laughed, the movement of her lips. . . . But the contents of the letter did not satisfy me. . . . In the first place, poetical letters are not answered in that way, and in the second, why should I go to Sasha's house to wait till it should occur to her stout mamma, her brothers, and poor relations to leave us alone together? It would never enter their heads, and nothing is more hateful than to have to restrain one's raptures simply because of the intrusion of some animate trumpery in the shape of a half-deaf old woman or little girl pestering one with questions. I sent an answer by the maid asking Sasha to select some park or boulevard for a rendezvous. My suggestion was readily accepted. I had struck the right chord, as the saying is.

Between four and five o'clock in the afternoon I made my way to the furthest and most overgrown part of the park. There was not a soul in the park, and the tryst might have taken place somewhere nearer in one of the avenues or arbours, but women don't like doing it by halves in romantic affairs; in for a penny, in for a pound—if you are in for a tryst, let it be in the furthest and most impenetrable thicket, where one runs the risk of stumbling upon some rough or drunken man. When I went up to Sasha she was standing with her back to me, and in that back I could read a devilish lot of mystery. It seemed as though that back and the nape of her neck, and the black spots on her dress were saying: Hush! . . . The girl was wearing a simple cotton dress over which she had thrown a light cape. To add to the air of mysterious secrecy, her face was covered with a white veil. Not to spoil the effect, I had to approach on tiptoe and speak in a half whisper.

From what I remember now, I was not so much the essential point of the rendezvous as a detail of it. Sasha was not so much absorbed in the interview itself as in its romantic mysteriousness, my kisses, the silence of the gloomy trees, my vows. . . . There was not a minute in which she forgot herself, was overcome, or let the mysterious expression drop from her face, and really if there had been any Ivan

Sidoritch or Sidor Ivanitch in my place she would have felt just as happy. How is one to make out in such circumstances whether one is loved or not? Whether the love is "the real thing" or not?

From the park I took Sasha home with me. The presence of the beloved woman in one's bachelor quarters affects one like wine and music. Usually one begins to speak of the future, and the confidence and self-reliance with which one does so is beyond bounds. You make plans and projects, talk fervently of the rank of general though you have not yet reached the rank of a lieutenant, and altogether you fire off such high-flown nonsense that your listener must have a great deal of love and ignorance of life to assent to it. Fortunately for men, women in love are always blinded by their feelings and never know anything of life. Far from not assenting, they actually turn pale with holy awe, are full of reverence and hang greedily on the maniac's words. Sasha listened to me with attention, but I soon detected an absent-minded expression on her face, she did not understand me. The future of which I talked interested her only in its external aspect and I was wasting time in displaying my plans and projects before her. She was keenly interested in knowing which would be her room, what paper she would have in the room, why I had an upright piano instead of a grand piano, and so on. She examined carefully all the little things on my table, looked at the photographs, sniffed at the bottles, peeled the old stamps off the envelopes, saying she wanted them for something.

"Please collect old stamps for me!" she said, making a grave face. "Please do."

Then she found a nut in the window, noisily cracked it and ate it.

"Why don't you stick little labels on the backs of your books?" she asked, taking a look at the bookcase.

"What for?"

"Oh, so that each book should have its number. . . . And where am I to put my books? I've got books too, you know."

"What books have you got?" I asked.

Sasha raised her eyebrows, thought a moment and said:

"All sorts."

And if it had entered my head to ask her what thoughts, what convictions, what aims she had, she would no doubt have raised her eyebrows, thought a minute, and have said in the same way: "All sorts."

Later I saw Sasha home and left her house regularly, officially engaged, and was so reckoned till our wedding. If the reader will allow me to judge merely from my personal experience, I maintain that to be engaged is very dreary, far more so than to be a husband or nothing at all. An engaged man is neither one thing nor the other, he has left one side of the river and not reached the other, he is not married and yet he can't be said to be a bachelor, but is in something not unlike the condition of the porter whom I have mentioned above.

Every day as soon as I had a free moment I hastened to my fiancée. As I went I usually bore within me a multitude of hopes, desires, intentions, suggestions, phrases. I always fancied that as soon as the maid opened the door I should, from feeling oppressed and stifled, plunge at once up to my neck into a sea of refreshing happiness. But it always turned out otherwise in fact. Every time I went to see my fiancée I found all her family and other members of the household busy over the silly trousseau. (And by the way, they were hard at work sewing for two months and then they had less than a hundred roubles' worth of things). There was a smell of irons, candle grease and fumes. Bugles scrunched under one's feet. The two most important rooms were piled up with billows of linen, calico, and muslin and from among the billows peeped out Sasha's little head with a thread between her teeth. All the sewing party welcomed me with cries of delight but at once led me off into the dining-room where I could not hinder them nor see what only husbands are permitted to behold. In spite of my feelings, I had to sit in the dining-room and converse with Pimenovna, one of the poor relations. Sasha, looking worried and excited, kept running by me with a thimble, a skein of wool or some other boring object.

"Wait, wait, I shan't be a minute," she would say when I raised imploring eyes to her. "Only fancy that wretch Stepanida has spoilt the bodice of the barège dress!"

And after waiting in vain for this grace, I lost my temper, went out of the house and walked about the streets in the company of the new cane I had bought. Or I would want to go for a walk or a drive with my fiancée, would go round and find her already standing in the hall with her mother, dressed to go out and playing with her parasol.

"Oh, we are going to the Arcade," she would say. "We have got to buy some more cashmere and change the hat."

My outing is knocked on the head. I join the ladies and go with them to the Arcade. It is revoltingly dull to listen to women shopping, haggling and trying to outdo the sharp shopman. I felt ashamed when Sasha, after turning over masses of material and knocking down the prices to a minimum, walked out of the shop without buying anything, or else told the shopman to cut her some half rouble's worth.

When they came out of the shop, Sasha and her mamma with scared and worried faces would discuss at length having made a mistake, having bought the wrong thing, the flowers in the chintz being too dark, and so on.

Yes, it is a bore to be engaged! I'm glad it's over.

Now I am married. It is evening. I am sitting in my study reading. Behind me on the sofa Sasha is sitting munching something noisily. I want a glass of beer.

"Sasha, look for the corkscrew. . . ." I say. "It's lying about somewhere."

Sasha leaps up, rummages in a disorderly way among two or three heaps of papers, drops the matches, and without finding the corkscrew, sits down in silence. . . . Five minutes pass—ten . . . I begin to be fretted both by thirst and vexation.

"Sasha, do look for the corkscrew," I say.

Sasha leaps up again and rummages among the papers near me. Her munching and rustling of the papers affects me like the sound of sharpening knives against each other. . . . I get up and begin looking for the corkscrew myself. At last it is found and the beer is uncorked. Sasha remains by the table and begins telling me something at great length.

"You'd better read something, Sasha," I say.

She takes up a book, sits down facing me and begins moving her lips. . . . I look at her little forehead, moving lips, and sink into thought.

"She is getting on for twenty. . . ." I reflect. "If one takes a boy of the educated class and of that age and compares them, what a difference!

The boy would have knowledge and convictions and some intelligence."

But I forgive that difference just as the low forehead and moving lips are forgiven. I remember in my old Lovelace days I have cast off women for a stain on their stockings, or for one foolish word, or for not cleaning their teeth, and now I forgive everything: the munching, the muddling about after the corkscrew, the slovenliness, the long talking about nothing that matters; I forgive it all almost unconsciously, with no effort of will, as though Sasha's mistakes were my mistakes, and many things which would have made me wince in old days move me to tenderness and even rapture. The explanation of this forgiveness of everything lies in my love for Sasha, but what is the explanation of the love itself, I really don't know.

A Gentleman Friend

The charming Vanda, or, as she was described in her passport, the "Honourable Citizen Nastasya Kanavkin," found herself, on leaving the hospital, in a position she had never been in before: without a home to go to or a farthing in her pocket. What was she to do?

The first thing she did was to visit a pawn-broker's and pawn her turquoise ring, her one piece of jewellery. They gave her a rouble for the ring . . . but what can you get for a rouble? You can't buy for that sum a fashionable short jacket, nor a big hat, nor a pair of bronze shoes, and without those things she had a feeling of being, as it were, undressed. She felt as though the very horses and dogs were staring and laughing at the plainness of her dress. And clothes were all she thought about: the question what she should eat and where she should sleep did not trouble her in the least.

"If only I could meet a gentleman friend," she thought to herself, "I could get some money. . . . There isn't one who would refuse me, I know. . . ."

But no gentleman she knew came her way. It would be easy enough to meet them in the evening at the "Renaissance," but they wouldn't let her in at the "Renaissance" in that shabby dress and with no hat. What was she to do?

After long hesitation, when she was sick of walking and sitting and thinking, Vanda made up her mind to fall back on her last resource: to go straight to the lodgings of some gentleman friend and ask for money.

She pondered which to go to. "Misha is out of the question; he's a married man. . . . The old chap with the red hair will be at his office at this time. . . ."

Vanda remembered a dentist, called Finkel, a converted Jew, who six months ago had given her a bracelet, and on whose head she had once emptied a glass of beer at the supper at the German Club. She was awfully pleased at the thought of Finkel.

"He'll be sure to give it me, if only I find him at home," she thought, as she walked in his direction. "If he doesn't, I'll smash all the lamps in the house."

Before she reached the dentist's door she thought out her plan of action: she would run laughing up the stairs, dash into the dentist's room and demand twenty-five roubles. But as she touched the bell, this plan seemed to vanish from her mind of itself. Vanda began suddenly feeling frightened and nervous, which was not at all her way. She was bold and saucy enough at drinking parties, but now, dressed in everyday clothes, feeling herself in the position of an ordinary person asking a favour, who might be refused admittance, she felt suddenly timid and humiliated. She was ashamed and frightened.

"Perhaps he has forgotten me by now," she thought, hardly daring to pull the bell. "And how can I go up to him in such a dress, looking like a beggar or some working girl?"

And she rang the bell irresolutely.

She heard steps coming: it was the porter.

"Is the doctor at home?" she asked.

She would have been glad now if the porter had said "No," but the latter, instead of answering ushered her into the hall, and helped her off with her coat. The staircase impressed her as luxurious, and magnificent, but of all its splendours what caught her eye most was an immense looking-glass, in which she saw a ragged figure without a fashionable jacket, without a big hat, and without bronze shoes. And it seemed strange to Vanda that, now that she was humbly dressed and looked like a laundress or sewing girl, she felt ashamed, and no trace of her usual boldness and sauciness remained, and in her own mind she no longer thought of herself as Vanda, but as the Nastasya Kanavkin she used to be in the old days. . . .

"Walk in, please," said a maidservant, showing her into the consulting-room. "The doctor will be here in a minute. Sit down."

Vanda sank into a soft arm-chair.

"I'll ask him to lend it me," she thought; "that will be quite proper, for, after all, I do know him. If only that servant would go. I don't like to ask before her. What does she want to stand there for?"

Five minutes later the door opened and Finkel came in. He was a tall, dark Jew, with fat cheeks and bulging eyes. His cheeks, his eyes, his chest, his body, all of him was so well fed, so loathsome and repellent! At the "Renaissance" and the German Club he had usually been rather tipsy, and would spend his money freely on women, and be very long-suffering and patient with their pranks (when Vanda, for instance, poured the beer over his head, he simply smiled and shook his finger at her): now he had a cross, sleepy expression and looked solemn and frigid like a police captain, and he kept chewing something.

"What can I do for you?" he asked, without looking at Vanda.

Vanda looked at the serious countenance of the maid and the smug figure of Finkel, who apparently did not recognize her, and she turned red.

"What can I do for you?" repeated the dentist a little irritably.

"I've got toothache," murmured Vanda.

"Aha! . . . Which is the tooth? Where?"

Vanda remembered she had a hole in one of her teeth.

"At the bottom . . . on the right . . ." she said.

"Hm! . . . Open your mouth."

Finkel frowned and, holding his breath, began examining the tooth.

"Does it hurt?" he asked, digging into it with a steel instrument.

"Yes," Vanda replied, untruthfully.

"Shall I remind him?" she was wondering. "He would be sure to remember me. But that servant! Why will she stand there?"

Finkel suddenly snorted like a steam-engine right into her mouth, and said:

"I don't advise you to have it stopped. That tooth will never be worth keeping anyhow."

After probing the tooth a little more and soiling Vanda's lips and gums with his tobacco-stained fingers, he held his breath again, and put something cold into her mouth. Vanda suddenly felt a sharp pain, cried out, and clutched at Finkel's hand.

"It's all right, it's all right," he muttered; "don't you be frightened! That tooth would have been no use to you, anyway . . . you must be brave. . . ."

And his tobacco-stained fingers, smeared with blood, held up the tooth to her eyes, while the maid approached and put a basin to her mouth.

"You wash out your mouth with cold water when you get home, and that will stop the bleeding," said Finkel.

He stood before her with the air of a man expecting her to go, waiting to be left in peace.

"Good-day," she said, turning towards the door.

"Hm! . . . and how about my fee?" enquired Finkel, in a jesting tone.

"Oh, yes!" Vanda remembered, blushing, and she handed the Jew the rouble that had been given her for her ring.

When she got out into the street she felt more overwhelmed with shame than before, but now it was not her poverty she was ashamed of. She was unconscious now of not having a big hat and a fashionable jacket. She walked along the street, spitting blood, and brooding on her life, her ugly, wretched life, and the insults she had endured, and would have to endure to-morrow, and next week, and all her life, up to the very day of her death.

"Oh! how awful it is! My God, how fearful!"

Next day, however, she was back at the "Renaissance," and dancing there. She had on an enormous new red hat, a new fashionable jacket, and bronze shoes. And she was taken out to supper by a young merchant up from Kazan.

The Privy Councillor

At the beginning of April in 1870 my mother, Klavdia Arhipovna, the widow of a lieutenant, received from her brother Ivan, a privy councillor in Petersburg, a letter in which, among other things, this passage occurred: "My liver trouble forces me to spend every summer abroad, and as I have not at the moment the money in hand for a trip to Marienbad, it is very possible, dear sister, that I may spend this summer with you at Kotchuevko...."

On reading the letter my mother turned pale and began trembling all over; then an expression of mingled tears and laughter came into her face. She began crying and laughing. This conflict of tears and laughter always reminds me of the flickering and spluttering of a brightly burning candle when one sprinkles it with water. Reading the letter once more, mother called together all the household, and in a voice broken with emotion began explaining to us that there had been four Gundasov brothers: one Gundasov had died as a baby; another had gone to the war, and he, too, was dead; the third, without offence to him be it said, was an actor; the fourth ...

"The fourth has risen far above us," my mother brought out tearfully. "My own brother, we grew up together; and I am all of a tremble, all of a tremble! ... A privy councillor with the rank of a general!

How shall I meet him, my angel brother? What can I, a foolish, uneducated woman, talk to him about? It's fifteen years since I've seen him! Andryushenka," my mother turned to me, "you must rejoice, little stupid! It's a piece of luck for you that God is sending him to us!"

After we had heard a detailed history of the Gundasovs, there followed a fuss and bustle in the place such as I had been accustomed to see only before Christmas and Easter. The sky above and the water in the river were all that escaped; everything else was subjected to a merciless cleansing, scrubbing, painting. If the sky had been lower and smaller and the river had not flowed so swiftly, they would have scoured them, too, with bath-brick and rubbed them, too, with tow. Our walls were as white as snow, but they were whitewashed; the floors were bright and shining, but they were washed every day. The cat Bobtail (as a small child I had cut off a good quarter of his tail with the knife used for chopping the sugar, and that was why he was called Bobtail) was carried off to the kitchen and put in charge of Anisya; Fedka was told that if any of the dogs came near the front-door "God would punish him." But no one was so badly treated as the poor sofas, easychairs, and rugs! They had never before been so violently beaten as on this occasion in preparation for our visitor. My pigeons took fright at the loud thud of the sticks, and were continually flying up into the sky.

The tailor Spiridon, the only tailor in the whole district who ventured to make for the gentry, came over from Novostroevka. He was a hard-working capable man who did not drink and was not without a certain fancy and feeling for form, but yet he was an atrocious tailor. His work was ruined by hesitation. . . . The idea that his cut was not fashionable enough made him alter everything half a dozen times, walk all the way to the town simply to study the dandies, and in the end dress us in suits that even a caricaturist would have called *outré* and grotesque. We cut a dash in impossibly narrow trousers and in such short jackets that we always felt quite abashed in the presence of young ladies.

This Spiridon spent a long time taking my measure. He measured me all over lengthways and crossways, as though he meant to put hoops round me like a barrel; then he spent a long time noting down my measurements with a thick pencil on a bit of paper, and ticked off all the measurements with triangular signs. When he had finished with me he set to work on my tutor, Yegor Alexyevitch Pobyedimsky. My beloved tutor was then at the stage when young men watch the growth of their moustache and are critical of their clothes, and so you can imagine the devout awe with which Spiridon approached him. Yegor Alexyevitch had to throw back his head, to straddle his legs like an inverted V, first lift up his arms, then let them fall. Spiridon measured him several times, walking round him during the process like a love-sick pigeon round its mate, going down on one knee, bending double. . . . My mother, weary, exhausted by her exertions and heated by ironing, watched these lengthy proceedings, and said:

"Mind now, Spiridon, you will have to answer for it to God if you spoil the cloth! And it will be the worse for you if you don't make them fit!"

Mother's words threw Spiridon first into a fever, then into a perspiration, for he was convinced that he would not make them fit. He received one rouble twenty kopecks for making my suit, and for Pobyedimsky's two roubles, but we provided the cloth, the lining, and the buttons. The price cannot be considered excessive, as Novostroevka was about seven miles from us, and the tailor came to fit us four times. When he came to try the things on and we squeezed ourselves into the tight trousers and jackets adorned with basting threads, mother always frowned contemptuously and expressed her surprise:

"Goodness knows what the fashions are coming to nowadays! I am positively ashamed to look at them. If brother were not used to Petersburg I would not get you fashionable clothes!"

Spiridon, relieved that the blame was thrown on the fashion and not on him, shrugged his shoulders and sighed, as though to say:

"There's no help for it; it's the spirit of the age!"

The excitement with which we awaited the arrival of our guest can only be compared with the strained suspense with which spiritualists wait from minute to minute the appearance of a ghost. Mother went about with a sick headache, and was continually melting into tears. I lost my appetite, slept badly, and did not learn my lessons. Even in my dreams I was haunted by an impatient longing to see a general—that is, a man with epaulettes and an embroidered collar sticking up to his ears, and with a naked sword in his hands, exactly like the one who hung over the sofa in the drawing-room and glared with terrible black eyes at everybody who dared to look at him. Pobyedimsky was the only one who felt himself in his element. He was neither terrified nor delighted, and merely from time to time, when he heard the history of the Gundasov family, said:

"Yes, it will be pleasant to have some one fresh to talk to."

My tutor was looked upon among us as an exceptional nature. He was a young man of twenty, with a pimply face, shaggy locks, a low forehead, and an unusually long nose. His nose was so big that when he wanted to look close at anything he had to put his head on one side like a bird. To our thinking, there was not a man in the province cleverer, more cultivated, or more stylish. He had left the high-school in the class next to the top, and had then entered a veterinary college, from which he was expelled before the end of the first half-year. The reason of his expulsion he carefully concealed, which enabled any one who wished to do so to look upon my instructor as an injured and to some extent a mysterious person. He spoke little, and only of intellectual subjects; he ate meat during the fasts, and looked with contempt and condescension on the life going on around him, which did not prevent him, however, from taking presents, such as suits of clothes, from my mother, and drawing funny faces with red teeth on my kites. Mother disliked him for his "pride," but stood in awe of his cleverness.

Our visitor did not keep us long waiting. At the beginning of May two wagon-loads of big boxes arrived from the station. These boxes looked so majestic that the drivers instinctively took off their hats as they lifted them down.

"There must be uniforms and gunpowder in those boxes," I thought.

Why "gunpowder"? Probably the conception of a general was closely connected in my mind with cannons and gunpowder.

When I woke up on the morning of the tenth of May, nurse told me in a whisper that "my uncle had come." I dressed rapidly, and, washing after a fashion, flew out of my bedroom without saying my prayers. In the vestibule I came upon a tall, solid gentleman with fashionable whiskers and a foppish-looking overcoat. Half dead with devout awe,

I went up to him and, remembering the ceremonial mother had impressed upon me, I scraped my foot before him, made a very low bow, and craned forward to kiss his hand; but the gentleman did not allow me to kiss his hand: he informed me that he was not my uncle, but my uncle's footman, Pyotr. The appearance of this Pyotr, far better dressed than Pobyedimsky or me, excited in me the utmost astonishment, which, to tell the truth, has lasted to this day. Can such dignified, respectable people with stern and intellectual faces really be footmen? And what for?

Pyotr told me that my uncle was in the garden with my mother. I rushed into the garden.

Nature, knowing nothing of the history of the Gundasov family and the rank of my uncle, felt far more at ease and unconstrained than I. There was a clamour going on in the garden such as one only hears at fairs. Masses of starlings flitting through the air and hopping about the walks were noisily chattering as they hunted for cockchafers. There were swarms of sparrows in the lilac-bushes, which threw their tender, fragrant blossoms straight in one's face. Wherever one turned, from every direction came the note of the golden oriole and the shrill cry of the hoopoe and the red-legged falcon. At any other time I should have begun chasing dragon-flies or throwing stones at a crow which was sitting on a low mound under an aspen-tree, with its blunt beak turned away; but at that moment I was in no mood for mischief. My heart was throbbing, and I felt a cold sinking at my stomach; I was preparing myself to confront a gentleman with epaulettes, with a naked sword, and with terrible eyes!

But imagine my disappointment! A dapper little foppish gentleman in white silk trousers, with a white cap on his head, was walking beside my mother in the garden. With his hands behind him and his head thrown back, every now and then running on ahead of mother, he looked quite young. There was so much life and movement in his whole figure that I could only detect the treachery of age when I came close up behind and saw beneath his cap a fringe of close-cropped silver hair. Instead of the staid dignity and stolidity of a general, I saw an almost schoolboyish nimbleness; instead of a collar sticking up to his ears, an ordinary light blue necktie. Mother and my uncle were walking in the avenue talking together. I went softly up to them from behind, and waited for one of them to look round.

"What a delightful place you have here, Klavdia!" said my uncle. "How charming and lovely it is! Had I known before that you had such a charming place, nothing would have induced me to go abroad all these years."

My uncle stooped down rapidly and sniffed at a tulip. Everything he saw moved him to rapture and excitement, as though he had never been in a garden on a sunny day before. The queer man moved about as though he were on springs, and chattered incessantly, without allowing mother to utter a single word. All of a sudden Pobyedimsky came into sight from behind an elder-tree at the turn of the avenue. His appearance was so unexpected that my uncle positively started and stepped back a pace. On this occasion my tutor was attired in his best Inverness cape with sleeves, in which, especially backview, he looked remarkably like a windmill. He had a solemn and majestic air. Pressing his hat to his bosom in Spanish style, he took a step towards my uncle and made a bow such as a marquis makes in a melodrama, bending forward, a little to one side.

"I have the honour to present myself to your high excellency," he said aloud: "the teacher and instructor of your nephew, formerly a pupil of the veterinary institute, and a nobleman by birth, Pobyedimsky!"

This politeness on the part of my tutor pleased my mother very much. She gave a smile, and waited in thrilled suspense to hear what clever thing he would say next; but my tutor, expecting his dignified address to be answered with equal dignity—that is, that my uncle would say "H'm!" like a general and hold out two fingers—was greatly confused and abashed when the latter laughed genially and shook hands with him. He muttered something incoherent, cleared his throat, and walked away.

"Come! isn't that charming?" laughed my uncle. "Just look! he has made his little flourish and thinks he's a very clever fellow! I do like that—upon my soul I do! What youthful aplomb, what life in that foolish flourish! And what boy is this?" he asked, suddenly turning and looking at me.

"That is my Andryushenka," my mother introduced me, flushing crimson. "My consolation. . . ."

I made a scrape with my foot on the sand and dropped a low bow.

"A fine fellow . . . a fine fellow . . ." muttered my uncle, taking his hand from my lips and stroking me on the head. "So your name is Andrusha? Yes, yes. . . . H'm! . . . upon my soul! . . . Do you learn lessons?"

My mother, exaggerating and embellishing as all mothers do, began to describe my achievements in the sciences and the excellence of my behaviour, and I walked round my uncle and, following the ceremonial laid down for me, I continued making low bows. Then my mother began throwing out hints that with my remarkable abilities it would not be amiss for me to get a government nomination to the cadet school; but at the point when I was to have burst into tears and begged for my uncle's protection, my uncle suddenly stopped and flung up his hands in amazement.

"My goo-oodness! What's that?" he asked.

Tatyana Ivanovna, the wife of our bailiff, Fyodor Petrovna, was coming towards us. She was carrying a starched white petticoat and a long ironing-board. As she passed us she looked shyly at the visitor through her eyelashes and flushed crimson.

"Wonders will never cease . . ." my uncle filtered through his teeth, looking after her with friendly interest. "You have a fresh surprise at every step, sister . . . upon my soul!"

"She's a beauty . . ." said mother. "They chose her as a bride for Fyodor, though she lived over seventy miles from here. . . ."

Not every one would have called Tatyana a beauty. She was a plump little woman of twenty, with black eyebrows and a graceful figure, always rosy and attractive-looking, but in her face and in her whole person there was not one striking feature, not one bold line to catch the eye, as though nature had lacked inspiration and confidence when creating her. Tatyana Ivanovna was shy, bashful, and modest in her behaviour; she moved softly and smoothly, said little, seldom laughed, and her whole life was as regular as her face and as flat as her smooth, tidy hair. My uncle screwed up his eyes looking after her, and smiled. Mother looked intently at his smiling face and grew serious.

"And so, brother, you've never married!" she sighed.

"No; I've not married."

"Why not?" asked mother softly.

"How can I tell you? It has happened so. In my youth I was too hard at work, I had no time to live, and when I longed to live—I looked round—and there I had fifty years on my back already. I was too late! However, talking about it . . . is depressing."

My mother and my uncle both sighed at once and walked on, and I left them and flew off to find my tutor, that I might share my impressions with him. Pobyedimsky was standing in the middle of the yard, looking majestically at the heavens.

"One can see he is a man of culture!" he said, twisting his head round. "I hope we shall get on together."

An hour later mother came to us.

"I am in trouble, my dears!" she began, sighing. "You see brother has brought a valet with him, and the valet, God bless him, is not one you can put in the kitchen or in the hall; we must give him a room apart. I can't think what I am to do! I tell you what, children, couldn't you move out somewhere—to Fyodor's lodge, for instance—and give your room to the valet? What do you say?"

We gave our ready consent, for living in the lodge was a great deal more free than in the house, under mother's eye.

"It's a nuisance, and that's a fact!" said mother. "Brother says he won't have dinner in the middle of the day, but between six and seven, as they do in Petersburg. I am simply distracted with worry! By seven o'clock the dinner will be done to rags in the oven. Really, men don't understand anything about housekeeping, though they have so much intellect. Oh, dear! we shall have to cook two dinners every day! You will have dinner at midday as before, children, while your poor old mother has to wait till seven, for the sake of her brother."

Then my mother heaved a deep sigh, bade me try and please my uncle, whose coming was a piece of luck for me for which we must thank God, and hurried off to the kitchen. Pobyedimsky and I moved into the lodge the same day. We were installed in a room which formed the passage from the entry to the bailiff's bedroom.

Contrary to my expectations, life went on just as before, drearily and monotonously, in spite of my uncle's arrival and our move into new quarters. We were excused lessons "on account of the visitor." Pobyedimsky, who never read anything or occupied himself in any way, spent most of his time sitting on his bed, with his long nose thrust into the air, thinking. Sometimes he would get up, try on his new suit, and sit down again to relapse into contemplation and silence. Only one thing worried him, the flies, which he used mercilessly to squash between his hands. After dinner he usually "rested," and his snores were a cause of annoyance to the whole household. I ran about the garden from morning to night, or sat in the lodge sticking my kites together. For the first two or three weeks we did not see my uncle often. For days together he sat in his own room working, in spite of the flies and the heat. His extraordinary capacity for sitting as though glued to his table produced upon us the effect of an inexplicable conjuring trick. To us idlers, knowing nothing of systematic work, his industry seemed simply miraculous. Getting up at nine, he sat down to his table, and did not leave it till dinner-time; after dinner he set to work again, and went on till late at night. Whenever I peeped through the keyhole I invariably saw the same thing: my uncle sitting at the table working. The work consisted in his writing with one hand while he turned over the leaves of a book with the other, and, strange to say, he kept moving all over—swinging his leg as though it were a pendulum, whistling, and nodding his head in time. He had an extremely careless and frivolous expression all the while, as though he were not working, but playing at noughts and crosses. I always saw him wearing a smart short jacket and a jauntily tied cravat, and he always smelt, even through the keyhole, of delicate feminine perfumery. He only left his room for dinner, but he ate little.

"I can't make brother out!" mother complained of him. "Every day we kill a turkey and pigeons on purpose for him, I make a *compote* with my own hands, and he eats a plateful of broth and a bit of meat the size of a finger and gets up from the table. I began begging him to eat; he comes back and drinks a glass of milk. And what is there in that, in a glass of milk? It's no better than washing up water! You may die of a diet like that. . . . If I try to persuade him, he laughs and makes a joke of it. . . . No; he does not care for our fare, poor dear!"

We spent the evenings far more gaily than the days. As a rule, by the time the sun was setting and long shadows were lying across the yard, we—that is, Tatyana Ivanovna, Pobyedimsky, and I—were sitting on the steps of the lodge. We did not talk till it grew quite dusk. And, indeed, what is one to talk of when every subject has been talked over already? There was only one thing new, my uncle's arrival, and even that subject was soon exhausted. My tutor never took his eyes off Tatyana Ivanovna's face, and frequently heaved deep sighs.... At the time I did not understand those sighs, and did not try to fathom their significance; now they explain a great deal to me.

When the shadows merged into one thick mass of shade, the bailiff Fyodor would come in from shooting or from the field. This Fyodor gave me the impression of being a fierce and even a terrible man. The son of a Russianized gipsy from Izyumskoe, swarthy-faced and curly-headed, with big black eyes and a matted beard, he was never called among our Kotchuevko peasants by any name but "The Devil." And, indeed, there was a great deal of the gipsy about him apart from his appearance. He could not, for instance, stay at home, and went off for days together into the country or into the woods to shoot. He was gloomy, ill-humoured, taciturn, was afraid of nobody, and refused to recognize any authority. He was rude to mother, addressed me familiarly, and was contemptuous of Pobyedimsky's learning. All this we forgave him, looking upon him as a hot-tempered and nervous man; mother liked him because, in spite of his gipsy nature, he was ideally honest and industrious. He loved his Tatyana Ivanovna passionately, like a gipsy, but this love took in him a gloomy form, as though it cost him suffering. He was never affectionate to his wife in our presence, but simply rolled his eyes angrily at her and twisted his mouth.

When he came in from the fields he would noisily and angrily put down his gun, would come out to us on the steps, and sit down beside his wife. After resting a little, he would ask his wife a few questions about household matters, and then sink into silence.

"Let us sing," I would suggest.

My tutor would tune his guitar, and in a deep deacon's bass strike up "In the midst of the valley." We would begin singing. My tutor took the bass, Fyodor sang in a hardly audible tenor, while I sang soprano in unison with Tatyana Ivanovna.

When the whole sky was covered with stars and the frogs had left off croaking, they would bring in our supper from the kitchen. We went into the lodge and sat down to the meal. My tutor and the gipsy ate greedily, with such a sound that it was hard to tell whether it was the bones crunching or their jaws, and Tatyana Ivanovna and I scarcely succeeded in getting our share. After supper the lodge was plunged in deep sleep.

One evening, it was at the end of May, we were sitting on the steps, waiting for supper. A shadow suddenly fell across us, and Gundasov stood before us as though he had sprung out of the earth. He looked at us for a long time, then clasped his hands and laughed gaily.

"An idyll!" he said. "They sing and dream in the moonlight! It's charming, upon my soul! May I sit down and dream with you?"

We looked at one another and said nothing. My uncle sat down on the bottom step, yawned, and looked at the sky. A silence followed. Pobyedimsky, who had for a long time been wanting to talk to somebody fresh, was delighted at the opportunity, and was the first to break the silence. He had only one subject for intellectual conversation, the epizootic diseases. It sometimes happens that after one has been in an immense crowd, only some one countenance of the thousands remains long imprinted on the memory; in the same way, of all that Pobyedimsky had heard, during his six months at the veterinary institute, he remembered only one passage:

"The epizootics do immense damage to the stock of the country. It is the duty of society to work hand in hand with the government in waging war upon them."

Before saying this to Gundasov, my tutor cleared his throat three times, and several times, in his excitement, wrapped himself up in his Inverness. On hearing about the epizootics, my uncle looked intently at my tutor and made a sound between a snort and a laugh.

"Upon my soul, that's charming!" he said, scrutinizing us as though we were mannequins. "This is actually life. . . . This is really what reality is bound to be. Why are you silent, Pelagea Ivanovna?" he said, addressing Tatyana Ivanovna.

She coughed, overcome with confusion.

"Talk, my friends, sing . . . play! . . . Don't lose time. You know, time, the rascal, runs away and waits for no man! Upon my soul, before you have time to look round, old age is upon you. . . . Then it is too late to live! That's how it is, Pelagea Ivanovna. . . . We mustn't sit still and be silent. . . ."

At that point supper was brought out from the kitchen. Uncle went into the lodge with us, and to keep us company ate five curd fritters and the wing of a duck. He ate and looked at us. He was touched and delighted by us all. Whatever silly nonsense my precious tutor talked, and whatever Tatyana Ivanovna did, he thought charming and delightful. When after supper Tatyana Ivanovna sat quietly down and took up her knitting, he kept his eyes fixed on her fingers and chatted away without ceasing.

"Make all the haste you can to live, my friends . . ." he said. "God forbid you should sacrifice the present for the future! There is youth, health, fire in the present; the future is smoke and deception! As soon as you are twenty begin to live."

Tatyana Ivanovna dropped a knitting-needle. My uncle jumped up, picked up the needle, and handed it to Tatyana Ivanovna with a bow, and for the first time in my life I learnt that there were people in the world more refined than Pobyedimsky.

"Yes . . ." my uncle went on, "love, marry, do silly things. Foolishness is a great deal more living and healthy than our straining and striving after rational life."

My uncle talked a great deal, so much that he bored us; I sat on a box listening to him and dropping to sleep. It distressed me that he did not once all the evening pay attention to me. He left the lodge at two o'clock, when, overcome with drowsiness, I was sound asleep.

From that time forth my uncle took to coming to the lodge every evening. He sang with us, had supper with us, and always stayed on till two o'clock in the morning, chatting incessantly, always about the same subject. His evening and night work was given up, and by the end of June, when the privy councillor had learned to eat mother's turkey and *compote,* his work by day was abandoned too. My uncle tore himself away from his table and plunged into "life." In the daytime he walked up and down the garden, he whistled to the workmen and hin-

dered them from working, making them tell him their various histo-
ries. When his eye fell on Tatyana Ivanovna he ran up to her, and, if
she were carrying anything, offered his assistance, which embarrassed
her dreadfully.

As the summer advanced my uncle grew more and more frivolous,
volatile, and careless. Pobyedimsky was completely disillusioned in regard to him.

"He is too one-sided," he said. "There is nothing to show that he is
in the very foremost ranks of the service. And he doesn't even know
how to talk. At every word it's 'upon my soul.' No, I don't like him!"

From the time that my uncle began visiting the lodge there was a
noticeable change both in Fyodor and my tutor. Fyodor gave up going
out shooting, came home early, sat more taciturn than ever, and stared
with particular ill-humour at his wife. In my uncle's presence my tutor
gave up talking about epizootics, frowned, and even laughed sarcastically.

"Here comes our little bantam cock!" he growled on one occasion
when my uncle was coming into the lodge.

I put down this change in them both to their being offended with
my uncle. My absent-minded uncle mixed up their names, and to the
very day of his departure failed to distinguish which was my tutor and
which was Tatyana Ivanovna's husband. Tatyana Ivanovna herself he
sometimes called Nastasya, sometimes Pelagea, and sometimes Yev-
dokia. Touched and delighted by us, he laughed and behaved exactly
as though in the company of small children. . . . All this, of course,
might well offend young men. It was not a case of offended pride,
however, but, as I realize now, subtler feelings.

I remember one evening I was sitting on the box struggling with
sleep. My eyelids felt glued together and my body, tired out by running about all day, drooped sideways. But I struggled against sleep and
tried to look on. It was about midnight. Tatyana Ivanovna, rosy and
unassuming as always, was sitting at a little table sewing at her husband's shirt. Fyodor, sullen and gloomy, was staring at her from one
corner, and in the other sat Pobyedimsky, snorting angrily and retreating into the high collar of his shirt. My uncle was walking up and down

the room thinking. Silence reigned; nothing was to be heard but the rustling of the linen in Tatyana Ivanovna's hands. Suddenly my uncle stood still before Tatyana Ivanovna, and said:

"You are all so young, so fresh, so nice, you live so peacefully in this quiet place, that I envy you. I have become attached to your way of life here; my heart aches when I remember I have to go away. . . . You may believe in my sincerity!"

Sleep closed my eyes and I lost myself. When some sound waked me, my uncle was standing before Tatyana Ivanovna, looking at her with a softened expression. His cheeks were flushed.

"My life has been wasted," he said. "I have not lived! Your young face makes me think of my own lost youth, and I should be ready to sit here watching you to the day of my death. It would be a pleasure to me to take you with me to Petersburg."

"What for?" Fyodor asked in a husky voice.

"I should put her under a glass case on my worktable. I should admire her and show her to other people. You know, Pelagea Ivanovna, we have no women like you there. Among us there is wealth, distinction, sometimes beauty, but we have not this true sort of life, this healthy serenity. . . ."

My uncle sat down facing Tatyana Ivanovna and took her by the hand.

"So you won't come with me to Petersburg?" he laughed. "In that case give me your little hand. . . . A charming little hand! . . . You won't give it? Come, you miser! let me kiss it, anyway. . . ."

At that moment there was the scrape of a chair. Fyodor jumped up, and with heavy, measured steps went up to his wife. His face was pale, grey, and quivering. He brought his fist down on the table with a bang, and said in a hollow voice:

"I won't allow it!"

At the same moment Pobyedimsky jumped up from his chair. He, too, pale and angry, went up to Tatyana Ivanovna, and he, too, struck the table with his fist.

"I . . . I won't allow it!" he said.

"What, what's the matter?" asked my uncle in surprise.

"I won't allow it!" repeated Fyodor, banging on the table.

My uncle jumped up and blinked nervously. He tried to speak, but in his amazement and alarm could not utter a word; with an embarrassed smile, he shuffled out of the lodge with the hurried step of an old man, leaving his hat behind. When, a little later, my mother ran into the lodge, Fyodor and Pobyedimsky were still hammering on the table like blacksmiths and repeating, "I won't allow it!"

"What has happened here?" asked mother. "Why has my brother been taken ill? What's the matter?"

Looking at Tatyana's pale, frightened face and at her infuriated husband, mother probably guessed what was the matter. She sighed and shook her head.

"Come! give over banging on the table!" she said. "Leave off, Fyodor! And why are you thumping, Yegor Alexyevitch? What have you got to do with it?"

Pobyedimsky was startled and confused. Fyodor looked intently at him, then at his wife, and began walking about the room. When mother had gone out of the lodge, I saw what for long afterwards I looked upon as a dream. I saw Fyodor seize my tutor, lift him up in the air, and thrust him out of the door.

When I woke up in the morning my tutor's bed was empty. To my question where he was nurse told me in a whisper that he had been taken off early in the morning to the hospital, as his arm was broken. Distressed at this intelligence and remembering the scene of the previous evening, I went out of doors. It was a grey day. The sky was covered with storm-clouds and there was a wind blowing dust, bits of paper, and feathers along the ground. . . . It felt as though rain were coming. There was a look of boredom in the servants and in the animals. When I went into the house I was told not to make such a noise with my feet, as mother was ill and in bed with a migraine. What was I to do? I went outside the gate, sat down on the little bench there, and fell to trying to discover the meaning of what I had seen and heard the day before. From our gate there was a road which, passing the forge and the pool which never dried up, ran into the main road. I looked at the telegraph-posts, about which clouds of dust were whirling, and at the sleepy birds sitting on the wires, and I suddenly felt so dreary that I began to cry.

A dusty wagonette crammed full of townspeople, probably going to visit the shrine, drove by along the main road. The wagonette was hardly out of sight when a light chaise with a pair of horses came into view. In it was Akim Nikititch, the police inspector, standing up and holding on to the coachman's belt. To my great surprise, the chaise turned into our road and flew by me in at the gate. While I was puzzling why the police inspector had come to see us, I heard a noise, and a carriage with three horses came into sight on the road. In the carriage stood the police captain, directing his coachman towards our gate.

"And why is he coming?" I thought, looking at the dusty police captain. "Most probably Pobyedimsky has complained of Fyodor to him, and they have come to take him to prison."

But the mystery was not so easily solved. The police inspector and the police captain were only the first instalment, for five minutes had scarcely passed when a coach drove in at our gate. It dashed by me so swiftly that I could only get a glimpse of a red beard.

Lost in conjecture and full of misgivings, I ran to the house. In the passage first of all I saw mother; she was pale and looking with horror towards the door, from which came the sounds of men's voices. The visitors had taken her by surprise in the very throes of migraine.

"Who has come, mother?" I asked.

"Sister," I heard my uncle's voice, "will you send in something to eat for the governor and me?"

"It is easy to say 'something to eat,' " whispered my mother, numb with horror. "What have I time to get ready now? I am put to shame in my old age!"

Mother clutched at her head and ran into the kitchen. The governor's sudden visit stirred and overwhelmed the whole household. A ferocious slaughter followed. A dozen fowls, five turkeys, eight ducks, were killed, and in the fluster the old gander, the progenitor of our whole flock of geese and a great favourite of mother's, was beheaded. The coachmen and the cook seemed frenzied, and slaughtered birds at random, without distinction of age or breed. For the sake of some wretched sauce a pair of valuable pigeons, as dear to me as the gander was to mother, were sacrificed. It was a long while before I could forgive the governor their death.

In the evening, when the governor and his suite, after a sumptuous dinner, had got into their carriages and driven away, I went into the house to look at the remains of the feast. Glancing into the drawing-room from the passage, I saw my uncle and my mother. My uncle, with his hands behind his back, was walking nervously up and down close to the wall, shrugging his shoulders. Mother, exhausted and looking much thinner, was sitting on the sofa and watching his movements with heavy eyes.

"Excuse me, sister, but this won't do at all," my uncle grumbled, wrinkling up his face. "I introduced the governor to you, and you didn't offer to shake hands. You covered him with confusion, poor fellow! No, that won't do. . . . Simplicity is a very good thing, but there must be limits to it. . . . Upon my soul! And then that dinner! How can one give people such things? What was that mess, for instance, that they served for the fourth course?"

"That was duck with sweet sauce . . ." mother anwered softly.

"Duck! Forgive me, sister, but . . . but here I've got heartburn! I am ill!"

My uncle made a sour, tearful face, and went on:

"It was the devil sent that governor! As though I wanted his visit! Pff! . . . heartburn! I can't work or sleep . . . I am completely out of sorts. . . . And I can't understand how you can live here without anything to do . . . in this boredom! Here I've got a pain coming under my shoulder-blade! . . ."

My uncle frowned, and walked about more rapidly than ever.

"Brother," my mother inquired softly, "what would it cost to go abroad?"

"At least three thousand . . ." my uncle answered in a tearful voice. "I would go, but where am I to get it? I haven't a farthing. Pff! . . . heartburn!"

My uncle stopped to look dejectedly at the grey, overcast prospect from the window, and began pacing to and fro again.

A silence followed.... Mother looked a long while at the ikon, pondering something, then she began crying, and said:

"I'll give you the three thousand, brother...."

———

Three days later the majestic boxes went off to the station, and the privy councillor drove off after them. As he said good-bye to mother he shed tears, and it was a long time before he took his lips from her hands, but when he got into his carriage his face beamed with child-like pleasure.... Radiant and happy, he settled himself comfortably, kissed his hand to my mother, who was crying, and all at once his eye was caught by me. A look of the utmost astonishment came into his face.

"What boy is this?" he asked.

My mother, who had declared my uncle's coming was a piece of luck for which I must thank God, was bitterly mortified at this question. I was in no mood for questions. I looked at my uncle's happy face, and for some reason I felt fearfully sorry for him. I could not resist jumping up to the carriage and hugging that frivolous man, weak as all men are. Looking into his face and wanting to say something pleasant, I asked:

"Uncle, have you ever been in a battle?"

"Ah, the dear boy ..." laughed my uncle, kissing me. "A charming boy, upon my soul! How natural, how living it all is, upon my soul!..."

The carriage set off.... I looked after him, and long afterwards that farewell "upon my soul" was ringing in my ears.

A Day in the Country

Between eight and nine o'clock in the morning.

A dark leaden-coloured mass is creeping over the sky towards the sun. Red zigzags of lightning gleam here and there across it. There is a sound of far-away rumbling. A warm wind frolics over the grass, bends the trees, and stirs up the dust. In a minute there will be a spurt of May rain and a real storm will begin.

Fyokla, a little beggar-girl of six, is running through the village, looking for Terenty the cobbler. The white-haired, barefoot child is pale. Her eyes are wide-open, her lips are trembling.

"Uncle, where is Terenty?" she asks every one she meets. No one answers. They are all preoccupied with the approaching storm and take refuge in their huts. At last she meets Silanty Silitch, the sacristan, Terenty's bosom friend. He is coming along, staggering from the wind.

"Uncle, where is Terenty?"

"At the kitchen-gardens," answers Silanty.

The beggar-girl runs behind the huts to the kitchen-gardens and there finds Terenty; the tall old man with a thin, pock-marked face, very long legs, and bare feet, dressed in a woman's tattered jacket, is standing near the vegetable plots, looking with drowsy, drunken eyes at the dark storm-cloud. On his long crane-like legs he sways in the wind like a starling-cote.

"Uncle Terenty!" the white-headed beggar-girl addresses him. "Uncle, darling!"

Terenty bends down to Fyokla, and his grim, drunken face is overspread with a smile, such as come into people's faces when they look at something little, foolish, and absurd, but warmly loved.

"Ah! servant of God, Fyokla," he says, lisping tenderly, "where have you come from?"

"Uncle Terenty," says Fyokla, with a sob, tugging at the lapel of the cobbler's coat. "Brother Danilka has had an accident! Come along!"

"What sort of accident? Ough, what thunder! Holy, holy, holy. . . . What sort of accident?"

"In the count's copse Danilka stuck his hand into a hole in a tree, and he can't get it out. Come along, uncle, do be kind and pull his hand out!"

"How was it he put his hand in? What for?"

"He wanted to get a cuckoo's egg out of the hole for me."

"The day has hardly begun and already you are in trouble. . . ." Terenty shook his head and spat deliberately. "Well, what am I to do with you now? I must come . . . I must, may the wolf gobble you up, you naughty children! Come, little orphan!"

Terenty comes out of the kitchen-garden and, lifting high his long legs, begins striding down the village street. He walks quickly without stopping or looking from side to side, as though he were shoved from behind or afraid of pursuit. Fyokla can hardly keep up with him.

They come out of the village and turn along the dusty road towards the count's copse that lies dark blue in the distance. It is about a mile and a half away. The clouds have by now covered the sun, and soon afterwards there is not a speck of blue left in the sky. It grows dark.

"Holy, holy, holy . . ." whispers Fyokla, hurrying after Terenty. The first rain-drops, big and heavy, lie, dark dots on the dusty road. A big drop falls on Fyokla's cheek and glides like a tear down her chin.

"The rain has begun," mutters the cobbler, kicking up the dust with his bare, bony feet. "That's fine, Fyokla, old girl. The grass and the trees are fed by the rain, as we are by bread. And as for the thunder, don't you be frightened, little orphan. Why should it kill a little thing like you?"

As soon as the rain begins, the wind drops. The only sound is the patter of rain dropping like fine shot on the young rye and the parched road.

"We shall get soaked, Fyokla," mutters Terenty. "There won't be a dry spot left on us. . . . Ho-ho, my girl! It's run down my neck! But don't be frightened, silly. . . . The grass will be dry again, the earth will be dry again, and we shall be dry again. There is the same sun for us all."

A flash of lightning, some fourteen feet long, gleams above their heads. There is a loud peal of thunder, and it seems to Fyokla that something big, heavy, and round is rolling over the sky and tearing it open, exactly over her head.

"Holy, holy, holy . . ." says Terenty, crossing himself. "Don't be afraid, little orphan! It is not from spite that it thunders."

Terenty's and Fyokla's feet are covered with lumps of heavy, wet clay. It is slippery and difficult to walk, but Terenty strides on more and more rapidly. The weak little beggar-girl is breathless and ready to drop.

But at last they go into the count's copse. The washed trees, stirred by a gust of wind, drop a perfect waterfall upon them. Terenty stumbles over stumps and begins to slacken his pace.

"Whereabouts is Danilka?" he asks. "Lead me to him."

Fyokla leads him into a thicket, and, after going a quarter of a mile, points to Danilka. Her brother, a little fellow of eight, with hair as red as ochre and a pale sickly face, stands leaning against a tree, and, with his head on one side, looking sideways at the sky. In one hand he holds his shabby old cap, the other is hidden in an old lime tree. The boy is gazing at the stormy sky, and apparently not thinking of his trouble. Hearing footsteps and seeing the cobbler he gives a sickly smile and says:

"A terrible lot of thunder, Terenty. . . . I've never heard so much thunder in all my life."

"And where is your hand?"

"In the hole. . . . Pull it out, please, Terenty!"

The wood had broken at the edge of the hole and jammed Danilka's hand: he could push it farther in, but could not pull it out. Terenty snaps off the broken piece, and the boy's hand, red and crushed, is released.

"It's terrible how it's thundering," the boy says again, rubbing his hand. "What makes it thunder, Terenty?"

"One cloud runs against the other," answers the cobbler. The party come out of the copse, and walk along the edge of it towards the darkened road. The thunder gradually abates, and its rumbling is heard far away beyond the village.

"The ducks flew by here the other day, Terenty," says Danilka, still rubbing his hand. "They must be nesting in the Gniliya Zaimishtcha marshes. . . . Fyokla, would you like me to show you a nightingale's nest?"

"Don't touch it, you might disturb them," says Terenty, wringing the water out of his cap. "The nightingale is a singing-bird, without sin. He has had a voice given him in his throat, to praise God and gladden the heart of man. It's a sin to disturb him."

"What about the sparrow?"

"The sparrow doesn't matter, he's a bad, spiteful bird. He is like a pickpocket in his ways. He doesn't like man to be happy. When Christ was crucified it was the sparrow brought nails to the Jews, and called 'alive! alive!' "

A bright patch of blue appears in the sky.

"Look!" says Terenty. "An ant-heap burst open by the rain! They've been flooded, the rogues!"

They bend over the ant-heap. The downpour has damaged it; the insects are scurrying to and fro in the mud, agitated, and busily trying to carry away their drowned companions.

"You needn't be in such a taking, you won't die of it!" says Terenty, grinning. "As soon as the sun warms you, you'll come to your senses again. . . . It's a lesson to you, you stupids. You won't settle on low ground another time."

They go on.

"And here are some bees," cries Danilka, pointing to the branch of a young oak tree.

The drenched and chilled bees are huddled together on the branch.

There are so many of them that neither bark nor leaf can be seen. Many of them are settled on one another.

"That's a swarm of bees," Terenty informs them. "They were flying looking for a home, and when the rain came down upon them they settled. If a swarm is flying, you need only sprinkle water on them to make them settle. Now if, say, you wanted to take the swarm, you would bend the branch with them into a sack and shake it, and they all fall in."

Little Fyokla suddenly frowns and rubs her neck vigorously. Her brother looks at her neck, and sees a big swelling on it.

"Hey-hey!" laughs the cobbler. "Do you know where you got that from, Fyokla, old girl? There are Spanish flies on some tree in the wood. The rain has trickled off them, and a drop has fallen on your neck—that's what has made the swelling."

The sun appears from behind the clouds and floods the wood, the fields, and the three friends with its warm light. The dark menacing cloud has gone far away and taken the storm with it. The air is warm and fragrant. There is a scent of bird-cherry, meadowsweet, and lilies-of-the-valley.

"That herb is given when your nose bleeds," says Terenty, pointing to a woolly-looking flower. "It does good."

They hear a whistle and a rumble, but not such a rumble as the storm-clouds carried away. A goods train races by before the eyes of Terenty, Danilka, and Fyokla. The engine, panting and puffing out black smoke, drags more than twenty vans after it. Its power is tremendous. The children are interested to know how an engine, not alive and without the help of horses, can move and drag such weights, and Terenty undertakes to explain it to them:

"It's all the steam's doing, children. . . . The steam does the work. . . . You see, it shoves under that thing near the wheels, and it . . . you see . . . it works. . . ."

They cross the railway line, and, going down from the embankment, walk towards the river. They walk not with any object, but just at random, and talk all the way. . . . Danilka asks questions, Terenty answers them. . . .

Terenty answers all his questions, and there is no secret in Nature which baffles him. He knows everything. Thus, for example, he knows the names of all the wild flowers, animals, and stones. He knows what herbs cure diseases, he has no difficulty in telling the age of a horse or a cow. Looking at the sunset, at the moon, or the birds, he can tell what sort of weather it will be next day. And indeed, it is not only Terenty who is so wise. Silanty Silitch, the innkeeper, the market-gardener, the shepherd, and all the villagers, generally speaking, know as much as he does. These people have learned not from books, but in the fields, in the wood, on the river bank. Their teachers have been the birds them-selves, when they sang to them, the sun when it left a glow of crimson behind it at setting, the very trees, and wild herbs.

Danilka looks at Terenty and greedily drinks in every word. In spring, before one is weary of the warmth and the monotonous green of the fields, when everything is fresh and full of fragrance, who would not want to hear about the golden may-beetles, about the cranes, about the gurgling streams, and the corn mounting into ear?

The two of them, the cobbler and the orphan, walk about the fields, talk unceasingly, and are not weary. They could wander about the world endlessly. They walk, and in their talk of the beauty of the earth do not notice the frail little beggar-girl tripping after them. She is breathless and moves with a lagging step. There are tears in her eyes; she would be glad to stop these inexhaustible wanderers, but to whom and where can she go? She has no home or people of her own; whether she likes it or not, she must walk and listen to their talk.

Towards midday, all three sit down on the river bank. Danilka takes out of his bag a piece of bread, soaked and reduced to a mash, and they begin to eat. Terenty says a prayer when he has eaten the bread, then stretches himself on the sandy bank and falls asleep. While he is asleep, the boy gazes at the water, pondering. He has many different things to think of. He has just seen the storm, the bees, the ants, the train. Now, before his eyes, fishes are whisking about. Some are two inches long and more, others are no bigger than one's nail. A viper, with its head held high, is swimming from one bank to the other.

Only towards the evening our wanderers return to the village. The children go for the night to a deserted barn, where the corn of the commune used to be kept, while Terenty, leaving them, goes to the tavern. The children lie huddled together on the straw, dozing.

The boy does not sleep. He gazes into the darkness, and it seems to him that he is seeing all that he has seen in the day: the storm-clouds, the bright sunshine, the birds, the fish, lanky Terenty. The number of his impressions, together with exhaustion and hunger, are too much for him; he is as hot as though he were on fire, and tosses from side to side. He longs to tell someone all that is haunting him now in the darkness and agitating his soul, but there is no one to tell. Fyokla is too little and could not understand.

"I'll tell Terenty to-morrow," thinks the boy.

The children fall asleep thinking of the homeless cobbler, and, in the night, Terenty comes to them, makes the sign of the cross over them, and puts bread under their heads. And no one sees his love. It is seen only by the moon which floats in the sky and peeps caressingly through the holes in the wall of the deserted barn.

The Chorus Girl

One day when she was younger and better-looking, and when her voice was stronger, Nikolay Petrovitch Kolpakov, her adorer, was sitting in the outer room in her summer villa. It was intolerably hot and stifling. Kolpakov, who had just dined and drunk a whole bottle of inferior port, felt ill-humoured and out of sorts. Both were bored and waiting for the heat of the day to be over in order to go for a walk.

All at once there was a sudden ring at the door. Kolpakov, who was sitting with his coat off, in his slippers, jumped up and looked inquiringly at Pasha.

"It must be the postman or one of the girls," said the singer.

Kolpakov did not mind being found by the postman or Pasha's lady friends, but by way of precaution gathered up his clothes and went into the next room, while Pasha ran to open the door. To her great surprise in the doorway stood, not the postman and not a girl friend, but an unknown woman, young and beautiful, who was dressed like a lady, and from all outward signs was one.

The stranger was pale and was breathing heavily as though she had been running up a steep flight of stairs.

"What is it?" asked Pasha.

The lady did not at once answer. She took a step forward, slowly looked about the room, and sat down in a way that suggested that from fatigue, or perhaps illness, she could not stand; then for a long time her pale lips quivered as she tried in vain to speak.

"Is my husband here?" she asked at last, raising to Pasha her big eyes with their red tear-stained lids.

"Husband?" whispered Pasha, and was suddenly so frightened that her hands and feet turned cold. "What husband?" she repeated, beginning to tremble.

"My husband, . . . Nikolay Petrovitch Kolpakov."

"N . . . no, madam. . . . I . . . I don't know any husband."

A minute passed in silence. The stranger several times passed her handkerchief over her pale lips and held her breath to stop her inward trembling, while Pasha stood before her motionless, like a post, and looked at her with astonishment and terror.

"So you say he is not here?" the lady asked, this time speaking with a firm voice and smiling oddly.

"I . . . I don't know who it is you are asking about."

"You are horrid, mean, vile . . ." the stranger muttered, scanning Pasha with hatred and repulsion. "Yes, yes . . . you are horrid. I am very, very glad that at last I can tell you so!"

Pasha felt that on this lady in black with the angry eyes and white slender fingers she produced the impression of something horrid and unseemly, and she felt ashamed of her chubby red cheeks, the pockmark on her nose, and the fringe on her forehead, which never could be combed back. And it seemed to her that if she had been thin, and had had no powder on her face and no fringe on her forehead, then she could have disguised the fact that she was not "respectable," and she would not have felt so frightened and ashamed to stand facing this unknown, mysterious lady.

"Where is my husband?" the lady went on. "Though I don't care whether he is here or not, but I ought to tell you that the money has been missed, and they are looking for Nikolay Petrovitch. . . . They mean to arrest him. That's your doing!"

The lady got up and walked about the room in great excitement. Pasha looked at her and was so frightened that she could not understand.

"He'll be found and arrested to-day," said the lady, and she gave a sob, and in that sound could be heard her resentment and vexation. "I know who has brought him to this awful position! Low, horrid creature! Loathsome, mercenary hussy!" The lady's lips worked and her nose wrinkled up with disgust. "I am helpless, do you hear, you low woman? . . . I am helpless; you are stronger than I am, but there is One to defend me and my children! God sees all! He is just! He will punish you for every tear I have shed, for all my sleepless nights! The time will come; you will think of me! . . ."

Silence followed again. The lady walked about the room and wrung her hands, while Pasha still gazed blankly at her in amazement, not understanding and expecting something terrible.

"I know nothing about it, madam," she said, and suddenly burst into tears.

"You are lying!" cried the lady, and her eyes flashed angrily at her. "I know all about it! I've known you a long time. I know that for the last month he has been spending every day with you!"

"Yes. What then? What of it? I have a great many visitors, but I don't force anyone to come. He is free to do as he likes."

"I tell you they have discovered that money is missing! He has embezzled money at the office! For the sake of such a . . . creature as you, for your sake he has actually committed a crime. Listen," said the lady in a resolute voice, stopping short, facing Pasha. "You can have no principles; you live simply to do harm—that's your object; but one can't imagine you have fallen so low that you have no trace of human feeling left! He has a wife, children. . . . If he is condemned and sent into exile we shall starve, the children and I. . . . Understand that! And yet there is a chance of saving him and us from destitution and disgrace. If I take them nine hundred roubles to-day they will let him alone. Only nine hundred roubles!"

"What nine hundred roubles?" Pasha asked softly. "I . . . I don't know. . . . I haven't taken it."

"I am not asking you for nine hundred roubles. . . . You have no money, and I don't want your money. I ask you for something else. . . . Men usually give expensive things to women like you. Only give me back the things my husband has given you!"

"Madam, he has never made me a present of anything!" Pasha wailed, beginning to understand.

"Where is the money? He has squandered his own and mine and other people's. . . . What has become of it all? Listen, I beg you! I was carried away by indignation and have said a lot of nasty things to you, but I apologize. You must hate me, I know, but if you are capable of sympathy, put yourself in my position! I implore you to give me back the things!"

"H'm!" said Pasha, and she shrugged her shoulders. "I would with pleasure, but God is my witness, he never made me a present of anything. Believe me, on my conscience. However, you are right, though," said the singer in confusion, "he did bring me two little things. Certainly I will give them back, if you wish it."

Pasha pulled out one of the drawers in the toilet-table and took out of it a hollow gold bracelet and a thin ring with a ruby in it.

"Here, madam!" she said, handing the visitor these articles.

The lady flushed and her face quivered. She was offended.

"What are you giving me?" she said. "I am not asking for charity, but for what does not belong to you . . . what you have taken advantage of your position to squeeze out of my husband . . . that weak, unhappy man. . . . On Thursday, when I saw you with my husband at the harbour you were wearing expensive brooches and bracelets. So it's no use your playing the innocent lamb to me! I ask you for the last time: will you give me the things, or not?"

"You are a queer one, upon my word," said Pasha, beginning to feel offended. "I assure you that, except the bracelet and this little ring, I've never seen a thing from your Nikolay Petrovitch. He brings me nothing but sweet cakes."

"Sweet cakes!" laughed the stranger. "At home the children have nothing to eat, and here you have sweet cakes. You absolutely refuse to restore the presents?"

Receiving no answer, the lady sat down and stared into space, pondering.

"What's to be done now?" she said. "If I don't get nine hundred roubles, he is ruined, and the children and I am ruined, too. Shall I kill this low woman or go down on my knees to her?"

The lady pressed her handkerchief to her face and broke into sobs.

"I beg you!" Pasha heard through the stranger's sobs. "You see you have plundered and ruined my husband. Save him. . . . You have no feeling for him, but the children . . . the children . . . What have the children done?"

Pasha imagined little children standing in the street, crying with hunger, and she, too, sobbed.

"What can I do, madam?" she said. "You say that I am a low woman and that I have ruined Nikolay Petrovitch, and I assure you . . . before God Almighty, I have had nothing from him whatever. . . . There is only one girl in our chorus who has a rich admirer; all the rest of us live from hand to mouth on bread and kvass. Nikolay Petrovitch is a highly educated, refined gentleman, so I've made him welcome. We are bound to make gentlemen welcome."

"I ask you for the things! Give me the things! I am crying. . . . I am humiliating myself. . . . If you like I will go down on my knees! If you wish it!"

Pasha shrieked with horror and waved her hands. She felt that this pale, beautiful lady who expressed herself so grandly, as though she were on the stage, really might go down on her knees to her, simply from pride, from grandeur, to exalt herself and humiliate the chorus girl.

"Very well, I will give you things!" said Pasha, wiping her eyes and bustling about. "By all means. Only they are not from Nikolay Petrovitch. . . . I got these from other gentlemen. As you please. . . ."

Pasha pulled out the upper drawer of the chest, took out a diamond brooch, a coral necklace, some rings and bracelets, and gave them all to the lady.

"Take them if you like, only I've never had anything from your husband. Take them and grow rich," Pasha went on, offended at the threat to go down on her knees. "And if you are a lady . . . his lawful wife, you should keep him to yourself. I should think so! I did not ask him to come; he came of himself."

Through her tears the lady scrutinized the articles given her and said:

"This isn't everything. . . . There won't be five hundred roubles' worth here."

Pasha impulsively flung out of the chest a gold watch, a cigar-case and studs, and said, flinging up her hands:

"I've nothing else left. . . . You can search!"

The visitor gave a sigh, with trembling hands twisted the things up in her handkerchief, and went out without uttering a word, without even nodding her head.

The door from the next room opened and Kolpakov walked in. He was pale and kept shaking his head nervously, as though he had swallowed something very bitter; tears were glistening in his eyes.

"What presents did you make me?" Pasha asked, pouncing upon him. "When did you, allow me to ask you?"

"Presents . . . that's no matter!" said Kolpakov, and he tossed his head. "My God! She cried before you, she humbled herself. . . ."

"I am asking you, what presents did you make me?" Pasha cried.

"My God! She, a lady, so proud, so pure. . . . She was ready to go down on her knees to . . . to this wench! And I've brought her to this! I've allowed it!"

He clutched his head in his hands and moaned.

"No, I shall never forgive myself for this! I shall never forgive myself! Get away from me . . . you low creature!" he cried with repulsion, backing away from Pasha, and thrusting her off with trembling hands. "She would have gone down on her knees, and . . . and to you! Oh, my God!"

He rapidly dressed, and pushing Pasha aside contemptuously, made for the door and went out.

Pasha lay down and began wailing aloud. She was already regretting her things which she had given away so impulsively, and her feelings were hurt. She remembered how three years ago a merchant had beaten her for no sort of reason, and she wailed more loudly than ever.

A Misfortune

Sofya Petrovna, the wife of Lubyantsev the notary, a handsome young woman of five-and-twenty, was walking slowly along a track that had been cleared in the wood, with Ilyin, a lawyer who was spending the summer in the neighbourhood. It was five o'clock in the evening. Feathery-white masses of cloud stood overhead; patches of bright blue sky peeped out between them. The clouds stood motionless, as though they had caught in the tops of the tall old pine-trees. It was still and sultry.

Farther on, the track was crossed by a low railway embankment on which a sentinel with a gun was for some reason pacing up and down. Just beyond the embankment there was a large white church with six domes and a rusty roof.

"I did not expect to meet you here," said Sofya Petrovna, looking at the ground and prodding at the last year's leaves with the tip of her parasol, "and now I am glad we have met. I want to speak to you seriously and once for all. I beg you, Ivan Mihalovitch, if you really love and respect me, please make an end of this pursuit of me! You follow me about like a shadow, you are continually looking at me not in a nice way, making love to me, writing me strange letters, and . . . and I don't know where it's all going to end! Why, what can come of it?"

Ilyin said nothing. Sofya Petrovna walked on a few steps and continued:

"And this complete transformation in you all came about in the course of two or three weeks, after five years' friendship. I don't know you, Ivan Mihalovitch!"

Sofya Petrovna stole a glance at her companion. Screwing up his eyes, he was looking intently at the fluffy clouds. His face looked angry, ill-humoured, and preoccupied, like that of a man in pain forced to listen to nonsense.

"I wonder you don't see it yourself," Madame Lubyantsev went on, shrugging her shoulders. "You ought to realize that it's not a very nice part you are playing. I am married; I love and respect my husband. . . . I have a daughter. . . . Can you think all that means nothing? Besides, as an old friend you know my attitude to family life and my views as to the sanctity of marriage."

Ilyin cleared his throat angrily and heaved a sigh.

"Sanctity of marriage . . ." he muttered. "Oh, Lord!"

"Yes, yes. . . . I love my husband, I respect him; and in any case I value the peace of my home. I would rather let myself be killed than be a cause of unhappiness to Andrey and his daughter. . . . And I beg you, Ivan Mihalovitch, for God's sake, leave me in peace! Let us be as good, true friends as we used to be, and give up these sighs and groans, which really don't suit you. It's settled and over! Not a word more about it. Let us talk of something else."

Sofya Petrovna again stole a glance at Ilyin's face. Ilyin was looking up; he was pale, and was angrily biting his quivering lips. She could not understand why he was angry and why he was indignant, but his pallor touched her.

"Don't be angry; let us be friends," she said affectionately. "Agreed? Here's my hand."

Ilyin took her plump little hand in both of his, squeezed it, and slowly raised it to his lips.

"I am not a schoolboy," he muttered. "I am not in the least tempted by friendship with the woman I love."

"Enough, enough! It's settled and done with. We have reached the seat; let us sit down."

Sofya Petrovna's soul was filled with a sweet sense of relief: the most difficult and delicate thing had been said, the painful question was settled and done with. Now she could breathe freely and look Ilyin straight in the face. She looked at him, and the egoistic feeling of the superiority of the woman over the man who loves her, agreeably flattered her. It pleased her to see this huge, strong man, with his manly, angry face and his big black beard—clever, cultivated, and, people said, talented—sit down obediently beside her and bow his head dejectedly. For two or three minutes they sat without speaking.

"Nothing is settled or done with," began Ilyin. "You repeat copybook maxims to me. 'I love and respect my husband . . . the sanctity of marriage. . . .' I know all that without your help, and I could tell you more, too. I tell you truthfully and honestly that I consider the way I am behaving as criminal and immoral. What more can one say than that? But what's the good of saying what everybody knows? Instead of feeding nightingales with paltry words, you had much better tell me what I am to do."

"I've told you already—go away."

"As you know perfectly well, I have gone away five times, and every time I turned back on the way. I can show you my through tickets—I've kept them all. I have not will enough to run away from you! I am struggling. I am struggling horribly; but what the devil am I good for if I have no backbone, if I am weak, cowardly! I can't struggle with Nature! Do you understand? I cannot! I run away from here, and she holds on to me and pulls me back. Contemptible, loathsome weakness!"

Ilyin flushed crimson, got up, and walked up and down by the seat.

"I feel as cross as a dog," he muttered, clenching his fists. "I hate and despise myself! My God! like some depraved schoolboy, I am making love to another man's wife, writing idiotic letters, degrading myself . . . ugh!"

Ilyin clutched at his head, grunted, and sat down.

"And then your insincerity!" he went on bitterly. "If you do dislike my disgusting behaviour, why have you come here? What drew you here? In my letters I only ask you for a direct, definite answer—yes or no; but instead of a direct answer, you contrive every day these 'chance' meetings with me and regale me with copy-book maxims!"

Madame Lubyantsev was frightened and flushed. She suddenly felt the awkwardness which a decent woman feels when she is accidentally discovered undressed.

"You seem to suspect I am playing with you," she muttered. "I have always given you a direct answer, and . . . only today I've begged you . . ."

"Ough! as though one begged in such cases! If you were to say straight out 'Get away,' I should have been gone long ago; but you've never said that. You've never once given me a direct answer. Strange indecision! Yes, indeed; either you are playing with me, or else . . ."

Ilyin leaned his head on his fists without finishing. Sofya Petrovna began going over in her own mind the way she had behaved from beginning to end. She remembered that not only in her actions, but even in her secret thoughts, she had always been opposed to Ilyin's lovemaking; but yet she felt there was a grain of truth in the lawyer's words. But not knowing exactly what the truth was, she could not find answers to make to Ilyin's complaint, however hard she thought. It was awkward to be silent, and, shrugging her shoulders, she said:

"So I am to blame, it appears."

"I don't blame you for your insincerity," sighed Ilyin. "I did not mean that when I spoke of it. . . . Your insincerity is natural and in the order of things. If people agreed together and suddenly became sincere, everything would go to the devil."

Sofya Petrovna was in no mood for philosophical reflections, but she was glad of a chance to change the conversation, and asked:

"But why?"

"Because only savage women and animals are sincere. Once civilization has introduced a demand for such comforts as, for instance, feminine virtue, sincerity is out of place. . . ."

Ilyin jabbed his stick angrily into the sand. Madame Lubyantsev listened to him and liked his conversation, though a great deal of it she did not understand. What gratified her most was that she, an ordinary woman, was talked to by a talented man on "intellectual" subjects; it afforded her great pleasure, too, to watch the working of his mobile, young face, which was still pale and angry. She failed to understand a great deal that he said, but what was clear to her in his words was the attractive boldness with which the modern man without hesitation or doubt decides great questions and draws conclusive deductions.

She suddenly realized that she was admiring him, and was alarmed.

"Forgive me, but I don't understand," she said hurriedly. "What makes you talk of insincerity? I repeat my request again: be my good, true friend; let me alone! I beg you most earnestly!"

"Very good; I'll try again," sighed Ilyin. "Glad to do my best. . . . Only I doubt whether anything will come of my efforts. Either I shall put a bullet through my brains or take to drink in an idiotic way. I shall come to a bad end! There's a limit to everything—to struggles with Nature, too. Tell me, how can one struggle against madness? If you drink wine, how are you to struggle against intoxication? What am I to do if your image has grown into my soul, and day and night stands persistently before my eyes, like that pine there at this moment? Come, tell me, what hard and difficult thing can I do to get free from this abominable, miserable condition, in which all my thoughts, desires, and dreams are no longer my own, but belong to some demon who has taken possession of me? I love you, love you so much that I am completely thrown out of gear; I've given up my work and all who are dear to me; I've forgotten my God! I've never been in love like this in my life."

Sofya Petrovna, who had not expected such a turn to their conversation, drew away from Ilyin and looked into his face in dismay. Tears came into his eyes, his lips were quivering, and there was an imploring, hungry expression in his face.

"I love you!" he muttered, bringing his eyes near her big, frightened eyes. "You are so beautiful! I am in agony now, but I swear I would sit here all my life, suffering and looking in your eyes. But . . . be silent, I implore you!"

Sofya Petrovna, feeling utterly disconcerted, tried to think as quickly as possible of something to say to stop him. "I'll go away," she decided, but before she had time to make a movement to get up, Ilyin was on his knees before her. . . . He was clasping her knees, gazing into her face and speaking passionately, hotly, eloquently. In her terror and confusion she did not hear his words; for some reason now, at this dangerous moment, while her knees were being agreeably squeezed and felt as though they were in a warm bath, she was trying, with a sort of angry spite, to interpret her own sensations. She was angry that instead of brimming over with protesting virtue, she was entirely over-whelmed with weakness, apathy, and emptiness, like a drunken man utterly reckless; only at the bottom of her soul a remote bit of herself was malignantly taunting her: "Why don't you go? Is this as it should be? Yes?"

Seeking for some explanation, she could not understand how it was she did not pull away the hand to which Ilyin was clinging like a leech, and why, like Ilyin, she hastily glanced to right and to left to see whether any one was looking. The clouds and the pines stood motion-less, looking at them severely, like old ushers seeing mischief, but bribed not to tell the school authorities. The sentry stood like a post on the embankment and seemed to be looking at the seat.

"Let him look," thought Sofya Petrovna.

"But ... but listen," she said at last, with despair in her voice. "What can come of this? What will be the end of this?"

"I don't know, I don't know," he whispered, waving off the dis-agreeable questions.

They heard the hoarse, discordant whistle of the train. This cold, irrelevant sound from the everyday world of prose made Sofya Petro-vna rouse herself.

"I can't stay ... it's time I was at home," she said, getting up quickly. "The train is coming in. . . . Andrey is coming by it! He will want his dinner."

Sofya Petrovna turned towards the embankment with a burning face. The engine slowly crawled by, then came the carriages. It was not the local train, as she had supposed, but a goods train. The trucks filed by against the background of the white church in a long string like the days of a man's life, and it seemed as though it would never end.

But at last the train passed, and the last carriage with the guard and a light in it had disappeared behind the trees. Sofya Petrovna turned round sharply, and without looking at Ilyin, walked rapidly back along the track. She had regained her self-possession. Crimson with shame, humiliated not by Ilyin—no, but by her own cowardice, by the shamelessness with which she, a chaste and high-principled woman, had allowed a man, not her husband, to hug her knees—she had only one thought now: to get home as quickly as possible to her villa, to her family. The lawyer could hardly keep pace with her. Turning from the clearing into a narrow path, she turned round and glanced at him so quickly that she saw nothing but the sand on his knees, and waved to him to drop behind.

Reaching home, Sofya Petrovna stood in the middle of her room for five minutes without moving, and looked first at the window and then at her writing-table.

"You low creature!" she said, upbraiding herself. "You low creature!"

To spite herself, she recalled in precise detail, keeping nothing back—she recalled that though all this time she had been opposed to Ilyin's love-making, something had impelled her to seek an interview with him; and what was more, when he was at her feet she had enjoyed it enormously. She recalled it all without sparing herself, and now, breathless with shame, she would have liked to slap herself in the face.

"Poor Andrey!" she said to herself, trying as she thought of her husband to put into her face as tender an expression as she could. "Varya, my poor little girl, doesn't know what a mother she has! Forgive me, my dear ones! I love you so much . . . so much!"

And anxious to prove to herself that she was still a good wife and mother, and that corruption had not yet touched that "sanctity of marriage" of which she had spoken to Ilyin, Sofya Petrovna ran to the kitchen and abused the cook for not having yet laid the table for Andrey Ilyitch. She tried to picture her husband's hungry and exhausted appearance, commiserated him aloud, and laid the table for him with her own hands, which she had never done before. Then she found her daughter Varya, picked her up in her arms and hugged her warmly; the child seemed to her cold and heavy, but she was unwilling to acknowledge this to herself, and she began explaining to the child how good, kind, and honourable her papa was.

But when Andrey Ilyitch arrived soon afterwards she hardly greeted him. The rush of false feeling had already passed off without proving anything to her, only irritating and exasperating her by its falsity. She was sitting by the window, feeling miserable and cross. It is only by being in trouble that people can understand how far from easy it is to be the master of one's feelings and thoughts. Sofya Petrovna said afterwards that there was a tangle within her which it was as difficult to unravel as to count a flock of sparrows rapidly flying by. From the fact that she was not overjoyed to see her husband, that she did not like his manner at dinner, she concluded all of a sudden that she was beginning to hate her husband.

Andrey Ilyitch, languid with hunger and exhaustion, fell upon the sausage while waiting for the soup to be brought in, and ate it greedily, munching noisily and moving his temples.

"My goodness!" thought Sofya Petrovna. "I love and respect him, but ... why does he munch so repulsively?"

The disorder in her thoughts was no less than the disorder in her feelings. Like all persons inexperienced in combating unpleasant ideas, Madame Lubyantsev did her utmost not to think of her trouble, and the harder she tried the more vividly Ilyin, the sand on his knees, the fluffy clouds, the train, stood out in her imagination.

"And why did I go there this afternoon like a fool?" she thought, tormenting herself. "And am I really so weak that I cannot depend upon myself?"

Fear magnifies danger. By the time Andrey Ilyitch was finishing the last course, she had firmly made up her mind to tell her husband everything and to flee from danger!

"I've something serious to say to you, Andrey," she began after dinner while her husband was taking off his coat and boots to lie down for a nap.

"Well?"

"Let us leave this place!"

"H'm! ... Where shall we go? It's too soon to go back to town."

"No; for a tour or something of that sort. ..."

"For a tour ..." repeated the notary, stretching. "I dream of that myself, but where are we to get the money, and to whom am I to leave the office?"

And thinking a little he added:

"Of course, you must be bored. Go by yourself if you like."

Sofya Petrovna agreed, but at once reflected that Ilyin would be delighted with the opportunity, and would go with her in the same train, in the same compartment. . . . She thought and looked at her husband, now satisfied but still languid. For some reason her eyes rested on his feet—miniature, almost feminine feet, clad in striped socks; there was a thread standing out at the tip of each sock.

Behind the blind a bumble-bee was beating itself against the window-pane and buzzing. Sofya Petrovna looked at the threads on the socks, listened to the bee, and pictured how she would set off. . . . _Vis-à-vis_ Ilyin would sit, day and night, never taking his eyes off her, wrathful at his own weakness and pale with spiritual agony. He would call himself an immoral schoolboy, would abuse her, tear his hair, but when darkness came on and the passengers were asleep or got out at a station, he would seize the opportunity to kneel before her and embrace her knees as he had at the seat in the wood. . . .

She caught herself indulging in this day-dream.

"Listen. I won't go alone," she said. "You must come with me."

"Nonsense, Sofotchka!" sighed Lubyantsev. "One must be sensible and not want the impossible."

"You will come when you know all about it," thought Sofya Petrovna.

Making up her mind to go at all costs, she felt that she was out of danger. Little by little her ideas grew clearer; her spirits rose and she allowed herself to think about it all, feeling that however much she thought, however much she dreamed, she would go away. While her husband was asleep, the evening gradually came on. She sat in the drawing-room and played the piano. The greater liveliness out of doors, the sound of music, but above all the thought that she was a sensible person, that she had surmounted her difficulties, completely restored her spirits. Other women, her appeased conscience told her, would probably have been carried off their feet in her position, and would have lost their balance, while she had almost died of shame, had been miserable, and was now running out of the danger which perhaps did not exist! She was so touched by her own virtue and determination that she even looked at herself two or three times in the looking-glass.

When it got dark, visitors arrived. The men sat down in the dining-room to play cards; the ladies remained in the drawing-room and the verandah. The last to arrive was Ilyin. He was gloomy, morose, and looked ill. He sat down in the corner of the sofa and did not move the whole evening. Usually good-humoured and talkative, this time he remained silent, frowned, and rubbed his eyebrows. When he had to answer some question, he gave a forced smile with his upper lip only, and answered jerkily and irritably. Four or five times he made some jest, but his jests sounded harsh and cutting. It seemed to Sofya Petrovna that he was on the verge of hysterics. Only now, sitting at the piano, she recognized fully for the first time that this unhappy man was in deadly earnest, that his soul was sick, and that he could find no rest. For her sake he was wasting the best days of his youth and his career, spending the last of his money on a summer villa, abandoning his mother and sisters, and, worst of all, wearing himself out in an agonizing struggle with himself. From mere common humanity he ought to be treated seriously.

She recognized all this clearly till it made her heart ache, and if at that moment she had gone up to him and said to him, "No," there would have been a force in her voice hard to disobey. But she did not go up to him and did not speak—indeed, never thought of doing so. The pettiness and egoism of youth had never been more patent in her than that evening. She realized that Ilyin was unhappy, and that he was sitting on the sofa as though he were on hot coals; she felt sorry for him, but at the same time the presence of a man who loved her to distraction, filled her soul with triumph and a sense of her own power. She felt her youth, her beauty, and her unassailable virtue, and, since she had decided to go away, gave herself full licence for that evening. She flirted, laughed incessantly, sang with peculiar feeling and gusto. Everything delighted and amused her. She was amused at the memory of what had happened at the seat in the wood, of the sentinel who had looked on. She was amused by her guests, by Ilyin's cutting jests, by the pin in his cravat, which she had never noticed before. There was a red snake with diamond eyes on the pin; this snake struck her as so amusing that she could have kissed it on the spot.

Sofya Petrovna sang nervously, with defiant recklessness as though half intoxicated, and she chose sad, mournful songs which dealt with wasted hopes, the past, old age, as though in mockery of another's grief. " 'And old age comes nearer and nearer' . . ." she sang. And what was old age to her?

"It seems as though there is something going wrong with me," she thought from time to time through her laughter and singing.

The party broke up at twelve o'clock. Ilyin was the last to leave. Sofya Petrovna was still reckless enough to accompany him to the bottom step of the verandah. She wanted to tell him that she was going away with her husband, and to watch the effect this news would produce on him.

The moon was hidden behind the clouds, but it was light enough for Sofya Petrovna to see how the wind played with the skirts of his overcoat and with the awning of the verandah. She could see, too, how white Ilyin was, and how he twisted his upper lip in the effort to smile.

"Sonia, Sonitchka . . . my darling woman!" he muttered, preventing her from speaking. "My dear! my sweet!"

In a rush of tenderness, with tears in his voice, he showered caressing words upon her, that grew tenderer and tenderer, and even called her "thou," as though she were his wife or mistress. Quite unexpectedly he put one arm round her waist and with the other hand took hold of her elbow.

"My precious! my delight!" he whispered, kissing the nape of her neck; "be sincere; come to me at once!"

She slipped out of his arms and raised her head to give vent to her indignation and anger, but the indignation did not come off, and all her vaunted virtue and chastity was only sufficient to enable her to utter the phrase used by all ordinary women on such occasions:

"You must be mad."

"Come, let us go," Ilyin continued. "I felt just now, as well as at the seat in the wood, that you are as helpless as I am, Sonia. . . . You are in the same plight! You love me and are fruitlessly trying to appease your conscience. . . ."

Seeing that she was moving away, he caught her by her lace cuff and said rapidly:

"If not today, then tomorrow you will have to give in! Why, then, this waste of time? My precious, darling Sonia, the sentence is passed; why put off the execution? Why deceive yourself?"

Sofya Petrovna tore herself from him and darted in at the door. Returning to the drawing-room, she mechanically shut the piano, looked for a long time at the music-stand, and sat down. She could not stand up nor think. All that was left of her excitement and recklessness was a fearful weakness, apathy, and dreariness. Her conscience whispered to her that she had behaved badly, foolishly, that evening, like some mad-cap girl—that she had just been embraced on the verandah, and still had an uneasy feeling in her waist and her elbow. There was not a soul in the drawing-room; there was only one candle burning. Madame Lubyantsev sat on the round stool before the piano, motionless, as though expecting something. And as though taking advantage of the darkness and her extreme lassitude, an oppressive, overpowering desire began to assail her. Like a boa-constrictor it gripped her limbs and her soul, and grew stronger every second, and no longer menaced her as it had done, but stood clear before her in all its nakedness.

She sat for half an hour without stirring, not restraining herself from thinking of Ilyin, then she got up languidly and dragged herself to her bedroom. Andrey Ilyitch was already in bed. She sat down by the open window and gave herself up to desire. There was no "tangle" now in her head; all her thoughts and feelings were bent with one accord upon a single aim. She tried to struggle against it, but instantly gave it up. . . . She understood now how strong and relentless was the foe. Strength and fortitude were needed to combat him, and her birth, her education, and her life had given her nothing to fall back upon.

"Immoral wretch! Low creature!" she nagged at herself for her weakness. "So that's what you're like!"

Her outraged sense of propriety was moved to such indignation by this weakness that she lavished upon herself every term of abuse she knew, and told herself many offensive and humiliating truths. So, for instance, she told herself that she never had been moral, that she had not come to grief before simply because she had had no opportunity, that her inward conflict during that day had all been a farce. . . .

"And even if I have struggled," she thought, "what sort of struggle was it? Even the woman who sells herself struggles before she brings herself to it, and yet she sells herself. A fine struggle! Like milk, I've turned in a day! In one day!"

She convicted herself of being tempted, not by feeling, not by Ilyin personally, but by sensations which awaited her . . . an idle lady, having her fling in the summer holidays, like so many!

" 'Like an unfledged bird when the mother has been slain,' " sang a husky tenor outside the window.

"If I am to go, it's time," thought Sofya Petrovna. Her heart suddenly began beating violently.

"Andrey!" she almost shrieked. "Listen! we . . . we are going? Yes?"

"Yes, I've told you already: you go alone."

"But listen," she began. "If you don't go with me, you are in danger of losing me. I believe I am . . . in love already."

"With whom?" asked Andrey Ilyitch.

"It can't make any difference to you who it is!" cried Sofya Petrovna.

Andrey Ilyitch sat up with his feet out of bed and looked wonderingly at his wife's dark figure.

"It's a fancy!" he yawned.

He did not believe her, but yet he was frightened. After thinking a little and asking his wife several unimportant questions, he delivered himself of his opinions on the family, on infidelity . . . spoke listlessly for about ten minutes and got into bed again. His moralizing produced no effect. There are a great many opinions in the world, and a good half of them are held by people who have never been in trouble!

In spite of the late hour, summer visitors were still walking outside. Sofya Petrovna put on a light cape, stood a little, thought a little. . . . She still had resolution enough to say to her sleeping husband:

"Are you asleep? I am going for a walk. . . . Will you come with me?"

That was her last hope. Receiving no answer, she went out. . . . It was fresh and windy. She was conscious neither of the wind nor the darkness, but went on and on. . . . An overmastering force drove her on, and it seemed as though, if she had stopped, it would have pushed her in the back.

"Immoral creature!" she muttered mechanically. "Low wretch!"

She was breathless, hot with shame, did not feel her legs under her, but what drove her on was stronger than shame, reason, or fear.

A Trifle from Life

A well-fed, red-cheeked young man called Nikolay Ilyitch Belyaev, of thirty-two, who was an owner of house property in Petersburg, and a devotee of the race-course, went one evening to see Olga Ivanovna Irnin, with whom he was living, or, to use his own expression, was dragging out a long, wearisome romance. And, indeed, the first interesting and enthusiastic pages of this romance had long been perused; now the pages dragged on, and still dragged on, without presenting anything new or of interest.

Not finding Olga Ivanovna at home, my hero lay down on the lounge chair and proceeded to wait for her in the drawing-room.

"Good-evening, Nikolay Ilyitch!" he heard a child's voice. "Mother will be here directly. She has gone with Sonia to the dressmaker's."

Olga Ivanovna's son, Alyosha—a boy of eight who looked graceful and very well cared for, who was dressed like a picture, in a black velvet jacket and long black stockings—was lying on the sofa in the same room. He was lying on a satin cushion and, evidently imitating an acrobat he had lately seen at the circus, stuck up in the air first one leg and then the other. When his elegant legs were exhausted, he brought his arms into play or jumped up impulsively and went on all fours, trying to stand with his legs in the air. All this he was doing with the utmost gravity, gasping and groaning painfully as though he regretted that God had given him such a restless body.

"Ah, good-evening, my boy," said Belyaev. "It's you! I did not notice you. Is your mother well?"

Alyosha, taking hold of the tip of his left toe with his right hand and falling into the most unnatural attitude, turned over, jumped up, and peeped at Belyaev from behind the big fluffy lampshade.

"What shall I say?" he said, shrugging his shoulders. "In reality mother's never well. You see, she is a woman, and women, Nikolay Ilyitch, have always something the matter with them."

Belyaev, having nothing better to do, began watching Alyosha's face. He had never before during the whole of his intimacy with Olga Ivanovna paid any attention to the boy, and had completely ignored his existence; the boy had been before his eyes, but he had not cared to think why he was there and what part he was playing.

In the twilight of the evening, Alyosha's face, with his white forehead and black, unblinking eyes, unexpectedly reminded Belyaev of Olga Ivanovna as she had been during the first pages of their romance. And he felt disposed to be friendly to the boy.

"Come here, insect," he said; "let me have a closer look at you."

The boy jumped off the sofa and skipped up to Belyaev.

"Well," began Nikolay Ilyitch, putting a hand on the boy's thin shoulder. "How are you getting on?"

"How shall I say! We used to get on a great deal better."

"Why?"

"It's very simple. Sonia and I used only to learn music and reading, and now they give us French poetry to learn. Have you been shaved lately?"

"Yes."

"Yes, I see you have. Your beard is shorter. Let me touch it. . . . Does that hurt?"

"No."

"Why is it that if you pull one hair it hurts, but if you pull a lot at once it doesn't hurt a bit? Ha, ha! And, you know, it's a pity you don't have whiskers. Here ought to be shaved . . . but here at the sides the hair ought to be left. . . ."

The boy nestled up to Belyaev and began playing with his watch-chain.

"When I go to the high-school," he said, "mother is going to buy me a watch. I shall ask her to buy me a watch-chain like this. . . . Wh—at a loc—ket! Father's got a locket like that, only yours has little bars on it and his has letters. . . . There's mother's portrait in the middle of his. Father has a different sort of chain now, not made with rings, but like ribbon. . . ."

"How do you know? Do you see your father?"

"I? M'm . . . no. . . . I . . ."

Alyosha blushed, and in great confusion, feeling caught in a lie, began zealously scratching the locket with his nail. . . . Belyaev looked steadily into his face and asked:

"Do you see your father?"

"N-no!"

"Come, speak frankly, on your honour. . . . I see from your face you are telling a fib. Once you've let a thing slip out it's no good wriggling about it. Tell me, do you see him? Come, as a friend."

Alyosha hesitated.

"You won't tell mother?" he said.

"As though I should!"

"On your honour?"

"On my honour."

"Do you swear?"

"Ah, you provoking boy! What do you take me for?"

Alyosha looked round him, then with wide-open eyes, whispered to him:

"Only, for goodness' sake, don't tell mother. . . . Don't tell any one at all, for it is a secret. I hope to goodness mother won't find out, or we should all catch it—Sonia, and I, and Pelagea. . . . Well, listen. . . . Sonia and I see father every Tuesday and Friday. When Pelagea takes us for a walk before dinner we go to the Apfel Restaurant, and there is father waiting for us. . . . He is always sitting in a room apart, where you know there's a marble table and an ash-tray in the shape of a goose without a back. . . ."

"What do you do there?"

"Nothing! First we say how-do-you-do, then we all sit round the table, and father treats us with coffee and pies. You know Sonia eats the meat-pies, but I can't endure meat-pies! I like the pies made of cabbage and eggs. We eat such a lot that we have to try hard to eat as much as we can at dinner, for fear mother should notice."

"What do you talk about?"

"With father? About anything. He kisses us, he hugs us, tells us all sorts of amusing jokes. Do you know, he says when we are grown up he is going to take us to live with him. Sonia does not want to go, but I agree. Of course, I should miss mother; but, then, I should write her letters! It's a queer idea, but we could come and visit her on holidays—couldn't we? Father says, too, that he will buy me a horse. He's an awfully kind man! I can't understand why mother does not ask him to come and live with us, and why she forbids us to see him. You know he loves mother very much. He is always asking us how she is and what she is doing. When she was ill he clutched his head like this, and . . . and kept running about. He always tells us to be obedient and respectful to her. Listen. Is it true that we are unfortunate?"

"H'm! . . . Why?"

"That's what father says. 'You are unhappy children,' he says. It's strange to hear him, really. 'You are unhappy,' he says, 'I am unhappy, and mother's unhappy. You must pray to God,' he says; 'for yourselves and for her.' "

Alyosha let his eyes rest on a stuffed bird and sank into thought.

"So . . ." growled Belyaev. "So that's how you are going on. You arrange meetings at restaurants. And mother does not know?"

"No-o. . . . How should she know? Pelagea would not tell her for anything, you know. The day before yesterday he gave us some pears. As sweet as jam! I ate two."

"H'm! . . . Well, and I say . . . Listen. Did father say anything about me?"

"About you? What shall I say?"

Alyosha looked searchingly into Belyaev's face and shrugged his shoulders.

"He didn't say anything particular."

"For instance, what did he say?"

"You won't be offended?"

"What next? Why, does he abuse me?"

"He doesn't abuse you, but you know he is angry with you. He says mother's unhappy owing to you . . . and that you have ruined mother. You know he is so queer! I explain to him that you are kind, that you never scold mother; but he only shakes his head."

"So he says I have ruined her?"

"Yes; you mustn't be offended, Nikolay Ilyitch."

Belyaev got up, stood still a moment, and walked up and down the drawing-room.

"That's strange and . . . ridiculous!" he muttered, shrugging his shoulders and smiling sarcastically. "He's entirely to blame, and I have ruined her, eh? An innocent lamb, I must say. So he told you I ruined your mother?"

"Yes, but . . . you said you would not be offended, you know."

"I am not offended, and . . . and it's not your business. Why, it's . . . why, it's positively ridiculous! I have been thrust into it like a chicken in the broth, and now it seems I'm to blame!"

A ring was heard. The boy sprang up from his place and ran out. A minute later a lady came into the room with a little girl; this was Olga Ivanovna, Alyosha's mother. Alyosha followed them in, skipping and jumping, humming aloud and waving his hands. Belyaev nodded, and went on walking up and down.

"Of course, whose fault is it if not mine?" he muttered with a snort. "He is right! He is an injured husband."

"What are you talking about?" asked Olga Ivanovna.

"What about? . . . Why, just listen to the tales your lawful spouse is spreading now! It appears that I am a scoundrel and a villain, that I have ruined you and the children. All of you are unhappy, and I am the only happy one! Wonderfully, wonderfully happy!"

"I don't understand, Nikolay. What's the matter?"

"Why, listen to this young gentleman!" said Belyaev, pointing to Alyosha.

Alyosha flushed crimson, then turned pale, and his whole face began working with terror.

"Nikolay Ilyitch," he said in a loud whisper. "Sh-sh!"

Olga Ivanovna looked in surprise at Alyosha, then at Belyaev, then at Alyosha again.

"Just ask him," Belyaev went on. "Your Pelagea, like a regular fool, takes them about to restaurants and arranges meetings with their papa. But that's not the point: the point is that their dear papa is a victim, while I'm a wretch who has broken up both your lives. . . ."

"Nikolay Ilyitch," moaned Alyosha. "Why, you promised on your word of honour!"

"Oh, get away!" said Belyaev, waving him off. "This is more important than any word of honour. It's the hypocrisy revolts me, the lying! . . ."

"I don't understand it," said Olga Ivanovna, and tears glistened in her eyes. "Tell me, Alyosha," she turned to her son. "Do you see your father?"

Alyosha did not hear her; he was looking with horror at Belyaev.

"It's impossible," said his mother; "I will go and question Pelagea."

Olga Ivanovna went out.

"I say, you promised on your word of honour!" said Alyosha, trembling all over.

Belyaev dismissed him with a wave of his hand, and went on walking up and down. He was absorbed in his grievance and was oblivious of the boy's presence, as he always had been. He, a grown-up, serious person, had no thought to spare for boys. And Alyosha sat down in the corner and told Sonia with horror how he had been deceived. He was trembling, stammering, and crying. It was the first time in his life that he had been brought into such coarse contact with lying; till then he had not known that there are in the world, besides sweet pears, pies, and expensive watches, a great many things for which the language of children has no expression.

Difficult People

Yevgraf Ivanovitch Shiryaev, a small farmer, whose father, a parish priest, now deceased, had received a gift of three hundred acres of land from Madame Kuvshinnikov, a general's widow, was standing in a corner before a copper washing-stand, washing his hands. As usual, his face looked anxious and ill-humoured, and his beard was uncombed.

"What weather!" he said. "It's not weather, but a curse laid upon us. It's raining again!"

He grumbled on, while his family sat waiting at table for him to have finished washing his hands before beginning dinner. Fedosya Semyonovna, his wife, his son Pyotr, a student, his eldest daughter Varvara, and three small boys, had been sitting waiting a long time. The boys—Kolka, Vanka, and Arhipka—grubby, snub-nosed little fellows with chubby faces and tousled hair that wanted cutting, moved their chairs impatiently, while their elders sat without stirring, and apparently did not care whether they ate their dinner or waited. . . .

As though trying their patience, Shiryaev deliberately dried his hands, deliberately said his prayer, and sat down to the table without hurrying himself. Cabbage-soup was served immediately. The sound of carpenters' axes (Shiryaev was having a new barn built) and the laughter of Fomka, their labourer, teasing the turkey, floated in from the courtyard.

Big, sparse drops of rain pattered on the window.

Pyotr, a round-shouldered student in spectacles, kept exchanging glances with his mother as he ate his dinner. Several times he laid down his spoon and cleared his throat, meaning to begin to speak, but after an intent look at his father he fell to eating again. At last, when the porridge had been served, he cleared his throat resolutely and said:

"I ought to go tonight by the evening train. I ought to have gone before; I have missed a fortnight as it is. The lectures begin on the first of September."

"Well, go," Shiryaev assented; "why are you lingering on here? Pack up and go, and good luck to you."

A minute passed in silence.

"He must have money for the journey, Yevgraf Ivanovitch," the mother observed in a low voice.

"Money? To be sure, you can't go without money. Take it at once, since you need it. You could have had it long ago!"

The student heaved a faint sight and looked with relief at his mother. Deliberately Shiryaev took a pocket-book out of his coat-pocket and put on his spectacles.

"How much do you want?" he asked.

"The fare to Moscow is eleven roubles forty-two kopecks. . . ."

"Ah, money, money!" sighed the father. (He always sighed when he saw money, even when he was receiving it.) "Here are twelve roubles for you. You will have change out of that which will be of use to you on the journey."

"Thank you."

After waiting a little, the student said:

"I did not get lessons quite at first last year. I don't know how it will be this year; most likely it will take me a little time to find work. I ought to ask you for fifteen roubles for my lodging and dinner."

Shiryaev thought a little and heaved a sigh.

"You will have to make ten do," he said. "Here, take it."

The student thanked him. He ought to have asked him for something more, for clothes, for lecture fees, for books, but after an intent look at his father he decided not to pester him further.

The mother, lacking in diplomacy and prudence, like all mothers, could not restrain herself, and said:

"You ought to give him another six roubles, Yevgraf Ivanovitch, for a pair of boots. Why, just see, how can he go to Moscow in such wrecks?"

"Let him take my old ones; they are still quite good."

"He must have trousers, anyway; he is a disgrace to look at."

And immediately after that a storm-signal showed itself, at the sight of which all the family trembled.

Shiryaev's short, fat neck turned suddenly red as a beetroot. The colour mounted slowly to his ears, from his ears to his temples, and by degrees suffused his whole face. Yevgraf Ivanovitch shifted in his chair and unbuttoned his shirt-collar to save himself from choking. He was evidently struggling with the feeling that was mastering him. A death-like silence followed. The children held their breath. Fedosya Semyonovna, as though she did not grasp what was happening to her husband, went on:

"He is not a little boy now, you know; he is ashamed to go about without clothes."

Shiryaev suddenly jumped up, and with all his might flung down his fat pocket-book in the middle of the table, so that a hunk of bread flew off a plate. A revolting expression of anger, resentment, avarice—all mixed together—flamed on his face.

"Take everything!" he shouted in an unnatural voice; "plunder me! Take it all! Strangle me!"

He jumped up from the table, clutched at his head, and ran staggering about the room.

"Strip me to the last thread!" he shouted in a shrill voice. "Squeeze out the last drop! Rob me! Wring my neck!"

The student flushed and dropped his eyes. He could not go on eating. Fedosya Semyonovna, who had not after twenty-five years grown used to her husband's difficult character, shrank into herself and muttered something in self-defence. An expression of amazement and dull terror came into her wasted and birdlike face, which at all times looked dull and scared. The little boys and the elder daughter Varvara, a girl in her teens, with a pale ugly face, laid down their spoons and sat mute.

Shiryaev, growing more and more ferocious, uttering words each more terrible than the one before, dashed up to the table and began shaking the notes out of his pocket-book.

"Take them!" he muttered, shaking all over. "You've eaten and drunk your fill, so here's money for you too! I need nothing! Order yourself new boots and uniforms!"

The student turned pale and got up.

"Listen, papa," he began, gasping for breath. "I . . . I beg you to end this, for . . ."

"Hold your tongue!" the father shouted at him, and so loudly that the spectacles fell off his nose; "hold your tongue!"

"I used . . . I used to be able to put up with such scenes, but . . . but now I have got out of the way of it. Do you understand? I have got out of the way of it!"

"Hold your tongue!" cried the father, and he stamped with his feet. "You must listen to what I say! I shall say what I like, and you hold your tongue. At your age I was earning my living, while you . . . Do you know what you cost me, you scoundrel? I'll turn you out! Wastrel!"

"Yevgraf Ivanovitch," muttered Fedosya Semyonovna, moving her fingers nervously; "you know he . . . you know Petya . . . !"

"Hold your tongue!" Shiryaev shouted out to her, and tears actually came into his eyes from anger. "It is you who have spoilt them—you! It's all your fault! He has no respect for us, does not say his prayers, and earns nothing! I am only one against the ten of you! I'll turn you out of the house!"

The daughter Varvara gazed fixedly at her mother with her mouth open, moved her vacant-looking eyes to the window, turned pale, and, uttering a loud shriek, fell back in her chair. The father, with a curse and a wave of the hand, ran out into the yard.

This was how domestic scenes usually ended at the Shiryaevs'. But on this occasion, unfortunately, Pyotr the student was carried away by overmastering anger. He was just as hasty and ill-tempered as his father and his grandfather the priest, who used to beat his parishioners about the head with a stick. Pale and clenching his fists, he went up to his mother and shouted in the very highest tenor note his voice could reach:

"These reproaches are loathsome! sickening to me! I want nothing from you! Nothing! I would rather die of hunger than eat another mouthful at your expense! Take your nasty money back! take it!"

The mother huddled against the wall and waved her hands, as though it were not her son, but some phantom before her.

"What have I done?" she wailed. "What?"

Like his father, the boy waved his hands and ran into the yard. Shiryaev's house stood alone on a ravine which ran like a furrow for four miles along the steppe. Its sides were overgrown with oak saplings and alders, and a stream ran at the bottom. On one side the house looked towards the ravine, on the other towards the open country, there were no fences nor hurdles. Instead there were farm-buildings of all sorts close to one another, shutting in a small space in front of the house which was regarded as the yard, and in which hens, ducks, and pigs ran about.

Going out of the house, the student walked along the muddy road towards the open country. The air was full of a penetrating autumn dampness. The road was muddy, puddles gleamed here and there, and in the yellow fields autumn itself seemed looking out from the grass, dismal, decaying, dark. On the right-hand side of the road was a vegetable-garden cleared of its crops and gloomy-looking, with here and there sunflowers standing up in it with hanging heads already black.

Pyotr thought it would not be a bad thing to walk to Moscow on foot; to walk just as he was, with holes in his boots, without a cap, and without a farthing of money. When he had gone eighty miles his father, frightened and aghast, would overtake him, would begin begging him to turn back or take the money, but he would not even look at him, but would go on and on.... Bare forests would be followed by desolate fields, fields by forests again; soon the earth would be white with the first snow, and the streams would be coated with ice.... Somewhere near Kursk or near Serpuhovo, exhausted and dying of hunger, he would sink down and die. His corpse would be found, and there would be a paragraph in all the papers saying that a student called Shiryaev had died of hunger. . . .

A white dog with a muddy tail who was wandering about the vegetable-garden looking for something gazed at him and sauntered after him. . . .

He walked along the road and thought of death, of the grief of his family, of the moral sufferings of his father, and then pictured all sorts of adventures on the road, each more marvellous than the one before—picturesque places, terrible nights, chance encounters. He imagined a string of pilgrims, a hut in the forest with one little window shining in the darkness; he stands before the window, begs for a night's lodging. . . . They let him in, and suddenly he sees that they are robbers. Or, better still, he is taken into a big manor-house, where, learning who he is, they give him food and drink, play to him on the piano, listen to his complaints, and the daughter of the house, a beauty, falls in love with him.

Absorbed in his bitterness and such thoughts, young Shiryaev walked on and on. Far, far ahead he saw the inn, a dark patch against the grey background of cloud. Beyond the inn, on the very horizon, he could see a little hillock; this was the railway-station. That hillock reminded him of the connection existing between the place where he was now standing and Moscow, where street-lamps were burning and carriages were rattling in the streets, where lectures were being given. And he almost wept with depression and impatience. The solemn landscape, with its order and beauty, the deathlike stillness all around, revolted him and moved him to despair and hatred!

"Look out!" He heard behind him a loud voice.

An old lady of his acquaintance, a landowner of the neighbourhood, drove past him in a light, elegant landau. He bowed to her, and smiled all over his face. And at once he caught himself in that smile, which was so out of keeping with his gloomy mood. Where did it come from if his whole heart was full of vexation and misery? And he thought nature itself had given man this capacity for lying, that even in difficult moments of spiritual strain he might be able to hide the secrets of his nest as the fox and the wild duck do. Every family has its

joys and its horrors, but however great they may be, it's hard for an outsider's eye to see them; they are a secret. The father of the old lady
who had just driven by, for instance, had for some offence lain for half
his lifetime under the ban of the wrath of Tsar Nicolas I; her husband
had been a gambler; of her four sons, not one had turned out well. One
could imagine how many terrible scenes there must have been in her
life, how many tears must have been shed. And yet the old lady seemed
happy and satisfied, and she had answered his smile by smiling too.
The student thought of his comrades, who did not like talking about
their families; he thought of his mother, who almost always lied when
she had to speak of her husband and children. . . .

Pyotr walked about the roads far from home till dusk, abandoning
himself to dreary thoughts. When it began to drizzle with rain he
turned homewards. As he walked back he made up his mind at all costs
to talk to his father, to explain to him, once and for all, that it was
dreadful and oppressive to live with him.

He found perfect stillness in the house. His sister Varvara was lying
behind a screen with a headache, moaning faintly. His mother, with a
look of amazement and guilt upon her face, was sitting beside her on
a box, mending Arhipka's trousers. Yevgraf Ivanovitch was pacing
from one window to another, scowling at the weather. From his walk,
from the way he cleared his throat, and even from the back of his head,
it was evident he felt himself to blame.

"I suppose you have changed your mind about going today?" he
asked.

The student felt sorry for him, but immediately suppressing that
feeling, he said:

"Listen . . . I must speak to you seriously . . . yes, seriously. I have always respected you, and . . . and have never brought myself to speak to
you in such a tone, but your behaviour . . . your last action . . ."

The father looked out of the window and did not speak. The student, as though considering his words, rubbed his forehead and went
on in great excitement:

"Not a dinner or tea passes without your making an uproar. Your
bread sticks in our throat . . . nothing is more bitter, more humiliating,
than bread that sticks in one's throat. . . . Though you are my father, no

one, neither God nor nature, has given you the right to insult and humiliate us so horribly, to vent your ill-humour on the weak. You have
worn my mother out and made a slave of her, my sister is hopelessly
crushed, while I . . ."

"It's not your business to teach me," said his father.

"Yes, it is my business! You can quarrel with me as much as you like,
but leave my mother in peace! I will not allow you to torment my
mother!" the student went on, with flashing eyes. "You are spoilt because no one has yet dared to oppose you. They tremble and are mute
towards you, but now that is over! Coarse, ill-bred man! You are coarse
. . . do you understand? You are coarse, ill-humoured, unfeeling. And
the peasants can't endure you!"

The student had by now lost his thread, and was not so much speaking as firing off detached words. Yevgraf Ivanovitch listened in silence,
as though stunned; but suddenly his neck turned crimson, the colour
crept up his face, and he made a movement.

"Hold your tongue!" he shouted.

"That's right!" the son persisted; "you don't like to hear the truth!
Excellent! Very good! begin shouting! Excellent!"

"Hold your tongue, I tell you!" roared Yevgraf Ivanovitch.

Fedosya Semyonovna appeared in the doorway, very pale, with an
astonished face; she tried to say something, but she could not, and
could only move her fingers.

"It's all your fault!" Shiryaev shouted at her. "You have brought him
up like this!"

"I don't want to go on living in this house!" shouted the student, crying, and looking angrily at his mother. "I don't want to live with you!"

Varvara uttered a shriek behind the screen and broke into loud sobs.
With a wave of his hand, Shiryaev ran out of the house.

The student went to his own room and quietly lay down. He lay till
midnight without moving or opening his eyes. He felt neither anger
nor shame, but a vague ache in his soul. He neither blamed his father
nor pitied his mother, nor was he tormented by stings of conscience;
he realized that every one in the house was feeling the same ache, and
God only knew which was most to blame, which was suffering most. . . .

At midnight he woke the labourer, and told him to have the horse ready at five o'clock in the morning for him to drive to the station; he undressed and got into bed, but could not get to sleep. He heard how his father, still awake, paced slowly from window to window, sighing, till early morning. No one was asleep; they spoke rarely, and only in whispers. Twice his mother came to him behind the screen. Always with the same look of vacant wonder, she slowly made the cross over him, shaking nervously.

At five o'clock in the morning he said good-bye to them all affectionately, and even shed tears. As he passed his father's room, he glanced in at the door. Yevgraf Ivanovitch, who had not taken off his clothes or gone to bed, was standing by the window, drumming on the panes.

"Good-bye; I am going," said his son.

"Good-bye . . . the money is on the round table . . ." his father answered, without turning round.

A cold, hateful rain was falling as the labourer drove him to the station. The sunflowers were drooping their heads still lower, and the grass seemed darker than ever.

In the Court

At the district town of N. in the cinnamon-coloured government house in which the Zemstvo, the sessional meetings of the justices of the peace, the Rural Board, the Liquor Board, the Military Board, and many others sit by turns, the Circuit Court was in session on one of the dull days of autumn. Of the above-mentioned cinnamon-coloured house a local official had wittily observed:

"Here is Justitia, here is Policia, here is Militia—a regular boarding school of high-born young ladies."

But, as the saying is, "Too many cooks spoil the broth," and probably that is why the house strikes, oppresses, and overwhelms a fresh unofficial visitor with its dismal barrack-like appearance, its decrepit condition, and the complete absence of any kind of comfort, external or internal. Even on the brightest spring days it seems wrapped in a dense shade, and on clear moonlight nights, when the trees and the little dwelling-houses merged in one blur of shadow seem plunged in quiet slumber, it alone absurdly and inappropriately towers, an oppressive mass of stone, above the modest landscape, spoils the general harmony, and keeps sleepless vigil as though it could not escape from burdensome memories of past unforgiven sins. Inside it is like a barn and extremely unattractive. It is strange to see how readily these elegant lawyers, members of committees, and marshals of nobility, who in their own homes will make a scene over the slightest fume from the stove, or stain on the floor, resign themselves here to whirring ventilation wheels, the disgusting smell of fumigating candles, and the filthy, forever perspiring walls.

The sitting of the circuit court began between nine and ten. The programme of the day was promptly entered upon, with noticeable haste. The cases came on one after another and ended quickly, like a church service without a choir, so that no mind could form a complete picture of all this parti-coloured mass of faces, movements, words, misfortunes, true sayings and lies, all racing by like a river in flood.... By two o'clock a great deal had been done: two prisoners had been sentenced to service in convict battalions, one of the privileged class had been sentenced to deprivation of rights and imprisonment, one had been acquitted, one case had been adjourned.

At precisely two o'clock the presiding judge announced that the case "of the peasant Nikolay Harlamov, charged with the murder of his wife," would next be heard. The composition of the court remained the same as it had been for the preceding case, except that the place of the defending counsel was filled by a new personage, a beardless young graduate in a coat with bright buttons. The president gave the order—"Bring in the prisoner!"

But the prisoner, who had been got ready beforehand, was already walking to his bench. He was a tall, thick-set peasant of about fifty-five, completely bald, with an apathetic, hairy face and a big red beard. He was followed by a frail-looking little soldier with a gun.

Just as he was reaching the bench the escort had a trifling mishap. He stumbled and dropped the gun out of his hands, but caught it at once before it touched the ground, knocking his knee violently against the butt end as he did so. A faint laugh was audible in the audience. Either from the pain or perhaps from shame at his awkwardness the soldier flushed a dark red.

After the customary questions to the prisoner, the shuffling of the jury, the calling over and swearing in of the witnesses, the reading of the charge began. The narrow-chested, pale-faced secretary, far too thin for his uniform, and with sticking plaster on his cheek, read it in a low, thick bass, rapidly like a sacristan, without raising or dropping his voice, as though afraid of exerting his lungs; he was seconded by the ventilation wheel whirring indefatigably behind the judge's table, and the result was a sound that gave a drowsy, narcotic character to the stillness of the hall.

The president, a short-sighted man, not old but with an extremely exhausted face, sat in his armchair without stirring and held his open hand near his brow as though screening his eyes from the sun. To the droning of the ventilation wheel and the secretary he meditated. When the secretary paused for an instant to take breath on beginning a new page, he suddenly started and looked round at the court with lustreless eyes, then bent down to the ear of the judge next to him and asked with a sigh:

"Are you putting up at Demyanov's, Matvey Petrovitch?"

"Yes, at Demyanov's," answered the other, starting too.

"Next time I shall probably put up there too. It's really impossible to put up at Tipyakov's! There's noise and uproar all night! Knocking, coughing, children crying.... It's impossible!"

The assistant prosecutor, a fat, well-nourished, dark man with gold spectacles, with a handsome, well-groomed beard, sat motionless as a statue, with his cheek propped on his fist, reading Byron's "Cain." His eyes were full of eager attention and his eyebrows rose higher and higher with wonder.... From time to time he dropped back in his chair, gazed without interest straight before him for a minute, and then buried himself in his reading again. The council for the defence moved the blunt end of his pencil about the table and mused with his head on one side. . . . His youthful face expressed nothing but the frigid, immovable boredom which is commonly seen on the face of schoolboys and men on duty who are forced from day to day to sit in the same place, to see the same faces, the same walls. He felt no excitement about the speech he was to make, and indeed what did that speech amount to? On instructions from his superiors in accordance with long-established routine he would fire it off before the jurymen, without passion or ardour, feeling that it was colourless and boring, and then—gallop through the mud and the rain to the station, thence to the town, shortly to receive instructions to go off again to some district to deliver another speech. . . . It was a bore!

At first the prisoner turned pale and coughed nervously into his sleeve, but soon the stillness, the general monotony and boredom infected him too. He looked with dull-witted respectfulness at the judges' uniforms, at the weary faces of the jurymen, and blinked calmly. The surroundings and procedure of the court, the expectation of which had so weighed on his soul while he was awaiting them in prison, now had the most soothing effect on him. What he met here was not at all what he could have expected. The charge of murder hung over him, and yet here he met with neither threatening faces nor indignant looks nor loud phrases about retribution nor sympathy for his extraordinary fate; not one of those who were judging him looked at him with interest or for long. . . . The dingy windows and walls, the voice of the secretary, the attitude of the prosecutor were all saturated with official indifference and produced an atmosphere of frigidity, as though the murderer were simply an official property, or as though he were not being judged by living men, but by some unseen machine, set going, goodness knows how or by whom. . . .

The peasant, reassured, did not understand that the men here were as accustomed to the dramas and tragedies of life and were as blunted by the sight of them as hospital attendants are at the sight of death, and that the whole horror and hopelessness of his position lay just in this mechanical indifference. It seemed that if he were not to sit quietly but to get up and begin beseeching, appealing with tears for their mercy, bitterly repenting, that if he were to die of despair—it would all be shattered against blunted nerves and the callousness of custom, like waves against a rock.

When the secretary finished, the president for some reason passed his hands over the table before him, looked for some time with his eyes screwed up towards the prisoner, and then asked, speaking languidly:

"Prisoner at the bar, do you plead guilty to having murdered your wife on the evening of the ninth of June?"

"No, sir," answered the prisoner, getting up and holding his gown over his chest.

After this the court proceeded hurriedly to the examination of witnesses. Two peasant women and five men and the village policeman who had made the enquiry were questioned. All of them, mud-bespattered, exhausted with their long walk and waiting in the witnesses' room, gloomy and dispirited, gave the same evidence. They testified that Harlamov lived "well" with his old woman, like anyone else; that he never beat her except when he had had a drop; that on the ninth of June when the sun was setting the old woman had been found in the porch with her skull broken; that beside her in a pool of blood lay an axe. When they looked for Nikolay to tell him of the calamity he was not in his hut or in the streets. They ran all over the village, looking for him. They went to all the pothouses and huts, but could not find him. He had disappeared, and two days later came of his own accord to the police office, pale, with his clothes torn, trembling all over. He was bound and put in the lock-up.

"Prisoner," said the president, addressing Harlamov, "cannot you explain to the court where you were during the three days following the murder?"

"I was wandering about the fields.... Neither eating nor drinking...."

"Why did you hide yourself, if it was not you that committed the murder?"

"I was frightened.... I was afraid I might be judged guilty...."

"Aha!... Good, sit down!"

The last to be examined was the district doctor who had made a post-mortem on the old woman. He told the court all that he remembered of his report at the post-mortem and all that he had succeeded in thinking of on his way to the court that morning. The president screwed up his eyes at his new glossy black suit, at his foppish cravat, at his moving lips; he listened and in his mind the languid thought seemed to spring up of itself:

"Everyone wears a short jacket nowadays, why has he had his made long? Why long and not short?"

The circumspect creak of boots was audible behind the president's back. It was the assistant prosecutor going up to the table to take some papers.

"Mihail Vladimirovitch," said the assistant prosecutor, bending down to the president's ear, "amazingly slovenly the way that Koreisky conducted the investigation. The prisoner's brother was not examined, the village elder was not examined, there's no making anything out of his description of the hut. . . ."

"It can't be helped, it can't be helped," said the president, sinking back in his chair. "He's a wreck . . . dropping to bits!"

"By the way," whispered the assistant prosecutor, "look at the audience, in the front row, the third from the right . . . a face like an actor's . . . that's the local Croesus. He has a fortune of something like fifty thousand."

"Really? You wouldn't guess it from his appearance. . . . Well, dear boy, shouldn't we have a break?"

"We will finish the case for the prosecution, and then. . . ."

"As you think best. . . . Well?" the president raised his eyes to the doctor. "So you consider that death was instantaneous?"

"Yes, in consequence of the extent of the injury to the brain substance. . . ."

When the doctor had finished, the president gazed into the space between the prosecutor and the counsel for the defence and suggested:

"Have you any questions to ask?"

The assistant prosecutor shook his head negatively, without lifting his eyes from "Cain"; the counsel for the defence unexpectedly stirred and, clearing his throat, asked:

"Tell me, doctor, can you from the dimensions of the wound form any theory as to . . . as to the mental condition of the criminal? That is, I mean, does the extent of the injury justify the supposition that the accused was suffering from temporary aberration?"

The president raised his drowsy indifferent eyes to the counsel for the defence. The assistant prosecutor tore himself from "Cain," and looked at the president. They merely looked, but there was no smile, no surprise, no perplexity—their faces expressed nothing.

"Perhaps," the doctor hesitated, "if one considers the force with which . . . er—er—er . . . the criminal strikes the blow. . . . However, excuse me, I don't quite understand your question. . . ."

The counsel for the defence did not get an answer to his question, and indeed he did not feel the necessity of one. It was clear even to himself that that question had strayed into his mind and found utterance simply through the effect of the stillness, the boredom, the whirring ventilator wheels.

When they had got rid of the doctor the court rose to examine the "material evidences." The first thing examined was the full-skirted coat, upon the sleeve of which there was a dark brownish stain of blood. Harlamov on being questioned as to the origin of the stain stated:

"Three days before my old woman's death Penkov bled his horse. I was there; I was helping to be sure, and ... and got smeared with it...."

"But Penkov has just given evidence that he does not remember that you were present at the bleeding...."

"I can't tell about that."

"Sit down."

They proceeded to examine the axe with which the old woman had been murdered.

"That's not my axe," the prisoner declared.

"Whose is it, then?"

"I can't tell ... I hadn't an axe...."

"A peasant can't get on for a day without an axe. And your neighbour Ivan Timofeyitch, with whom you mended a sledge, has given evidence that it is your axe...."

"I can't say about that, but I swear before God (Harlamov held out his hand before him and spread out the fingers), before the living God. And I don't remember how long it is since I did have an axe of my own. I did have one like that only a bit smaller, but my son Prohor lost it. Two years before he went into the army, he drove off to fetch wood, got drinking with the fellows, and lost it...."

"Good, sit down."

This systematic distrust and disinclination to hear him probably irritated and offended Harlamov. He blinked and red patches came out on his cheekbones.

"I swear in the sight of God," he went on, craning his neck forward. "If you don't believe me, be pleased to ask my son Prohor. Proshka, what did you do with the axe?" he suddenly asked in a rough voice, turning abruptly to the soldier escorting him. "Where is it?"

It was a painful moment! Everyone seemed to wince and as it were shrink together. The same fearful, incredible thought flashed like lightning through every head in the court, the thought of possibly fatal coincidence, and not one person in the court dared to look at the soldier's face. Everyone refused to trust his thought and believed that he had heard wrong.

"Prisoner, conversation with the guards is forbidden . . ." the president made haste to say.

No one saw the escort's face, and horror passed over the hall unseen as in a mask. The usher of the court got up quietly from his place and tiptoeing with his hand held out to balance himself went out of the court. Half a minute later there came the muffled sounds and footsteps that accompany the change of guard.

All raised their heads and, trying to look as though nothing had happened, went on with their work. . . .

An Incident

Morning. Brilliant sunshine is piercing through the frozen lacework on the window-panes into the nursery. Vanya, a boy of six, with a cropped head and a nose like a button, and his sister Nina, a short, chubby, curly-headed girl of four, wake up and look crossly at each other through the bars of their cots.

"Oo-oo-oo! naughty children!" grumbles their nurse. "Good people have had their breakfast already, while you can't get your eyes open."

The sunbeams frolic over the rugs, the walls, and nurse's skirts, and seem inviting the children to join in their play, but they take no notice. They have woken up in a bad humour. Nina pouts, makes a grimace, and begins to whine:

"Brea-eakfast, nurse, breakfast!"

Vanya knits his brows and ponders what to pitch upon to howl over. He has already begun screwing up his eyes and opening his mouth, but at that instant the voice of mamma reaches them from the drawing-room, saying: "Don't forget to give the cat her milk, she has a family now!"

The children's puckered countenances grow smooth again as they look at each other in astonishment. Then both at once begin shouting, jump out of their cots, and filling the air with piercing shrieks, run barefoot, in their nightgowns, to the kitchen.

"The cat has puppies!" they cry. "The cat has got puppies!"

Under the bench in the kitchen there stands a small box, the one in which Stepan brings coal when he lights the fire. The cat is peeping out of the box. There is an expression of extreme exhaustion on her grey face; her green eyes, with their narrow black pupils, have a languid, sentimental look. . . . From her face it is clear that the only thing lacking to complete her happiness is the presence in the box of "him," the father of her children, to whom she had abandoned herself so recklessly! She wants to mew, and opens her mouth wide, but nothing but a hiss comes from her throat; the squealing of the kittens is audible.

The children squat on their heels before the box, and, motionless, holding their breath, gaze at the cat. . . . They are surprised, impressed, and do not hear nurse grumbling as she pursues them. The most genuine delight shines in the eyes of both.

Domestic animals play a scarcely noticed but undoubtedly beneficial part in the education and life of children. Which of us does not remember powerful but magnanimous dogs, lazy lapdogs, birds dying in captivity, dull-witted but haughty turkeys, mild old tabby cats, who forgave us when we trod on their tails for fun and caused them agonising pain? I even fancy, sometimes, that the patience, the fidelity, the readiness to forgive, and the sincerity which are characteristic of our domestic animals have a far stronger and more definite effect on the mind of a child than the long exhortations of some dry, pale Karl Karlovitch, or the misty expositions of a governess, trying to prove to children that water is made up of hydrogen and oxygen.

"What little things!" says Nina, opening her eyes wide and going off into a joyous laugh. "They are like mice!"

"One, two, three," Vanya counts. "Three kittens. So there is one for you, one for me, and one for somebody else, too."

"Murrm . . . murrm . . ." purrs the mother, flattered by their attention. "Murrm."

After gazing at the kittens, the children take them from under the cat, and begin squeezing them in their hands, then, not satisfied with this, they put them in the skirts of their nightgowns, and run into the other rooms.

"Mamma, the cat has got pups!" they shout.

Mamma is sitting in the drawing-room with some unknown gentleman. Seeing the children unwashed, undressed, with their nightgowns held up high, she is embarrassed, and looks at them severely.

"Let your nightgowns down, disgraceful children," she says. "Go out of the room, or I will punish you."

But the children do not notice either mamma's threats or the presence of a stranger. They put the kittens down on the carpet, and go off into deafening squeals. The mother walks round them, mewing imploringly. When, a little afterwards, the children are dragged off to the nursery, dressed, made to say their prayers, and given their breakfast, they are full of a passionate desire to get away from these prosaic duties as quickly as possible, and to run to the kitchen again.

Their habitual pursuits and games are thrown completely into the background.

The kittens throw everything into the shade by making their appearance in the world, and supply the great sensation of the day. If Nina or Vanya had been offered forty pounds of sweets or ten thousand kopecks for each kitten, they would have rejected such a barter without the slightest hesitation. In spite of the heated protests of the nurse and the cook, the children persist in sitting by the cat's box in the kitchen, busy with the kittens till dinner-time. Their faces are earnest and concentrated and express anxiety. They are worried not so much by the present as by the future of the kittens. They decide that one kitten shall remain at home with the old cat to be a comfort to her mother, while the second shall go to their summer villa, and the third shall live in the cellar, where there are ever so many rats.

"But why don't they look at us?" Nina wondered. "Their eyes are blind like the beggars'."

Vanya, too, is perturbed by this question. He tries to open one kitten's eyes, and spends a long time puffing and breathing hard over it, but his operation is unsuccessful. They are a good deal troubled, too, by the circumstance that the kittens obstinately refuse the milk and the meat that is offered to them. Everything that is put before their little noses is eaten by their grey mamma.

"Let's build the kittens little houses," Vanya suggests. "They shall live in different houses, and the cat shall come and pay them visits...."

Cardboard hat-boxes are put in the different corners of the kitchen and the kittens are installed in them. But this division turns out to be premature; the cat, still wearing an imploring and sentimental expression on her face, goes the round of all the hat-boxes, and carries off her children to their original position.

"The cat's their mother," observed Vanya, "but who is their father?"

"Yes, who is their father?" repeats Nina.

"They must have a father."

Vanya and Nina are a long time deciding who is to be the kittens' father, and, in the end, their choice falls on a big dark-red horse without a tail, which is lying in the store-cupboard under the stairs, together with other relics of toys that have outlived their day. They drag him up out of the store-cupboard and stand him by the box.

"Mind now!" they admonish him, "stand here and see they behave themselves properly."

All this is said and done in the gravest way, with an expression of anxiety on their faces. Vanya and Nina refuse to recognise the existence of any world but the box of kittens. Their joy knows no bounds. But they have to pass through bitter, agonising moments, too.

Just before dinner, Vanya is sitting in his father's study, gazing dreamily at the table. A kitten is moving about by the lamp, on stamped note paper. Vanya is watching its movements, and thrusting first a pencil, then a match into its little mouth. . . . All at once, as though he has sprung out of the floor, his father is beside the table.

"What's this?" Vanya hears, in an angry voice.

"It's . . . it's the kitty, papa. . . ."

"I'll give it you; look what you have done, you naughty boy! You've dirtied all my paper!"

To Vanya's great surprise his papa does not share his partiality for the kittens, and, instead of being moved to enthusiasm and delight, he pulls Vanya's ear and shouts:

"Stepan, take away this horrid thing."

At dinner, too, there is a scene. . . . During the second course there is suddenly the sound of a shrill mew. They begin to investigate its origin, and discover a kitten under Nina's pinafore.

"Nina, leave the table!" cries her father angrily. "Throw the kittens in the cesspool! I won't have the nasty things in the house! . . ."

Vanya and Nina are horrified. Death in the cesspool, apart from its cruelty, threatens to rob the cat and the wooden horse of their children, to lay waste the cat's box, to destroy their plans for the future, that fair future in which one cat will be a comfort to its old mother, another will live in the country, while the third will catch rats in the cellar. The children begin to cry and entreat that the kittens may be spared. Their father consents, but on the condition that the children do not go into the kitchen and touch the kittens.

After dinner, Vanya and Nina slouch about the rooms, feeling depressed. The prohibition of visits to the kitchen has reduced them to dejection. They refuse sweets, are naughty, and are rude to their mother. When their uncle Petrusha comes in the evening, they draw him aside, and complain to him of their father, who wanted to throw the kittens into the cesspool.

"Uncle Petrusha, tell mamma to have the kittens taken to the nursery," the children beg their uncle, "do-o tell her."

"There, there . . . very well," says their uncle, waving them off. "All right."

Uncle Petrusha does not usually come alone. He is accompanied by Nero, a big black dog of Danish breed, with drooping ears, and a tail as hard as a stick. The dog is silent, morose, and full of a sense of his own dignity. He takes not the slightest notice of the children, and when he passes them hits them with his tail as though they were chairs. The children hate him from the bottom of their hearts, but on this occasion, practical considerations override sentiment.

"I say, Nina," says Vanya, opening his eyes wide. "Let Nero be their father, instead of the horse! The horse is dead and he is alive, you see."

They are waiting the whole evening for the moment when papa will sit down to his cards and it will be possible to take Nero to the kitchen without being observed. . . . At last, papa sits down to cards, mamma is busy with the samovar and not noticing the children. . . .

The happy moment arrives.

"Come along!" Vanya whispers to his sister.

But, at that moment, Stepan comes in and, with a snigger, announces:

"Nero has eaten the kittens, madam."

Nina and Vanya turn pale and look at Stepan with horror.

"He really has..." laughs the footman, "he went to the box and gobbled them up."

The children expect that all the people in the house will be aghast and fall upon the miscreant Nero. But they all sit calmly in their seats, and only express surprise at the appetite of the huge dog. Papa and mamma laugh. Nero walks about by the table, wags his tail, and licks his lips complacently ... the cat is the only one who is uneasy. With her tail in the air she walks about the rooms, looking suspiciously at people and mewing plaintively.

"Children, it's past nine," cries mamma, "it's bedtime."

Vanya and Nina go to bed, shed tears, and spend a long time thinking about the injured cat, and the cruel, insolent, and unpunished Nero.

A Work of Art

Sasha Smirnov, the only son of his mother, holding under his arm, something wrapped up in No. 223 of the *Financial News*, assumed a sentimental expression, and went into Dr. Koshelkov's consulting-room.

"Ah, dear lad!" was how the doctor greeted him. "Well! how are we feeling? What good news have you for me?"

Sasha blinked, laid his hand on his heart and said in an agitated voice: "Mamma sends her greetings to you, Ivan Nikolaevitch, and told me to thank you.... I am the only son of my mother and you have saved my life ... you have brought me through a dangerous illness and ... we do not know how to thank you."

"Nonsense, lad!" said the doctor, highly delighted. "I only did what anyone else would have done in my place."

"I am the only son of my mother ... we are poor people and cannot of course repay you, and.... we are quite ashamed, doctor, although, however, mamma and I ... the only son of my mother, earnestly beg you to accept in token of our gratitude ... this object, which ... An object of great value, an antique bronze.... A rare work of art."

"You shouldn't!" said the doctor, frowning. "What's this for!"

"No, please do not refuse," Sasha went on muttering as he unpacked the parcel. "You will wound mamma and me by refusing.... It's a fine thing ... an antique bronze.... It was left us by my deceased father and we have kept it as a precious souvenir. My father used to buy antique bronzes and sell them to connoisseurs ... Mamma and I keep on the business now...."

Sasha undid the object and put it solemnly on the table. It was a not very tall candelabra of old bronze and artistic workmanship. It consisted of a group: on the pedestal stood two female figures in the costume of Eve and in attitudes for the description of which I have neither the courage nor the fitting temperament. The figures were smiling coquettishly and altogether looked as though, had it not been for the necessity of supporting the candlestick, they would have skipped off the pedestal and have indulged in an orgy such as is improper for the reader even to imagine.

Looking at the present, the doctor slowly scratched behind his ear, cleared his throat and blew his nose irresolutely.

"Yes, it certainly is a fine thing," he muttered, "but ... how shall I express it? ... it's ... h'm ... it's not quite for family reading. It's not simply decolleté but beyond anything, dash it all...."

"How do you mean?"

"The serpent-tempter himself could not have invented anything worse.... Why, to put such a phantasmagoria on the table would be defiling the whole flat."

"What a strange way of looking at art, doctor!" said Sasha, offended. "Why, it is an artistic thing, look at it! There is so much beauty and elegance that it fills one's soul with a feeling of reverence and brings a lump into one's throat! When one sees anything so beautiful one forgets everything earthly.... Only look, how much movement, what an atmosphere, what expression!"

"I understand all that very well, my dear boy," the doctor interposed, "but you know I am a family man, my children run in here, ladies come in."

"Of course if you look at it from the point of view of the crowd," said Sasha, "then this exquisitely artistic work may appear in a certain light.... But, doctor, rise superior to the crowd, especially as you will wound mamma and me by refusing it. I am the only son of my mother, you have saved my life.... We are giving you the thing most precious to us and ... and I only regret that I have not the pair to present to you...."

"Thank you, my dear fellow, I am very grateful ... Give my respects to your mother but really consider, my children run in here, ladies come.... However, let it remain! I see there's no arguing with you."

"And there is nothing to argue about," said Sasha, relieved. "Put the candlestick here, by this vase. What a pity we have not the pair to it! It is a pity! Well, good-bye, doctor."

After Sasha's departure the doctor looked for a long time at the candelabra, scratched behind his ear and meditated.

"It's a superb thing, there's no denying it," he thought, "and it would be a pity to throw it away.... But it's impossible for me to keep it.... H'm!... Here's a problem! To whom can I make a present of it, or to what charity can I give it?"

After long meditation he thought of his good friend, the lawyer Uhov, to whom he was indebted for the management of legal business.

"Excellent," the doctor decided, "it would be awkward for him as a friend to take money from me, and it will be very suitable for me to present him with this. I will take him the devilish thing! Luckily he is a bachelor and easy-going."

Without further procrastination the doctor put on his hat and coat, took the candelabra and went off to Uhov's.

"How are you, friend!" he said, finding the lawyer at home. "I've come to see you ... to thank you for your efforts.... You won't take money so you must at least accept this thing here.... See, my dear fellow.... The thing is magnificent!"

On seeing the bronze the lawyer was moved to indescribable delight.

"What a specimen!" he chuckled. "Ah, deuce take it, to think of them imagining such a thing, the devils! Exquisite! Ravishing! Where did you get hold of such a delightful thing?"

After pouring out his ecstasies the lawyer looked timidly towards the door and said: "Only you must carry off your present, my boy.... I can't take it...."

"Why?" cried the doctor, disconcerted.

"Why . . . because my mother is here at times, my clients . . . besides I should be ashamed for my servants to see it."

"Nonsense! Nonsense! Don't you dare to refuse!" said the doctor, gesticulating. "It's piggish of you! It's a work of art! . . . What movement . . . what expression! I won't even talk of it! You will offend me!"

"If one could plaster it over or stick on fig-leaves . . ."

But the doctor gesticulated more violently than before, and dashing out of the flat went home, glad that he had succeeded in getting the present off his hands.

When he had gone away the lawyer examined the candelabra, fingered it all over, and then, like the doctor, racked his brains over the question what to do with the present.

"It's a fine thing," he mused, "and it would be a pity to throw it away and improper to keep it. The very best thing would be to make a present of it to someone. . . . I know what! I'll take it this evening to Shashkin, the comedian. The rascal is fond of such things, and by the way it is his benefit tonight."

No sooner said than done. In the evening the candelabra, carefully wrapped up, was duly carried to Shashkin's. The whole evening the comic actor's dressing-room was besieged by men coming to admire the present; the dressing-room was filled with the hum of enthusiasm and laughter like the neighing of horses. If one of the actresses approached the door and asked: "May I come in?" the comedian's husky voice was heard at once: "No, no, my dear, I am not dressed!"

After the performance the comedian shrugged his shoulders, flung up his hands and said: "Well what am I to do with the horrid thing? Why, I live in a private flat! Actresses come and see me! It's not a photograph that you can put in a drawer!"

"You had better sell it, sir," the hairdresser who was disrobing the actor advised him. "There's an old woman living about here who buys antique bronzes. Go and enquire for Madame Smirnov . . . everyone knows her."

The actor followed his advice. . . . Two days later the doctor was sitting in his consulting-room, and with his finger to his brow was meditating on the acids of the bile. All at once the door opened and Sasha Smirnov flew into the room. He was smiling, beaming, and his whole figure was radiant with happiness. In his hands he held something wrapped up in newspaper.

"Doctor!" he began breathlessly, "imagine my delight! Happily for you we have succeeded in picking up the pair to your candelabra! Mamma is so happy. . . . I am the only son of my mother, you saved my life. . . ."

And Sasha, all of a tremor with gratitude, set the candelabra before the doctor. The doctor opened his mouth, tried to say something, but said nothing: he could not speak.

Vanka

Vanka Zhukov, a boy of nine, who had been for three months apprenticed to Alyahin the shoemaker, was sitting up on Christmas Eve. Waiting till his master and mistress and their workmen had gone to the midnight service, he took out of his master's cupboard a bottle of ink and a pen with a rusty nib, and, spreading out a crumpled sheet of paper in front of him, began writing. Before forming the first letter he several times looked round fearfully at the door and the windows, stole a glance at the dark ikon, on both sides of which stretched shelves full of lasts, and heaved a broken sigh. The paper lay on the bench while he knelt before it.

"Dear grandfather, Konstantin Makaritch," he wrote, "I am writing you a letter. I wish you a happy Christmas, and all blessings from God Almighty. I have neither father nor mother, you are the only one left me."

Vanka raised his eyes to the dark ikon on which the light of his candle was reflected, and vividly recalled his grandfather, Konstantin Makaritch, who was night watchman to a family called Zhivarev. He was a thin but extraordinarily nimble and lively little old man of sixty-five, with an everlastingly laughing face and drunken eyes. By day he slept in the servants' kitchen, or made jokes with the cooks; at night, wrapped in an ample sheepskin, he walked round the grounds and tapped with his little mallet. Old Kashtanka and Eel, so-called on account of his dark colour and his long body like a weasel's, followed him with hanging heads. This Eel was exceptionally polite and affectionate, and looked with equal kindness on strangers and his own masters, but had not a very good reputation. Under his politeness and meekness was hidden the most Jesuitical cunning. No one knew better how to creep up on occasion and snap at one's legs, to slip into the storeroom, or steal a hen from a peasant. His hind legs had been nearly pulled off more than once, twice he had been hanged, every week he was thrashed till he was half dead, but he always revived.

At this moment grandfather was, no doubt, standing at the gate, screwing up his eyes at the red windows of the church, stamping with his high felt boots, and joking with the servants. His little mallet was hanging on his belt. He was clasping his hands, shrugging with the cold, and, with an aged chuckle, pinching first the housemaid, then the cook.

"How about a pinch of snuff?" he was saying, offering the women his snuff-box.

The women would take a sniff and sneeze. Grandfather would be indescribably delighted, go off into a merry chuckle, and cry:

"Tear it off, it has frozen on!"

They give the dogs a sniff of snuff too. Kashtanka sneezes, wriggles her head, and walks away offended. Eel does not sneeze, from politeness, but wags his tail. And the weather is glorious. The air is still, fresh, and transparent. The night is dark, but one can see the whole village with its white roofs and coils of smoke coming from the chimneys, the trees silvered with hoar frost, the snowdrifts. The whole sky spangled with gay twinkling stars, and the Milky Way is as distinct as though it had been washed and rubbed with snow for a holiday. . . .

Vanka sighed, dipped his pen, and went on writing:

"And yesterday I had a wigging. The master pulled me out into the yard by my hair, and whacked me with a boot-stretcher because I accidentally fell asleep while I was rocking their brat in the cradle. And a week ago the mistress told me to clean a herring, and I began from the tail end, and she took the herring and thrust its head in my face.

The workmen laugh at me and send me to the tavern for vodka, and tell me to steal the master's cucumbers for them, and the master beats me with anything that comes to hand. And there is nothing to eat. In the morning they give me bread, for dinner, porridge, and in the evening, bread again; but as for tea, or soup, the master and mistress gobble it all up themselves. And I am put to sleep in the passage, and when their wretched brat cries I get no sleep at all, but have to rock the cradle. Dear grandfather, show the divine mercy, take me away from here, home to the village. It's more than I can bear. I bow down to your feet, and will pray to God for you for ever, take me away from here or I shall die."

Vanka's mouth worked, he rubbed his eyes with his black fist, and gave a sob.

"I will powder your snuff for you," he went on. "I will pray for you, and if I do anything you can thrash me like Sidor's goat. And if you think I've no job, then I will beg the steward for Christ's sake to let me clean his boots, or I'll go for a shepherd-boy instead of Fedka. Dear grandfather, it is more than I can bear, it's simply no life at all. I wanted to run away to the village, but I have no boots, and I am afraid of the frost. When I grow up big I will take care of you for this, and not let anyone annoy you, and when you die I will pray for the rest of your soul, just as for my mammy's.

"Moscow is a big town. It's all gentlemen's houses, and there are lots of horses, but there are no sheep, and the dogs are not spiteful. The lads here don't go out with the star, and they don't let anyone go into the choir, and once I saw in a shop window fishing-hooks for sale, fitted ready with the line and for all sorts of fish, awfully good ones, there was even one hook that would hold a forty-pound sheat-fish. And I have seen shops where there are guns of all sorts, after the pattern of the master's guns at home, so that I shouldn't wonder if they are a hundred roubles each. . . . And in the butchers' shops there are grouse and woodcocks and fish and hares, but the shopmen don't say where they shoot them.

"Dear grandfather, when they have the Christmas tree at the big house, get me a gilt walnut, and put it away in the green trunk. Ask the young lady Olga Ignatyevna, say it's for Vanka."

Vanka gave a tremulous sigh, and again stared at the window. He remembered how his grandfather always went into the forest to get the Christmas tree for his master's family, and took his grandson with him. It was a merry time! Grandfather made a noise in his throat, the forest crackled with the frost, and looking at them Vanka chortled too. Before chopping down the Christmas tree, grandfather would smoke a pipe, slowly take a pinch of snuff, and laugh at frozen Vanka. . . . The young fir trees, covered with hoar frost, stood motionless, waiting to see which of them was to die. Wherever one looked, a hare flew like an arrow over the snowdrifts. . . . Grandfather could not refrain from shouting: "Hold him, hold him . . . hold him! Ah, the bob-tailed devil!"

When he had cut down the Christmas tree, grandfather used to drag it to the big house, and there set to work to decorate it. . . . The young lady, who was Vanka's favourite, Olga Ignatyevna, was the busiest of all. When Vanka's mother Pelageya was alive, and a servant in the big house, Olga Ignatyevna used to give him goodies, and having nothing better to do, taught him to read and write, to count up to a hundred, and even to dance a quadrille. When Pelageya died, Vanka had been transferred to the servants' kitchen to be with his grandfather, and from the kitchen to the shoemaker's in Moscow.

"Do come, dear grandfather," Vanka went on with his letter. "For Christ's sake, I beg you, take me away. Have pity on an unhappy orphan like me; here everyone knocks me about, and I am fearfully hungry; I can't tell you what misery it is, I am always crying. And the other day the master hit me on the head with a last, so that I fell down. My life is wretched, worse than any dog's. . . . I send greetings to Alyona, one-eyed Yegorka, and the coachman, and don't give my concertina to anyone. I remain, your grandson, Ivan Zhukov. Dear grandfather, do come."

Vanka folded the sheet of writing-paper twice, and put it into an envelope he had bought the day before for a kopeck. . . . After thinking a little, he dipped the pen and wrote the address:

To grandfather in the village.

Then he scratched his head, thought a little, and added: *Konstantin Makaritch.* Glad that he had not been prevented from writing, he put on his cap and, without putting on his little greatcoat, ran out into the street as he was in his shirt. . . .

The shopmen at the butcher's, whom he had questioned the day before, told him that letters were put in post-boxes, and from the boxes were carried about all over the earth in mailcarts with drunken drivers and ringing bells. Vanka ran to the nearest post-box, and thrust the precious letter in the slit. . . .

An hour later, lulled by sweet hopes, he was sound asleep. . . . He dreamed of the stove. On the stove was sitting his grandfather, swinging his bare legs, and reading the letter to the cooks. . . .

By the stove was Eel, wagging his tail.

On the Road

*"Upon the breast of a gigantic crag,
A golden cloudlet rested for one night."*
LERMONTOV.

In the room which the tavern keeper, the Cossack Semyon Tchisto-pluy, called the "travellers' room," that is kept exclusively for travellers, a tall, broad-shouldered man of forty was sitting at the big unpainted table. He was asleep with his elbows on the table and his head leaning on his fist. An end of tallow candle, stuck into an old pomatum pot, lighted up his light brown beard, his thick, broad nose, his sunburnt cheeks, and the thick, black eyebrows overhanging his closed eyes. . . . The nose and the cheeks and the eyebrows, all the features, each taken separately, were coarse and heavy, like the furniture and the stove in the "travellers' room," but taken all together they gave the effect of something harmonious and even beautiful. Such is the lucky star, as it is called, of the Russian face: the coarser and harsher its features the softer and more good-natured it looks. The man was dressed in a gentleman's reefer jacket, shabby, but bound with wide new braid, a plush waistcoat, and full black trousers thrust into big high boots.

On one of the benches, which stood in a continuous row along the wall, a girl of eight, in a brown dress and long black stockings, lay asleep on a coat lined with fox. Her face was pale, her hair was flaxen, her shoulders were narrow, her whole body was thin and frail, but her nose stood out as thick and ugly a lump as the man's. She was sound asleep, and unconscious that her semi-circular comb had fallen off her head and was cutting her cheek.

The "travellers' room" had a festive appearance. The air was full of the smell of freshly scrubbed floors, there were no rags hanging as usual on the line that ran diagonally across the room, and a little lamp was burning in the corner over the table, casting a patch of red light on the ikon of St. George the Victorious. From the ikon stretched on each side of the corner a row of cheap oleographs, which maintained a strict and careful gradation in the transition from the sacred to the profane. In the dim light of the candle end and the red ikon lamp the pictures looked like one continuous stripe, covered with blurs of black. When the tiled stove, trying to sing in unison with the weather, drew in the air with a howl, while the logs, as though waking up, burst into bright flame and hissed angrily, red patches began dancing on the log walls, and over the head of the sleeping man could be seen first the Elder Seraphim, than the Shah Nasir-ed-Din, then a fat, brown baby with goggle eyes, whispering in the ear of a young girl with an extra-ordinarily blank, and indifferent face. . . .

Outside a storm was raging. Something frantic and wrathful, but profoundly unhappy, seemed to be flinging itself about the tavern with the ferocity of a wild beast and trying to break in. Banging at the doors, knocking at the windows and on the roof, scratching at the walls, it alternately threatened and besought, then subsided for a brief interval, and then with a gleeful, treacherous howl burst into the chimney, but the wood flared up, and the fire, like a chained dog, flew wrathfully to meet its foe, a battle began, and after it—sobs, shrieks, howls of wrath. In all of this there was the sound of angry misery and unsatisfied hate, and the mortified impatience of something accus-tomed to triumph.

Bewitched by this wild, inhuman music the "travellers' room" seemed spellbound for ever, but all at once the door creaked and the potboy, in a new print shirt, came in. Limping on one leg, and blinking his sleepy eyes, he snuffed the candle with his fingers, put some more wood on the fire and went out. At once from the church, which was three hundred paces from the tavern, the clock struck midnight. The wind played with the chimes as with the snowflakes; chasing the sounds of the clock it whirled them round and round over a vast space, so that some strokes were cut short or drawn out in long, vibrating notes, while others were completely lost in the general uproar. One stroke sounded as distinctly in the room as though it had chimed just under the window. The child, sleeping on the fox-skin, started and raised her head. For a minute she stared blankly at the dark window, at Nasir-ed-Din over whom a crimson glow from the fire flickered at that moment, then she turned her eyes upon the sleeping man.

"Daddy," she said.

But the man did not move. The little girl knitted her brow angrily, lay down, and curled up her legs. Someone in the tavern gave a loud, prolonged yawn. Soon afterwards there was the squeak of the swing door and the sound of indistinct voices. Someone came in, shaking the snow off, and stamping in felt boots which made a muffled thud.

"What is it?" a woman's voice asked languidly.

"Mademoiselle Ilovaisky has come, . . ." answered a bass voice.

Again there was the squeak of the swing door. Then came the roar of the wind rushing in. Someone, probably the lame boy, ran to the door leading to the "travellers' room," coughed deferentially, and lifted the latch.

"This way, lady, please," said a woman's voice in dulcet tones. "It's clean in here, my beauty. . . ."

The door was opened wide and a peasant with a beard appeared in the doorway, in the long coat of a coachman, plastered all over with snow from head to foot, and carrying a big trunk on his shoulder. He was followed into the room by a feminine figure, scarcely half his height, with no face and no arms, muffled and wrapped up like a bundle and also covered with snow. A damp chill, as from a cellar, seemed to come to the child from the coachman and the bundle, and the fire and the candles flickered.

"What nonsense!" said the bundle angrily, "We could go perfectly well. We have only nine more miles to go, mostly by the forest, and we should not get lost. . . ."

"As for getting lost, we shouldn't, but the horses can't go on, lady!" answered the coachman. "And it is Thy Will, O Lord! As though I had done it on purpose!"

"God knows where you have brought me. . . . Well, be quiet. . . . There are people asleep here, it seems. You can go. . . ."

The coachman put the portmanteau on the floor, and as he did so, a great lump of snow fell off his shoulders. He gave a sniff and went out.

Then the little girl saw two little hands come out from the middle of the bundle, stretch upwards and begin angrily disentangling the network of shawls, kerchiefs, and scarves. First a big shawl fell on the ground, then a hood, then a white knitted kerchief. After freeing her head, the traveller took off her pelisse and at once shrank to half the size. Now she was in a long, grey coat with big buttons and bulging pockets. From one pocket she pulled out a paper parcel, from the other a bunch of big, heavy keys, which she put down so carelessly that the sleeping man started and opened his eyes. For some time he looked blankly round him as though he didn't know where he was, then he shook his head, went to the corner and sat down. . . . The newcomer took off her great coat, which made her shrink to half her size again, she took off her big felt boots, and sat down, too.

By now she no longer resembled a bundle: she was a thin little brunette of twenty, as slim as a snake, with a long white face and curly hair. Her nose was long and sharp, her chin, too, was long and sharp, her eyelashes were long, the corners of her mouth were sharp, and, thanks to this general sharpness, the expression of her face was biting. Swathed in a closely fitting black dress with a mass of lace at her neck and sleeves, with sharp elbows and long pink fingers, she recalled the portraits of mediæval English ladies. The grave concentration of her face increased this likeness.

The lady looked round at the room, glanced sideways at the man and the little girl, shrugged her shoulders, and moved to the window. The dark windows were shaking from the damp west wind. Big flakes of snow glistening in their whiteness, lay on the window frame, but at once disappeared, borne away by the wind. The savage music grew louder and louder. . . .

After a long silence the little girl suddenly turned over, and said angrily, emphasizing each word:

"Oh, goodness, goodness, how unhappy I am! Unhappier than anyone!"

The man got up and moved with little steps to the child with a guilty air, which was utterly out of keeping with his huge figure and big beard.

"You are not asleep, dearie?" he said, in an apologetic voice. "What do you want?"

"I don't want anything, my shoulder aches! You are a wicked man, Daddy, and God will punish you! You'll see He will punish you."

"My darling, I know your shoulder aches, but what can I do, dearie?" said the man, in the tone in which men who have been drinking excuse themselves to their stern spouses. "It's the journey has made your shoulder ache, Sasha. To-morrow we shall get there and rest, and the pain will go away. . . ."

"To-morrow, to-morrow. . . . Every day you say to-morrow. We shall be going on another twenty days."

"But we shall arrive to-morrow, dearie, on your father's word of honour. I never tell a lie, but if we are detained by the snowstorm it is not my fault."

"I can't bear any more, I can't, I can't!"

Sasha jerked her leg abruptly and filled the room with an unpleasant wailing. Her father made a despairing gesture, and looked hopelessly towards the young lady. The latter shrugged her shoulders, and hesitatingly went up to Sasha.

"Listen, my dear," she said, "it is no use crying. It's really naughty; if your shoulder aches it can't be helped."

"You see, Madam," said the man quickly, as though defending himself, "we have not slept for two nights, and have been travelling in a revolting conveyance. Well, of course, it is natural she should be ill and miserable, . . . and then, you know, we had a drunken driver, our portmanteau has been stolen . . . the snowstorm all the time, but what's the use of crying, Madam? I am exhausted, though, by sleeping in a sitting position, and I feel as though I were drunk. Oh, dear! Sasha, and I feel sick as it is, and then you cry!"

The man shook his head, and with a gesture of despair sat down.

"Of course you mustn't cry," said the young lady. "It's only little babies cry. If you are ill, dear, you must undress and go to sleep. . . . Let us take off your things!"

When the child had been undressed and pacified a silence reigned again. The young lady seated herself at the window, and looked round wonderingly at the room of the inn, at the ikon, at the stove. . . . Apparently the room and the little girl with the thick nose, in her short boy's nightgown, and the child's father, all seemed strange to her. This strange man was sitting in a corner; he kept looking about him helplessly, as though he were drunk, and rubbing his face with the palm of his hand. He sat silent, blinking, and judging from his guilty-looking figure it was difficult to imagine that he would soon begin to speak. Yet he was the first to begin. Stroking his knees, he gave a cough, laughed, and said:

"It's a comedy, it really is. . . . I look and I cannot believe my eyes: for what devilry has destiny driven us to this accursed inn? What did she want to show by it? Life sometimes performs such '*salto mortale*,' one can only stare and blink in amazement. Have you come from far, Madam?"

"No, not from far," answered the young lady. "I am going from our estate, fifteen miles from here, to our farm, to my father and brother. My name is Ilovaisky, and the farm is called Ilovaiskoe. It's nine miles away. What unpleasant weather!"

"It couldn't be worse."

The lame boy came in and stuck a new candle in the pomatum pot.

"You might bring us the samovar, boy," said the man, addressing him.

"Who drinks tea now?" laughed the boy. "It is a sin to drink tea before mass. . . ."

"Never mind, boy, you won't burn in hell if we do. . . ."

Over the tea the new acquaintances got into conversation.

Mlle. Ilovaisky learned that her companion was called Grigory Petrovitch Liharev, that he was the brother of the Liharev who was Marshal of Nobility in one of the neighbouring districts, and he himself had once been a landowner, but had "run through everything in his time." Liharev learned that her name was Marya Mihailovna, that her father had a huge estate, but that she was the only one to look after it as her father and brother looked at life through their fingers, were irresponsible, and were too fond of harriers.

"My father and brother are all alone at the farm," she told him, brandishing her fingers (she had the habit of moving her fingers before her pointed face as she talked, and after every sentence moistened her lips with her sharp little tongue). "They, I mean men, are an irresponsible lot, and don't stir a finger for themselves. I can fancy there will be no one to give them a meal after the fast! We have no mother, and we have such servants that they can't lay the tablecloth properly when I am away. You can imagine their condition now! They will be left with nothing to break their fast, while I have to stay here all night. How strange it all is."

She shrugged her shoulders, took a sip from her cup, and said:

"There are festivals that have a special fragrance: at Easter, Trinity and Christmas there is a peculiar scent in the air. Even unbelievers are fond of those festivals. My brother, for instance, argues that there is no God, but he is the first to hurry to Matins at Easter."

Liharev raised his eyes to Mlle. Ilovaisky and laughed.

"They argue that there is no God," she went on, laughing too, "but why is it, tell me, all the celebrated writers, the learned men, clever people generally, in fact, believe towards the end of their life?"

"If a man does not know how to believe when he is young, Madam, he won't believe in his old age if he is ever so much of a writer."

Judging from Liharev's cough he had a bass voice, but, probably from being afraid to speak aloud, or from exaggerated shyness, he spoke in a tenor. After a brief pause he heaved a sign and said:

"The way I look at it is that faith is a faculty of the spirit. It is just the same as a talent, one must be born with it. So far as I can judge by myself, by the people I have seen in my time, and by all that is done around us, this faculty is present in Russians in its highest degree. Russian life presents us with an uninterrupted succession of convictions and aspirations, and if you care to know, it has not yet the faintest notion of lack of faith or scepticism. If a Russian does not believe in God, it means he believes in something else."

Liharev took a cup of tea from Mlle. Ilovaisky, drank off half in one gulp, and went on:

"I will tell you about myself. Nature has implanted in my breast an extraordinary faculty for belief. Whisper it not to the night, but half my life I was in the ranks of the Atheists and Nihilists, but there was not one hour in my life in which I ceased to believe. All talents, as a rule, show themselves in early childhood, and so my faculty showed itself when I could still walk upright under the table. My mother liked her children to eat a great deal, and when she gave me food she used to say: 'Eat! Soup is the great thing in life!' I believed, and ate the soup ten times a day, ate like a shark, ate till I was disgusted and stupefied. My nurse used to tell me fairy tales, and I believed in house-spirits, in wood-elves, and in goblins of all kinds. I used sometimes to steal corrosive sublimate from my father, sprinkle it on cakes, and carry them up to the attic that the house-spirits, you see, might eat them and be killed. And when I was taught to read and understand what I read, then there was a fine to-do. I ran away to America and went off to join the brigands, and wanted to go into a monastery, and hired boys to torture me for being a Christian. And note that my faith was always active, never dead. If I was running away to America I was not alone, but seduced someone else, as great a fool as I was, to go with me, and was delighted when I was nearly frozen outside the town gates and when I was thrashed; if I went to join the brigands I always came back with my face battered. A most restless childhood, I assure you! And when they sent me to the high school and pelted me with all sorts of truths—that is, that the earth goes round the sun, or that white light is not white, but is made up of seven colours—my poor little head began to go round! Everything was thrown into a whirl in me: Navin who made the sun stand still, and my mother who in the name of the Prophet Elijah disapproved of lightning conductors, and my father who was indifferent to the truths I had learned. My enlightenment inspired me. I wandered about the house and stables like one possessed, preaching my truths, was horrified by ignorance, glowed with hatred for anyone who saw in white light nothing but white light. . . . But all that's nonsense and childishness. Serious, so to speak, manly enthusiasms began only at the university. You have, no doubt, Madam, taken your degree somewhere?"

"I studied at Novotcherkask at the Don Institute."

"Then you have not been to a university? So you don't know what science means. All the sciences in the world have the same passport, without which they regard themselves as meaningless . . . the striving towards truth! Every one of them, even pharmacology, has for its aim not utility, not the alleviation of life, but truth. It's remarkable! When you set to work to study any science, what strikes you first of all is its beginning. I assure you there is nothing more attractive and grander, nothing is so staggering, nothing takes a man's breath away like the beginning of any science. From the first five or six lectures you are soaring on wings of the brightest hopes, you already seem to yourself to be welcoming truth with open arms. And I gave myself up to science, heart and soul, passionately, as to the woman one loves. I was its slave; I found it the sun of my existence, and asked for no other. I studied day and night without rest, ruined myself over books, wept when before my eyes men exploited science for their own personal ends. But my enthusiasm did not last long. The trouble is that every science has a beginning but not an end, like a recurring decimal. Zoology has discovered 35,000 kinds of insects, chemistry reckons 60 elements. If in time tens of noughts can be written after these figures, Zoology and chemistry will be just as far from their end as now, and all contemporary scientific work consists in increasing these numbers. I saw through this trick when I discovered the 35,001-st and felt no satisfaction. Well, I had no time to suffer from disillusionment, as I was soon possessed by a new faith. I plunged into Nihilism, with its manifestoes, its 'black divisions,' and all the rest of it. I 'went to the people,' worked in factories, worked as an oiler, as a barge hauler. Afterwards, when wandering over Russia, I had a taste of Russian life, I turned into a fervent devotee of that life. I loved the Russian people with poignant intensity; I loved their God and believed in Him, and in their language, their creative genius. . . . And so on, and so on. . . . I have been a Slavophile in my time, I used to pester Aksakov with letters, and I was a Ukrainophile, and an archæologist, and a collector of specimens of peasant art. . . . I was enthusiastic over ideas, people, events, places . . . my enthusiasm was endless! Five years ago I was working for the abolition of private property; my last creed was non-resistance to evil."

Sasha gave an abrupt sigh and began moving. Liharev got up and went to her.

"Won't you have some tea, dearie?" he asked tenderly.

"Drink it yourself," the child answered rudely.

Liharev was disconcerted, and went back to the table with a guilty step.

"Then you have had a lively time," said Mlle. Ilovaisky; "you have something to remember."

"Well, yes, it's all very lively when one sits over tea and chatters to a kind listener, but you should ask what that liveliness has cost me! What price have I paid for the variety of my life? You see, Madam, I have not held my convictions like a German doctor of philosophy, *zierlichmännerlich,* I have not lived in solitude, but every conviction I have had has bound my back to the yoke, has torn my body to pieces. Judge, for yourself. I was wealthy like my brothers, but now I am a beggar. In the delirium of my enthusiasm I smashed up my own fortune and my wife's—a heap of other people's money. Now I am forty-two, old age is close upon me, and I am homeless, like a dog that has dropped behind its waggon at night. All my life I have not known what peace meant, my soul has been in continual agitation, distressed even by its hopes . . . I have been wearied out with heavy irregular work, have endured privation, have five times been in prison, have dragged myself across the provinces of Archangel and of Tobolsk . . . it's painful to think of it! I have lived, but in my fever I have not even been conscious of the process of life itself. Would you believe it, I don't remember a single spring, I never noticed how my wife loved me, how my children were born. What more can I tell you? I have been a misfortune to all who have loved me. . . . My mother has worn mourning for me all these fifteen years, while my proud brothers, who have had to wince, to blush, to bow their heads, to waste their money on my account, have come in the end to hate me like poison."

Liharev got up and sat down again.

"If I were simply unhappy I should thank God," he went on without looking at his listener. "My personal unhappiness sinks into the background when I remember how often in my enthusiasms I have been absurd, far from the truth, unjust, cruel, dangerous! How often I have hated and despised those whom I ought to have loved, and *vice versa*, I have changed a thousand times. One day I believe, fall down and worship, the next I flee like a coward from the gods and friends of yesterday, and swallow in silence the 'scoundrel!' they hurl after me. God alone has seen how often I have wept and bitten my pillow in shame for my enthusiasms. Never once in my life have I intentionally lied or done evil, but my conscience is not clear! I cannot even boast, Madam, that I have no one's life upon my conscience, for my wife died before my eyes, worn out by my reckless activity. Yes, my wife! I tell you they have two ways of treating women nowadays. Some measure women's skulls to prove woman is inferior to man, pick out her defects to mock at her, to look original in her eyes, and to justify their sensuality. Others do their utmost to raise women to their level, that is, force them to learn by heart the 35,000 species, to speak and write the same foolish things as they speak and write themselves."

Liharev's face darkened.

"I tell you that woman has been and always will be the slave of man," he said in a bass voice, striking his fist on the table. "She is the soft, tender wax which a man always moulds into anything he likes.... My God! for the sake of some trumpery masculine enthusiasm she will cut off her hair, abandon her family, die among strangers! ... among the ideas for which she has sacrificed herself there is not a single feminine one.... An unquestioning, devoted slave! I have not measured skulls, but I say this from hard, bitter experience: the proudest, most independent women, if I have succeeded in communicating to them my enthusiasm, have followed me without criticism, without question, and done anything I chose; I have turned a nun into a Nihilist who, as I heard afterwards, shot a gendarme; my wife never left me for a minute in my wanderings, and like a weathercock changed her faith in step with my changing enthusiasms."

Liharev jumped up and walked up and down the room.

"A noble, sublime slavery!" he said, clasping his hands. "It is just in it that the highest meaning of woman's life lies! Of all the fearful medley of thoughts and impressions accumulated in my brain from my association with women my memory, like a filter, has retained no ideas, no clever saying, no philosophy, nothing but that extraordinary, resignation to fate, that wonderful mercifulness, forgiveness of everything."

Liharev clenched his fists, stared at a fixed point, and with a sort of passionate intensity, as though he were savouring each word as he uttered it, hissed through his clenched teeth:

"That . . . that great-hearted fortitude, faithfulness unto death, poetry of the heart. . . . The meaning of life lies in just that unrepining martyrdom, in the tears which would soften a stone, in the boundless, all-forgiving love which brings light and warmth into the chaos of life. . . ."

Mlle. Ilovaisky got up slowly, took a step towards Liharev, and fixed her eyes upon his face. From the tears that glittered on his eyelashes, from his quivering, passionate voice, from the flush on his cheeks, it was clear to her that women were not a chance, not a simple subject of conversation. They were the object of his new enthusiasm, or, as he said himself, his new faith! For the first time in her life she saw a man carried away, fervently believing. With his gesticulations, with his flashing eyes he seemed to her mad, frantic, but there was a feeling of such beauty in the fire of his eyes, in his words, in all the movements of his huge body, that without noticing what she was doing she stood facing him as though rooted to the spot, and gazed into his face with delight.

"Take my mother," he said, stretching out his hand to her with an imploring expression on his face, "I poisoned her existence, according to her ideas disgraced the name of Liharev, did her as much harm as the most malignant enemy, and what do you think? My brothers give her little sums for holy bread and church services, and outraging her religious feelings, she saves that money and sends it in secret to her erring Grigory. This trifle alone elevates and ennobles the soul far more than all the theories, all the clever sayings and the 35,000 species. I can give you thousands of instances. Take you, even, for instance! With tempest and darkness outside you are going to your father and your brother to cheer them with your affection in the holiday, though very likely they have forgotten and are not thinking of you. And, wait a bit, and you will love a man and follow him to the North Pole. You would, wouldn't you?"

"Yes, if I loved him."

"There, you see," cried Liharev delighted, and he even stamped with his foot. "Oh dear! How glad I am that I have met you! Fate is kind to me, I am always meeting splendid people. Not a day passes but one makes acquaintance with somebody one would give one's soul for. There are ever so many more good people than bad in this world. Here, see, for instance, how openly and from our hearts we have been talking as though we had known each other a hundred years. Sometimes, I assure you, one restrains oneself for ten years and holds one's tongue, is reserved with one's friends and one's wife, and meets some cadet in a train and babbles one's whole soul out to him. It is the first time I have the honour of seeing you, and yet I have confessed to you as I have never confessed in my life. Why is it?"

Rubbing his hands and smiling good-humouredly Liharev walked up and down the room, and fell to talking about women again. Meanwhile they began ringing for matins.

"Goodness," wailed Sasha. "He won't let me sleep with his talking!"

"Oh, yes!" said Liharev, startled. "I am sorry, darling, sleep, sleep. . . . I have two boys besides her," he whispered. "They are living with their uncle, Madam, but this one can't exist a day without her father. She's wretched, she complains, but she sticks to me like a fly to honey. I have been chattering too much, Madam, and it would do you no harm to sleep. Wouldn't you like me to make up a bed for you?"

Without waiting for permission he shook the wet pelisse, stretched it on a bench, fur side upwards, collected various shawls and scarves, put the overcoat folded up into a roll for a pillow, and all this he did in silence with a look of devout reverence, as though he were not handling a woman's rags, but the fragments of holy vessels. There was something apologetic, embarrassed about his whole figure, as though in the presence of a weak creature he felt ashamed of his height and strength. . . .

When Mlle. Ilovaisky had lain down, he put out the candle and sat down on a stool by the stove.

"So, Madam," he whispered, lighting a fat cigarette and puffing the smoke into the stove. "Nature has put into the Russian an extraordinary faculty for belief, a searching intelligence, and the gift of speculation, but all that is reduced to ashes by irresponsibility, laziness, and dreamy frivolity.... Yes...."

She gazed wonderingly into the darkness, and saw only a spot of red on the ikon and the flicker of the light of the stove on Liharev's face. The darkness, the chime of the bells, the roar of the storm, the lame boy, Sasha with her fretfulness, unhappy Liharev and his sayings—all this was mingled together, and seemed to grow into one huge impression, and God's world seemed to her fantastic, full of marvels and magical forces. All that she had heard was ringing in her ears, and human life presented itself to her as a beautiful poetic fairy-tale without an end.

The immense impression grew and grew, clouded consciousness, and turned into a sweet dream. She was asleep, though she saw the little ikon lamp and a big nose with the light playing on it.

She heard the sound of weeping.

"Daddy, darling," a child's voice was tenderly entreating, "let's go back to uncle! There is a Christmas-tree there! Styopa and Kolya are there!"

"My darling, what can I do?" a man's bass persuaded softly. "Understand me! Come, understand!"

And the man's weeping blended with the child's. This voice of human sorrow, in the midst of the howling of the storm, touched the girl's ear with such sweet human music that she could not bear the delight of it, and wept too. She was conscious afterwards of a big, black shadow coming softly up to her, picking up a shawl that had dropped on to the floor and carefully wrapping it round her feet.

Mlle. Ilovaisky was awakened by a strange uproar. She jumped up and looked about her in astonishment. The deep blue dawn was looking in at the window half-covered with snow. In the room there was a grey twilight, through which the stove and the sleeping child and Nasir-ed-Din stood out distinctly. The stove and the lamp were both out. Through the wide-open door she could see the big tavern room with a counter and chairs. A man, with a stupid, gipsy face and astonished eyes, was standing in the middle of the room in a puddle of melting snow, holding a big red star on a stick. He was surrounded by a group of boys, motionless as statues, and plastered over with snow. The light shone through the red paper of the star, throwing a glow of red on their wet faces. The crowd was shouting in disorder, and from its uproar Mlle. Ilovaisky could make out only one couplet:

> "Hi, you Little Russian lad,
>   Bring your sharp knife,
>   We will kill the Jew, we will kill him,
>   The son of tribulation. . . ."

Liharev was standing near the counter, looking feelingly at the singers and tapping his feet in time. Seeing Mlle. Ilovaisky, he smiled all over his face and came up to her. She smiled too.

"A happy Christmas!" he said. "I saw you slept well."

She looked at him, said nothing, and went on smiling.

After the conversation in the night he seemed to her not tall and broad shouldered, but little, just as the biggest steamer seems to us a little thing when we hear that it has crossed the ocean.

"Well, it is time for me to set off," she said. "I must put on my things. Tell me where you are going now?"

"I? To the station of Klinushki, from there to Sergievo, and from Sergievo, with horses, thirty miles to the coal mines that belong to a horrid man, a general called Shashkovsky. My brothers have got me the post of superintendent there. . . . I am going to be a coal miner."

"Stay, I know those mines. Shashkovsky is my uncle, you know. But . . . what are you going there for?" asked Mlle. Ilovaisky, looking at Liharev in surprise.

"As superintendent. To superintend the coal mines."

"I don't understand!" she shrugged her shoulders. "You are going to the mines. But you know, it's the bare steppe, a desert, so dreary that you couldn't exist a day there! It's horrible coal, no one will buy it, and my uncle's a maniac, a despot, a bankrupt. . . . You won't get your salary!"

"No matter," said Liharev, unconcernedly, "I am thankful even for coal mines."

She shrugged her shoulders, and walked about the room in agitation.

"I don't understand, I don't understand," she said, moving her fingers before her face. "It's impossible, and . . . and irrational! You must understand that it's . . . it's worse than exile. It is a living tomb! O Heavens!" she said hotly, going up to Liharev and moving her fingers before his smiling face; her upper lip was quivering, and her sharp face turned pale, "Come, picture it, the bare steppe, solitude. There is no one to say a word to there, and you . . . are enthusiastic over women! Coal mines . . . and women!"

Mlle. Ilovaisky was suddenly ashamed of her heat and, turning away from Liharev, walked to the window.

"No, no, you can't go there," she said, moving her fingers rapidly over the pane.

Not only in her heart, but even in her spine she felt that behind her stood an infinitely unhappy man, lost and outcast, while he, as though he were unaware of his unhappiness, as though he had not shed tears in the night, was looking at her with a kindly smile. Better he should go on weeping! She walked up and down the room several times in agitation, then stopped short in a corner and sank into thought. Liharev was saying something, but she did not hear him. Turning her back on him she took out of her purse a money note, stood for a long time crumpling it in her hand, and looking round at Liharev, blushed and put it in her pocket.

The coachman's voice was heard through the door. With a stern, concentrated face she began putting on her things in silence. Liharev wrapped her up, chatting gaily, but every word he said lay on her heart like a weight. It is not cheering to hear the unhappy or the dying jest.

When the transformation of a live person into a shapeless bundle had been completed, Mlle. Ilovaisky looked for the last time round the "travellers' room," stood a moment in silence, and slowly walked out. Liharev went to see her off. . . .

Outside, God alone knows why, the winter was raging still. Whole clouds of big soft snowflakes were whirling restlessly over the earth, unable to find a resting-place. The horses, the sledge, the trees, a bull tied to a post, all were white and seemed soft and fluffy.

"Well, God help you," muttered Liharev, tucking her into the sledge. "Don't remember evil against me. . . ."

She was silent. When the sledge started, and had to go round a huge snowdrift, she looked back at Liharev with an expression as though she wanted to say something to him. He ran up to her, but she did not say a word to him, she only looked at him through her long eyelashes with little specks of snow on them.

Whether his finely intuitive soul were really able to read that look, or whether his imagination deceived him, it suddenly began to seem to him that with another touch or two that girl would have forgiven him his failures, his age, his desolate position, and would have followed him without question or reasonings. He stood a long while as though rooted to the spot, gazing at the tracks left by the sledge runners. The snowflakes greedily settled on his hair, his beard, his shoulders. . . . Soon the track of the runners had vanished, and he himself covered with snow, began to look like a white rock, but still his eyes kept seeking something in the clouds of snow.

Easter Eve

I was standing on the bank of the River Goltva, waiting for the ferry-boat from the other side. At ordinary times the Goltva is a humble stream of moderate size, silent and pensive, gently glimmering from behind thick reeds; but now a regular lake lay stretched out before me. The waters of spring, running riot, had overflowed both banks and flooded both sides of the river for a long distance, submerging vegetable gardens, hayfields and marshes, so that it was no unusual thing to meet poplars and bushes sticking out above the surface of the water and looking in the darkness like grim solitary crags.

The weather seemed to me magnificent. It was dark, yet I could see the trees, the water and the people. . . . The world was lighted by the stars, which were scattered thickly all over the sky. I don't remember ever seeing so many stars. Literally one could not have put a finger in between them. There were some as big as a goose's egg, others tiny as hempseed. . . . They had come out for the festival procession, every one of them, little and big, washed, renewed and joyful, and every one of them was softly twinkling its beams. The sky was reflected in the water; the stars were bathing in its dark depths and trembling with the quivering eddies. The air was warm and still. . . . Here and there, far away on the further bank in the impenetrable darkness, several bright red lights were gleaming. . . .

A couple of paces from me I saw the dark silhouette of a peasant in a high hat, with a thick knotted stick in his hand.

"How long the ferry-boat is in coming!" I said.

"It is time it was here," the silhouette answered.

"You are waiting for the ferry-boat, too?"

"No, I am not," yawned the peasant—"I am waiting for the illumination. I should have gone, but, to tell you the truth, I haven't the five kopecks for the ferry."

"I'll give you the five kopecks."

"No; I humbly thank you. . . . With that five kopecks put up a candle for me over there in the monastery. . . . That will be more interesting, and I will stand here. What can it mean, no ferry-boat, as though it had sunk in the water!"

The peasant went up to the water's edge, took the rope in his hands, and shouted: "Ieronim! Ieron—im!"

As though in answer to his shout, the slow peal of a great bell floated across from the further bank. The note was deep and low, as from the thickest string of a double bass; it seemed as though the darkness itself had hoarsely uttered it. At once there was the sound of a cannon shot. It rolled away in the darkness and ended somewhere in the far distance behind me. The peasant took off his hat and crossed himself.

"Christ is risen," he said.

Before the vibrations of the first peal of the bell had time to die away in the air a second sounded, after it at once a third, and the darkness was filled with an unbroken quivering clamour. Near the red lights fresh lights flashed, and all began moving together and twinkling restlessly.

"Ieron—im!" we heard a hollow prolonged shout.

"They are shouting from the other bank," said the peasant, "so there is no ferry there either. Our Ieronim has gone to sleep."

The lights and the velvety chimes of the bell drew one towards them. . . . I was already beginning to lose patience and grow anxious, but behold at last, staring into the dark distance, I saw the outline of something very much like a gibbet. It was the long-expected ferry. It moved towards us with such deliberation that if it had not been that its lines grew gradually more definite, one might have supposed that it was standing still or moving to the other bank.

"Make haste! Ieronim!" shouted my peasant. "The gentleman's tired of waiting!"

The ferry crawled to the bank, gave a lurch and stopped with a creak. A tall man in a monk's cassock and a conical cap stood on it, holding the rope.

"Why have you been so long?" I asked, jumping upon the ferry.

"Forgive me, for Christ's sake," Ieronim answered gently. "Is there no one else?"

"No one. . . ."

Ieronim took hold of the rope in both hands, bent himself to the figure of a mark of interrogation, and gasped. The ferry-boat creaked and gave a lurch. The outline of the peasant in the high hat began slowly retreating from me—so the ferry was moving off. Ieronim soon drew himself up and began working with one hand only. We were silent, gazing towards the bank to which we were floating. There the illumination for which the peasant was waiting had begun. At the water's edge barrels of tar were flaring like huge camp fires. Their reflections, crimson as the rising moon, crept to meet us in long broad streaks. The burning barrels lighted up their own smoke and the long shadows of men flitting about the fire; but further to one side and behind them from where the velvety chime floated there was still the same unbroken black gloom. All at once, cleaving the darkness, a rocket zigzagged in a golden ribbon up the sky; it described an arc and, as though broken to pieces against the sky, was scattered crackling into sparks. There was a roar from the bank like a far-away hurrah.

"How beautiful!" I said.

"Beautiful beyond words!" sighed Ieronim. "Such a night, sir! Another time one would pay no attention to the fireworks, but to-day one rejoices in every vanity. Where do you come from?"

I told him where I came from.

"To be sure . . . a joyful day to-day. . . ." Ieronim went on in a weak sighing tenor like the voice of a convalescent. "The sky is rejoicing and the earth, and what is under the earth. All the creatures are keeping holiday. Only tell me, kind sir, why, even in the time of great rejoicing, a man cannot forget his sorrows?"

I fancied that this unexpected question was to draw me into one of those endless religious conversations which bored and idle monks are so fond of. I was not disposed to talk much, and so I only asked:

"What sorrows have you, father?"

"As a rule only the same as all men, kind sir, but to-day a special sorrow has happened in the monastery: at mass, during the reading of the Bible, the monk and deacon Nikolay died."

"Well, it's God's will!" I said, falling into the monastic tone. "We must all die. To my mind, you ought to rejoice indeed. . . . They say if anyone dies at Easter he goes straight to the kingdom of heaven."

"That's true."

We sank into silence. The figure of the peasant in the high hat melted into the lines of the bank. The tar barrels were flaring up more and more.

"The Holy Scripture points clearly to the vanity of sorrow, and so does reflection," said Ieronim, breaking the silence; "but why does the heart grieve and refuse to listen to reason? Why does one want to weep bitterly?"

Ieronim shrugged his shoulders, turned to me and said quickly:

"If I died, or anyone else, it would not be worth notice, perhaps; but, you see, Nikolay is dead! No one else but Nikolay! Indeed, it's hard to believe that he is no more! I stand here on my ferry-boat and every minute I keep fancying that he will lift up his voice from the bank. He always used to come to the bank and call to me that I might not be afraid on the ferry. He used to get up from his bed at night on purpose for that. He was a kind soul. My God! how kindly and gracious! Many a mother is not so good to her child as Nikolay was to me! Lord, save his soul!"

Ieronim took hold of the rope, but turned to me again at once.

"And such a lofty intelligence, your honour," he said in a vibrating voice. "Such a sweet and harmonious tongue! Just as they will sing immediately at early matins: 'Oh lovely! oh sweet is Thy Voice!' Besides all other human qualities, he had, too, an extraordinary gift!"

"What gift?" I asked.

The monk scrutinized me, and as though he had convinced himself that he could trust me with a secret, he laughed good-humouredly.

"He had a gift for writing hymns of praise," he said. "It was a marvel, sir; you couldn't call it anything else! You will be amazed if I tell you about it. Our Father Archimandrite comes from Moscow, the Father Sub-Prior studied at the Kazan academy, we have wise monks and elders, but, would you believe it, no one could write them; while Nikolay, a simple monk, a deacon, had not studied anywhere, and had not even any outer appearance of it, but he wrote them! A marvel! a real marvel!" Ieronim clasped his hands and, completely forgetting the rope, went on eagerly:

"The Father Sub-Prior has great difficulty in composing sermons; when he wrote the history of the monastery he worried all the brotherhood and drove a dozen times to town, while Nikolay wrote canticles! Hymns of praise! That's a very different thing from a sermon or a history!"

"Is it difficult to write them?" I asked.

"There's great difficulty!" Ieronim wagged his head. "You can do nothing by wisdom and holiness if God has not given you the gift. The monks who don't understand argue that you only need to know the life of the saint for whom you are writing the hymn, and to make it harmonize with the other hymns of praise. But that's a mistake, sir. Of course, anyone who writes canticles must know the life of the saint to perfection, to the least trivial detail. To be sure, one must make them harmonize with the other canticles and know where to begin and what to write about. To give you an instance, the first response begins everywhere with 'the chosen' or 'the elect.' . . . The first line must always begin with the 'angel.' In the canticle of praise to Jesus the Most Sweet, if you are interested in the subject, it begins like this: 'Of angels Creator and Lord of all powers!' In the canticle to the Holy Mother of God: 'Of angels the foremost sent down from on high,' to Nikolay, the Wonder-worker—'an angel in semblance, though in substance a man,' and so on. Everywhere you begin with the angel. Of course, it would be impossible without making them harmonize, but the lives of the saints and conformity with the others is not what matters; what matters is the beauty and sweetness of it. Everything must be harmonious, brief and complete. There must be in every line softness, graciousness and tenderness; not one word should be harsh or rough or unsuitable. It must be written so that the worshipper may rejoice at heart and weep, while his mind is stirred and he is thrown into a tremor. In the canticle to the Holy Mother are the words: 'Rejoice, O Thou too high for human thought to reach! Rejoice, O Thou too deep for angels' eyes to fathom!' In another place in the same canticle: 'Rejoice, O tree that bearest the fair fruit of light that is the food of the faithful! Rejoice, O tree of gracious spreading shade, under which there is shelter for multitudes!' "

Ieronim hid his face in his hands, as though frightened at something or overcome with shame, and shook his head.

"Tree that bearest the fair fruit of light . . . tree of gracious spreading shade, . . ." he muttered. "To think that a man should find words like those! Such a power is a gift from God! For brevity he packs many thoughts into one phrase, and how smooth and complete it all is! 'Light-radiating torch to all that be . . .' comes in the canticle to Jesus the Most Sweet. 'Light-radiating!' There is no such word in conversation or in books, but you see he invented it, he found it in his mind! Apart from the smoothness and grandeur of language, sir, every line must be beautified in every way; there must be flowers and lightning and wind and sun and all the objects of the visible world. And every exclamation ought to be put so as to be smooth and easy for the ear. 'Rejoice, thou flower of heavenly growth!' comes in the hymn to Nikolay the Wonder-worker. It's not simply 'heavenly flower,' but 'flower of heavenly growth.' It's smoother so and sweet to the ear. That was just as Nikolay wrote it! exactly like that! I can't tell you how he used to write!"

"Well, in that case it is a pity he is dead," I said; "but let us get on, father, or we shall be late."

Ieronim started and ran to the rope; they were beginning to peal all the bells. Probably the procession was already going on near the monastery, for all the dark space behind the tar barrels was now dotted with moving lights.

"Did Nikolay print his hymns?" I asked Ieronim.

"How could he print them?" he sighed. "And, indeed, it would be strange to print them. What would be the object? No one in the monastery takes any interest in them. They don't like them. They knew Nikolay wrote them, but they let it pass unnoticed. No one esteems new writings nowadays, sir!"

"Were they prejudiced against him?"

"Yes, indeed. If Nikolay had been an elder perhaps the brethren would have been interested, but he wasn't forty, you know. There were some who laughed and even thought his writing a sin."

"What did he write them for?"

"Chiefly for his own comfort. Of all the brotherhood, I was the only one who read his hymns. I used to go to him in secret, that no one else might know of it, and he was glad that I took an interest in them. He would embrace me, stroke my head, speak to me in caressing words as to a little child. He would shut his cell, make me sit down beside him, and begin to read. . . ."

Ieronim left the rope and came up to me.

"We were dear friends in a way," he whispered, looking at me with shining eyes. "Where he went I would go. If I were not there he would miss me. And he cared more for me than for anyone, and all because I used to weep over his hymns. It makes me sad to remember. Now I feel just like an orphan or a widow. You know, in our monastery they are all good people, kind and pious, but . . . there is no one with softness and refinement, they are just like peasants. They all speak loudly, and tramp heavily when they walk; they are noisy, they clear their throats, but Nikolay always talked softly, caressingly, and if he noticed that anyone was asleep or praying he would slip by like a fly or a gnat. His face was tender, compassionate. . . ."

Ieronim heaved a deep sigh and took hold of the rope again. We were by now approaching the bank. We floated straight out of the darkness and stillness of the river into an enchanted realm, full of stifling smoke, crackling lights and uproar. By now one could distinctly see people moving near the tar barrels. The flickering of the lights gave a strange, almost fantastic, expression to their figures and red faces. From time to time one caught among the heads and faces a glimpse of a horse's head motionless as though cast in copper.

"They'll begin singing the Easter hymn directly, . . ." said Ieronim, "and Nikolay is gone; there is no one to appreciate it. . . . There was nothing written dearer to him than that hymn. He used to take in every word! You'll be there, sir, so notice what is sung; it takes your breath away!"

"Won't you be in church, then?"

"I can't; . . . I have to work the ferry. . . ."

"But won't they relieve you?"

"I don't know. . . . I ought to have been relieved at eight; but, as you see, they don't come! . . . And I must own I should have liked to be in the church. . . ."

"Are you a monk?"

"Yes . . . that is, I am a lay brother."

The ferry ran into the bank and stopped. I thrust a five kopeck piece into Ieronim's hand for taking me across, and jumped on land. Immediately a cart with a boy and a sleeping woman in it drove creaking onto the ferry. Ieronim, with a faint glow from the lights on his figure, pressed on the rope, bent down to it, and started the ferry back. . . .

I took a few steps through mud, but a little farther walked on a soft freshly trodden path. This path led to the dark monastery gates, that looked like a cavern through a cloud of smoke, through a disorderly crowd of people, unharnessed horses, carts and chaises. All this crowd was rattling, snorting, laughing, and the crimson light and wavering shadows from the smoke flickered over it all. . . . A perfect chaos! And in this subbub the people yet found room to load a little cannon and to sell cakes. There was no less commotion on the other side of the wall in the monastery precincts, but there was more regard for decorum and order. Here there was a smell of juniper and incense. They talked loudly, but there was no sound of laughter or snorting. Near the tombstones and crosses people pressed close to one another with Easter cakes and bundles in their arms. Apparently many had come from a long distance for their cakes to be blessed and now were exhausted. Young lay brothers, making a metallic sound with their boots, ran busily along the iron slabs that paved the way from the monastery gates to the church door. They were busy and shouting on the belfry, too.

"What a restless night!" I thought. "How nice!"

One was tempted to see the same unrest and sleeplessness in all nature, from the night darkness to the iron slabs, the crosses on the tombs and the trees under which the people were moving to and fro. But nowhere was the excitement and restlessness so marked as in the church. An unceasing struggle was going on in the entrance between the inflowing stream and the outflowing stream. Some were going in, others going out and soon coming back again to stand still for a little and begin moving again. People were scurrying from place to place, lounging about as though they were looking for something. The stream flowed from the entrance all round the church, disturbing even the front rows, where persons of weight and dignity were standing. There could be no thought of concentrated prayer. There were no prayers at all, but a sort of continuous, childishly irresponsible joy, seeking a pretext to break out and vent itself in some movement, even in senseless jostling and shoving.

The same unaccustomed movement is striking in the Easter service itself. The altar gates are flung wide open, thick clouds of incense float in the air near the candelabra; wherever one looks there are lights, the gleam and splutter of candles. . . . There is no reading; restless and light-hearted singing goes on to the end without ceasing. After each hymn the clergy change their vestments and come out to burn incense, which is repeated every ten minutes.

I had no sooner taken a place, when a wave rushed from in front and forced me back. A tall thick-set deacon walked before me with a long red candle; the grey-headed archimandrite in his golden mitre hurried after him with the censer. When they had vanished from sight the crowd squeezed me back to my former position. But ten minutes had not passed before a new wave burst on me, and again the deacon appeared. This time he was followed by the Father Sub-Prior, the man who, as Ieronim had told me, was writing the history of the monastery.

As I mingled with the crowd and caught the infection of the universal joyful excitement, I felt unbearably sore on Ieronim's account. Why did they not send someone to relieve him? Why could not someone of less feeling and less susceptibility go on the ferry? "Lift up thine eyes, O Sion, and look around," they sang in the choir, "for thy children have come to thee as to a beacon of divine light from north and south, and from east and from the sea. . . ."

I looked at the faces; they all had a lively expression of triumph, but not one was listening to what was being sung and taking it in, and not one was "holding his breath." Why was not Ieronim released? I could fancy Ieronim standing meekly somewhere by the wall, bending forward and hungrily drinking in the beauty of the holy phrase. All this that glided by the ears of people standing by me he would have eagerly drunk in with his delicately sensitive soul, and would have been spell-bound to ecstasy, to holding his breath, and there would not have been a man happier than he in all the church. Now he was plying to and fro over the dark river and grieving for his dead friend and brother.

The wave surged back. A stout smiling monk, playing with his rosary and looking round behind him, squeezed sideways by me, making way for a lady in a hat and velvet cloak. A monastery servant hurried after the lady, holding a chair over our heads.

I came out of the church. I wanted to have a look at the dead Nikolay, the unknown canticle writer. I walked about the monastery wall, where there was a row of cells, peeped into several windows, and, seeing nothing, came back again. I do not regret now that I did not see Nikolay; God knows, perhaps if I had seen him I should have lost the picture my imagination paints for me now. I imagine that lovable poetical figure, solitary and not understood, who went out at nights to call to Ieronim over the water, and filled his hymns with flowers, stars and sunbeams, as a pale timid man with soft, mild, melancholy features. His eyes must have shone, not only with intelligence, but with kindly tenderness and that hardly restrained childlike enthusiasm which I could hear in Ieronim's voice when he quoted to me passages from the hymns.

When we came out of church after mass it was no longer night. The morning was beginning. The stars had gone out and the sky was a morose greyish blue. The iron slabs, the tombstones and the buds on the trees were covered with dew. There was a sharp freshness in the air. Outside the precincts I did not find the same animated scene as I had beheld in the night. Horses and men looked exhausted, drowsy, scarcely moved, while nothing was left of the tar barrels but heaps of black ash. When anyone is exhausted and sleepy he fancies that nature, too, is in the same condition. It seemed to me that the trees and the young grass were asleep. It seemed as though even the bells were not pealing so loudly and gaily as at night. The restlessness was over, and of the excitement nothing was left but a pleasant weariness, a longing for sleep and warmth.

Now I could see both banks of the river; a faint mist hovered over it in shifting masses. There was a harsh cold breath from the water. When I jumped on to the ferry, a chaise and some two dozen men and women were standing on it already. The rope, wet and as I fancied drowsy, stretched far away across the broad river and in places disappeared in the white mist.

"Christ is risen! Is there no one else?" asked a soft voice.

I recognized the voice of Ieronim. There was no darkness now to hinder me from seeing the monk. He was a tall narrow-shouldered man of five-and-thirty, with large rounded features, with half-closed listless-looking eyes and an unkempt wedge-shaped beard. He had an extraordinarily sad and exhausted look.

"They have not relieved you yet?" I asked in surprise.

"Me?" he answered, turning to me his chilled and dewy face with a smile. "There is no one to take my place now till morning. They'll all be going to the Father Archimandrite's to break the fast directly."

With the help of a little peasant in a hat of reddish fur that looked like the little wooden tubs in which honey is sold, he threw his weight on the rope; they gasped simultaneously, and the ferry started.

We floated across, disturbing on the way the lazily rising mist. Everyone was silent. Ieronim worked mechanically with one hand. He slowly passed his mild lustreless eyes over us; then his glance rested on the rosy face of a young merchant's wife with black eyebrows, who was standing on the ferry beside me silently shrinking from the mist that wrapped her about. He did not take his eyes off her face all the way.

There was little that was masculine in that prolonged gaze. It seemed to me that Ieronim was looking in the woman's face for the soft and tender features of his dead friend.

The Beggar

"Kind sir, be so good as to notice a poor, hungry man. I have not tasted food for three days. ... I have not a five-kopeck piece for a night's lodging. ... I swear by God! For five years I was a village schoolmaster and lost my post through the intrigues of the Zemstvo. I was the victim of false witness. I have been out of a place for a year now."

Skvortsov, a Petersburg lawyer, looked at the speaker's tattered dark blue overcoat, at his muddy, drunken eyes, at the red patches on his cheeks, and it seemed to him that he had seen the man before.

"And now I am offered a post in the Kaluga province," the beggar continued, "but I have not the means for the journey there. Graciously help me! I am ashamed to ask, but ... I am compelled by circumstances."

Skvortsov looked at his goloshes, of which one was shallow like a shoe, while the other came high up the leg like a boot, and suddenly remembered.

"Listen, the day before yesterday I met you in Sadovoy Street," he said, "and then you told me, not that you were a village schoolmaster, but that you were a student who had been expelled. Do you remember?"

"N-o. No, that cannot be so!" the beggar muttered in confusion. "I am a village schoolmaster, and if you wish it I can show you documents to prove it."

"That's enough lies! You called yourself a student, and even told me what you were expelled for. Do you remember?"

Skvortsov flushed, and with a look of disgust on his face turned away from the ragged figure.

"It's contemptible, sir!" he cried angrily. "It's a swindle! I'll hand you over to the police, damn you! You are poor and hungry, but that does not give you the right to lie so shamelessly!"

The ragged figure took hold of the door-handle and, like a bird in a snare, looked round the hall desperately.

"I . . . I am not lying," he muttered. "I can show documents."

"Who can believe you?" Skvortsov went on, still indignant. "To exploit the sympathy of the public for village schoolmasters and students—it's so low, so mean, so dirty! It's revolting!"

Skvortsov flew into a rage and gave the beggar a merciless scolding. The ragged fellow's insolent lying aroused his disgust and aversion, was an offence against what he, Skvortsov, loved and prized in himself: kindliness, a feeling heart, sympathy for the unhappy. By his lying, by his treacherous assault upon compassion, the individual had, as it were, defiled the charity which he liked to give to the poor with no misgivings in his heart. The beggar at first defended himself, protested with oaths, then he sank into silence and hung his head, overcome with shame.

"Sir!" he said, laying his hand on his heart, "I really was . . . lying! I am not a student and not a village schoolmaster. All that's mere invention! I used to be in the Russian choir, and I was turned out of it for drunkenness. But what can I do? Believe me, in God's name, I can't get on without lying—when I tell the truth no one will give me anything. With the truth one may die of hunger and freeze without a night's lodging! What you say is true, I understand that, but . . . what am I to do?"

"What are you to do? You ask what are you to do?" cried Skvortsov, going close up to him. "Work—that's what you must do! You must work!"

"Work. . . . I know that myself, but where can I get work?"

"Nonsense. You are young, strong, and healthy, and could always find work if you wanted to. But you know you are lazy, pampered, drunken! You reek of vodka like a pothouse! You have become false and corrupt to the marrow of your bones and fit for nothing but begging and lying! If you do graciously condescend to take work, you must have a job in an office, in the Russian choir, or as a billiard-marker, where you will have a salary and have nothing to do! But how would you like to undertake manual labour? I'll be bound, you wouldn't be a house porter or a factory hand! You are too genteel for that!"

"What things you say, really . . ." said the beggar, and he gave a bitter smile. "How can I get manual work? It's rather late for me to be a shopman, for in trade one has to begin from a boy; no one would take me as a house porter, because I am not of that class. . . . And I could not get work in a factory; one must know a trade, and I know nothing."

"Nonsense! You always find some justification! Wouldn't you like to chop wood?"

"I would not refuse to, but the regular woodchoppers are out of work now."

"Oh, all idlers argue like that! As soon as you are offered anything you refuse it. Would you care to chop wood for me?"

"Certainly I will. . . ."

"Very good, we shall see. . . . Excellent. . . . We'll see!" Skvortsov, in nervous haste, and not without malignant pleasure, rubbing his hands, summoned his cook from the kitchen.

"Here, Olga," he said to her, "take this gentleman to the shed and let him chop some wood."

The beggar shrugged his shoulders as though puzzled, and irresolutely followed the cook. It was evident from his demeanour that he had consented to go and chop wood, not because he was hungry and wanted to earn money, but simply from shame and *amour propre*, because he had been taken at his word. It was clear, too, that he was suffering from the effects of vodka, that he was unwell, and felt not the faintest inclination to work.

Skvortsov hurried into the dining-room. There from the window which looked out into the yard he could see the woodshed and everything that happened in the yard. Standing at the window, Skvortsov saw the cook and the beggar come by the back way into the yard and go through the muddy snow to the woodshed. Olga scrutinized her companion angrily, and jerking her elbow unlocked the woodshed and angrily banged the door open.

"Most likely we interrupted the woman drinking her coffee," thought Skvortsov. "What a cross creature she is!"

Then he saw the pseudo-schoolmaster and pseudo-student seat himself on a block of wood, and, leaning his red cheeks upon his fists, sink into thought. The cook flung an axe at his feet, spat angrily on the ground, and, judging by the expression of her lips, began abusing him. The beggar drew a log of wood towards him irresolutely, set it up between his feet, and diffidently drew the axe across it. The log toppled and fell over. The beggar drew it towards him, breathed on his frozen hands, and again drew the axe along it as cautiously as though he were afraid of its hitting his golosh or chopping off his fingers. The log fell over again.

Skvortsov's wrath had passed off by now, he felt sore and ashamed at the thought that he had forced a pampered, drunken, and perhaps sick man to do hard, rough work in the cold.

"Never mind, let him go on . . ." he thought, going from the dining-room into his study. "I am doing it for his good!"

An hour later Olga appeared and announced that the wood had been chopped up.

"Here, give him half a rouble," said Skvortsov. "If he likes, let him come and chop wood on the first of every month. . . . There will always be work for him."

On the first of the month the beggar turned up and again earned half a rouble, though he could hardly stand. From that time forward he took to turning up frequently, and work was always found for him: sometimes he would sweep the snow into heaps, or clear up the shed, at another he used to beat the rugs and the mattresses. He always received thirty to forty kopecks for his work, and on one occasion an old pair of trousers was sent out to him.

When he moved, Skvortsov engaged him to assist in packing and moving the furniture. On this occasion the beggar was sober, gloomy, and silent; he scarcely touched the furniture, walked with hanging head behind the furniture vans, and did not even try to appear busy; he merely shivered with the cold, and was overcome with confusion when the men with the vans laughed at his idleness, feebleness, and ragged coat that had once been a gentleman's. After the removal Skvortsov sent for him.

"Well, I see my words have had an effect upon you," he said, giving him a rouble. "This is for your work. I see that you are sober and not disinclined to work. What is your name?"

"Lushkov."

"I can offer you better work, not so rough, Lushkov. Can you write?"

"Yes, sir."

"Then go with this note to-morrow to my colleague and he will give you some copying to do. Work, don't drink, and don't forget what I said to you. Good-bye."

Skvortsov, pleased that he had put a man in the path of rectitude, patted Lushkov genially on the shoulder, and even shook hands with him at parting. Lushkov took the letter, departed, and from that time forward did not come to the back-yard for work.

Two years passed. One day as Skvortsov was standing at the ticket-office of a theatre, paying for his ticket, he saw beside him a little man with a lambskin collar and a shabby cat's-skin cap. The man timidly asked the clerk for a gallery ticket and paid for it with kopecks.

"Lushkov, is it you?" asked Skvortsov, recognizing in the little man his former woodchopper. "Well, what are you doing? Are you getting on all right?"

"Pretty well. . . . I am in a notary's office now. I earn thirty-five roubles."

"Well, thank God, that's capital. I rejoice for you. I am very, very glad, Lushkov. You know, in a way, you are my godson. It was I who shoved you into the right way. Do you remember what a scolding I gave you, eh? You almost sank through the floor that time. Well, thank you, my dear fellow, for remembering my words."

"Thank you too," said Lushkov. "If I had not come to you that day, maybe I should be calling myself a schoolmaster or a student still. Yes, in your house I was saved, and climbed out of the pit."

"I am very, very glad."

"Thank you for your kind words and deeds. What you said that day was excellent. I am grateful to you and to your cook, God bless that kind, noble-hearted woman. What you said that day was excellent; I am indebted to you as long as I live, of course, but it was your cook, Olga, who really saved me."

"How was that?"

"Why, it was like this. I used to come to you to chop wood and she would begin: 'Ah, you drunkard! You God-forsaken man! And yet death does not take you!' and then she would sit opposite me, lamenting, looking into my face and wailing: 'You unlucky fellow! You have no gladness in this world, and in the next you will burn in hell, poor drunkard! You poor sorrowful creature!' and she always went on in that style, you know. How often she upset herself, and how many tears she shed over me I can't tell you. But what affected me most—she chopped the wood for me! Do you know, sir, I never chopped a single log for you—she did it all! How it was she saved me, how it was I changed, looking at her, and gave up drinking, I can't explain. I only know that what she said and the noble way she behaved brought about a change in my soul, and I shall never forget it. It's time to go up, though, they are just going to ring the bell."

Lushkov bowed and went off to the gallery.

An Inadvertence

Pyotr Petrovitch Strizhin, the nephew of Madame Ivanov, the colonel's widow—the man whose new goloshes were stolen last year,—came home from a christening party at two o'clock in the morning. To avoid waking the household he took off his things in the lobby, made his way on tiptoe to his room, holding his breath, and began getting ready for bed without lighting a candle.

Strizhin leads a sober and regular life. He has a sanctimonious expression of face, he reads nothing but religious and edifying books, but at the christening party, in his delight that Lyubov Spiridonovna had passed through her confinement successfully, he had permitted himself to drink four glasses of vodka and a glass of wine, the taste of which suggested something midway between vinegar and castor oil. Spirituous liquors are like sea-water and glory: the more you imbibe of them the greater your thirst. And now as he undressed, Strizhin was aware of an overwhelming craving for drink.

"I believe Dashenka has some vodka in the cupboard in the right-hand corner," he thought. "If I drink one wine-glassful, she won't notice it."

After some hesitation, overcoming his fears, Strizhin went to the cupboard. Cautiously opening the door he felt in the right-hand corner for a bottle and poured out a wine-glassful, put the bottle back in its place, then, making the sign of the cross, drank it off. And immediately something like a miracle took place. Strizhin was flung back from the cupboard to the chest with fearful force like a bomb. There were flashes before his eyes, he felt as though he could not breathe, and all over his body he had a sensation as though he had fallen into a marsh full of leeches. It seemed to him as though, instead of vodka, he had swallowed dynamite, which blew up his body, the house, and the whole street. . . . His head, his arms, his legs—all seemed to be torn off and to be flying away somewhere to the devil, into space.

For some three minutes he lay on the chest, not moving and scarcely breathing, then he got up and asked himself:

"Where am I?"

The first thing of which he was clearly conscious on coming to himself was the pronounced smell of paraffin.

"Holy saints," he thought in horror, "it's paraffin I have drunk instead of vodka."

The thought that he had poisoned himself threw him into a cold shiver, then into a fever. That it was really poison that he had taken was proved not only by the smell in the room but also by the burning taste in his mouth, the flashes before his eyes, the ringing in his head, and the colicky pain in his stomach. Feeling the approach of death and not buoying himself up with false hopes, he wanted to say good-bye to those nearest to him, and made his way to Dashenka's bedroom (being a widower he had his sister-in-law called Dashenka, an old maid, living in the flat to keep house for him).

"Dashenka," he said in a tearful voice as he went into the bedroom, "dear Dashenka!"

Something grumbled in the darkness and uttered a deep sigh.

"Dashenka."

"Eh? What?" A woman's voice articulated rapidly. "Is that you, Pyotr Petrovitch? Are you back already? Well, what is it? What has the baby been christened? Who was godmother?"

"The godmother was Natalya Andreyevna Velikosvyetsky, and the godfather Pavel Ivanitch Bezsonnitsin. . . . I . . . I believe, Dashenka, I am dying. And the baby has been christened Olimpiada, in honour of their kind patroness. . . . I . . . I have just drunk paraffin, Dashenka!"

"What next! You don't say they gave you paraffin there?"

"I must own I wanted to get a drink of vodka without asking you, and . . . and the Lord chastised me: by accident in the dark I took paraffin. . . . What am I to do?"

Dashenka, hearing that the cupboard had been opened without her permission, grew more wide-awake. . . . She quickly lighted a candle, jumped out of bed, and in her nightgown, a freckled, bony figure in curl-papers, padded with bare feet to the cupboard.

"Who told you you might?" she asked sternly, as she scrutinized the inside of the cupboard. "Was the vodka put there for you?"

"I . . . I haven't drunk vodka but paraffin, Dashenka . . ." muttered Strizhin, mopping the cold sweat on his brow.

"And what did you want to touch the paraffin for? That's nothing to do with you, is it? Is it put there for you? Or do you suppose paraffin costs nothing? Eh? Do you know what paraffin is now? Do you know?"

"Dear Dashenka," moaned Strizhin, "it's a question of life and death, and you talk about money!"

"He's drunk himself tipsy and now he pokes his nose into the cupboard!" cried Dashenka, angrily slamming the cupboard door. "Oh, the monsters, the tormentors! I'm a martyr, a miserable woman, no peace day or night! Vipers, basilisks, accursed Herods, may you suffer the same in the world to come! I am going to-morrow! I am a maiden lady and I won't allow you to stand before me in your underclothes! How dare you look at me when I am not dressed!"

And she went on and on. . . . Knowing that when Dashenka was enraged there was no moving her with prayers or vows or even by firing a cannon, Strizhin waved his hand in despair, dressed, and made up his mind to go to the doctor. But a doctor is only readily found when he is not wanted. After running through three streets and ringing five times at Dr. Tchepharyants's, and seven times at Dr. Bultyhin's, Strizhin raced off to a chemist's shop, thinking possibly the chemist could help him. There, after a long interval, a little dark and curly-headed chemist came out to him in his dressing gown, with drowsy eyes, and such a wise and serious face that it was positively terrifying.

"What do you want?" he asked in a tone in which only very wise and dignified chemists of Jewish persuasion can speak.

"For God's sake ... I entreat you ..." said Strizhin breathlessly, "give me something. I have just accidentally drunk paraffin, I am dying!"

"I beg you not to excite yourself and to answer the questions I am about to put to you. The very fact that you are excited prevents me from understanding you. You have drunk paraffin. Yes?"

"Yes, paraffin! Please save me!"

The chemist went coolly and gravely to the desk, opened a book, became absorbed in reading it. After reading a couple of pages he shrugged one shoulder and then the other, made a contemptuous grimace and, after thinking for a minute, went into the adjoining room. The clock struck four, and when it pointed to ten minutes past the chemist came back with another book and again plunged into reading.

"H'm," he said as though puzzled, "the very fact that you feel unwell shows you ought to apply to a doctor, not a chemist."

"But I have been to the doctors already. I could not ring them up."

"H'm ... you don't regard us chemists as human beings, and disturb our rest even at four o'clock at night, though every dog, every cat, can rest in peace. ... You don't try to understand anything, and to your thinking we are not people and our nerves are like cords."

Strizhin listened to the chemist, heaved a sigh, and went home.

"So I am fated to die," he thought.

And in his mouth was a burning and a taste of paraffin, there were twinges in his stomach, and a sound of boom, boom, boom in his ears. Every moment it seemed to him that his end was near, that his heart was no longer beating.

Returning home he made haste to write: "Let no one be blamed for my death," then he said his prayers, lay down and pulled the bedclothes over his head. He lay awake till morning expecting death, and all the time he kept fancying how his grave would be covered with fresh green grass and how the birds would twitter over it. ...

And in the morning he was sitting on his bed, saying with a smile to Dashenka:

"One who leads a steady and regular life, dear sister, is unaffected by any poison. Take me, for example. I have been on the verge of death. I was dying and in agony, yet now I am all right. There is only a burning in my mouth and a soreness in my throat, but I am all right all over, thank God. . . . And why? It's because of my regular life."

"No, it's because it's inferior paraffin!" sighed Dashenka, thinking of the household expenses and gazing into space. "The man at the shop could not have given me the best quality, but that at three farthings. I am a martyr, I am a miserable woman. You monsters! May you suffer the same, in the world to come, accursed Herods. . . ."

And she went on and on. . . .

Verotchka

Ivan Alexeyitch Ognev remembers how on that August evening he opened the glass door with a rattle and went out on to the verandah. He was wearing a light Inverness cape and a wide-brimmed straw hat, the very one that was lying with his top-boots in the dust under his bed. In one hand he had a big bundle of books and notebooks, in the other a thick knotted stick.

Behind the door, holding the lamp to show the way, stood the master of the house, Kuznetsov, a bald old man with a long grey beard, in a snow-white piqué jacket. The old man was smiling cordially and nodding his head.

"Good-bye, old fellow!" said Ognev.

Kuznetsov put the lamp on a little table and went out to the verandah. Two long narrow shadows moved down the steps towards the flower-beds, swayed to and fro, and leaned their heads on the trunks of the lime-trees.

"Good-bye and once more thank you, my dear fellow!" said Ivan Alexeyitch. "Thank you for your welcome, for your kindness, for your affection. . . . I shall never forget your hospitality as long as I live. You are so good, and your daughter is so good, and everyone here is so kind, so good-humoured and friendly . . . Such a splendid set of people that I don't know how to say what I feel!"

From excess of feeling and under the influence of the home-made wine he had just drunk, Ognev talked in a singing voice like a divinity student, and was so touched that he expressed his feelings not so much by words as by the blinking of his eyes and the twitching of his shoulders. Kuznetsov, who had also drunk a good deal and was touched, craned forward to the young man and kissed him.

"I've grown as fond of you as if I were your dog," Ognev went on. "I've been turning up here almost every day; I've stayed the night a dozen times. It's dreadful to think of all the home-made wine I've drunk. And thank you most of all for your co-operation and help. Without you I should have been busy here over my statistics till October. I shall put in my preface: 'I think it my duty to express my gratitude to the President of the District Zemstvo of N——, Kuznetsov, for his kind co-operation.' There is a brilliant future before statistics! My humble respects to Vera Gavrilovna, and tell the doctors, both the lawyers and your secretary, that I shall never forget their help! And now, old fellow, let us embrace one another and kiss for the last time!"

Ognev, limp with emotion, kissed the old man once more and began going down the steps. On the last step he looked round and asked: "Shall we meet again some day?"

"God knows!" said the old man. "Most likely not!"

"Yes, that's true! Nothing will tempt you to Petersburg and I am never likely to turn up in this district again. Well, good-bye!"

"You had better leave the books behind!" Kuznetsov called after him. "You don't want to drag such a weight with you. I would send them by a servant to-morrow!"

But Ognev was rapidly walking away from the house and was not listening. His heart, warmed by the wine, was brimming over with good-humour, friendliness, and sadness. He walked along thinking how frequently one met with good people, and what a pity it was that nothing was left of those meetings but memories. At times one catches a glimpse of cranes on the horizon, and a faint gust of wind brings their plaintive, ecstatic cry, and a minute later, however greedily one scans the blue distance, one cannot see a speck nor catch a sound; and like that, people with their faces and their words flit through our lives and are drowned in the past, leaving nothing except faint traces in the memory. Having been in the N—— District from the early spring, and having been almost every day at the friendly Kuznetsovs', Ivan Alexeyitch had become as much at home with the old man, his daughter, and the servants as though they were his own people; he had grown familiar with the whole house to the smallest detail, with the cosy verandah, the windings of the avenues, the silhouettes of the trees over the kitchen and the bath-house; but as soon as he was out of the gate all this would be changed to memory and would lose its meaning as reality for ever, and in a year or two all these dear images would grow as dim in his consciousness as stories he had read or things he had imagined.

"Nothing in life is so precious as people!" Ognev thought in his emotion, as he strode along the avenue to the gate. "Nothing!"

It was warm and still in the garden. There was a scent of the mignonette, of the tobacco-plants, and of the heliotrope, which were not yet over in the flower-beds. The spaces between the bushes and the tree-trunks were filled with a fine soft mist soaked through and through with moonlight, and, as Ognev long remembered, coils of mist that looked like phantoms slowly but perceptibly followed one another across the avenue. The moon stood high above the garden, and below it transparent patches of mist were floating eastward. The whole world seemed to consist of nothing but black silhouettes and wandering white shadows. Ognev, seeing the mist on a moonlight August evening almost for the first time in his life, imagined he was seeing, not nature, but a stage effect in which unskilful workmen, trying to light up the garden with white Bengal fire, hid behind the bushes and let off clouds of white smoke together with the light.

When Ognev reached the garden gate a dark shadow moved away from the low fence and came towards him.

"Vera Gavrilovna!" he said, delighted. "You here? And I have been looking everywhere for you; wanted to say good-bye. . . . Good-bye; I am going away!"

"So early? Why, it's only eleven o'clock."

"Yes, it's time I was off. I have a four-mile walk and then my packing. I must be up early to-morrow."

Before Ognev stood Kuznetsov's daughter Vera, a girl of one-and-twenty, as usual melancholy, carelessly dressed, and attractive. Girls who are dreamy and spend whole days lying down, lazily reading whatever they come across, who are bored and melancholy, are usually careless in their dress. To those of them who have been endowed by nature with taste and an instinct of beauty, the slight carelessness adds a special charm. When Ognev later on remembered her, he could not picture pretty Verotchka except in a full blouse which was crumpled in deep folds at the belt and yet did not touch her waist; without her hair done up high and a curl that had come loose from it on her forehead; without the knitted red shawl with ball fringe at the edge which hung disconsolately on Vera's shoulders in the evenings, like a flag on a windless day, and in the daytime lay about, crushed up, in the hall near the men's hats or on a box in the dining-room, where the old cat did not hesitate to sleep on it. This shawl and the folds of her blouse suggested a feeling of freedom and laziness, of good-nature and sitting at home. Perhaps because Vera attracted Ognev he saw in every frill and button something warm, naïve, cosy, something nice and poetical, just what is lacking in cold, insincere women that have no instinct for beauty.

Verotchka had a good figure, a regular profile, and beautiful curly hair. Ognev, who had seen few women in his life, thought her a beauty.

"I am going away," he said as he took leave of her at the gate. "Don't remember evil against me! Thank you for everything!"

In the same singing divinity student's voice in which he had talked to her father, with the same blinking and twitching of his shoulders, he began thanking Vera for her hospitality, kindness, and friendliness.

"I've written about you in every letter to my mother," he said. "If everyone were like you and your dad, what a jolly place the world would be! You are such a splendid set of people! All such genuine, friendly people with no nonsense about you."

"Where are you going to now?" asked Vera.

"I am going now to my mother's at Oryol; I shall be a fortnight with her, and then back to Petersburg and work."

"And then?"

"And then? I shall work all the winter and in the spring go somewhere into the provinces again to collect material. Well, be happy, live a hundred years ... don't remember evil against me. We shall not see each other again."

Ognev stooped down and kissed Vera's hand. Then, in silent emotion, he straightened his cape, shifted his bundle of books to a more comfortable position, paused, and said:

"What a lot of mist!"

"Yes. Have you left anything behind?"

"No, I don't think so. . . ."

For some seconds Ognev stood in silence, then he moved clumsily towards the gate and went out of the garden.

"Stay; I'll see you as far as our wood," said Vera, following him out.

They walked along the road. Now the trees did not obscure the view, and one could see the sky and the distance. As though covered with a veil all nature was hidden in a transparent, colourless haze through which her beauty peeped gaily; where the mist was thicker and whiter it lay heaped unevenly about the stones, stalks, and bushes or drifted in coils over the road, clung close to the earth and seemed trying not to conceal the view. Through the haze they could see all the road as far as the wood, with dark ditches at the sides and tiny bushes which grew in the ditches and caught the straying wisps of mist. Half a mile from the gate they saw the dark patch of Kuznetsov's wood.

"Why has she come with me? I shall have to see her back," thought Ognev, but looking at her profile he gave a friendly smile and said: "One doesn't want to go away in such lovely weather. It's quite a romantic evening, with the moon, the stillness, and all the etceteras. Do you know, Vera Gavrilovna, here I have lived twenty-nine years in the world and never had a romance. No romantic episode in my whole life, so that I only know by hearsay of rendezvous, 'avenues of sighs,' and kisses. It's not normal! In town, when one sits in one's lodgings, one does not notice the blank, but here in the fresh air one feels it. . . . One resents it!"

"Why is it?"

"I don't know. I suppose I've never had time, or perhaps it was I have never met women who. . . . In fact, I have very few acquaintances and never go anywhere."

For some three hundred paces the young people walked on in silence. Ognev kept glancing at Verotchka's bare head and shawl, and days of spring and summer rose to his mind one after another. It had been a period when far from his grey Petersburg lodgings, enjoying the friendly warmth of kind people, nature, and the work he loved, he had not had time to notice how the sunsets followed the glow of dawn, and how, one after another foretelling the end of summer, first the nightingale ceased singing, then the quail, then a little later the landrail. The days slipped by unnoticed, so that life must have been happy and easy. He began calling aloud how reluctantly he, poor and unaccustomed to change of scene and society, had come at the end of April to the N—— District, where he had expected dreariness, loneliness, and indifference to statistics, which he considered was now the foremost among the sciences. When he arrived on an April morning at the little town of N—— he had put up at the inn kept by Ryabuhin, the Old Believer, where for twenty kopecks a day they had given him a light, clean room on condition that he should not smoke indoors. After resting and finding who was the president of the District Zemstvo, he had set off at once on foot to Kuznetsov. He had to walk three miles through lush meadows and young copses. Larks were hovering in the clouds, filling the air with silvery notes, and rooks flapping their wings with sedate dignity floated over the green cornland.

"Good heavens!" Ognev had thought in wonder; "can it be that there's always air like this to breathe here, or is this scent only to-day, in honour of my coming?"

Expecting a cold business-like reception, he went in to Kuznetsov's diffidently, looking up from under his eyebrows and shyly pulling his beard. At first Kuznetsov wrinkled up his brows and could not understand what use the Zemstvo could be to the young man and his statistics; but when the latter explained at length what was material for statistics and how such material was collected, Kuznetsov brightened, smiled, and with childish curiosity began looking at his notebooks. On the evening of the same day Ivan Alexeyitch was already sitting at supper with the Kuznetsovs, was rapidly becoming exhilarated by their strong home-made wine, and looking at the calm faces and lazy movements of his new acquaintances, felt all over that sweet, drowsy indolence which makes one want to sleep and stretch and smile; while his new acquaintances looked at him good-naturedly and asked him whether his father and mother were living, how much he earned a month, how often he went to the theatre. . . .

Ognev recalled his expeditions about the neighbourhood, the picnics, the fishing parties, the visit of the whole party to the convent to see the Mother Superior Marfa, who had given each of the visitors a bead purse; he recalled the hot, endless typically Russian arguments in which the opponents, spluttering and banging the table with their fists, misunderstand and interrupt one another, unconsciously contradict themselves at every phrase, continually change the subject, and after arguing for two or three hours, laugh and say:

"Goodness knows what we have been arguing about! Beginning with one thing and going on to another!"

"And do you remember how the doctor and you and I rode to Shestovo?" said Ivan Alexeyitch to Vera as they reached the copse. "It was there that the crazy saint met us: I gave him a five-kopeck piece, and he crossed himself three times and flung it into the rye. Good heavens! I am carrying away such a mass of memories that if I could gather them together into a whole it would make a good nugget of gold! I don't understand why clever, perceptive people crowd into Petersburg and Moscow and don't come here. Is there more truth and freedom in the Nevsky and in the big damp houses than here? Really, the idea of artists, scientific men, and journalists all living crowded together in furnished rooms has always seemed to me a mistake."

Twenty paces from the copse the road was crossed by a small narrow bridge with posts at the corners, which had always served as a resting-place for the Kuznetsovs and their guests on their evening walks. From there those who liked could mimic the forest echo, and one could see the road vanish in the dark woodland track.

"Well, here is the bridge!" said Ognev. "Here you must turn back."

Vera stopped and drew a breath.

"Let us sit down," she said, sitting down on one of the posts. "People generally sit down when they say good-bye before starting on a journey."

Ognev settled himself beside her on his bundle of books and went on talking. She was breathless from the walk, and was looking, not at Ivan Alexeyitch, but away into the distance so that he could not see her face.

"And what if we meet in ten years' time?" he said. "What shall we be like then? You will be by then the respectable mother of a family, and I shall be the author of some weighty statistical work of no use to anyone, as thick as forty thousand such works. We shall meet and think of old days. . . . Now we are conscious of the present; it absorbs and excites us, but when we meet we shall not remember the day, nor the month, nor even the year in which we saw each other for the last time on this bridge. You will be changed, perhaps. . . . Tell me, will you be different?"

Vera started and turned her face towards him.

"What?" she asked.

"I asked you just now. . . ."

"Excuse me, I did not hear what you were saying."

Only then Ognev noticed a change in Vera. She was pale, breathing fast, and the tremor in her breathing affected her hands and lips and head, and not one curl as usual, but two, came loose and fell on her forehead. . . . Evidently she avoided looking him in the face, and, trying to mask her emotion, at one moment fingered her collar, which seemed to be rasping her neck, at another pulled her red shawl from one shoulder to the other.

"I am afraid you are cold," said Ognev. "It's not at all wise to sit in the mist. Let me see you back *nach-haus*."

Vera sat mute.

"What is the matter?" asked Ognev, with a smile. "You sit silent and don't answer my questions. Are you cross, or don't you feel well? Eh?"

Vera pressed the palm of her hand to the cheek nearest to Ognev, and then abruptly jerked it away.

"An awful position!" she murmured, with a look of pain on her face. "Awful!"

"How is it awful?" asked Ognev, shrugging his shoulders and not concealing his surprise. "What's the matter?"

Still breathing hard and twitching her shoulders, Vera turned her back to him, looked at the sky for half a minute, and said:

"There is something I must say to you, Ivan Alexeyitch. . . ."

"I am listening."

"It may seem strange to you. . . . You will be surprised, but I don't care. . . ."

Ognev shrugged his shoulders once more and prepared himself to listen.

"You see . . ." Verotchka began, bowing her head and fingering a ball on the fringe of her shawl. "You see . . . this is what I wanted to tell you. . . . You'll think it strange . . . and silly, but I . . . can't bear it any longer."

Vera's words died away in an indistinct mutter and were suddenly cut short by tears. The girl hid her face in her handkerchief, bent lower than ever, and wept bitterly. Ivan Alexeyitch cleared his throat in confusion and looked about him hopelessly, at his wits' end, not knowing what to say or do. Being unused to the sight of tears, he felt his own eyes, too, beginning to smart.

"Well, what next!" he muttered helplessly. "Vera Gavrilovna, what's this for, I should like to know? My dear girl, are you . . . are you ill? Or has someone been nasty to you? Tell me, perhaps I could, so to say . . . help you. . . ."

When, trying to console her, he ventured cautiously to remove her hands from her face, she smiled at him through her tears and said:

"I . . . love you!"

These words, so simple and ordinary, were uttered in ordinary human language, but Ognev, in acute embarrassment, turned away from Vera, and got up, while his confusion was followed by terror.

The sad, warm, sentimental mood induced by leave-taking and the home-made wine suddenly vanished, and gave place to an acute and unpleasant feeling of awkwardness. He felt an inward revulsion; he looked askance at Vera, and now that by declaring her love for him she had cast off the aloofness which so adds to a woman's charm, she seemed to him, as it were, shorter, plainer, more ordinary.

"What's the meaning of it?" he thought with horror. "But I . . . do I love her or not? That's the question!"

And she breathed easily and freely now that the worst and most difficult thing was said. She, too, got up, and looking Ivan Alexeyitch straight in the face, began talking rapidly, warmly, irrepressibly.

As a man suddenly panic-stricken cannot afterwards remember the succession of sounds accompanying the catastrophe that overwhelmed him, so Ognev cannot remember Vera's words and phrases. He can only recall the meaning of what she said, and the sensation her words evoked in him. He remembers her voice, which seemed stifled and husky with emotion, and the extraordinary music and passion of her intonation. Laughing, crying with tears glistening on her eyelashes, she told him that from the first day of their acquaintance he had struck her by his originality, his intelligence, his kind intelligent eyes, by his work and objects in life; that she loved him passionately, deeply, madly; that when coming into the house from the garden in the summer she saw his cape in the hall or heard his voice in the distance, she felt a cold shudder at her heart, a foreboding of happiness; even his slightest jokes had made her laugh; in every figure in his notebooks she saw something extraordinarily wise and grand; his knotted stick seemed to her more beautiful than the trees.

The copse and the wisps of mist and the black ditches at the side of the road seemed hushed listening to her, whilst something strange and unpleasant was passing in Ognev's heart. . . . Telling him of her love, Vera was enchantingly beautiful; she spoke eloquently and passionately, but he felt neither pleasure nor gladness, as he would have liked to; he felt nothing but compassion for Vera, pity and regret that a good girl should be distressed on his account. Whether he was affected by generalizations from reading or by the insuperable habit of looking at things objectively, which so often hinders people from living, but Vera's ecstasies and suffering struck him as affected, not to be taken seriously, and at the same time rebellious feeling whispered to him that all he was hearing and seeing now, from the point of view of nature and personal happiness, was more important than any statistics and books and truths. . . . And he raged and blamed himself, though he did not understand exactly where he was in fault.

To complete his embarrassment, he was absolutely at a loss what to say, and yet something he must say. To say bluntly, "I don't love you," was beyond him, and he could not bring himself to say "Yes," because however much he rummaged in his heart he could not find one spark of feeling in it. . . .

He was silent, and she meanwhile was saying that for her there was no greater happiness than to see him, to follow him wherever he liked this very moment, to be his wife and helper, and that if he went away from her she would die of misery.

"I cannot stay here!" she said, wringing her hands. "I am sick of the house and this wood and the air. I cannot bear the everlasting peace and aimless life, I can't endure our colourless, pale people, who are all as like one another as two drops of water! They are all good-natured and warm-hearted because they are all well-fed and know nothing of struggle or suffering. . . . I want to be in those big damp houses where people suffer, embittered by work and need. . . ."

And this, too, seemed to Ognev affected and not to be taken seriously. When Vera had finished he still did not know what to say, but it was impossible to be silent, and he muttered:

"Vera Gavrilovna, I am very grateful to you, though I feel I've done nothing to deserve such . . . feeling . . . on your part. Besides, as an honest man I ought to tell you that . . . happiness depends on equality— that is, when both parties are . . . equally in love. . . ."

But he was immediately ashamed of his mutterings and ceased. He felt that his face at that moment looked stupid, guilty, blank, that it was strained and affected. . . . Vera must have been able to read the truth on his countenance, for she suddenly became grave, turned pale, and bent her head.

"You must forgive me," Ognev muttered, not able to endure the silence. "I respect you so much that . . . it pains me. . . ."

Vera turned sharply and walked rapidly homewards. Ognev followed her.

"No, don't!" said Vera, with a wave of her hand. "Don't come; I can go alone."

"Oh, yes . . . I must see you home anyway."

Whatever Ognev said, it all to the last word struck him as loathsome and flat. The feeling of guilt grew greater at every step. He raged inwardly, clenched his fists, and cursed his coldness and his stupidity with women. Trying to stir his feelings, he looked at Verotchka's beautiful figure, at her hair and the traces of her little feet on the dusty road; he remembered her words and her tears, but all that only touched his heart and did not quicken his pulse.

"Ach! one can't force oneself to love," he assured himself, and at the same time he thought, "But shall I ever fall in love without? I am nearly thirty! I have never met anyone better than Vera and I never shall. . . . Oh, this premature old age! Old age at thirty!"

Vera walked on in front more and more rapidly, without looking back at him or raising her head. It seemed to him that sorrow had made her thinner and narrower in the shoulders.

"I can imagine what's going on in her heart now!" he thought, looking at her back. "She must be ready to die with shame and mortification! My God, there's so much life, poetry, and meaning in it that it would move a stone, and I . . . I am stupid and absurd!"

At the gate Vera stole a glance at him, and, shrugging and wrapping her shawl round her walked rapidly away down the avenue.

Ivan Alexeyitch was left alone. Going back to the copse, he walked slowly, continually standing still and looking round at the gate with an expression in his whole figure that suggested that he could not believe his own memory. He looked for Vera's footprints on the road, and could not believe that the girl who had so attracted him had just declared her love, and that he had so clumsily and bluntly "refused" her. For the first time in his life it was his lot to learn by experience how little that a man does depends on his own will, and to suffer in his own person the feelings of a decent kindly man who has against his will caused his neighbour cruel, undeserved anguish.

His conscience tormented him, and when Vera disappeared he felt as though he had lost something very precious, something very near and dear which he could never find again. He felt that with Vera a part of his youth had slipped away from him, and that the moments which he had passed through so fruitlessly would never be repeated.

When he reached the bridge he stopped and sank into thought. He wanted to discover the reason of his strange coldness. That it was due to something within him and not outside himself was clear to him. He frankly acknowledged to himself that it was not the intellectual coldness of which clever people so often boast, not the coldness of a conceited fool, but simply impotence of soul, incapacity for being moved by beauty, premature old age brought on by education, his casual existence, struggling for a livelihood, his homeless life in lodgings. From the bridge he walked slowly, as it were reluctantly, into the wood. Here, where in the dense black darkness glaring patches of moonlight gleamed here and there, where he felt nothing except his thoughts, he longed passionately to regain what he had lost.

And Ivan Alexeyitch remembers that he went back again. Urging himself on with his memories, forcing himself to picture Vera, he strode rapidly towards the garden. There was no mist by then along the road or in the garden, and the bright moon looked down from the sky as though it had just been washed; only the eastern sky was dark and misty. . . . Ognev remembers his cautious steps, the dark windows, the heavy scent of heliotrope and mignonette. His old friend Karo, wagging his tail amicably, came up to him and sniffed his hand. This was the one living creature who saw him walk two or three times round the house, stand near Vera's dark window, and with a deep sigh and a wave of his hand walk out of the garden.

An hour later he was in the town, and, worn out and exhausted, leaned his body and hot face against the gatepost of the inn as he knocked at the gate. Somewhere in the town a dog barked sleepily, and as though in response to his knock, someone clanged the hour on an iron plate near the church.

"You prowl about at night," grumbled his host, the Old Believer, opening the door to him, in a long nightgown like a woman's. "You had better be saying your prayers instead of prowling about."

When Ivan Alexeyitch reached his room he sank on the bed and gazed a long, long time at the light. Then he tossed his head and began packing.

Shrove Tuesday

"Pavel Vassilitch!" cries Pelageya Ivanovna, waking her husband. "Pavel Vassilitch! You might go and help Styopa with his lessons, he is sitting crying over his book. He can't understand something again!"

Pavel Vassilitch gets up, makes the sign of the cross over his mouth as he yawns, and says softly: "In a minute, my love!"

The cat who has been asleep beside him gets up too, straightens out its tail, arches its spine, and half-shuts its eyes. There is stillness. . . . Mice can be heard scurrying behind the wall-paper. Putting on his boots and his dressing-gown, Pavel Vassilitch, crumpled and frowning from sleepiness, comes out of his bedroom into the dining-room; on his entrance another cat, engaged in sniffing a marinade of fish in the window, jumps down to the floor, and hides behind the cupboard.

"Who asked you to sniff that!" he says angrily, covering the fish with a sheet of newspaper. "You are a pig to do that, not a cat. . . ."

From the dining-room there is a door leading into the nursery. There, at a table covered with stains and deep scratches, sits Styopa, a high-school boy in the second class, with a peevish expression of face and tear-stained eyes. With his knees raised almost to his chin, and his hands clasped round them, he is swaying to and fro like a Chinese idol and looking crossly at a sum book.

"Are you working?" asks Pavel Vassilitch, sitting down to the table and yawning. "Yes, my boy. . . . We have enjoyed ourselves, slept, and eaten pancakes, and to-morrow comes Lenten fare, repentance, and going to work. Every period of time has its limits. Why are your eyes so red? Are you sick of learning your lessons? To be sure, after pancakes, lessons are nasty to swallow. That's about it."

"What are you laughing at the child for?" Pelageya Ivanovna calls from the next room. "You had better show him instead of laughing at him. He'll get a one again to-morrow, and make me miserable."

"What is it you don't understand?" Pavel Vassilitch asks Styopa.

"Why this . . . division of fractions," the boy answers crossly. "The division of fractions by fractions. . . ."

"H'm . . . queer boy! What is there in it? There's nothing to understand in it. Learn the rules, and that's all. . . . To divide a fraction by a fraction you must multiply the numerator of the first fraction by the denominator of the second, and that will be the numerator of the quotient. . . . In this case, the numerator of the first fraction . . ."

"I know that without your telling me," Styopa interrupts him, flicking a walnut shell off the table. "Show me the proof."

"The proof? Very well, give me a pencil. Listen. . . . Suppose we want to divide seven eighths by two fifths. Well, the point of it is, my boy, that it's required to divide these fractions by each other. . . . Have they set the samovar?"

"I don't know."

"It's time for tea. . . . It's past seven. Well, now listen. We will look at it like this. . . . Suppose we want to divide seven eighths not by two fifths but by two, that is, by the numerator only. We divide it, what do we get?"

"Seven sixteenths."

"Right. Bravo! Well, the trick of it is, my boy, that if we . . . so if we have divided it by two then. . . . Wait a bit, I am getting muddled. I remember when I was at school, the teacher of arithmetic was called Sigismund Urbanitch, a Pole. He used to get into a muddle over every lesson. He would begin explaining some theory, get in a tangle, and turn crimson all over and race up and down the class-room as though someone were sticking an awl in his back, then he would blow his nose half a dozen times and begin to cry. But you know we were magnanimous to him, we pretended not to see it. 'What is it, Sigismund Urbanitch?' we used to ask him. 'Have you got toothache?' And what a set of young ruffians, regular cut-throats, we were, but yet we were magnanimous, you know! There weren't any boys like you in my day, they were all great hulking fellows, great strapping louts, one taller than another. For instance, in our third class, there was Mamahin. My goodness, he was a solid chap! You know, a regular maypole, seven feet high. When he moved, the floor shook; when he brought his great fist down on your back, he would knock the breath out of your body! Not only we boys, but even the teachers were afraid of him. So this Mamahin used to . . ."

Pelageya Ivanovna's footsteps are heard through the door. Pavel Vassilitch winks towards the door and says:

"There's mother coming. Let's get to work. Well, so you see, my boy," he says, raising his voice. "This fraction has to be multiplied by that one. Well, and to do that you have to take the numerator of the first fraction . . ."

"Come to tea!" cries Pelageya Ivanovna. Pavel Vassilitch and his son abandon arithmetic and go in to tea. Pelageya Ivanovna is already sitting at the table with an aunt who never speaks, another aunt who is deaf and dumb, and Granny Markovna, a midwife who had helped Styopa into the world. The samovar is hissing and puffing out steam which throws flickering shadows on the ceiling. The cats come in from the entry sleepy and melancholy with their tails in the air. . . .

"Have some jam with your tea, Markovna," says Pelageya Ivanovna, addressing the midwife. "To-morrow the great fast begins. Eat well to-day."

Markovna takes a heaped spoonful of jam hesitatingly as though it were a powder, raises it to her lips, and with a sidelong look at Pavel Vassilitch, eats it; at once her face is overspread with a sweet smile, as sweet as the jam itself.

"The jam is particularly good," she says. "Did you make it yourself, Pelageya Ivanovna, ma'am?"

"Yes. Who else is there to do it? I do everything myself. Styopotchka, have I given you your tea too weak? Ah, you have drunk it already. Pass your cup, my angel; let me give you some more."

"So this Mamahin, my boy, could not bear the French master," Pavel Vassilitch goes on, addressing his son. " 'I am a nobleman,' he used to shout, 'and I won't allow a Frenchman to lord it over me! We beat the French in 1812!' Well, of course they used to thrash him for it . . . thrash him dre-ead-fully, and sometimes when he saw they were meaning to thrash him, he would jump out of window, and off he would go! Then for five or six days afterwards he would not show himself at the school. His mother would come to the head-master and beg him for God's sake: 'Be so kind, sir, as to find my Mishka, and flog him, the rascal!' And the head-master would say to her: 'Upon my word, madam, our five porters aren't a match for him!' "

"Good heavens, to think of such ruffians being born," whispers Pelageya Ivanovna, looking at her husband in horror. "What a trial for the poor mother!"

A silence follows. Styopa yawns loudly, and scrutinises the China-man on the tea-caddy whom he has seen a thousand times already. Markovna and the two aunts sip tea carefully out of their saucers. The air is still and stifling from the stove. . . . Faces and gestures betray the sloth and repletion that comes when the stomach is full, and yet one must go on eating. The samovar, the cups, and the table-cloth are cleared away, but still the family sits on at the table. . . . Pelageya Ivanovna is continually jumping up and, with an expression of alarm on her face, running off into the kitchen, to talk to the cook about the supper. The two aunts go on sitting in the same position immov-ably, with their arms folded across their bosoms and doze, staring with their pewtery little eyes at the lamp. Markovna hiccups every minute and asks:

"Why is it I have the hiccups? I don't think I have eaten anything to account for it . . . nor drunk anything either. . . . Hic!"

Pavel Vassilitch and Styopa sit side by side, with their heads touch-ing, and, bending over the table, examine a volume of the "Neva" for 1878.

" 'The monument of Leonardo da Vinci, facing the gallery of

Victor Emmanuel at Milan.' I say! . . . After the style of a triumphal arch. . . . A cavalier with his lady. . . . And there are little men in the distance. . . ."

"That little man is like a schoolfellow of mine called Niskubin," says Styopa.

"Turn over. . . . 'The proboscis of the common house-fly seen under the microscope.' So that's a proboscis! I say—a fly. Whatever would a bug look like under a microscope, my boy? Wouldn't it be horrid!"

The old-fashioned clock in the drawing-room does not strike, but coughs ten times huskily as though it had a cold. The cook, Anna, comes into the dining-room, and plumps down at the master's feet.

"Forgive me, for Christ's sake, Pavel Vassilitch!" she says, getting up, flushed all over.

"You forgive me, too, for Christ's sake," Pavel Vassilitch responds unconcernedly.

In the same manner, Anna goes up to the other members of the family, plumps down at their feet, and begs forgiveness. She only misses out Markovna to whom, not being one of the gentry, she does not feel it necessary to bow down.

Another half-hour passes in stillness and tranquillity. The "Neva" is by now lying on the sofa, and Pavel Vassilitch, holding up his finger, repeats by heart some Latin verses he has learned in his childhood. Styopa stares at the finger with the wedding ring, listens to the unintelligible words, and dozes; he rubs his eyelids with his fists, and they shut all the tighter.

"I am going to bed . . ." he says, stretching and yawning.

"What, to bed?" says Pelageya Ivanovna. "What about supper before the fast?"

"I don't want any."

"Are you crazy?" says his mother in alarm. "How can you go without your supper before the fast? You'll have nothing but Lenten food all through the fast!"

Pavel Vassilitch is scared too.

"Yes, yes, my boy," he says. "For seven weeks mother will give you nothing but Lenten food. You can't miss the last supper before the fast."

"Oh dear, I am sleepy," says Styopa peevishly.

"Since that is how it is, lay the supper quickly," Pavel Vassilitch cries in a fluster. "Anna, why are you sitting there, silly? Make haste and lay the table."

Pelageya Ivanovna clasps her hands and runs into the kitchen with an expression as though the house were on fire.

"Make haste, make haste," is heard all over the house. "Styopotchka is sleepy. Anna! Oh dear me, what is one to do? Make haste."

Five minutes later the table is laid. Again the cats, arching their spines, and stretching themselves with their tails in the air, come into the dining-room. . . . The family begin supper. . . . No one is hungry, everyone's stomach is overfull, but yet they must eat.

A Bad Business

"Who goes there?"

No answer. The watchman sees nothing, but through the roar of the wind and the trees distinctly hears someone walking along the avenue ahead of him. A March night, cloudy and foggy, envelopes the earth, and it seems to the watchman that the earth, the sky, and he himself with his thoughts are all merged together into something vast and impenetrably black. He can only grope his way.

"Who goes there?" the watchman repeats, and he begins to fancy that he hears whispering and smothered laughter. "Who's there?"

"It's I, friend . . ." answers an old man's voice.

"But who are you?"

"I . . . a traveller."

"What sort of traveller?" the watchman cries angrily, trying to disguise his terror by shouting. "What the devil do you want here? You go prowling about the graveyard at night, you ruffian!"

"You don't say it's a graveyard here?"

"Why, what else? Of course it's the graveyard! Don't you see it is?"

"O-o-oh . . . Queen of Heaven!" there is a sound of an old man sighing. "I see nothing, my good soul, nothing. Oh the darkness, the darkness! You can't see your hand before your face, it is dark, friend. O-o-oh...."

"But who are you?"

"I am a pilgrim, friend, a wandering man."

"The devils, the nightbirds. . . . Nice sort of pilgrims! They are drunkards..." mutters the watchman, reassured by the tone and sighs of the stranger. "One's tempted to sin by you. They drink the day away and prowl about at night. But I fancy I heard you were not alone; it sounded like two or three of you."

"I am alone, friend, alone. Quite alone.... O-o-oh our sins...."

The watchman stumbles up against the man and stops.

"How did you get here?" he asks.

"I have lost my way, good man. I was walking to the Mitrievsky Mill and I lost my way."

"Whew! Is this the road to Mitrievsky Mill? You sheepshead! For the Mitrievsky Mill you must keep much more to the left, straight out of the town along the high road. You have been drinking and have gone a couple of miles out of your way. You must have had a drop in the town."

"I did, friend ... Truly I did; I won't hide my sins. But how am I to go now?"

"Go straight on and on along this avenue till you can go no farther, and then turn at once to the left and go till you have crossed the whole graveyard right to the gate. There will be a gate there.... Open it and go with God's blessing. Mind you don't fall into the ditch. And when you are out of the graveyard you go all the way by the fields till you come out on the main road."

"God give you health, friend. May the Queen of Heaven save you and have mercy on you. You might take me along, good man! Be merciful! Lead me to the gate."

"As though I had the time to waste! Go by yourself!"

"Be merciful! I'll pray for you. I can't see anything; one can't see one's hand before one's face, friend. . . . It's so dark, so dark! Show me the way, sir!"

"As though I had the time to take you about; if I were to play the nurse to everyone I should never have done."

"For Christ's sake, take me! I can't see, and I am afraid to go alone through the graveyard. It's terrifying, friend, it's terrifying; I am afraid, good man."

"There's no getting rid of you," sighs the watchman. "All right then, come along."

The watchman and the traveller go on together. They walk shoulder to shoulder in silence. A damp, cutting wind blows straight into their faces and the unseen trees murmuring and rustling scatter big drops upon them. . . . The path is almost entirely covered with puddles.

"There is one thing passes my understanding," says the watchman after a prolonged silence—"how you got here. The gate's locked. Did you climb over the wall? If you did climb over the wall, that's the last thing you would expect of an old man."

"I don't know, friend, I don't know. I can't say myself how I got here. It's a visitation. A chastisement of the Lord. Truly a visitation, the evil one confounded me. So you are a watchman here, friend?"

"Yes."

"The only one for the whole graveyard?"

There is such a violent gust of wind that both stop for a minute. Waiting till the violence of the wind abates, the watchman answers:

"There are three of us, but one is lying ill in a fever and the other's asleep. He and I take turns about."

"Ah, to be sure, friend. What a wind! The dead must hear it! It howls like a wild beast! O-o-oh."

"And where do you come from?"

"From a distance, friend. I am from Vologda, a long way off. I go from one holy place to another and pray for people. Save me and have mercy upon me, O Lord."

The watchman stops for a minute to light his pipe. He stoops down behind the traveller's back and lights several matches. The gleam of the first match lights up for one instant a bit of the avenue on the right, a white tombstone with an angel, and a dark cross; the light of the second match, flaring up brightly and extinguished by the wind, flashes like lightning on the left side, and from the darkness nothing stands out but the angle of some sort of trellis; the third match throws light to right and to left, revealing the white tombstone, the dark cross, and the trellis round a child's grave.

"The departed sleep; the dear ones sleep!" the stranger mutters, sighing loudly. "They all sleep alike, rich and poor, wise and foolish, good and wicked. They are of the same value now. And they will sleep till the last trump. The Kingdom of Heaven and peace eternal be theirs."

"Here we are walking along now, but the time will come when we shall be lying here ourselves," says the watchman.

"To be sure, to be sure, we shall all. There is no man who will not die. O-o-oh. Our doings are wicked, our thoughts are deceitful! Sins, sins! My soul accursed, ever covetous, my belly greedy and lustful! I have angered the Lord and there is no salvation for me in this world and the next. I am deep in sins like a worm in the earth."

"Yes, and you have to die."

"You are right there."

"Death is easier for a pilgrim than for fellows like us," says the watchman.

"There are pilgrims of different sorts. There are the real ones who are God-fearing men and watch over their own souls, and there are such as stray about the graveyard at night and are a delight to the devils. . . . Ye-es! There's one who is a pilgrim could give you a crack on the pate with an axe if he liked and knock the breath out of you."

"What are you talking like that for?"

"Oh, nothing . . . Why, I fancy here's the gate. Yes, it is. Open it, good man."

The watchman, feeling his way, opens the gate, leads the pilgrim out by the sleeve, and says:

"Here's the end of the graveyard. Now you must keep on through the open fields till you get to the main road. Only close here there will be the boundary ditch—don't fall in. . . . And when you come out on to the road, turn to the right, and keep on till you reach the mill. . . ."

"O-o-oh!" sighs the pilgrim after a pause, "and now I am thinking that I have no cause to go to Mitrievsky Mill. . . . Why the devil should I go there? I had better stay a bit with you here, sir. . . ."

"What do you want to stay with me for?"

"Oh . . . it's merrier with you! . . ."

"So you've found a merry companion, have you? You, pilgrim, are fond of a joke I see. . . ."

"To be sure I am," says the stranger, with a hoarse chuckle. "Ah, my dear good man, I bet you will remember the pilgrim many a long year!"

"Why should I remember you?"

"Why I've got round you so smartly. . . . Am I a pilgrim? I am not a pilgrim at all."

"What are you then?"

"A dead man. . . . I've only just got out of my coffin. . . . Do you remember Gubaryev, the locksmith, who hanged himself in carnival week? Well, I am Gubaryev himself! . . ."

"Tell us something else!"

The watchman does not believe him, but he feels all over such a cold, oppressive terror that he starts off and begins hurriedly feeling for the gate.

"Stop, where are you off to?" says the stranger, clutching him by the arm. "Aie, aie, aie . . . what a fellow you are! How can you leave me all alone?"

"Let go!" cries the watchman, trying to pull his arm away.

"Sto-op! I bid you stop and you stop. Don't struggle, you dirty dog! If you want to stay among the living, stop and hold your tongue till I tell you. It's only that I don't care to spill blood or you would have been a dead man long ago, you scurvy rascal. . . . Stop!"

The watchman's knees give way under him. In his terror he shuts his eyes, and trembling all over huddles close to the wall. He would like to call out, but he knows his cries would not reach any living thing. The stranger stands beside him and holds him by the arm. . . . Three minutes pass in silence.

"One's in a fever, another's asleep, and the third is seeing pilgrims on their way," mutters the stranger. "Capital watchmen, they are worth their salary! Ye-es, brother, thieves have always been cleverer than watchmen! Stand still, don't stir. . . ."

Five minutes, ten minutes pass in silence. All at once the wind brings the sound of a whistle.

"Well, now you can go," says the stranger, releasing the watchman's arm. "Go and thank God you are alive!"

The stranger gives a whistle too, runs away from the gate, and the watchman hears him leap over the ditch.

With a foreboding of something very dreadful in his heart, the watchman, still trembling with terror, opens the gate irresolutely and runs back with his eyes shut.

At the turning into the main avenue he hears hurried footsteps, and someone asks him, in a hissing voice: "Is that you, Timofey? Where is Mitka?"

And after running the whole length of the main avenue he notices a little dim light in the darkness. The nearer he gets to the light the more frightened he is and the stronger his foreboding of evil.

"It looks as though the light were in the church," he thinks. "And how can it have come there? Save me and have mercy on me, Queen of Heaven! And that it is."

The watchman stands for a minute before the broken window and looks with horror towards the altar. . . . A little wax candle which the thieves had forgotten to put out flickers in the wind that bursts in at the window and throws dim red patches of light on the vestments flung about and a cupboard overturned on the floor, on numerous footprints near the high altar and the altar of offerings.

A little time passes and the howling wind sends floating over the churchyard the hurried uneven clangs of the alarm-bell. . . .

Home

"Someone came from the Grigoryevs' to fetch a book, but I said you were not at home. The postman brought the newspaper and two letters. By the way, Yevgeny Petrovitch, I should like to ask you to speak to Seryozha. To-day, and the day before yesterday, I have noticed that he is smoking. When I began to expostulate with him, he put his fingers in his ears as usual, and sang loudly to drown my voice."

Yevgeny Petrovitch Bykovsky, the prosecutor of the circuit court, who had just come back from a session and was taking off his gloves in his study, looked at the governess as she made her report, and laughed.

"Seryozha smoking . . ." he said, shrugging his shoulders. "I can picture the little cherub with a cigarette in his mouth! Why, how old is he?"

"Seven. You think it is not important, but at his age smoking is a bad and pernicious habit, and bad habits ought to be eradicated in the beginning."

"Perfectly true. And where does he get the tobacco?"

"He takes it from the drawer in your table."

"Yes? In that case, send him to me."

When the governess had gone out, Bykovsky sat down in an arm-chair before his writing-table, shut his eyes, and fell to thinking. He pictured his Seryozha with a huge cigar, a yard long, in the midst of clouds of tobacco smoke, and this caricature made him smile; at the same time, the grave, troubled face of the governess called up memories of the long past, half-forgotten time when smoking aroused in his teachers and parents a strange, not quite intelligible horror. It really was horror. Children were mercilessly flogged and expelled from school, and their lives were made a misery on account of smoking, though not a single teacher or father knew exactly what was the harm or sinfulness of smoking. Even very intelligent people did not scruple to wage war on a vice which they did not understand. Yevgeny Petrovitch remembered the head-master of the high school, a very cultured and good-natured old man, who was so appalled when he found a high-school boy with a cigarette in his mouth that he turned pale, immediately summoned an emergency committee of the teachers, and sentenced the sinner to expulsion. This was probably a law of social life: the less an evil was understood, the more fiercely and coarsely it was attacked.

The prosecutor remembered two or three boys who had been expelled and their subsequent life, and could not help thinking that very often the punishment did a great deal more harm than the crime itself. The living organism has the power of rapidly adapting itself, growing accustomed and inured to any atmosphere whatever, otherwise man would be bound to feel at every moment what an irrational basis there often is underlying his rational activity, and how little of established truth and certainty there is even in work so responsible and so terrible in its effects as that of the teacher, of the lawyer, of the writer. . . .

And such light and discursive thoughts as visit the brain only when it is weary and resting began straying through Yevgeny Petrovitch's head; there is no telling whence and why they come, they do not remain long in the mind, but seem to glide over its surface without sinking deeply into it. For people who are forced for whole hours, and even days, to think by routine in one direction, such free private thinking affords a kind of comfort, an agreeable solace.

It was between eight and nine o'clock in the evening. Overhead, on the second storey, someone was walking up and down, and on the floor above that four hands were playing scales. The pacing of the man overhead who, to judge from his nervous step, was thinking of something harassing, or was suffering from toothache, and the monotonous scales gave the stillness of the evening a drowsiness that disposed to lazy reveries. In the nursery, two rooms away, the governess and Seryozha were talking.

"Pa-pa has come!" carolled the child. "Papa has co-ome. Pa! Pa! Pa!"

"Votre père vous appelle, allez vite!" cried the governess, shrill as a frightened bird. "I am speaking to you!"

"What am I to say to him, though?" Yevgeny Petrovitch wondered.

But before he had time to think of anything whatever his son Seryozha, a boy of seven, walked into the study.

He was a child whose sex could only have been guessed from his dress: weakly, white-faced, and fragile. He was limp like a hot-house plant, and everything about him seemed extraordinarily soft and tender: his movements, his curly hair, the look in his eyes, his velvet jacket.

"Good evening, papa!" he said, in a soft voice, clambering on to his father's knee and giving him a rapid kiss on his neck. "Did you send for me?"

"Excuse me, Sergey Yevgenitch," answered the prosecutor, removing him from his knee. "Before kissing we must have a talk, and a serious talk . . . I am angry with you, and don't love you any more. I tell you, my boy, I don't love you, and you are no son of mine. . . ."

Seryozha looked intently at his father, then shifted his eyes to the table, and shrugged his shoulders.

"What have I done to you?" he asked in perplexity, blinking. "I haven't been in your study all day, and I haven't touched anything."

"Natalya Semyonovna has just been complaining to me that you have been smoking. . . . Is it true? Have you been smoking?"

"Yes, I did smoke once. . . . That's true. . . ."

"Now you see you are lying as well," said the prosecutor, frowning to disguise a smile. "Natalya Semyonovna has seen you smoking twice. So you see you have been detected in three misdeeds: smoking, taking someone else's tobacco, and lying. Three faults."

"Oh yes," Seryozha recollected, and his eyes smiled. "That's true, that's true; I smoked twice: to-day and before."

"So you see it was not once, but twice. . . . I am very, very much displeased with you! You used to be a good boy, but now I see you are spoilt and have become a bad one."

Yevgeny Petrovitch smoothed down Seryozha's collar and thought: "What more am I to say to him!"

"Yes, it's not right," he continued. "I did not expect it of you. In the first place, you ought not to take tobacco that does not belong to you. Every person has only the right to make use of his own property; if he takes anyone else's . . . he is a bad man!" ("I am not saying the right thing!" thought Yevgeny Petrovitch.) "For instance, Natalya Semyonovna has a box with her clothes in it. That's her box, and we—that is, you and I—dare not touch it, as it is not ours. That's right, isn't it? You've got toy horses and pictures. . . . I don't take them, do I? Perhaps I might like to take them, but . . . they are not mine, but yours!"

"Take them if you like!" said Seryozha, raising his eyebrows. "Please don't hesitate, papa, take them! That yellow dog on your table is mine, but I don't mind. . . . Let it stay."

"You don't understand me," said Bykovsky. "You have given me the dog, it is mine now and I can do what I like with it; but I didn't give you the tobacco! The tobacco is mine." ("I am not explaining properly!" thought the prosecutor. "It's wrong! Quite wrong!") "If I want to smoke someone else's tobacco, I must first of all ask his permission. . . ."

Languidly linking one phrase on to another and imitating the language of the nursery, Bykovsky tried to explain to his son the meaning of property. Seryozha gazed at his chest and listened attentively (he liked talking to his father in the evening), then he leaned his elbow on the edge of the table and began screwing up his short-sighted eyes at the papers and the inkstand. His eyes strayed over the table and rested on the gum-bottle.

"Papa, what is gum made of?" he asked suddenly, putting the bottle to his eyes.

Bykovsky took the bottle out of his hands and set it in its place and went on:

"Secondly, you smoke. . . . That's very bad. Though I smoke it does not follow that you may. I smoke and know that it is stupid, I blame myself and don't like myself for it." ("A clever teacher, I am!" he thought.) "Tobacco is very bad for the health, and anyone who smokes dies earlier than he should. It's particularly bad for boys like you to smoke. Your chest is weak, you haven't reached your full strength yet, and smoking leads to consumption and other illness in weak people. Uncle Ignat died of consumption, you know. If he hadn't smoked, perhaps he would have lived till now."

Seryozha looked pensively at the lamp, touched the lamp-shade with his finger, and heaved a sigh.

"Uncle Ignat played the violin splendidly!" he said. "His violin is at the Grigoryevs' now."

Seryozha leaned his elbows on the edge of the table again, and sank into thought. His white face wore a fixed expression, as though he were listening or following a train of thought of his own; distress and something like fear came into his big staring eyes. He was most likely thinking now of death, which had so lately carried off his mother and Uncle Ignat. Death carries mothers and uncles off to the other world, while their children and violins remain upon the earth. The dead live somewhere in the sky beside the stars, and look down from there upon the earth. Can they endure the parting?

"What am I to say to him?" thought Yevgeny Petrovitch. "He's not listening to me. Obviously he does not regard either his misdoings or my arguments as serious. How am I to drive it home?"

The prosecutor got up and walked about the study.

"Formerly, in my time, these questions were very simply settled," he reflected. "Every urchin who was caught smoking was thrashed. The cowardly and faint-hearted did actually give up smoking, any who were somewhat more plucky and intelligent, after the thrashing took to carrying tobacco in the legs of their boots, and smoking in the barn. When they were caught in the barn and thrashed again, they would go away to smoke by the river ... and so on, till the boy grew up. My mother used to give me money and sweets not to smoke. Now that method is looked upon as worthless and immoral. The modern teacher, taking his stand on logic, tries to make the child form good principles, not from fear, nor from desire for distinction or reward, but consciously."

While he was walking about, thinking, Seryozha climbed up with his legs on a chair sideways to the table, and began drawing. That he might not spoil official paper nor touch the ink, a heap of half-sheets, cut on purpose for him, lay on the table together with a blue pencil.

"Cook was chopping up cabbage to-day and she cut her finger," he said, drawing a little house and moving his eyebrows. "She gave such a scream that we were all frightened and ran into the kitchen. Stupid thing! Natalya Semyonovna told her to dip her finger in cold water, but she sucked it. . . . And how could she put a dirty finger in her mouth! That's not proper, you know, papa!"

Then he went on to describe how, while they were having dinner, a man with a hurdy-gurdy had come into the yard with a little girl, who had danced and sung to the music.

"He has his own train of thought!" thought the prosecutor. "He has a little world of his own in his head, and he has his own ideas of what is important and unimportant. To gain possession of his attention, it's not enough to imitate his language, one must also be able to think in the way he does. He would understand me perfectly if I really were sorry for the loss of the tobacco, if I felt injured and cried. . . . That's why no one can take the place of a mother in bringing up a child, because she can feel, cry, and laugh together with the child. One can do nothing by logic and morality. What more shall I say to him? What?"

And it struck Yevgeny Petrovitch as strange and absurd that he, an experienced advocate, who spent half his life in the practice of reducing people to silence, forestalling what they had to say, and punishing them, was completely at a loss and did not know what to say to the boy.

"I say, give me your word of honour that you won't smoke again," he said.

"Word of hon-nour!" carolled Seryozha, pressing hard on the pencil and bending over the drawing. "Word of hon-nour!"

"Does he know what is meant by word of honour?" Bykovsky asked himself. "No, I am a poor teacher of morality! If some schoolmaster or one of our legal fellows could peep into my brain at this moment he would call me a poor stick, and would very likely suspect me of unnecessary subtlety. . . . But in school and in court, of course, all these wretched questions are far more simply settled than at home; here one has to do with people whom one loves beyond everything, and love is exacting and complicates the question. If this boy were not my son, but my pupil, or a prisoner on his trial, I should not be so cowardly, and my thoughts would not be racing all over the place!"

Yevgeny Petrovitch sat down to the table and pulled one of Seryozha's drawings to him. In it there was a house with a crooked roof, and smoke which came out of the chimney like a flash of lightning in zigzags up to the very edge of the paper; beside the house stood a soldier with dots for eyes and a bayonet that looked like the figure 4.

"A man can't be taller than a house," said the prosecutor.

Seryozha got on his knee, and moved about for some time to get comfortably settled there.

"No, papa!" he said, looking at his drawing. "If you were to draw the soldier small you would not see his eyes."

Ought he to argue with him? From daily observation of his son the prosecutor had become convinced that children, like savages, have their own artistic standpoints and requirements peculiar to them, beyond the grasp of grown-up people. Had he been attentively observed, Seryozha might have struck a grown-up person as abnormal. He thought it possible and reasonable to draw men taller than houses, and to represent in pencil, not only objects, but even his sensations. Thus he would depict the sounds of an orchestra in the form of smoke like spherical blurs, a whistle in the form of a spiral thread.... To his mind sound was closely connected with form and colour, so that when he painted letters he invariably painted the letter L yellow, M red, A black, and so on.

Abandoning his drawing, Seryozha shifted about once more, got into a comfortable attitude, and busied himself with his father's beard. First he carefully smoothed it, then he parted it and began combing it into the shape of whiskers.

"Now you are like Ivan Stepanovitch," he said, "and in a minute you will be like our porter. Papa, why is it porters stand by doors? Is it to prevent thieves getting in?"

The prosecutor felt the child's breathing on his face, he was continually touching his hair with his cheek, and there was a warm soft feeling in his soul, as soft as though not only his hands but his whole soul were lying on the velvet of Seryozha's jacket. He looked at the boy's big dark eyes, and it seemed to him as though from those wide pupils there looked out at him his mother and his wife and everything that he had ever loved.

"To think of thrashing him . . ." he mused. "A nice task to devise a punishment for him! How can we undertake to bring up the young? In old days people were simpler and thought less, and so settled problems boldly. But we think too much, we are eaten up by logic. . . . The more developed a man is, the more he reflects and gives himself up to subtleties, the more undecided and scrupulous he becomes, and the more timidity he shows in taking action. How much courage and self-confidence it needs, when one comes to look into it closely, to undertake to teach, to judge, to write a thick book. . . ."

It struck ten.

"Come, boy, it's bedtime," said the prosecutor. "Say good-night and go."

"No, papa," said Seryozha, "I will stay a little longer. Tell me something! Tell me a story. . . ."

"Very well, only after the story you must go to bed at once."

Yevgeny Petrovitch on his free evenings was in the habit of telling Seryozha stories. Like most people engaged in practical affairs, he did not know a single poem by heart, and could not remember a single fairy tale, so he had to improvise. As a rule he began with the stereotyped: "In a certain country, in a certain kingdom," then he heaped up all kinds of innocent nonsense and had no notion as he told the beginning how the story would go on, and how it would end. Scenes, characters, and situations were taken at random, impromptu, and the plot and the moral came of itself as it were, with no plan on the part of the story-teller. Seryozha was very fond of this improvisation, and the prosecutor noticed that the simpler and the less ingenious the plot, the stronger the impression it made on the child.

"Listen," he said, raising his eyes to the ceiling. "Once upon a time, in a certain country, in a certain kingdom, there lived an old, very old emperor with a long grey beard, and . . . and with great grey moustaches like this. Well, he lived in a glass palace which sparkled and glittered in the sun, like a great piece of clear ice. The palace, my boy, stood in a huge garden, in which there grew oranges, you know . . . bergamots, cherries . . . tulips, roses, and lilies-of-the-valley were in flower in it, and birds of different colours sang there.... Yes.... On the trees there hung little glass bells, and, when the wind blew, they rang so sweetly that one was never tired of hearing them. Glass gives a softer, tenderer note than metals. . . . Well, what next? There were fountains in the garden.... Do you remember you saw a fountain at Auntie Sonya's summer villa? Well, there were fountains just like that in the emperor's garden, only ever so much bigger, and the jets of water reached to the top of the highest poplar."

Yevgeny Petrovitch thought a moment, and went on:

"The old emperor had an only son and heir of his kingdom—a boy as little as you. He was a good boy. He was never naughty, he went to bed early, he never touched anything on the table, and altogether he was a sensible boy. He had only one fault, he used to smoke. . . ."

Seryozha listened attentively, and looked into his father's eyes without blinking. The prosecutor went on, thinking: "What next?" He spun out a long rigmarole, and ended like this:

"The emperor's son fell ill with consumption through smoking, and died when he was twenty. His infirm and sick old father was left without anyone to help him. There was no one to govern the kingdom and defend the palace. Enemies came, killed the old man, and destroyed the palace, and now there are neither cherries, nor birds, nor little bells in the garden.... That's what happened."

This ending struck Yevgeny Petrovitch as absurd and naïve, but the whole story made an intense impression on Seryozha. Again his eyes were clouded by mournfulness and something like fear; for a minute he looked pensively at the dark window, shuddered, and said, in a sinking voice:

"I am not going to smoke any more...."

When he had said good-night and gone away his father walked up and down the room and smiled to himself.

"They would tell me it was the influence of beauty, artistic form," he meditated. "It may be so but that's no comfort. It's not the right way, all the same.... Why must morality and truth never be offered in their crude form, but only with embellishments, sweetened and gilded like pills? It's not normal.... It's falsification ... deception ... tricks...."

He thought of the jurymen to whom it was absolutely necessary to make a "speech," of the general public who absorb history only from legends and historical novels, and of himself and how he had gathered an understanding of life not from sermons and laws, but from fables, novels, poems.

"Medicine should be sweet, truth beautiful, and man has had this foolish habit since the days of Adam . . . though, indeed, perhaps it is all natural, and ought to be so. . . . There are many deceptions and delusions in nature that serve a purpose."

He set to work, but lazy, intimate thoughts still strayed through his mind for a good while. Overhead the scales could no longer be heard, but the inhabitant of the second storey was still pacing from one end of the room to another.

Typhus

A young lieutenant called Klimov was travelling from Petersburg to Moscow in a smoking carriage of the mail train. Opposite him was sitting an elderly man with a shaven face like a sea captain's, by all appearances a well-to-do Finn or Swede. He pulled at his pipe the whole journey and kept talking about the same subject:

"Ha, you are an officer! I have a brother an officer too, only he is a naval officer. . . . He is a naval officer, and he is stationed at Kronstadt. Why are you going to Moscow?"

"I am serving there."

"Ha! And are you a family man?"

"No, I live with my sister and aunt."

"My brother's an officer, only he is a naval officer; he has a wife and three children. Ha!"

The Finn seemed continually surprised at something, and gave a broad idiotic grin when he exclaimed "Ha!" and continually puffed at his stinking pipe. Klimov, who for some reason did not feel well, and found it burdensome to answer questions, hated him with all his heart. He dreamed of how nice it would be to snatch the wheezing pipe out of his hand and fling it under the seat, and drive the Finn himself into another compartment.

"Detestable people these Finns and . . . Greeks," he thought. "Absolutely superfluous, useless, detestable people. They simply fill up space on the earthly globe. What are they for?"

And the thought of Finns and Greeks produced a feeling akin to sickness all over his body. For the sake of comparison he tried to think of the French, of the Italians, but his efforts to think of these people evoked in his mind, for some reason, nothing but images of organ-grinders, naked women, and the foreign oleographs which hung over the chest of drawers at home, at his aunt's.

Altogether the officer felt in an abnormal state. He could not arrange his arms and legs comfortably on the seat, though he had the whole seat to himself. His mouth felt dry and sticky; there was a heavy fog in his brain; his thoughts seemed to be straying, not only within his head, but outside his skull, among the seats and the people that were shrouded in the darkness of night. Through the mist in his brain, as through a dream, he heard the murmur of voices, the rumble of wheels, the slamming of doors. The sounds of the bells, the whistles, the guards, the running to and fro of passengers on the platforms, seemed more frequent than usual. The time flew by rapidly, imperceptibly, and so it seemed as though the train were stopping at stations every minute, and metallic voices crying continually:

"Is the mail ready?"

"Yes!" was repeatedly coming from outside.

It seemed as though the man in charge of the heating came in too often to look at the thermometer, that the noise of trains going in the opposite direction and the rumble of the wheels over the bridges was incessant. The noise, the whistles, the Finn, the tobacco smoke—all this mingling with the menace and flickering of the misty images in his brain, the shape and character of which a man in health can never recall, weighed upon Klimov like an unbearable nightmare. In horrible misery he lifted his heavy head, looked at the lamp in the rays of which shadows and misty blurs seemed to be dancing. He wanted to ask for water, but his parched tongue would hardly move, and he scarcely had strength to answer the Finn's questions. He tried to lie down more comfortably and go to sleep, but he could not succeed. The Finn several times fell asleep, woke up again, lighted his pipe, addressed him with his "Ha!" and went to sleep again; and still the lieutenant's legs could not get into a comfortable position, and still the menacing images stood facing him.

At Spirovo he went out into the station for a drink of water. He saw people sitting at the table and hurriedly eating.

"And how can they eat!" he thought, trying not to sniff the air, that smelt of roast meat, and not to look at the munching mouths—they both seemed to him sickeningly disgusting.

A good-looking lady was conversing loudly with a military man in a red cap, and showing magnificent white teeth as she smiled; and the smile, and the teeth, and the lady herself made on Klimov the same revolting impression as the ham and the rissoles. He could not understand how it was the military man in the red cap was not ill at ease, sitting beside her and looking at her healthy, smiling face.

When after drinking some water he went back to his carriage, the Finn was sitting smoking; his pipe was wheezing and squelching like a golosh with holes in it in wet weather.

"Ha!" he said, surprised; "what station is this?"

"I don't know," answered Klimov, lying down and shutting his mouth that he might not breathe the acrid tobacco smoke.

"And when shall we reach Tver?"

"I don't know. Excuse me, I . . . I can't answer. I am ill. I caught cold today."

The Finn knocked his pipe against the window-frame and began talking of his brother, the naval officer. Klimov no longer heard him; he was thinking miserably of his soft, comfortable bed, of a bottle of cold water, of his sister Katya, who was so good at making one comfortable, soothing, giving one water. He even smiled when the vision of his orderly Pavel, taking off his heavy stifling boots and putting water on the little table, flitted through his imagination. He fancied that if he could only get into his bed, have a drink of water, his nightmare would give place to sound healthy sleep.

"Is the mail ready?" a hollow voice reached him from the distance.

"Yes," answered a bass voice almost at the window.

It was already the second or third station from Spirovo.

The time was flying rapidly in leaps and bounds, and it seemed as though the bells, whistles, and stoppings would never end. In despair Klimov buried his face in the corner of the seat, clutched his head in his hands, and began again thinking of his sister Katya and his orderly Pavel, but his sister and his orderly were mixed up with the misty images in his brain, whirled round, and disappeared. His burning breath, reflected from the back of the seat, seemed to scald his face; his legs were uncomfortable; there was a draught from the window on his back; but, however wretched he was, he did not want to change his position.... A heavy nightmarish lethargy gradually gained possession of him and fettered his limbs.

When he brought himself to raise his head, it was already light in the carriage. The passengers were putting on their fur coats and moving about. The train was stopping. Porters in white aprons and with discs on their breasts were bustling among the passengers and snatching up their boxes. Klimov put on his great-coat, mechanically followed the other passengers out of the carriage, and it seemed to him that not he, but some one else was moving, and he felt that his fever, his thirst, and the menacing images which had not let him sleep all night, came out of the carriage with him. Mechanically he took his luggage and engaged a sledge-driver. The man asked him for a rouble and a quarter to drive to Povarsky Street, but he did not haggle, and without protest got submissively into the sledge. He still understood the difference of numbers, but money had ceased to have any value to him.

At home Klimov was met by his aunt and his sister Katya, a girl of eighteen. When Katya greeted him she had a pencil and exercise book in her hand, and he remembered that she was preparing for an examination as a teacher. Gasping with fever, he walked aimlessly through all the rooms without answering their questions or greetings, and when he reached his bed he sank down on the pillow. The Finn, the red cap, the lady with the white teeth, the smell of roast meat, the flickering blurs, filled his consciousness, and by now he did not know where he was and did not hear the agitated voices.

When he recovered consciousness he found himself in bed, undressed, saw a bottle of water and Pavel, but it was no cooler, nor softer, nor more comfortable for that. His arms and legs, as before, refused to lie comfortably; his tongue stuck to the roof of his mouth, and he heard the wheezing of the Finn's pipe. . . . A stalwart, black-bearded doctor was busy doing something beside the bed, brushing against Pavel with his broad back.

"It's all right, it's all right, young man," he muttered. "Excellent, excellent . . . goo-od, goo-od . . . !"

The doctor called Klimov "young man," said "goo-od" instead of "good" and "so-o" instead of "so."

"So-o . . . so-o . . . so-o," he murmured. "Goo-od, goo-od . . . ! Excellent, young man. . . . You mustn't lose heart!"

The doctor's rapid, careless talk, his well-fed countenance, and condescending "young man," irritated Klimov.

"Why do you call me 'young man'?" he moaned. "What familiarity! Damn it all!"

And he was frightened by his own voice. The voice was so dried up, so weak and peevish, that he would not have known it.

"Excellent, excellent!" muttered the doctor, not in the least offended. . . . "You mustn't get angry, so-o, so-o, so-o. . . ."

And the time flew by at home with the same startling swiftness as in the railway carriage. . . . The daylight was continually being replaced by the dusk of evening. The doctor seemed never to leave his bedside, and he heard at every moment his "so-o, so-o, so-o." A continual succession of people was incessantly crossing the bedroom. Among them were: Pavel, the Finn, Captain Yaroshevitch, Lance-Corporal Maximenko, the red cap, the lady with the white teeth, the doctor. They were all talking and waving their arms, smoking and eating. Once by daylight Klimov saw the chaplain of the regiment, Father Alexandr, who was standing before the bed, wearing a stole and with a prayer-book in his hand. He was muttering something with a grave face such as Klimov had never seen in him before. The lieutenant remembered that Father Alexandr used in a friendly way to call all the Catholic officers "Poles," and wanting to amuse him, he cried:

"Father, Yaroshevitch the Pole has climbed up a pole!"

But Father Alexandr, a light-hearted man who loved a joke, did not smile, but became graver than ever, and made the sign of the cross over Klimov. At night-time by turn two shadows came noiselessly in and out; they were his aunt and sister. His sister's shadow knelt down and prayed; she bowed down to the ikon, and her grey shadow on the wall bowed down too, so that two shadows were praying. The whole time there was a smell of roast meat and the Finn's pipe, but once Klimov smelt the strong smell of incense. He felt so sick he could not lie still, and began shouting:

"The incense! Take away the incense!"

There was no answer. He could only hear the subdued singing of the priest somewhere and some one running upstairs.

When Klimov came to himself there was not a soul in his bed-room. The morning sun was streaming in at the window through the lower blind, and a quivering sunbeam, bright and keen as the sword's edge, was flashing on the glass bottle. He heard the rattle of wheels— so there was no snow now in the street. The lieutenant looked at the ray, at the familiar furniture, at the door, and the first thing he did was to laugh. His chest and stomach heaved with delicious, happy, tickling laughter. His whole body from head to foot was overcome by a sensation of infinite happiness and joy in life, such as the first man must have felt when he was created and first saw the world. Klimov felt a passionate desire for movement, people, talk. His body lay a motionless block; only his hands stirred, but that he hardly noticed, and his whole attention was concentrated on trifles. He rejoiced in his breathing, in his laughter, rejoiced in the existence of the water-bottle, the ceiling, the sunshine, the tape on the curtains. God's world, even in the narrow space of his bedroom, seemed beautiful, varied, grand. When the doctor made his appearance, the lieutenant was thinking what a delicious thing medicine was, how charming and pleasant the doctor was, and how nice and interesting people were in general.

"So-o, so, so. . . . Excellent, excellent! . . . Now we are well again. . . . Goo-od, goo-od!" the doctor pattered.

The lieutenant listened and laughed joyously; he remembered the

Finn, the lady with the white teeth, the train, and he longed to smoke, to eat.

"Doctor," he said, "tell them to give me a crust of rye bread and salt, and . . . and sardines."

The doctor refused; Pavel did not obey the order, and did not go for the bread. The lieutenant could not bear this and began crying like a naughty child.

"Baby!" laughed the doctor. "Mammy, bye-bye!"

Klimov laughed, too, and when the doctor went away he fell into a sound sleep. He woke up with the same joyfulness and sensation of happiness. His aunt was sitting near the bed.

"Well, aunt," he said joyfully. "What has been the matter?"

"Spotted typhus."

"Really. But now I am well, quite well! Where is Katya?"

"She is not at home. I suppose she has gone somewhere from her examination."

The old lady said this and looked at her stocking; her lips began quivering, she turned away, and suddenly broke into sobs. Forgetting the doctor's prohibition in her despair, she said:

"Ah, Katya, Katya! Our angel is gone! Is gone!"

She dropped her stocking and bent down to it, and as she did so her cap fell off her head. Looking at her grey head and understanding nothing, Klimov was frightened for Katya, and asked:

"Where is she, aunt?"

The old woman, who had forgotten Klimov and was thinking only of her sorrow, said:

"She caught typhus from you, and is dead. She was buried the day before yesterday."

This terrible, unexpected news was fully grasped by Klimov's consciousness; but terrible and startling as it was, it could not overcome the animal joy that filled the convalescent. He cried and laughed, and soon began scolding because they would not let him eat.

Only a week later when, leaning on Pavel, he went in his dressing-gown to the window, looked at the overcast spring sky and listened to the unpleasant clang of the old iron rails which were being carted by, his heart ached, he burst into tears, and leaned his forehead against the window-frame.

"How miserable I am!" he muttered. "My God, how miserable!"

And joy gave way to the boredom of everyday life and the feeling of his irrevocable loss.

The Cossack

Maxim Tortchakov, a farmer in southern Russia, was driving home from church with his young wife and bringing back an Easter cake which had just been blessed. The sun had not yet risen, but the east was all tinged with red and gold and had dissipated the haze which usually, in the early morning, screens the blue of the sky from the eyes. It was quiet.... The birds were hardly yet awake.... The corncrake uttered its clear note, and far away above a little tumulus, a sleepy kite floated, heavily flapping its wings, and no other living creature could be seen all over the steppe.

Tortchakov drove on and thought that there was no better nor happier holiday than the Feast of Christ's Resurrection. He had only lately been married, and was now keeping his first Easter with his wife. Whatever he looked at, whatever he thought about, it all seemed to him bright, joyous, and happy. He thought about his farming, and thought that it was all going well, that the furnishing of his house was all the heart could desire—there was enough of everything and all of it good; he looked at his wife, and she seemed to him lovely, kind, and gentle. He was delighted by the glow in the east, and the young grass, and his squeaking chaise, and the kite.... And when on the way, he ran into a tavern to light his cigarette and drank a glass, he felt happier still.

"It is said, 'Great is the day,'" he chattered. "Yes, it is great! Wait a bit, Lizaveta, the sun will begin to dance. It dances every Easter. So it rejoices too!"

"It is not alive," said his wife.

"But there are people on it!" exclaimed Tortchakov, "there are really! Ivan Stepanitch told me that there are people on all the planets—on the sun, and on the moon! Truly . . . but maybe the learned men tell lies—the devil only knows! Stay, surely that's not a horse? Yes, it is!"

At the Crooked Ravine, which was just half-way on the journey home, Tortchakov and his wife saw a saddled horse standing motionless, and sniffing last year's dry grass. On a hillock beside the roadside a red-haired Cossack was sitting doubled up, looking at his feet.

"Christ is risen!" Maxim shouted to him. "Wo-o-o!"

"Truly He is risen," answered the Cossack, without raising his head.

"Where are you going?"

"Home on leave."

"Why are you sitting here, then?"

"Why . . . I have fallen ill . . . I haven't the strength to go on."

"What is wrong?"

"I ache all over."

"H'm. What a misfortune! People are keeping holiday, and you fall sick! But you should ride on to a village or an inn, what's the use of sitting here!"

The Cossack raised his head, and with big, exhausted eyes, scanned Maxim, his wife, and the horse.

"Have you come from church?" he asked.

"Yes."

"The holiday found me on the high road. It was not God's will for me to reach home. I'd get on my horse at once and ride off, but I haven't the strength. . . . You might, good Christians, give a wayfarer some Easter cake to break his fast!"

"Easter cake?" Tortchakov repeated, "That we can, to be sure. . . . Stay, I'll. . . ."

Maxim fumbled quickly in his pockets, glanced at his wife, and said:

"I haven't a knife, nothing to cut it with. And I don't like to break it, it would spoil the whole cake. There's a problem! You look and see if you haven't a knife?"

The Cossack got up groaning, and went to his saddle to get a knife.

"What an idea," said Tortchakov's wife angrily. "I won't let you slice up the Easter cake! What should I look like, taking it home already cut! Ride on to the peasants in the village, and break your fast there!"

The wife took the napkin with the Easter cake in it out of her husband's hands and said:

"I won't allow it! One must do things properly; it's not a loaf, but a holy Easter cake. And it's a sin to cut it just anyhow."

"Well, Cossack, don't be angry," laughed Tortchakov. "The wife forbids it! Good-bye. Good luck on your journey!"

Maxim shook the reins, clicked to his horse, and the chaise rolled on squeaking. For some time his wife went on grumbling, and declaring that to cut the Easter cake before reaching home was a sin and not the proper thing. In the east the first rays of the rising sun shone out, cutting their way through the feathery clouds, and the song of the lark was heard in the sky. Now not one but three kites were hovering over the steppe at a respectful distance from one another. Grasshoppers began churring in the young grass.

When they had driven three-quarters of a mile from the Crooked Ravine, Tortchakov looked round and stared intently into the distance.

"I can't see the Cossack," he said. "Poor, dear fellow, to take it into his head to fall ill on the road. There couldn't be a worse misfortune, to have to travel and not have the strength.... I shouldn't wonder if he dies by the roadside. We didn't give him any Easter cake, Lizaveta, and we ought to have given it. I'll be bound he wants to break his fast too."

The sun had risen, but whether it was dancing or not Tortchakov did not see. He remained silent all the way home, thinking and keeping his eyes fixed on the horse's black tail. For some unknown reason he felt overcome by depression, and not a trace of the holiday gladness was left in his heart. When he had arrived home and said, "Christ is risen" to his workmen, he grew cheerful again and began talking, but when he had sat down to break the fast and had taken a bite from his piece of Easter cake, he looked regretfully at his wife, and said:

"It wasn't right of us, Lizaveta, not to give that Cossack something to eat."

"You are a queer one, upon my word," said Lizaveta, shrugging her shoulders in surprise. "Where did you pick up such a fashion as giving away the holy Easter cake on the high road? Is it an ordinary loaf? Now that it is cut and lying on the table, let anyone eat it that likes—your Cossack too! Do you suppose I grudge it?"

"That's all right, but we ought to have given the Cossack some. . . . Why, he was worse off than a beggar or an orphan. On the road, and far from home, and sick too."

Tortchakov drank half a glass of tea, and neither ate nor drank anything more. He had no appetite, the tea seemed to choke him, and he felt depressed again. After breaking their fast, his wife and he lay down to sleep. When Lizaveta woke two hours later, he was standing by the window, looking into the yard.

"Are you up already?" asked his wife.

"I somehow can't sleep. . . . Ah, Lizaveta," he sighed. "We were unkind, you and I, to that Cossack!"

"Talking about that Cossack again!" yawned his wife. "You have got him on the brain."

"He has served his Tsar, shed his blood maybe, and we treated him as though he were a pig. We ought to have brought the sick man home and fed him, and we did not even give him a morsel of bread."

"Catch me letting you spoil the Easter cake for nothing! And one that has been blessed too! You would have cut it on the road, and shouldn't I have looked a fool when I got home?"

Without saying anything to his wife, Maxim went into the kitchen, wrapped a piece of cake up in a napkin, together with half a dozen eggs, and went to the labourers in the barn.

"Kuzma, put down your concertina," he said to one of them. "Saddle the bay, or Ivantchik, and ride briskly to the Crooked Ravine. There you will see a sick Cossack with a horse, so give him this. Maybe he hasn't ridden away yet."

Maxim felt cheerful again, but after waiting for Kuzma for some hours, he could bear it no longer, so he saddled a horse and went off to meet him. He met him just at the Ravine.

"Well, have you seen the Cossack?"

"I can't find him anywhere, he must have ridden on."

"H'm . . . a queer business."

Tortchakov took the bundle from Kuzma, and galloped on farther. When he reached Shustrovo he asked the peasants:

"Friends, have you seen a sick Cossack with a horse? Didn't he ride by here? A red-headed fellow on a bay horse."

The peasants looked at one another, and said they had not seen the Cossack.

"The returning postman drove by, it's true, but as for a Cossack or anyone else, there has been no such."

Maxim got home at dinner time.

"I can't get that Cossack out of my head, do what you will!" he said to his wife. "He gives me no peace. I keep thinking: what if God meant to try us, and sent some saint or angel in the form of a Cossack? It does happen, you know. It's bad, Lizaveta; we were unkind to the man!"

"What do you keep pestering me with that Cossack for?" cried Lizaveta, losing patience at last. "You stick to it like tar!"

"You are not kind, you know . . ." said Maxim, looking into his wife's face.

And for the first time since his marriage he perceived that he wife was not kind.

"I may be unkind," cried Lizaveta, tapping angrily with her spoon, "but I am not going to give away the holy Easter cake to every drunken man in the road."

"The Cossack wasn't drunk!"

"He was drunk!"

"Well, you are a fool then!"

Maxim got up from the table and began reproaching his young wife for hard-heartedness and stupidity. She, getting angry too, answered his reproaches with reproaches, burst into tears, and went away into their bedroom, declaring she would go home to her father's. This was the first matrimonial squabble that had happened in the Tortchakov's married life. He walked about the yard till the evening, picturing his wife's face, and it seemed to him now spiteful and ugly. And as though to torment him the Cossack haunted his brain, and Maxim seemed to see now his sick eyes, now his unsteady walk.

"Ah, we were unkind to the man," he muttered.

When it got dark, he was overcome by an insufferable depression such as he had never felt before. Feeling so dreary, and being angry with his wife, he got drunk, as he had sometimes done before he was married. In his drunkenness he used bad language and shouted to his wife that she had a spiteful, ugly face, and that next day he would send her packing to her father's. On the morning of Easter Monday, he drank some more to sober himself, and got drunk again.

And with that his downfall began.

His horses, cows, sheep, and hives disappeared one by one from the yard; Maxim was more and more often drunk, debts mounted up, he felt an aversion for his wife. Maxim put down all his misfortunes to the fact that he had an unkind wife, and above all, that God was angry with him on account of the sick Cossack.

Lizaveta saw their ruin, but who was to blame for it she did not understand.

Volodya

At five o'clock one Sunday afternoon in summer, Volodya, a plain, shy, sickly-looking lad of seventeen, was sitting in the arbour of the Shumihins' country villa, feeling dreary. His despondent thoughts flowed in three directions. In the first place, he had next day, Monday, an examination in mathematics; he knew that if he did not get through the written examination on the morrow, he would be expelled, for he had already been two years in the sixth form and had two and three-quarter marks for algebra in his annual report. In the second place, his presence at the villa of the Shumihins, a wealthy family with aristocratic pretensions, was a continual source of mortification to his amour-propre. It seemed to him that Madame Shumihin looked upon him and his *maman* as poor relations and dependents, that they laughed at his *maman* and did not respect her. He had on one occasion accidentally overheard Madame Shumihin, in the verandah, telling her cousin Anna Fyodorovna that his *maman* still tried to look young and got herself up, that she never paid her losses at cards, and had a partiality for other people's shoes and tobacco. Every day Volodya besought his *maman* not to go to the Shumihins', and drew a picture of the humiliating part she played with these gentlefolk. He tried to persuade her, said rude things, but she—a frivolous, pampered woman, who had run through two fortunes, her own and her husband's, in her time, and always gravitated towards acquaintances of high rank—did not understand him, and twice a week Volodya had to accompany her to the villa he hated.

In the third place, the youth could not for one instant get rid of a strange, unpleasant feeling which was absolutely new to him. . . . It seemed to him that he was in love with Anna Fyodorovna, the Shumihins' cousin, who was staying with them. She was a vivacious, loud-voiced, laughter-loving, healthy, and vigorous lady of thirty, with rosy cheeks, plump shoulders, a plump round chin and a continual smile on her thin lips. She was neither young nor beautiful—Volodya knew that perfectly well; but for some reason he could not help thinking of her, looking at her while she shrugged her plump shoulders and moved her flat back as she played croquet, or after prolonged laughter and running up and down stairs, sank into a low chair, and, half closing her eyes and gasping for breath, pretended that she was stifling and could not breathe. She was married. Her husband, a staid and dignified architect, came once a week to the villa, slept soundly, and returned to town. Volodya's strange feeling had begun with his conceiving an unaccountable hatred for the architect, and feeling relieved every time he went back to town.

Now, sitting in the arbour, thinking of his examination next day, and of his *maman,* at whom they laughed, he felt an intense desire to see Nyuta (that was what the Shumihins called Anna Fyodorovna), to hear her laughter and the rustle of her dress. . . . This desire was not like the pure, poetic love of which he read in novels and about which he dreamed every night when he went to bed; it was strange, incomprehensible; he was ashamed of it, and afraid of it as of something very wrong and impure, something which it was disagreeable to confess even to himself.

"It's not love," he said to himself. "One can't fall in love with women of thirty who are married. It is only a little intrigue. . . . Yes, an intrigue. . . ."

Pondering on the "intrigue," he thought of his uncontrollable shyness, his lack of moustache, his freckles, his narrow eyes, and put himself in his imagination side by side with Nyuta, and the juxtaposition seemed to him impossible; then he made haste to imagine himself bold, handsome, witty, dressed in the latest fashion.

When his dreams were at their height, as he sat huddled together and looking at the ground in a dark corner of the arbour, he heard the sound of light footsteps. Some one was coming slowly along the avenue. Soon the steps stopped and something white gleamed in the entrance.

"Is there any one here?" asked a woman's voice.

Volodya recognised the voice, and raised his head in a fright.

"Who is here?" asked Nyuta, going into the arbour. "Ah, it is you, Volodya? What are you doing here? Thinking? And how can you go on thinking, thinking, thinking? . . . That's the way to go out of your mind!"

Volodya got up and looked in a dazed way at Nyuta. She had only just come back from bathing. Over her shoulder there was hanging a sheet and a rough towel, and from under the white silk kerchief on her head he could see the wet hair sticking to her forehead. There was the cool damp smell of the bath-house and of almond soap still hanging about her. She was out of breath from running quickly. The top button of her blouse was undone, so that the boy saw her throat and bosom.

"Why don't you say something?" said Nyuta, looking Volodya up and down. "It's not polite to be silent when a lady talks to you. What a clumsy seal you are though, Volodya! You always sit, saying nothing, thinking like some philosopher. There's not a spark of life or fire in you! You are really horrid! . . . At your age you ought to be living, skipping, and jumping, chattering, flirting, falling in love."

Volodya looked at the sheet that was held by a plump white hand, and thought. . . .

"He's mute," said Nyuta, with wonder; "it is strange, really. . . . Listen! Be a man! Come, you might smile at least! Phew, the horrid philosopher!" she laughed. "But do you know, Volodya, why you are such a clumsy seal? Because you don't devote yourself to the ladies. Why don't you? It's true there are no girls here, but there is nothing to prevent your flirting with the married ladies! Why don't you flirt with me, for instance?"

Volodya listened and scratched his forehead in acute and painful irresolution.

"It's only very proud people who are silent and love solitude," Nyuta went on, pulling his hand away from his forehead. "You are proud, Volodya. Why do you look at me like that from under your brows? Look me straight in the face, if you please! Yes, now then, clumsy seal!"

Volodya made up his mind to speak. Wanting to smile, he twitched his lower lip, blinked, and again put his hand to his forehead.

"I . . . I love you," he said.

Nyuta raised her eyebrows in surprise, and laughed.

"What do I hear?" she sang, as prima-donnas sing at the opera when they hear something awful. "What? What did you say? Say it again, say it again. . . ."

"I . . . I love you!" repeated Volodya.

And without his will's having any part in his action, without reflection or understanding, he took half a step towards Nyuta and clutched her by the arm. Everything was dark before his eyes, and tears came into them. The whole world was turned into one big, rough towel which smelt of the bath-house.

"Bravo, bravo!" he heard a merry laugh. "Why don't you speak? I want you to speak! Well?"

Seeing that he was not prevented from holding her arm, Volodya glanced at Nyuta's laughing face, and clumsily, awkwardly, put both arms round her waist, his hands meeting behind her back. He held her round the waist with both arms, while, putting her hands up to her head, showing the dimples in her elbows, she set her hair straight under the kerchief and said in a calm voice:

"You must be tactful, polite, charming, and you can only become that under feminine influence. But what a wicked, angry face you have! You must talk, laugh. . . . Yes, Volodya, don't be surly; you are young and will have plenty of time for philosophising. Come, let go of me; I am going. Let go."

Without effort she released her waist, and, humming something, walked out of the arbour. Volodya was left alone. He smoothed his hair, smiled, and walked three times to and fro across the arbour, then he sat down on the bench and smiled again. He felt insufferably ashamed, so much so that he wondered that human shame could reach such a pitch of acuteness and intensity. Shame made him smile, gesticulate, and whisper some disconnected words.

He was ashamed that he had been treated like a small boy, ashamed of his shyness, and, most of all, that he had had the audacity to put his arms round the waist of a respectable married woman, though, as it seemed to him, he had neither through age nor by external quality, nor by social position any right to do so.

He jumped up, went out of the arbour, and, without looking round, walked into the recesses of the garden furthest from the house.

"Ah! only to get away from here as soon as possible," he thought, clutching his head. "My God! as soon as possible."

The train by which Volodya was to go back with his _maman_ was at eight-forty. There were three hours before the train started, but he would with pleasure have gone to the station at once without waiting for his _maman._

At eight o'clock he went to the house. His whole figure was expressive of determination: what would be, would be! He made up his mind to go in boldly, to look them straight in the face, to speak in a loud voice, regardless of everything.

He crossed the terrace, the big hall and the drawing-room, and there stopped to take breath. He could hear them in the dining-room, drinking tea. Madame Shumihin, _maman,_ and Nyuta were talking and laughing about something.

Volodya listened.

"I assure you!" said Nyuta. "I could not believe my eyes! When he began declaring his passion and—just imagine!—put his arms round my waist, I should not have recognised him. And you know he has a way with him! When he told me he was in love with me, there was something brutal in his face, like a Circassian."

"Really!" gasped _maman,_ going off into a peal of laughter. "Really! How he does remind me of his father!"

Volodya ran back and dashed out into the open air.

"How could they talk of it aloud!" he wondered in agony, clasping his hands and looking up to the sky in horror. "They talk aloud in cold blood . . . and *maman* laughed! . . . *Maman!* My God, why didst Thou give me such a mother? Why?"

But he had to go to the house, come what might. He walked three times up and down the avenue, grew a little calmer, and went into the house.

"Why didn't you come in in time for tea?" Madame Shumihin asked sternly.

"I am sorry, it's . . . it's time for me to go," he muttered, not raising his eyes. "*Maman,* it's eight o'clock!"

"You go alone, my dear," said his *maman* languidly. "I am staying the night with Lili. Good-bye, my dear. . . . Let me make the sign of the cross over you."

She made the sign of the cross over her son, and said in French, turning to Nyuta:

"He's rather like Lermontov . . . isn't he?"

Saying good-bye after a fashion, without looking any one in the face, Volodya went out of the dining-room. Ten minutes later he was walking along the road to the station, and was glad of it. Now he felt neither frightened nor ashamed; he breathed freely and easily.

About half a mile from the station, he sat down on a stone by the side of the road, and gazed at the sun, which was half hidden behind a barrow. There were lights already here and there at the station, and one green light glimmered dimly, but the train was not yet in sight. It was pleasant to Volodya to sit still without moving, and to watch the evening coming little by little. The darkness of the arbour, the footsteps, the smell of the bath-house, the laughter, and the waist—all these rose with amazing vividness before his imagination, and all this was no longer so terrible and important as before.

"It's of no consequence. . . . She did not pull her hand away, and laughed when I held her by the waist," he thought. "So she must have liked it. If she had disliked it she would have been angry. . . ."

And now Volodya felt sorry that he had not had more boldness there in the arbour. He felt sorry that he was so stupidly going away, and he was by now persuaded that if the same thing happened again he would be bolder and look at it more simply.

And it would not be difficult for the opportunity to occur again. They used to stroll about for a long time after supper at the Shumihins'. If Volodya went for a walk with Nyuta in the dark garden, there would be an opportunity!

"I will go back," he thought, "and will go by the morning train to-morrow.... I will say I have missed the train."

And he turned back.... Madame Shumihin, *maman,* Nyuta, and one of the nieces were sitting on the verandah, playing *vint.* When Volodya told them the lie that he had missed the train, they were uneasy that he might be late for the examination next day, and advised him to get up early. All the while they were playing he sat on one side, greedily watching Nyuta and waiting.... He already had a plan prepared in his mind: he would go up to Nyuta in the dark, would take her by the hand, then would embrace her; there would be no need to say anything, as both of them would understand without words.

But after supper the ladies did not go for a walk in the garden, but went on playing cards. They played till one o'clock at night, and then broke up to go to bed.

"How stupid it all is!" Volodya thought with vexation as he got into bed. "But never mind; I'll wait till to-morrow ... to-morrow in the arbour. It doesn't matter...."

He did not attempt to go to sleep, but sat in bed, hugging his knees and thinking. All thought of the examination was hateful to him. He had already made up his mind that they would expel him, and that there was nothing terrible about his being expelled. On the contrary, it was a good thing—a very good thing, in fact. Next day he would be as free as a bird; he would put on ordinary clothes instead of his school uniform, would smoke openly, come out here, and make love to Nyuta when he liked; and he would not be a schoolboy but "a young man." And as for the rest of it, what is called a career, a future, that was clear; Volodya would go into the army or the telegraph service, or he would go into a chemist's shop and work his way up till he was a dispenser.... There were lots of callings. An hour or two passed, and he was still sitting and thinking....

Towards three o'clock, when it was beginning to get light, the door creaked cautiously and his *maman* came into the room.

"Aren't you asleep?" she asked, yawning. "Go to sleep; I have only come in for a minute. . . . I am only fetching the drops. . . ."

"What for?"

"Poor Lili has got spasms again. Go to sleep, my child, your examination's to-morrow. . . ."

She took a bottle of something out of the cupboard, went to the window, read the label, and went away.

"Marya Leontyevna, those are not the drops!" Volodya heard a woman's voice, a minute later. "That's convallaria, and Lili wants morphine. Is your son asleep? Ask him to look for it. . . ."

It was Nyuta's voice. Volodya turned cold. He hurriedly put on his trousers, flung his coat over his shoulders, and went to the door.

"Do you understand? Morphine," Nyuta explained in a whisper. "There must be a label in Latin. Wake Volodya; he will find it."

Maman opened the door and Volodya caught sight of Nyuta. She was wearing the same loose wrapper in which she had gone to bathe. Her hair hung loose and disordered on her shoulders, her face looked sleepy and dark in the half-light. . . .

"Why, Volodya is not asleep," she said. "Volodya, look in the cupboard for the morphine, there's a dear! What a nuisance Lili is! She has always something the matter."

Maman muttered something, yawned, and went away.

"Look for it," said Nyuta. "Why are you standing still?"

Volodya went to the cupboard, knelt down, and began looking through the bottles and boxes of medicine. His hands were trembling, and he had a feeling in his chest and stomach as though cold waves were running all over his inside. He felt suffocated and giddy from the smell of ether, carbolic acid, and various drugs, which he quite unnecessarily snatched up with his trembling fingers and spilled in so doing.

"I believe *maman* has gone," he thought. "That's a good thing . . . a good thing. . . ."

"Will you be quick?" said Nyuta, drawling.

"In a minute. . . . Here, I believe this is morphine," said Volodya, reading on one of the labels the word "morph . . ." "Here it is!"

Nyuta was standing in the doorway in such a way that one foot was in his room and one was in the passage. She was tidying her hair, which was difficult to put in order because it was so thick and long, and looked absent-mindedly at Volodya. In her loose wrap, with her sleepy face and her hair down, in the dim light that came into the white sky not yet lit by the sun, she seemed to Volodya captivating, magnificent. . . . Fascinated, trembling all over, and remembering with relish how he had held that exquisite body in his arms in the arbour, he handed her the bottle and said:

"How wonderful you are!"

"What?"

She came into the room.

"What?" she asked, smiling.

He was silent and looked at her, then, just as in the arbour, he took her hand, and she looked at him with a smile and waited for what would happen next.

"I love you," he whispered.

She left off smiling, thought a minute, and said:

"Wait a little; I think somebody is coming. Oh, these schoolboys!" she said in an undertone, going to the door and peeping out into the passage. "No, there is no one to be seen. . . ."

She came back.

Then it seemed to Volodya that the room, Nyuta, the sunrise and himself—all melted together in one sensation of acute, extraordinary, incredible bliss, for which one might give up one's whole life and face eternal torments. . . . But half a minute passed and all that vanished. Volodya saw only a fat, plain face, distorted by an expression of repulsion, and he himself suddenly felt a loathing for what had happened.

"I must go away, though," said Nyuta, looking at Volodya with disgust. "What a wretched, ugly . . . fie, ugly duckling!"

How unseemly her long hair, her loose wrap, her steps, her voice seemed to Volodya now! . . .

" 'Ugly duckling' . . ." he thought after she had gone away. "I really am ugly . . . everything is ugly."

The sun was rising, the birds were singing loudly; he could hear the gardener walking in the garden and the creaking of his wheelbarrow . . . and soon afterwards he heard the lowing of the cows and the sounds of the shepherd's pipe. The sunlight and the sounds told him that somewhere in this world there is a pure, refined, poetical life. But where was it? Volodya had never heard a word of it from his *maman* or any of the people round about him.

When the footman came to wake him for the morning train, he pretended to be asleep. . . .

"Bother it! Damn it all!" he thought.

He got up between ten and eleven.

Combing his hair before the looking-glass, and looking at his ugly face, pale from his sleepless night, he thought:

"It's perfectly true . . . an ugly duckling!"

When *maman* saw him and was horrified that he was not at his examination, Volodya said:

"I overslept myself, *maman*. . . . But don't worry, I will get a medical certificate."

Madame Shumihin and Nyuta waked up at one o'clock. Volodya heard Madame Shumihin open her window with a bang, heard Nyuta go off into a peal of laughter in reply to her coarse voice. He saw the door open and a string of nieces and other toadies (among the latter was his *maman*) file into lunch, caught a glimpse of Nyuta's freshly washed laughing face, and, beside her, the black brows and beard of her husband the architect, who had just arrived.

Nyuta was wearing a Little Russian dress which did not suit her at all, and made her look clumsy; the architect was making dull and vulgar jokes. The rissoles served at lunch had too much onion in them— so it seemed to Volodya. It also seemed to him that Nyuta laughed loudly on purpose, and kept glancing in his direction to give him to understand that the memory of the night did not trouble her in the least, and that she was not aware of the presence at table of the "ugly duckling."

At four o'clock Volodya drove to the station with his *maman*. Foul memories, the sleepless night, the prospect of expulsion from school, the stings of conscience—all roused in him now an oppressive, gloomy anger. He looked at *maman's* sharp profile, at her little nose, and at the raincoat which was a present from Nyuta, and muttered:

"Why do you powder? It's not becoming at your age! You make yourself up, don't pay your debts at cards, smoke other people's tobacco. . . . It's hateful! I don't love you . . . I don't love you!"

He was insulting her, and she moved her little eyes about in alarm, flung up her hands, and whispered in horror:

"What are you saying, my dear! Good gracious! the coachman will hear! Be quiet or the coachman will hear! He can overhear everything."

"I don't love you . . . I don't love you!" he went on breathlessly. "You've no soul and no morals. . . . Don't dare to wear that raincoat! Do you hear? Or else I will tear it into rags. . . ."

"Control yourself, my child," *maman* wept; "the coachman can hear!"

"And where is my father's fortune? Where is your money? You have wasted it all. I am not ashamed of being poor, but I am ashamed of having such a mother. . . . When my schoolfellows ask questions about you, I always blush."

In the train they had to pass two stations before they reached the town. Volodya spent all the time on the little platform between two carriages and shivered all over. He did not want to go into the compartment because there the mother he hated was sitting. He hated himself, hated the ticket collectors, the smoke from the engine, the cold to which he attributed his shivering. And the heavier the weight on his heart, the more strongly he felt that somewhere in the world, among some people, there was a pure, honourable, warm, refined life, full of love, affection, gaiety, and serenity. . . . He felt this and was so intensely miserable that one of the passengers, after looking in his face attentively, actually asked:

"You have the toothache, I suppose?"

In the town *maman* and Volodya lived with Marya Petrovna, a lady of noble rank, who had a large flat and let rooms to boarders. *Maman* had two rooms, one with windows and two pictures in gold frames hanging on the walls, in which her bed stood and in which she lived, and a little dark room opening out of it in which Volodya lived. Here there was a sofa on which he slept, and, except that sofa, there was no other furniture; the rest of the room was entirely filled up with wicker baskets full of clothes, cardboard hat-boxes, and all sorts of rubbish, which *maman* preserved for some reason or other. Volodya prepared his lessons either in his mother's room or in the "general room," as the large room in which the boarders assembled at dinner-time and in the evening was called.

On reaching home he lay down on his sofa and put the quilt over him to stop his shivering. The cardboard hat-boxes, the wicker baskets, and the other rubbish, reminded him that he had not a room of his own, that he had no refuge in which he could get away from his mother, from her visitors, and from the voices that were floating up from the "general room." The satchel and the books lying about in the corners reminded him of the examination he had missed.... For some reason there came into his mind, quite inappropriately, Mentone, where he had lived with his father when he was seven years old; he thought of Biarritz and two little English girls with whom he ran about on the sand.... He tried to recall to his memory the colour of the sky, the sea, the height of the waves, and his mood at the time, but he could not succeed. The English girls flitted before his imagination as though they were living; all the rest was a medley of images that floated away in confusion....

"No; it's cold here," thought Volodya. He got up, put on his overcoat, and went into the "general room."

There they were drinking tea. There were three people at the samovar: *maman;* an old lady with tortoiseshell pince-nez, who gave music lessons; and Avgustin Mihalitch, an elderly and very stout Frenchman, who was employed at a perfumery factory.

"I have had no dinner to-day," said *maman.* "I ought to send the maid to buy some bread."

"Dunyasha!" shouted the Frenchman.

It appeared that the maid had been sent out somewhere by the lady of the house.

"Oh, that's of no consequence," said the Frenchman, with a broad smile. "I will go for some bread myself at once. Oh, it's nothing."

He laid his strong, pungent cigar in a conspicuous place, put on his hat and went out. After he had gone away *maman* began telling the music teacher how she had been staying at the Shumihins', and how warmly they welcomed her.

"Lili Shumihin is a relation of mine, you know," she said. "Her late husband, General Shumihin, was a cousin of my husband. And she was a Baroness Kolb by birth. . . ."

"*Maman*, that's false!" said Volodya irritably. "Why tell lies?"

He knew perfectly well that what his mother said was true; in what she was saying about General Shumihin and about Baroness Kolb there was not a word of lying, but nevertheless he felt that she was lying. There was a suggestion of falsehood in her manner of speaking, in the expression of her face, in her eyes, in everything.

"You are lying," repeated Volodya; and he brought his fist down on the table with such force that all the crockery shook and *maman's* tea was spilt over. "Why do you talk about generals and baronesses? It's all lies!"

The music teacher was disconcerted, and coughed into her hand-kerchief, affecting to sneeze, and *maman* began to cry.

"Where can I go?" thought Volodya.

He had been in the street already; he was ashamed to go to his schoolfellows. Again, quite incongruously, he remembered the two little English girls. . . . He paced up and down the "general room," and went into Avgustin Mihalitch's room. Here there was a strong smell of ethereal oils and glycerine soap. On the table, in the window, and even on the chairs, there were a number of bottles, glasses, and wineglasses containing fluids of various colours. Volodya took up from the table a newspaper, opened it and read the title *Figaro*. . . . There was a strong and pleasant scent about the paper. Then he took a revolver from the table. . . .

"There, there! Don't take any notice of it." The music teacher was comforting *maman* in the next room. "He is young! Young people of his age never restrain themselves. One must resign oneself to that."

"No, Yevgenya Andreyevna; he's too spoilt," said *maman* in a singsong voice. "He has no one in authority over him, and I am weak and can do nothing. Oh, I am unhappy!"

Volodya put the muzzle of the revolver to his mouth, felt something like a trigger or spring, and pressed it with his finger. . . . Then felt something else projecting, and once more pressed it. Taking the muzzle out of his mouth, he wiped it with the lapel of his coat, looked at the lock. He had never in his life taken a weapon in his hand before. . . .

"I believe one ought to raise this . . ." he reflected. "Yes, it seems so."

Avgustin Mihalitch went into the "general room," and with a laugh began telling them about something. Volodya put the muzzle in his mouth again, pressed it with his teeth, and pressed something with his fingers. There was a sound of a shot. . . . Something hit Volodya in the back of his head with terrible violence, and he fell on the table with his face downwards among the bottles and glasses. Then he saw his father, as in Mentone, in a top-hat with a wide black band on it, wearing mourning for some lady, suddenly seize him by both hands, and they fell headlong into a very deep, dark pit.

Then everything was blurred and vanished.

Happiness

A flock of sheep was spending the night on the broad steppe road that is called the great highway. Two shepherds were guarding it. One, a toothless old man of eighty, with a tremulous face, was lying on his stomach at the very edge of the road, leaning his elbows on the dusty leaves of a plantain; the other, a young fellow with thick black eyebrows and no moustache, dressed in the coarse canvas of which cheap sacks are made, was lying on his back, with his arms under his head, looking upwards at the sky, where the stars were slumbering and the Milky Way lay stretched exactly above his face.

The shepherds were not alone. A couple of yards from them in the dusk that shrouded the road a horse made a patch of darkness, and, beside it, leaning against the saddle, stood a man in high boots and a short full-skirted jacket who looked like an overseer on some big estate. Judging from his upright and motionless figure, from his manners, and his behaviour to the shepherds and to his horse, he was a serious, reasonable man who knew his own value; even in the darkness signs could be detected in him of military carriage and of the majestically condescending expression gained by frequent intercourse with the gentry and their stewards.

The sheep were asleep. Against the grey background of the dawn, already beginning to cover the eastern part of the sky, the silhouettes of sheep that were not asleep could be seen here and there; they stood with drooping heads, thinking. Their thoughts, tedious and oppressive, called forth by images of nothing but the broad steppe and the sky, the days and the nights, probably weighed upon them themselves, crushing them into apathy; and, standing there as though rooted to the earth, they noticed neither the presence of a stranger nor the uneasiness of the dogs.

The drowsy, stagnant air was full of the monotonous noise inseparable from a summer night on the steppes; the grasshoppers chirruped incessantly; the quails called, and the young nightingales trilled languidly half a mile away in a ravine where a stream flowed and willows grew.

The overseer had halted to ask the shepherds for a light for his pipe. He lighted it in silence and smoked the whole pipe; then, still without uttering a word, stood with his elbow on the saddle, plunged in thought. The young shepherd took no notice of him, he still lay gazing at the sky while the old man slowly looked the overseer up and down and then asked:

"Why, aren't you Panteley from Makarov's estate?"

"That's myself," answered the overseer.

"To be sure, I see it is. I didn't know you—that is a sign you will be rich. Where has God brought you from?"

"From the Kovylyevsky fields."

"That's a good way. Are you letting the land on the part-crop system?"

"Part of it. Some like that, and some we are letting on lease, and some for raising melons and cucumbers. I have just come from the mill."

A big shaggy old sheep-dog of a dirty white colour with woolly tufts about its nose and eyes walked three times quietly round the horse, trying to seem unconcerned in the presence of strangers, then all at once dashed suddenly from behind at the overseer with an angry aged growl; the other dogs could not refrain from leaping up too.

"Lie down, you damned brute," cried the old man, raising himself on his elbow; "blast you, you devil's creature."

When the dogs were quiet again, the old man resumed his former attitude and said quietly:

"It was at Kovyli on Ascension Day that Yefim Zhmenya died. Don't speak of it in the dark, it is a sin to mention such people. He was a wicked old man. I dare say you have heard."

"No, I haven't."

"Yefim Zhmenya, the uncle of Styopka, the blacksmith. The whole district round knew him. Aye, he was a cursed old man, he was! I knew him for sixty years, ever since Tsar Alexander who beat the French was brought from Taganrog to Moscow. We went together to meet the dead Tsar, and in those days the great highway did not run to Bahmut, but from Esaulovka to Gorodishtche, and where Kovyli is now, there were bustards' nests—there was a bustard's nest at every step. Even then I had noticed that Yefim had given his soul to damnation, and that the Evil One was in him. I have observed that if any man of the peasant class is apt to be silent, takes up with old women's jobs, and tries to live in solitude, there is no good in it, and Yefim from his youth up was always one to hold his tongue and look at you sideways, he always seemed to be sulky and bristling like a cock before a hen. To go to church or to the tavern or to lark in the street with the lads was not his fashion, he would rather sit alone or be whispering with old women. When he was still young he took jobs to look after the bees and the market gardens. Good folks would come to his market garden sometimes and his melons were whistling. One day he caught a pike, when folks were looking on, and it laughed aloud, 'Ho-ho-ho-ho!'"

"It does happen," said Panteley.

The young shepherd turned on his side and, lifting his black eyebrows, stared intently at the old man.

"Did you hear the melons whistling?" he asked.

"Hear them I didn't, the Lord spared me," sighed the old man, "but folks told me so. It is no great wonder . . . the Evil One will begin whistling in a stone if he wants to. Before the Day of Freedom a rock was humming for three days and three nights in our parts. I heard it myself. The pike laughed because Yefim caught a devil instead of a pike."

The old man remembered something. He got up quickly on to his knees and, shrinking as though from the cold, nervously thrusting his hands into his sleeves, he muttered in a rapid womanish gabble:

"Lord save us and have mercy upon us! I was walking along the river bank one day to Novopavlovka. A storm was gathering, such a tempest it was, preserve us Holy Mother, Queen of Heaven. . . . I was hurrying on as best I could, I looked, and beside the path between the thorn bushes—the thorn was in flower at the time—there was a white bullock coming along. I wondered whose bullock it was, and what the devil had sent it there for. It was coming along and swinging its tail and moo-oo-oo! but would you believe it, friends, I overtake it, I come up close—and it's not a bullock, but Yefim—holy, holy, holy! I make the sign of the cross while he stares at me and mutters, showing the whites of his eyes; wasn't I frightened! We came alongside, I was afraid to say a word to him—the thunder was crashing, the sky was streaked with lightning, the willows were bent right down to the water—all at once, my friends, God strike me dead that I die impenitent, a hare ran across the path . . . it ran and stopped, and said like a man: 'Good-evening, peasants.' Lie down, you brute!" the old man cried to the shaggy dog, who was moving round the horse again. "Plague take you!"

"It does happen," said the overseer, still leaning on the saddle and not stirring; he said this in the hollow, toneless voice in which men speak when they are plunged in thought.

"It does happen," he repeated, in a tone of profundity and conviction.

"Ugh, he was a nasty old fellow," the old shepherd went on with somewhat less fervour. "Five years after the Freedom he was flogged by the commune at the office, so to show his spite he took and sent the throat illness upon all Kovyli. Folks died out of number, lots and lots of them, just as in cholera. . . ."

"How did he send the illness?" asked the young shepherd after a brief silence.

"We all know how, there is no great cleverness needed where there is a will to it. Yefim murdered people with viper's fat. That is such a poison that folks will die from the mere smell of it, let alone the fat."

"That's true," Panteley agreed.

"The lads wanted to kill him at the time, but the old people would not let them. It would never have done to kill him; he knew the place where the treasure is hidden, and not another soul did know. The treasures about here are charmed so that you may find them and not see them, but he did see them. At times he would walk along the river bank or in the forest, and under the bushes and under the rocks there would be little flames, little flames . . . little flames as though from brimstone. I have seen them myself. Everyone expected that Yefim would show people the places or dig the treasure up himself, but he—as the saying is, like a dog in the manger—so he died without digging it up himself or showing other people."

The overseer lit a pipe, and for an instant lighted up his big moustaches and his sharp, stern-looking, and dignified nose. Little circles of light danced from his hands to his cap, raced over the saddle along the horse's back, and vanished in its mane near its ears.

"There are lots of hidden treasures in these parts," he said.

And slowly stretching, he looked round him, resting his eyes on the whitening east and added:

"There must be treasures."

"To be sure," sighed the old man, "one can see from every sign there are treasures, only there is no one to dig them, brother. No one knows the real places; besides, nowadays, you must remember, all the treasures are under a charm. To find them and see them you must have a talisman, and without a talisman you can do nothing, lad. Yefim had talismans, but there was no getting anything out of him, the bald devil. He kept them, so that no one could get them."

The young shepherd crept two paces nearer to the old man and, propping his head on his fists, fastened his fixed stare upon him. A childish expression of terror and curiosity gleamed in his dark eyes, and seemed in the twilight to stretch and flatten out the large features of his coarse young face. He was listening intently.

"It is even written in the Scriptures that there are lots of treasures hidden here," the old man went on; "it is so for sure . . . and no mistake about it. An old soldier of Novopavlovka was shown at Ivanovka a writing, and in this writing it was printed about the place of the treasure and even how many pounds of gold was in it and the sort of vessel it was in; they would have found the treasures long ago by that writing, only the treasure is under a spell, you can't get at it."

"Why can't you get at it, grandfather?" asked the young man.

"I suppose there is some reason, the soldier didn't say. It is under a spell . . . you need a talisman."

The old man spoke with warmth, as though he were pouring out his soul before the overseer. He talked through his nose and, being unaccustomed to talk much and rapidly, stuttered; and, conscious of his defects, he tried to adorn his speech with gesticulations of the hands and head and thin shoulders, and at every movement his hempen shirt crumpled into folds, slipped upwards and displayed his back, black with age and sunburn. He kept pulling it down, but it slipped up again at once. At last, as though driven out of all patience by the rebellious shirt, the old man leaped up and said bitterly:

"There is fortune, but what is the good of it if it is buried in the earth? It is just riches wasted with no profit to anyone, like chaff or sheep's dung, and yet there are riches there, lad, fortune enough for all the country round, but not a soul sees it! It will come to this, that the gentry will dig it up or the government will take it away. The gentry have begun digging the barrows. . . . They scented something! They are envious of the peasants' luck! The government, too, is looking after itself. It is written in the law that if any peasant finds the treasure he is to take it to the authorities! I dare say, wait till you get it! There is a brew but not for you!"

The old man laughed contemptuously and sat down on the ground. The overseer listened with attention and agreed, but from his silence and the expression of his figure it was evident that what the old man told him was not new to him, that he had thought it all over long ago, and knew much more than was known to the old shepherd.

"In my day, I must own, I did seek for fortune a dozen times," said the old man, scratching himself nervously. "I looked in the right places, but I must have come on treasures under a charm. My father looked for it, too, and my brother, too—but not a thing did they find, so they died without luck. A monk revealed to my brother Ilya—the Kingdom of Heaven be his—that in one place in the fortress of

Taganrog there was a treasure under three stones, and that that treasure was under a charm, and in those days—it was, I remember, in the year '38—an Armenian used to live at Matvyeeev Barrow who sold talismans. Ilya bought a talisman, took two other fellows with him, and went to Taganrog. Only when he got to the place in the fortress, brother, there was a soldier with a gun, standing at the very spot. . . ."

A sound suddenly broke on the still air, and floated in all directions over the steppe. Something in the distance gave a menacing bang, crashed against stone, and raced over the steppe, uttering, "Tah! tah! tah! tah!" When the sound had died away the old man looked inquiringly at Panteley, who stood motionless and unconcerned.

"It's a bucket broken away at the pits," said the young shepherd after a moment's thought.

It was by now getting light. The Milky Way had turned pale and gradually melted like snow, losing its outlines; the sky was becoming dull and dingy so that you could not make out whether it was clear or covered thickly with clouds, and only from the bright leaden streak in the east and from the stars that lingered here and there could one tell what was coming.

The first noiseless breeze of morning, cautiously stirring the spurges and the brown stalks of last year's grass, fluttered along the road.

The overseer roused himself from his thoughts and tossed his head. With both hands he shook the saddle, touched the girth and, as though he could not make up his mind to mount the horse, stood still again, hesitating.

"Yes," he said, "your elbow is near, but you can't bite it. There is fortune, but there is not the wit to find it."

And he turned facing the shepherds. His stern face looked sad and mocking, as though he were a disappointed man.

"Yes, so one dies without knowing what happiness is like . . ." he said emphatically, lifting his left leg into the stirrup. "A younger man may live to see it, but it is time for us to lay aside all thought of it."

Stroking his long moustaches covered with dew, he seated himself heavily on the horse and screwed up his eyes, looking into the distance, as though he had forgotten something or left something unsaid. In the bluish distance where the furthest visible hillock melted into the mist nothing was stirring; the ancient barrows, once watch-mounds and tombs, which rose here and there above the horizon and the boundless steppe had a sullen and death-like look; there was a feeling of endless time and utter indifference to man in their immobility and silence; another thousand years would pass, myriads of men would die, while they would still stand as they had stood, with no regret for the dead nor interest in the living, and no soul would ever know why they stood there, and what secret of the steppes was hidden under them.

The rooks awakening, flew one after another in silence over the earth. No meaning was to be seen in the languid flight of those long-lived birds, nor in the morning which is repeated punctually every twenty-four hours, nor in the boundless expanse of the steppe.

The overseer smiled and said:

"What space, Lord have mercy upon us! You would have a hunt to find treasure in it! Here," he went on, dropping his voice and making a serious face, "here there are two treasures buried for a certainty. The gentry don't know of them, but the old peasants, particularly the soldiers, know all about them. Here, somewhere on that ridge [the overseer pointed with his whip] robbers one time attacked a caravan of gold; the gold was being taken from Petersburg to the Emperor Peter who was building a fleet at the time at Voronezh. The robbers killed the men with the caravan and buried the gold, but did not find it again afterwards. Another treasure was buried by our Cossacks of the Don. In the year '12 they carried off lots of plunder of all sorts from the French, goods and gold and silver. When they were going homewards they heard on the way that the government wanted to take away all the gold and silver from them. Rather than give up their plunder like that to the government for nothing, the brave fellows took and buried it, so that their children, anyway, might get it; but where they buried it no one knows."

"I have heard of those treasures," the old man muttered grimly.

"Yes . . ." Panteley pondered again. "So it is. . . ."

A silence followed. The overseer looked dreamily into the distance, gave a laugh and pulled the rein, still with the same expression as though he had forgotten something or left something unsaid. The horse reluctantly started at a walking pace. After riding a hundred paces Panteley shook his head resolutely, roused himself from his thoughts and, lashing his horse, set off at a trot.

The shepherds were left alone.

"That was Panteley from Makarov's estate," said the old man. "He gets a hundred and fifty a year and provisions found, too. He is a man of education. . . ."

The sheep, waking up—there were about three thousand of them—began without zest to while away the time, nipping at the low, half-trampled grass. The sun had not yet risen, but by now all the barrows could be seen and, like a cloud in the distance, Saur's Grave with its peaked top. If one clambered up on that tomb one could see the plain from it, level and boundless as the sky, one could see villages, manor-houses, the settlements of the Germans and of the Molokani, and a long-sighted Kalmuck could even see the town and the railway-station. Only from there could one see that there was something else in the world besides the silent steppe and the ancient barrows, that there was another life that had nothing to do with buried treasure and the thoughts of sheep.

The old man felt beside him for his crook—a long stick with a hook at the upper end—and got up. He was silent and thoughtful. The young shepherd's face had not lost the look of childish terror and curiosity. He was still under the influence of what he had heard in the night, and impatiently awaiting fresh stories.

"Grandfather," he asked, getting up and taking his crook, "what did your brother Ilya do with the soldier?"

The old man did not hear the question. He looked absent-mindedly at the young man, and answered, mumbling with his lips:

"I keep thinking, Sanka, about that writing that was shown to that soldier at Ivanovka. I didn't tell Panteley—God be with him—but you know in that writing the place was marked out so that even a woman could find it. Do you know where it is? At Bogata Bylotchka at the spot, you know, where the ravine parts like a goose's foot into three little ravines; it is the middle one."

"Well, will you dig?"

"I will try my luck . . ."

"And, grandfather, what will you do with the treasure when you find it?"

"Do with it?" laughed the old man. "H'm! . . . If only I could find it then. . . . I would show them all. . . . H'm! . . . I should know what to do. . . ."

And the old man could not answer what he would do with the treasure if he found it. That question had presented itself to him that morning probably for the first time in his life, and judging from the expression of his face, indifferent and uncritical, it did not seem to him important and deserving of consideration. In Sanka's brain another puzzled question was stirring: why was it only old men searched for hidden treasure, and what was the use of earthly happiness to people who might die any day of old age? But Sanka could not put this perplexity into words, and the old man could scarcely have found an answer to it.

An immense crimson sun came into view surrounded by a faint haze. Broad streaks of light, still cold, bathing in the dewy grass, lengthening out with a joyous air as though to prove they were not weary of their task, began spreading over the earth. The silvery wormwood, the blue flowers of the pig's onion, the yellow mustard, the corn-flowers—all burst into gay colours, taking the sunlight for their own smile.

The old shepherd and Sanka parted and stood at the further sides of the flock. Both stood like posts, without moving, staring at the ground and thinking. The former was haunted by thoughts of fortune, the latter was pondering on what had been said in the night; what interested him was not the fortune itself, which he did not want and could not imagine, but the fantastic, fairy-tale character of human happiness.

A hundred sheep started and, in some inexplicable panic as at a signal, dashed away from the flock; and as though the thoughts of the sheep—tedious and oppressive—had for a moment infected Sanka also, he, too, dashed aside in the same inexplicable animal panic, but at once he recovered himself and shouted:

"You crazy creatures! You've gone mad, plague take you!"

When the sun, promising long hours of overwhelming heat, began to bake the earth, all living things that in the night had moved and uttered sounds were sunk in drowsiness. The old shepherd and Sanka stood with their crooks on opposite sides of the flock, stood without stirring, like fakirs at their prayers, absorbed in thought. They did not heed each other; each of them was living in his own life. The sheep were pondering, too.

Zinotchka

The party of sportsmen spent the night in a peasant's hut on some newly mown hay. The moon peeped in at the window; from the street came the mournful wheezing of a concertina; from the hay came a sickly sweet, faintly troubling scent. The sportsmen talked about dogs, about women, about first love, and about snipe. After all the ladies of their acquaintance had been picked to pieces, and hundreds of stories had been told, the stoutest of the sportsmen, who looked in the darkness like a haycock, and who talked in the mellow bass of a staff officer, gave a loud yawn and said:

"It is nothing much to be loved; the ladies are created for the purpose of loving us men. But, tell me, has any one of you fellows been hated—passionately, furiously hated? Has any one of you watched the ecstasies of hatred? Eh?"

No answer followed.

"Has no one, gentlemen?" asked the staff officer's bass voice. "But I, now, have been hated, hated by a pretty girl, and have been able to study the symptoms of first hatred directed against myself. It was the first, because it was something exactly the converse of first love. What I am going to tell, however, happened when I knew nothing about love or hate. I was eight at the time, but that made no difference; in this case it was not *he* but *she* that mattered. Well, I beg your attention. One fine summer evening, just before sunset, I was sitting in the nursery, doing my lesson with my governess, Zinotchka, a very charming and poetical creature who had left boarding school not long before. Zinotchka looked absent-mindedly towards the window and said:

" 'Yes. We breathe in oxygen; now tell me, Petya, what do we breathe out?"

" 'Carbonic acid gas,' I answered, looking towards the same window.

" 'Right,' assented Zinotchka. 'Plants, on the contrary, breathe in carbonic acid gas, and breathe out oxygen. Carbonic acid gas is contained in seltzer water, and in the fumes from the samovar. . . . It is a very noxious gas. Near Naples there is the so-called Cave of Dogs, which contains carbonic acid gas; a dog dropped into it is suffocated and dies.'

"This luckless Cave of Dogs near Naples is a chemical marvel beyond which no governess ventures to go. Zinotchka always hotly maintained the usefulness of natural science, but I doubt if she knew any chemistry beyond this Cave.

"Well, she told me to repeat it. I repeated it. She asked me what was meant by the horizon. I answered. And meantime, while we were ruminating over the horizon and the Cave, in the yard below, my father was just getting ready to go shooting. The dogs yapped, the trace horses shifted from one leg to another impatiently and coquetted with the coachman, the footman packed the waggonette with parcels and all sorts of things. Beside the waggonette stood a brake in which my mother and sisters were sitting to drive to a name-day party at the Ivanetskys'. No one was left in the house but Zinotchka, me, and my eldest brother, a student, who had toothache. You can imagine my envy and my boredom.

" 'Well, what do we breathe in?' asked Zinotchka, looking at the window.

" 'Oxygen. . . .'

" 'Yes. And the horizon is the name given to the place where it seems to us as though the earth meets the sky . . .'

"Then the waggonette drove off, and after it the brake. . . . I saw Zinotchka take a note out of her pocket, crumple it up convulsively and press it to her temple, then she flushed crimson and looked at her watch.

" 'So, remember,' she said, 'that near Naples is the so-called Cave of Dogs. . . .' She glanced at her watch again and went on: 'where the sky seems to us to meet the earth. . . .'

"The poor girl in violent agitation walked about the room, and once more glanced at her watch. There was another half-hour before the end of our lesson.

" 'Now arithmetic,' she said, breathing hard and turning over the pages of the sum-book with a trembling hand. 'Come, you work out problem 325 and I . . . will be back directly.'

"She went out. I heard her scurry down the stairs, and then I saw her dart across the yard in her blue dress and vanish through the garden gate. The rapidity of her movements, the flush on her cheeks and her excitement, aroused my curiosity. Where had she run, and what for? Being intelligent beyond my years I soon put two and two together, and understood it all: she had run into the garden, taking advantage of the absence of my stern parents, to steal in among the raspberry bushes, or to pick herself some cherries. If that were so, dash it all, I would go and have some cherries too. I threw aside the sum-book and ran into the garden. I ran to the cherry orchard, but she was not there. Passing by the raspberries, the gooseberries, and the watchman's shanty, she crossed the kitchen garden and reached the pond, pale, and starting at every sound. I stole after her, and what I saw, my friends, was this. At the edge of the pond, between the thick stumps of two old willows, stood my elder brother, Sasha; one could not see from his face that he had toothache. He looked towards Zinotchka as she approached him, and his whole figure was lighted up by an expression of happiness as though by sunshine. And Zinotchka, as though she were being driven into the Cave of Dogs, and were being forced to breathe carbonic acid gas, walked towards him, scarcely able to move one leg before the other, breathing hard, with her head thrown back. . . . To judge from appearances she was going to a rendezous for the first time in her life. But at last she reached him. . . . For half a minute they gazed at each other in silence, as though they could not believe their eyes. Thereupon some force seemed to shove Zinotchka; she laid her hands on Sasha's shoulders and let her head droop upon his waistcoat. Sasha laughed, muttered something incoherent, and with the clumsiness of a man head over ears in love, laid both hands on Zinotchka's face. And the weather, gentlemen, was exquisite. . . . The hill behind which the sun was setting, the two willows, the green bank, the sky—all together with Sasha and Zinotchka were reflected in the pond . . . perfect stillness . . . you can imagine it. Millions of butterflies with long whiskers gleamed golden above the reeds; beyond the garden they were driving the cattle. In fact, it was a perfect picture.

"Of all I had seen the only thing I understood was that Sasha was kissing Zinotchka. That was improper. If *maman* heard of it they would both catch it. Feeling for some reason ashamed I went back to the nursery, not waiting for the end of the rendezvous. There I sat over the sum-book, pondered and reflected. A triumphant smile strayed upon my countenance. On one side it was agreeable to be the possessor of another person's secret; on the other it was also very agreeable that such authorities as Sasha and Zinotchka might at any moment be convicted by me of ignorance of the social proprieties. Now they were in my power, and their peace was entirely dependent on my magnanimity. I'd let them know.

"When I went to bed, Zinotchka came into the nursery as usual to find out whether I had dropped asleep without undressing and whether I had said my prayers. I looked at her pretty, happy face and grinned. I was bursting with my secret and itching to let it out. I had to drop a hint and enjoy the effect.

" 'I know,' I said, grinning. 'Gy—y.'

" 'What do you know?'

" 'Gy—y! I saw you near the willows kissing Sasha. I followed you and saw it all. . . .'

"Zinotchka started, flushed all over, and overwhelmed by 'my hint' she sank down on the chair, on which stood a glass of water and a candlestick.

" 'I saw you . . . kissing . . .' I repeated, sniggering and enjoying her confusion. 'Aha! I'll tell mamma!'

"Cowardly Zinotchka gazed at me intently, and convincing herself that I really did know all about it, clutched my hand in despair and muttered in a trembling whisper:

" 'Petya, it is low. . . . I beg of you, for God's sake. . . . Be a man . . . don't tell anyone. . . . Decent people don't spy. . . . It's low. . . . I entreat you.'

"The poor girl was terribly afraid of my mother, a stern and virtuous lady—that was one thing; and the second was that my grinning countenance could not but outrage her first love so pure and poetical, and you can imagine the state of her heart. Thanks to me, she did not sleep a wink all night, and in the morning she appeared at breakfast with blue rings round her eyes. When I met Sasha after breakfast I could not refrain from grinning and boasting:

" 'I know! I saw you yesterday kissing Mademoiselle Zina!'

"Sasha looked at me and said:

" 'You are a fool.'

"He was not so cowardly as Zinotchka, and so my effect did not come off. That provoked me to further efforts. If Sasha was not frightened it was evident that he did not believe that I had seen and knew all about it; wait a bit, I would show him.

"At our lessons before dinner Zinotchka did not look at me, and her voice faltered. Instead of trying to scare me she tried to propitiate me in every way, giving me full marks, and not complaining to my father of my naughtiness. Being intelligent beyond my years I exploited her secret: I did not learn my lessons, walked into the schoolroom on my head, and said all sorts of rude things. In fact, if I had remained in that vein till to-day I should have become a famous blackmailer. Well, a week passed. Another person's secret irritated and fretted me like a splinter in my soul. I longed at all costs to blurt it out and gloat over the effect. And one day at dinner, when we had a lot of visitors, I gave a stupid snigger, looked fiendishly at Zinotchka and said:

" 'I know. Gy—y! I saw! . . .'

" 'What do you know?' asked my mother.

"I looked still more fiendishly at Zinotchka and Sasha. You ought to have seen how the girl flushed up, and how furious Sasha's eyes were! I bit my tongue and did not go on. Zinotchka gradually turned pale, clenched her teeth, and ate no more dinner. At our evening lessons that day I noticed a striking change in Zinotchka's face. It looked sterner, colder, as it were, more like marble, while her eyes gazed strangely straight into my face, and I give you my word of honour I have never seen such terrible, annihilating eyes, even in hounds when they overtake the wolf. I understood their expression perfectly, when in the middle of a lesson she suddenly clenched her teeth and hissed through them:

" 'I hate you! Oh, you vile, loathsome creature, if you knew how I hate you, how I detest your cropped head, your vulgar, prominent ears!'

"But at once she took fright and said:

" 'I am not speaking to you, I am repeating a part out of a play. . . .'

"Then, my friends, at night I saw her come to my bedside and gaze a long time into my face. She hated me passionately, and could not exist away from me. The contemplation of my hated pug of a face had become a necessity to her. I remember a lovely summer evening . . . with the scent of hay, perfect stillness, and so on. The moon was shining. I was walking up and down the avenue, thinking of cherry jam. Suddenly Zinotchka, looking pale and lovely, came up to me, she caught hold of my hand, and breathlessly began expressing herself:

" 'Oh, how I hate you! I wish no one harm as I do you! Let me tell you that! I want you to understand that!'

"You understand, moonlight, her pale face, breathless with passion, the stillness . . . little pig as I was I actually enjoyed it. I listened to her, looked at her eyes. . . . At first I liked it, and enjoyed the novelty. Then I was suddenly seized with terror, I gave a scream, and ran into the house at breakneck speed.

"I made up my mind that the best thing to do was to complain to *maman*. And I did complain, mentioning incidentally how Sasha had kissed Zinotchka. I was stupid, and did not know what would follow, or I should have kept the secret to myself. . . . After hearing my story *maman* flushed with indignation and said:

" 'It is not your business to speak about that, you are still very young. . . . But, what an example for children.'

"My *maman* was not only virtuous but diplomatic. To avoid a scandal she did not get rid of Zinotchka at once, but set to work gradually, systematically, to pave the way for her departure, as one does with well-bred but intolerable people. I remember that when Zinotchka did leave us the last glance she cast at the house was directed at the window at which I was sitting, and I assure you, I remember that glance to this day.

"Zinotchka soon afterwards became my brother's wife. She is the Zinaida Nikolaevna whom you know. The next time I met her I was already an ensign. In spite of all her efforts she could not recognize the hated Petya in the ensign with his moustache, but still she did not treat me quite like a relation. . . . And even now, in spite of my good-humoured baldness, meek corpulence, and unassuming air, she still looks askance at me, and feels put out when I go to see my brother. Hatred it seems can no more be forgotten than love. . . .

"Tchoo! I hear the cock crowing! Good-night. Milord! Lie down!"

The Doctor

It was still in the drawing-room, so still that a house-fly that had flown in from outside could be distinctly heard brushing against the ceiling. Olga Ivanovna, the lady of the villa, was standing by the window, looking out at the flower-beds and thinking. Dr. Tsvyetkov, who was her doctor as well as an old friend, and had been sent for to treat her son Misha, was sitting in an easy chair and swinging his hat, which he held in both hands, and he too was thinking. Except them, there was not a soul in the drawing-room or in the adjoining rooms. The sun had set, and the shades of evening began settling in the corners under the furniture and on the cornices.

The silence was broken by Olga Ivanovna.

"No misfortune more terrible can be imagined," she said, without turning from the window. "You know that life has no value for me whatever apart from the boy."

"Yes, I know that," said the doctor.

"No value whatever," said Olga Ivanovna, and her voice quivered. "He is everything to me. He is my joy, my happiness, my wealth. And if, as you say, I cease to be a mother, if he . . . dies, there will be nothing left of me but a shadow. I cannot survive it."

Wringing her hands, Olga Ivanovna walked from one window to the other and went on:

"When he was born, I wanted to send him away to the Foundling Hospital, you remember that, but, my God, how can that time be compared with now? Then I was vulgar, stupid, feather-headed, but now I am a mother, do you understand? I am a mother, and that's all I care to know. Between the present and the past there is an impassable gulf."

Silence followed again. The doctor shifted his seat from the chair to the sofa and impatiently playing with his hat, kept his eyes fixed upon Olga Ivanovna. From his face it could be seen that he wanted to speak, and was waiting for a fitting moment.

"You are silent, but still I do not give up hope," said the lady, turning round. "Why are you silent?"

"I should be as glad of any hope as you, Olga, but there is none," Tsvyetkov answered, "we must look the hideous truth in the face. The boy has a tumour on the brain, and we must try to prepare ourselves for his death, for such cases never recover."

"Nikolay, are you certain you are not mistaken?"

"Such questions lead to nothing. I am ready to answer as many as you like, but it will make it no better for us."

Olga Ivanovna pressed her face into the window curtains, and began weeping bitterly. The doctor got up and walked several times up and down the drawing-room, then went to the weeping woman, and lightly touched her arm. Judging from his uncertain movements, from the expression of his gloomy face, which looked dark in the dusk of the evening, he wanted to say something.

"Listen, Olga," he began. "Spare me a minute's attention; there is something I must ask you. You can't attend to me now, though. I'll come later, afterwards. . . ." He sat down again, and sank into thought. The bitter, imploring weeping, like the weeping of a little girl, continued. Without waiting for it to end, Tsvyetkov heaved a sigh and walked out of the drawing-room. He went into the nursery to Misha. The boy was lying on his back as before, staring at one point as though he were listening. The doctor sat down on his bed and felt his pulse.

"Misha, does your head ache?" he asked.

Misha answered, not at once: "Yes. I keep dreaming."

"What do you dream?"

"All sorts of things. . . ."

The doctor, who did not know how to talk with weeping women or with children, stroked his burning head, and muttered:

"Never mind, poor boy, never mind. . . . One can't go through life without illness. . . . Misha, who am I—do you know me?"

Misha did not answer.

"Does your head ache very badly?"

"Ve-ery. I keep dreaming."

After examining him and putting a few questions to the maid who was looking after the sick child, the doctor went slowly back to the drawing-room. There it was by now dark, and Olga Ivanovna, standing by the window, looked like a silhouette.

"Shall I light up?" asked Tsvyetkov.

No answer followed. The house-fly was still brushing against the ceiling. Not a sound floated in from outside as though the whole world, like the doctor, were thinking, and could not bring itself to speak. Olga Ivanovna was not weeping now, but as before, staring at the flower-bed in profound silence. When Tsvyetkov went up to her, and through the twilight glanced at her pale face, exhausted with grief, her expression was such as he had seen before during her attacks of acute, stupefying, sick headache.

"Nikolay Trofimitch!" she addressed him, "and what do you think about a consultation?"

"Very good; I'll arrange it to-morrow."

From the doctor's tone it could be easily seen that he put little faith in the benefit of a consultation. Olga Ivanovna would have asked him something else, but her sobs prevented her. Again she pressed her face into the window curtain. At that moment, the strains of a band playing at the club floated in distinctly. They could hear not only the wind instruments, but even the violins and the flutes.

"If he is in pain, why is he silent?" asked Olga Ivanovna. "All day long, not a sound, he never complains, and never cries. I know God will take the poor boy from us because we have not known how to prize him. Such a treasure!"

The band finished the march, and a minute later began playing a lively waltz for the opening of the ball.

"Good God, can nothing really be done?" moaned Olga Ivanovna. "Nikolay, you are a doctor and ought to know what to do! You must understand that I can't bear the loss of him! I can't survive it."

The doctor, who did not know how to talk to weeping women, heaved a sigh, and paced slowly about the drawing-room. There followed a succession of oppressive pauses interspersed with weeping and the questions which lead to nothing. The band had already played a quadrille, a polka, and another quadrille. It got quite dark. In the adjoining room, the maid lighted the lamp; and all the while the doctor kept his hat in his hands, and seemed trying to say something. Several times Olga Ivanovna went off to her son, sat by him for half an hour, and came back again into the drawing-room; she was continually breaking into tears and lamentations. The time dragged agonisingly, and it seemed as though the evening had no end.

At midnight, when the band had played the cotillion and ceased altogether, the doctor got ready to go.

"I will come again to-morrow," he said, pressing the mother's cold hand. "You go to bed."

After putting on his greatcoat in the passage and picking up his walking-stick, he stopped, thought a minute, and went back into the drawing-room.

"I'll come to-morrow, Olga," he repeated in a quivering voice. "Do you hear?"

She did not answer, and it seemed as though grief had robbed her of all power of speech. In his greatcoat and with his stick still in his hand, the doctor sat down beside her, and began in a soft, tender half-whisper, which was utterly out of keeping with his heavy, dignified figure:

"Olga! For the sake of your sorrow which I share. . . . Now, when falsehood is criminal, I beseech you to tell me the truth. You have always declared that the boy is my son. Is that the truth?"

Olga Ivanovna was silent.

"You have been the one attachment in my life," the doctor went on, "and you cannot imagine how deeply my feeling is wounded by falsehood. . . . Come, I entreat you, Olga, for once in your life, tell me the truth. . . . At these moments one cannot lie. Tell me that Misha is not my son. I am waiting."

"He is."

Olga Ivanovna's face could not be seen, but in her voice the doctor could hear hesitation. He sighed.

"Even at such moments you can bring yourself to tell a lie," he said in his ordinary voice. "There is nothing sacred to you! Do listen, do understand me. . . . You have been the one only attachment in my life. Yes, you were depraved, vulgar, but I have loved no one else but you in my life. That trivial love, now that I am growing old, is the one solitary bright spot in my memories. Why do you darken it with deception? What is it for?"

"I don't understand you."

"Oh my God!" cried Tsvyetkov. "You are lying, you understand very well!" he cried more loudly, and he began pacing about the drawing-room, angrily waving his stick. "Or have you forgotten? Then I will remind you! A father's rights to the boy are equally shared with me by Petrov and Kurovsky the lawyer, who still make you an allowance for their son's education, just as I do! Yes, indeed! I know all that quite well! I forgive your lying in the past, what does it matter? But now when you have grown older, at this moment when the boy is dying, your lying stifles me! How sorry I am that I cannot speak, how sorry I am!"

The doctor unbuttoned his overcoat, and still pacing about, said:

"Wretched woman! Even such moments have no effect on her! Even now she lies as freely as nine years ago in the Hermitage Restaurant! She is afraid if she tells me the truth I shall leave off giving her money, she thinks that if she did not lie I should not love the boy! You are lying! It's contemptible!"

The doctor rapped the floor with his stick, and cried:

"It's loathsome. Warped, corrupted creature! I must despise you, and I ought to be ashamed of my feeling. Yes! Your lying has stuck in my throat these nine years, I have endured it, but now it's too much—too much."

From the dark corner where Olga Ivanovna was sitting there came the sound of weeping. The doctor ceased speaking and cleared his throat. A silence followed. The doctor slowly buttoned up his overcoat, and began looking for his hat which he had dropped as he walked about.

"I lost my temper," he muttered, bending down to the floor. "I quite lost sight of the fact that you cannot attend to me now. . . . God knows what I have said. . . . Don't take any notice of it, Olga."

He found his hat and went towards the dark corner.

"I have wounded you," he said in a soft, tender half-whisper, "but once more I entreat you, tell me the truth; there should not be lying between us. . . . I blurted it out, and now you know that Petrov and Kurovsky are no secret to me. So now it is easy for you to tell me the truth."

Olga Ivanovna thought a moment, and with perceptible hesitation, said:

"Nikolay, I am not lying—Misha is your child."

"My God," moaned the doctor, "then I will tell you something more: I have kept your letter to Petrov in which you call him Misha's father! Olga, I know the truth, but I want to hear it from you! Do you hear?"

Olga Ivanovna made no reply, but went on weeping. After waiting for an answer the doctor shrugged his shoulders and went out.

"I will come to-morrow," he called from the passage.

All the way home, as he sat in his carriage, he was shrugging his shoulders and muttering:

"What a pity that I don't know how to speak! I haven't the gift of persuading and convincing. It's evident she does not understand me since she lies! It's evident! How can I make her see? How?"

The Runaway

It had been a long business. At first Pashka had walked with his mother in the rain, at one time across a mown field, then by forest paths, where the yellow leaves stuck to his boots; he had walked until it was daylight. Then he had stood for two hours in the dark passage, waiting for the door to open. It was not so cold and damp in the passage as in the yard, but with the high wind spurts of rain flew in even there. When the passage gradually became packed with people Pashka, squeezed among them, leaned his face against somebody's sheepskin which smelt strongly of salt fish, and sank into a doze. But at last the bolt clicked, the door flew open, and Pashka and his mother went into the waiting-room. All the patients sat on benches without stirring or speaking. Pashka looked round at them, and he too was silent, though he was seeing a great deal that was strange and funny. Only once, when a lad came into the waiting-room hopping on one leg, Pashka longed to hop too; he nudged his mother's elbow, giggled in his sleeve, and said: "Look, mammy, a sparrow."

"Hush, child, hush!" said his mother.

A sleepy-looking hospital assistant appeared at the little window.

"Come and be registered!" he boomed out.

All of them, including the funny lad who hopped, filed up to the window. The assistant asked each one his name, and his father's name, where he lived, how long he had been ill, and so on. From his mother's answers, Pashka learned that his name was not Pashka, but Pavel Galaktionov, that he was seven years old, that he could not read or write, and that he had been ill ever since Easter.

Soon after the registration, he had to stand up for a little while; the doctor in a white apron, with a towel round his waist, walked across the waiting-room. As he passed by the boy who hopped, he shrugged his shoulders, and said in a sing-song tenor:

"Well, you are an idiot! Aren't you an idiot? I told you to come on Monday, and you come on Friday. It's nothing to me if you don't come at all, but you know, you idiot, your leg will be done for!"

The lad made a pitiful face, as though he were going to beg for alms, blinked, and said:

"Kindly do something for me, Ivan Mikolaitch!"

"It's no use saying 'Ivan Mikolaitch,' " the doctor mimicked him. "You were told to come on Monday, and you ought to obey. You are an idiot, and that is all about it."

The doctor began seeing the patients. He sat in his little room, and called up the patients in turn. Sounds were continually coming from the little room, piercing wails, a child's crying, or the doctor's angry words:

"Come, why are you bawling? Am I murdering you, or what? Sit quiet!"

Pashka's turn came.

"Pavel Galaktionov!" shouted the doctor.

His mother was aghast, as though she had not expected this summons, and taking Pashka by the hand, she led him into the room.

The doctor was sitting at the table, mechanically tapping on a thick book with a little hammer.

"What's wrong?" he asked, without looking at them.

"The little lad has an ulcer on his elbow, sir," answered his mother, and her face assumed an expression as though she really were terribly grieved at Pashka's ulcer.

"Undress him!"

Pashka, panting, unwound the kerchief from his neck, then wiped his nose on his sleeve, and began deliberately pulling off his sheepskin.

"Woman, you have not come here on a visit!" said the doctor angrily. "Why are you dawdling? You are not the only one here."

Pashka hurriedly flung the sheepskin on the floor, and with his mother's help took off his shirt.... The doctor looked at him lazily, and patted him on his bare stomach.

"You have grown quite a respectable corporation, brother Pashka," he said, and heaved a sigh. "Come, show me your elbow."

Pashka looked sideways at the basin full of bloodstained slops, looked at the doctor's apron, and began to cry.

"May-ay!" the doctor mimicked him. "Nearly old enough to be married, spoilt boy, and here he is blubbering! For shame!"

Pashka, trying not to cry, looked at his mother, and in that look could be read the entreaty: "Don't tell them at home that I cried at the hospital."

The doctor examined his elbow, pressed it, heaved a sigh, clicked with his lips, then pressed it again.

"You ought to be beaten, woman, but there is no one to do it," he said. "Why didn't you bring him before? Why, the whole arm is done for. Look, foolish woman. You see, the joint is diseased!"

"You know best, kind sir . . ." sighed the woman.

"Kind sir. . . . She's let the boy's arm rot, and now it is 'kind sir.' What kind of workman will he be without an arm? You'll be nursing him and looking after him for ages. I bet if you had had a pimple on your nose, you'd have run to the hospital quick enough, but you have left your boy to rot for six months. You are all like that."

The doctor lighted a cigarette. While the cigarette smoked, he scolded the woman, and shook his head in time to the song he was humming inwardly, while he thought of something else. Pashka stood naked before him, listening and looking at the smoke. When the cigarette went out, the doctor started, and said in a lower tone:

"Well, listen, woman. You can do nothing with ointments and drops in this case. You must leave him in the hospital."

"If necessary, sir, why not?"

"We must operate on him. You stop with me, Pashka," said the doctor, slapping Pashka on the shoulder. "Let mother go home, and you and I will stop here, old man. It's nice with me, old boy, it's first-rate

here. I'll tell you what we'll do, Pashka, we will go catching finches together. I will show you a fox! We will go visiting together! Shall we?
And mother will come for you to-morrow! Eh?"

Pashka looked inquiringly at his mother.

"You stay, child!" she said.

"He'll stay, he'll stay!" cried the doctor gleefully. "And there is no
need to discuss it. I'll show him a live fox! We will go to the fair together to buy candy! Marya Denisovna, take him upstairs!"

The doctor, apparently a light-hearted and friendly fellow, seemed
glad to have company; Pashka wanted to oblige him, especially as he
had never in his life been to a fair, and would have been glad to have a
look at a live fox, but how could he do without his mother?

After a little reflection he decided to ask the doctor to let his mother
stay in the hospital too, but before he had time to open his mouth the
lady assistant was already taking him upstairs. He walked up and
looked about him with his mouth open. The staircase, the floors, and
the doorposts—everything huge, straight, and bright—were painted a
splendid yellow colour, and had a delicious smell of Lenten oil. On all
sides lamps were hanging, strips of carpet stretched along the floor,
copper taps stuck out on the walls. But best of all Pashka liked the bedstead upon which he was made to sit down, and the grey woollen coverlet. He touched the pillows and the coverlet with his hands, looked
round the ward, and made up his mind that it was very nice at the
doctor's.

The ward was not a large one, it consisted of only three beds. One
bed stood empty, the second was occupied by Pashka, and on the third
sat an old man with sour eyes, who kept coughing and spitting into a
mug. From Pashka's bed part of another ward could be seen with two
beds; on one a very pale wasted-looking man with an india-rubber
bottle on his head was asleep; on the other a peasant with his head tied
up, looking very like a woman, was sitting with his arms spread out.

After making Pashka sit down, the assistant went out and came back
a little later with a bundle of clothes under her arm.

"These are for you," she said, "put them on."

Pashka undressed and, not without satisfaction, began attiring himself in his new array. When he had put on the shirt, the drawers, and

the little grey dressing-gown, he looked at himself complacently, and thought that it would not be bad to walk through the village in that costume. His imagination pictured his mother's sending him to the kitchen garden by the river to gather cabbage leaves for the little pig; he saw himself walking along, while the boys and girls surrounded him and looked with envy at his little dressing-gown.

A nurse came into the ward, bringing two tin bowls, two spoons, and two pieces of bread. One bowl she set before the old man, the other before Pashka.

"Eat!" she said.

Looking into his bowl, Pashka saw some rich cabbage soup, and in the soup a piece of meat, and thought again that it was very nice at the doctor's, and that the doctor was not nearly so cross as he had seemed at first. He spent a long time swallowing the soup, licking the spoon after each mouthful, then when there was nothing left in the bowl but the meat he stole a look at the old man, and felt envious that he was still eating the soup. With a sigh Pashka attacked the meat, trying to make it last as long as possible, but his efforts were fruitless; the meat, too, quickly vanished. There was nothing left but the piece of bread. Plain bread without anything on it was not appetising, but there was no help for it. Pashka thought a little, and ate the bread. At that moment the nurse came in with another bowl. This time there was roast meat with potatoes in the bowl.

"And where is the bread?" asked the nurse.

Instead of answering, Pashka puffed out his cheeks, and blew out the air.

"Why did you gobble it all up?" said the nurse reproachfully. "What are you going to eat your meat with?"

She went and fetched another piece of bread. Pashka had never eaten roast meat in his life, and trying it now found it very nice. It vanished quickly, and then he had a piece of bread left bigger than the first. When the old man had finished his dinner, he put away the remains of his bread in a little table. Pashka meant to do the same, but on second thoughts ate his piece.

When he had finished he went for a walk. In the next ward, besides the two he had seen from the door, there were four other people. Of these only one drew his attention. This was a tall, extremely emaciated peasant with a morose-looking, hairy face. He was sitting on the bed, nodding his head and swinging his right arm all the time like a pendulum. Pashka could not take his eyes off him for a long time. At first the man's regular pendulum-like movements seemed to him curious, and he thought they were done for the general amusement, but when he looked into the man's face he felt frightened, and realised that he was terribly ill. Going into a third ward he saw two peasants with dark red faces as though they were smeared with clay. They were sitting motionless on their beds, and with their strange faces, in which it was hard to distinguish their features, they looked like heathen idols.

"Auntie, why do they look like that?" Pashka asked the nurse.

"They have got smallpox, little lad."

Going back to his own ward, Pashka sat down on his bed and began waiting for the doctor to come and take him to catch finches, or to go to the fair. But the doctor did not come. He got a passing glimpse of a hospital assistant at the door of the next ward. He bent over the patient on whose head lay a bag of ice, and cried: "Mihailo!"

But the sleeping man did not stir. The assistant made a gesture and went away. Pashka scrutinised the old man, his next neighbour. The old man coughed without ceasing and spat into a mug. His cough had a long-drawn-out, creaking sound. Pashka liked one peculiarity about him; when he drew the air in as he coughed, something in his chest whistled and sang on different notes.

"Grandfather, what is it whistles in you?" Pashka asked.

The old man made no answer. Pashka waited a little and asked:

"Grandfather, where is the fox?"

"What fox?"

"The live one."

"Where should it be? In the forest!"

A long time passed, but the doctor still did not appear. The nurse brought in tea, and scolded Pashka for not having saved any bread for his tea; the assistant came once more and set to work to wake Mihailo. It turned blue outside the windows, the wards were lighted up, but the doctor did not appear. It was too late now to go to the fair and catch finches; Pashka stretched himself on his bed and began thinking. He remembered the candy promised him by the doctor, the face and voice of his mother, the darkness in his hut at home, the stove, peevish granny Yegorovna . . . and he suddenly felt sad and dreary. He remembered that his mother was coming for him next day, smiled, and shut his eyes.

He was awakened by a rustling. In the next ward someone was stepping about and speaking in a whisper. Three figures were moving about Mihailo's bed in the dim light of the night-light and the ikon lamp.

"Shall we take him, bed and all, or without?" asked one of them.

"Without. You won't get through the door with the bed."

"He's died at the wrong time, the Kingdom of Heaven be his!"

One took Mihailo by his shoulders, another by his legs and lifted him up: Mihailo's arms and the skirt of his dressing-gown hung limply to the ground. A third—it was the peasant who looked like a woman—crossed himself, and all three tramping clumsily with their feet and stepping on Mihailo's skirts, went out of the ward.

There came the whistle and humming on different notes from the chest of the old man who was asleep. Pashka listened, peeped at the dark windows, and jumped out of bed in terror.

"Ma-a-mka!" he moaned in a deep bass.

And without waiting for an answer, he rushed into the next ward. There the darkness was dimly lighted up by a night-light and the ikon lamp; the patients, upset by the death of Mihailo, were sitting on their bedsteads: their dishevelled figures, mixed up with the shadows, looked broader, taller, and seemed to be growing bigger and bigger; on the furthest bedstead in the corner, where it was darkest, there sat the peasant moving his head and his hand.

Pashka, without noticing the doors, rushed into the smallpox ward, from there into the corridor, from the corridor he flew into a big room where monsters, with long hair and the faces of old women, were lying and sitting on the beds. Running through the women's wing he found himself again in the corridor, saw the banisters of the staircase he knew already, and ran downstairs. There he recognised the waiting-room in which he had sat that morning, and began looking for the door into the open air.

The latch creaked, there was a whiff of cold wind, and Pashka, stumbling, ran out into the yard. He had only one thought—to run, to run! He did not know the way, but felt convinced that if he ran he would be sure to find himself at home with his mother. The sky was overcast, but there was a moon behind the clouds. Pashka ran from the steps straight forward, went round the barn and stumbled into some thick bushes; after stopping for a minute and thinking, he dashed back again to the hospital, ran round it, and stopped again undecided; behind the hospital there were white crosses.

"Ma-a-mka!" he cried, and dashed back.

Running by the dark sinister buildings, he saw one lighted window.

The bright red patch looked dreadful in the darkness, but Pashka, frantic with terror, not knowing where to run, turned towards it. Beside the window was a porch with steps, and a front door with a white board on it; Pashka ran up the steps, looked in at the window, and was at once possessed by intense overwhelming joy. Through the window he saw the merry affable doctor sitting at the table reading a book. Laughing with happiness, Pashka stretched out his hands to the person he knew and tried to call out, but some unseen force choked him and struck at his legs; he staggered and fell down on the steps unconscious.

When he came to himself it was daylight, and a voice he knew very well, that had promised him a fair, finches, and a fox, was saying beside him:

"Well, you are an idiot, Pashka! Aren't you an idiot? You ought to be beaten, but there's no one to do it."

The Cattle-Dealers

The long goods train has been standing for hours in the little station.
The engine is as silent as though its fire had gone out; there is not a
soul near the train or in the station yard.

A pale streak of light comes from one of the vans and glides over
the rails of a siding. In that van two men are sitting on an outspread
cape: one is an old man with a big gray beard, wearing a sheepskin coat
and a high lambskin hat, somewhat like a busby; the other a beardless
youth in a threadbare cloth reefer jacket and muddy high boots. They
are the owners of the goods. The old man sits, his legs stretched out
before him, musing in silence; the young man half reclines and softly
strums on a cheap accordion. A lantern with a tallow candle in it is
hanging on the wall near them.

The van is quite full. If one glances in through the dim light of the
lantern, for the first moment the eyes receive an impression of something shapeless, monstrous, and unmistakably alive, something very
much like gigantic crabs which move their claws and feelers, crowd together, and noiselessly climb up the walls to the ceiling; but if one
looks more closely, horns and their shadows, long lean backs, dirty
hides, tails, eyes begin to stand out in the dusk. They are cattle and

their shadows. There are eight of them in the van. Some turn round and stare at the men and swing their tails. Others try to stand or lie down more comfortably. They are crowded. If one lies down the others must stand and huddle closer. No manger, no halter, no litter, not a wisp of hay. . . .*

At last the old man pulls out of his pocket a silver watch and looks at the time: a quarter past two.

"We have been here nearly two hours," he says, yawning. "Better go and stir them up, or we may be here till morning. They have gone to sleep, or goodness knows what they are up to."

The old man gets up and, followed by his long shadow, cautiously gets down from the van into the darkness. He makes his way along beside the train to the engine, and after passing some two dozen vans sees a red open furnace; a human figure sits motionless facing it; its peaked cap, nose, and knees are lighted up by the crimson glow, all the rest is black and can scarcely be distinguished in the darkness.

"Are we going to stay here much longer?" asks the old man.

No answer. The motionless figure is evidently asleep. The old man clears his throat impatiently and, shrinking from the penetrating damp, walks round the engine, and as he does so the brilliant light of the two engine lamps dazzles his eyes for an instant and makes the night even blacker to him; he goes to the station.

The platform and steps of the station are wet. Here and there are white patches of freshly fallen melting snow. In the station itself it is light and as hot as a steam-bath. There is a smell of paraffin. Except for the weighing-machine and a yellow seat on which a man wearing a guard's uniform is asleep, there is no furniture in the place at all. On the left are two wide-open doors. Through one of them the telegraphic apparatus and a lamp with a green shade on it can be seen; through the other, a small room, half of it taken up by a dark cupboard. In this room the head guard and the engine-driver are sitting on the window-sill. They are both feeling a cap with their fingers and disputing.

---

* On many railway lines, in order to avoid accidents, it is against the regulations to carry hay on the trains, and so live stock are without fodder on the journey.—*Author's note.*

"That's not real beaver, it's imitation," says the engine-driver. "Real beaver is not like that. Five roubles would be a high price for the whole cap, if you care to know!"

"You know a great deal about it, . . ." the head guard says, offended. "Five roubles, indeed! Here, we will ask the merchant. Mr. Malahin," he says, addressing the old man, "what do you say: is this imitation beaver or real?"

Old Malahin takes the cap into his hand, and with the air of a connoisseur pinches the fur, blows on it, sniffs at it, and a contemptuous smile lights up his angry face.

"It must be imitation!" he says gleefully. "Imitation it is."

A dispute follows. The guard maintains that the cap is real beaver, and the engine-driver and Malahin try to persuade him that it is not. In the middle of the argument the old man suddenly remembers the object of his coming.

"Beaver and cap is all very well, but the train's standing still, gentlemen!" he says. "Who is it we are waiting for? Let us start!"

"Let us," the guard agrees. "We will smoke another cigarette and go on. But there is no need to be in a hurry. . . . We shall be delayed at the next station anyway!"

"Why should we?"

"Oh, well. . . . We are too much behind time. . . . If you are late at one station you can't help being delayed at the other stations to let the trains going the opposite way pass. Whether we set off now or in the morning we shan't be number fourteen. We shall have to be number twenty-three."

"And how do you make that out?"

"Well, there it is."

Malahin looks at the guard, reflects, and mutters mechanically as though to himself:

"God be my judge, I have reckoned it and even jotted it down in a notebook; we have wasted thirty-four hours standing still on the journey. If you go on like this, either the cattle will die, or they won't pay me two roubles for the meat when I do get there. It's not traveling, but ruination."

The guard raises his eyebrows and sighs with an air that seems to say: "All that is unhappily true!" The engine-driver sits silent, dreamily looking at the cap. From their faces one can see that they have a secret thought in common, which they do not utter, not because they want to conceal it, but because such thoughts are much better expressed by signs than by words. And the old man understands. He feels in his pocket, takes out a ten-rouble note, and without preliminary words, without any change in the tone of his voice or the expression of his face, but with the confidence and directness with which probably only Russians give and take bribes, he gives the guard the note. The latter takes it, folds it in four, and without undue haste puts it in his pocket. After that all three go out of the room, and waking the sleeping guard on the way, go on to the platform.

"What weather!" grumbles the head guard, shrugging his shoulders. "You can't see your hand before your face."

"Yes, it's vile weather."

From the window they can see the flaxen head of the telegraph clerk appear beside the green lamp and the telegraphic apparatus; soon after another head, bearded and wearing a red cap, appears beside it—no doubt that of the station-master. The station-master bends down to the table, reads something on a blue form, rapidly passing his cigarette along the lines. . . . Malahin goes to his van.

The young man, his companion, is still half reclining and hardly audibly strumming on the accordion. He is little more than a boy, with no trace of a mustache; his full white face with its broad cheek-bones is childishly dreamy; his eyes have a melancholy and tranquil look unlike that of a grown-up person, but he is broad, strong, heavy and rough like the old man; he does not stir nor shift his position, as though he is not equal to moving his big body. It seems as though any movement he made would tear his clothes and be so noisy as to frighten both him and the cattle. From under his big fat fingers that clumsily pick out the stops and keys of the accordion comes a steady flow of thin, tinkling sounds which blend into a simple, monotonous little tune; he listens to it, and is evidently much pleased with his performance.

A bell rings, but with such a muffled note that it seems to come from far away. A hurried second bell soon follows, then a third and the guard's whistle. A minute passes in profound silence; the van does not move, it stands still, but vague sounds begin to come from beneath it, like the crunch of snow under sledge-runners; the van begins to shake and the sounds cease. Silence reigns again. But now comes the clank of buffers, the violent shock makes the van start and, as it were, give a lurch forward, and all the cattle fall against one another.

"May you be served the same in the world to come," grumbles the old man, setting straight his cap, which had slipped on the back of his head from the jolt. "He'll maim all my cattle like this!"

Yasha gets up without a word and, taking one of the fallen beasts by the horns, helps it to get on to its legs. . . . The jolt is followed by a stillness again. The sounds of crunching snow come from under the van again, and it seems as though the train had moved back a little.

"There will be another jolt in a minute," says the old man. And the convulsive quiver does, in fact, run along the train, there is a crashing sound and the bullocks fall on one another again.

"It's a job!" says Yasha, listening. "The train must be heavy. It seems it won't move."

"It was not heavy before, but now it has suddenly got heavy. No, my lad, the guard has not gone shares with him, I expect. Go and take him something, or he will be jolting us till morning."

Yasha takes a three-rouble note from the old man and jumps out of the van. The dull thud of his heavy footsteps resounds outside the van and gradually dies away. Stillness. . . . In the next van a bullock utters a prolonged subdued "moo," as though it were singing.

Yasha comes back. A cold damp wind darts into the van.

"Shut the door, Yasha, and we will go to bed," says the old man. "Why burn a candle for nothing?"

Yasha moves the heavy door; there is a sound of a whistle, the engine and the train set off.

"It's cold," mutters the old man, stretching himself on the cape and laying his head on a bundle. "It is very different at home! It's warm and clean and soft, and there is room to say your prayers, but here we are worse off than any pigs. It's four days and nights since I have taken off my boots."

Yasha, staggering from the jolting of the train, opens the lantern and snuffs out the wick with his wet fingers. The light flares up, hisses like a frying-pan and goes out.

"Yes, my lad," Malahin goes on, as he feels Yasha lie down beside him and the young man's huge back huddle against his own, "it's cold. There is a draught from every crack. If your mother or your sister were to sleep here for one night they would be dead by morning. There it is, my lad, you wouldn't study and go to the high school like your brothers, so you must take the cattle with your father. It's your own fault, you have only yourself to blame. . . . Your brothers are asleep in their beds now, they are snug under the bedclothes, but you, the careless and lazy one, are in the same box as the cattle. . . . Yes. . . ."

The old man's words are inaudible in the noise of the train, but for a long time he goes on muttering, sighing and clearing his throat. . . . The cold air in the railway van grows thicker and more stifling. The pungent odor of fresh dung and smoldering candle makes it so repulsive and acrid that it irritates Yasha's throat and chest as he falls asleep. He coughs and sneezes, while the old man, being accustomed to it, breathes with his whole chest as though nothing were amiss, and merely clears his throat.

To judge from the swaying of the van and the rattle of the wheels the train is moving rapidly and unevenly. The engine breathes heavily, snorting out of time with the pulsation of the train, and altogether there is a medley of sounds. The bullocks huddle together uneasily and knock their horns against the walls.

When the old man wakes up, the deep blue sky of early morning is peeping in at the cracks and at the little uncovered window. He feels unbearably cold, especially in the back and the feet. The train is standing still; Yasha, sleepy and morose, is busy with the cattle.

The old man wakes up out of humor. Frowning and gloomy, he clears his throat angrily and looks from under his brows at Yasha who, supporting a bullock with his powerful shoulder and slightly lifting it, is trying to disentangle its leg.

"I told you last night that the cords were too long," mutters the old man; "but no, 'It's not too long, Daddy.' There's no making you do anything, you will have everything your own way. . . . Block-head!"

He angrily moves the door open and the light rushes into the van. A passenger train is standing exactly opposite the door, and behind it a red building with a roofed-in platform—a big station with a refreshment bar. The roofs and bridges of the trains, the earth, the sleepers, all are covered with a thin coating of fluffy, freshly fallen snow. In the spaces between the carriages of the passenger train the passengers can be seen moving to and fro, and a red-haired, red-faced gendarme walking up and down; a waiter in a frock-coat and a snow-white shirt-front, looking cold and sleepy, and probably very much dissatisfied with his fate, is running along the platform carrying a glass of tea and two rusks on a tray.

The old man gets up and begins saying his prayers towards the east. Yasha, having finished with the bullock and put down the spade in the corner, stands beside him and says his prayers also. He merely moves his lips and crosses himself; the father prays in a loud whisper and pronounces the end of each prayer aloud and distinctly.

". . . And the life of the world to come. Amen," the old man says aloud, draws in a breath, and at once whispers another prayer, rapping out clearly and firmly at the end: ". . . and lay calves upon Thy altar!"

After saying his prayers, Yasha hurriedly crosses himself and says: "Five kopecks, please."

And on being given the five-kopeck piece, he takes a red copper teapot and runs to the station for boiling water. Taking long jumps over the rails and sleepers, leaving huge tracks in the feathery snow, and pouring away yesterday's tea out of the teapot, he runs to the refreshment room and jingles his five-kopeck piece against his teapot. From the van the bar-keeper can be seen pushing away the big teapot and refusing to give half of his samovar for five kopecks, but Yasha turns the tap himself and, spreading wide his elbows so as not to be interfered with, fills his teapot with boiling water.

"Damned blackguard!" the bar-keeper shouts after him as he runs back to the railway van.

The scowling face of Malahin grows a little brighter over the tea.

"We know how to eat and drink, but we don't remember our work. Yesterday we could do nothing all day but eat and drink, and I'll be bound we forgot to put down what we spent. What a memory! Lord have mercy on us!"

The old man recalls aloud the expenditure of the day before, and writes down in a tattered notebook where and how much he had given to guards, engine-drivers, oilers. . . .

Meanwhile the passenger train has long ago gone off, and an engine runs backwards and forwards on the empty line, apparently without any definite object, but simply enjoying its freedom. The sun has risen and is playing on the snow; bright drops are falling from the station roof and the tops of the vans.

Having finished his tea, the old man lazily saunters from the van to the station. Here in the middle of the first-class waiting-room he sees the familiar figure of the guard standing beside the station-master, a young man with a handsome beard and in a magnificent rough woollen overcoat. The young man, probably new to his position, stands in the same place, gracefully shifting from one foot to the other like a good racehorse, looks from side to side, salutes everyone that passes by, smiles and screws up his eyes. . . . He is red-cheeked, sturdy, and good-humored; his face is full of eagerness, and is as fresh as though he had just fallen from the sky with the feathery snow. Seeing Malahin, the guard sighs guiltily and throws up his hands.

"We can't go number fourteen," he says. "We are very much behind time. Another train has gone with that number."

The station-master rapidly looks through some forms, then turns his beaming blue eyes upon Malahin, and, his face radiant with smiles and freshness, showers questions on him:

"You are Mr. Malahin? You have the cattle? Eight vanloads? What is to be done now? You are late and I let number fourteen go in the night. What are we to do now?"

The young man discreetly takes hold of the fur of Malahin's coat with two pink fingers and, shifting from one foot to the other, explains affably and convincingly that such and such numbers have gone already, and that such and such are going, and that he is ready to do for Malahin everything in his power. And from his face it is evident that he is ready to do anything to please not only Malahin, but the whole world—he is so happy, so pleased, and so delighted! The old man listens, and though he can make absolutely nothing of the intricate system of numbering the trains, he nods his head approvingly, and he, too, puts two fingers on the soft wool of the rough coat. He enjoys seeing and hearing the polite and genial young man. To show goodwill on his side also, he takes out a ten-rouble note and, after a moment's thought, adds a couple of rouble notes to it, and gives them to the station-master. The latter takes them, puts his finger to his cap, and gracefully thrusts them into his pocket.

"Well, gentlemen, can't we arrange it like this?" he says, kindled by a new idea that has flashed on him. "The troop train is late, . . . as you see, it is not here, . . . so why shouldn't you go as the troop train?* And I will let the troop train go as twenty-eight. Eh?"

"If you like," agrees the guard.

"Excellent!" the station-master says, delighted. "In that case there is no need for you to wait here; you can set off at once. I'll dispatch you immediately. Excellent!"

He salutes Malahin and runs off to his room, reading forms as he goes. The old man is very much pleased by the conversation that has just taken place; he smiles and looks about the room as though looking for something else agreeable.

"We'll have a drink, though," he says, taking the guard's arm.

"It seems a little early for drinking."

"No, you must let me treat you to a glass in a friendly way."

They both go to the refreshment bar. After having a drink the guard spends a long time selecting something to eat.

He is a very stout, elderly man, with a puffy and discolored face. His fatness is unpleasant, flabby-looking, and he is sallow as people are who drink too much and sleep irregularly.

"And now we might have a second glass," says Malahin. "It's cold now, it's no sin to drink. Please take some. So I can rely upon you, Mr. Guard, that there will be no hindrance or unpleasantness for the rest of the journey. For you know in moving cattle every hour is precious.

---

* The train destined especially for the transport of troops is called the troop train; when there are no troops it takes goods, and goes more rapidly than ordinary goods train.—*Author's Note.*

To-day meat is one price; and to-morrow, look you, it will be another. If you are a day or two late and don't get your price, instead of a profit you get home—excuse my saying it—without your breeches. Pray take a little.... I rely on you, and as for standing you something or what you like, I shall be pleased to show you my respect at any time."

After having fed the guard, Malahin goes back to the van.

"I have just got hold of the troop train," he says to his son. "We shall go quickly. The guard says if we go all the way with that number we shall arrive at eight o'clock to-morrow evening. If one does not bestir oneself, my boy, one gets nothing.... That's so.... So you watch and learn...."

After the first bell a man with a face black with soot, in a blouse and filthy frayed trousers hanging very slack, comes to the door of the van. This is the oiler, who had been creeping under the carriages and tapping the wheels with a hammer.

"Are these your vans of cattle?" he asks.

"Yes. Why?"

"Why, because two of the vans are not safe. They can't go on, they must stay here to be repaired."

"Oh, come, tell us another! You simply want a drink, to get something out of me.... You should have said so."

"As you please, only it is my duty to report it at once."

Without indignation or protest, simply, almost mechanically, the old man takes two twenty-kopeck pieces out of his pocket and gives them to the oiler. He takes them very calmly, too, and looking good-naturedly at the old man enters into conversation.

"You are going to sell your cattle, I suppose.... It's good business!"

Malahin sighs and, looking calmly at the oiler's black face, tells him that trading in cattle used certainly to be profitable, but now it has become a risky and losing business.

"I have a mate here," the oiler interrupts him. "You merchant gentlemen might make him a little present...."

Malahin gives something to the mate too. The troop train goes quickly and the waits at the stations are comparatively short. The old man is pleased. The pleasant impression made by the young man in the rough overcoat has gone deep, the vodka he has drunk slightly clouds his brain, the weather is magnificent, and everything seems to be going well. He talks without ceasing, and at every stopping place runs to the refreshment bar. Feeling the need of a listener, he takes with him first the guard, and then the engine-driver, and does not simply drink, but makes a long business of it, with suitable remarks and clinking of glasses.

"You have your job and we have ours," he says with an affable smile. "May God prosper us and you, and not our will but His be done."

The vodka gradually excites him and he is worked up to a great pitch of energy. He wants to bestir himself, to fuss about, to make inquiries, to talk incessantly. At one minute he fumbles in his pockets and bundles and looks for some form. Then he thinks of something and cannot remember it; then takes out his pocketbook, and with no sort of object counts over his money. He bustles about, sighs and groans, clasps his hands. . . . Laying out before him the letters and telegrams from the meat salesmen in the city, bills, post office and telegraphic receipt forms, and his notebook, he reflects aloud and insists on Yasha's listening.

And when he is tired of reading over forms and talking about prices, he gets out at the stopping places, runs to the vans where his cattle are, does nothing, but simply clasps his hands and exclaims in horror.

"Oh, dear! oh, dear!" he says in a complaining voice. "Holy Martyr Vlassy! Though they are bullocks, though they are beasts, yet they want to eat and drink as men do. . . . It's four days and nights since they have drunk or eaten. Oh, dear! oh, dear!"

Yasha follows him and does what he is told like an obedient son. He does not like the old man's frequent visits to the refreshment bar. Though he is afraid of his father, he cannot refrain from remarking on it.

"So you have begun already!" he says, looking sternly at the old man. "What are you rejoicing at? Is it your name-day or what?"

"Don't you dare teach your father."

"Fine goings on!"

When he has not to follow his father along the other vans Yasha sits on the cape and strums on the accordion. Occasionally he gets out and walks lazily beside the train; he stands by the engine and turns a prolonged, unmoving stare on the wheels or on the workmen tossing blocks of wood into the tender; the hot engine wheezes, the falling blocks come down with the mellow, hearty thud of fresh wood; the engine-driver and his assistant, very phlegmatic and imperturbable persons, perform incomprehensible movements and don't hurry themselves. After standing for a while by the engine, Yasha saunters lazily to the station; here he looks at the eatables in the refreshment bar, reads aloud some quite uninteresting notice, and goes back slowly to the cattle van. His face expresses neither boredom nor desire; apparently he does not care where he is, at home, in the van, or by the engine.

Towards evening the train stops near a big station. The lamps have only just been lighted along the line; against the blue background in the fresh limpid air the lights are bright and pale like stars; they are only red and glowing under the station roof, where it is already dark. All the lines are loaded up with carriages, and it seems that if another train came in there would be no place for it. Yasha runs to the station for boiling water to make the evening tea. Well-dressed ladies and high-school boys are walking on the platform. If one looks into the distance from the platform there are far-away lights twinkling in the evening dusk on both sides of the station—that is the town. What town? Yasha does not care to know. He sees only the dim lights and wretched buildings beyond the station, hears the cabmen shouting, feels a sharp, cold wind on his face, and imagines that the town is probably disagreeable, uncomfortable, and dull.

While they are having tea, when it is quite dark and a lantern is hanging on the wall again as on the previous evening, the train quivers from a slight shock and begins moving backwards. After going a little way it stops; they hear indistinct shouts, someone sets the chains clanking near the buffers, and shouts, "Ready!" The train moves and goes forward. Ten minutes later it is dragged back again.

Getting out of the van, Malahin does not recognize his train. His eight vans of bullocks are standing in the same row with some trolleys which were not a part of the train before. Two or three of these are loaded with rubble and the others are empty. The guards running to and fro on the platform are strangers. They give unwilling and indistinct answers to his questions. They have no thoughts to spare for Malahin; they are in a hurry to get the train together so as to finish as soon as possible and be back in the warmth.

"What number is this?" asks Malahin.

"Number eighteen."

"And where is the troop train? Why have you taken me off the troop train?"

Getting no answer, the old man goes to the station. He looks first for the familiar figure of the head guard and, not finding him, goes to the station-master. The station-master is sitting at a table in his own room, turning over a bundle of forms. He is busy, and affects not to see the newcomer. His appearance is impressive: a cropped black head, prominent ears, a long hooked nose, a swarthy face; he has a forbidding and, as it were, offended expression. Malahin begins making his complaint at great length.

"What?" queries the station-master. "How is this?" He leans against the back of his chair and goes on, growing indignant: "What is it? and why shouldn't you go by number eighteen? Speak more clearly, I don't understand! How is it? Do you want me to be everywhere at once?"

He showers questions on him, and for no apparent reason grows sterner and sterner. Malahin is already feeling in his pocket for his pocketbook, but in the end the station-master, aggrieved and indignant, for some unknown reason jumps up from his seat and runs out of the room. Malahin shrugs his shoulders, and goes out to look for someone else to speak to.

From boredom or from a desire to put the finishing stroke to a busy day, or simply that a window with the inscription "Telegraph!" on it catches his eye, he goes to the window and expresses a desire to send off a telegram. Taking up a pen, he thinks for a moment, and writes on a blue form: "Urgent. Traffic Manager. Eight vans of live stock. Delayed at every station. Kindly send an express number. Reply paid. Malahin."

Having sent off the telegram, he goes back to the station-master's room. There he finds, sitting on a sofa covered with gray cloth, a benevolent-looking gentleman in spectacles and a cap of racoon fur; he is wearing a peculiar overcoat very much like a lady's, edged with fur, with frogs and slashed sleeves. Another gentleman, dried-up and sinewy, wearing the uniform of a railway inspector, stands facing him.

"Just think of it," says the inspector, addressing the gentleman in the queer overcoat. "I'll tell you an incident that really is A1! The Z. railway line in the coolest possible way stole three hundred trucks from the N. line. It's a fact, sir! I swear it! They carried them off, repainted them, put their letters on them, and that's all about it. The N. line sends its agents everywhere, they hunt and hunt. And then—can you imagine it?—the Company happen to come upon a broken-down carriage of the Z. line. They repair it at their depot, and all at once, bless my soul! see their own mark on the wheels. What do you say to that? Eh? If I did it they would send me to Siberia, but the railway companies simply snap their fingers at it!"

It is pleasant to Malahin to talk to educated, cultured people. He strokes his beard and joins in the conversation with dignity.

"Take this case, gentlemen, for instance," he says. "I am transporting cattle to X. Eight vanloads. Very good. . . . Now let us say they charge me for each vanload as a weight of ten tons; eight bullocks don't weigh ten tons, but much less, yet they don't take any notice of that. . . ."

At that instant Yasha walks into the room, looking for his father. He listens and is about to sit down on a chair, but probably thinking of his weight goes and sits on the window-sill.

"They don't take any notice of that," Malahin goes on, "and charge me and my son the third-class fare, too, forty-two roubles, for going in the van with the bullocks. This is my son Yakov. I have two more at home, but they have gone in for study. Well, and apart from that it is my opinion that the railways have ruined the cattle trade. In old days when they drove them in herds it was better."

The old man's talk is lengthy and drawn out. After every sentence he looks at Yasha as though he would say: "See how I am talking to clever people."

"Upon my word!" the inspector interrupts him. "No one is indignant, no one criticizes. And why? It is very simple. An abomination strikes the eye and arouses indignation only when it is exceptional, when the established order is broken by it. Here, where, saving your presence, it constitutes the long-established program and forms and enters into the basis of the order itself, where every sleeper on the line bears the trace of it and stinks of it, one too easily grows accustomed to it! Yes, sir!"

The second bell rings, the gentlemen in the queer overcoat gets up. The inspector takes him by the arm and, still talking with heat, goes off with him to the platform. After the third bell the station-master runs into his room, and sits down at his table.

"Listen, with what number am I to go?" asks Malahin.

The station-master looks at a form and says indignantly:

"Are you Malahin, eight vanloads? You must pay a rouble a van and six roubles and twenty kopecks for stamps. You have no stamps. Total, fourteen roubles, twenty kopecks."

Receiving the money, he writes something down, dries it with sand, and, hurriedly snatching up a bundle of forms, goes quickly out of the room.

At ten o'clock in the evening Malahin gets an answer from the traffic manager: "Give precedence."

Reading the telegram through, the old man winks significantly and, very well pleased with himself, puts it in his pocket.

"Here," he says to Yasha, "look and learn."

At midnight his train goes on. The night is dark and cold like the previous one; the waits at the stations are long. Yasha sits on the cape and imperturbably strums on the accordion, while the old man is still more eager to exert himself. At one of the stations he is overtaken by a desire to lodge a complaint. At his request a gendarme sits down and writes:

"*November* 10, 188–.—I, non-commissioned officer of the Z. section of the N. police department of railways, Ilya Tchered, in accordance with article II of the statute of May 19, 1871, have drawn up this protocol at the station of X. as herewith follows. . . ."

"What am I to write next?" asks the gendarme.

Malahin lays out before him forms, postal and telegraph receipts, accounts.... He does not know himself definitely what he wants of the gendarme; he wants to describe in the protocol not any separate episode but his whole journey, with all his losses and conversations with station-masters—to describe it lengthily and vindictively.

"At the station of Z.," he says, "write that the station-master unlinked my vans from the troop train because he did not like my countenance."

And he wants the gendarme to be sure to mention his countenance. The latter listens wearily, and goes on writing without hearing him to the end. He ends his protocol thus:

"The above desposition I, non-commissioned officer Tchered, have written down in this protocol with a view to present it to the head of the Z. section, and have handed a copy thereof to Gavril Malahin."

The old man takes the copy, adds it to the papers with which his side pocket is stuffed, and, much pleased, goes back to his van.

In the morning Malahin wakes up again in a bad humor, but his wrath vents itself not on Yasha but the cattle.

"The cattle are done for!" he grumbles. "They are done for! They are at the last gasp! God be my judge! they will all die. Tfoo!"

The bullocks, who have had nothing to drink for many days, tortured by thirst, are licking the hoar frost on the walls, and when Malachin goes up to them they begin licking his cold fur jacket. From their clear, tearful eyes it can be seen that they are exhausted by thirst and the jolting of the train, that they are hungry and miserable.

"It's a nice job taking you by rail, you wretched brutes!" mutters Malahin. "I could wish you were dead to get it over! It makes me sick to look at you!"

At midday the train stops at a big station where, according to the regulations, there was drinking water provided for cattle.

Water is given to the cattle, but the bullocks will not drink it: the water is too cold....

———

Two more days and nights pass, and at last in the distance in the murky fog the city comes into sight. The journey is over. The train comes to a standstill before reaching the town, near a goods' station. The bullocks, released from the van, stagger and stumble as though they were walking on slippery ice.

Having got through the unloading and veterinary inspection, Malahin and Yasha take up their quarters in a dirty, cheap hotel in the outskirts of the town, in the square in which the cattle-market is held. Their lodgings are filthy and their food is disgusting, unlike what they ever have at home; they sleep to the harsh strains of a wretched steam hurdy-gurdy which plays day and night in the restaurant under their lodging.

The old man spends his time from morning till night going about looking for purchasers, and Yasha sits for days in the hotel room, or goes out into the street to look at the town. He sees the filthy square heaped up with dung, the signboards of restaurants, the turreted walls of a monastery in the fog. Sometimes he runs across the street and looks into the grocer's shop, admires the jars of cakes of different colors, yawns, and lazily saunters back to his room. The city does not interest him.

At last the bullocks are sold to a dealer. Malahin hires drovers. The cattle are divided into herds, ten in each, and driven to the other end of the town. The bullocks, exhausted, go with drooping heads through the noisy streets, and look indifferently at what they see for the first and last time in their lives. The tattered drovers walk after them, their heads drooping too. They are bored. . . . Now and then some drover starts out of his brooding, remembers that there are cattle in front of him intrusted to his charge, and to show that he is doing his duty brings a stick down full swing on a bullock's back. The bullock staggers with the pain, runs forward a dozen paces, and looks about him as though he were ashamed at being beaten before people.

After selling the bullocks and buying for his family presents such as they could perfectly well have bought at home, Malahin and Yasha get ready for their journey back. Three hours before the train goes the old man, who has already had a drop too much with the purchaser and so is fussy, goes down with Yasha to the restaurant and sits down to drink tea. Like all provincials, he cannot eat and drink alone: he must have company as fussy and as fond of sedate conversation as himself.

"Call the host!" he says to the waiter; "tell him I should like to entertain him."

The hotel-keeper, a well-fed man, absolutely indifferent to his lodgers, comes and sits down to the table.

"Well, we have sold our stock," Malahin says, laughing. "I have swapped my goat for a hawk. Why, when we set off the price of meat was three roubles ninety kopecks, but when we arrived it had dropped to three roubles twenty-five. They tell us we are too late, we should have been here three days earlier, for now there is not the same demand for meat, St. Philip's fast has come. . . . Eh? It's a nice how-do-you-do! It meant a loss of fourteen roubles on each bullock. Yes. But only think what it costs to bring the stock! Fifteen roubles carriage, and you must put down six roubles for each bullock, tips, bribes, drinks, and one thing and another. . . ."

The hotel-keeper listens out of politeness and reluctantly drinks tea. Malahin sighs and groans, gesticulates, jests about his ill-luck, but everything shows that the loss he has sustained does not trouble him much. He doesn't mind whether he has lost or gained as long as he has listeners, has something to make a fuss about, and is not late for his train.

An hour later Malahin and Yasha, laden with bags and boxes, go downstairs from the hotel room to the front door to get into a sledge and drive to the station. They are seen off by the hotel-keeper, the waiter, and various women. The old man is touched. He thrusts ten-kopeck pieces in all directions, and says in a sing-song voice:

"Good-by, good health to you! God grant that all may be well with you. Please God if we are alive and well we shall come again in Lent. Good-by. Thank you. God bless you!"

Getting into the sledge, the old man spends a long time crossing himself in the direction in which the monastery walls make a patch of darkness in the fog. Yasha sits beside him on the very edge of the seat with his legs hanging over the side. His face as before shows no sign of emotion and expresses neither boredom nor desire. He is not glad that he is going home, nor sorry that he has not had time to see the sights of the city.

"Drive on!"

The cabman whips up the horse and, turning round, begins swearing at the heavy and cumbersome luggage.

In Trouble

Pyotr Semyonitch, the bank manager, together with the book-keeper, his assistant, and two members of the board, were taken in the night to prison. The day after the upheaval the merchant Avdeyev, who was one of the committee of auditors, was sitting with his friends in the shop saying:

"So it is God's will, it seems. There is no escaping your fate. Here to-day we are eating caviare and to-morrow, for aught we know, it will be prison, beggary, or maybe death. Anything may happen. Take Pyotr Semyonitch, for instance. . . ."

He spoke, screwing up his drunken eyes, while his friends went on drinking, eating caviare, and listening. Having described the disgrace and helplessness of Pyotr Semyonitch, who only the day before had been powerful and respected by all, Avdeyev went on with a sigh:

"The tears of the mouse come back to the cat. Serve them right, the scoundrels! They could steal, the rooks, so let them answer for it!"

"You'd better look out, Ivan Danilitch, that you don't catch it too!" one of his friends observed.

"What has it to do with me?"

"Why, they were stealing, and what were you auditors thinking about? I'll be bound, you signed the audit."

"It's all very well to talk!" laughed Avdeyev: "Signed it, indeed! They used to bring the accounts to my shop and I signed them. As though I understood! Give me anything you like, I'll scrawl my name to it. If you were to write that I murdered someone I'd sign my name to it. I haven't time to go into it; besides, I can't see without my spectacles."

After discussing the failure of the bank and the fate of Pyotr Semyonitch, Avdeyev and his friends went to eat pie at the house of a friend whose wife was celebrating her name-day. At the name-day party everyone was discussing the bank failure. Avdeyev was more excited than anyone, and declared that he had long foreseen the crash and knew two years before that things were not quite right at the bank. While they were eating pie he described a dozen illegal operations which had come to his knowledge.

"If you knew, why did you not give information?" asked an officer who was present.

"I wasn't the only one: the whole town knew of it," laughed Avdeyev. "Besides, I haven't the time to hang about the law courts, damn them!"

He had a nap after the pie and then had dinner, then had another nap, then went to the evening service at the church of which he was a warden; after the service he went back to the name-day party and played preference till midnight. Everything seemed satisfactory.

But when Avdeyev hurried home after midnight the cook, who opened the door to him, looked pale, and was trembling so violently that she could not utter a word. His wife, Elizaveta Trofimovna, a flabby, overfed woman, with her grey hair hanging loose, was sitting on the sofa in the drawing-room quivering all over, and vacantly rolling her eyes as though she were drunk. Her elder son, Vassily, a high-school boy, pale too, and extremely agitated, was fussing round her with a glass of water.

"What's the matter?" asked Avdeyev, and looked angrily sideways at the stove (his family was constantly being upset by the fumes from it).

"The examining magistrate has just been with the police," answered Vassily; "they've made a search."

Avdeyev looked round him. The cupboards, the chests, the tables—everything bore traces of the recent search. For a minute Avdeyev stood motionless as though petrified, unable to understand; then his whole inside quivered and seemed to grow heavy, his left leg went numb, and, unable to endure his trembling, he lay down flat on the sofa. He felt his inside heaving and his rebellious left leg tapping against the back of the sofa.

In the course of two or three minutes he recalled the whole of his past, but could not remember any crime deserving of the attention of the police.

"It's all nonsense," he said, getting up. "They must have slandered me. To-morrow I must lodge a complaint of their having dared to do such a thing."

Next morning after a sleepless night Avdeyev, as usual, went to his shop. His customers brought him the news that during the night the public prosecutor had sent the deputy manager and the head-clerk to prison as well. This news did not disturb Avdeyev. He was convinced that he had been slandered, and that if he were to lodge a complaint to-day the examining magistrate would get into trouble for the search of the night before.

Between nine and ten o'clock he hurried to the town hall to see the secretary, who was the only educated man in the town council.

"Vladimir Stepanitch, what's this new fashion?" he said, bending down to the secretary's ear. "People have been stealing, but how do I come in? What has it to do with me? My dear fellow," he whispered, "there has been a search at my house last night! Upon my word! Have they gone crazy? Why touch me?"

"Because one shouldn't be a sheep," the secretary answered calmly. "Before you sign you ought to look."

"Look at what? But if I were to look at those accounts for a thousand years I could not make head or tail of them! It's all Greek to me! I am no book-keeper. They used to bring them to me and I signed them."

"Excuse me. Apart from that you and your committee are seriously compromised. You borrowed nineteen thousand from the bank, giving no security."

"Lord have mercy upon us!" cried Avdeyev in amazement. "I am not the only one in debt to the bank! The whole town owes it money. I pay the interest and I shall repay the debt. What next! And besides, to tell the honest truth, it wasn't I myself borrowed the money. Pyotr Semyonitch forced it upon me. 'Take it,' he said, 'take it. If you don't take it,' he said, 'it means that you don't trust us and fight shy of us. You take it,' he said, 'and build your father a mill.' So I took it."

"Well, you see, none but children or sheep can reason like that. In any case, *signor,* you need not be anxious. You can't escape trial, of course, but you are sure to be acquitted."

The secretary's indifference and calm tone restored Avdeyev's composure. Going back to his shop and finding friends there, he again began drinking, eating caviare, and airing his views. He almost forgot the police search, and he was only troubled by one circumstance which he could not help noticing: his left leg was strangely numb, and his stomach for some reason refused to do its work.

That evening destiny dealt another overwhelming blow at Avdeyev: at an extraordinary meeting of the town council all members who were on the staff of the bank, Avdeyev among them, were asked to resign, on the ground that they were charged with a criminal offence. In the morning he received a request to give up immediately his duties as churchwarden.

After that Avdeyev lost count of the blows dealt him by fate, and strange, unprecedented days flitted rapidly by, one after another, and every day brought some new, unexpected surprise. Among other things, the examining magistrate sent him a summons, and he returned home after the interview, insulted and red in the face.

"He gave me no peace, pestering me to tell him why I had signed. I signed, that's all about it. I didn't do it on purpose. They brought the papers to the shop and I signed them. I am no great hand at reading writing."

Young men with unconcerned faces arrived, sealed up the shop, and made an inventory of all the furniture of the house. Suspecting some intrigue behind this, and, as before, unconscious of any wrongdoing, Avdeyev in his mortification ran from one Government office to another lodging complaints. He spent hours together in waiting-rooms, composed long petitions, shed tears, swore. To his complaints the public prosecutor and the examining magistrate made the indifferent and rational reply: "Come to us when you are summoned: we have not time to attend to you now." While others answered: "It is not our business."

The secretary, an educated man, who, Avdeyev thought, might have helped him, merely shrugged his shoulders and said:

"It's your own fault. You shouldn't have been a sheep."

The old man exerted himself to the utmost, but his left leg was still numb, and his digestion was getting worse and worse. When he was weary of doing nothing and was getting poorer and poorer, he made up his mind to go to his father's mill, or to his brother, and begin dealing in corn. His family went to his father's and he was left alone. The days flitted by, one after another. Without a family, without a shop, and without money, the former churchwarden, an honoured and respected man, spent whole days going the round of his friends' shops, drinking, eating, and listening to advice. In the mornings and in the evenings, to while away the time, he went to church. Looking for hours together at the ikons, he did not pray, but pondered. His conscience was clear, and he ascribed his position to mistake and misunderstanding; to his mind, it was all due to the fact that the officials and the examining magistrates were young men and inexperienced. It seemed to him that if he were to talk it over in detail and open his heart to some elderly judge, everything would go right again. He did not understand his judges, and he fancied they did not understand him.

The days raced by, and at last, after protracted, harassing delays, the day of the trial came. Avdeyev borrowed fifty roubles, and providing himself with spirit to rub on his leg and a decoction of herbs for his digestion, set off for the town where the circuit court was being held.

The trial lasted for ten days. Throughout the trial Avdeyev sat among his companions in misfortune with the stolid composure and dignity befitting a respectable and innocent man who is suffering for no fault of his own: he listened and did not understand a word. He was in an antagonistic mood. He was angry at being detained so long in the court, at being unable to get Lenten food anywhere, at his defending counsel's not understanding him, and, as he thought, saying the wrong thing. He thought that the judges did not understand their business. They took scarcely any notice of Avdeyev, they only addressed him once in three days, and the questions they put to him were of such a character that Avdeyev raised a laugh in the audience each time he answered them. When he tried to speak of the expenses he had incurred, of his losses, and of his meaning to claim his costs from the court, his counsel turned round and made an incomprehensible grimace, the public laughed, and the judge announced sternly that that had nothing to do with the case. The last words that he was allowed to say were not what his counsel had instructed him to say, but something quite different, which raised a laugh again.

During the terrible hour when the jury were consulting in their room he sat angrily in the refreshment bar, not thinking about the jury at all. He did not understand why they were so long deliberating when everything was so clear, and what they wanted of him.

Getting hungry, he asked the waiter to give him some cheap Lenten dish. For forty kopecks they gave him some cold fish and carrots. He ate it and felt at once as though the fish were heaving in a chilly lump in his stomach; it was followed by flatulence, heartburn, and pain.

Afterwards, as he listened to the foreman of the jury reading out the questions point by point, there was a regular revolution taking place in his inside, his whole body was bathed in a cold sweat, his left leg was numb; he did not follow, understood nothing, and suffered unbearably at not being able to sit or lie down while the foreman was reading. At last, when he and his companions were allowed to sit down, the public prosecutor got up and said something unintelligible, and all at once, as though they had sprung out of the earth, some police officers appeared on the scene with drawn swords and surrounded all the prisoners. Avdeyev was told to get up and go.

Now he understood that he was found guilty and in charge of the police, but he was not frightened nor amazed; such a turmoil was going on in his stomach that he could not think about his guards.

"So they won't let us go back to the hotel?" he asked one of his companions. "But I have three roubles and an untouched quarter of a pound of tea in my room there."

He spent the night at the police station; all night he was aware of a loathing for fish, and was thinking about the three roubles and the quarter of a pound of tea. Early in the morning, when the sky was beginning to turn blue, he was told to dress and set off. Two soldiers with bayonets took him to prison. Never before had the streets of the town seemed to him so long and endless. He walked not on the pavement but in the middle of the road in the muddy, thawing snow. His inside was still at war with the fish, his left leg was numb; he had forgotten his goloshes either in the court or in the police station, and his feet felt frozen.

Five days later all the prisoners were brought before the court again to hear their sentence. Avdeyev learnt that he was sentenced to exile in the province of Tobolsk. And that did not frighten nor amaze him either. He fancied for some reason that the trial was not yet over, that there were more adjournments to come, and that the final decision had not been reached yet. . . . He went on in the prison expecting this final decision every day.

Only six months later, when his wife and his son Vassily came to say good-bye to him, and when in the wasted, wretchedly dressed old woman he scarcely recognized his once fat and dignified Elizaveta Trofimovna, and when he saw his son wearing a short, shabby reefer-jacket and cotton trousers instead of the high-school uniform, he realized that his fate was decided, and that whatever new "decision" there might be, his past would never come back to him. And for the first time since the trial and his imprisonment the angry expression left his face, and he wept bitterly.

The Kiss

At eight o'clock on the evening of the twentieth of May all the six batteries of the N—— Reserve Artillery Brigade halted for the night in the village of Myestetchki on their way to camp. When the general commotion was at its height, while some officers were busily occupied around the guns, while others, gathered together in the square near the church enclosure, were listening to the quartermasters, a man in civilian dress, riding a strange horse, came into sight round the church. The little dun-coloured horse with a good neck and a short tail came, moving not straight forward, but as it were sideways, with a sort of dance step, as though it were being lashed about the legs. When he reached the officers the man on the horse took off his hat and said:

"His Excellency Lieutenant-General von Rabbek invites the gentlemen to drink tea with him this minute. . . ."

The horse turned, danced, and retired sideways; the messenger raised his hat once more, and in an instant disappeared with his strange horse behind the church.

"What the devil does it mean?" grumbled some of the officers, dispersing to their quarters. "One is sleepy, and here this Von Rabbek with his tea! We know what tea means."

The officers of all the six batteries remembered vividly an incident of the previous year, when during manœuvres they, together with the officers of a Cossack regiment, were in the same way invited to tea by a count who had an estate in the neighbourhood and was a retired army officer: the hospitable and genial count made much of them, fed them, and gave them drink, refused to let them go to their quarters in the village and made them stay the night. All that, of course, was very nice—nothing better could be desired, but the worst of it was, the old army officer was so carried away by the pleasure of the young men's company that till sunrise he was telling the officers anecdotes of his glorious past, taking them over the house, showing them expensive pictures, old engravings, rare guns, reading them autograph letters from great people, while the weary and exhausted officers looked and listened, longing for their beds and yawning in their sleeves; when at last their host let them go, it was too late for sleep.

Might not this Von Rabbek be just such another? Whether he were or not, there was no help for it. The officers changed their uniforms, brushed themselves, and went all together in search of the gentleman's house. In the square by the church they were told they could get to His Excellency's by the lower path—going down behind the church to the river, going along the bank to the garden, and there an avenue would taken them to the house; or by the upper way—straight from the church by the road which, half a mile from the village, led right up to His Excellency's granaries. The officers decided to go by the upper way.

"What Von Rabbek is it?" they wondered on the way. "Surely not the one who was in command of the N—— cavalry division at Plevna?"

"No, that was not Von Rabbek, but simply Rabbe and no 'von.' "

"What lovely weather!"

At the first of the granaries the road divided in two: one branch went straight on and vanished in the evening darkness, the other led to the owner's house on the right. The officers turned to the right and began to speak more softly. . . . On both sides of the road stretched stone granaries with red roofs, heavy and sullen-looking, very much like barracks of a district town. Ahead of them gleamed the windows of the manor-house.

"A good omen, gentlemen," said one of the officers. "Our setter is the foremost of all; no doubt he scents game ahead of us! ..."

Lieutenant Lobytko, who was walking in front, a tall and stalwart fellow, though entirely without moustache (he was over five-and-twenty, yet for some reason there was no sign of hair on his round, well-fed face), renowned in the brigade for his peculiar faculty for divining the presence of women at a distance, turned round and said:

"Yes, there must be women here; I feel that by instinct."

On the threshold the officers were met by Von Rabbek himself, a comely-looking man of sixty in civilian dress. Shaking hands with his guests, he said that he was very glad and happy to see them, but begged them earnestly for God's sake to excuse him for not asking them to stay the night; two sisters with their children, some brothers, and some neighbours, had come on a visit to him, so that he had not one spare room left.

The General shook hands with every one, made his apologies, and smiled, but it was evident by his face that he was by no means so delighted as their last year's count, and that he had invited the officers simply because, in his opinion, it was a social obligation to do so. And the officers themselves, as they walked up the softly carpeted stairs, as they listened to him, felt that they had been invited to this house simply because it would have been awkward not to invite them; and at the sight of the footmen, who hastened to light the lamps in the entrance below and in the anteroom above, they began to feel as though they had brought uneasiness and discomfort into the house with them. In a house in which two sisters and their children, brothers, and neighbours were gathered together, probably on account of some family festivity, or event, how could the presence of nineteen unknown officers possibly be welcome?

At the entrance to the drawing-room the officers were met by a tall, graceful old lady with black eyebrows and a long face, very much like the Empress Eugénie. Smiling graciously and majestically, she said she was glad and happy to see her guests, and apologized that her husband and she were on this occasion unable to invite *messieurs les officers* to stay the night. From her beautiful majestic smile, which instantly vanished from her face every time she turned away from her guests, it was evident that she had seen numbers of officers in her day, that she was in no humour for them now, and if she invited them to her house and apologized for not doing more, it was only because her breeding and position in society required it of her.

When the officers went into the big dining-room, there were about a dozen people, men and ladies, young and old, sitting at tea at the end of a long table. A group of men was dimly visible behind their chairs, wrapped in a haze of cigar smoke; and in the midst of them stood a lanky young man with red whiskers, talking loudly, with a lisp, in English. Through a door beyond the group could be seen a light room with pale blue furniture.

"Gentlemen, there are so many of you that it is impossible to introduce you all!" said the General in a loud voice, trying to sound very cheerful. "Make each other's acquaintance, gentlemen, without any ceremony!"

The officers—some with very serious and even stern faces, others with forced smiles, and all feeling extremely awkward—somehow made their bows and sat down to tea.

The most ill at ease of them all was Ryabovitch—a little officer in spectacles, with sloping shoulders, and whiskers like a lynx's. While some of his comrades assumed a serious expression, while others wore forced smiles, his face, his lynx-like whiskers, and spectacles seemed to say: "I am the shyest, most modest, and most undistinguished officer in the whole brigade!" At first, on going into the room and sitting down to the table, he could not fix his attention on any one face or object. The faces, the dresses, the cut-glass decanters of brandy, the steam from the glasses, the moulded cornices—all blended in one general impression that inspired in Ryabovitch alarm and a desire to hide his head. Like a lecturer making his first appearance before the public, he saw everything that was before his eyes, but apparently only had a dim understanding of it (among physiologists this condition, when the subject sees but does not understand, is called psychical blindness). After a little while, growing accustomed to his surroundings, Ryabovitch saw clearly and began to observe. As a shy man, unused to society, what struck him first was that in which he had always been deficient—namely, the extraordinary boldness of his new acquaintances. Von Rabbek, his wife, two elderly ladies, a young lady in a lilac dress, and the young man with the red whiskers, who was, it appeared, a younger son of Von Rabbek, very cleverly, as though they had rehearsed it beforehand, took seats between the officers, and at once got up a heated discussion in which the visitors could not help taking part. The lilac young lady hotly asserted that the artillery had a much better time than the cavalry and the infantry, while Von Rabbek and the elderly ladies maintained the opposite. A brisk interchange of talk followed. Ryabovitch watched the lilac young lady who argued so hotly about what was unfamiliar and utterly uninteresting to her, and watched artificial smiles come and go on her face.

Von Rabbek and his family skilfully drew the officers into the discussion, and meanwhile kept a sharp lookout over their glasses and mouths, to see whether all of them were drinking, whether all had enough sugar, why some one was not eating cakes or not drinking brandy. And the longer Ryabovitch watched and listened, the more he was attracted by this insincere but splendidly disciplined family.

After tea the officers went into the drawing-room. Lieutenant Lobytko's instinct had not deceived him. There were a great number of girls and young married ladies. The "setter" lieutenant was soon standing by a very young, fair girl in a black dress, and, bending down to her jauntily, as though leaning on an unseen sword, smiled and shrugged his shoulders coquettishly. He probably talked very interesting nonsense, for the fair girl looked at his well-fed face condescendingly and asked indifferently, "Really?" And from that uninterested "Really?" the setter, had he been intelligent, might have concluded that she would never call him to heel.

The piano struck up; the melancholy strains of a valse floated out of the wide open windows, and every one, for some reason, remembered that it was spring, a May evening. Every one was conscious of the fragrance of roses, of lilac, and of the young leaves of the poplar. Ryabovitch, in whom the brandy he had drunk made itself felt, under the influence of the music stole a glance towards the window, smiled, and began watching the movements of the women, and it seemed to him that the smell of roses, of poplars, and lilac came not from the garden, but from the ladies' faces and dresses.

Von Rabbek's son invited a scraggy-looking young lady to dance, and waltzed round the room twice with her. Lobytko, gliding over the parquet floor, flew up to the lilac young lady and whirled her away. Dancing began. . . . Ryabovitch stood near the door among those who were not dancing and looked on. He had never once danced in his whole life, and he had never once in his life put his arm round the waist of a respectable woman. He was highly delighted that a man should in the sight of all take a girl he did not know round the waist and offer her his shoulder to put her hand on, but he could not imagine himself in the position of such a man. There were times when he envied the boldness and swagger of his companions and was inwardly wretched; the consciousness that he was timid, that he was round-shouldered and uninteresting, that he had a long waist and lynx-like whiskers, had deeply mortified him, but with years he had grown used to this feeling, and now, looking at his comrades dancing or loudly talking, he no longer envied them, but only felt touched and mournful.

When the quadrille began, young Von Rabbek came up to those who were not dancing and invited two officers to have a game at billiards. The officers accepted and went with him out of the drawing-room. Ryabovitch, having nothing to do and wishing to take part in the general movement, slouched after them. From the big drawing-room they went into the little drawing-room, then into a narrow corridor with a glass roof, and thence into a room in which on their entrance three sleepy-looking footmen jumped up quickly from the sofa. At last, after passing through a long succession of rooms, young Von Rabbek and the officers came into a small room where there was a billiard-table. They began to play.

Ryabovitch, who had never played any game but cards, stood near the billiard-table and looked indifferently at the players, while they in unbuttoned coats, with cues in their hands, stepped about, made puns, and kept shouting out unintelligible words.

The players took no notice of him, and only now and then one of them, shoving him with his elbow or accidentally touching him with the end of his cue, would turn round and say "Pardon!" Before the first game was over he was weary of it, and began to feel he was not wanted and in the way.... He felt disposed to return to the drawing-room, and he went out.

On his way back he met with a little adventure. When he had gone half-way he noticed he had taken a wrong turning. He distinctly remembered that he ought to meet three sleepy footmen on his way, but he had passed five or six rooms, and those sleepy figures seemed to have vanished into the earth. Noticing his mistake, he walked back a little way and turned to the right; he found himself in a little dark room which he had not seen on his way to the billiard-room. After standing there a little while, he resolutely opened the first door that met his eyes and walked into an absolutely dark room. Straight in front could be seen the crack in the doorway through which there was a gleam of vivid light; from the other side of the door came the muffled sound of a melancholy mazurka. Here, too, as in the drawing-room, the windows were wide open and there was a smell of poplars, lilac and roses....

Ryabovitch stood still in hesitation.... At that moment, to his surprise, he heard hurried footsteps and the rustling of a dress, a breathless feminine voice whispered "At last!" And two soft, fragrant, unmistakably feminine arms were clasped about his neck; a warm cheek was pressed to his cheek, and simultaneously there was the sound of a kiss. But at once the bestower of the kiss uttered a faint shriek and skipped back from him, as it seemed to Ryabovitch, with aversion. He, too, almost shrieked and rushed towards the gleam of light at the door....

When he went back into the drawing-room his heart was beating and his hands were trembling so noticeably that he made haste to hide them behind his back. At first he was tormented by shame and dread that the whole drawing-room knew that he had just been kissed and embraced by a woman. He shrank into himself and looked uneasily about him, but as he became convinced that people were dancing and talking as calmly as ever, he gave himself up entirely to the new sensation which he had never experienced before in his life. Something strange was happening to him. . . . His neck, round which soft, fragrant arms had so lately been clasped, seemed to him to be anointed with oil; on his left cheek near his moustache where the unknown had kissed him there was a faint chilly tingling sensation as from peppermint drops, and the more he rubbed the place the more distinct was the chilly sensation; all over, from head to foot, he was full of a strange new feeling which grew stronger and stronger. . . . He wanted to dance, to talk, to run into the garden, to laugh aloud. . . . He quite forgot that he was round-shouldered and uninteresting, that he had lynx-like whiskers and an "undistinguished appearance" (that was how his appearance had been described by some ladies whose conversation he had accidentally overheard). When Von Rabbek's wife happened to pass by him, he gave her such a broad and friendly smile that she stood still and looked at him inquiringly.

"I like your house immensely!" he said, setting his spectacles straight.

The General's wife smiled and said that the house had belonged to her father; then she asked whether his parents were living, whether he had long been in the army, why he was so thin, and so on. . . . After receiving answers to her questions, she went on, and after his conversation with her his smiles were more friendly than ever, and he thought he was surrounded by splendid people. . . .

At supper Ryabovitch ate mechanically everything offered him, drank, and without listening to anything, tried to understand what had just happened to him. . . . The adventure was of a mysterious and romantic character, but it was not difficult to explain it. No doubt some girl or young married lady had arranged a tryst with some one in the dark room; had waited a long time, and being nervous and excited had taken Ryabovitch for her hero; this was the more probable as Ryabovitch had stood still hesitating in the dark room, so that he, too, had seemed like a person expecting something. . . . This was how Ryabovitch explained to himself the kiss he had received.

"And who is she?" he wondered, looking round at the women's faces. "She must be young, for elderly ladies don't give rendezvous. That she was a lady, one could tell by the rustle of her dress, her perfume, her voice. . . ."

His eyes rested on the lilac young lady, and he thought her very attractive; she had beautiful shoulders and arms, a clever face, and a delightful voice. Ryabovitch, looking at her, hoped that she and no one else was his unknown. . . . But she laughed somehow artificially and wrinkled up her long nose, which seemed to him to make her look old. Then he turned his eyes upon the fair girl in a black dress. She was younger, simpler, and more genuine, had a charming brow, and drank very daintily out of her wineglass. Ryabovitch now hoped that it was she. But soon he began to think her face flat, and fixed his eyes upon the one next her.

"It's difficult to guess," he thought, musing. "If one takes the shoulders and arms of the lilac one only, adds the brow of the fair one and the eyes of the one on the left of Lobytko, then . . ."

He made a combination of these things in his mind and so formed the image of the girl who had kissed him, the image that he wanted her to have, but could not find at the table. . . .

After supper, replete and exhilarated, the officers began to take leave and say thank you. Von Rabbek and his wife began again apologizing that they could not ask them to stay the night.

"Very, very glad to have met you, gentlemen," said Von Rabbek, and this time sincerely (probably because people are far more sincere and good-humoured at speeding their parting guests than on meeting them). "Delighted. I hope you will come on your way back! Don't stand on ceremony! Where are you going? Do you want to go by the upper way? No, go across the garden; it's nearer here by the lower way."

The officers went out into the garden. After the bright light and the noise the garden seemed very dark and quiet. They walked in silence all the way to the gate. They were a little drunk, pleased, and in good spirits, but the darkness and silence made them thoughtful for a minute. Probably the same idea occurred to each one of them as to Ryabovitch: would there ever come a time for them when, like Von Rabbek, they would have a large house, a family, a garden—when they, too, would be able to welcome people, even though insincerely, feed them, make them drunk and contented?

Going out of the garden gate, they all began talking at once and laughing loudly about nothing. They were walking now along the little path that led down to the river, and then ran along the water's edge, winding round the bushes on the bank, the pools, and the willows that overhung the water. The bank and the path were scarcely visible, and the other bank was entirely plunged in darkness. Stars were reflected here and there on the dark water; they quivered and were broken up on the surface—and from that alone it could be seen that the river was flowing rapidly. It was still. Drowsy curlews cried plaintively on the further bank, and in one of the bushes on the nearest side a nightingale was trilling loudly, taking no notice of the crowd of officers. The officers stood round the bush, touched it, but the nightingale went on singing.

"What a fellow!" they exclaimed approvingly. "We stand beside him and he takes not a bit of notice! What a rascal!"

At the end of the way the path went uphill, and, skirting the church enclosure, turned into the road. Here the officers, tired with walking uphill, sat down and lighted their cigarettes. On the other side of the river a murky red fire came into sight, and having nothing better to do, they spent a long time in discussing whether it was a camp fire or a light in a window, or something else. . . . Ryabovitch, too, looked at the light, and he fancied that the light looked and winked at him, as though it knew about the kiss.

On reaching his quarters, Ryabovitch undressed as quickly as possible and got into bed. Lobytko and Lieutenant Merzlyakov—a peaceable, silent fellow, who was considered in his own circle a highly educated officer, and was always, whenever it was possible, reading the "Vyestnik Evropi," which he carried about with him everywhere— were quartered in the same hut with Ryabovitch. Lobytko undressed, walked up and down the room for a long while with the air of a man who has not been satisfied, and sent his orderly for beer. Merzlyakov got into bed, put a candle by his pillow and plunged into reading the "Vyestnik Evropi."

"Who was she?" Ryabovitch wondered, looking at the smoky ceiling.

His neck still felt as though he had been anointed with oil, and there was still the chilly sensation near his mouth as though from peppermint drops. The shoulders and arms of the young lady in lilac, the brow and the truthful eyes of the fair girl in black, waists, dresses, and brooches, floated through his imagination. He tried to fix his attention on these images, but they danced about, broke up and flickered. When these images vanished altogether from the broad dark background which every man sees when he closes his eyes, he began to hear hurried footsteps, the rustle of skirts, the sound of a kiss and—an intense groundless joy took possession of him. . . . Abandoning himself to this joy, he heard the orderly return and announce that there was no beer. Lobytko was terribly indignant, and began pacing up and down again.

"Well, isn't he an idiot?" he kept saying, stopping first before Ryabovitch and then before Merzlyakov. "What a fool and a dummy a man must be not to get hold of any beer! Eh? Isn't he a scoundrel?"

"Of course you can't get beer here," said Merzlyakov, not removing his eyes from the "Vyestnik Evropi."

"Oh! Is that your opinion?" Lobytko persisted. "Lord have mercy upon us, if you dropped me on the moon I'd find you beer and women directly! I'll go and find some at once. . . . You may call me an impostor if I don't!"

He spent a long time in dressing and pulling on his high boots, then finished smoking his cigarette in silence and went out.

"Rabbek, Grabbek, Labbek," he muttered, stopping in the outer room. "I don't care to go alone, damn it all! Ryabovitch, wouldn't you like to go for a walk? Eh?"

Receiving no answer, he returned, slowly undressed and got into bed. Merzlyakov sighed, put the "Vyestnik Evropi" away, and put out the light.

"H'm! . . . ." muttered Lobytko, lighting a cigarette in the dark.

Ryabovitch pulled the bed-clothes over his head, curled himself up in bed, and tried to gather together the floating images in his mind and to combine them into one whole. But nothing came of it. He soon fell asleep, and his last thought was that some one had caressed him and made him happy—that something extraordinary, foolish, but joyful and delightful, had come into his life. The thought did not leave him even in his sleep.

When he woke up the sensations of oil on his neck and the chill of peppermint about his lips had gone, but joy flooded his heart just as the day before. He looked enthusiastically at the window-frames, gilded by the light of the rising sun, and listened to the movement of the passers-by in the street. People were talking loudly close to the window. Lebedetsky, the commander of Ryabovitch's battery, who had only just overtaken the brigade, was talking to his sergeant at the top of his voice, being always accustomed to shout.

"What else?" shouted the commander.

"When they were shoeing yesterday, your high nobility, they drove a nail into Pigeon's hoof. The vet. put on clay and vinegar; they are leading him apart now. And also, your honour, Artemyev got drunk yesterday, and the lieutenant ordered him to be put in the limber of a spare gun-carriage."

The sergeant reported that Karpov had forgotten the new cords for the trumpets and the rings for the tents, and that their honours, the officers, had spent the previous evening visiting General Von Rabbek. In the middle of this conversation the red-bearded face of Lebedetsky appeared in the window. He screwed up his short-sighted eyes, looking at the sleepy faces of the officers, and said good-morning to them.

"Is everything all right?" he asked.

"One of the horses has a sore neck from the new collar," answered Lobytko, yawning.

The commander sighed, thought a moment, and said in a loud voice:

"I am thinking of going to see Alexandra Yevgrafovna. I must call on her. Well, good-bye. I shall catch you up in the evening."

A quarter of an hour later the brigade set off on its way. When it was moving along the road by the granaries, Ryabovitch looked at the house on the right. The blinds were down in all the windows. Evidently the household was still asleep. The one who had kissed Ryabovitch the day before was asleep, too. He tried to imagine her asleep. The wide-open windows of the bedroom, the green branches peeping in, the morning freshness, the scent of the poplars, lilac, and roses, the bed, a chair, and on it the skirts that had rustled the day before, the little slippers, the little watch on the table—all this he pictured to himself clearly and distinctly, but the features of the face, the sweet sleepy smile, just what was characteristic and important, slipped through his imagination like quicksilver through the fingers. When he had ridden on half a mile, he looked back: the yellow church, the house, and the river, were all bathed in light; the river with its bright green banks, with the blue sky reflected in it and glints of silver in the sunshine here and there, was very beautiful. Ryabovitch gazed for the last time at Myestetchki, and he felt as sad as though he were parting with something very near and dear to him.

And before him on the road lay nothing but long familiar, uninteresting pictures. . . . To right and to left, fields of young rye and buckwheat with rooks hopping about in them. If one looked ahead, one saw dust and the backs of men's heads; if one looked back, one saw the same dust and faces. . . . Foremost of all marched four men with sabres—this was the vanguard. Next, behind, the crowd of singers, and behind them the trumpeters on horseback. The vanguard and the chorus of singers, like torch-bearers in a funeral procession, often forgot to keep the regulation distance and pushed a long way ahead. . . . Ryabovitch was with the first cannon of the fifth battery. He could see all the four batteries moving in front of him. For any one not a military man this long tedious procession of a moving brigade seems an intricate and unintelligible muddle; one cannot understand why there are so many people round one cannon, and why it is drawn by so many horses in such a strange network of harness, as though it really were so terrible and heavy. To Ryabovitch it was all perfectly comprehensible and therefore uninteresting. He had known for ever so long why at the head of each battery there rode a stalwart bombardier, and why he was called a bombardier; immediately behind this bombardier could be seen the horsemen of the first and then of the middle units. Ryabovitch knew that the horses on which they rode, those on the left, were called one name, while those on the right were called another—it was extremely uninteresting. Behind the horsemen came two shaft-horses. On one of them sat a rider with the dust of yesterday on his back and a clumsy and funny-looking piece of wood on his leg. Ryabovitch knew the object of this piece of wood, and did not think it funny. All the riders waved their whips mechanically and shouted from time to time. The cannon itself was ugly. On the fore part lay sacks of oats covered with canvas, and the cannon itself was hung all over with kettles, soldiers' knapsacks, bags, and looked like some small harmless animal surrounded for some unknown reason by men and horses. To the leeward of it marched six men, the gunners, swinging their arms. After the cannon there came again more bombardiers, riders, shaft-horses, and behind them another cannon, as ugly and unimpressive as the first. After the second followed a third, a fourth; near the fourth an officer, and so on. There were six batteries in all in the brigade, and four cannons in each battery. The procession covered half a mile; it ended in a string of wagons near which an extremely attractive creature—the ass, Magar, brought by a battery commander from Turkey—paced pensively with his long-eared head drooping.

Ryabovitch looked indifferently before and behind, at the backs of heads and at faces; at any other time he would have been half asleep, but now he was entirely absorbed in his new agreeable thoughts. At first when the brigade was setting off on the march he tried to persuade himself that the incident of the kiss could only be interesting as a mysterious little adventure, that it was in reality trivial, and to think of it seriously, to say the least of it, was stupid; but now he bade farewell to logic and gave himself up to dreams. . . . At one moment he imagined himself in Von Rabbek's drawing-room beside a girl who was like the young lady in lilac and the fair girl in black; then he would close his eyes and see himself with another, entirely unknown girl, whose features were very vague. In his imagination he talked, caressed her, leaned on her shoulder, pictured war, separation, then meeting again, supper with his wife, children. . . .

"Brakes on!" the word of command rang out every time they went downhill.

He, too, shouted "Brakes on!" and was afraid this shout would disturb his reverie and bring him back to reality. . . .

As they passed by some landowner's estate Ryabovitch looked over the fence into the garden. A long avenue, straight as a ruler, strewn with yellow sand and bordered with young birch-trees, met his eyes.... With the eagerness of a man given up to dreaming, he pictured to himself little feminine feet tripping along yellow sand, and quite unexpectedly had a clear vision in his imagination of the girl who had kissed him and whom he had succeeded in picturing to himself the evening before at supper. This image remained in his brain and did not desert him again.

At midday there was a shout in the rear near the string of wagons:

"Easy! Eyes to the left! Officers!"

The general of the brigade drove by in a carriage with a pair of white horses. He stopped near the second battery, and shouted something which no one understood. Several officers, among them Ryabovitch, galloped up to them.

"Well?" asked the general, blinking his red eyes. "Are there any sick?"

Receiving an answer, the general, a little skinny man, chewed, thought for a moment and said, addressing one of the officers:

"One of your drivers of the third cannon has taken off his leg-guard and hung it on the fore part of the cannon, the rascal. Reprimand him."

He raised his eyes to Ryabovitch and went on:

"It seems to me your front strap is too long."

Making a few other tedious remarks, the general looked at Lobytko and grinned.

"You look very melancholy today, Lieutenant Lobytko," he said. "Are you pining for Madame Lopuhov? Eh? Gentlemen, he is pining for Madame Lopuhov."

The lady in question was a very stout and tall person who had long passed her fortieth year. The general, who had a predilection for solid ladies, whatever their ages, suspected a similar taste in his officers. The officers smiled respectfully. The general, delighted at having said something very amusing and biting, laughed loudly, touched his coachman's back, and saluted. The carriage rolled on....

"All I am dreaming about now which seems to me so impossible and unearthly is really quite an ordinary thing," thought Ryabovitch, looking at the clouds of dust racing after the general's carriage. "It's all very ordinary, and every one goes through it.... That general, for instance, has once been in love; now he is married and has children. Captain Vahter, too, is married and beloved, though the nape of his neck is very red and ugly and he has no waist. . . . Salmanov is coarse and very Tatar, but he has had a love affair that has ended in marriage. . . . I am the same as every one else, and I, too, shall have the same experience as every one else, sooner or later. . . ."

And the thought that he was an ordinary person, and that his life was ordinary, delighted him and gave him courage. He pictured *her* and his happiness as he pleased, and put no rein on his imagination. . . .

When the brigade reached their halting-place in the evening, and the officers were resting in their tents, Ryabovitch, Merzlyakov, and Lobytko were sitting round a box having supper. Merzlyakov ate without haste, and, as he munched deliberately, read the "Vyestnik Evropi," which he held on his knees. Lobytko talked incessantly and kept filling up his glass with beer, and Ryabovitch, whose head was confused from dreaming all day long, drank and said nothing. After three glasses he got a little drunk, felt weak, and had an irresistible desire to impart his new sensations to his comrades.

"A strange thing happened to me at those Von Rabbeks'," he began, trying to put an indifferent and ironical tone into his voice. "You know I went into the billiard-room. . . ."

He began describing very minutely the incident of the kiss, and a moment later relapsed into silence. . . . In the course of that moment he had told everything, and it surprised him dreadfully to find how short a time it took him to tell it. He had imagined that he could have been telling the story of the kiss till next morning. Listening to him, Lobytko, who was a great liar and consequently believed no one, looked at him sceptically and laughed. Merzlyakov twitched his eyebrows and, without removing his eyes from the "Vyestnik Evropi," said:

"That's an odd thing! How strange! . . . throws herself on a man's neck, without addressing him by name. . . . She must be some sort of hysterical neurotic."

"Yes, she must," Ryabovitch agreed.

"A similar thing once happened to me," said Lobytko, assuming a scared expression. "I was going last year to Kovno.... I took a second-class ticket. The train was crammed, and it was impossible to sleep. I gave the guard half a rouble; he took my luggage and led me to another compartment.... I lay down and covered myself with a rug.... It was dark, you understand. Suddenly I felt some one touch me on the shoulder and breathe in my face. I made a movement with my hand and felt somebody's elbow.... I opened my eyes and only imagine—a woman. Black eyes, lips red as a prime salmon, nostrils breathing passionately—a bosom like a buffer...."

"Excuse me," Merzlyakov interrupted calmly, "I understand about the bosom, but how could you see the lips if it was dark?"

Lobytko began trying to put himself right and laughing at Merzlyakov's unimaginativeness. It made Ryabovitch wince. He walked away from the box, got into bed, and vowed never to confide again.

Camp life began.... The days flowed by, one very much like another. All those days Ryabovitch felt, thought, and behaved as though he were in love. Every morning when his orderly handed him water to wash with, and he sluiced his head with cold water, he thought there was something warm and delightful in his life.

In the evenings when his comrades began talking of love and women, he would listen, and draw up closer; and he wore the expression of a soldier when he hears the description of a battle in which he has taken part. And on the evenings when the officers, out on the spree with the setter—Lobytko—at their head, made Don Juan excursions to the "suburb," and Ryabovitch took part in such excursions, he always was sad, felt profoundly guilty, and inwardly begged *her* forgiveness.... In hours of leisure or on sleepless nights, when he felt moved to recall his childhood, his father and mother—everything near and dear, in fact, he invariably thought of Myestetchki, the strange horse, Von Rabbek, his wife who was like the Empress Eugénie, the dark room, the crack of light at the door....

On the thirty-first of August he went back from the camp, not with the whole brigade, but with only two batteries of it. He was dreaming and excited all the way, as though he were going back to his native place. He had an intense longing to see again the strange horse, the church, the insincere family of the Von Rabbeks, the dark room. The "inner voice," which so often deceives lovers, whispered to him for some reason that he would be sure to see her ... and he was tortured by the questions, How he should meet her? What he would talk to her about? Whether she had forgotten the kiss? If the worst came to the worst, he thought, even if he did not meet her, it would be a pleasure to him merely to go through the dark room and recall the past. . . .

Towards evening there appeared on the horizon the familiar church and white granaries. Ryabovitch's heart beat. . . . He did not hear the officer who was riding beside him and saying something to him, he forgot everything, and looked eagerly at the river shining in the distance, at the roof of the house, at the dovecote round which the pigeons were circling in the light of the setting sun.

When they reached the church and were listening to the billeting orders, he expected every second that a man on horseback would come round the church enclosure and invite the officers to tea, but ... the billeting orders were read, the officers were in haste to go on to the village, and the man on horseback did not appear.

"Von Rabbek will hear at once from the peasants that we have come and will send for us," thought Ryabovitch, as he went into the hut, unable to understand why a comrade was lighting a candle and why the orderlies were hurriedly setting samovars. . . .

A painful uneasiness took possession of him. He lay down, then got up and looked out of the window to see whether the messenger were coming. But there was no sign of him.

He lay down again, but half an hour later he got up, and, unable to restrain his uneasiness, went into the street and strode towards the church. It was dark and deserted in the square near the church. . . . Three soldiers were standing silent in a row where the road began to go downhill. Seeing Ryabovitch, they roused themselves and saluted. He returned the salute and began to go down the familiar path.

On the further side of the river the whole sky was flooded with crimson: the moon was rising; two peasant women, talking loudly, were picking cabbage in the kitchen garden; behind the kitchen garden there were some dark huts. . . . And everything on the near side of the river was just as it had been in May: the path, the bushes, the willows overhanging the water . . . but there was no sound of the brave nightingale, and no scent of poplar and fresh grass.

Reaching the garden, Ryabovitch looked in at the gate. The garden was dark and still. . . . He could see nothing but the white stems of the nearest birch-trees and a little bit of the avenue; all the rest melted together into a dark blur. Ryabovitch looked and listened eagerly, but after waiting for a quarter of an hour without hearing a sound or catching a glimpse of a light, he trudged back. . . .

He went down to the river. The General's bath-house and the bath-sheets on the rail of the little bridge showed white before him. . . . He went on to the bridge, stood a little, and, quite unnecessarily, touched the sheets. They felt rough and cold. He looked down at the water. . . . The river ran rapidly and with a faintly audible gurgle round the piles of the bath-house. The red moon was reflected near the left bank; little ripples ran over the reflection, stretching it out, breaking it into bits, and seemed trying to carry it away. . . .

"How stupid, how stupid!" thought Ryabovitch, looking at the running water. "How unintelligent it all is!"

Now that he expected nothing, the incident of the kiss, his impatience, his vague hopes and disappointment, presented themselves in a clear light. It no longer seemed to him strange that he had not seen the General's messenger, and that he would never see the girl who had accidentally kissed him instead of some one else; on the contrary, it would have been strange if he had seen her. . . .

The water was running, he knew not where or why, just as it did in May. In May it had flowed into the great river, from the great river into the sea; then it had risen in vapour, turned into rain, and perhaps the very same water was running now before Ryabovitch's eyes again. . . . What for? Why?

And the whole world, the whole of life, seemed to Ryabovitch an unintelligible, aimless jest. . . . And turning his eyes from the water and looking at the sky, he remembered again how fate in the person of an unknown woman had by chance caressed him, he remembered his summer dreams and fancies, and his life struck him as extraordinarily meagre, poverty-stricken, and colourless. . . .

When he went back to his hut he did not find one of his comrades. The orderly informed him that they had all gone to "General von Rabbek's, who had sent a messenger on horseback to invite them. . . ."

For an instant there was a flash of joy in Ryabovitch's heart, but he quenched it at once, got into bed, and in his wrath with his fate, as though to spite it, did not go to the General's.

Boys

"Volodya's come!" someone shouted in the yard.

"Master Volodya's here!" bawled Natalya the cook, running into the dining-room. "Oh, my goodness!"

The whole Korolyov family, who had been expecting their Volodya from hour to hour, rushed to the windows. At the front door stood a wide sledge, with three white horses in a cloud of steam. The sledge was empty, for Volodya was already in the hall, untying his hood with red and chilly fingers. His school overcoat, his cap, his snowboots, and the hair on his temples were all white with frost, and his whole figure from head to foot diffused such a pleasant, fresh smell of the snow that the very sight of him made one want to shiver and say "brrr!"

His mother and aunt ran to kiss and hug him. Natalya plumped down at his feet and began pulling off his snowboots, his sisters shrieked with delight, the doors creaked and banged, and Volodya's father, in his waistcoat and shirt-sleeves, ran out into the hall with scissors in his hand, and cried out in alarm:

"We were expecting you all yesterday? Did you come all right? Had a good journey? Mercy on us! you might let him say 'how do you do' to his father! I am his father after all!"

"Bow-wow!" barked the huge black dog, Milord, in a deep bass, tapping with his tail on the walls and furniture.

For two minutes there was nothing but a general hubbub of joy. After the first outburst of delight was over the Korolyovs noticed that there was, besides their Volodya, another small person in the hall, wrapped up in scarves and shawls and white with frost. He was standing perfectly still in a corner, in the shadow of a big fox-lined overcoat.

"Volodya darling, who is it?" asked his mother, in a whisper.

"Oh!" cried Volodya. "This is—let me introduce my friend Lentilov, a schoolfellow in the second class. . . . I have brought him to stay with us."

"Delighted to hear it! You are very welcome," the father said cordially. "Excuse me, I've been at work without my coat. . . . Please come in! Natalya, help Mr. Lentilov off with his things. Mercy on us, do turn that dog out! He is unendurable!"

A few minutes later, Volodya and his friend Lentilov, somewhat dazed by their noisy welcome, and still red from the outside cold, were sitting down to tea. The winter sun, making its way through the snow and the frozen tracery on the window-panes, gleamed on the samovar, and plunged its pure rays in the tea-basin. The room was warm, and the boys felt as though the warmth and the frost were struggling together with a tingling sensation in their bodies.

"Well, Christmas will soon be here," the father said in a pleasant sing-song voice, rolling a cigarette of dark reddish tobacco. "It doesn't seem long since the summer, when mamma was crying at your going . . . and here you are back again. . . . Time flies, my boy. Before you have time to cry out, old age is upon you. Mr. Lentilov, take some more, please help yourself! We don't stand on ceremony!"

Volodya's three sisters, Katya, Sonya, and Masha (the eldest was eleven), sat at the table and never took their eyes off the newcomer.

Lentilov was of the same height and age as Volodya, but not as round-faced and fair-skinned. He was thin, dark, and freckled; his hair stood up like a brush, his eyes were small, and his lips were thick. He was, in fact, distinctly ugly, and if he had not been wearing the school uniform, he might have been taken for the son of a cook. He seemed morose, did not speak, and never once smiled. The little girls, staring at him, immediately came to the conclusion that he must be a very clever and learned person. He seemed to be thinking about something all the time, and was so absorbed in his own thoughts, that, whenever he was spoken to, he started, threw his head back, and asked to have the question repeated.

The little girls noticed that Volodya, who had always been so merry and talkative, also said very little, did not smile at all, and hardly seemed to be glad to be home. All the time they were at tea he only once addressed his sisters, and then he said something so strange. He pointed to the samovar and said:

"In California they don't drink tea, but gin."

He, too, seemed absorbed in his own thoughts, and, to judge by the looks that passed between him and his friend Lentilov, their thoughts were the same.

After tea, they all went into the nursery. The girls and their father took up the work that had been interrupted by the arrival of the boys. They were making flowers and frills for the Christmas tree out of paper of different colours. It was an attractive and noisy occupation. Every fresh flower was greeted by the little girls with shrieks of delight, even of awe, as though the flower had dropped straight from heaven; their father was in ecstasies too, and every now and then he threw the scissors on the floor, in vexation at their bluntness. Their mother kept running into the nursery with an anxious face, asking:

"Who has taken my scissors? Ivan Nikolaitch, have you taken my scissors again?"

"Mercy on us! I'm not even allowed a pair of scissors!" their father would respond in a lachrymose voice, and, flinging himself back in his chair, he would pretend to be a deeply injured man; but a minute later, he would be in ecstasies again.

On his former holidays Volodya, too, had taken part in the preparations for the Christmas tree, or had been running in the yard to look at the snow mountain that the watchman and the shepherd were building. But this time Volodya and Lentilov took no notice whatever of the coloured paper, and did not once go into the stable. They sat in the window and began whispering to one another; then they opened an atlas and looked carefully at a map.

"First to Perm . . ." Lentilov said, in an undertone, "from there to Tiumen, then Tomsk . . . then . . . then . . . Kamchatka. There the Samoyedes take one over Behring's Straits in boats . . . And then we are in America. . . . There are lots of furry animals there. . . ."

"And California?" asked Volodya.

"California is lower down. . . . We've only to get to America and California is not far off. . . . And one can get a living by hunting and plunder."

All day long Lentilov avoided the little girls, and seemed to look at them with suspicion. In the evening he happened to be left alone with them for five minutes or so. It was awkward to be silent. He cleared his throat morosely, rubbed his left hand against his right, looked sullenly at Katya and asked:

"Have you read Mayne Reid?"

"No, I haven't. . . . I say, can you skate?"

Absorbed in his own reflections, Lentilov made no reply to this question; he simply puffed out his cheeks, and gave a long sigh as though he were very hot. He looked up at Katya once more and said:

"When a herd of bisons stampedes across the prairie the earth trembles, and the frightened mustangs kick and neigh."

He smiled impressively and added:

"And the Indians attack the trains, too. But worst of all are the mosquitoes and the termites."

"Why, what's that?"

"They're something like ants, but with wings. They bite fearfully. Do you know who I am?"

"Mr. Lentilov."

"No, I am Montehomo, the Hawk's Claw, Chief of the Ever Victorious."

Masha, the youngest, looked at him, then into the darkness out of window and said, wondering:

"And we had lentils for supper yesterday."

Lentilov's incomprehensible utterances, and the way he was always whispering with Volodya, and the way Volodya seemed now to be always thinking about something instead of playing . . . all this was strange and mysterious. And the two elder girls, Katya and Sonya, began to keep a sharp look-out on the boys. At night, when the boys had gone to bed, the girls crept to their bedroom door, and listened to what they were saying. Ah, what they discovered! The boys were planning to run away to America to dig for gold: they had everything ready for the journey, a pistol, two knives, biscuits, a burning glass to serve instead of matches, a compass, and four roubles in cash. They learned that the boys would have to walk some thousands of miles, and would have to fight tigers and savages on the road: then they would get gold and ivory, slay their enemies, become pirates, drink gin, and finally marry beautiful maidens, and make a plantation.

The boys interrupted each other in their excitement. Throughout the conversation, Lentilov called himself "Montehomo, the Hawk's Claw," and Volodya was "my pale-face brother!"

"Mind you don't tell mamma," said Katya, as they went back to bed. "Volodya will bring us gold and ivory from America, but if you tell mamma he won't be allowed to go."

The day before Christmas Eve, Lentilov spent the whole day poring over the map of Asia and making notes, while Volodya, with a languid and swollen face that looked as though it had been stung by a bee, walked about the rooms and ate nothing. And once he stood still before the holy image in the nursery, crossed himself, and said:

"Lord, forgive me a sinner; Lord, have pity on my poor unhappy mamma!"

In the evening he burst out crying. On saying good-night he gave his father a long hug, and then hugged his mother and sisters. Katya and Sonya knew what was the matter, but little Masha was puzzled, completely puzzled. Every time she looked at Lentilov she grew thoughtful and said with a sigh:

"When Lent comes, nurse says we shall have to eat peas and lentils."

Early in the morning of Christmas Eve, Katya and Sonya slipped quietly out of bed, and went to find out how the boys meant to run away to America. They crept to their door.

"Then you don't mean to go?" Lentilov was saying angrily. "Speak out: aren't you going?"

"Oh dear," Volodya wept softly. "How can I go? I feel so unhappy about mamma."

"My pale-face brother, I pray you, let us set off. You declared you were going, you egged me on, and now the time comes, you funk it!"

"I . . . I . . . I'm not funking it, but I . . . I . . . I'm sorry for mamma."

"Say once and for all, are you going or are you not?"

"I am going, only . . . wait a little . . . I want to be at home a little."

"In that case I will go by myself," Lentilov declared. "I can get on without you. And you wanted to hunt tigers and fight! Since that's how it is, give me back my cartridges!"

At this Volodya cried so bitterly that his sisters could not help crying too. Silence followed.

"So you are not coming?" Lentilov began again.

"I . . . I . . . I am coming!"

"Well, put on your things, then."

And Lentilov tried to cheer Volodya up by singing the praises of America, growling like a tiger, pretending to be a steamer, scolding him, and promising to give him all the ivory and lions' and tigers' skins.

And this thin, dark boy, with his freckles and his bristling shock of hair, impressed the little girls as an extraordinary remarkable person. He was a hero, a determined character, who knew no fear, and he growled so ferociously, that, standing at the door, they really might imagine there was a tiger or lion inside. When the little girls went back to their room and dressed, Katya's eyes were full of tears, and she said:

"Oh, I feel so frightened!"

Everything was as usual till two o'clock, when they sat down to dinner. Then it appeared that the boys were not in the house. They sent to the servants' quarters, to the stables, to the bailiff's cottage. They were not to be found. They sent into the village—they were not there.

At tea, too, the boys were still absent, and by supper-time Volodya's mother was dreadfully uneasy, and even shed tears.

Late in the evening they sent again to the village, they searched everywhere, and walked along the river bank with lanterns. Heavens! what a fuss there was!

Next day the police officer came, and a paper of some sort was written out in the dining-room. Their mother cried. . . .

All of a sudden a sledge stopped at the door, with three white horses in a cloud of steam.

"Volodya's come," someone shouted in the yard.

"Master Volodya's here!" bawled Natalya, running into the dining-room. And Milford barked his deep bass, "bow-wow."

It seemed that the boys had been stopped in the Arcade, where they had gone from shop to shop asking where they could get gunpowder.

Volodya burst into sobs as soon as he came into the hall, and flung himself on his mother's neck. The little girls, trembling, wondered with terror what would happen next. They saw their father take Volodya and Lentilov into his study, and there he talked to them a long while.

"Is this a proper thing to do?" their father said to them. "I only pray they won't hear of it at school, you would both be expelled. You ought to be ashamed, Mr. Lentilov, really. It's not at all the thing to do! You began it, and I hope you will be punished by your parents. How could you? Where did you spend the night?"

"At the station," Lentilov answered proudly.

Then Volodya went to bed, and had a compress, steeped in vinegar, on his forehead.

A telegram was sent off, and next day a lady, Lentilov's mother, made her appearance and bore off her son.

Lentilov looked morose and haughty to the end, and he did not utter a single word at taking leave of the little girls. But he took Katya's book and wrote in it as a souvenir: "Montehomo, the Hawk's Claw, Chief of the Ever Victorious."

Kashtanka

(A Story)

I

Misbehaviour

A young dog, a reddish mongrel, between a dachshund and a "yard-dog," very like a fox in face, was running up and down the pavement looking uneasily from side to side. From time to time she stopped and, whining and lifting first one chilled paw and then another, tried to make up her mind how it could have happened that she was lost.

She remembered very well how she had passed the day, and how, in the end, she had found herself on this unfamiliar pavement.

The day had begun by her master Luka Alexandritch's putting on his hat, taking something wooden under his arm wrapped up in a red handkerchief, and calling: "Kashtanka, come along!"

Hearing her name the mongrel had come out from under the work-table, where she slept on the shavings, stretched herself voluptuously and run after her master. The people Luka Alexandritch worked for lived a very long way off, so that, before he could get to any one of them, the carpenter had several times to step into a tavern to fortify himself. Kashtanka remembered that on the way she had behaved extremely improperly. In her delight that she was being taken for a walk she jumped about, dashed barking after the trams, ran into yards, and chased other dogs. The carpenter was continually losing sight of her, stopping, and angrily shouting at her. Once he had even, with an expression of fury in his face, taken her fox-like ear in his fist, smacked her, and said emphatically: "Pla-a-ague take you, you pest!"

After having left the work where it had been bespoken, Luka Alexandritch went into his sister's and there had something to eat and drink; from his sister's he had gone to see a bookbinder he knew; from the bookbinder's to a tavern, from the tavern to another crony's, and so on. In short, by the time Kashtanka found herself on the unfamiliar pavement, it was getting dusk, and the carpenter was as drunk as a cobbler. He was waving his arms and, breathing heavily, muttered:

"In sin my mother bore me! Ah, sins, sins! Here now we are walking along the street and looking at the street lamps, but when we die, we shall burn in a fiery Gehenna. . . ."

Or he fell into a good-natured tone, called Kashtanka to him, and said to her: "You, Kashtanka, are an insect of a creature, and nothing else. Beside a man, you are much the same as a joiner beside a cabinet-maker. . . ."

While he talked to her in that way, there was suddenly a burst of music. Kashtanka looked round and saw that a regiment of soldiers was coming straight towards her. Unable to endure the music, which unhinged her nerves, she turned round and round and wailed. To her great surprise, the carpenter, instead of being frightened, whining and barking, gave a broad grin, drew himself up to attention, and saluted with all his five fingers. Seeing that her master did not protest, Kashtanka whined louder than ever, and dashed across the road to the opposite pavement.

When she recovered herself, the band was not playing and the regiment was no longer there. She ran across the road to the spot where she had left her master, but alas, the carpenter was no longer there. She dashed forward, then back again and ran across the road once more, but the carpenter seemed to have vanished into the earth. Kashtanka began sniffing the pavement, hoping to find her master by the scent of his tracks, but some wretch had been that way just before in new rubber goloshes, and now all delicate scents were mixed with an acute stench of india-rubber, so that it was impossible to make out anything.

Kashtanka ran up and down and did not find her master, and meanwhile it had got dark. The street lamps were lighted on both sides of the road, and lights appeared in the windows. Big, fluffy snow-flakes were falling and painting white the pavement, the horses' backs and the cabmen's caps, and the darker the evening grew the whiter were all these objects. Unknown customers kept walking incessantly to and fro, obstructing her field of vision and shoving against her with their feet. (All mankind Kashtanka divided into two uneven parts: masters and customers; between them there was an essentail difference: the first had the right to beat her, and the second she had the right to nip by the calves of their legs.) These customers were hurrying off somewhere and paid no attention to her.

When it got quite dark, Kashtanka was overcome by despair and horror. She huddled up in an entrance and began whining piteously. The long day's journeying with Luka Alexandritch had exhausted her, her ears and her paws were freezing, and, what was more, she was terribly hungry. Only twice in the whole day had she tasted a morsel: she had eaten a little paste at the bookbinder's, and in one of the taverns she had found a sausage skin on the floor, near the counter—that was all. If she had been a human being she would have certainly thought: "No, it is impossible to live like this! I must shoot myself!"

II

A Mysterious Stranger

But she thought of nothing, she simply whined. When her head and back were entirely plastered over with the soft feathery snow, and she had sunk into a painful doze of exhaustion, all at once the door of the entrance clicked, creaked, and struck her on the side. She jumped up. A man belonging to the class of customers came out. As Kashtanka whined and got under his feet, he could not help noticing her. He bent down to her and asked:

"Doggy, where do you come from? Have I hurt you? O, poor thing, poor thing. . . . Come, don't be cross, don't be cross. . . . I am sorry."

Kashtanka looked at the stranger through the snow-flakes that hung on her eyelashes, and saw before her a short, fat little man, with a plump, shaven face wearing a top hat and a fur coat that swung open.

"What are you whining for?" he went on, knocking the snow off her back with his fingers. "Where is your master? I suppose you are lost? Ah, poor doggy! What are we going to do now?"

Catching in the stranger's voice a warm, cordial note, Kashtanka licked his hand, and whined still more pitifully.

"Oh, you nice funny thing!" said the stranger. "A regular fox! Well, there's nothing for it, you must come along with me! Perhaps you will be of use for something. . . . Well!"

He clicked with his lips, and made a sign to Kashtanka with his hand, which could only mean one thing: "Come along!" Kashtanka went.

Not more than half an hour later she was sitting on the floor in a big, light room, and, leaning her head against her side, was looking with tenderness and curiosity at the stranger who was sitting at the table, dining. He ate and threw pieces to her. . . . At first he gave her bread and the green rind of cheese, then a piece of meat, half a pie and chicken bones, while through hunger she ate so quickly that she had not time to distinguish the taste, and the more she ate the more acute was the feeling of hunger.

"Your masters don't feed you properly," said the stranger, seeing with what ferocious greediness she swallowed the morsels without munching them. "And how thin you are! Nothing but skin and bones. . . ."

Kashtanka ate a great deal and yet did not satisfy her hunger, but was simply stupefied with eating. After dinner she lay down in the middle of the room, stretched her legs and, conscious of an agreeable weariness all over her body, wagged her tail. While her new master, lounging in an easy-chair, smoked a cigar, she wagged her tail and considered the question, whether it was better at the stranger's or at the carpenter's. The stranger's surroundings were poor and ugly; besides the easy-chairs, the sofa, the lamps and the rugs, there was nothing, and the room seemed empty. At the carpenter's the whole place was stuffed full of things: he had a table, a bench, a heap of shavings, planes, chisels, saws, a cage with a goldfinch, a basin. . . . The stranger's room smelt of nothing, while there was always a thick fog in the carpenter's room, and a glorious smell of glue, varnish, and shavings. On the other hand, the stranger had one great superiority—he gave her a great deal to eat and, to do him full justice, when Kashtanka sat facing the table and looking wistfully at him, he did not once hit or kick her, and did not once shout: "Go away, damned brute!"

When he had finished his cigar her new master went out, and a minute later came back holding a little mattress in his hands.

"Hey, you dog, come here!" he said, laying the mattress in the corner near the dog. "Lie down here, go to sleep!"

Then he put out the lamp and went away. Kashtanka lay down on the mattress and shut her eyes; the sound of a bark rose from the street, and she would have liked to answer it, but all at once she was overcome with unexpected melancholy. She thought of Luka Alexandritch, of his son Fedyushka, and her snug little place under the bench. . . . She remembered on the long winter evenings, when the carpenter was planing or reading the paper aloud, Fedyushka usually played with her. . . . He used to pull her from under the bench by her hind legs, and play such tricks with her, that she saw green before her eyes, and ached in every joint. He would make her walk on her hind legs, use her as a bell, that is, shake her violently by the tail so that she squealed and barked, and give her tobacco to sniff. . . . The following trick was particularly agonising: Fedyushka would tie a piece of meat to a thread and give it to Kashtanka, and then, when she had swallowed it he would, with a loud laugh, pull it back again from her stomach, and the more lurid were her memories the more loudly and miserably Kashtanka whined.

But soon exhaustion and warmth prevailed over melancholy. She began to fall asleep. Dogs ran by in her imagination: among them a shaggy old poodle, whom she had seen that day in the street with a white patch on his eye and tufts of wool by his nose. Fedyushka ran after the poodle with a chisel in his hand, then all at once he too was covered with shaggy wool, and began merrily barking beside Kashtanka. Kashtanka and he good-naturedly sniffed each other's noses and merrily ran down the street....

III

New and Very Agreeable Acquaintances

When Kashtanka woke up it was already light, and a sound rose from the street, such as only comes in the day-time. There was not a soul in the room. Kashtanka stretched, yawned and, cross and ill-humoured, walked about the room. She sniffed the corners and the furniture, looked into the passage and found nothing of interest there. Besides the door that led into the passage there was another door. After thinking a little Kashtanka scratched on it with both paws, opened it, and went into the adjoining room. Here on the bed, covered with a rug, a customer, in whom she recognised the stranger of yesterday, lay asleep.

"Rrrrr..." she growled, but recollecting yesterday's dinner, wagged her tail, and began sniffing.

She sniffed the stranger's clothes and boots and thought they smelt of horses. In the bedroom was another door, also closed. Kashtanka scratched at the door, leaned her chest against it, opened it, and was instantly aware of a strange and very suspicious smell. Foreseeing an unpleasant encounter, growling and looking about her, Kashtanka walked into a little room with a dirty wall-paper and drew back in alarm. She saw something surprising and terrible. A grey gander came straight towards her, hissing, with its neck bowed down to the floor and its wings outspread. Not far from him, on a little mattress, lay a white tom-cat; seeing Kashtanka, he jumped up, arched his back, wagged his tail with his hair standing on end and he, too, hissed at her. The dog was frightened in earnest, but not caring to betray her alarm, began barking loudly and dashed at the cat.... The cat arched his back more than ever, mewed and gave Kashtanka a smack on the head with his paw.

Kashtanka jumped back, squatted on all four paws, and craning her nose towards the cat, went off into loud, shrill barks; meanwhile the gander came up behind and gave her a painful peck in the back. Kashtanka leapt up and dashed at the gander.

"What's this?" They heard a loud angry voice, and the stranger came into the room in his dressing-gown, with a cigar between his teeth. "What's the meaning of this? To your places!"

He went up to the cat, flicked him on his arched back, and said:

"Fyodor Timofeyitch, what's the meaning of this? Have you got up a fight? Ah, you old rascal! Lie down!"

And turning to the gander he shouted: "Ivan Ivanitch, go home!"

The cat obediently lay down on his mattress and closed his eyes. Judging from the expression of his face and whiskers, he was displeased with himself for having lost his temper and got into a fight. Kashtanka began whining resentfully, while the gander craned his neck and began saying something rapidly, excitedly, distinctly, but quite unintelligibly.

"All right, all right," said his master, yawning. "You must live in peace and friendship." He stroked Kashtanka and went on: "And you, red-hair, don't be frightened. . . . They are capital company, they won't annoy you. Stay, what are we to call you? You can't go on without a name, my dear."

The stranger thought a moment and said: "I tell you what . . . you shall be Auntie. . . . Do you understand? Auntie!"

And repeating the word "Auntie" several times he went out. Kashtanka sat down and began watching. The cat sat motionless on his little mattress, and pretended to be asleep. The gander, craning his neck and stamping, went on talking rapidly and excitedly about something. Apparently it was a very clever gander; after every long tirade, he always stepped back with an air of wonder and made a show of being highly delighted with his own speech. . . . Listening to him and answering "R-r-r-r," Kashtanka fell to sniffing the corners. In one of the corners she found a little trough in which she saw some soaked peas and a sop of rye crusts. She tried the peas; they were not nice; she tried the sopped bread and began eating it. The gander was not at all offended that the strange dog was eating his food, but, on the contrary, talked even more excitedly, and to show his confidence went to the trough and ate a few peas himself.

IV

Marvels on a Hurdle

A little while afterwards the stranger came in again, and brought a strange thing with him like a hurdle, or like the figure II. On the crosspiece on the top of this roughly made wooden frame hung a bell, and a pistol was also tied to it; there were strings from the tongue of the bell, and the trigger of the pistol. The stranger put the frame in the middle of the room, spent a long time tying and untying something, then looked at the gander and said: "Ivan Ivanitch, if you please!"

The gander went up to him and stood in an expectant attitude.

"Now then," said the stranger, "let us begin at the very beginning. First of all, bow and make a curtsey! Look sharp!"

Ivan Ivanitch craned his neck, nodded in all directions, and scraped with his foot.

"Right. Bravo. . . . Now die!"

The gander lay on his back and stuck his legs in the air. After performing a few more similar, unimportant tricks, the stranger suddenly clutched at his head, and assuming an expression of horror, shouted: "Help! Fire! We are burning!"

Ivan Ivanitch ran to the frame, took the string in his beak, and set the bell ringing.

The stranger was very much pleased. He stroked the gander's neck and said:

"Bravo, Ivan Ivanitch! Now pretend that you are a jeweller selling gold and diamonds. Imagine now that you go to your shop and find thieves there. What would you do in that case?"

The gander took the other string in his beak and pulled it, and at once a deafening report was heard. Kashtanka was highly delighted with the bell ringing, and the shot threw her into so much ecstasy that she ran round the frame barking.

"Auntie, lie down!" cried the stranger; "be quiet!"

Ivan Ivanitch's task was not ended with the shooting. For a whole hour afterwards the stranger drove the gander round him on a cord, cracking a whip, and the gander had to jump over barriers and through hoops; he had to rear, that is, sit on his tail and wave his legs in the air. Kashtanka could not take her eyes off Ivan Ivanitch, wriggled with delight, and several times fell to running after him with shrill barks. After exhausting the gander and himself, the stranger wiped the sweat from his brow and cried:

"Marya, fetch Havronya Ivanovna here!"

A minute later there was the sound of grunting. . . . Kashtanka growled, assumed a very valiant air, and to be on the safe side, went nearer to the stranger. The door opened, an old woman looked in, and, saying something, led in a black and very ugly sow. Paying no attention to Kashtanka's growls, the sow lifted up her little hoof and grunted good-humouredly. Apparently it was very agreeable to her to see her master, the cat, and Ivan Ivanitch. When she went up to the cat and gave him a light tap on the stomach with her hoof, and then made some remark to the gander, a great deal of good-nature was expressed in her movements, and the quivering of her tail. Kashtanka realised at once that to growl and bark at such a character was useless.

The master took away the frame and cried: "Fyodor Timofeyitch, if you please!"

The cat stretched lazily, and reluctantly, as though performing a duty, went up to the sow.

"Come, let us begin with the Egyptian pyramid," began the master.

He spent a long time explaining something, then gave the word of command, "One . . . two . . . three!" At the word "three" Ivan Ivanitch flapped his wings and jumped on to the sow's back. . . . When, balancing himself with his wings and his neck, he got a firm foothold on the bristly back, Fyodor Timofeyitch listlessly and lazily, with manifest disdain, and with an air of scorning his art and not caring a pin for it, climbed on to the sow's back, then reluctantly mounted on to the gander, and stood on his hind legs. The result was what the stranger called the Egyptian pyramid. Kashtanka yapped with delight, but at that moment the old cat yawned and, losing his balance, rolled off the gander.

Ivan Ivanitch lurched and fell off too. The stranger shouted, waved his hands, and began explaining something again. After spending an hour over the pyramid their indefatigable master proceeded to teach Ivan Ivanitch to ride on the cat, then began to teach the cat to smoke, and so on.

The lesson ended in the stranger's wiping the sweat off his brow and going away. Fyodor Timofeyitch gave a disdainful sniff, lay down on his mattress, and closed his eyes; Ivan Ivanitch went to the trough, and the pig was taken away by the old woman. Thanks to the number of her new impressions, Kashtanka hardly noticed how the day passed, and in the evening she was installed with her mattress in the room with the dirty wall-paper, and spent the night in the society of Fyodor Timofeyitch and the gander.

V

Talent! Talent!

A month passed.

Kashtanka had grown used to having a nice dinner every evening, and being called Auntie. She had grown used to the stranger too, and to her new companions. Life was comfortable and easy.

Every day began in the same way. As a rule, Ivan Ivanitch was the first to wake up, and at once went up to Auntie or to the cat, twisting his neck, and beginning to talk excitedly and persuasively, but, as before, unintelligibly. Sometimes he would crane up his head in the air and utter a long monologue. At first Kashtanka thought he talked so much because he was very clever, but after a little time had passed, she lost all her respect for him; when he went up to her with his long speeches she no longer wagged her tail, but treated him as a tiresome chatterbox, who would not let anyone sleep and, without the slightest ceremony, answered him with "R-r-r-r!"

Fyodor Timofeyitch was a gentleman of a very different sort. When he woke he did not utter a sound, did not stir, and did not even open his eyes. He would have been glad not to wake, for, as was evident, he was not greatly in love with life. Nothing interested him, he showed an

apathetic and nonchalant attitude to everything, he disdained everything and, even while eating his delicious dinner, sniffed contemptuously.

When she woke Kashtanka began walking about the room and
sniffing the corners. She and the cat were the only ones allowed to go
all over the flat; the gander had not the right to cross the threshold of
the room with the dirty wall-paper, and Havronya Ivanovna lived
somewhere in a little outhouse in the yard and made her appearance
only during the lessons. Their master got up late, and immediately
after drinking his tea began teaching them their tricks. Every day the
frame, the whip, and the hoop were brought in, and every day almost
the same performance took place. The lesson lasted three or four
hours, so that sometimes Fyodor Timofeyitch was so tired that he
staggered about like a drunken man, and Ivan Ivanitch opened his beak
and breathed heavily, while their master became red in the face and
could not mop the sweat from his brow fast enough.

The lesson and the dinner made the day very interesting, but the
evenings were tedious. As a rule, their master went off somewhere in
the evening and took the cat and the gander with him. Left alone, Auntie lay down on her little mattress and began to feel sad. . . .

Melancholy crept on her imperceptibly and took possession of her
by degrees, as darkness does of a room. It began with the dog's losing
every inclination to bark, to eat, to run about the rooms, and even to
look at things; then vague figures, half dogs, half human beings, with
countenances attractive, pleasant, but incomprehensible, would appear in her imagination; when they came Auntie wagged her tail, and
it seemed to her that she had somewhere, at some time, seen them and
loved them. . . . And as she dropped asleep, she always felt that those
figures smelt of glue, shavings, and varnish.

When she had grown quite used to her new life, and from a thin,
long mongrel, had changed into a sleek, well-groomed dog, her master looked at her one day before the lesson and said:

"It's high time, Auntie, to get to business. You have kicked up your
heels in idleness long enough. I want to make an artiste of you. . . . Do
you want to be an artiste?"

And he began teaching her various accomplishments. At the first lesson he taught her to stand and walk on her hind legs, which she liked extremely. At the second lesson she had to jump on her hind legs and catch some sugar, which her teacher held high above her head. After that, in the following lessons she danced, ran tied to a cord, howled to music, rang the bell, and fired the pistol, and in a month could successfully replace Fyodor Timofeyitch in the "Egyptian Pyramid." She learned very eagerly and was pleased with her own success; running with her tongue out on the cord, leaping through the hoop, and riding on old Fyodor Timofeyitch, gave her the greatest enjoyment. She accompanied every successful trick with a shrill, delighted bark, while her teacher wondered, was also delighted, and rubbed his hands.

"It's talent! It's talent!" he said. "Unquestionable talent! You will certainly be successful!"

And Auntie grew so used to the word talent, that every time her master pronounced it, she jumped up as if it had been her name.

VI

An Uneasy Night

Auntie had a doggy dream that a porter ran after her with a broom, and she woke up in a fright.

It was quite dark and very stuffy in the room. The fleas were biting. Auntie had never been afraid of darkness before, but now, for some reason, she felt frightened and inclined to bark.

Her master heaved a loud sigh in the next room, then soon afterwards the sow grunted in her sty, and then all was still again. When one thinks about eating one's heart grows lighter, and Auntie began thinking how that day she had stolen the leg of a chicken from Fyodor Timofeyitch, and had hidden it in the drawing-room, between the cupboard and the wall, where there were a great many spiders' webs and a great deal of dust. Would it not be as well to go now and look whether the chicken leg were still there or not? It was very possible that her master had found it and eaten it. But she must not go out of the room before morning, that was the rule. Auntie shut her eyes to go to sleep as quickly as possible, for she knew by experience that the sooner you go to sleep the sooner the morning comes. But all at once there was a strange scream not far from her which made her start and jump up on all four legs. It was Ivan Ivanitch, and his cry was not babbling and persuasive as usual, but a wild, shrill, unnatural scream, like the squeak of a door opening. Unable to distinguish anything in the darkness, and not understanding what was wrong, Auntie felt still more frightened and growled: "R-r-r-r. . . ."

Some time passed, as long as it takes to eat a good bone; the scream was not repeated. Little by little Auntie's uneasiness passed off and she began to doze. She dreamed of two big black dogs with tufts of last year's coat left on their haunches and sides; they were eating out of a big basin some swill, from which there came a white steam and a most appetising smell; from time to time they looked round at Auntie, showed their teeth and growled: "We are not going to give you any!" But a peasant in a fur-coat ran out of the house and drove them away with a whip; then Auntie went up to the basin and began eating, but as soon as the peasant went out of the gate, the two black dogs rushed at her growling, and all at once there was again a shrill scream.

"K-gee! K-gee-gee!" cried Ivan Ivanitch.

Auntie woke, jumped up and, without leaving her mattress, went off into a yelping bark. It seemed to her that it was not Ivan Ivanitch that was screaming but someone else, and for some reason the sow again grunted in her sty.

Then there was the sound of shuffling slippers, and the master came into the room in his dressing-gown with a candle in his hand. The flickering light danced over the dirty wall-paper and the ceiling, and chased away the darkness. Auntie saw that there was no stranger in the room. Ivan Ivanitch was sitting on the floor and was not asleep. His wings were spread out and his beak was open, and altogether he looked as though he were very tired and thirsty. Old Fyodor Timofeyitch was not asleep either. He, too, must have been awakened by the scream.

"Ivan Ivanitch, what's the matter with you?" the master asked the gander. "Why are you screaming? Are you ill?"

The gander did not answer. The master touched him on the neck, stroked his back, and said: "You are a queer chap. You don't sleep your-self, and you don't let other people. . . ."

When the master went out, carrying the candle with him, there was darkness again. Auntie felt frightened. The gander did not scream, but again she fancied that there was some stranger in the room. What was most dreadful was that this stranger could not be bitten, as he was unseen and had no shape. And for some reason she thought that some-thing very bad would certainly happen that night. Fyodor Timofey-itch was uneasy too. Auntie could hear him shifting on his mattress, yawning and shaking his head.

Somewhere in the street there was a knocking at a gate and the sow grunted in her sty. Auntie began to whine, stretched out her front-paws and laid her head down upon them. She fancied that in the knocking at the gate, in the grunting of the sow, who was for some rea-son awake, in the darkness and the stillness, there was something as miserable and dreadful as in Ivan Ivanitch's scream. Everything was in agitation and anxiety, but why? Who was the stranger who could not be seen? Then two dim flashes of green gleamed for a minute near Auntie. It was Fyodor Timofeyitch, for the first time of their whole ac-quaintance coming up to her. What did he want? Auntie licked his paw, and not asking why he had come, howled softly and on various notes.

"K-gee!" cried Ivan Ivanitch, "K-g-ee!"

The door opened again and the master came in with a candle.

The gander was sitting in the same attitude as before, with his beak open, and his wings spread out, his eyes were closed.

"Ivan Ivanitch!" his master called him.

The gander did not stir. His master sat down before him on the floor, looked at him in silence for a minute, and said:

"Ivan Ivanitch, what is it? Are you dying? Oh, I remember now, I re-member!" he cried out, and clutched at his head. "I know why it is! It's because the horse stepped on you to-day! My God! My God!

Auntie did not understand what her master was saying, but she saw from his face that he, too, was expecting something dreadful. She stretched out her head towards the dark window, where it seemed to her some stranger was looking in, and howled.

"He is dying, Auntie!" said her master, and wrung his hands. "Yes, yes, he is dying! Death has come into your room. What are we to do?"

Pale and agitated, the master went back into his room, sighing and shaking his head. Auntie was afraid to remain in the darkness, and followed her master into his bedroom. He sat down on the bed and repeated several times: "My God, what's to be done?"

Auntie walked about round his feet, and not understanding why she was wretched and why they were all so uneasy, and trying to understand, watched every movement he made. Fyodor Timofeyitch, who rarely left his little mattress, came into the master's bedroom too, and began rubbing himself against his feet. He shook his head as though he wanted to shake painful thoughts out of it, and kept peeping suspiciously under the bed.

The master took a saucer, poured some water from his wash-stand into it, and went to the gander again.

"Drink, Ivan Ivanitch!" he said tenderly, setting the saucer before him; "drink, darling."

But Ivan Ivanitch did not stir and did not open his eyes. His master bent his head down to the saucer and dipped his beak into the water, but the gander did not drink, he spread his wings wider than ever, and his head remained lying in the saucer.

"No, there's nothing to be done now," sighed his master. "It's all over. Ivan Ivanitch is gone!"

And shining drops, such as one sees on the window-pane when it rains, trickled down his cheeks. Not understanding what was the matter, Auntie and Fyodor Timofeyitch snuggled up to him and looked with horror at the gander.

"Poor Ivan Ivanitch!" said the master, sighing mournfully. "And I was dreaming I would take you in the spring into the country, and would walk with you on the green grass. Dear creature, my good comrade, you are no more! How shall I do without you now?"

It seemed to Auntie that the same thing would happen to her, that is, that she too, there was no knowing why, would close her eyes, stretch out her paws, open her mouth, and everyone would look at her with horror. Apparently the same reflections were passing through the brain of Fyodor Timofeyitch. Never before had the old cat been so morose and gloomy.

It began to get light, and the unseen stranger who had so frightened Auntie was no longer in the room. When it was quite daylight, the porter came in, took the gander, and carried him away. And soon afterwards the old woman came in and took away the trough.

Auntie went into the drawing-room and looked behind the cupboard: her master had not eaten the chicken bone, it was lying in its place among the dust and spiders' webs. But Auntie felt sad and dreary and wanted to cry. She did not even sniff at the bone, but went under the sofa, sat down there, and began softly whining in a thin voice.

VII

An Unsuccessful Début

One fine evening the master came into the room with the dirty wall-paper, and, rubbing his hands, said:

"Well. . . ."

He meant to say something more, but went away without saying it. Auntie, who during her lessons had thoroughly studied his face and intonations, divined that he was agitated, anxious and, she fancied, angry. Soon afterwards he came back and said:

"To-day I shall take with me Auntie and Fyodor Timofeyitch. To-day, Auntie, you will take the place of poor Ivan Ivanitch in the 'Egyptian Pyramid.' Goodness knows how it will be! Nothing is ready, nothing has been thoroughly studied, there have been few rehearsals! We shall be disgraced, we shall come to grief!"

Then he went out again, and a minute later, came back in his fur-coat and top hat. Going up to the cat he took him by the fore-paws and put him inside the front of his coat, while Fyodor Timofeyitch appeared completely unconcerned, and did not even trouble to open his eyes. To him it was apparently a matter of absolute indifference whether he remained lying down, or were lifted up by his paws, whether he rested on his mattress or under his master's fur-coat. . . .

"Come along, Auntie," said her master.

Wagging her tail, and understanding nothing, Auntie followed him. A minute later she was sitting in a sledge by her master's feet and heard him, shrinking with cold and anxiety, mutter to himself:

"We shall be disgraced! We shall come to grief!"

The sledge stopped at a big strange-looking house, like a soup-ladle turned upside down. The long entrance to this house, with its three glass doors, was lighted up with a dozen brilliant lamps. The doors opened with a resounding noise and, like jaws, swallowed up the people who were moving to and fro at the entrance. There were a great many people, horses, too, often ran up to the entrance, but no dogs were to be seen.

The master took Auntie in his arms and thrust her in his coat, where Fyodor Timofeyitch already was. It was dark and stuffy there, but warm. For an instant two green sparks flashed at her; it was the cat, who opened his eyes on being disturbed by his neighbour's cold rough paws. Auntie licked his ear, and, trying to settle herself as comfortably as possible, moved uneasily, crushed him under her cold paws, and casually poked her head out from under the coat, but at once growled angrily, and tucked it in again. It seemed to her that she had seen a huge, badly lighted room, full of monsters; from behind screens and gratings, which stretched on both sides of the room, horrible faces looked out: faces of horses with horns, with long ears, and one fat, huge countenance with a tail instead of a nose, and two long gnawed bones sticking out of his mouth.

The cat mewed huskily under Auntie's paws, but at that moment the coat was flung open, the master said, "Hop!" and Fyodor Timofeyitch and Auntie jumped to the floor. They were now in a little room with grey plank walls; there was no other furniture in it but a little table with a looking-glass on it, a stool, and some rags hung about the corners, and instead of a lamp or candles, there was a bright fan-shaped light attached to a little pipe fixed in the wall. Fyodor Timofeyitch licked his coat which had been ruffled by Auntie, went under the stool, and lay down. Their master, still agitated and rubbing his hands, began undressing. . . . He undressed as he usually did at home when he was preparing to get under the rug, that is, took off everything but his underlinen, then he sat down on the stool, and, looking in the looking-glass, began playing the most surprising tricks with himself.... First of all he put on his head a wig, with a parting and with two tufts of hair standing up like horns, then he smeared his face thickly with something white, and over the white colour painted his eyebrows, his moustaches, and red on his cheeks. His antics did not end with that. After smearing his face and neck, he began putting himself into an extraordinary and incongruous costume, such as Auntie had never seen before, either in houses or in the street. Imagine very full trousers, made of chintz covered with big flowers, such as is used in working-class houses for curtains and covering furniture, trousers which buttoned up just under his armpits. One trouser leg was made of brown chintz, the other of bright yellow. Almost lost in these, he then put on a short chintz jacket, with a big scalloped collar, and a gold star on the back, stockings of different colours, and green slippers....

Everything seemed going round before Auntie's eyes and in her soul. The white-faced, sack-like figure smelt like her master, its voice, too, was the familiar master's voice, but there were moments when Auntie was tortured by doubts, and then she was ready to run away from the parti-coloured figure and to bark. The new place, the fan-shaped light, the smell, the transformation that had taken place in her master—all this aroused in her a vague dread and a foreboding that she would certainly meet with some horror such as the big face with the tail instead of a nose. And then, somewhere through the wall, some hateful band was playing, and from time to time she heard an incomprehensible roar. Only one thing reassured her—that was the imperturbability of Fyodor Timofeyitch. He dozed with the utmost tranquillity under the stool, and did not open his eyes even when it was moved.

A man in a dress coat and a white waistcoat peeped into the little room and said:

"Miss Arabella has just gone on. After her—you."

Their master made no answer. He drew a small box from under the table, sat down, and waited. From his lips and his hands it could be seen that he was agitated, and Auntie could hear how his breathing came in gasps.

"Monsieur George, come on!" someone shouted behind the door.

Their master got up and crossed himself three times, then took the cat from under the stool and put him in the box.

"Come, Auntie," he said softly.

Auntie, who could make nothing out of it, went up to his hands, he kissed her on the head, and put her beside Fyodor Timofeyitch. Then followed darkness. . . . Auntie trampled on the cat, scratched at the walls of the box, and was so frightened that she could not utter a sound, while the box swayed and quivered, as though it were on the waves. . . .

"Here we are again!" her master shouted aloud: "here we are again!"

Auntie felt that after that shout the box struck against something hard and left off swaying. There was a loud deep roar, someone was being slapped, and that someone, probably the monster with the tail instead of a nose, roared and laughed so loud that the locks of the box trembled. In response to the roar, there came a shrill, squeaky laugh from her master, such as he never laughed at home.

"Ha!" he shouted, trying to shout above the roar. "Honoured friends! I have only just come from the station! My granny's kicked the bucket and left me a fortune! There is something very heavy in the box, it must be gold, ha! ha! I bet there's a million here! We'll open it and look. . . ."

The lock of the box clicked. The bright light dazzled Auntie's eyes, she jumped out of the box, and, deafened by the roar, ran quickly round her master, and broke into a shrill bark.

"Ha!" exclaimed her master. "Uncle Fyodor Timofeyitch! Beloved Aunt, dear relations! The devil take you!"

He fell on his stomach on the sand, seized the cat and Auntie, and fell to embracing them. While he held Auntie tight in his arms, she glanced round into the world into which fate had brought her and, impressed by its immensity, was for a minute dumbfounded with amazement and delight, then jumped out of her master's arms, and to express the intensity of her emotions, whirled round and round on one spot like a top. This new world was big and full of bright light; wherever she looked, on all sides, from floor to ceiling there were faces, faces, faces, and nothing else.

"Auntie, I beg you to sit down!" shouted her master. Remembering what that meant, Auntie jumped on to a chair, and sat down. She looked at her master. His eyes looked at her gravely and kindly as always, but his face, especially his mouth and teeth, were made grotesque by a broad immovable grin. He laughed, skipped about, twitched his shoulders, and made a show of being very merry in the presence of the thousands of faces. Auntie believed in his merriment, all at once felt all over her that those thousands of faces were looking at her, lifted up her fox-like head, and howled joyously.

"You sit there, Auntie," her master said to her, "while Uncle and I will dance the Kamarinsky."

Fyodor Timofeyitch stood looking about him indifferently, waiting to be made to do something silly. He danced listlessly, carelessly, sullenly, and one could see from his movements, his tail and his ears, that he had a profound contempt for the crowd, the bright light, his master and himself. When he had performed his allotted task, he gave a yawn and sat down.

"Now, Auntie!" said her master, "we'll have first a song, and then a dance, shall we?"

He took a pipe out of his pocket, and began playing. Auntie, who could not endure music, began moving uneasily in her chair and howled. A roar of applause rose from all sides. Her master bowed, and when all was still again, went on playing.... Just as he took one very high note, someone high up among the audience uttered a loud exclamation:

"Auntie!" cried a child's voice, "why it's Kashtanka!"

"Kashtanka it is!" declared a cracked drunken tenor. "Kashtanka! Strike me dead, Fedyushka, it is Kashtanka. Kashtanka! here!"

Someone in the gallery gave a whistle, and two voices, one a boy's and one a man's, called loudly: "Kashtanka! Kashtanka!"

Auntie started, and looked where the shouting came from. Two faces, one hairy, drunken and grinning, the other chubby, rosy-cheeked and frightened-looking, dazed her eyes as the bright light had dazed them before.... She remembered, fell off the chair, struggled on the sand, then jumped up, and with a delighted yap dashed towards those faces. There was a deafening roar, interspersed with whistles and a shrill childish shout: "Kashtanka! Kashtanka!"

Auntie leaped over the barrier, then across someone's shoulders.

She found herself in a box: to get into the next tier she had to leap over a high wall. Auntie jumped, but did not jump high enough, and slipped back down the wall. Then she was passed from hand to hand, licked hands and faces, kept mounting higher and higher, and at last got into the gallery. . . .

———

Half an hour afterwards, Kashtanka was in the street, following the people who smelt of glue and varnish. Luka Alexandritch staggered and instinctively, taught by experience, tried to keep as far from the gutter as possible.

"In sin my mother bore me," he muttered. "And you, Kashtanka, are a thing of little understanding. Beside a man, you are like a joiner beside a cabinet-maker."

Fedyushka walked beside him, wearing his father's cap. Kashtanka looked at their backs, and it seemed to her that she had been following them for ages, and was glad that there had not been a break for a minute in her life.

She remembered the little room with dirty wall-paper, the gander, Fyodor Timofeyitch, the delicious dinners, the lessons, the circus, but all that seemed to her now like a long, tangled, oppressive dream.

A Lady's Story

Nine years ago Pyotr Sergeyitch, the deputy prosecutor, and I were riding towards evening in haymaking time to fetch the letters from the station.

The weather was magnificent, but on our way back we heard a peal of thunder, and saw an angry black storm-cloud which was coming straight towards us. The storm-cloud was approaching us and we were approaching it.

Against the background of it our house and church looked white and the tall poplars shone like silver. There was a scent of rain and mown hay. My companion was in high spirits. He kept laughing and talking all sorts of nonsense. He said it would be nice if we could suddenly come upon a medieval castle with turreted towers, with moss on it and owls, in which we could take shelter from the rain and in the end be killed by a thunderbolt. . . .

Then the first wave raced through the rye and a field of oats, there was a gust of wind, and the dust flew round and round in the air. Pyotr Sergeyitch laughed and spurred on his horse.

"It's fine!" he cried, "it's splendid!"

Infected by his gaiety, I too began laughing at the thought that in a minute I should be drenched to the skin and might be struck by lightning.

Riding swiftly in a hurricane when one is breathless with the wind, and feels like a bird, thrills one and puts one's heart in a flutter. By the time we rode into our courtyard the wind had gone down, and big drops of rain were pattering on the grass and on the roofs. There was not a soul near the stable.

Pyotr Sergeyitch himself took the bridles off, and led the horses to their stalls. I stood in the doorway waiting for him to finish, and watching the slanting streaks of rain; the sweetish, exciting scent of hay was even stronger here than in the fields; the storm-clouds and the rain made it almost twilight.

"What a crash!" said Pyotr Sergeyitch, coming up to me after a very loud rolling peal of thunder when it seemed as though the sky were split in two. "What do you say to that?"

He stood beside me in the doorway and, still breathless from his rapid ride, looked at me. I could see that he was admiring me.

"Natalya Vladimirovna," he said, "I would give anything only to stay here a little longer and look at you. You are lovely to-day."

His eyes looked at me with delight and supplication, his face was pale. On his beard and mustache were glittering raindrops, and they, too, seemed to be looking at me with love.

"I love you," he said. "I love you, and I am happy at seeing you. I know you cannot be my wife, but I want nothing, I ask nothing; only know that I love you. Be silent, do not answer me, take no notice of it, but only know that you are dear to me and let me look at you."

His rapture affected me too; I looked at his enthusiastic face, listened to his voice which mingled with the patter of the rain, and stood as though spellbound, unable to stir.

I longed to go on endlessly looking at his shining eyes and listening.

"You say nothing, and that is splendid," said Pyotr Sergeyitch. "Go on being silent."

I felt happy. I laughed with delight and ran through the drenching rain to the house; he laughed too, and, leaping as he went, ran after me.

Both drenched, panting, noisily clattering up the stairs like children, we dashed into the room. My father and brother, who were not used to seeing me laughing and light-hearted, looked at me in surprise and began laughing too.

The storm-clouds had passed over and the thunder had ceased, but the raindrops still glittered on Pyotr Sergeyitch's beard. The whole evening till supper-time he was singing, whistling, playing noisily with the dog and racing about the room after it, so that he nearly upset the servant with the samovar. And at supper he ate a great deal, talked nonsense, and maintained that when one eats fresh cucumbers in winter there is the fragrance of spring in one's mouth.

When I went to bed I lighted a candle and threw my window wide open, and an undefined feeling took possession of my soul. I remembered that I was free and healthy, that I had rank and wealth, that I was beloved; above all, that I had rank and wealth, rank and wealth, my God! how nice that was!... Then, huddling up in bed at a touch of cold which reached me from the garden with the dew, I tried to discover whether I loved Pyotr Sergeyitch or not, ... and fell asleep unable to reach any conclusion.

And when in the morning I saw quivering patches of sunlight and the shadows of the lime trees on my bed, what had happened yesterday rose vividly in my memory. Life seemed to me rich, varied, full of charm. Humming, I dressed quickly and went out into the garden....

And what happened afterwards? Why—nothing. In the winter when we lived in town Pyotr Sergeyitch came to see us from time to time. Country acquaintances are charming only in the country and in summer; in the town and in winter they lose their charm. When you pour out tea for them in the town it seems as though they are wearing other people's coats, and as though they stirred their tea too long. In the town, too, Pyotr Sergeyitch spoke sometimes of love, but the effect was not at all the same as in the country. In the town we were more vividly conscious of the wall that stood between us: I had rank and wealth, while he was poor, and he was not even a nobleman, but only the son of a deacon and a deputy public prosecutor; we both of us—I through my youth and he for some unknown reason—thought of that wall as very high and thick, and when he was with us in the town he would criticize aristocratic society with a forced smile, and maintain a sullen silence when there was anyone else in the drawing-room. There is no wall that cannot be broken through, but the heroes of the modern romance, so far as I know them, are too timid, spiritless, lazy, and oversensitive, and are too ready to resign themselves to the thought that they are doomed to failure, that personal life has disappointed them; instead of struggling they merely criticize, calling the world vulgar and forgetting that their criticism passes little by little into vulgarity.

I was loved, happiness was not far away, and seemed to be almost touching me; I went on living in careless ease without trying to understand myself, not knowing what I expected or what I wanted from life, and time went on and on. . . . People passed by me with their love, bright days and warm nights flashed by, the nightingales sang, the hay smelt fragrant, and all this, sweet and overwhelming in remembrance, passed with me as with everyone rapidly, leaving no trace, was not prized, and vanished like mist. . . . Where is it all?

My father is dead, I have grown older; everything that delighted me, caressed me, gave me hope—the patter of the rain, the rolling of the thunder, thoughts of happiness, talk of love—all that has become nothing but a memory, and I see before me a flat desert distance; on the plain not one living soul, and out there on the horizon it is dark and terrible. . . .

A ring at the bell. . . . It is Pyotr Sergeyitch. When in the winter I see the trees and remember how green they were for me in the summer I whisper:

"Oh, my darlings!"

And when I see people with whom I spent my spring-time, I feel sorrowful and warm and whisper the same thing.

He has long ago by my father's good offices been transferred to town. He looks a little older, a little fallen away. He has long given up declaring his love, has left off talking nonsense, dislikes his official work, is ill in some way and disillusioned; he has given up trying to get anything out of life, and takes no interest in living. Now he has sat down by the hearth and looks in silence at the fire. . . .

Not knowing what to say I ask him:

"Well, what have you to tell me?"

"Nothing," he answers.

And silence again. The red glow of the fire plays about his melancholy face.

I thought of the past, and all at once my shoulders began quivering, my head dropped, and I began weeping bitterly. I felt unbearably sorry for myself and for this man, and passionately longed for what had passed away and what life refused us now. And now I did not think about rank and wealth.

I broke into loud sobs, pressing my temples, and muttered:

"My God! my God! my life is wasted!"

And he sat and was silent, and did not say to me: "Don't weep." He understood that I must weep, and that the time for this had come.

I saw from his eyes that he was sorry for me; and I was sorry for him, too, and vexed with this timid, unsuccessful man who could not make a life for me, nor for himself.

When I saw him to the door, he was, I fancied, purposely a long while putting on his coat. Twice he kissed my hand without a word, and looked a long while into my tear-stained face. I believe at that moment he recalled the storm, the streaks of rain, our laughter, my face that day; he longed to say something to me, and he would have been glad to say it; but he said nothing, he merely shook his head and pressed my hand. God help him!

After seeing him out, I went back to my study and again sat on the carpet before the fireplace; the red embers were covered with ash and began to grow dim. The frost tapped still more angrily at the windows, and the wind droned in the chimney.

The maid came in and, thinking I was asleep, called my name.

A Story
Without a Title

In the fifth century, just as now, the sun rose every morning and every evening retired to rest. In the morning, when the first rays kissed the dew, the earth revived, the air was filled with the sounds of rapture and hope; while in the evening the same earth subsided into silence and plunged into gloomy darkness. One day was like another, one night like another. From time to time a storm-cloud raced up and there was the angry rumble of thunder, or a negligent star fell out of the sky, or a pale monk ran to tell the brotherhood that not far from the monastery he had seen a tiger—and that was all, and then each day was like the next.

The monks worked and prayed, and their Father Superior played on the organ, made Latin verses, and wrote music. The wonderful old man possessed an extraordinary gift. He played on the organ with such art that even the oldest monks, whose hearing had grown somewhat dull towards the end of their lives, could not restrain their tears when the sounds of the organ floated from his cell. When he spoke of anything, even of the most ordinary things—for instance of the trees, of the wild beasts, or of the sea—they could not listen to him without a smile or tears, and it seemed that the same chords vibrated in his soul as in the organ. If he were moved to anger or abandoned himself to intense joy, or began speaking of something terrible or grand, then a passionate inspiration took possession of him, tears came into his flashing eyes, his face flushed, and his voice thundered, and as the monks listened to him they felt that their souls were spell-bound by his inspiration; at such marvellous, splendid moments his power over them was boundless, and if he had bidden his elders fling themselves into the sea, they would all, every one of them, have hastened to carry out his wishes.

His music, his voice, his poetry in which he glorified God, the heavens and the earth, were a continual source of joy to the monks. It sometimes happened that through the monotony of their lives they grew weary of the trees, the flowers, the spring, the autumn, their ears were tired of the sound of the sea, and the song of the birds seemed tedious to them, but the talents of their Father Superior were as necessary to them as their daily bread.

Dozens of years passed by, and every day was like every other day, every night was like every other night. Except the birds and the wild beasts, not one soul appeared near the monastery. The nearest human habitation was far away, and to reach it from the monastery, or to reach the monastery from it, meant a journey of over seventy miles across the desert. Only men who despised life, who had renounced it, and who came to the monastery as to the grave, ventured to cross the desert.

What was the amazement of the monks, therefore, when one night there knocked at their gate a man who turned out to be from the town, and the most ordinary sinner who loved life. Before saying his prayers and asking for the Father Superior's blessing, this man asked for wine and food. To the question how he had come from the town into the desert, he answered by a long story of hunting; he had gone out hunting, had drunk too much, and lost his way. To the suggestion that he should enter the monastery and save his soul, he replied with a smile: "I am not a fit companion for you!"

When he had eaten and drunk he looked at the monks who were serving him, shook his head reproachfully, and said:

"You don't do anything, you monks. You are good for nothing but eating and drinking. Is that the way to save one's soul? Only think, while you sit here in peace, eat and drink and dream of beatitude, your neighbours are perishing and going to hell. You should see what is going on in the town! Some are dying of hunger, others, not knowing what to do with their gold, sink into profligacy and perish like flies stuck in honey. There is no faith, no truth in men. Whose task is it to save them? Whose work is it to preach to them? It is not for me, drunk from morning till night as I am. Can a meek spirit, a loving heart, and faith in God have been given you for you to sit here within four walls doing nothing?"

The townsman's drunken words were insolent and unseemly, but they had a strange effect upon the Father Superior. The old man exchanged glances with his monks, turned pale, and said:

"My brothers, he speaks the truth, you know. Indeed, poor people in their weakness and lack of understanding are perishing in vice and infidelity, while we do not move, as though it did not concern us. Why should I not go and remind them of the Christ whom they have forgotten?"

The townsman's words had carried the old man away. The next day he took his staff, said farewell to the brotherhood, and set off for the town. And the monks were left without music, and without his speeches and verses. They spent a month drearily, then a second, but the old man did not come back. At last after three months had passed the familiar tap of his staff was heard. The monks flew to meet him and showered questions upon him, but instead of being delighted to see them he wept bitterly and did not utter a word. The monks noticed that he looked greatly aged and had grown thinner; his face looked exhausted and wore an expression of profound sadness, and when he wept he had the air of a man who has been outraged.

The monks fell to weeping too, and began with sympathy asking him why he was weeping, why his face was so gloomy, but he locked himself in his cell without uttering a word. For seven days he sat in his cell, eating and drinking nothing, weeping and not playing on his organ. To knocking at his door and to the entreaties of the monks to come out and share his grief with them he replied with unbroken silence.

At last he came out. Gathering all the monks around him, with a tear-stained face and with an expression of grief and indignation, he began telling them of what had befallen him during those three months. His voice was calm and his eyes were smiling while he described his journey from the monastery to the town. On the road, he told them, the birds sang to him, the brooks gurgled, and sweet youthful hopes agitated his soul; he marched on and felt like a soldier going to battle and confident of victory; he walked on dreaming, and composed poems and hymns, and reached the end of his journey without noticing it.

But his voice quivered, his eyes flashed, and he was full of wrath when he came to speak of the town and of the men in it. Never in his life had he seen or even dared to imagine what he met with when he went into the town. Only then for the first time in his life, in his old age, he saw and understood how powerful was the devil, how fair was evil and how weak and faint-hearted and worthless were men. By an unhappy chance the first dwelling he entered was the abode of vice. Some fifty men in possession of much money were eating and drinking wine beyond measure. Intoxicated by the wine, they sang songs and boldly uttered terrible, revolting words such as a God-fearing man could not bring himself to pronounce; boundlessly free, self-confident, and happy, they feared neither God nor the devil, nor death, but said and did what they liked, and went whither their lust led them. And the wine, clear as amber, flecked with sparks of gold, must have been irresistibly sweet and fragrant, for each man who drank it smiled blissfully and wanted to drink more. To the smile of man it responded with a smile and sparkled joyfully when they drank it, as though it knew the devilish charm it kept hidden in its sweetness.

The old man, growing more and more incensed and weeping with wrath, went on to describe what he had seen. On a table in the midst of the revellers, he said, stood a sinful, half-naked woman. It was hard to imagine or to find in nature anything more lovely and fascinating. This reptile, young, long-haired, dark-skinned, with black eyes and full lips, shameless and insolent, showed her snow-white teeth and smiled as though to say: "Look how shameless, how beautiful I am." Silk and brocade fell in lovely folds from her shoulders, but her beauty would not hide itself under her clothes, but eagerly thrust itself through the folds, like the young grass through the ground in spring. The shameless woman drank wine, sang songs, and abandoned herself to anyone who wanted her.

Then the old man, wrathfully brandishing his arms, described the horse-races, the bull-fights, the theatres, the artists' studios where they painted naked women or moulded them of clay. He spoke with inspiration, with sonorous beauty, as though he were playing on unseen chords, while the monks, petrified, greedily drank in his words and gasped with rapture. . . .

After describing all the charms of the devil, the beauty of evil, and the fascinating grace of the dreadful female form, the old man cursed the devil, turned and shut himself up in his cell. . . .

When he came out of his cell in the morning there was not a monk left in the monastery; they had all fled to the town.

The Steppe

The Story of a Journey

I

Early one morning in July a shabby covered chaise, one of those ante-diluvian chaises without springs in which no one travels in Russia nowadays, except merchant's clerks, dealers and the less well-to-do among priests, drove out of N., the principal town of the province of Z., and rumbled noisily along the posting-track. It rattled and creaked at every movement; the pail, hanging on behind, chimed in gruffly, and from these sounds alone and from the wretched rags of leather hanging loose about its peeling body one could judge of its decrepit age and readiness to drop to pieces.

Two of the inhabitants of N. were sitting in the chaise; they were a merchant of N. called Ivan Ivanitch Kuzmitchov, a man with a shaven face wearing glasses and a straw hat, more like a government clerk than a merchant, and Father Christopher Sireysky, the priest of the Church of St. Nikolay at N., a little old man with long hair, in a grey canvas cassock, a wide-brimmed top-hat and a coloured embroidered girdle. The former was absorbed in thought, and kept tossing his head to shake off drowsiness; in his countenance an habitual business-like reserve was struggling with the genial expression of a man who has just said good-bye to his relatives and has had a good drink at parting. The latter gazed with moist eyes wonderingly at God's world, and his smile was so broad that it seemed to embrace even the brim of his hat; his face was red and looked frozen. Both of them, Father Christopher as well as Kuzmitchov, were going to sell wool. At parting with their families they had just eaten heartily of pastry puffs and cream, and although it was so early in the morning had had a glass or two.... Both were in the best of humours.

Apart from the two persons described above and the coachman Deniska, who lashed the pair of frisky bay horses, there was another figure in the chaise—a boy of nine with a sunburnt face, wet with tears. This was Yegorushka, Kuzmitchov's nephew. With the sanction of his uncle and the blessing of Father Christopher, he was now on his way to go to school. His mother, Olga Ivanovna, the widow of a collegiate secretary, and Kuzmitchov's sister, who was fond of educated people and refined society, had entreated her brother to take Yegorushka with him when he went to sell wool and to put him to school; and now the boy was sitting on the box beside the coachman Deniska, holding on to his elbow to keep from falling off, and dancing up and down like a kettle on the hob, with no notion where he was going or what he was going for. The rapid motion through the air blew out his red shirt like a balloon on his back and made his new hat with a peacock's feather in it, like a coachman's, keep slipping on to the back of his head. He felt himself an intensely unfortunate person, and had an inclination to cry.

When the chaise drove past the prison, Yegorushka glanced at the sentinels pacing slowly by the high white walls, at the little barred windows, at the cross shining on the roof, and remembered how the week before, on the day of the Holy Mother of Kazan, he had been with his mother to the prison church for the Dedication Feast, and how before that, at Easter, he had gone to the prison with Deniska and Ludmila the cook, and had taken the prisoners Easter bread, eggs, cakes and roast beef. The prisoners had thanked them and made the sign of the cross, and one of them had given Yegorushka a pewter buckle of his own making.

The boy gazed at the familiar places, while the hateful chaise flew

by and left them all behind. After the prison he caught glimpses of
black grimy foundries, followed by the snug green cemetery surrounded by a wall of cobblestones; white crosses and tombstones,
nestling among green cherry-trees and looking in the distance like
patches of white, peeped out gaily from behind the wall. Yegorushka
remembered that when the cherries were in blossom those white
patches melted with the flowers into a sea of white; and that when the
cherries were ripe the white tombstones and crosses were dotted with
splashes of red like bloodstains. Under the cherry-trees in the cemetery Yegorushka's father and granny, Zinaida Danilovna, lay sleeping
day and night. When Granny had died she had been put in a long narrow coffin and two pennies had been put upon her eyes, which would
not keep shut. Up to the time of her death she had been brisk, and used
to bring soft rolls covered with poppy seeds from the market. Now she
did nothing but sleep and sleep....

Beyond the cemetery came the smoking brickyards. From under the
long roofs of reeds that looked as though pressed flat to the ground, a
thick black smoke rose in great clouds and floated lazily upwards. The
sky was murky above the brickyards and the cemetery, and great shadows from the clouds of smoke crept over the fields and across the
roads. Men and horses covered with red dust were moving about in the
smoke near the roofs....

The town ended with the brickyards and the open country began.
Yegorushka looked at the town for the last time, pressed his face
against Deniska's elbow, and wept bitterly....

"Come, not done howling yet, cry-baby!" cried Kuzmitchov. "You
are blubbering again, little milksop! If you don't want to go, stay behind; no one is taking you by force!"

"Never mind, never mind, Yegor boy, never mind," Father Christopher muttered rapidly—"never mind, my boy.... Call upon God....
You are not going for your harm, but for your good. Learning is light,
as the saying is, and ignorance is darkness.... That is so, truly."

"Do you want to go back?" asked Kuzmitchov.

"Yes,... yes,..." answered Yegorushka, sobbing.

"Well, you'd better go back then. Anyway, you are going for nothing; it's a day's journey for a spoonful of porridge."

"Never mind, never mind, my boy," Father Christopher went on. "Call upon God.... Lomonosov set off with the fishermen in the same way, and he became a man famous all over Europe. Learning in conjunction with faith brings forth fruit pleasing to God. What are the words of the prayer? For the glory of our Maker, for the comfort of our parents, for the benefit of our Church and our country.... Yes, indeed!"

"The benefit is not the same in all cases," said Kuzmitchov, lighting a cheap cigar; "some will study twenty years and get no sense from it."

"That does happen."

"Learning is a benefit to some, but others only muddle their brains. My sister is a woman who does not understand; she is set upon refinement, and wants to turn Yegorka into a learned man, and she does not understand that with my business I could settle Yegorka happily for the rest of his life. I tell you this, that if everyone were to go in for being learned and refined there would be no one to sow the corn and do the trading; they would all die of hunger."

"And if all go in for trading and sowing corn there will be no one to acquire learning."

And considering that each of them had said something weighty and convincing, Kuzmitchov and Father Christopher both looked serious and cleared their throats simultaneously.

Deniska, who had been listening to their conversation without understanding a word of it, shook his head and, rising in his seat, lashed at both the bays. A silence followed.

Meanwhile a wide boundless plain encircled by a chain of low hills lay stretched before the travellers' eyes. Huddling together and peeping out from behind one another, these hills melted together into rising ground, which stretched right to the very horizon and disappeared into the lilac distance; one drives on and on and cannot discern where it begins or where it ends.... The sun had already peeped out from beyond the town behind them, and quietly, without fuss, set to its accustomed task. At first in the distance before them a broad, bright, yellow streak of light crept over the ground where the earth met the sky, near the little barrows and the windmills, which in the distance looked like tiny men waving their arms. A minute later a similar streak gleamed a little nearer, crept to the right and embraced the hills. Something warm touched Yegorushka's spine; the streak of light, stealing up from behind, darted between the chaise and the horses, moved to meet the other streak, and soon the whole wide steppe flung off the twilight of early morning, and was smiling and sparkling with dew.

The cut rye, the coarse steppe grass, the milkwort, the wild hemp, all withered from the sultry heat, turned brown and half dead, now washed by the dew and caressed by the sun, revived, to fade again. Arctic petrels flew across the road with joyful cries; marmots called to one another in the grass. Somewhere, far away to the left, lapwings uttered their plaintive notes. A covey of partridges, scared by the chaise, fluttered up and with their soft "trrrr!" flew off to the hills. In the grass crickets, locusts and grasshoppers kept up their churring, monotonous music.

But a little time passed, the dew evaporated, the air grew stagnant, and the disillusioned steppe began to wear its jaded July aspect. The grass drooped, everything living was hushed. The sun-baked hills, brownish-green and lilac in the distance, with their quiet shadowy tones, the plain with the misty distance and, arched above them, the sky, which seems terribly deep and transparent in the steppes, where there are no woods or high hills, seemed now endless, petrified with dreariness. . . .

How stifling and oppressive it was! The chaise raced along, while Yegorushka saw always the same—the sky, the plain, the low hills. . . . The music in the grass was hushed, the petrels had flown away, the partridges were out of sight, rooks hovered idly over the withered grass; they were all alike and made the steppe even more monotonous.

A hawk flew just above the ground, with an even sweep of its wings, suddenly halted in the air as though pondering on the dreariness of life, then fluttered its wings and flew like an arrow over the steppe, and there was no telling why it flew off and what it wanted. In the distance a windmill waved its sails. . . .

Now and then a glimpse of a white potsherd or a heap of stones broke the monotony; a grey stone stood out for an instant or a parched willow with a blue crow on its top branch; a marmot would run across the road and—again there flitted before the eyes only the high grass, the low hills, the rooks. . . .

But at last, thank God, a waggon loaded with sheaves came to meet them; a peasant wench was lying on the very top. Sleepy, exhausted by the heat, she lifted her head and looked at the travellers. Deniska gaped, looking at her; the horses stretched out their noses towards the sheaves; the chaise, squeaking, kissed the waggon, and the pointed ears passed over Father Christopher's hat like a brush.

"You are driving over folks, fatty!" cried Deniska. "What a swollen lump of a face, as though a bumble-bee had stung it!"

The girl smiled drowsily, and moving her lips lay down again; then a solitary poplar came into sight on the low hill. Someone had planted it, and God only knows why it was there. It was hard to tear the eyes away from its graceful figure and green drapery. Was that lovely creature happy? Sultry heat in summer, in winter frost and snowstorms, terrible nights in autumn when nothing is to be seen but darkness and nothing is to be heard but the senseless angry howling wind, and, worst of all, alone, alone for the whole of life. . . . Beyond the poplar stretches of wheat extended like a bright yellow carpet from the road to the top of the hills. On the hills the corn was already cut and laid up in sheaves, while at the bottom they were still cutting. . . . Six mowers were standing in a row swinging their scythes, and the scythes gleamed gaily and uttered in unison together "Vzhee, vzhee!" From the movements of the peasant women binding the sheaves, from the faces of the mowers, from the glitter of the scythes, it could be seen that the sultry heat was baking and stifling. A black dog with its tongue hanging out ran from the mowers to meet the chaise, probably with the intention of barking, but stopped halfway and stared indifferently at Deniska, who shook his whip at him; it was too hot to bark! One peasant woman got up and, putting both hands to her aching back, followed Yegorushka's red shirt with her eyes. Whether it was that the colour pleased her or that he reminded her of her children, she stood a long time motionless staring after him. . . .

But now the wheat, too, had flashed by; again the parched plain, the sunburnt hills, the sultry sky stretched before them; again a hawk hovered over the earth. In the distance, as before, a windmill whirled its sails, and still it looked like a little man waving his arms. It was wearisome to watch, and it seemed as though one would never reach it, as though it were running away from the chaise.

Father Christopher and Kuzmitchov were silent. Deniska lashed the horses and kept shouting to them, while Yegorushka had left off crying, and gazed about him listlessly. The heat and the tedium of the steppes overpowered him. He felt as though he had been travelling and jolting up and down for a very long time, that the sun had been baking his back a long time. Before they had gone eight miles he began to feel "It must be time to rest." The geniality gradually faded out of his uncle's face and nothing else was left but the air of business reserve; and to a gaunt shaven face, especially when it is adorned with spectacles and the nose and temples are covered with dust, this reserve gives a relentless, inquisitorial appearance. Father Christopher never left off gazing with wonder at God's world, and smiling. Without speaking, he brooded over something pleasant and nice, and a kindly, genial smile remained imprinted on his face. It seemed as though some nice and pleasant thought were imprinted on his brain by the heat. . . .

"Well, Deniska, shall we overtake the waggons to-day?" asked Kuzmitchov.

Deniska looked at the sky, rose in his seat, lashed at his horses and then answered:

"By nightfall, please God, we shall overtake them."

There was a sound of dogs barking. Half a dozen steppe sheep-dogs, suddenly leaping out as though from ambush, with ferocious howling barks, flew to meet the chaise. All of them, extraordinarily furious, surrounded the chaise, with their shaggy spider-like muzzles and their eyes red with anger, and jostling against one another in their anger, raised a hoarse howl. They were filled with passionate hatred of the horses, of the chaise, and of the human beings, and seemed ready to tear them into pieces. Deniska, who was fond of teasing and beating, was delighted at the chance of it, and with a malignant expression bent over and lashed at the sheep-dogs with his whip. The brutes growled more than ever, the horses flew on; and Yegorushka, who had difficulty in keeping his seat on the box, realized, looking at the dogs' eyes and teeth, that if he fell down they would instantly tear him to bits; but he felt no fear and looked at them as malignantly as Deniska, and regretted that he had no whip in his hand.

The chaise came upon a flock of sheep.

"Stop!" cried Kuzmitchov. "Pull up! Woa!"

Deniska threw his whole body backwards and pulled up the horses.

"Come here!" Kuzmitchov shouted to the shepherd. "Call off the dogs, curse them!"

The old shepherd, tattered and barefoot, wearing a fur cap, with a dirty sack round his loins and a long crook in his hand—a regular figure from the Old Testament—called off the dogs, and taking off his cap, went up to the chaise. Another similar Old Testament figure was standing motionless at the other end of the flock, staring without interest at the travellers.

"Whose sheep are these?" asked Kuzmitchov.

"Varlamov's," the old man answered in a loud voice.

"Varlamov's," repeated the shepherd standing at the other end of the flock.

"Did Varlamov come this way yesterday or not?"

"He did not; his clerk came...."

"Drive on!"

The chaise rolled on and the shepherds, with their angry dogs, were left behind. Yegorushka gazed listlessly at the lilac distance in front, and it began to seem as though the windmill, waving its sails, were getting nearer. It became bigger and bigger, grew quite large, and now he could distinguish clearly its two sails. One sail was old and patched, the other had only lately been made of new wood and glistened in the sun. The chaise drove straight on, while the windmill, for some reason, began retreating to the left. They drove on and on, and the windmill kept moving away to the left, and still did not disappear.

"A fine windmill Boltva has put up for his son," observed Deniska.

"And how is it we don't see his farm?"

"It is that way, beyond the creek."

Boltva's farm, too, soon came into sight, but yet the windmill did not retreat, did not drop behind; it still watched Yegorushka with its shining sail and waved. What a sorcerer!

II

Towards midday the chaise turned off the road to the right; it went on a little way at walking pace and then stopped. Yegorushka heard a soft, very caressing gurgle, and felt a different air breathe on his face with a cool velvety touch. Through a little pipe of hemlock stuck there by some unknown benefactor, water was running in a thin trickle from a low hill, put together by nature of huge monstrous stones. It fell to the ground, and limpid, sparkling gaily in the sun, and softly murmuring as though fancying itself a great tempestuous torrent, flowed swiftly away to the left. Not far from its source the little stream spread itself out into a pool; the burning sunbeams and the parched soil greedily drank it up and sucked away its strength; but a little further on it must have mingled with another rivulet, for a hundred paces away thick reeds showed green and luxuriant along its course, and three snipe flew up from them with a loud cry as the chaise drove by.

The travellers got out to rest by the stream and feed the horses. Kuzmitchov, Father Christopher and Yegorushka sat down on a mat in the narrow strip of shade cast by the chaise and the unharnessed horses. The nice pleasant thought that the heat had imprinted in Father Christopher's brain craved expression after he had had a drink of water and eaten a hard-boiled egg. He bent a friendly look upon Yegorushka, munched, and began:

"I studied too, my boy; from the earliest age God instilled into me good sense and understanding, so that while I was just such a lad as you I was beyond others, a comfort to my parents and preceptors by my good sense. Before I was fifteen I could speak and make verses in Latin, just as in Russian. I was the crosier-bearer to his Holiness Bishop Christopher. After mass one day, as I remember it was the patron saint's day of His Majesty Tsar Alexandr Pavlovitch of blessed memory, he unrobed at the altar, looked kindly at me and asked, 'Puer bone, quam appelaris?' And I answered, 'Christopherus sum;' and he said,

'Ergo connominati sumus'—that is, that we were namesakes.... Then he asked in Latin, 'Whose son are you?' To which I answered, also in Latin, that I was the son of deacon Sireysky of the village of Lebedin- skoe. Seeing my readiness and the clearness of my answers, his Holi- ness blessed me and said, 'Write to your father that I will not forget him, and that I will keep you in view.' The holy priests and fathers who were standing round the altar, hearing our discussion in Latin, were not a little surprised, and everyone expressed his pleasure in praise of me. Before I had moustaches, my boy, I could read Latin, Greek, and French; I knew philosophy, mathematics, secular history, and all the sciences. The Lord gave me a marvellous memory. Sometimes, if I read a thing once or twice, I knew it by heart. My preceptors and pa- trons were amazed, and so they expected I should make a learned man, a luminary of the Church. I did think of going to Kiev to continue my studies, but my parents did not approve. 'You'll be studying all your life,' said my father; 'when shall we see you finished?' Hearing such words, I gave up study and took a post.... Of course, I did not become a learned man, but then I did not disobey my parents; I was a comfort to them in their old age and gave them a creditable funeral. Obedience is more than fasting and prayer."

"I suppose you have forgotten all your learning?" observed Kuzmitchov.

"I should think so! Thank God, I have reached my eightieth year! Something of philosophy and rhetoric I do remember, but languages and mathematics I have quite forgotten."

Father Christopher screwed up his eyes, thought a minute and said in an undertone:

"What is a substance? A creature is a self-existing object, not re- quiring anything else for its completion."

He shook his head and laughed with feeling.

"Spiritual nourishment!" he said. "Of a truth matter nourishes the flesh and spiritual nourishment the soul!"

"Learning is all very well," sighed Kuzmitchov, "but if we don't overtake Varlamov, learning won't do much for us."

"A man isn't a needle—we shall find him. He must be going his rounds in these parts."

Among the sedge were flying the three snipe they had seen before, and in their plaintive cries there was a note of alarm and vexation at having been driven away from the stream. The horses were steadily munching and snorting. Deniska walked about by them and, trying to appear indifferent to the cucumbers, pies, and eggs that the gentry were eating, he concentrated himself on the gadflies and horseflies that were fastening upon the horses' backs and bellies; he squashed his victims apathetically, emitting a peculiar, fiendishly triumphant, guttural sound, and when he missed them cleared his throat with an air of vexation and looked after every lucky one that escaped death.

"Deniska, where are you? Come and eat," said Kuzmitchov, heaving a deep sigh, a sign that he had had enough.

Deniska diffidently approached the mat and picked out five thick and yellow cucumbers (he did not venture to take the smaller and fresher ones), took two hard-boiled eggs that looked dark and were cracked, then irresolutely, as though afraid he might get a blow on his outstretched hand, touched a pie with his finger.

"Take them, take them," Kuzmitchov urged him on.

Deniska took the pies resolutely, and, moving some distance away, sat down on the grass with his back to the chaise. At once there was such a sound of loud munching that even the horses turned round to look suspiciously at Deniska.

After his meal Kuzmitchov took a sack containing something out of the chaise and said to Yegorushka:

"I am going to sleep, and you mind that no one takes the sack from under my head."

Father Christopher took off his cassock, his girdle, and his full coat, and Yegorushka, looking at him, was dumb with astonishment. He had never imagined that priests wore trousers, and Father Christopher had on real canvas trousers thrust into high boots, and a short striped jacket. Looking at him, Yegorushka thought that in this costume, so unsuitable to his dignified position, he looked with his long hair and beard very much like Robinson Crusoe. After taking off their outer garments Kuzmitchov and Father Christopher lay down in the shade under the chaise, facing one another, and closed their eyes. Deniska, who had finished munching, stretched himself out on his back and also closed his eyes.

"You look out that no one takes away the horses!" he said to Yegorushka, and at once fell asleep.

Stillness reigned. There was no sound except the munching and snorting of the horses and the snoring of the sleepers; somewhere far away a lapwing wailed, and from time to time there sounded the shrill cries of the three snipe who had flown up to see whether their uninvited visitors had gone away; the rivulet babbled, lisping softly, but all these sounds did not break the stillness, did not stir the stagnation, but, on the contrary, lulled all nature to slumber.

Yegorushka, gasping with the heat, which was particularly oppressive after a meal, ran to the sedge and from there surveyed the country. He saw exactly the same as he had in the morning: the plain, the low hills, the sky, the lilac distance; only the hills stood nearer; and he could not see the windmill, which had been left far behind. From behind the rocky hill from which the stream flowed rose another, smoother and broader; a little hamlet of five or six homesteads clung to it. No people, no trees, no shade were to be seen about the huts; it looked as though the hamlet had expired in the burning air and was dried up. To while away the time Yegorushka caught a grasshopper in the grass, held it in his closed hand to his ear, and spent a long time listening to the creature playing on its instrument. When he was weary of its music he ran after a flock of yellow butterflies who were flying towards the sedge on the watercourse, and found himself again beside the chaise, without noticing how he came there. His uncle and Father Christopher were sound asleep; their sleep would be sure to last two or three hours till the horses had rested. . . . How was he to get through that long time, and where was he to get away from the heat? A hard problem. . . . Mechanically Yegorushka put his lips to the trickle that ran from the waterpipe; there was a chilliness in his mouth and there was the smell of hemlock. He drank at first eagerly, then went on with effort till the sharp cold had run from his mouth all over his body and the water was spilt on his shirt. Then he went up to the chaise and began looking at the sleeping figures. His uncle's face wore, as before, an expression of business-like reserve. Fanatically devoted to his work, Kuzmitchov always, even in his sleep and at church when they were singing, "Like the cherubim," thought about his business and could never forget it for a moment; and now he was probably dreaming about bales of wool, waggons, prices, Varlamov.... Father Christopher, now, a soft, frivolous and absurd person, had never all his life been conscious of anything which could, like a boa-constrictor, coil about his soul and hold it tight. In all the numerous enterprises he had undertaken in his day what attracted him was not so much the business itself, but the bustle and the contact with other people involved in every undertaking. Thus, in the present expedition, he was not so much interested in wool, in Varlamov, and in prices, as in the long journey, the conversations on the way, the sleeping under a chaise, and the meals at odd times.... And now, judging from his face, he must have been dreaming of Bishop Christopher, of the Latin discussion, of his wife, of puffs and cream and all sorts of things that Kuzmitchov could not possibly dream of.

While Yegorushka was watching their sleeping faces he suddenly heard a soft singing; somewhere at a distance a woman was singing, and it was difficult to tell where and in what direction. The song was subdued, dreary and melancholy, like a dirge, and hardly audible, and seemed to come first from the right, then from the left, then from above, and then from underground, as though an unseen spirit were hovering over the steppe and singing. Yegorushka looked about him, and could not make out where the strange song came from. Then as he listened he began to fancy that the grass was singing; in its song, withered and half-dead, it was without words, but plaintively and passionately, urging that it was not to blame, that the sun was burning it for no fault of its own; it urged that it ardently longed to live, that it was young and might have been beautiful but for the heat and the drought; it was guiltless, but yet it prayed forgiveness and protested that it was in anguish, sad and sorry for itself....

Yegorushka listened for a little, and it began to seem as though this dreary, mournful song made the air hotter, more suffocating and more stagnant.... To drown the singing he ran to the sedge, humming to himself and trying to make a noise with his feet. From there he looked about in all directions and found out who was singing. Near the furthest hut in the hamlet stood a peasant woman in a short petticoat, with long thin legs like a heron. She was sowing something. A white dust floated languidly from her sieve down the hillock. Now it was evident that she was singing. A couple of yards from her a little bareheaded boy in nothing but a smock was standing motionless. As though fascinated by the song, he stood stock-still, staring away into the distance, probably at Yegorushka's crimson shirt.

The song ceased. Yegorushka sauntered back to the chaise, and to while away the time went again to the trickle of water.

And again there was the sound of the dreary song. It was the same long-legged peasant woman in the hamlet over the hill. Yegorushka's boredom came back again. He left the pipe and looked upwards. What he saw was so unexpected that he was a little frightened. Just above his head on one of the big clumsy stones stood a chubby little boy, wearing nothing but a shirt, with a prominent stomach and thin legs, the same boy who had been standing before by the peasant woman. He was gazing with open mouth and unblinking eyes at Yegorushka's crimson shirt and at the chaise, with a look of blank astonishment and even fear, as though he saw before him creatures of another world. The red colour of the shirt charmed and allured him. But the chaise and the men sleeping under it excited his curiosity; perhaps he had not noticed how the agreeable red colour and curiosity had attracted him down from the hamlet, and now probably he was surprised at his own boldness. For a long while Yegorushka stared at him, and he at Yegorushka. Both were silent and conscious of some awkwardness. After a long silence Yegorushka asked:

"What's your name?"

The stranger's cheeks puffed out more than ever; he pressed his back against the rock, opened his eyes wide, moved his lips, and answered in a husky bass: "Tit!"

The boys said not another word to each other; after a brief silence, still keeping his eyes fixed on Yegorushka, the mysterious Tit kicked up one leg, felt with his heel for a niche and clambered up the rock; from that point he ascended to the next rock, staggering backwards and looking intently at Yegorushka, as though afraid he might hit him from behind, and so made his way upwards till he disappeared altogether behind the crest of the hill.

After watching him out of sight, Yegorushka put his arms round his knees and leaned his head on them. . . . The burning sun scorched the back of his head, his neck, and his spine. The melancholy song died away, then floated again on the stagnant stifling air. The rivulet gurgled monotonously, the horses munched, and time dragged on endlessly, as though it, too, were stagnant and had come to a standstill. It seemed as though a hundred years had passed since the morning. Could it be that God's world, the chaise and the horses would come to a standstill in that air, and, like the hills, turn to stone and remain for ever in one spot? Yegorushka raised his head, and with smarting eyes looked before him; the lilac distance, which till then had been motionless, began heaving, and with the sky floated away into the distance. . . . It drew after it the brown grass, the sedge, and with extraordinary swiftness Yegorushka floated after the flying distance. Some force noiselessly drew him onwards, and the heat and the wearisome song flew after in pursuit. Yegorushka bent his head and shut his eyes. . . .

Deniska was the first to wake up. Something must have bitten him, for he jumped up, quickly scratched his shoulder and said:

"Plague take you, cursed idolater!"

Then he went to the brook, had a drink and slowly washed. His splashing and puffing roused Yegorushka from his lethargy. The boy looked at his wet face with drops of water and big freckles which made it look like marble, and asked:

"Shall we soon be going?"

Deniska looked at the height of the sun and answered:

"I expect so."

He dried himself with the tail of his shirt and, making a very serious face, hopped on one leg.

"I say, which of us will get to the sedge first?" he said.

Yegorushka was exhausted by the heat and drowsiness, but he raced off after him all the same. Deniska was in his twentieth year, was a coachman and going to be married, but he had not left off being a boy. He was very fond of flying kites, chasing pigeons, playing knuckle-bones, running races, and always took part in children's games and disputes. No sooner had his master turned his back or gone to sleep than Deniska would begin doing something such as hopping on one leg or throwing stones. It was hard for any grown-up person, seeing the genuine enthusiasm with which he frolicked about in the society of children, to resist saying, "What a baby!" Children, on the other hand, saw nothing strange in the invasion of their domain by the big coachman. "Let him play," they thought, "as long as he doesn't fight!" In the same way little dogs see nothing strange in it when a simple-hearted big dog joins their company uninvited and begins playing with them.

Deniska outstripped Yegorushka, and was evidently very much pleased at having done so. He winked at him, and to show that he could hop on one leg any distance, suggested to Yegorushka that he should hop with him along the road and from there, without resting, back to the chaise. Yegorushka declined this suggestion, for he was very much out of breath and exhausted.

All at once Deniska looked very grave, as he did not look even when Kuzmitchov gave him a scolding or threatened him with a stick; listening intently, he dropped quietly to one knee and an expression of sternness and alarm came into his face, such as one sees in people who hear heretical talk. He fixed his eyes on one spot, raised his hand curved into a hollow, and suddenly fell on his stomach on the ground and slapped the hollow of his hand down upon the grass.

"Caught!" he wheezed triumphantly, and, getting up, lifted a big grasshopper to Yegorushka's eyes.

The two boys stroked the grasshopper's broad green back with their fingers and touched his antennæ, supposing that this would please the creature. Then Deniska caught a fat fly that had been sucking blood and offered it to the grasshopper. The latter moved his huge jaws, that were like the visor of a helmet, with the utmost unconcern, as though he had been long acquainted with Deniska, and bit off the fly's stomach. They let him go. With a flash of the pink lining of his wings, he flew down into the grass and at once began his churring notes again. They let the fly go, too. It preened its wings, and without its stomach flew off to the horses.

A loud sigh was heard from under the chaise. It was Kuzmitchov waking up. He quickly raised his head, looked uneasily into the distance, and from that look, which passed by Yegorushka and Deniska without sympathy or interest, it could be seen that his thought on awaking was of the wool and of Varlamov.

"Father Christopher, get up; it is time to start," he said anxiously. "Wake up; we've slept too long as it is! Deniska, put the horses in."

Father Christopher woke up with the same smile with which he had fallen asleep; his face looked creased and wrinkled from sleep, and seemed only half the size. After washing and dressing, he proceeded without haste to take out of his pocket a little greasy psalter; and standing with his face towards the east, began in a whisper repeating the psalms of the day and crossing himself.

"Father Christopher," said Kuzmitchov reproachfully, "it's time to start; the horses are ready, and here are you, . . . upon my word."

"In a minute, in a minute," muttered Father Christopher. "I must read the psalms. . . . I haven't read them to-day."

"The psalms can wait."

"Ivan Ivanitch, that is my rule every day. . . . I can't . . ."

"God will overlook it."

For a full quarter of an hour Father Christopher stood facing the east and moving his lips, while Kuzmitchov looked at him almost with hatred and impatiently shrugged his shoulders. He was particularly irritated when, after every "Hallelujah," Father Christopher drew a long breath, rapidly crossed himself and repeated three times, intentionally raising his voice so that the others might cross themselves, "Hallelujah, hallelujah, hallelujah! Glory be to Thee, O Lord!" At last he smiled, looked upwards at the sky, and, putting the psalter in his pocket, said:

"Finis!"

A minute later the chaise had started on the road. As though it were going backwards and not forwards, the travellers saw the same scene as they had before midday.

The low hills were still plunged in the lilac distance, and no end could be seen to them. There were glimpses of high grass and heaps of stones; strips of stubble land passed by them and still the same rooks, the same hawk, moving its wings with slow dignity, moved over the steppe. The air was more sultry than ever; from the sultry heat and the stillness submissive nature was spellbound into silence. . . . No wind, no fresh cheering sound, no cloud.

But at last, when the sun was beginning to sink into the west, the steppe, the hills and the air could bear the oppression no longer, and, driven out of all patience, exhausted, tried to fling off the yoke. A fleecy ashen-grey cloud unexpectedly appeared behind the hills. It exchanged glances with the steppe, as though to say, "Here I am," and frowned. Suddenly something burst in the stagnant air; there was a violent squall of wind which whirled round and round, roaring and whistling over the steppe. At once a murmur rose from the grass and last year's dry herbage, the dust curled in spiral eddies over the road, raced over the steppe, and carrying with it straws, dragon flies and feathers, rose up in a whirling black column towards the sky and darkened the sun. Prickly uprooted plants ran stumbling and leaping in all directions over the steppe, and one of them got caught in the whirlwind, turned round and round like a bird, flew towards the sky, and turning into a little black speck, vanished from sight. After it flew another, and then a third, and Yegorushka saw two of them meet in the blue height and clutch at one another as though they were wrestling.

A bustard flew up by the very road. Fluttering his wings and his tail, he looked, bathed in the sunshine, like an angler's glittering tin fish or a waterfly flashing so swiftly over the water that its wings cannot be told from its antennæ, which seem to be growing before, behind and on all sides. . . . Quivering in the air like an insect with a shimmer of bright colours, the bustard flew high up in a straight line, then, probably frightened by a cloud of dust, swerved to one side, and for a long time the gleam of his wings could be seen. . . .

Then a corncrake flew up from the grass, alarmed by the hurricane and not knowing what was the matter. It flew with the wind and not against it, like all the other birds, so that all its feathers were ruffled up and it was puffed out to the size of a hen and looked very angry and impressive. Only the rooks who had grown old on the steppe and were accustomed to its vagaries hovered calmly over the grass, or taking no notice of anything, went on unconcernedly pecking with their stout beaks at the hard earth.

There was a dull roll of thunder beyond the hills; there came a whiff of fresh air. Deniska gave a cheerful whistle and lashed his horses. Father Christopher and Kuzmitchov held their hats and looked intently towards the hills. . . . How pleasant a shower of rain would have been!

One effort, one struggle more, and it seemed the steppe would have got the upper hand. But the unseen oppressive force gradually riveted its fetters on the wind and the air, laid the dust, and the stillness came back again as though nothing had happened, the cloud hid, the sun-baked hills frowned submissively, the air grew calm, and only some-where the troubled lapwings wailed and lamented their destiny. . . .

Soon after that the evening came on.

III

In the dusk of evening a big house of one storey, with a rusty iron roof and with dark windows, came into sight. This house was called a posting-inn, though it had nothing like a stableyard, and it stood in the middle of the steppe, with no kind of enclosure round it. A little to one side of it a wretched little cherry orchard shut in by a hurdle fence made a dark patch, and under the windows stood sleepy sunflowers drooping their heavy heads. From the orchard came the clatter of a lit-tle toy windmill, set there to frighten away hares by the rattle. Noth-ing more could be seen near the house, and nothing could be heard but the steppe. The chaise had scarcely stopped at the porch with an awning over it, when from the house there came the sound of cheer-ful voices, one a man's, another a woman's; there was the creak of a swing-door, and in a flash a tall gaunt figure, swinging its arms and flut-tering its coat, was standing by the chaise. This was the innkeeper, Moisey Moisevitch, a man no longer young, with a very pale face and a handsome beard as black as charcoal. He was wearing a threadbare black coat, which hung flapping on his narrow shoulders as though on a hatstand, and fluttered its skirts like wings every time Moisey Moisevitch flung up his hands in delight or horror. Besides his coat the innkeeper was wearing full white trousers, not stuck into his boots, and a velvet waistcoat with brown flowers on it that looked like gigantic bugs.

Moisey Moisevitch was at first dumb with excess of feeling on recognizing the travellers, then he clasped his hands and uttered a moan. His coat swung its skirts, his back bent into a bow, and his pale face twisted into a smile that suggested that to see the chaise was not merely a pleasure to him, but actually a joy so sweet as to be painful.

"Oh dear! oh dear!" he began in a thin sing-song voice, breathless, fussing about and preventing the travellers from getting out of the chaise by his antics. "What a happy day for me! Oh, what am I to do now? Ivan Ivanitch! Father Christopher! What a pretty little gentleman sitting on the box, God strike me dead! Oh, my goodness! why am I standing here instead of asking the visitors indoors? Please walk in, I humbly beg you. . . . You are kindly welcome! Give me all your things. . . . Oh, my goodness me!"

Moisey Moisevitch, who was rummaging in the chaise and assisting the travellers to alight, suddenly turned back and shouted in a voice as frantic and choking as though he were drowning and calling for help:

"Solomon! Solomon!"

"Solomon! Solomon!" a woman's voice repeated indoors.

The swing-door creaked, and in the doorway appeared a rather short young Jew with a big beak-like nose, with a bald patch surrounded by rough red curly hair; he was dressed in a short and very shabby reefer jacket, with rounded lappets and short sleeves, and in short serge trousers, so that he looked skimpy and short-tailed like an unfledged bird. This was Solomon, the brother of Moisey Moisevitch. He went up to the chaise, smiling rather queerly, and did not speak or greet the travellers.

"Ivan Ivanitch and Father Christopher have come," said Moisey Moisevitch in a tone as though he were afraid his brother would not believe him. "Dear, dear! What a surprise! Such honoured guests to have come us so suddenly! Come, take their things, Solomon. Walk in, honoured guests."

A little later Kuzmitchov, Father Christopher, and Yegorushka were sitting in a big gloomy empty room at an old oak table. The table was almost in solitude, for, except a wide sofa covered with torn American leather and three chairs, there was no other furniture in the room. And, indeed, not everybody would have given the chairs that name. They were a pitiful semblance of furniture, covered with American leather that had seen its best days, and with backs bent backwards at an unnaturally acute angle, so that they looked like children's sledges. It was hard to imagine what had been the unknown carpenter's object in bending the chairbacks so mercilessly, and one was tempted to imagine that it was not the carpenter's fault, but that some athletic visitor had bent the chairs like this as a feat, then had tried to bend them back again and had made them worse. The room looked gloomy, the walls were grey, the ceilings and the cornices were grimy; on the floor were chinks and yawning holes that were hard to account for (one might have fancied they were made by the heel of the same athlete), and it seemed as though the room would still have been dark if a dozen lamps had hung in it. There was nothing approaching an ornament on the walls or the windows. On one wall, however, there hung a list of regulations of some sort under a two-headed eagle in a grey wooden frame, and on another wall in the same sort of frame an engraving with the inscription, "The Indifference of Man." What it was to which men were indifferent it was impossible to make out, as the engraving was very dingy with age and was extensively flyblown. There was a smell of something decayed and sour in the room.

As he led the visitors into the room, Moisey Moisevitch went on wriggling, gesticulating, shrugging and uttering joyful exclamations; he considered these antics necessary in order to seem polite and agreeable.

"When did our waggons go by?" Kuzmitchov asked.

"One party went by early this morning, and the other, Ivan Ivanitch, put up here for dinner and went on towards evening."

"Ah! . . . Has Varlamov been by or not?"

"No, Ivan Ivanitch. His clerk, Grigory Yegoritch, went by yesterday morning and said that he had to be to-day at the Molokans' farm."

"Good! so we will go after the waggons directly and then on to the Molokans'."

"Mercy on us, Ivan Ivanitch!" Moisey Moisevitch cried in horror, flinging up his hands. "Where are you going for the night? You will have a nice little supper and stay the night, and to-morrow morning, please God, you can go on and overtake anyone you like."

"There is no time for that. . . . Excuse me, Moisey Moisevitch, another time; but now I must make haste. We'll stay a quarter of an hour and then go on; we can stay the night at the Molokans'."

"A quarter of an hour!" squealed Moisey Moisevitch. "Have you no fear of God, Ivan Ivanitch? You will compel me to hide your caps and lock the door! You must have a cup of tea and a snack of something, anyway."

"We have no time for tea," said Kuzmitchov.

Moisey Moisevitch bent his head on one side, crooked his knees, and put his open hands before him as though warding off a blow, while with a smile of agonized sweetness he began imploring:

"Ivan Ivanitch! Father Christopher! Do be so good as to take a cup of tea with me. Surely I am not such a bad man that you can't even drink tea in my house? Ivan Ivanitch!"

"Well, we may just as well have a cup of tea," said Father Christopher, with a sympathetic smile; "that won't keep us long."

"Very well," Kuzmitchov assented.

Moisey Moisevitch, in a fluster uttered an exclamation of joy, and shrugging as though he had just stepped out of cold weather into warm, ran to the door and cried in the same frantic voice in which he had called Solomon:

"Rosa! Rosa! Bring the samovar!"

A minute later the door opened, and Solomon came into the room carrying a large tray in his hands. Setting the tray on the table, he looked away sarcastically with the same queer smile as before. Now, by the light of the lamp, it was possible to see his smile distinctly; it was very complex, and expressed a variety of emotions, but the predominant element in it was undisguised contempt. He seemed to be thinking of something ludicrous and silly, to be feeling contempt and dislike, to be pleased at something and waiting for the favourable moment to turn something into ridicule and to burst into laughter. His long nose, his thick lips, and his sly prominent eyes seemed tense with the desire to laugh. Looking at his face, Kuzmitchov smiled ironically and asked:

"Solomon, why did you not come to our fair at N. this summer, and act some Jewish scenes?"

Two years before, as Yegorushka remembered very well, at one of the booths at the fair at N., Solomon had performed some scenes of Jewish life, and his acting had been a great success. The allusion to this made no impression whatever upon Solomon. Making no answer, he went out and returned a little later with the samovar.

When he had done what he had to do at the table he moved a little aside, and, folding his arms over his chest and thrusting out one leg, fixed his sarcastic eyes on Father Christopher. There was something defiant, haughty, and contemptuous in his attitude, and at the same time it was comic and pitiful in the extreme, because the more impressive his attitude the more vividly it showed up his short trousers, his bobtail coat, his caricature of a nose, and his bird-like plucked-looking little figure.

Moisey Moisevitch brought a footstool from the other room and sat down a little way from the table.

"I wish you a good appetite! Tea and sugar!" he began, trying to entertain his visitors. "I hope you will enjoy it. Such rare guests, such rare ones; it is years since I last saw Father Christopher. And will no one tell me who is this nice little gentleman?" he asked, looking tenderly at Yegorushka.

"He is the son of my sister, Olga Ivanovna," answered Kuzmitchov.

"And where is he going?"

"To school. We are taking him to a high school."

In his politeness, Moisey Moisevitch put on a look of wonder and wagged his head expressively.

"Ah, that is a fine thing," he said, shaking his finger at the samovar. "That's a fine thing. You will come back from the high school such a gentleman that we shall all take off our hats to you. You will be wealthy and wise and so grand that your mamma will be delighted. Oh, that's a fine thing!"

He paused a little, stroked his knees, and began again in a jocose and deferential tone.

"You must excuse me, Father Christopher, but I am thinking of writing to the bishop to tell him you are robbing the merchants of their living. I shall take a sheet of stamped paper and write that I suppose Father Christopher is short of pence, as he has taken up with trade and begun selling wool."

"H'm, yes... it's a queer notion in my old age," said Father Christopher, and he laughed. "I have turned from priest to merchant, brother. I ought to be at home now saying my prayers, instead of galloping about the country like a Pharaoh in his chariot.... Vanity!"

"But it will mean a lot of pence!"

"Oh, I dare say! More kicks than halfpence, and serve me right. The wool's not mine, but my son-in-law Mihail's!"

"Why doesn't he go himself?"

"Why, because . . . His mother's milk is scarcely dry upon his lips. He can buy wool all right, but when it comes to selling, he has no sense; he is young yet. He has wasted all his money; he wanted to grow rich and cut a dash, but he tried here and there, and no one would give him his price. And so the lad went on like that for a year, and then he came to me and said, 'Daddy, you sell the wool for me; be kind and do it! I am no good at the business!' And that is true enough. As soon as there is anything wrong then it's 'Daddy,' but till then they could get on without their dad. When he was buying he did not consult me, but now when he is in difficulties it's Daddy's turn. And what does his dad know about it? If it were not for Ivan Ivanitch, his dad could do nothing. I have a lot of worry with them."

"Yes; one has a lot of worry with one's children, I can tell you that," sighed Moisey Moisevitch. "I have six of my own. One needs schooling, another needs doctoring, and a third needs nursing, and when they grow up they are more trouble still. It is not only nowadays, it was the same in Holy Scripture. When Jacob had little children he wept, and when they grew up he wept still more bitterly."

"H'm, yes..." Father Christopher assented pensively, looking at his glass. "I have no cause myself to rail against the Lord. I have lived to the end of my days as any man might be thankful to live.... I have married my daughters to good men, my sons I have set up in life, and now I am free; I have done my work and can go where I like. I live in peace with my wife. I eat and drink and sleep and rejoice in my grandchildren, and say my prayers and want nothing more. I live on the fat of the land, and don't need to curry favour with anyone. I have never had any trouble from childhood, and now suppose the Tsar were to ask me, 'What do you need? What would you like?' why, I don't need anything. I have everything I want and everything to be thankful for. In the whole town there is no happier man than I am. My only trouble is I have so many sins, but there—only God is without sin. That's right, isn't it?"

"No doubt it is."

"I have no teeth, of course; my poor old back aches; there is one thing and another,... asthma and that sort of thing.... I ache.... The flesh is weak, but then think of my age! I am in the eighties! One can't go on for ever; one mustn't outstay one's welcome."

Father Christopher suddenly thought of something, spluttered into his glass and choked with laughter. Moisey Moisevitch laughed, too, from politeness, and he, too, cleared his throat.

"So funny!" said Father Christopher, and he waved his hand. "My eldest son Gavrila came to pay me a visit. He is in the medical line, and is a district doctor in the province of Tchernigov.... 'Very well...' I said to him, 'here I have asthma and one thing and another.... You are a doctor; cure your father!' He undressed me on the spot, tapped me, listened, and all sorts of tricks,... kneaded my stomach, and then he said, 'Dad, you ought to be treated with compressed air.'" Father Christopher laughed convulsively, till the tears came into his eyes, and got up.

"And I said to him, 'God bless your compressed air!'" he brought out through his laughter, waving both hands. "God bless your compressed air!"

Moisey Moisevitch got up, too, and with his hands on his stomach, went off into shrill laughter like the yap of a lap-dog.

"God bless the compressed air!" repeated Father Christopher, laughing.

Moisey Moisevitch laughed two notes higher and so violently that he could hardly stand on his feet.

"Oh dear!" he moaned through his laughter. "Let me get my breath.... You'll be the death of me."

He laughed and talked, though at the same time he was casting timorous and suspicious looks at Solomon. The latter was standing in the same attitude and still smiling. To judge from his eyes and his smile, his contempt and hatred were genuine, but that was so out of keeping with his plucked-looking figure that it seemed to Yegorushka as though he were putting on his defiant attitude and biting sarcastic smile to play the fool for the entertainment of their honoured guests.

After drinking six glasses of tea in silence, Kuzmitchov cleared a space before him on the table, took his bag, the one which he kept under his head when he slept under the chaise, untied the string and shook it. Rolls of paper notes were scattered out of the bag on the table.

"While we have the time, Father Christopher, let us reckon up," said Kuzmitchov.

Moisey Moisevitch was embarrassed at the sight of the money. He got up, and, as a man of delicate feeling unwilling to pry into other people's secrets, he went out of the room on tiptoe, swaying his arms. Solomon remained where he was.

"How many are there in the rolls of roubles?" Father Christopher began.

"The rouble notes are done up in fifties, ... the three-rouble notes in nineties, the twenty-five and hundred roubles in thousands. You count out seven thousand eight hundred for Varlamov, and I will count out for Gusevitch. And mind you don't make a mistake...."

Yegorushka had never in his life seen so much money as was lying on the table before him. There must have been a great deal of money, for the roll of seven thousand eight hundred, which Father Christopher put aside for Varlamov, seemed very small compared with the whole heap. At any other time such a mass of money would have impressed Yegorushka, and would have moved him to reflect how many cracknels, buns and poppy-cakes could be bought for that money. Now he looked at it listlessly, only conscious of the disgusting smell of kerosene and rotten apples that came from the heap of notes. He was exhausted by the jolting ride in the chaise, tired out and sleepy. His head was heavy, his eyes would hardly keep open and his thoughts were tangled like threads. If it had been possible he would have been relieved to lay his head on the table, so as not to see the lamp and the fingers moving over the heaps of notes, and to have let his tired sleepy thoughts go still more at random. When he tried to keep awake, the light of the lamp, the cups and the fingers grew double, the samovar heaved and the smell of rotten apples seemed even more acrid and disgusting.

"Ah, money, money!" sighed Father Christopher, smiling. "You bring trouble! Now I expect my Mihailo is asleep and dreaming that I am going to bring him a heap of money like this."

"Your Mihailo Timofevitch is a man who doesn't understand business," said Kuzmitchov in an undertone; "he undertakes what isn't his work, but you understand and can judge. You had better hand over your wool to me, as I have said already, and I would give you half a rouble above my own price—yes, I would, simply out of regard for you. . . ."

"No, Ivan Ivanitch." Father Christopher sighed. "I thank you for your kindness. . . . Of course, if it were for me to decide, I shouldn't think twice about it; but as it is, the wool is not mine, as you know. . . ."

Moisey Moisevitch came in on tiptoe. Trying from delicacy not to look at the heaps of money, he stole up to Yegorushka and pulled at his shirt from behind.

"Come along, little gentleman," he said in an undertone, "come and see the little bear I can show you! Such a queer, cross little bear. Oo-oo!"

The sleepy boy got up and listlessly dragged himself after Moisey Moisevitch to see the bear. He went into a little room, where, before he saw anything, he felt he could not breathe from the smell of something sour and decaying, which was much stronger here than in the big room and probably spread from this room all over the house. One part of the room was occupied by a big bed, covered with a greasy quilt and another by a chest of drawers and heaps of rags of all kinds from a woman's stiff petticoat to children's little breeches and braces. A tallow candle stood on the chest of drawers.

Instead of the promised bear, Yegorushka saw a big fat Jewess with her hair hanging loose, in a red flannel skirt with black sprigs on it; she turned with difficulty in the narrow space between the bed and the chest of drawers and uttered drawn-out moaning as though she had toothache. On seeing Yegorushka, she made a doleful, woe-begone face, heaved a long-drawn-out sigh, and before he had time to look round, put to his lips a slice of bread smeared with honey.

"Eat it, dearie, eat it!" she said. "You are here without your mamma, and no one to look after you. Eat it up."

Yegorushka did eat it, though after the goodies and poppy-cakes he had every day at home, he did not think very much of the honey, which was mixed with wax and bees' wings. He ate while Moisey Moisevitch and the Jewess looked at him and sighed.

"Where are you going, dearie?" asked the Jewess.

"To school," answered Yegorushka.

"And how many brothers and sisters have you got?"

"I am the only one; there are no others."

"O-oh!" sighed the Jewess, and turned her eyes upward. "Poor mamma, poor mamma! How she will weep and miss you! We are going to send our Nahum to school in a year. O-oh!"

"Ah, Nahum, Nahum!" sighed Moisey Moisevitch, and the skin of his pale face twitched nervously. "And he is so delicate."

The greasy quilt quivered, and from beneath it appeared a child's curly head on a very thin neck; two black eyes gleamed and stared with curiosity at Yegorushka. Still sighing, Moisey Moisevitch and the Jewess went to the chest of drawers and began talking in Yiddish. Moisey Moisevitch spoke in a low bass undertone, and altogether his talk in Yiddish was like a continual "ghaal-ghaal-ghaal-ghaal, . . ." while his wife answered him in a shrill voice like a turkeycock's, and the whole effect of her talk was something like "Too-too-too-too!" While they were consulting, another little curly head on a thin neck peeped out of the greasy quilt, then a third, then a fourth. . . . If Yegorushka had had a fertile imagination he might have imagined that the hundred-headed hydra was hiding under the quilt.

"Ghaal-ghaal-ghaal-ghaal!" said Moisey Moisevitch.

"Too-too-too-too!" answered the Jewess.

The consultation ended in the Jewess's diving with a deep sigh into the chest of drawers, and, unwrapping some sort of green rag there, she took out a big rye cake made in the shape of a heart.

"Take it, dearie," she said, giving Yegorushka the cake; "you have no mamma now—no one to give you nice things."

Yegorushka stuck the cake in his pocket and staggered to the door, as he could not go on breathing the foul, sour air in which the inn-keeper and his wife lived. Going back to the big room, he settled him-self more comfortably on the sofa and gave up trying to check his straying thoughts.

As soon as Kuzmitchov had finished counting out the notes he put them back into the bag. He did not treat them very respectfully and stuffed them into the dirty sack without ceremony, as indifferently as though they had not been money but waste paper.

Father Christopher was talking to Solomon.

"Well, Solomon the Wise!" he said, yawning and making the sign of the cross over his mouth. "How is business?"

"What sort of business are you talking about?" asked Solomon, and he looked as fiendish, as though it were a hint of some crime on his part.

"Oh, things in general. What are you doing?"

"What am I doing?" Solomon repeated, and he shrugged his shoul-ders. "The same as everyone else. . . . You see, I am a menial, I am my brother's servant; my brother's the servant of the visitors; the visitors are Varlamov's servants; and if I had ten millions, Varlamov would be my servant."

"Why would he be your servant?"

"Why, because there isn't a gentleman or millionaire who isn't ready to lick the hand of a scabby Jew for the sake of making a kopeck. Now, I am a scabby Jew and a beggar. Everybody looks at me as though

I were a dog, but if I had money Varlamov would play the fool before me just as Moisey does before you."

Father Christopher and Kuzmitchov looked at each other. Neither of them understood Solomon. Kuzmitchov looked at him sternly and dryly, and asked:

"How can you compare yourself with Varlamov, you blockhead?"

"I am not such a fool as to put myself on a level with Varlamov," answered Solomon, looking sarcastically at the speaker. "Though Varlamov is a Russian, he is at heart a scabby Jew; money and gain are all he lives for, but I threw my money in the stove! I don't want money, or land, or sheep, and there is no need for people to be afraid of me and to take off their hats when I pass. So I am wiser than your Varlamov and more like a man!"

A little later Yegorushka, half asleep, heard Solomon in a hoarse hollow voice choked with hatred, in hurried stuttering phrases, talking about the Jews. At first he talked correctly in Russian, then he fell into the tone of a Jewish recitation, and began speaking as he had done at the fair with an exaggerated Jewish accent.

"Stop! . . ." Father Christopher said to him. "If you don't like your religion you had better change it, but to laugh at it is a sin; it is only the lowest of the low who will make fun of his religion."

"You don't understand," Solomon cut him short rudely. "I am talking of one thing and you are talking of something else. . . ."

"One can see you are a foolish fellow," sighed Father Christopher. "I admonish you to the best of my ability, and you are angry. I speak to you like an old man quietly, and you answer like a turkeycock: 'Bla—bla—bla!' You really are a queer fellow. . . ."

Moisey Moisevitch came in. He looked anxiously at Solomon and at his visitors, and again the skin on his face quivered nervously. Yegorushka shook his head and looked about him; he caught a passing glimpse of Solomon's face at the very moment when it was turned three-quarters towards him and when the shadow of his long nose divided his left cheek in half; the contemptuous smile mingled with that shadow; the gleaming sarcastic eyes, the haughty expression, and the whole plucked-looking little figure, dancing and doubling itself before

Yegorushka's eyes, made him now not like a buffoon, but like something one sometimes dreams of, like an evil spirit.

"What a ferocious fellow you've got here, Moisey Moisevitch! God bless him!" said Father Christopher with a smile. "You ought to find him a place or a wife or something. . . . There's no knowing what to make of him. . . ."

Kuzmitchov frowned angrily. Moisey Moisevitch looked uneasily and inquiringly at his brother and the visitors again.

"Solomon, go away!" he said shortly. "Go away!" and he added something in Yiddish. Solomon gave an abrupt laugh and went out.

"What was it?" Moisey Moisevitch asked Father Christopher anxiously.

"He forgets himself," answered Kuzmitchov. "He's rude and thinks too much of himself."

"I knew it!" Moisey Moisevitch cried in horror, clasping his hands. "Oh dear, oh dear!" he muttered in a low voice. "Be so kind as to excuse it, and don't be angry. He is such a queer fellow, such a queer fellow! Oh dear, oh dear! He is my own brother, but I have never had anything but trouble from him. You know he's . . ."

Moisey Moisevitch crooked his finger by his forehead and went on:

"He is not in his right mind; . . . he's hopeless. And I don't know what I am to do with him! He cares for nobody, he respects nobody, and is afraid of nobody. . . . You know he laughs at everybody, he says silly things, speaks familiarly to anyone. You wouldn't believe it, Varlamov came here one day and Solomon said such things to him that he gave us both a taste of his whip. . . . But why whip me? Was it my fault? God has robbed him of his wits, so it is God's will, and how am I to blame?"

Ten minutes passed and Moisey Moisevitch was still muttering in an undertone and sighing:

"He does not sleep at night, and is always thinking and thinking and thinking, and what he is thinking about God only knows. If you go to him at night he is angry and laughs. He doesn't like me either. . . . And there is nothing he wants! When our father died he left us each six thousand roubles. I bought myself an inn, married, and now I have children; and he burnt all his money in the stove. Such a pity, such a pity! Why burn it? If he didn't want it he could give it to me, but why burn it?"

Suddenly the swing-door creaked and the floor shook under footsteps. Yegorushka felt a draught of cold air, and it seemed to him as though some big black bird had passed by him and had fluttered its wings close in his face. He opened his eyes. . . . His uncle was standing by the sofa with his sack in his hands ready for departure; Father Christopher, holding his broad-brimmed top-hat, was bowing to someone and smiling—not his usual soft kindly smile, but a respectful forced smile which did not suit his face at all—while Moisey Moisevitch looked as though his body had been broken into three parts, and he were balancing and doing his utmost not to drop to pieces. Only Solomon stood in the corner with his arms folded, as though nothing had happened, and smiled contemptuously as before.

"Your Excellency must excuse us for not being tidy," moaned Moisey Moisevitch with the agonizingly sweet smile, taking no more notice of Kuzmitchov or Father Christopher, but swaying his whole person so as to avoid dropping to pieces. "We are plain folks, your Excellency."

Yegorushka rubbed his eyes. In the middle of the room there really was standing an Excellency, in the form of a young plump and very beautiful woman in a black dress and a straw hat. Before Yegorushka had time to examine her features the image of the solitary graceful poplar he had seen that day on the hill for some reason came into his mind.

"Has Varlamov been here to-day?" a woman's voice inquired.

"No, your Excellency," said Moisey Moisevitch.

"If you see him to-morrow, ask him to come and see me for a minute."

All at once, quite unexpectedly, Yegorushka saw half an inch from his eyes velvety black eyebrows, big brown eyes, delicate feminine cheeks with dimples, from which smiles seemed radiating all over the face like sunbeams. There was a glorious scent.

"What a pretty boy!" said the lady. "Whose boy is it? Kazimir Mihalovitch, look what a charming fellow! Good heavens, he is asleep!"

And the lady kissed Yegorushka warmly on both cheeks, and he smiled and, thinking he was asleep, shut his eyes. The swing-door squeaked, and there was the sound of hurried footsteps, coming in and going out.

"Yegorushka, Yegorushka!" he heard two bass voices whisper. "Get up; it is time to start."

Somebody, it seemed to be Deniska, set him on his feet and led him by the arm. On the way he half-opened his eyes and once more saw the beautiful lady in the black dress who had kissed him. She was standing in the middle of the room and watched him go out, smiling at him and nodding her head in a friendly way. As he got near the door he saw a handsome, stoutly built, dark man in a bowler hat and in leather gaiters. This must have been the lady's escort.

"Woa!" he heard from the yard.

At the front door Yegorushka saw a splendid new carriage and a pair of black horses. On the box sat a groom in livery, with a long whip in his hands. No one but Solomon came to see the travellers off. His face was tense with a desire to laugh; he looked as though he were waiting impatiently for the visitors to be gone, so that he might laugh at them without restraint.

"The Countess Dranitsky," whispered Father Christopher, clambering into the chaise.

"Yes, Countess Dranitsky," repeated Kuzmitchov, also in a whisper.

The impression made by the arrival of the countess was probably very great, for even Deniska spoke in a whisper, and only ventured to lash his bays and shout when the chaise had driven a quarter of a mile away and nothing could be seen of the inn but a dim light.

IV

Who was this elusive, mysterious Varlamov of whom people talked so much, whom Solomon despised, and whom even the beautiful countess needed? Sitting on the box beside Deniska, Yegorushka, half asleep, thought about this person. He had never seen him. But he had often heard of him and pictured him in his imagination. He knew that Varlamov possessed several tens of thousands of acres of land, about a hundred thousand sheep, and a great deal of money. Of his manner of life and occupation Yegorushka knew nothing, except that he was always "going his rounds in these parts," and he was always being looked for.

At home Yegorushka had heard a great deal of the Countess Dranitsky, too. She, too, had some tens of thousands of acres, a great many sheep, a stud farm and a great deal of money, but she did not "go rounds," but lived at home in a splendid house and grounds, about which Ivan Ivanitch, who had been more than once at the countess's on business, and other acquaintances told many marvellous tales; thus, for instance, they said that in the countess's drawing-room, where the portraits of all the kings of Poland hung on the walls, there was a big table-clock in the form of a rock, on the rock a gold horse with diamond eyes, rearing, and on the horse the figure of a rider also of gold, who brandished his sword to right and to left whenever the clock struck. They said, too, that twice a year the countess used to give a ball, to which the gentry and officials of the whole province were invited, and to which even Varlamov used to come; all the visitors drank tea from silver samovars, ate all sorts of extraordinary things (they had strawberries and raspberries, for instance, in winter at Christmas), and danced to a band which played day and night. . . .

"And how beautiful she is," thought Yegorushka, remembering her face and smile.

Kuzmitchov, too, was probably thinking about the countess. For when the chaise had driven a mile and a half he said:

"But doesn't that Kazimir Mihalovitch plunder her right and left! The year before last when, do you remember, I bought some wool from her, he made over three thousand from my purchase alone."

"That is just what you would expect from a Pole," said Father Christopher.

"And little does it trouble her. Young and foolish, as they say, her head is full of nonsense."

Yegorushka, for some reason, longed to think of nothing but Varlamov and the countess, particularly the latter. His drowsy brain utterly refused ordinary thoughts, was in a cloud and retained only fantastic fairy-tale images, which have the advantage of springing into the brain of themselves without any effort on the part of the thinker, and completely vanishing of themselves at a mere shake of the head; and, indeed, nothing that was around him disposed to ordinary thoughts. On the right there were the dark hills which seemed to be screening something unseen and terrible; on the left the whole sky about the horizon was covered with a crimson glow, and it was hard to tell whether there was a fire somewhere, or whether it was the moon about to rise. As by day the distance could be seen, but its tender lilac tint had gone, quenched by the evening darkness, in which the whole steppe was hidden like Moisey Moisevitch's children under the quilt.

Corncakes and quails do not call in the July nights, the nightingale does not sing in the woodland marsh, and there is no scent of flowers, but still the steppe is lovely and full of life. As soon as the sun goes down and the darkness enfolds the earth, the day's weariness is forgotten, everything is forgiven, and the steppe breathes a light sigh from its broad bosom. As though because the grass cannot see in the dark that it has grown old, a gay youthful twitter rises up from it, such as is not heard by day; chirruping, twittering, whistling, scratching, the basses, tenors and sopranos of the steppe all mingle in an incessant, monotonous roar of sound in which it is sweet to brood on memories and sorrows. The monotonous twitter soothes to sleep like a lullaby; you drive and feel you are falling asleep, but suddenly there comes the abrupt agitated cry of a wakeful bird, or a vague sound like a voice crying out in wonder "A-ah, a-ah!" and slumber closes one's eyelids again. Or you drive by a little creek where there are bushes and hear the bird, called by the steppe dwellers "the sleeper," call "Asleep, asleep, asleep!" while another laughs or breaks into trills of hysterical weeping—that is the owl. For whom do they call and who hears them on that plain, God only knows, but there is deep sadness and lamentation in their cry. . . . There is a scent of hay and dry grass and belated flowers, but the scent is heavy, sweetly mawkish and soft.

Everything can be seen through the mist, but it is hard to make out the colours and the outlines of objects. Everything looks different from what it is. You drive on and suddenly see standing before you right in the roadway a dark figure like a monk; it stands motionless, waiting, holding something in its hands. . . . Can it be a robber? The figure comes closer, grows bigger; now it is on a level with the chaise, and you see it is not a man, but a solitary bush or a great stone. Such motionless expectant figures stand on the low hills, hide behind the old barrows, peep out from the high grass, and they all look like human beings and arouse suspicion.

And when the moon rises the night becomes pale and dim. The mist seems to have passed away. The air is transparent, fresh and warm; one can see well in all directions and even distinguish the separate stalks of grass by the wayside. Stones and bits of pots can be seen at a long distance. The suspicious figures like monks look blacker against the light background of the night, and seem more sinister. More and more often in the midst of the monotonous chirruping there comes the sound of the "A-ah, a-ah!" of astonishment troubling the motionless air, and the cry of a sleepless or delirious bird. Broad shadows move across the plain like clouds across the sky, and in the inconceivable distance, if you look long and intently at it, misty monstrous shapes rise up and huddle one against another. . . . It is rather uncanny. One glances at the pale green, star-spangled sky on which there is no cloudlet, no spot, and understands why the warm air is motionless, why nature is on her guard, afraid to stir: she is afraid and reluctant to lose one instant of life. Of the unfathomable depth and infinity of the sky one can only form a conception at sea and on the steppe by night when the moon is shining. It is terribly lonely and caressing; it looks down languid and alluring, and its caressing sweetness makes one giddy.

You drive on for one hour, for a second. . . . You meet upon the way a silent old barrow or a stone figure put up God knows when and by whom; a nightbird floats noiselessly over the earth, and little by little those legends of the steppes, the tales of men you have met, the stories of some old nurse from the steppe, and all the things you have managed to see and treasure in your soul, come back to your mind. And then in the churring of insects, in the sinister figures, in the ancient barrows, in the blue sky, in the moonlight, in the flight of the nightbird, in everything you see and hear, triumphant beauty, youth, the fulness of power, and the passionate thirst for life begin to be apparent; the soul responds to the call of her lovely austere fatherland,

and longs to fly over the steppes with the nightbird. And in the triumph of beauty, in the exuberance of happiness you are conscious of yearning and grief, as though the steppe knew she was solitary, knew that her wealth and her inspiration were wasted for the world, not glorified in song, not wanted by anyone; and through the joyful clamour one hears her mournful, hopeless call for singers, singers!

"Woa! Good-evening, Panteley! Is everything all right?"

"First-rate, Ivan Ivanitch!"

"Haven't you seen Varlamov, lads?"

"No, we haven't."

Yegorushka woke up and opened his eyes. The chaise had stopped. On the right the train of waggons stretched for a long way ahead on the road, and men were moving to and fro near them. All the waggons being loaded up with great bales of wool looked very high and fat, while the horses looked short-legged and little.

"Well, then, we shall go on to the Molokans'!" Kuzmitchov said aloud. "The Jew told us that Varlamov was putting up for the night at the Molokans'. So good-bye, lads! Good luck to you!"

"Good-bye, Ivan Ivanitch," several voices replied.

"I say, lads," Kuzmitchov cried briskly, "you take my little lad along with you! Why should he go jolting off with us for nothing? You put him on the bales, Panteley, and let him come on slowly, and we shall overtake you. Get down, Yegor! Go on; it's all right. . . ."

Yegorushka got down from the box-seat. Several hands caught him, lifted him high into the air, and he found himself on something big, soft, and rather wet with dew. It seemed to him now as though the sky were quite close and the earth far away.

"Hey, take his little coat!" Deniska shouted from somewhere far below.

His coat and bundle flung up from far below fell close to Yegorushka. Anxious not to think of anything, he quickly put his bundle under his head and covered himself with his coat, and stretching his legs out and shrinking a little from the dew, he laughed with content.

"Sleep, sleep, sleep, . . ." he thought.

"Don't be unkind to him, you devils!" he heard Deniska's voice below.

"Good-bye, lads; good luck to you," shouted Kuzmitchov. "I rely upon you!"

"Don't you be uneasy, Ivan Ivanitch!"

Deniska shouted to the horses, the chaise creaked and started, not along the road, but somewhere off to the side. For two minutes there was silence, as though the waggons were asleep and there was no sound except the clanking of the pails tied on at the back of the chaise as it slowly died away in the distance. Then someone at the head of the waggons shouted:

"Kiruha! Sta-art!"

The foremost of the waggons creaked, then the second, then the third. . . . Yegorushka felt the waggon he was on sway and creak also. The waggons were moving. Yegorushka took a tighter hold of the cord with which the bales were tied on, laughed again with content, shifted the cake in his pocket, and fell asleep just as he did in his bed at home. . . .

When he woke up the sun had risen, it was screened by an ancient barrow, and, trying to shed its light upon the earth, it scattered its beams in all directions and flooded the horizon with gold. It seemed to Yegorushka that it was not in its proper place, as the day before it had risen behind his back, and now it was much more to his left. . . . And the whole landscape was different. There were no hills now, but on all sides, wherever one looked, there stretched the brown cheerless plain; here and there upon it small barrows rose up and rooks flew as they had done the day before. The belfries and huts of some village showed white in the distance ahead; as it was Sunday the Little Russians were at home baking and cooking—that could be seen by the smoke which rose from every chimney and hung, a dark blue transparent veil, over the village. In between the huts and beyond the church there were blue glimpses of a river, and beyond the river a misty distance. But nothing was so different from yesterday as the road. Something extraordinarily broad, spread out and titanic, stretched over the steppe by way of a road. It was a grey streak well trodden down and covered with dust, like all roads. Its width puzzled Yegorushka and brought thoughts of fairy tales to his mind. Who travelled along that road? Who needed so much space? It was strange and unintelligible. It might have been supposed that giants with immense strides, such as Ilya Muromets and Solovy the Brigand, were still surviving in Russia, and that their gigantic steeds were still alive. Yegorushka, looking at the road, imagined some half a dozen high chariots racing along side by side, like some he used to see in pictures in his Scripture history; these chariots were each drawn by six wild furious horses, and their great wheels raised a cloud of dust to the sky, while the horses were driven by men such as one may see in one's dreams or in imagination brooding over fairy tales. And if those figures had existed, how perfectly in keeping with the steppe and the road they would have been!

Telegraph-poles with two wires on them stretched along the right side of the road to its furthermost limit. Growing smaller and smaller they disappeared near the village behind the huts and green trees, and then again came into sight in the lilac distance in the form of very small thin sticks that looked like pencils stuck into the ground. Hawks, falcons, and crows sat on the wires and looked indifferently at the moving waggons.

Yegorushka was lying in the last of the waggons, and so could see the whole string. There were about twenty waggons, and there was a driver to every three waggons. By the last waggon, the one in which Yegorushka was, there walked an old man with a grey beard, as short and lean as Father Christopher, but with a sunburnt, stern and brooding face. It is very possible that the old man was not stern and not brooding, but his red eyelids and his sharp long nose gave his face a stern frigid expression such as is common with people in the habit of continually thinking of serious things in solitude. Like Father Christopher he was wearing a wide-brimmed top-hat, not like a gentleman's, but made of brown felt, and in shape more like a cone with the top cut off than a real top-hat. Probably from a habit acquired in cold winters, when he must more than once have been nearly frozen as he trudged beside the waggons, he kept slapping his thighs and stamping with his feet as he walked. Noticing that Yegorushka was awake, he looked at him and said, shrugging his shoulders as though from the cold:

"Ah, you are awake, youngster! So you are the son of Ivan Ivanitch?"

"No; his nephew. . . ."

"Nephew of Ivan Ivanitch? Here I have taken off my boots and am hopping along barefoot. My feet are bad; they are swollen, and it's easier without my boots . . . easier, youngster . . . without boots, I mean. . . . So you are his nephew? He is a good man; no harm in him. . . . God give him health. . . . No harm in him . . . I mean Ivan Ivanitch. . . . He has gone to the Molokans'. . . . O Lord, have mercy upon us!"

The old man talked, too, as though it were very cold, pausing and not opening his mouth properly; and he mispronounced the labial consonants, stuttering over them as though his lips were frozen. As he talked to Yegorushka he did not once smile, and he seemed stern.

Two waggons ahead of them there walked a man wearing a long reddish-brown coat, a cap and high boots with sagging bootlegs and carrying a whip in his hand. This was not an old man, only about forty. When he looked round Yegorushka saw a long red face with a scanty goat-beard and a spongy looking swelling under his right eye. Apart from this very ugly swelling, there was another peculiar thing about him which caught the eye at once: in his left hand he carried a whip, while he waved the right as though he were conducting an unseen choir; from time to time he put the whip under his arm, and then he conducted with both hands and hummed something to himself.

The next driver was a long rectilinear figure with extremely sloping shoulders and a back as flat as a board. He held himself as stiffly erect as though he were marching or had swallowed a yard measure. His hands did not swing as he walked, but hung down as if they were straight sticks, and he strode along in a wooden way, after the manner of toy soldiers, almost without bending his knees, and trying to take as long steps as possible. While the old man or the owner of the spongy swelling were taking two steps he succeeded in taking only one, and so it seemed as though he were walking more slowly than any of them, and would drop behind. His face was tied up in a rag, and on his head something stuck up that looked like a monk's peaked cap; he was dressed in a short Little Russian coat, with full dark blue trousers and bark shoes.

Yegorushka did not even distinguish those that were farther on. He lay on his stomach, picked a little hole in the bale, and, having nothing better to do, began twisting the wool into a thread. The old man trudging along below him turned out not to be so stern as one might have supposed from his face. Having begun a conversation, he did not let it drop.

"Where are you going?" he asked, stamping with his feet.

"To school," answered Yegorushka.

"To school? Aha! . . . Well, may the Queen of Heaven help you. Yes. One brain is good, but two are better. To one man God gives one brain, to another two brains, and to another three. . . . To another three, that is true. . . . One brain you are born with, one you get from learning, and a third with a good life. So you see, my lad, it is a good thing if a man has three brains. Living is easier for him, and, what's more, dying is, too. Dying is, too. . . . And we shall all die for sure."

The old man scratched his forehead, glanced upwards at Yegorushka with his red eyes, and went on:

"Maxim Nikolaitch, the gentleman from Slavyanoserbsk, brought a little lad to school, too, last year. I don't know how he is getting on there in studying the sciences, but he was a nice good little lad. . . . God give them help, they are nice gentlemen. Yes, he, too, brought his boy to school. . . . In Slavyanoserbsk there is no establishment, I suppose, for study. No. . . . But it is a nice town. . . . There's an ordinary school for simple folks, but for the higher studies there is nothing. No, that's true. What's your name? . . ."

"Yegorushka."

"Yegory, then. . . . The holy martyr Yegory, the Bearer of Victory, whose day is the twenty-third of April. And my christian name is Panteley, . . . Panteley Zaharov Holodov. . . . We are Holodovs. . . . I am a native of—maybe you've heard of it—Tim in the province of Kursk. My brothers are artisans and work at trades in the town, but I am a peasant. . . . I have remained a peasant. Seven years ago I went there—home, I mean. I went to the village and to the town. . . . To Tim, I mean. Then, thank God, they were all alive and well; . . . but now I don't know. . . . Maybe some of them are dead. . . . And it's time they did die, for some of them are older than I am. Death is all right; it is good so long, of course, as one does not die without repentance. There is no worse evil than an impenitent death; an impenitent death is a joy to the devil. And if you want to die penitent, so that you may not be forbidden to enter the mansions of the Lord, pray to the holy martyr Varvara. She is the intercessor. She is, that's the truth.... For God has given her such a place in the heavens that everyone has the right to pray to her for penitence."

Panteley went on muttering, and apparently did not trouble whether Yegorushka heard him or not. He talked listlessly, mumbling to himself, without raising or dropping his voice, but succeeded in telling him a great deal in a short time. All he said was made up of fragments that had very little connection with one another, and quite uninteresting for Yegorushka. Possibly he talked only in order to reckon over his thoughts aloud after the night spent in silence, in order to see if they were all there. After talking of repentance, he spoke about a certain Maxim Nikolaitch from Slavyanoserbsk.

"Yes, he took his little lad; . . . he took him, that's true . . ."

One of the waggoners walking in front darted from his place, ran to one side and began lashing on the ground with his whip. He was a stalwart, broad-shouldered man of thirty, with curly flaxen hair and a look of great health and vigour. Judging from the movements of his shoulders and the whip, and the eagerness expressed in his attitude, he was beating something alive. Another waggoner, a short stubby little man with a bushy black beard, wearing a waistcoat and a shirt outside his trousers, ran up to him. The latter broke into a deep guffaw of laughter and coughing and said: "I say, lads, Dymov has killed a snake!"

There are people whose intelligence can be gauged at once by their voice and laughter. The man with the black beard belonged to that class of fortunate individuals; impenetrable stupidity could be felt in his voice and laugh. The flaxen-headed Dymov had finished, and lifting from the ground with his whip something like a cord, flung it with a laugh into the cart.

"That's not a viper; it's a grass snake!" shouted someone.

The man with the wooden gait and the bandage round his face

strode up quickly to the dead snake, glanced at it and flung up his stick-like arms.

"You jail-bird!" he cried in a hollow wailing voice. "What have you killed a grass snake for? What had he done to you, you damned brute? Look, he has killed a grass snake; how would you like to be treated so?"

"Grass snakes ought not to be killed, that's true," Panteley muttered placidly, "they ought not.... They are not vipers; though it looks like a snake, it is a gentle, innocent creature.... It's friendly to man, the grass snake is."

Dymov and the man with the black beard were probably ashamed, for they laughed loudly, and not answering, slouched lazily back to their waggons. When the hindmost waggon was level with the spot where the dead snake lay, the man with his face tied up standing over it turned to Panteley and asked in a tearful voice:

"Grandfather, what did he want to kill the grass snake for?"

His eyes, as Yegorushka saw now, were small and dingy looking; his face was grey, sickly and looked somehow dingy too while his chin was red and seemed very much swollen.

"Grandfather, what did he kill it for?" he repeated, striding along beside Panteley.

"A stupid fellow. His hands itch to kill, and that is why he does it," answered the old man; "but he oughtn't to kill a grass snake, that's true. ... Dymov is a ruffian, we all know, he kills everything he comes across, and Kiruha did not interfere. He ought to have taken its part, but instead of that, he goes off into 'Ha-ha-ha!' and 'Ho-ho-ho!' ... But don't be angry, Vassya.... Why be angry? They've killed it—well, never mind them. Dymov is a ruffian and Kiruha acted from foolishness— never mind.... They are foolish people without understanding—but there, don't mind them. Emelyan here never touches what he shouldn't; ... he never does; ... that is true, ... because he is a man of education, while they are stupid.... Emelyan, he doesn't touch things."

The waggoner in the reddish-brown coat and the spongy swelling on his face, who was conducting an unseen choir, stopped. Hearing his name, and waiting till Panteley and Vassya came up to him, he walked beside them.

"What are you talking about?" he asked in a husky muffled voice.

"Why, Vassya here is angry," said Panteley. "So I have been saying things to him to stop his being angry. . . . Oh, how my swollen feet hurt! Oh, oh! They are more inflamed than ever for Sunday, God's holy day!"

"It's from walking," observed Vassya.

"No, lad, no. It's not from walking. When I walk it seems easier; when I lie down and get warm, . . . it's deadly. Walking is easier for me."

Emelyan, in his reddish-brown coat, walked between Panteley and Vassya and waved his arms, as though they were going to sing. After waving them a little while he dropped them, and croaked out hopelessly:

"I have no voice. It's a real misfortune. All last night and this morning I have been haunted by the trio 'Lord, have Mercy' that we sang at the wedding at Marionovsky's. It's in my head and in my throat. It seems as though I could sing it, but I can't; I have no voice."

He paused for a minute, thinking, then went on:

"For fifteen years I was in the choir. In all the Lugansky works there was, maybe, no one with a voice like mine. But, confound it, I bathed two years ago in the Donets, and I can't get a single note true ever since. I took cold in my throat. And without a voice I am like a workman without hands."

"That's true," Panteley agreed.

"I think of myself as a ruined man and nothing more."

At that moment Vassya chanced to catch sight of Yegorushka. His eyes grew moist and smaller than ever.

"There's a little gentleman driving with us," and he covered his nose with his sleeve as though he were bashful. "What a grand driver! Stay with us and you shall drive the waggons and sell wool."

The incongruity of one person being at once a little gentleman and a waggon driver seemed to strike him as very queer and funny, for he burst into a loud guffaw, and went on enlarging upon the idea. Emelyan glanced upwards at Yegorushka, too, but coldly and cursorily. He was absorbed in his own thoughts, and had it not been for Vassya, would not have noticed Yegorushka's presence. Before five minutes had passed he was waving his arms again, then describing to his companions the beauties of the wedding anthem, "Lord, have Mercy," which he had remembered in the night. He put the whip under his arm and waved both hands.

A mile from the village the waggons stopped by a well with a crane. Letting his pail down into the well, black-bearded Kiruha lay on his stomach on the framework and thrust his shaggy head, his shoulders, and part of his chest into the black hole, so that Yegorushka could see nothing but his short legs, which scarcely touched the ground. Seeing the reflection of his head far down at the bottom of the well, he was delighted and went off into his deep bass stupid laugh, and the echo from the well answered him. When he got up his neck and face were as red as beetroot. The first to run up and drink was Dymov. He drank laughing, often turning from the pail to tell Kiruha something funny, then he turned round, and uttered aloud, to be heard all over the steppe, five very bad words. Yegorushka did not understand the meaning of such words, but he knew very well they were bad words. He knew the repulsion his friends and relations silently felt for such words. He himself, without knowing why, shared that feeling and was accustomed to think that only drunk and disorderly people enjoy the privilege of uttering such words aloud. He remembered the murder of the grass snake, listened to Dymov's laughter, and felt something like hatred for the man. And as ill-luck would have it, Dymov at that moment caught sight of Yegorushka, who had climbed down from the waggon and gone up to the well. He laughed aloud and shouted:

"I say, lads, the old man has been brought to bed of a boy in the night!"

Kiruha laughed his bass laugh till he coughed. Someone else laughed too, while Yegorushka crimsoned and made up his mind finally that Dymov was a very wicked man.

With his curly flaxen head, with his shirt opened on his chest and no hat on, Dymov looked handsome and exceptionally strong; in every movement he made one could see the reckless dare-devil and athlete, knowing his value. He shrugged his shoulders, put his arms akimbo, talked and laughed louder than any of the rest, and looked as though he were going to lift up something very heavy with one hand and astonish the whole world by doing so. His mischievous mocking eyes

glided over the road, the waggons, and the sky without resting on anything, and seemed looking for someone to kill, just as a pastime, and
something to laugh at. Evidently he was afraid of no one, would stick
at nothing, and most likely was not in the least interested in Yegorushka's opinion of him. . . . Yegorushka meanwhile hated his flaxen
head, his clear face, and his strength with his whole heart, listened
with fear and loathing to his laughter, and kept thinking what word of
abuse he could pay him out with.

Panteley, too, went up to the pail. He took out of his pocket a little
green glass of an ikon lamp, wiped it with a rag, filled it from the pail
and drank from it, then filled it again, wrapped the little glass in the
rag, and then put it back into his pocket.

"Grandfather, why do you drink out of a lamp?" Yegorushka asked
him, surprised.

"One man drinks out of a pail and another out of a lamp," the old
man answered evasively. "Every man to his own taste. . . . You drink out
of the pail—well, drink, and may it do you good. . . ."

"You darling, you beauty!" Vassya said suddenly, in a caressing,
plaintive voice. "You darling!"

His eyes were fixed on the distance; they were moist and smiling,
and his face wore the same expression as when he had looked at
Yegorushka.

"Who is it you are talking to?" asked Kiruha.

"A darling fox, . . . lying on her back, playing like a dog."

Everyone began staring into the distance, looking for the fox, but no
one could see it, only Vassya with his grey muddy-looking eyes, and he
was enchanted by it. His sight was extraordinarily keen, as Yegorushka
learnt afterwards. He was so long-sighted that the brown steppe was
for him always full of life and interest. He had only to look into the
distance to see a fox, a hare, a bustard, or some other animal keeping
at a distance from men. There was nothing strange in seeing a hare
running away or a flying bustard—everyone crossing the steppes
could see them; but it was not vouchsafed to everyone to see wild animals in their own haunts when they were not running nor hiding, nor
looking about them in alarm. Yet Vassya saw foxes playing, hares washing themselves with their paws, bustards preening their wings and

hammering out their hollow nests. Thanks to this keenness of sight, Vassya had, besides the world seen by everyone, another world of his own, accessible to no one else, and probably a very beautiful one, for when he saw something and was in raptures over it it was impossible not to envy him.

When the waggons set off again, the church bells were ringing for service.

V

The train of waggons drew up on the bank of a river on one side of a village. The sun was blazing, as it had been the day before; the air was stagnant and depressing. There were a few willows on the bank, but the shade from them did not fall on the earth, but on the water, where it was wasted; even in the shade under the waggon it was stifling and wearisome. The water, blue from the reflection of the sky in it, was alluring.

Styopka, a waggoner whom Yegorushka noticed now for the first time, a Little Russian lad of eighteen, in a long shirt without a belt, and full trousers that flapped like flags as he walked, undressed quickly, ran along the steep bank and plunged into the water. He dived three times, then swam on his back and shut his eyes in his delight. His face was smiling and wrinkled up as though he were being tickled, hurt and amused.

On a hot day when there is nowhere to escape from the sultry, stifling heat, the splash of water and the loud breathing of a man bathing sounds like good music to the ear. Dymov and Kiruha, looking at Styopka, undressed quickly and one after the other, laughing loudly in eager anticipation of their enjoyment, dropped into the water, and the quiet, modest little river resounded with snorting and splashing and shouting. Kiruha coughed, laughed and shouted as though they were trying to drown him, while Dymov chased him and tried to catch him by the leg.

"Ha-ha-ha!" he shouted. "Catch him! Hold him!"

Kiruha laughed and enjoyed himself, but his expression was the same as it had been on dry land, stupid, with a look of astonishment on it as though someone had, unnoticed, stolen up behind him and hit him on the head with the butt-end of an axe. Yegorushka undressed, too, but did not let himself down by the bank, but took a run and a flying leap from the height of about ten feet. Describing an arc in the air, he fell into the water, sank deep, but did not reach the bottom; some force, cold and pleasant to the touch, seemed to hold him up and bring him back to the surface. He popped out and, snorting and blowing bubbles, opened his eyes; but the sun was reflected in the water quite close to his face. At first blinding spots of light, then rainbow colours and dark patches, flitted before his eyes. He made haste to dive again, opened his eyes in the water and saw something cloudy-green like a sky on a moonlight night. Again the same force would not let him touch the bottom and stay in the coolness, but lifted him to the surface. He popped out and heaved a sigh so deep that he had a feeling of space and freshness, not only in his chest, but in his stomach. Then, to get from the water everything he possibly could get, he allowed himself every luxury; he lay on his back and basked, splashed, frolicked, swam on his face, on his side, on his back and standing up—just as he pleased till he was exhausted. The other bank was thickly overgrown with reeds; it was golden in the sun, and the flowers of the reeds hung drooping to the water in lovely tassels. In one place the reeds were shaking and nodding, with their flowers rustling—Styopka and Kiruha were hunting crayfish.

"A crayfish, look, lads! A crayfish!" Kiruha cried triumphantly and actually showed a crayfish.

Yegorushka swam up to the reeds, dived, and began fumbling among their roots. Burrowing in the slimy, liquid mud, he felt something sharp and unpleasant—perhaps it really was a crayfish. But at that minute someone seized him by the leg and pulled him to the surface. Spluttering and coughing, Yegorushka opened his eyes and saw before him the wet grinning face of the dare-devil Dymov. The impudent fellow was breathing hard, and from a look in his eyes he seemed inclined for further mischief. He held Yegorushka tight by the leg, and was lifting his hand to take hold of his neck. But Yegorushka tore himself away with repulsion and terror, as though disgusted at being touched and afraid that the bully would drown him, and said:

"Fool! I'll punch you in the face."

Feeling that this was not sufficient to express his hatred, he thought a minute and added:

"You blackguard! You son of a bitch!"

But Dymov, as though nothing were the matter, took no further notice of Yegorushka, but swam off to Kiruha, shouting:

"Ha-ha-ha! Let us catch fish! Mates, let us catch fish."

"To be sure," Kiruha agreed; "there must be a lot of fish here."

"Styopka, run to the village and ask the peasants for a net!"

"They won't give it to me."

"They will, you ask them. Tell them that they should give it to us for Christ's sake, because we are just the same as pilgrims."

"That's true."

Styopka clambered out of the water, dressed quickly, and without a cap on he ran, his full trousers flapping, to the village. The water lost all its charm for Yegorushka after his encounter with Dymov. He got out and began dressing. Panteley and Vassya were sitting on the steep bank, with their legs hanging down, looking at the bathers. Emelyan was standing naked, up to his knees in the water, holding on to the grass with one hand to prevent himself from falling while the other stroked his body. With his bony shoulder-blades, with the swelling under his eye, bending down and evidently afraid of the water, he made a ludicrous figure. His face was grave and severe. He looked angrily at the water, as though he were just going to upbraid it for having given him cold in the Donets and robbed him of his voice.

"And why don't you bathe?" Yegorushka asked Vassya.

"Oh, I don't care for it, . . ." answered Vassya.

"How is it your chin is swollen?"

"It's bad. . . . I used to work at the match factory, little sir. . . . The doctor used to say that it would make my jaw rot. The air is not healthy there. There were three chaps beside me who had their jaws swollen, and with one of them it rotted away altogether."

Styopka soon came back with the net. Dymov and Kiruha were already turning blue and getting hoarse by being so long in the water, but they set about fishing eagerly. First they went to a deep place beside the reeds; there Dymov was up to his neck, while the water went over squat Kiruha's head. The latter spluttered and blew bubbles, while Dymov, stumbling on the prickly roots, fell over and got caught in the net; both flopped about in the water, and made a noise, and nothing but mischief came of their fishing.

"It's deep," croaked Kiruha. "You won't catch anything."

"Don't tug, you devil!" shouted Dymov trying to put the net in the proper position. "Hold it up."

"You won't catch anything here," Panteley shouted from the bank. "You are only frightening the fish, you stupids! Go more to the left! It's shallower there!"

Once a big fish gleamed above the net; they all drew a breath, and Dymov struck the place where it had vanished with his fist, and his face expressed vexation.

"Ugh!" cried Panteley, and he stamped his foot. "You've let the perch slip! It's gone!"

Moving more to the left, Dymov and Kiruha picked out a shallower place, and then fishing began in earnest. They had wandered off some hundred paces from the waggons; they could be seen silently trying to go as deep as they could and as near the reeds, moving their legs a little at a time, drawing out the nets, beating the water with their fists to drive them towards the nets. From the reeds they got to the further bank; they drew the net out, then, with a disappointed air, lifting their knees high as they walked, went back into the reeds. They were talking about something, but what it was no one could hear. The sun was scorching their backs, the flies were stinging them, and their bodies had turned from purple to crimson. Styopka was walking after them with a pail in his hands; he had tucked his shirt right up under his armpits, and was holding it up by the hem with his teeth. After every successful catch he lifted up some fish, and letting it shine in the sun, shouted:

"Look at this perch! We've five like that!"

Every time Dymov, Kiruha and Styopka pulled out the net they could be seen fumbling about in the mud in it, putting some things into the pail and throwing other things away; sometimes they passed something that was in the net from hand to hand, examined it inquisitively, then threw that, too, away.

"What is it?" they shouted to them from the bank.

Styopka made some answer, but it was hard to make out his words. Then he climbed out of the water and, holding the pail in both hands, forgetting to let his shirt drop, ran to the waggons.

"It's full!" he shouted, breathing hard. "Give us another!"

Yegorushka looked into the pail: it was full. A young pike poked its ugly nose out of the water, and there were swarms of crayfish and little fish round about it. Yegorushka put his hand down to the bottom and stirred up the water; the pike vanished under the crayfish and a perch and a tench swam to the surface instead of it. Vassya, too, looked into the pail. His eyes grew moist and his face looked as caressing as before when he saw the fox. He took something out of the pail, put it to his mouth and began chewing it.

"Mates," said Styopka in amazement, "Vassya is eating a live gudgeon! Phoo!"

"It's not a gudgeon, but a minnow," Vassya answered calmly, still munching.

He took a fish's tail out of his mouth, looked at it caressingly, and put it back again. While he was chewing and crunching with his teeth it seemed to Yegorushka that he saw before him something not human. Vassya's swollen chin, his lustreless eyes, his extraordinary sharp sight, the fish's tail in his mouth, and the caressing friendliness with which he crunched the gudgeon made him like an animal.

Yegorushka felt dreary beside him. And the fishing was over, too. He walked about beside the waggons, thought a little, and, feeling bored, strolled off to the village.

Not long afterwards he was standing in the church, and with his forehead leaning on somebody's back, listened to the singing of the choir. The service was drawing to a close. Yegorushka did not understand church singing and did not care for it. He listened a little, yawned, and began looking at the backs and heads before him. In one head, red and wet from his recent bathe, he recognized Emelyan. The back of his head had been cropped in a straight line higher than is usual; the hair in front had been cut unbecomingly high, and Emelyan's ears stood out like two dock leaves, and seemed to feel themselves out of place. Looking at the back of his head and his ears,

Yegorushka, for some reason, thought that Emelyan was probably very unhappy. He remembered the way he conducted with his hands, his husky voice, his timid air when he was bathing, and felt intense pity for him. He longed to say something friendly to him.

"I am here, too," he said, putting out his hand.

People who sing tenor or bass in the choir, especially those who have at any time in their lives conducted, are accustomed to look with a stern and unfriendly air at boys. They do not give up this habit, even when they leave off being in a choir. Turning to Yegorushka, Emelyan looked at him from under his brows and said:

"Don't play in church!"

Then Yegorushka moved forwards nearer to the ikon-stand. Here he saw interesting people. On the right side, in front of everyone, a lady and a gentleman were standing on a carpet. There were chairs behind them. The gentleman was wearing newly ironed shantung trousers; he stood as motionless as a soldier saluting, and held high his bluish shaven chin. There was a very great air of dignity in his stand-up collar, in his blue chin, in his small bald patch and his cane. His neck was so strained from excess of dignity, and his chin was drawn up so tensely, that it looked as though his head were ready to fly off and soar upwards any minute. The lady, who was stout and elderly and wore a white silk shawl, held her head on one side and looked as though she had done someone a favour, and wanted to say: "Oh, don't trouble yourself to thank me; I don't like it. . . ." A thick wall of Little Russian heads stood all round the carpet.

Yegorushka went up to the ikon-stand and began kissing the local ikons. Before each image he slowly bowed down to the ground, without getting up, looked round at the congregation, then got up and kissed the ikon. The contact of his forehead with the cold floor afforded him great satisfaction. When the beadle came from the altar with a pair of long snuffers to put out the candles, Yegorushka jumped up quickly from the floor and ran up to him.

"Have they given out the holy bread?" he asked.

"There is none; there is none," the beadle muttered gruffly. "It is no use your . . ."

The service was over; Yegorushka walked out of the church in a leisurely way, and began strolling about the market-place. He had seen a good many villages, market-places, and peasants in his time, and everything that met his eyes was entirely without interest for him. At a loss for something to do, he went into a shop over the door of which hung a wide strip of red cotton. The shop consisted of two roomy, badly lighted parts; in one half they sold drapery and groceries, in the other there were tubs of tar, and there were horse-collars hanging from the ceiling; from both came the savoury smell of leather and tar. The floor of the shop had been watered; the man who watered it must have been a very whimsical and original person, for it was sprinkled in patterns and mysterious symbols. The shopkeeper, an overfed-looking man with a broad face and round beard, apparently a Great Russian, was standing, leaning his person over the counter. He was nibbling a piece of sugar as he drank his tea, and heaved a deep sigh at every sip. His face expressed complete indifference, but each sigh seemed to be saying:

"Just wait a minute; I will give it you."

"Give me a farthing's worth of sunflower seeds," Yegorushka said, addressing him.

The shopkeeper raised his eyebrows, came out from behind the counter, and poured a farthing's worth of sunflower seeds into Yegorushka's pocket, using an empty pomatum pot as a measure. Yegorushka did not want to go away. He spent a long time in examining the box of cakes, thought a little and asked, pointing to some little cakes covered with the mildew of age:

"How much are these cakes?"

"Two for a farthing."

Yegorushka took out of his pocket the cake given him the day before by the Jewess, and asked him:

"And how much do you charge for cakes like this?"

The shopman took the cake in his hands, looked at it from all sides, and raised one eyebrow.

"Like that?" he asked.

Then he raised the other eyebrow, thought a minute, and answered:

"Two for three farthings. . . ."

A silence followed.

"Whose boy are you?" the shopman asked, pouring himself out some tea from a red copper teapot.

"The nephew of Ivan Ivanitch."

"There are all sorts of Ivan Ivanitchs," the shopkeeper sighed. He looked over Yegorushka's head towards the door, paused a minute and asked: "Would you like some tea?"

"Please...." Yegorushka assented not very readily, though he felt an intense longing for his usual morning tea.

The shopkeeper poured him out a glass and gave him with it a bit of sugar that looked as though it had been nibbled. Yegorushka sat down on the folding chair and began drinking it. He wanted to ask the price of a pound of sugar almonds, and had just broached the subject when a customer walked in, and the shopkeeper, leaving his glass of tea, attended to his business. He led the customer into the other half, where there was a smell of tar, and was there a long time discussing something with him. The customer, a man apparently very obstinate and pig-headed, was continually shaking his head to signify his disapproval, and retreating towards the door. The shopkeeper tried to persuade him of something and began pouring some oats into a big sack for him.

"Do you call those oats?" the customer said gloomily. "Those are not oats, but chaff. It's a mockery to give that to the hens; enough to make the hens laugh.... No, I will go to Bondarenko."

When Yegorushka went back to the river a small camp fire was smoking on the bank. The waggoners were cooking their dinner. Styopka was standing in the smoke, stirring the cauldron with a big notched spoon. A little on one side Kiruha and Vassya, with eyes reddened from the smoke, were sitting cleaning the fish. Before them lay the net covered with slime and water weeds, and on it lay gleaming fish and crawling crayfish.

Emelyan, who had not long been back from the church, was sitting beside Panteley, waving his arm and humming just audibly in a husky voice: "To Thee we sing...." Dymov was moving about by the horses.

When they had finished cleaning them, Kiruha and Vassya put the fish and the living crayfish together in the pail, rinsed them, and from the pail poured them all into the boiling water.

"Shall I put in some fat?" asked Styopka, skimming off the froth.

"No need. The fish will make its own gravy," answered Kiruha.

Before taking the cauldron off the fire Styopka scattered into the water three big handfuls of millet and a spoonful of salt; finally he tried it, smacked his lips, licked the spoon, and gave a self-satisfied grunt, which meant that the grain was done.

All except Panteley sat down near the cauldron and set to work with their spoons.

"You there! Give the little lad a spoon!" Panteley observed sternly. "I dare say he is hungry too!"

"Ours is peasant fare," sighed Kiruha.

"Peasant fare is welcome, too, when one is hungry."

They gave Yegorushka a spoon. He began eating, not sitting, but standing close to the cauldron and looking down into it as in a hole. The grain smelt of fish and fish-scales were mixed up with the millet. The crayfish could not be hooked out with a spoon, and the men simply picked them out of the cauldron with their hands; Vassya did so particularly freely, and wetted his sleeves as well as his hands in the mess. But yet the stew seemed to Yegorushka very nice, and reminded him of the crayfish soup which his mother used to make at home on fast-days. Panteley was sitting apart munching bread.

"Grandfather, why aren't you eating?" Emelyan asked him.

"I don't eat crayfish. . . . Nasty things," the old man said, and turned away with disgust.

While they were eating they all talked. From this conversation Yegorushka gathered that all his new acquaintances, in spite of the differences of their ages and their characters, had one point in common which made them all alike: they were all people with a splendid past and a very poor present. Of their past they all—every one of them— spoke with enthusiasm; their attitude to the present was almost one of contempt. The Russian loves recalling life, but he does not love living. Yegorushka did not yet know that, and before the stew had been all eaten he firmly believed that the men sitting round the cauldron were the injured victims of fate. Panteley told them that in the past, before there were railways, he used to go with trains of waggons to Moscow and to Nizhni, and used to earn so much that he did not know what to do with his money; and what merchants there used to be in those days! what fish! how cheap everything was! Now the roads were shorter, the merchants were stingier, the peasants were poorer, the bread was dearer, everything had shrunk and was on a smaller scale. Emelyan told them that in old days he had been in the choir in the Lugansky works, and that he had a remarkable voice and read music splendidly, while now he had become a peasant and lived on the charity of his brother, who sent him out with his horses and took half his earnings. Vassya had once worked in a match factory; Kiruha had been a coachman in a good family, and had been reckoned the smartest driver of a three-in-hand in the whole district. Dymov, the son of a well-to-do peasant, lived at ease, enjoyed himself and had known no trouble till he was twenty, when his stern harsh father, anxious to train him at work, and afraid he would be spoiled at home, had sent him to a carrier's to work as a hired labourer. Styopka was the only one who said nothing, but from his beardless face it was evident that his life had been a much better one in the past.

Thinking of his father, Dymov frowned and left off eating. Sullenly from under his brows he looked round at his companions and his eye rested upon Yegorushka.

"You heathen, take off your cap," he said rudely. "You can't eat with your cap on, and you a gentleman too!"

Yegorushka took off his hat and did not say a word, but the stew lost all savour for him, and he did not hear Panteley and Vassya intervening on his behalf. A feeling of anger with the insulting fellow was rankling oppressively in his breast, and he made up his mind that he would do him some injury, whatever it cost him.

After dinner everyone sauntered to the waggons and lay down in the shade.

"Are we going to start soon, grandfather?" Yegorushka asked Panteley.

"In God's good time we shall set off. . . . There's no starting yet; it is too hot. . . . O Lord, Thy will be done. Holy Mother. . . . Lie down, little lad."

Soon there was a sound of snoring from under the waggons. Yegorushka meant to go back to the village, but on consideration, yawned and lay down by the old man.

VI

The waggons remained by the river the whole day, and set off again when the sun was setting.

Yegorushka was lying on the bales again; the waggon creaked softly and swayed from side to side. Panteley walked below, stamping his feet, slapping himself on his thighs and muttering. The air was full of the churring music of the steppes, as it had been the day before.

Yegorushka lay on his back, and, putting his hands under his head, gazed upwards at the sky. He watched the glow of sunset kindle, then fade away; guardian angels covering the horizon with their gold wings disposed themselves to slumber. The day had passed peacefully; the quiet peaceful night had come, and they could stay tranquilly at home in heaven. . . . Yegorushka saw the sky by degrees grow dark and the mist fall over the earth—saw the stars light up, one after the other. . . .

When you gaze a long while fixedly at the deep sky thoughts and feelings for some reason merge in a sense of loneliness. One begins to feel hopelessly solitary, and everything one used to look upon as near and akin becomes infinitely remote and valueless; the stars that have looked down from the sky thousands of years already, the mists and the incomprehensible sky itself, indifferent to the brief life of man, oppress the soul with their silence when one is left face to face with them and tries to grasp their significance. One is reminded of the solitude awaiting each one of us in the grave, and the reality of life seems awful . . . full of despair. . . .

Yegorushka thought of his grandmother, who was sleeping now under the cherry-trees in the cemetery. He remembered how she lay in her coffin with pennies on her eyes, how afterwards she was shut in and let down into the grave; he even recalled the hollow sound of the clods of earth on the coffin lid. . . . He pictured his granny in the dark and narrow coffin, helpless and deserted by everyone. His imagination pictured his granny suddenly awakening, not understanding where she was, knocking upon the lid and calling for help, and in the end swooning with horror and dying again. He imagined his mother dead, Father Christopher, Countess Dranitsky, Solomon. But however much he tried to imagine himself in the dark tomb, far from home, outcast, helpless and dead, he could not succeed; for himself personally he could not admit the possibility of death, and felt that he would never die. . . .

Panteley, for whom death could not be far away, walked below and went on reckoning up his thoughts.

"All right. . . . Nice gentlefolk, . . ." he muttered. "Took his little lad to school—but how he is doing now I haven't heard say—in Slavyanoserbsk. I say there is no establishment for teaching them to be very clever. . . . No, that's true—a nice little lad, no harm in him. . . . He'll grow up and be a help to his father. . . . You, Yegory, are little now, but you'll grow big and will keep your father and mother. . . . So it is ordained of God, 'Honour your father and your mother.' . . . I had children myself, but they were burnt. . . . My wife was burnt and my children, . . . that's true. . . . The hut caught fire on the night of Epiphany. . . . I was not at home, I was driving in Oryol. In Oryol. . . . Marya dashed out into the street, but remembering that the children were asleep in the hut, ran back and was burnt with her children. . . . Next day they found nothing but bones."

About midnight Yegorushka and the waggoners were again sitting round a small camp fire. While the dry twigs and stems were burning up, Kiruha and Vassya went off somewhere to get water from a creek; they vanished into the darkness, but could be heard all the time talking and clinking their pails; so the creek was not far away. The light from the fire lay a great flickering patch on the earth; though the moon was bright, yet everything seemed impenetrably black beyond that red patch. The light was in the waggoners' eyes, and they saw only part of the great road; almost unseen in the darkness the waggons with the bales and the horses looked like a mountain of undefined shape. Twenty paces from the camp fire at the edge of the road stood a wooden cross that had fallen aslant. Before the camp fire had been lighted, when he could still see things at a distance, Yegorushka had noticed that there was a similar old slanting cross on the other side of the great road.

Coming back with the water, Kiruha and Vassya filled the cauldron and fixed it over the fire. Styopka, with the notched spoon in his hand, took his place in the smoke by the cauldron, gazing dreamily into the water for the scum to rise. Panteley and Emelyan were sitting side by side in silence, brooding over something. Dymov was lying on his stomach, with his head propped on his fists, looking into the fire. . . . Styopka's shadow was dancing over him, so that his handsome face was at one minute covered with darkness, at the next lighted up. . . . Kiruha and Vassya were wandering about at a little distance gathering dry grass and bark for the fire. Yegorushka, with his hands in his pockets, was standing by Panteley, watching how the fire devoured the grass.

All were resting, musing on something, and they glanced cursorily at the cross over which patches of red light were dancing. There is something melancholy, pensive, and extremely poetical about a solitary tomb; one feels its silence, and the silence gives one the sense of the presence of the soul of the unknown man who lies under the cross. Is that soul at peace on the steppe? Does it grieve in the moonlight? Near the tomb the steppe seems melancholy, dreary and mournful; the grass seems more sorrowful, and one fancies the grasshoppers chirrup less freely, and there is no passer-by who would not remember that lonely soul and keep looking back at the tomb, till it was left far behind and hidden in the mists. . . .

"Grandfather, what is that cross for?" asked Yegorushka.

Panteley looked at the cross and then at Dymov and asked:

"Nikola, isn't this the place where the mowers killed the merchants?"

Dymov not very readily raised himself on his elbow, looked at the road and said:

"Yes, it is. . . ."

A silence followed. Kiruha broke up some dry stalks, crushed them up together and thrust them under the cauldron. The fire flared up brightly; Styopka was enveloped in black smoke, and the shadow cast by the cross danced along the road in the dusk beside the waggons.

"Yes, they were killed," Dymov said reluctantly. "Two merchants, father and son, were travelling, selling holy images. They put up in the inn not far from here that is now kept by Ignat Fomin. The old man had a drop too much, and began boasting that he had a lot of money with him. We all know merchants are a boastful set, God preserve us. . . . They can't resist showing off before the likes of us. And at the time some mowers were staying the night at the inn. So they overheard what the merchants said and took note of it."

"O Lord! . . . Holy Mother!" sighed Panteley.

"Next day, as soon as it was light," Dymov went on, "the merchants were preparing to set off and the mowers tried to join them. 'Let us go together, your worships. It will be more cheerful and there will be less danger, for this is an out-of-the-way place. . . .' The merchants had to travel at a walking pace to avoid breaking the images, and that just suited the mowers. . . ."

Dymov rose into a kneeling position and stretched.

"Yes," he went on, yawning. "Everything went all right till they reached this spot, and then the mowers let fly at them with their scythes. The son, he was a fine young fellow, snatched the scythe from one of them, and he used it, too. . . . Well, of course, they got the best of it because there were eight of them. They hacked at the merchants so that there was not a sound place left on their bodies; when they had finished they dragged both of them off the road, the father to one side and the son to the other. Opposite that cross there is another cross on this side. . . . Whether it is still standing, I don't know. . . . I can't see from here. . . ."

"It is," said Kiruha.

"They say they did not find much money afterwards."

"No," Panteley confirmed; "they only found a hundred roubles."

"And three of them died afterwards, for the merchant had cut them badly with the scythe, too. They died from loss of blood. One had his hand cut off, so that they say he ran three miles without his hand, and they found him on a mound close to Kurikovo. He was squatting on his heels, with his head on his knees, as though he were lost in thought, but when they looked at him there was no life in him and he was dead. . . ."

"They found him by the track of blood," said Panteley.

Everyone looked at the cross, and again there was a hush. From somewhere, most likely from the creek, floated the mournful cry of the bird: "Sleep! sleep! sleep!"

"There are a great many wicked people in the world," said Emelyan.

"A great many," assented Panteley, and he moved up closer to the fire as though he were frightened. "A great many," he went on in a low voice. "I've seen lots and lots of them. . . . Wicked people! . . . I have seen a great many holy and just, too. . . . Queen of Heaven, save us and have mercy on us. I remember once thirty years ago, or maybe more, I was driving a merchant from Morshansk. The merchant was a jolly handsome fellow, with money, too . . . the merchant was . . . a nice man, no harm in him. . . . So we put up for the night at an inn. And in Russia the inns are not what they are in these parts. There the yards are roofed in and look like the ground floor, or let us say like barns in good farms. Only a barn would be a bit higher. So we put up there and were all right. My merchant was in a room, while I was with the horses, and everything was as it should be. So, lads, I said my prayers before going to sleep and began walking about the yard. And it was a dark night, I couldn't see anything; it was no good trying. So I walked about a bit up to the waggons, or nearly, when I saw a light gleaming. What could it mean? I thought the people of the inn had gone to bed long ago, and besides the merchant and me there were no other guests in the inn. . . . Where could the light have come from? I felt suspicious. . . . I went closer . . . towards the light. . . . The Lord have mercy upon me! and save me, Queen of Heaven! I looked and there was a little window with a grating, . . . close to the ground, in the house. . . . I lay down on the ground and looked in; as soon as I looked in a cold chill ran all down me. . . ."

Kiruha, trying not to make a noise, thrust a handful of twigs into the fire. After waiting for it to leave off crackling and hissing, the old man went on:

"I looked in and there was a big cellar, black and dark. . . . There was a lighted lantern on a tub. In the middle of the cellar were about a dozen men in red shirts with their sleeves turned up, sharpening long knives. . . . Ugh! So we had fallen into a nest of robbers. . . . What's to be done? I ran to the merchant, waked him up quietly, and said: 'Don't be frightened, merchant,' said I, 'but we are in a bad way. We have fallen into a nest of robbers,' I said. He turned pale and asked: 'What are we to do now, Panteley? I have a lot of money that belongs to orphans. As for my life,' he said, 'that's in God's hands. I am not afraid to die, but it's dreadful to lose the orphans' money,' said he. . . . What were we to do? The gates were locked; there was no getting out. If there had been a fence one could have climbed over it, but with the yard shut up! . . . 'Come, don't be frightened, merchant,' said I; 'but pray to God. Maybe the Lord will not let the orphans suffer. Stay still,' said I, 'and make no sign, and meanwhile, maybe, I shall think of something. . . .' Right! . . . I prayed to God and the Lord put the thought into my mind. . . . I clambered up on my chaise and softly, . . . softly so that no one should hear, began pulling out the straw in the thatch, made a hole and crept out, crept out. . . . Then I jumped off the roof and ran along the road as fast as I could. I ran and ran till I was nearly dead. . . . I ran maybe four miles without taking breath, if not more. Thank God I saw a village. I ran up to a hut and began tapping at a window. 'Good Christian people,' I said, and told them all about it, 'do not let a Christian soul perish. . . .' I waked them all up. . . . The peasants gathered together and went with me, . . . one with a cord, one with an oakstick, others with pitchforks. . . . We broke in the gates of the inn-yard and went straight to the cellar. . . . And the robbers had just finished sharpening their knives and were going to kill the merchant. The peasants took them, every one of them, bound them and carried them to the police. The merchant gave them three hundred roubles in his joy, and gave me five gold pieces and put my name down. They said that they found human bones in the cellar afterwards, heaps and heaps of them. . . . Bones! . . . So they robbed people and then buried them, so that there should be no traces. . . . Well, afterwards they were punished at Morshansk."

Panteley had finished his story, and he looked round at his listeners. They were gazing at him in silence. The water was boiling by now and Styopka was skimming off the froth.

"Is the fat ready?" Kiruha asked him in a whisper.

"Wait a little. . . . Directly."

Styopka, his eyes fixed on Panteley as though he were afraid that the latter might begin some story before he was back, ran to the waggons; soon he came back with a little wooden bowl and began pounding some lard in it.

"I went another journey with a merchant, too, . . ." Panteley went on again, speaking as before in a low voice and with fixed unblinking eyes. "His name, as I remember now, was Pyotr Grigoritch. He was a nice man, . . . the merchant was. We stopped in the same way at an inn. . . . He indoors and me with the horses. . . . The people of the house, the innkeeper and his wife, seemed friendly good sort of people; the labourers, too, seemed all right; but yet, lads, I couldn't sleep. I had a queer feeling in my heart, . . . a queer feeling, that was just it. The gates were open and there were plenty of people about, and yet I felt afraid and not myself. Everyone had been asleep long ago. It was the middle of the night; it would soon be time to get up, and I was lying alone in my chaise and could not close my eyes, as though I were some owl. And then, lads, I heard this sound, 'Toop! toop! toop!' Someone was creeping up to the chaise. I poke my head out, and there was a peasant woman in nothing but her shift and with her feet bare. . . . 'What do you want, good woman?' I asked. And she was all of a tremble; her face was terror-stricken. . . . 'Get up, good man,' said she; 'the people are plotting evil. . . . They mean to kill your merchant. With my own ears I heard the master whispering with his wife. . . .' So it was not for nothing, the foreboding of my heart! 'And who are you?' I asked. 'I am their cook,' she said. . . . Right! . . . So I got out of the chaise and went to the merchant. I waked him up and said: 'Things aren't quite right, Pyotr Grigoritch. . . . Make haste and rouse yourself from sleep, your worship, and dress now while there is still time,' I said; 'and to save our skins, let us get away from trouble.' He had no sooner begun dressing when the door opened and, mercy on us! I saw, Holy Mother! the innkeeper and his wife come into the room with three labourers. . . . So they had persuaded the labourers to join them. 'The merchant has a lot of money, and we'll go shares,' they told them. Every one of the five had a long knife in their hand . . . each a knife. The innkeeper locked the door and said: 'Say your prayers, travellers, . . . and if you begin screaming,' they said, 'we won't let you say your prayers before you die. . . .' As though we could scream! I had such a lump in my throat I could not cry out. . . . The merchant wept and said: 'Good Christian people! you have resolved to kill me because my money tempts you. Well, so be it; I shall not be the first nor shall I be the last. Many of us merchants have been murdered at inns. But why, good Christian brothers,' says he, 'murder my driver? Why should he have to suffer for my money?' And he said that so pitifully! And the innkeeper answered him: 'If we leave him alive,' said he, 'he will be the first to bear witness against us. One may just as well kill two as one. You can but answer once for seven misdeeds. . . . Say your prayers, that's all you can do, and it is no good talking!' The merchant and I knelt down side by side and wept and said our prayers. He thought of his children. I was young in those days; I wanted to live. . . . We looked at the images and prayed, and so pitifully that it brings a tear even now. . . . And the innkeeper's wife looks at us and says: 'Good people,' said she, 'don't bear a grudge against us in the other world and pray to God for our punishment, for it is want that drives us to it.' We prayed and wept and prayed and wept, and God heard us. He had pity on us, I suppose. . . . At the very minute when the innkeeper had taken the merchant by the beard to rip open his throat with his knife suddenly someone seemed to tap at the window from the yard! We all started, and the innkeeper's hands dropped. . . . Someone was tapping at the window and shouting: 'Pyotr Grigoritch,' he shouted, 'are you here? Get ready and let's go!' The people saw that someone had come for the merchant; they were terri-fied and took to their heels. . . . And we made haste into the yard, har-nessed the horses, and were out of sight in a minute. . . ."

"Who was it knocked at the window?" asked Dymov.

"At the window? It must have been a holy saint or angel, for there was no one else. . . . When we drove out of the yard there wasn't a soul in the street. . . . It was the Lord's doing."

Panteley told other stories, and in all of them "long knives" figured and all alike sounded made up. Had he heard these stories from some-one else, or had he made them up himself in the remote past, and af-terwards, as his memory grew weaker, mixed up his experiences with his imaginations and become unable to distinguish one from the other?

Anything is possible, but it is strange that on this occasion and for the rest of the journey, whenever he happened to tell a story, he gave unmistakable preference to fiction, and never told of what he really had experienced. At the time Yegorushka took it all for the genuine thing, and believed every word; later on it seemed to him strange that a man who in his day had travelled all over Russia and seen and known so much, whose wife and children had been burnt to death, so failed to appreciate the wealth of his life that whenever he was sitting by the camp fire he was either silent or talked of what had never been.

Over their porridge they were all silent, thinking of what they had just heard. Life is terrible and marvellous, and so, however terrible a story you tell in Russia, however you embroider it with nests of robbers, long knives and such marvels, it always finds an echo of reality in the soul of the listener, and only a man who has been a good deal affected by education looks askance distrustfully, and even he will be silent. The cross by the roadside, the dark bales of wool, the wide expanse of the plain, and the lot of the men gathered together by the camp fire—all this was of itself so marvellous and terrible that the fantastic colours of legend and fairy-tale were pale and blended with life.

All the others ate out of the cauldron, but Panteley sat apart and ate his porridge out of a wooden bowl. His spoon was not like those the others had, but was made of cypress wood, with a little cross on it. Yegorushka, looking at him, thought of the little ikon glass and asked Styopka softly:

"Why does Grandfather sit apart?"

"He is an Old Believer," Styopka and Vassya answered in a whisper. And as they said it they looked as though they were speaking of some secret vice or weakness.

All sat silent, thinking. After the terrible stories there was no inclination to speak of ordinary things. All at once in the midst of the silence Vassya drew himself up and, fixing his lustreless eyes on one point, pricked up his ears.

"What is it?" Dymov asked him.

"Someone is coming," answered Vassya.

"Where do you see him?"

"Yo-on-der! There's something white...."

There was nothing to be seen but darkness in the direction in which Vassya was looking; everyone listened, but they could hear no sound of steps.

"Is he coming by the highroad?" asked Dymov.

"No, over the open country.... He is coming this way."

A minute passed in silence.

"And maybe it's the merchant who was buried here walking over the steppe," said Dymov.

All looked askance at the cross, exchanged glances and suddenly broke into a laugh. They felt ashamed of their terror.

"Why should he walk?" asked Panteley. "It's only those walk at night whom the earth will not take to herself. And the merchants were all right.... The merchants have received the crown of martyrs."

But all at once they heard the sound of steps; someone was coming in haste.

"He's carrying something," said Vassya.

They could hear the grass rustling and the dry twigs crackling under the feet of the approaching wayfarer. But from the glare of the camp fire nothing could be seen. At last the steps sounded close by, and someone coughed. The flickering light seemed to part; a veil dropped from the waggoners' eyes, and they saw a man facing them.

Whether it was due to the flickering light or because everyone wanted to make out the man's face first of all, it happened, strangely enough, that at the first glance at him they all saw, first of all, not his face nor his clothes, but his smile. It was an extraordinarily good-natured, broad, soft smile, like that of a baby on waking, one of those infectious smiles to which it is difficult not to respond by smiling too. The stranger, when they did get a good look at him, turned out to be a man of thirty, ugly and in no way remarkable. He was a tall Little Russian, with a long nose, long arms and long legs; everything about him seemed long except his neck, which was so short that it made him seem stooping. He was wearing a clean white shirt with an embroidered collar, white trousers, and new high boots, and in comparison with the waggoners he looked quite a dandy. In his arms he was carrying something big, white, and at the first glance strange-looking, and the stock of a gun also peeped out from behind his shoulder.

Coming from the darkness into the circle of light, he stopped short as though petrified, and for half a minute looked at the waggoners as though he would have said: "Just look what a smile I have!"

Then he took a step towards the fire, smiled still more radiantly and said:

"Bread and salt, friends!"

"You are very welcome!" Panteley answered for them all.

The stranger put down by the fire what he was carrying in his arms—it was a dead bustard—and greeted them once more.

They all went up to the bustard and began examining it.

"A fine big bird; what did you kill it with?" asked Dymov.

"Grape-shot. You can't get him with small shot, he won't let you get near enough. Buy it, friends! I will let you have it for twenty kopecks."

"What use would it be to us? It's good roast, but I bet it would be tough boiled; you could not get your teeth into it. . . ."

"Oh, what a pity! I would take it to the gentry at the farm; they would give me half a rouble for it. But it's a long way to go—twelve miles!"

The stranger sat down, took off his gun and laid it beside him.

He seemed sleepy and languid; he sat smiling, and, screwing up his eyes at the firelight, apparently thinking of something very agreeable. They gave him a spoon; he began eating.

"Who are you?" Dymov asked him.

The stranger did not hear the question; he made no answer, and did not even glance at Dymov. Most likely this smiling man did not taste the flavour of the porridge either, for he seemed to eat it mechanically, lifting the spoon to his lips sometimes very full and sometimes quite empty. He was not drunk, but he seemed to have something nonsensical in his head.

"I ask you who you are?" repeated Dymov.

"I?" said the unknown, starting. "Konstantin Zvonik from Rovno. It's three miles from here."

And anxious to show straight off that he was not quite an ordinary peasant, but something better, Konstantin hastened to add:

"We keep bees and fatten pigs."

"Do you live with your father or in a house of your own?"

"No; now I am living in a house of my own. I have parted. This month, just after St. Peter's Day, I got married. I am a married man now!... It's eighteen days since the wedding."

"That's a good thing," said Panteley. "Marriage is a good thing.... God's blessing is on it."

"His young wife sits at home while he rambles about the steppe," laughed Kiruha. "Queer chap!"

As though he had been pinched on the tenderest spot, Konstantin started, laughed and flushed crimson.

"But, Lord, she is not at home!" he said quickly, taking the spoon out of his mouth and looking round at everyone with an expression of delight and wonder. "She is not; she has gone to her mother's for three days! Yes, indeed, she has gone away, and I feel as though I were not married...."

Konstantin waved his hand and turned his head; he wanted to go on thinking, but the joy which beamed in his face prevented him. As though he were not comfortable, he changed his attitude, laughed, and again waved his hand. He was ashamed to share his happy thoughts with strangers, but at the same time he had an irresistible longing to communicate his joy.

"She has gone to Demidovo to see her mother," he said, blushing and moving his gun. "She'll be back to-morrow.... She said she would be back to dinner."

"And do you miss her?" said Dymov.

"Oh, Lord, yes; I should think so. We have only been married such a little while, and she has gone away.... Eh! Oh, but she is a tricksy one, God strike me dead! She is such a fine, splendid girl, such a one for laughing and singing, full of life and fire! When she is there your brain is in a whirl, and now she is away I wander about the steppe like a fool, as though I had lost something. I have been walking since dinner."

Konstantin rubbed his eyes, looked at the fire and laughed.

"You love her, then, . . ." said Panteley.

"She is so fine and splendid," Konstantin repeated, not hearing him; "such a housewife, clever and sensible. You wouldn't find another like her among simple folk in the whole province. She has gone away. . . . But she is missing me, I kno-ow! I know the little magpie. She said she would be back to-morrow by dinner-time. . . . And just think how queer!" Konstantin almost shouted, speaking a note higher and shifting his position. "Now she loves me and is sad without me, and yet she would not marry me."

"But eat," said Kiruha.

"She would not marry me," Konstantin went on, not heeding him. "I have been struggling with her for three years! I saw her at the Kalatchik fair; I fell madly in love with her, was ready to hang myself. . . . I live at Rovno, she at Demidovo, more than twenty miles apart, and there was nothing I could do. I sent match-makers to her, and all she said was: 'I won't!' Ah, the magpie! I sent her one thing and another, earrings and cakes, and twenty pounds of honey—but still she said: 'I won't!' And there it was. If you come to think of it, I was not a match for her! She was young and lovely, full of fire, while I am old: I shall soon be thirty, and a regular beauty, too; a fine beard like a goat's, a clear complexion all covered with pimples—how could I be compared with her! The only thing to be said is that we are well off, but then the Vahramenkys are well off, too. They've six oxen, and they keep a couple of labourers. I was in love, friends, as though I were plague-stricken. I couldn't sleep or eat; my brain was full of thoughts, and in such a maze, Lord preserve us! I longed to see her, and she was in Demidovo. What do you think? God be my witness, I am not lying, three times a week I walked over there on foot just to have a look at her. I gave up my work! I was so frantic that I even wanted to get taken on as a labourer in Demidovo, so as to be near her. I was in misery! My mother called in a witch a dozen times; my father tried thrashing me. For three years I was in this torment, and then I made up my mind. 'Damn my soul!' I said. 'I will go to the town and be a cabman. . . . It seems it is fated not to be.' At Easter I went to Demidovo to have a last look at her. . . ."

Konstantin threw back his head and went off into a mirthful tinkling laugh, as though he had just taken someone in very cleverly.

"I saw her by the river with the lads," he went on. "I was overcome with anger. . . . I called her aside and maybe for a full hour I said all manner of things to her. She fell in love with me! For three years she did not like me! she fell in love with me for what I said to her. . . ."

"What did you say to her?" asked Dymov.

"What did I say? I don't remember. . . . How could one remember? My words flowed at the time like water from a tap, without stopping to take breath. Ta-ta-ta! And now I can't utter a word. . . . Well, so she married me. . . . She's gone now to her mother's, the magpie, and while she is away here I wander over the steppe. I can't stay at home. It's more than I can do!"

Konstantin awkwardly released his feet, on which he was sitting, stretched himself on the earth, and propped his head in his fists, then got up and sat down again. Everyone by now thoroughly understood that he was in love and happy, poignantly happy; his smile, his eyes, and every movement, expressed fervent happiness. He could not find a place for himself, and did not know what attitude to take to keep himself from being overwhelmed by the multitude of his delightful thoughts. Having poured out his soul before these strangers, he settled down quietly at last, and, looking at the fire, sank into thought.

At the sight of this happy man everyone felt depressed and longed to be happy, too. Everyone was dreamy. Dymov got up, walked about softly by the fire, and from his walk, from the movement of his shoulder-blades, it could be seen that he was weighed down by depression and yearning. He stood still for a moment, looked at Konstantin and sat down.

The camp fire had died down by now; there was no flicker, and the patch of red had grown small and dim. . . . And as the fire went out the moonlight grew clearer and clearer. Now they could see the full width of the road, the bales of wool, the shafts of the waggons, the munching horses; on the further side of the road there was the dim outline of the second cross. . . .

Dymov leaned his cheek on his hand and softly hummed some

plaintive song. Konstantin smiled drowsily and chimed in with a thin voice. They sang for half a minute, then sank into silence. Emelyan started, jerked his elbows and wriggled his fingers.

"Lads," he said in an imploring voice, "let's sing something sacred!" Tears came into his eyes. "Lads," he repeated, pressing his hands on his heart, "let's sing something sacred!"

"I don't know anything," said Konstantin.

Everyone refused, then Emelyan sang alone. He waved both arms, nodded his head, opened his mouth, but nothing came from his throat but a discordant gasp. He sang with his arms, with his head, with his eyes, even with the swelling on his face; he sang passionately with anguish, and the more he strained his chest to extract at least one note from it, the more discordant were his gasps.

Yegorushka, like the rest, was overcome with depression. He went to his waggon, clambered up on the bales and lay down. He looked at the sky, and thought of happy Konstantin and his wife. Why did people get married? What were women in the world for? Yegorushka put the vague questions to himself, and thought that a man would certainly be happy if he had an affectionate, merry and beautiful woman continually living at his side. For some reason he remembered the Countess Dranitsky, and thought it would probably be very pleasant to live with a woman like that; he would perhaps have married her with pleasure if that idea had not been so shameful. He recalled her eyebrows, the pupils of her eyes, her carriage, the clock with the horseman. . . . The soft warm night moved softly down upon him and whispered something in his ear, and it seemed to him that it was that lovely woman bending over him, looking at him with a smile and meaning to kiss him. . . .

Nothing was left of the fire but two little red eyes, which kept on growing smaller and smaller. Konstantin and the waggoners were sitting by it, dark motionless figures, and it seemed as though there were many more of them than before. The twin crosses were equally visible, and far, far away, somewhere by the highroad there gleamed a red light—other people cooking their porridge, most likely.

"Our Mother Russia is the he-ad of all the world!" Kiruha sang out suddenly in a harsh voice, choked and subsided. The steppe echo caught up his voice, carried it on, and it seemed as though stupidity itself were rolling on heavy wheels over the steppe.

"It's time to go," said Panteley. "Get up, lads."

While they were putting the horses in, Konstantin walked by the waggons and talked rapturously of his wife.

"Good-bye, mates!" he cried when the waggons started. "Thank you for your hospitality. I shall go on again towards that light. It's more than I can stand."

And he quickly vanished in the mist, and for a long time they could hear him striding in the direction of the light to tell those other strangers of his happiness.

When Yegorushka woke up next day it was early morning; the sun had not yet risen. The waggons were at a standstill. A man in a white cap and a suit of cheap grey material, mounted on a little Cossack stallion, was talking to Dymov and Kiruha beside the foremost waggon. A mile and a half ahead there were long low white barns and little houses with tiled roofs; there were neither yards nor trees to be seen beside the little houses.

"What village is that, Grandfather?" asked Yegorushka.

"That's the Armenian Settlement, youngster," answered Panteley. "The Armenians live there. They are a good sort of people, ... the Armenians are."

The man in grey had finished talking to Dymov and Kiruha; he pulled up his little stallion and looked across towards the settlement.

"What a business, only think!" sighed Panteley, looking towards the settlement, too, and shuddering at the morning freshness. "He has sent a man to the settlement for some papers, and he doesn't come. . . . He should have sent Styopka."

"Who is that, Grandfather?" asked Yegorushka.

"Varlamov."

My goodness! Yegorushka jumped up quickly, getting upon his knees, and looked at the white cap. It was hard to recognize the mysterious elusive Varlamov, who was sought by everyone, who was always "on his rounds," and who had far more money than Countess Dranitsky, in the short, grey little man in big boots, who was sitting on an ugly little nag and talking to peasants at an hour when all decent people were asleep.

"He is all right, a good man," said Panteley, looking towards the settlement. "God give him health—a splendid gentleman, Semyon Alexandritch. . . . It's people like that the earth rests upon. That's true. . . . The cocks are not crowing yet, and he is already up and about. . . . Another man would be asleep, or gallivanting with visitors at home, but he is on the steppe all day, . . . on his rounds. . . . He does not let things slip. . . . No-o! He's a fine fellow. . . ."

Varlamov was talking about something, while he kept his eyes fixed. The little stallion shifted from one leg to another impatiently.

"Semyon Alexandritch!" cried Panteley, taking off his hat. "Allow us to send Styopka! Emelyan, call out that Styopka should be sent."

But now at last a man on horseback could be seen coming from the settlement. Bending very much to one side and brandishing his whip above his head like a gallant young Caucasian, and wanting to astonish everyone by his horsemanship, he flew towards the waggons with the swiftness of a bird.

"That must be one of his circuit men," said Panteley. "He must have a hundred such horsemen or maybe more."

Reaching the first waggon, he pulled up his horse, and taking off his hat, handed Varlamov a little book. Varlamov took several papers out of the book, read them and cried:

"And where is Ivantchuk's letter?"

The horseman took the book back, looked at the papers and shrugged his shoulders. He began saying something, probably justifying himself and asking to be allowed to ride back to the settlement again. The little stallion suddenly stirred as though Varlamov had grown heavier. Varlamov stirred too.

"Go along!" he cried angrily, and he waved his whip at the man.

Then he turned his horse round and, looking through the papers in the book, moved at a walking pace alongside the waggons. When he reached the hindmost, Yegorushka strained his eyes to get a better look at him. Varlamov was an elderly man. His face, a simple Russian sunburnt face with a small grey beard, was red, wet with dew and covered with little blue veins; it had the same expression of business-like coldness as Ivan Ivanitch's face, the same look of fanatical zeal for business. But yet what a difference could be felt between him and Kuzmitchov! Uncle Ivan Ivanitch always had on his face, together with his business-like reserve, a look of anxiety and apprehension that he would not find Varlamov, that he would be late, that he would miss a good price; nothing of that sort, so characteristic of small and dependent persons, could be seen in the face or figure of Varlamov. This man made the price himself, was not looking for anyone, and did not depend on anyone; however ordinary his exterior, yet in everything, even in the manner of holding his whip, there was a sense of power and habitual authority over the steppe.

As he rode by Yegorushka he did not glance at him. Only the little stallion deigned to notice Yegorushka; he looked at him with his large foolish eyes, and even he showed no interest. Panteley bowed to Varlamov; the latter noticed it, and without taking his eyes off the sheets of paper, said lisping:

"How are you, old man?"

Varlamov's conversation with the horseman and the way he had brandished his whip had evidently made an overwhelming impression on the whole party. Everyone looked grave. The man on horseback, cast down at the anger of the great man, remained stationary, with his hat off, and the rein loose by the foremost waggon; he was silent, and seemed unable to grasp that the day had begun so badly for him.

"He is a harsh old man, . . ." muttered Panteley. "It's a pity he is so harsh! But he is all right, a good man. . . . He doesn't abuse men for nothing. . . . It's no matter. . . ."

After examining the papers, Varlamov thrust the book into his pocket; the little stallion, as though he knew what was in his mind, without waiting for orders, started and dashed along the highroad.

VII

On the following night the waggoners had halted and were cooking their porridge. On this occasion there was a sense of overwhelming oppression over everyone. It was sultry; they all drank a great deal, but could not quench their thirst. The moon was intensely crimson and sullen, as though it were sick. The stars, too, were sullen, the mist was thicker, the distance more clouded. Nature seemed as though languid and weighed down by some foreboding.

There was not the same liveliness and talk round the camp fire as there had been the day before. All were dreary and spoke listlessly and without interest. Panteley did nothing but sigh and complain of his feet, and continually alluded to impenitent deathbeds.

Dymov was lying on his stomach, chewing a straw in silence; there was an expression of disgust on his face as though the straw smelt unpleasant, a spiteful and exhausted look. . . . Vassya complained that his jaw ached, and prophesied bad weather; Emelyan was not waving his arms, but sitting still and looking gloomily at the fire. Yegorushka, too, was weary. This slow travelling exhausted him, and the sultriness of the day had given him a headache.

While they were cooking the porridge, Dymov, to relieve his boredom, began quarrelling with his companions.

"Here he lolls, the lumpy face, and is the first to put his spoon in," he said, looking spitefully at Emelyan. "Greedy! always contrives to sit next the cauldron. He's been a church-singer, so he thinks he is a gentleman! There are a lot of singers like you begging along the highroad!"

"What are you pestering me for?" asked Emelyan, looking at him angrily.

"To teach you not to be the first to dip into the cauldron. Don't think too much of yourself!"

"You are a fool, and that is all about it!" wheezed out Emelyan.

Knowing by experience how such conversations usually ended, Panteley and Vassya intervened and tried to persuade Dymov not to quarrel about nothing.

"A church-singer!" The bully would not desist, but laughed contemptuously. "Anyone can sing like that—sit in the church porch and sing 'Give me alms, for Christ's sake!' Ugh! you are a nice fellow!"

Emelyan did not speak. His silence had an irritating effect on Dymov. He looked with still greater hatred at the ex-singer and said:

"I don't care to have anything to do with you, or I would show you what to think of yourself."

"But why are you pushing me, you Mazeppa?" Emelyan cried, flaring up. "Am I interfering with you?"

"What did you call me?" asked Dymov, drawing himself up, and his eyes were suffused with blood. "Eh! I am a Mazeppa? Yes? Take that, then; go and look for it."

Dymov snatched the spoon out of Emelyan's hand and flung it far away. Kiruha, Vassya, and Styopka ran to look for it, while Emelyan fixed an imploring and questioning look on Panteley. His face suddenly became small and wrinkled; it began twitching, and the ex-singer began to cry like a child.

Yegorushka, who had long hated Dymov, felt as though the air all at once were unbearably stifling, as though the fire were scorching his face; he longed to run quickly to the waggons in the darkness, but the bully's angry bored eyes drew the boy to him. With a passionate desire to say something extremely offensive, he took a step towards Dymov and brought out, gasping for breath:

"You are the worst of the lot; I can't bear you!"

After this he ought to have run to the waggons, but he could not stir from the spot and went on:

"In the next world you will burn in hell! I'll complain to Ivan Ivanitch. Don't you dare insult Emelyan!"

"Say this too, please," laughed Dymov: " 'every little sucking-pig wants to lay down the law.' Shall I pull your ear?"

Yegorushka felt that he could not breathe; and something which had never happened to him before—he suddenly began shaking all over, stamping his feet and crying shrilly:

"Beat him, beat him!"

Tears gushed from his eyes; he felt ashamed, and ran staggering back to the waggon. The effect produced by his outburst he did not see. Lying on the bales and twitching his arms and legs, he whispered:

"Mother, mother!"

And these men and the shadows round the camp fire, and the dark bales and the far-away lightning, which was flashing every minute in the distance—all struck him now as terrible and unfriendly. He was overcome with terror and asked himself in despair why and how he had come into this unknown land in the company of terrible peasants? Where was his uncle now, where was Father Christopher, where was Deniska? Why were they so long in coming? Hadn't they forgotten him? At the thought that he was forgotten and cast out to the mercy of fate, he felt such a cold chill of dread that he had several times an impulse to jump off the bales of wool, and run back full speed along the road; but the thought of the huge dark crosses, which would certainly meet him on the way, and the lightning flashing in the distance, stopped him. . . . And only when he whispered, "Mother, mother!" he felt as it were a little better.

The waggoners must have been full of dread, too. After Yegorushka had run away from the camp fire they sat at first for a long time in silence, then they began speaking in hollow undertones about something, saying that it was coming and that they must make haste and get away from it. . . . They quickly finished supper, put out the fire and began harnessing the horses in silence. From their fluster and the broken phrases they uttered it was apparent they foresaw some trouble. Before they set off on their way, Dymov went up to Panteley and asked softly:

"What's his name?"

"Yegory," answered Panteley.

Dymov put one foot on the wheel, caught hold of the cord which was tied round the bales and pulled himself up. Yegorushka saw his face and curly head. The face was pale and looked grave and exhausted, but there was no expression of spite in it.

"Yera!" he said softly, "here, hit me!"

Yegorushka looked at him in surprise. At that instant there was a flash of lightning.

"It's all right, hit me," repeated Dymov. And without waiting for Yegorushka to hit him or to speak to him, he jumped down and said: "How dreary I am!"

Then, swaying from one leg to the other and moving his shoulder-blades, he sauntered lazily alongside the string of waggons and repeated in a voice half weeping, half angry:

"How dreary I am! O Lord! Don't you take offence, Emelyan," he said as he passed Emelyan. "Ours is a wretched cruel life!"

There was a flash of lightning on the right, and, like a reflection in the looking-glass, at once a second flash in the distance.

"Yegory, take this," cried Panteley, throwing up something big and dark.

"What is it?" asked Yegorushka.

"A mat. There will be rain, so cover yourself up."

Yegorushka sat up and looked about him. The distance had grown perceptibly blacker, and now oftener than every minute winked with a pale light. The blackness was being bent towards the right as though by its own weight.

"Will there be a storm, Grandfather?" asked Yegorushka.

"Ah, my poor feet, how they ache!" Panteley said in a high-pitched voice, stamping his feet and not hearing the boy.

On the left someone seemed to strike a match in the sky; a pale phosphorescent streak gleamed and went out. There was a sound as though someone very far away were walking over an iron roof, probably barefoot, for the iron gave a hollow rumble.

"It's set in!" cried Kiruha.

Between the distance and the horizon on the right there was a flash of lightning so vivid that it lighted up part of the steppe and the spot where the clear sky met the blackness. A terrible cloud was swooping down, without haste, a compact mass; big black shreds hung from its edge; similar shreds pressing one upon another were piling up on the right and left horizon. The tattered, ragged look of the storm-cloud gave it a drunken disorderly air. There was a distinct, not smothered, growl of thunder. Yegorushka crossed himself and began quickly putting on his great-coat.

"I am dreary!" Dymov's shout floated from the foremost waggon, and it could be told from his voice that he was beginning to be ill-humoured again. "I am so dreary!"

All at once there was a squall of wind, so violent that it almost snatched away Yegorushka's bundle and mat; the mat fluttered in all directions and flapped on the bale and on Yegorushka's face. The wind dashed whistling over the steppe, whirled round in disorder and raised such an uproar from the grass that neither the thunder nor the creaking of the wheels could be heard; it blew from the black storm-cloud, carrying with it clouds of dust and the scent of rain and wet earth. The moonlight grew mistier, as it were dirtier; the stars were even more overcast; and clouds of dust could be seen hurrying along the edge of the road, followed by their shadows. By now, most likely, the whirlwind eddying round and lifting from the earth dust, dry grass and feathers, was mounting to the very sky; uprooted plants must have been flying by that very black storm-cloud, and how frightened they must have been! But through the dust that clogged the eyes nothing could be seen but the flash of lightning.

Yegorushka, thinking it would pour with rain in a minute, knelt up and covered himself with the mat.

"Panteley-ey!" someone shouted in the front. "A . . . a . . . va!"

"I can't!" Panteley answered in a loud high voice. "A . . . a . . . va! Arya . . . a!"

There was an angry clap of thunder, which rolled across the sky from right to left, then back again, and died away near the foremost waggon.

"Holy, holy, holy, Lord of Sabaoth," whispered Yegorushka, crossing himself. "Fill heaven and earth with Thy glory."

The blackness in the sky yawned wide and breathed white fire. At once there was another clap of thunder. It had scarcely ceased when there was a flash of lightning so broad that Yegorushka suddenly saw through a slit in the mat the whole highroad to the very horizon, all the waggoners and even Kiruha's waistcoat. The black shreds had by now moved upwards from the left, and one of them, a coarse, clumsy monster like a claw with fingers, stretched to the moon. Yegorushka made up his mind to shut his eyes tight, to pay no attention to it, and to wait till it was all over.

The rain was for some reason long in coming. Yegorushka peeped out from the mat in the hope that perhaps the storm-cloud was passing over. It was fearfully dark. Yegorushka could see neither Panteley, nor the bale of wool, nor himself; he looked sideways towards the place where the moon had lately been, but there was the same black darkness there as over the waggons. And in the darkness the flashes of lightning seemed more violent and blinding, so that they hurt his eyes.

"Panteley!" called Yegorushka.

No answer followed. But now a gust of wind for the last time flung up the mat and hurried away. A quiet regular sound was heard. A big cold drop fell on Yegorushka's knee, another trickled over his hand. He noticed that his knees were not covered, and tried to rearrange the mat, but at that moment something began pattering on the road, then on the shafts and the bales. It was the rain. As though they understood one another, the rain and the mat began prattling of something rapidly, gaily and most annoyingly like two magpies.

Yegorushka knelt up or rather squatted on his boots. While the rain was pattering on the mat, he leaned forward to screen his knees, which were suddenly wet. He succeeded in covering his knees, but in less than a minute was aware of a penetrating, unpleasant dampness behind on his back and the calves of his legs. He returned to his former position, exposing his knees to the rain, and wondered what to do to rearrange the mat which he could not see in the darkness. But his arms were already wet, the water was trickling up his sleeves and down his collar, and his shoulder-blades felt chilly. And he made up his mind to do nothing but sit motionless and wait till it was all over.

"Holy, holy, holy!" he whispered.

Suddenly, exactly over his head, the sky cracked with a fearful deafening din; he huddled up and held his breath, waiting for the fragments to fall upon his head and back. He inadvertently opened his eyes and saw a blinding intense light flare out and flash five times on his fingers, his wet sleeves, and on the trickles of water running from the mat upon the bales and down to the ground. There was a fresh peal of thunder as violent and awful; the sky was not growling and rumbling now, but uttering short crashing sounds like the crackling of dry wood.

"Trrah! tah! tah! tah!" the thunder rang out distinctly, rolled over the sky, seemed to stumble, and somewhere by the foremost waggons or far behind to fall with an abrupt angry "Trrra!"

The flashes of lightning had at first been only terrible, but with such thunder they seemed sinister and menacing. Their magic light pierced through closed eyelids and sent a chill all over the body. What could he do not to see them? Yegorushka made up his mind to turn over on his face. Cautiously, as though afraid of being watched, he got on all fours, and his hands slipping on the wet bale, he turned back again.

"Trrah! tah! tah!" floated over his head, rolled under the waggons and exploded "Kraa!"

Again he inadvertently opened his eyes and saw a new danger: three huge giants with long pikes were following the waggon! A flash of lightning gleamed on the points of their pikes and lighted up their figures very distinctly. They were men of huge proportions, with covered faces, bowed heads, and heavy footsteps. They seemed gloomy and dispirited and lost in thought. Perhaps they were not following the waggons with any harmful intent, and yet there was something awful in their proximity.

Yegorushka turned quickly forward, and trembling all over cried: "Panteley! Grandfather!"

"Trrah! tah! tah!" the sky answered him.

He opened his eyes to see if the waggoners were there. There were flashes of lightning in two places, which lighted up the road to the far distance, the whole string of waggons and all the waggoners. Streams of water were flowing along the road and bubbles were dancing. Panteley was walking beside the waggon; his tall hat and his shoulder were covered with a small mat; his figure expressed neither terror nor uneasiness, as though he were deafened by the thunder and blinded by the lightning.

"Grandfather, the giants!" Yegorushka shouted to him in tears.

But the old man did not hear. Further away walked Emelyan. He was covered from head to foot with a big mat and was triangular in shape. Vassya, without anything over him, was walking with the same wooden step as usual, lifting his feet high and not bending his knees. In the flash of lightning it seemed as though the waggons were not moving and the men were motionless, that Vassya's lifted foot was rigid in the same position. . . .

Yegorushka called the old man once more. Getting no answer, he sat motionless, and no longer waited for it all to end. He was convinced that the thunder would kill him in another minute, that he would accidentally open his eyes and see the terrible giants, and he left off crossing himself, calling the old man and thinking of his mother, and was simply numb with cold and the conviction that the storm would never end.

But at last there was the sound of voices.

"Yegory, are you asleep?" Panteley cried below. "Get down! Is he deaf, the silly little thing? . . ."

"Something like a storm!" said an unfamiliar bass voice, and the stranger cleared his throat as though he had just tossed off a good glass of vodka.

Yegorushka opened his eyes. Close to the waggon stood Panteley, Emelyan, looking like a triangle, and the giants. The latter were by now much shorter, and when Yegorushka looked more closely at them they turned out to be ordinary peasants, carrying on their shoulders not pikes but pitchforks. In the space between Panteley and the triangular figure, gleamed the window of a low-pitched hut. So the waggons were halting in the village. Yegorushka flung off the mat, took his bundle and made haste to get off the waggon. Now when close to him there were people talking and a lighted window he no longer felt afraid, though the thunder was crashing as before and the whole sky was streaked with lightning.

"It was a good storm, all right, . . ." Panteley was muttering. "Thank God, . . . my feet are a little softened by the rain. It was all right. . . . Have you got down, Yegory? Well, go into the hut; it is all right. . . ."

"Holy, holy, holy!" wheezed Emelyan, "it must have struck something. . . . Are you of these parts?" he asked the giants.

"No, from Glinovo. We belong to Glinovo. We are working at the Platers'."

"Threshing?"

"All sorts. Just now we are getting in the wheat. The lightning, the lightning! It is long since we have had such a storm. . . ."

Yegorushka went into the hut. He was met by a lean hunchbacked old woman with a sharp chin. She stood holding a tallow candle in her hands, screwing up her eyes and heaving prolonged sighs.

"What a storm God has sent us!" she said. "And our lads are out for the night on the steppe; they'll have a bad time, poor dears! Take off your things, little sir, take off your things."

Shivering with cold and shrugging squeamishly, Yegorushka pulled off his drenched overcoat, then stretched out his arms and straddled his legs, and stood a long time without moving. The slightest movement caused an unpleasant sensation of cold and wetness. His sleeves and the back of his shirt were sopped, his trousers stuck to his legs, his head was dripping.

"What's the use of standing there, with your legs apart, little lad?" said the old woman. "Come, sit down."

Holding his legs wide apart, Yegorushka went up to the table and sat down on a bench near somebody's head. The head moved, puffed a stream of air through its nose, made a chewing sound and subsided. A mound covered with a sheepskin stretched from the head along the bench; it was a peasant woman asleep.

The old woman went out sighing, and came back with a big water melon and a little sweet melon.

"Have something to eat, my dear! I have nothing else to offer you, ..." she said, yawning. She rummaged in the table and took out a long sharp knife, very much like the one with which the brigands killed the merchants in the inn. "Have some, my dear!"

Yegorushka, shivering as though he were in a fever, ate a slice of sweet melon with black bread and then a slice of water melon, and that made him feel colder still.

"Our lads are out on the steppe for the night, ..." sighed the old woman while he was eating. "The terror of the Lord! I'd light the candle under the ikon, but I don't know where Stepanida has put it. Have some more, little sir, have some more...." The old woman gave a yawn and, putting her right hand behind her, scratched her left shoulder.

"It must be two o'clock now," she said; "it will soon be time to get up. Our lads are out on the steppe for the night; they are all wet through for sure...."

"Granny," said Yegorushka. "I am sleepy."

"Lie down, my dear, lie down," the old woman sighed, yawning. "Lord Jesus Christ! I was asleep, when I heard a noise as though someone were knocking. I woke up and looked, and it was the storm God had sent us.... I'd have lighted the candle, but I couldn't find it."

Talking to herself, she pulled some rags, probably her own bed, off the bench, took two sheepskins off a nail by the stove, and began laying them out for a bed for Yegorushka. "The storm doesn't grow less," she muttered. "If only nothing's struck in an unlucky hour. Our lads are out on the steppe for the night. Lie down and sleep, my dear. . . . Christ be with you, my child. . . . I won't take away the melon; maybe you'll have a bit when you get up."

The sighs and yawns of the old woman, the even breathing of the sleeping woman, the half-darkness of the hut, and the sound of the rain outside, made one sleepy. Yegorushka was shy of undressing before the old woman. He only took off his boots, lay down and covered himself with the sheepskin.

"Is the little lad lying down?" he heard Panteley whisper a little later.

"Yes," answered the old woman in a whisper. "The terror of the Lord! It thunders and thunders, and there is no end to it."

"It will soon be over," wheezed Panteley, sitting down; "it's getting quieter. . . . The lads have gone into the huts, and two have stayed with the horses. The lads have. . . . They can't; . . . the horses would be taken away. . . . I'll sit here a bit and then go and take my turn. . . . We can't leave them; they would be taken. . . ."

Panteley and the old woman sat side by side at Yegorushka's feet, talking in hissing whispers and interspersing their speech with sighs and yawns. And Yegorushka could not get warm. The warm heavy sheepskin lay on him, but he was trembling all over; his arms and legs were twitching, and his whole inside was shivering. . . . He undressed under the sheepskin, but that was no good. His shivering grew more and more acute.

Panteley went out to take his turn with the horses, and afterwards came back again, and still Yegorushka was shivering all over and could not get to sleep. Something weighed upon his head and chest and oppressed him, and he did not know what it was, whether it was the old people whispering, or the heavy smell of the sheepskin. The melon he had eaten had left an unpleasant metallic taste in his mouth. Moreover he was being bitten by fleas.

"Grandfather, I am cold," he said, and did not know his own voice.

"Go to sleep, my child, go to sleep," sighed the old woman.

Tit came up to the bedside on his thin little legs and waved his arms, then grew up to the ceiling and turned into a windmill. . . . Father Christopher, not as he was in the chaise, but in his full vestments with the sprinkler in his hand, walked round the mill, sprinkling it with holy water, and it left off waving. Yegorushka, knowing this was delirium, opened his eyes.

"Grandfather," he called, "give me some water."

No one answered. Yegorushka felt it insufferably stifling and uncomfortable lying down. He got up, dressed, and went out of the hut. Morning was beginning. The sky was overcast, but it was no longer raining. Shivering and wrapping himself in his wet overcoat, Yegorushka walked about the muddy yard and listened to the silence; he caught sight of a little shed with a half-open door made of reeds. He looked into this shed, went into it, and sat down in a dark corner on a heap of dry dung.

There was a tangle of thoughts in his heavy head; his mouth was dry and unpleasant from the metallic taste. He looked at his hat, straightened the peacock's feather on it, and thought how he had gone with his mother to buy the hat. He put his hand into his pocket and took out a lump of brownish sticky paste. How had that paste come into his pocket? He thought a minute, smelt it; it smelt of honey. Aha! it was the Jewish cake! How sopped it was, poor thing!

Yegorushka examined his coat. It was a little grey overcoat with big bone buttons, cut in the shape of a frock-coat. At home, being a new and expensive article, it had not been hung in the hall, but with his mother's dresses in her bedroom; he was only allowed to wear it on holidays. Looking at it, Yegorushka felt sorry for it. He thought that he and the great-coat were both abandoned to the mercy of destiny; he thought that he would never get back home, and began sobbing so violently that he almost fell off the heap of dung.

A big white dog with woolly tufts like curl-papers about its face, sopping from the rain, came into the shed and stared with curiosity at Yegorushka. It seemed to be hesitating whether to bark or not. Deciding that there was no need to bark, it went cautiously up to Yegorushka, ate the sticky plaster and went out again.

"There are Varlamov's men!" someone shouted in the street.

After having his cry out, Yegorushka went out of the shed and, walking round a big puddle, made his way towards the street. The waggons were standing exactly opposite the gateway. The drenched waggoners, with their muddy feet, were sauntering beside them or sitting on the shafts, as listless and drowsy as flies in autumn. Yegorushka looked at them and thought: "How dreary and comfortless to be a peasant!" He went up to Panteley and sat down beside him on the shaft.

"Grandfather, I'm cold," he said, shivering and thrusting his hands up his sleeves.

"Never mind, we shall soon be there," yawned Panteley. "Never mind, you will get warm."

It must have been early when the waggons set off, for it was not hot. Yegorushka lay on the bales of wool and shivered with cold, though the sun soon came out and dried his clothes, the bales, and the earth. As soon as he closed his eyes he saw Tit and the windmill again. Feeling a sickness and heaviness all over, he did his utmost to drive away these images, but as soon as they vanished the dare-devil Dymov, with red eyes and lifted fists, rushed at Yegorushka with a roar, or there was the sound of his complaint: "I am so dreary!" Varlamov rode by on his little Cossack stallion; happy Konstantin passed, with a smile and the bustard in his arms. And how tedious these people were, how sickening and unbearable!

Once—it was towards evening—he raised his head to ask for water. The waggons were standing on a big bridge across a broad river. There was black smoke below over the river, and through it could be seen a steamer with a barge in tow. Ahead of them, beyond the river, was a huge mountain dotted with houses and churches; at the foot of the mountain an engine was being shunted along beside some goods trucks. . . .

Yegorushka had never before seen steamers, nor engines, nor broad rivers. Glancing at them now, he was not alarmed or surprised; there was not even a look of anything like curiosity in his face. He merely felt sick, and made haste to turn over to the edge of the bale. He was sick. Panteley, seeing this, cleared his throat and shook his head.

"Our little lad's taken ill," he said. "He must have got a chill to the stomach. The little lad must . . . away from home; it's a bad lookout!"

VIII

The waggons stopped at a big inn for merchants, not far from the quay. As Yegorushka climbed down from the waggon he heard a very familiar voice. Someone was helping him to get down, and saying:

"We arrived yesterday evening. . . . We have been expecting you all day. We meant to overtake you yesterday, but it was out of our way; we came by the other road. I say, how you have crumpled your coat! You'll catch it from your uncle!"

Yegorushka looked into the speaker's mottled face and remembered that this was Deniska.

"Your uncle and Father Christopher are in the inn now, drinking tea; come along!"

And he led Yegorushka to a big two-storied building, dark and gloomy like the almshouse at N. After going across the entry, up a dark staircase and through a narrow corridor, Yegorushka and Deniska reached a little room in which Ivan Ivanitch and Father Christopher were sitting at the tea-table. Seeing the boy, both the old men showed surprise and pleasure.

"Aha! Yegor Ni-ko-la-aitch!" chanted Father Christopher. "Mr. Lomonosov!"

"Ah, our gentleman that is to be," said Kuzmitchov, "pleased to see you!"

Yegorushka took off his great-coat, kissed his uncle's hand and Father Christopher's, and sat down to the table.

"Well, how did you like the journey, *puer bone?*" Father Christopher pelted him with questions as he poured him out some tea, with his radiant smile. "Sick of it, I've no doubt? God save us all from having to travel by waggon or with oxen. You go on and on, God forgive us; you look ahead and the steppe is always lying stretched out the same as it was—you can't see the end of it! It's not travelling but regular torture. Why don't you drink your tea? Drink it up; and in your absence, while you have been trailing along with the waggons, we have settled all our business capitally. Thank God we have sold our wool to Tcherepahin, and no one could wish to have done better. . . . We have made a good bargain."

At the first sight of his own people Yegorushka felt an overwhelming desire to complain. He did not listen to Father Christopher, but thought how to begin and what exactly to complain of. But Father Christopher's voice, which seemed to him harsh and unpleasant, prevented him from concentrating his attention and confused his thoughts. He had not sat at the table five minutes before he got up, went to the sofa and lay down.

"Well, well," said Father Christopher in surprise. "What about your tea?"

Still thinking what to complain of, Yegorushka leaned his head against the wall and broke into sobs.

"Well, well!" repeated Father Christopher, getting up and going to the sofa. "Yegory, what is the matter with you? Why are you crying?"

"I'm . . . I'm ill," Yegorushka brought out.

"Ill?" said Father Christopher in amazement. "That's not the right thing, my boy. . . . One mustn't be ill on a journey. Aie, aie, what are you thinking about, boy . . . eh?"

He put his hand to Yegorushka's head, touched his cheek and said:

"Yes, your head's feverish. . . . You must have caught cold or else have eaten something. . . . Pray to God."

"Should we give him quinine? . . ." said Ivan Ivanitch, troubled.

"No; he ought to have something hot. . . . Yegory, have a little drop of soup? Eh?"

"I . . . don't want any," said Yegorushka.

"Are you feeling chilly?"

"I was chilly before, but now . . . now I am hot. And I ache all over. . . ."

Ivan Ivanitch went up to the sofa, touched Yegorushka on the head, cleared his throat with a perplexed air, and went back to the table.

"I tell you what, you undress and go to bed," said Father Christopher. "What you want is sleep now."

He helped Yegorushka to undress, gave him a pillow and covered him with a quilt, and over that Ivan Ivanitch's great-coat. Then he walked away on tiptoe and sat down to the table. Yegorushka shut his eyes, and at once it seemed to him that he was not in the hotel room, but on the highroad beside the camp fire. Emelyan waved his hands, and Dymov with red eyes lay on his stomach and looked mockingly at Yegorushka.

"Beat him, beat him!" shouted Yegorushka.

"He is delirious," said Father Christopher in an undertone.

"It's a nuisance!" sighed Ivan Ivanitch.

"He must be rubbed with oil and vinegar. Please God, he will be better to-morrow."

To be rid of bad dreams, Yegorushka opened his eyes and began looking towards the fire. Father Christopher and Ivan Ivanitch had now finished their tea and were talking in a whisper. The first was smiling with delight, and evidently could not forget that he had made a good bargain over his wool; what delighted him was not so much the actual profit he had made as the thought that on getting home he would gather round him his big family, wink slyly and go off into a chuckle; at first he would deceive them all, and say that he had sold the wool at a price below its value, then he would give his son-in-law, Mihail, a fat pocket-book and say: "Well, take it! that's the way to do business!" Kuzmitchov did not seem pleased; his face expressed, as before, a business-like reserve and anxiety.

"If I could have known that Tcherepahin would give such a price," he said in a low voice, "I wouldn't have sold Makarov those five tons at home. It is vexatious! But who could have told that the price had gone up here?"

A man in a white shirt cleared away the samovar and lighted the little lamp before the ikon in the corner. Father Christopher whispered something in his ear; the man looked, made a serious face like a conspirator, as though to say, "I understand," went out, and returned a little while afterwards and put something under the sofa. Ivan Ivanitch made himself a bed on the floor, yawned several times, said his prayers lazily, and lay down.

"I think of going to the cathedral to-morrow," said Father Christopher. "I know the sacristan there. I ought to go and see the bishop after mass, but they say he is ill."

He yawned and put out the lamp. Now there was no light in the room but the little lamp before the ikon.

"They say he can't receive visitors," Father Christopher went on, undressing. "So I shall go away without seeing him."

He took off his full coat, and Yegorushka saw Robinson Crusoe reappear. Robinson stirred something in a saucer, went up to Yegorushka and whispered:

"Lomonosov, are you asleep? Sit up; I'm going to rub you with oil and vinegar. It's a good thing, only you must say a prayer."

Yegorushka roused himself quickly and sat up. Father Christopher pulled down the boy's shirt, and shrinking and breathing jerkily, as though he were being tickled himself, began rubbing Yegorushka's chest.

"In the name of the Father, the Son, and the Holy Ghost," he whispered, "lie with your back upwards—that's it. . . . You'll be all right to-morrow, but don't do it again. . . . You are as hot as fire. I suppose you were on the road in the storm."

"Yes."

"You might well fall ill! In the name of the Father, the Son, and the Holy Ghost, . . . you might well fall ill!"

After rubbing Yegorushka, Father Christopher put on his shirt again, covered him, made the sign of the cross over him, and walked away. Then Yegorushka saw him saying his prayers. Probably the old man knew a great many prayers by heart, for he stood a long time before the ikon murmuring. After saying his prayers he made the sign of the cross over the window, the door, Yegorushka, and Ivan Ivanitch, lay down on the little sofa without a pillow, and covered himself with his full coat. A clock in the corridor struck ten. Yegorushka thought how long a time it would be before morning; feeling miserable, he pressed his forehead against the back of the sofa and left off trying to get rid of the oppressive misty dreams. But morning came much sooner than he expected.

It seemed to him that he had not been lying long with his head pressed to the back of the sofa, but when he opened his eyes slanting rays of sunlight were already shining on the floor through the two windows of the little hotel room. Father Christopher and Ivan Ivanitch were not in the room. The room had been tidied; it was bright, snug, and smelt of Father Christopher, who always smelt of cypress and dried cornflowers (at home he used to make the holy-water sprinklers and decorations for the ikon-stands out of cornflowers, and so he was saturated with the smell of them). Yegorushka looked at the pillow, at the slanting sunbeams, at his boots, which had been cleaned and were standing side by side near the sofa, and laughed. It seemed strange to him that he was not on the bales of wool, that everything was dry around him, and that there was no thunder and lightning on the ceiling.

He jumped off the sofa and began dressing. He felt splendid; nothing was left of his yesterday's illness but a slight weakness in his legs and neck. So the vinegar and oil had done good. He remembered the steamer, the railway engine, and the broad river, which he had dimly seen the day before, and now he made haste to dress, to run to the quay and have a look at them. When he had washed and was putting on his red shirt, the latch of the door clicked, and Father Christopher appeared in the doorway, wearing his top-hat and a brown silk cassock over his canvas coat and carrying his staff in his hand. Smiling and radiant (old men are always radiant when they come back from church), he put a roll of holy bread and a parcel of some sort on the table, prayed before the ikon, and said:

"God has sent us blessings—well, how are you?"

"Quite well now," answered Yegorushka, kissing his hand.

"Thank God.... I have come from mass.... I've been to see a sacristan I know. He invited me to breakfast with him, but I didn't go. I don't like visiting people too early, God bless them!"

He took off his cassock, stroked himself on the chest, and without haste undid the parcel. Yegorushka saw a little tin of caviare, a piece of dry sturgeon, and a French loaf.

"See; I passed a fish-shop and brought this," said Father Christopher. "There is no need to indulge in luxuries on an ordinary weekday; but I thought, I've an invalid at home, so it is excusable. And the caviare is good, real sturgeon. . . ."

The man in the white shirt brought in the samovar and a tray with tea-things.

"Eat some," said Father Christopher, spreading the caviare on a slice of bread and handing it to Yegorushka. "Eat now and enjoy yourself, but the time will soon come for you to be studying. Mind you study with attention and application, so that good may come of it. What you have to learn by heart, learn by heart, but when you have to tell the inner sense in your own words, without regard to the outer form, then say it in your own words. And try to master all subjects. One man knows mathematics excellently, but has never heard of Pyotr Mogila; another knows about Pyotr Mogila, but cannot explain about the moon. But you study so as to understand everything. Study Latin, French, German, . . . geography, of course, history, theology, philosophy, mathematics, . . . and when you have mastered everything, not with haste but with prayer and with zeal, then go into the service. When you know everything it will be easy for you in any line of life. . . . You study and strive for the divine blessing, and God will show you what to be. Whether a doctor, a judge or an engineer. . . ."

Father Christopher spread a little caviare on a piece of bread, put it in his mouth and said:

"The Apostle Paul says: 'Do not apply yourself to strange and diverse studies.' Of course, if it is black magic, unlawful arts, or calling up spirits from the other world, like Saul, or studying subjects that can be of no use to yourself or others, better not learn them. You must undertake only what God has blessed. Take example . . . the Holy Apostle spoke in all languages, so you study languages. Basil the Great studied mathematics and philosophy—so you study them; St. Nestor wrote history—so you study and write history. Take example from the saints."

Father Christopher sipped the tea from his saucer, wiped his moustaches, and shook his head.

"Good!" he said. "I was educated in the old-fashioned way; I have forgotten a great deal by now, but still I live differently from other people. Indeed, there is no comparison. For instance, in company at a dinner, or at an assembly, one says something in Latin, or makes some allusion from history or philosophy, and it pleases people, and it pleases me myself.... Or when the circuit court comes and one has to take the oath, all the other priests are shy, but I am quite at home with the judges, the prosecutors, and the lawyers. I talk intellectually, drink a cup of tea with them, laugh, ask them what I don't know, ... and they like it. So that's how it is, my boy. Learning is light and ignorance is darkness. Study! It's hard, of course; nowadays study is expensive.... Your mother is a widow; she lives on her pension, but there, of course ..."

Father Christopher glanced apprehensively towards the door, and went on in a whisper:

"Ivan Ivanitch will assist. He won't desert you. He has no children of his own, and he will help you. Don't be uneasy."

He looked grave, and whispered still more softly:

"Only mind, Yegory, don't forget your mother and Ivan Ivanitch, God preserve you from it. The commandment bids you honour your mother, and Ivan Ivanitch is your benefactor and takes the place of a father to you. If you become learned, God forbid you should be impatient and scornful with people because they are not so clever as you, then woe, woe to you!"

Father Christopher raised his hand and repeated in a thin voice:

"Woe to you! Woe to you!"

Father Christopher's tongue was loosened, and he was, as they say, warming to his subject; he would not have finished till dinner-time but the door opened and Ivan Ivanitch walked in. He said good-morning hurriedly, sat down to the table, and began rapidly swallowing his tea.

"Well, I have settled all our business," he said. "We might have gone home to-day, but we have still to think about Yegor. We must arrange for him. My sister told me that Nastasya Petrovna, a friend of hers, lives somewhere here, so perhaps she will take him in as a boarder."

He rummaged in his pocket-book, found a crumpled note and read:

" 'Little Lower Street: Nastasya Petrovna Toskunov, living in a house of her own.' We must go at once and try to find her. It's a nuisance!"

Soon after breakfast Ivan Ivanitch and Yegorushka left the inn.

"It's a nuisance," muttered his uncle. "You are sticking to me like a burr. You and your mother want education and gentlemanly breeding and I have nothing but worry with you both. . . ."

When they crossed the yard, the waggons and the drivers were not there. They had all gone off to the quay early in the morning. In a far-off dark corner of the yard stood the chaise.

"Good-bye, chaise!" thought Yegorushka.

At first they had to go a long way uphill by a broad street, then they had to cross a big market-place; here Ivan Ivanitch asked a policeman for Little Lower Street.

"I say," said the policeman, with a grin, "it's a long way off, out that way towards the town grazing ground."

They met several cabs but Ivan Ivanitch only permitted himself such a weakness as taking a cab in exceptional cases and on great holidays. Yegorushka and he walked for a long while through paved streets, then along streets where there were only wooden planks at the sides and no pavements, and in the end got to streets where there were neither planks nor pavements. When their legs and their tongues had brought them to Little Lower Street they were both red in the face, and taking off their hats, wiped away the perspiration.

"Tell me, please," said Ivan Ivanitch, addressing an old man sitting on a little bench by a gate, "where is Nastasya Petrovna Toskunov's house?"

"There is no one called Toskunov here," said the old man, after pondering a moment. "Perhaps it's Timoshenko you want."

"No, Toskunov. . . ."

"Excuse me, there's no one called Toskunov. . . ."

Ivan Ivanitch shrugged his shoulders and trudged on farther.

"You needn't look," the old man called after them. "I tell you there isn't, and there isn't."

"Listen, auntie," said Ivan Ivanitch, addressing an old woman who was sitting at a corner with a tray of pears and sunflower seeds, "where is Nastasya Petrovna Toskunov's house?"

The old woman looked at him with surprise and laughed.

"Why, Nastasya Petrovna live in her own house now!" she cried.

"Lord! it is eight years since she married her daughter and gave up the house to her son-in-law! It's her son-in-law lives there now."

And her eyes expressed: "How is it you didn't know a simple thing like that, you fools?"

"And where does she live now?" Ivan Ivanitch asked.

"Oh, Lord!" cried the old woman, flinging up her hands in surprise. "She moved ever so long ago! It's eight years since she gave up her house to her son-in-law! Upon my word!"

She probably expected Ivan Ivanitch to be surprised, too, and to exclaim: "You don't say so," but Ivan Ivanitch asked very calmly:

"Where does she live now?"

The old woman tucked up her sleeves and, stretching out her bare arm to point, shouted in a shrill piercing voice:

"Go straight on, straight on, straight on. You will pass a little red house, then you will see a little alley on your left. Turn down that little alley, and it will be the third gate on the right...."

Ivan Ivanitch and Yegorushka reached the little red house, turned to the left down the little alley, and made for the third gate on the right. On both sides of this very old grey gate there was a grey fence with big gaps in it. The first part of the fence was tilting forwards and threatened to fall, while on the left of the gate it sloped backwards towards the yard. The gate itself stood upright and seemed to be still undecided which would suit it best—to fall forwards or backwards. Ivan Ivanitch opened the little gate at the side, and he and Yegorushka saw a big yard overgrown with weeds and burdocks. A hundred paces from the gate stood a little house with a red roof and green shutters. A stout woman with her sleeves tucked up and her apron held out was standing in the middle of the yard, scattering something on the ground and shouting in a voice as shrill as that of the woman selling fruit:

"Chick!... Chick!... Chick!"

Behind her sat a red dog with pointed ears. Seeing the strangers, he ran to the little gate and broke into a tenor bark (all red dogs have a tenor bark).

"Whom do you want?" asked the woman, putting up her hand to shade her eyes from the sun.

"Good-morning!" Ivan Ivanitch shouted, too, waving off the red dog with his stick. "Tell me, please, does Nastasya Petrovna Toskunov live here?"

"Yes! But what do you want with her?"

"Perhaps you are Nastasya Petrovna?"

"Well, yes, I am!"

"Very pleased to see you.... You see, your old friend Olga Ivanovna Knyasev sends her love to you. This is her little son. And I, perhaps you remember, am her brother Ivan Ivanitch.... You are one of us from N.... You were born among us and married there...."

A silence followed. The stout woman stared blankly at Ivan Ivanitch, as though not believing or not understanding him, then she flushed all over, and flung up her hands; the oats were scattered out of her apron and tears spurted from her eyes.

"Olga Ivanovna!" she screamed, breathless with excitement. "My own darling! Ah, holy saints, why am I standing here like a fool? My pretty little angel...."

She embraced Yegorushka, wetted his face with her tears, and broke down completely.

"Heavens!" she said, wringing her hands, "Olga's little boy! How delightful! He is his mother all over! The image of his mother! But why are you standing in the yard? Come indoors."

Crying, gasping for breath and talking as she went, she hurried towards the house. Her visitors trudged after her.

"The room has not been done yet," she said, ushering the visitors into a stuffy little drawing-room adorned with many ikons and pots of flowers. "Oh, Mother of God! Vassilisa, go and open the shutters anyway! My little angel! My little beauty! I did not know that Olitchka had a boy like that!"

When she had calmed down and got over her first surprise Ivan Ivanitch asked to speak to her alone. Yegorushka went into another room; there was a sewing-machine; in the window was a cage with a starling in it, and there were as many ikons and flowers as in the drawing-room. Near the machine stood a little girl with a sunburnt face and chubby cheeks like Tit's, and a clean cotton dress. She stared at Yegorushka without blinking, and apparently felt very awkward. Yegorushka looked at her and after a pause asked:

"What's your name?"

The little girl moved her lips, looked as if she were going to cry, and answered softly:

"Atka...."

This meant Katka.

"He will live with you," Ivan Ivanitch was whispering in the drawing-room, "if you will be so kind, and we will pay ten roubles a month for his keep. He is not a spoilt boy; he is quiet...."

"I really don't know what to say, Ivan Ivanitch!" Nastasya Petrovna sighed tearfully. "Ten roubles a month is very good, but it is a dreadful thing to take another person's child! He may fall ill or something...."

When Yegorushka was summoned back to the drawing-room Ivan Ivanitch was standing with his hat in his hands, saying good-bye.

"Well, let him stay with you now, then," he said. "Good-bye! You stay, Yegor!" he said, addressing his nephew. "Don't be troublesome; mind you obey Nastasya Petrovna.... Good-bye; I am coming again to-morrow."

And he went away. Nastasya once more embraced Yegorushka, called him a little angel, and with a tear-stained face began preparing for dinner. Three minutes later Yegorushka was sitting beside her, answering her endless questions and eating hot savoury cabbage soup.

In the evening he sat again at the same table and, resting his head on his hand, listened to Nastasya Petrovna. Alternately laughing and crying, she talked of his mother's young days, her own marriage, her children.... A cricket chirruped in the stove, and there was a faint humming from the burner of the lamp. Nastasya Petrovna talked in a low voice, and was continually dropping her thimble in her excitement; and Katka her granddaughter, crawled under the table after it and each time sat a long while under the table, probably examining Yegorushka's feet; and Yegorushka listened, half dozing and looking at the old woman's face, her wart with hairs on it, and the stains of tears, ... and he felt sad, very sad. He was put to sleep on a chest and told that if he were hungry in the night he must go out into the little passage and take some chicken, put there under a plate in the window.

Next morning Ivan Ivanitch and Father Christopher came to say good-bye. Nastasya Petrovna was delighted to see them, and was about to set the samovar; but Ivan Ivanitch, who was in a great hurry, waved his hands and said:

"We have no time for tea! We are just setting off."

Before parting they all sat down and were silent for a minute. Nastasya Petrovna heaved a deep sigh and looked towards the ikon with tear-stained eyes.

"Well," began Ivan Ivanitch, getting up, "so you will stay...."

All at once the look of business-like reserve vanished from his face; he flushed a little and said with a mournful smile:

"Mind you work hard.... Don't forget your mother, and obey Nastasya Petrovna.... If you are diligent at school, Yegor, I'll stand by you."

He took his purse out of his pocket, turned his back to Yegorushka, fumbled for a long time among the smaller coins, and, finding a ten-kopeck piece, gave it to Yegorushka.

Father Christopher, without haste, blessed Yegorushka.

"In the name of the Father, the Son, and the Holy Ghost.... Study," he said. "Work hard, my lad. If I die, remember me in your prayers. Here is a ten-kopeck piece from me, too...."

Yegorushka kissed his hand, and shed tears; something whispered in his heart that he would never see the old man again.

"I have applied at the high school already," said Ivan Ivanitch in a voice as though there were a corpse in the room. "You will take him for the entrance examination on the seventh of August.... Well, good-bye; God bless you, good-bye, Yegor!"

"You might at least have had a cup of tea," wailed Nastasya Petrovna.

Through the tears that filled his eyes Yegorushka could not see his uncle and Father Christopher go out. He rushed to the window, but they were not in the yard, and the red dog, who had just been barking, was running back from the gate with the air of having done his duty.

When Yegorushka ran out of the gate Ivan Ivanitch and Father Christopher, the former waving his stick with the crook, the latter his staff, were just turning the corner. Yegorushka felt that with these people all that he had known till then had vanished from him for ever. He sank helplessly on to the little bench, and with bitter tears greeted the new unknown life that was beginning for him now. . . .

What would that life be like?

Lights

The dog was barking excitedly outside. And Ananyev the engineer, his assistant called Von Schtenberg, and I went out of the hut to see at whom it was barking. I was the visitor, and might have remained indoors, but I must confess my head was a little dizzy from the wine I had drunk, and I was glad to get a breath of fresh air.

"There is nobody here," said Ananyev when we went out. "Why are you telling stories, Azorka? You fool!"

There was not a soul in sight.

"The fool," Azorka, a black house-dog, probably conscious of his guilt in barking for nothing and anxious to propitiate us, approached us, diffidently wagging his tail. The engineer bent down and touched him between his ears.

"Why are you barking for nothing, creature?" he said in the tone in which good-natured people talk to children and dogs. "Have you had a bad dream or what? Here, doctor, let me commend to your attention," he said, turning to me, "a wonderfully nervous subject! Would you believe it, he can't endure solitude—he is always having terrible dreams and suffering from nightmares; and when you shout at him he has something like an attack of hysterics."

"Yes, a dog of refined feelings," the student chimed in.

Azorka must have understood that the conversation was concerning him. He turned his head upwards and grinned plaintively, as though to say, "Yes, at times I suffer unbearably, but please excuse it!"

It was an August night, there were stars, but it was dark. Owing to the fact that I had never in my life been in such exceptional surroundings, as I had chanced to come into now, the starry night seemed to me gloomy, inhospitable, and darker than it was in reality. I was on a railway line which was still in process of construction. The high, half-finished embankment, the mounds of sand, clay, and rubble, the holes, the wheel-barrows standing here and there, the flat tops of the mud huts in which the workmen lived—all this muddle, coloured to one tint by the darkness, gave the earth a strange, wild aspect that suggested the times of chaos. There was so little order in all that lay before me that it was somehow strange in the midst of the hideously excavated, grotesque-looking earth to see the silhouettes of human beings and the slender telegraph posts. Both spoiled the ensemble of the picture, and seemed to belong to a different world. It was still, and the only sound came from the telegraph wire droning its wearisome refrain somewhere very high above our heads.

We climbed up on the embankment and from its height looked down upon the earth. A hundred yards away where the pits, holes, and mounds melted into the darkness of the night, a dim light was twinkling. Beyond it gleamed another light, beyond that a third, then a hundred paces away two red eyes glowed side by side—probably the windows of some hut—and a long series of such lights, growing continually closer and dimmer, stretched along the line to the very horizon, then turned in a semicircle to the left and disappeared in the darkness of the distance. The lights were motionless. There seemed to be something in common between them and the stillness of the night and the disconsolate song of the telegraph wire. It seemed as though some weighty secret were buried under the embankment and only the lights, the night, and the wires knew of it.

"How glorious, O Lord!" sighed Ananyev; "such space and beauty that one can't tear oneself away! And what an embankment! It's not an embankment, my dear fellow, but a regular Mont Blanc. It's costing millions. . . ."

Going into ecstasies over the lights and the embankment that was costing millions, intoxicated by the wine and his sentimental mood, the engineer slapped Von Schtenberg on the shoulder and went on in a jocose tone:

"Well, Mihail Mihailitch, lost in reveries? No doubt it is pleasant to look at the work of one's own hands, eh? Last year this very spot was bare steppe, not a sight of human life, and now look: life . . . civilisation. . . . And how splendid it all is, upon my soul! You and I are building a railway, and after we are gone, in another century or two, good men will build a factory, a school, a hospital, and things will begin to move! Eh!"

The student stood motionless with his hands thrust in his pockets, and did not take his eyes off the lights. He was not listening to the engineer, but was thinking, and was apparently in the mood in which one does not want to speak or to listen. After a prolonged silence he turned to me and said quietly:

"Do you know what those endless lights are like? They make me think of something long dead, that lived thousands of years ago, something like the camps of the Amalekites or the Philistines. It is as though some people of the Old Testament had pitched their camp and were waiting for morning to fight with Saul or David. All that is wanting to complete the illusion is the blare of trumpets and sentries calling to one another in some Ethiopian language."

And, as though of design, the wind fluttered over the line and brought a sound like the clank of weapons. A silence followed. I don't know what the engineer and the student were thinking of, but it seemed to me already that I actually saw before me something long dead and even heard the sentry talking in an unknown tongue. My imagination hastened to picture the tents, the strange people, their clothes, their armour. . . .

"Yes," muttered the student pensively, "once Philistines and Amalekites were living in this world, making wars, playing their part, and now no trace of them remains. So it will be with us. Now we are making a railway, are standing here philosophising, but two thousand years will pass—and of this embankment and of all those men, asleep after their hard work, not one grain of dust will remain. In reality, it's awful!"

"You must drop those thoughts . . ." said the engineer gravely and admonishingly.

"Why?"

"Because. . . . Thoughts like that are for the end of life, not for the beginning of it. You are too young for them."

"Why so?" repeated the student.

"All these thoughts of the transitoriness, the insignificance and the aimlessness of life, of the inevitability of death, of the shadows of the grave, and so on, all such lofty thoughts, I tell you, my dear fellow, are good and natural in old age when they come as the product of years of inner travail, and are won by suffering and really are intellectual riches; for a youthful brain on the threshold of real life they are simply a calamity! A calamity!" Ananyev repeated with a wave of his hand. "To my mind it is better at your age to have no head on your shoulders at all than to think on these lines. I am speaking seriously, Baron. And I have been meaning to speak to you about it for a long time, for I noticed from the very first day of our acquaintance your partiality for these damnable ideas!"

"Good gracious, why are they damnable?" the student asked with a smile, and from his voice and his face I could see that he asked the question from simple politeness, and that the discussion raised by the engineer did not interest him in the least.

I could hardly keep my eyes open. I was dreaming that immediately after our walk we should wish each other good-night and go to bed, but my dream was not quickly realised. When we had returned to the hut the engineer put away the empty bottles and took out of a large wicker hamper two full ones, and uncorking them, sat down to his work-table with the evident intention of going on drinking, talking, and working. Sipping a little from his glass, he made pencil notes on some plans and went on pointing out to the student that the latter's way of thinking was not what it should be. The student sat beside him checking accounts and saying nothing. He, like me, had no inclination to speak or to listen. That I might not interfere with their work, I sat away from the table on the engineer's crooked-legged travelling bedstead, feeling bored and expecting every moment that they would suggest I should go to bed. It was going on for one o'clock.

Having nothing to do, I watched my new acquaintances. I had never seen Ananyev or the student before. I had only made their acquaintance on the night I have described. Late in the evening I was returning on horseback from a fair to the house of a landowner with whom I was staying, had got on the wrong road in the dark and lost my way. Going round and round by the railway line and seeing how dark the night was becoming, I thought of the "barefoot railway roughs," who lie in wait for travellers on foot and on horseback, was frightened, and knocked at the first hut I came to. There I was cordially received by Ananyev and the student. As is usually the case with strangers casually brought together, we quickly became acquainted, grew friendly and at first over the tea and afterward over the wine, began to feel as though we had known each other for years. At the end of an hour or so, I knew who they were and how fate had brought them from town to the far-away steppe; and they knew who I was, what my occupation and my way of thinking.

Nikolay Anastasyevitch Ananyev, the engineer, was a broad-shouldered, thick-set man, and, judging from his appearance, he had, like Othello, begun the "descent into the vale of years," and was growing rather too stout. He was just at that stage which old match-making women mean when they speak of "a man in the prime of his age," that is, he was neither young nor old, was fond of good fare, good liquor, and praising the past, panted a little as he walked, snored loudly when he was asleep, and in his manner with those surrounding him displayed that calm imperturbable good humour which is always acquired by decent people by the time they have reached the grade of a staff officer and begun to grow stout. His hair and beard were far from being grey, but already, with a condescension of which he was unconscious, he addressed young men as "my dear boy" and felt himself entitled to lecture them good-humouredly about their way of thinking. His movements and his voice were calm, smooth, and self-confident, as they are in a man who is thoroughly well aware that he has got his feet firmly planted on the right road, that he has definite work, a secure living, a settled outlook. . . . His sunburnt, thick-nosed face and muscular neck seemed to say: "I am well fed, healthy, satisfied with myself, and the time will come when you young people too, will be well fed, healthy, and satisfied with yourselves...." He was dressed in a cotton shirt with the collar awry and in full linen trousers thrust into his high boots. From certain trifles, as for instance, from his coloured worsted girdle, his embroidered collar, and the patch on his elbow, I was able to guess that he was married and in all probability tenderly loved by his wife.

Baron Von Schtenberg, a student of the Institute of Transport, was a young man of about three or four and twenty. Only his fair hair and scanty beard, and, perhaps, a certain coarseness and frigidity in his features showed traces of his descent from Barons of the Baltic provinces; everything else—his name, Mihail Mihailovitch, his religion, his ideas, his manners, and the expression of his face were purely Russian. Wearing, like Ananyev, a cotton shirt and high boots, with his round shoulders, his hair left uncut, and his sunburnt face, he did not look like a student or a Baron, but like an ordinary Russian workman. His words and gestures were few, he drank reluctantly without relish, checked the accounts mechanically, and seemed all the while to be thinking of something else. His movements and voice were calm, and smooth too, but his calmness was of a different kind from the engineer's. His sunburnt, slightly ironical, dreamy face, his eyes which looked up from under his brows, and his whole figure were expressive of spiritual stagnation—mental sloth. He looked as though it did not matter to him in the least whether the light were burning before him or not, whether the wine were nice or nasty, and whether the accounts he was checking were correct or not.... And on his intelligent, calm face I read: "I don't see so far any good in definite work, a secure living, and a settled outlook. It's all nonsense. I was in Petersburg, now I am sitting here in this hut, in the autumn I shall go back to Petersburg, then in the spring here again.... What sense there is in all that I don't know, and no one knows.... And so it's no use talking about it...."

He listened to the engineer without interest, with the condescending indifference with which cadets in the senior classes listen to an effusive and good-natured old attendant. It seemed as though there were nothing new to him in what the engineer said, and that if he had not himself been too lazy to talk, he would have said something newer and cleverer. Meanwhile Ananyev would not desist. He had by now laid aside his good-humoured, jocose tone and spoke seriously, even with a fervour which was quite out of keeping with his expression of calmness. Apparently he had no distaste for abstract subjects, was fond of them, indeed, but had neither skill nor practice in the handling of them. And this lack of practice was so pronounced in his talk that I did not always grasp his meaning at once.

"I hate those ideas with all my heart!" he said, "I was infected by them myself in my youth, I have not quite got rid of them even now, and I tell you—perhaps because I am stupid and such thoughts were not the right food for my mind—they did me nothing but harm. That's easy to understand! Thoughts of the aimlessness of life, of the insignificance and transitoriness of the visible world, Solomon's 'vanity of vanities' have been, and are to this day, the highest and final stage in the realm of thought. The thinker reaches that stage and—comes to a halt! There is nowhere further to go. The activity of the normal brain is completed with this, and that is natural and in the order of things. Our misfortune is that we begin thinking at that end. What normal people end with we begin with. From the first start, as soon as the brain begins working independently, we mount to the very topmost, final step and refuse to know anything about the steps below."

"What harm is there in that?" said the student.

"But you must understand that it's abnormal," shouted Ananyev, looking at him almost wrathfully. "If we find means of mounting to the topmost step without the help of the lower ones, then the whole long ladder, that is the whole of life, with its colours, sounds, and thoughts, loses all meaning for us. That at your age such reflections are harmful and absurd, you can see from every step of your rational independent life. Let us suppose you sit down this minute to read Darwin or Shakespeare, you have scarcely read a page before the poison shows itself; and your long life, and Shakespeare, and Darwin, seem to you nonsense, absurdity, because you know you will die, that Shakespeare and Darwin have died too, that their thoughts have not saved them, nor the earth, nor you, and that if life is deprived of meaning in that way, all science, poetry, and exalted thoughts seem only useless diversions, the idle playthings of grown up people; and you leave off reading at the second page. Now, let us suppose that people come to you as an intelligent man and ask your opinion about war, for instance: whether it is desirable, whether it is morally justifiable or not. In answer to that terrible question you merely shrug your shoulders and confine yourself to some commonplace, because for you, with your way of thinking, it makes absolutely no difference whether hundreds of thousands of people die a violent death, or a natural one: the results are the same— ashes and oblivion. You and I are building a railway line. What's the use, one may ask, of our worrying our heads, inventing, rising above the hackneyed thing, feeling for the workmen, stealing or not stealing, when we know that this railway line will turn to dust within two thousand years, and so on, and so on. . . . You must admit that with such a disastrous way of looking at things there can be no progress, no science, no art, nor even thought itself. We fancy that we are cleverer than the crowd, and than Shakespeare. In reality our thinking leads to nothing because we have no inclination to go down to the lower steps and there is nowhere higher to go, so our brain stands at the freezing point— neither up nor down; I was in bondage to these ideas for six years, and by all that is holy, I never read a sensible book all that time, did not gain a ha'porth of wisdom, and did not raise my moral standard an inch. Was not that disastrous? Moreover, besides being corrupted ourselves, we bring poison into the lives of those surrounding us. It would be all right if, with our pessimism, we renounced life, went to live in a cave, or made haste to die, but, as it is, in obedience to the universal law, we live, feel, love women, bring up children, construct railways!"

"Our thoughts make no one hot or cold," the student said reluctantly.

"Ah! there you are again!—do stop it! You have not yet had a good sniff at life. But when you have lived as long as I have you will know a thing or two! Our theory of life is not so innocent as you suppose. In practical life, in contact with human beings, it leads to nothing but horrors and follies. It has been my lot to pass through experiences which I would not wish a wicked Tatar to endure."

"For instance?" I asked.

"For instance?" repeated the engineer.

He thought a minute, smiled and said:

"For instance, take this example. More correctly, it is not an example, but a regular drama, with a plot and a dénouement. An excellent lesson! Ah, what a lesson!"

He poured out wine for himself and us, emptied his glass, stroked his broad chest with his open hands, and went on, addressing himself more to me than to the student.

"It was in the year 187—, soon after the war, and when I had just left the University. I was going to the Caucasus, and on the way stopped for five days in the seaside town of N. I must tell you that I was born and grew up in that town, and so there is nothing odd in my thinking N. extraordinarily snug, cosy, and beautiful, though for a man from Petersburg or Moscow, life in it would be as dreary and comfortless as in any Tchuhloma or Kashira. With melancholy I passed by the high school where I had been a pupil; with melancholy I walked about the very familiar park, I made a melancholy attempt to get a nearer look at people I had not seen for a long time—all with the same melancholy. . . .

"Among other things, I drove out one evening to the so-called Quarantine. It was a small mangy copse in which, at some forgotten time of plague, there really had been a quarantine station, and which was now the resort of summer visitors. It was a drive of three miles from the town along a good soft road. As one drove along one saw on the left the blue sea, on the right the unending gloomy steppe; there was plenty of air to breathe, and wide views for the eyes to rest on. The copse itself lay on the seashore. Dismissing my cabman, I went in at the familiar gates and first turned along an avenue leading to a little stone summer-house which I had been fond of in my childhood. In my opinion that round, heavy summer-house on its clumsy columns, which combined the romantic charm of an old tomb with the ungainliness of a Sobakevitch,* was the most poetical nook in the whole town. It stood at the edge above the cliff, and from it there was a splendid view of the sea.

"I sat down on the seat, and, bending over the parapet, looked down. A path ran from the summer-house along the steep, almost overhanging cliff, between the lumps of clay and tussocks of burdock. Where it ended, far below on the sandy shore, low waves were languidly foam-

* A character in Gogol's *Dead Souls.—Translator's Note.*

ing and softly purring. The sea was as majestic, as infinite, and as forbidding as seven years before when I left the high school and went from my native town to the capital; in the distance there was a dark streak of smoke—a steamer was passing—and except for this hardly visible and motionless streak and the sea-swallows that flitted over the water, there was nothing to give life to the monotonous view of sea and sky. To right and left of the summer-house stretched uneven clay cliffs.

"You know that when a man in a melancholy mood is left *tête-à-tête* with the sea, or any landscape which seems to him grandiose, there is always, for some reason, mixed with melancholy, a conviction that he will live and die in obscurity, and he reflectively snatches up a pencil and hastens to write his name on the first thing that comes handy. And that, I suppose, is why all convenient solitary nooks like my summer-house are always scrawled over in pencil or carved with penknives. I remember as though it were to-day; looking at the parapet I read: 'Ivan Korolkov, May 16, 1876.' Beside Korolkov some local dreamer had scribbled freely, adding:

> " 'He stood on the desolate ocean's strand,
> While his soul was filled with imaginings grand.'

And his handwriting was dreamy, limp like wet silk. An individual called Kross, probably an insignificant, little man, felt his unimportance so deeply that he gave full licence to his penknife and carved his name in deep letters an inch high. I took a pencil out of my pocket mechanically, and I too scribbled on one of the columns. All that is irrelevant, however. . . . You must forgive me—I don't know how to tell a story briefly.

"I was sad and a little bored. Boredom, the stillness, and the purring of the sea gradually brought me to the line of thought we have been discussing. At that period, towards the end of the 'seventies, it had begun to be fashionable with the public, and later, at the beginning of the 'eighties, it gradually passed from the general public into literature, science, and politics. I was no more than twenty-six at the time, but I knew perfectly well that life was aimless and had no meaning, that everything was a deception and an illusion, that in its essential nature and results a life of penal servitude in Sahalin was not in any way different from a life spent in Nice, that the difference between the brain of a Kant and the brain of a fly was of no real significance, that no one in this world is righteous or guilty, that everything was stuff and nonsense and damn it all! I lived as though I were doing a favour to some unseen power which compelled me to live, and to which I seemed to say: 'Look, I don't care a straw for life, but I am living!' I thought on one definite line, but in all sorts of keys, and in that respect I was like the subtle gourmand who could prepare a hundred appetising dishes from nothing but potatoes. There is no doubt that I was one-sided and even to some extent narrow, but I fancied at the time that my intellectual horizon had neither beginning nor end, and that my thought was as boundless as the sea. Well, as far as I can judge by myself, the philosophy of which we are speaking has something alluring, narcotic in its nature, like tobacco or morphia. It becomes a habit, a craving. You take advantage of every minute of solitude to gloat over thoughts of the aimlessness of life and the darkness of the grave. While I was sitting in the summer-house, Greek children with long noses were decorously walking about the avenues. I took advantage of the occasion and, looking at them, began reflecting in this style:

" 'Why are these children born, and what are they living for? Is there any sort of meaning in their existence? They grow up, without themselves knowing what for; they will live in this God-forsaken, comfortless hole for no sort of reason, and then they will die. . . .'

"And I actually felt vexed with those children because they were walking about decorously and talking with dignity, as though they did not hold their little colourless lives so cheap and knew what they were living for. . . . I remember that far away at the end of an avenue three feminine figures came into sight. Three young ladies, one in a pink dress, two in white, were walking arm-in-arm, talking and laughing. Looking after them, I thought:

" 'It wouldn't be bad to have an affair with some woman for a couple of days in this dull place.'

"I recalled by the way that it was three weeks since I had visited my Petersburg lady, and thought that a passing love affair would come in very appropriately for me just now. The young lady in white in the middle was rather younger and better looking than her companions, and judging by her manners and her laugh, she was a high-school girl in an upper form. I looked, not without impure thoughts, at her bust, and at the same time reflected about her: 'She will be trained in music and manners, she will be married to some Greek—God help us!—will lead a grey, stupid, comfortless life, will bring into the world a crowd of children without knowing why, and then will die. An absurd life!'

"I must say that as a rule I was a great hand at combining my lofty ideas with the lowest prose. Thoughts of the darkness of the grave did not prevent me from giving busts and legs their full due. Our dear Baron's exalted ideas do not prevent him from going on Saturdays to Vukolovka on amatory expeditions. To tell the honest truth, as far as I remember, my attitude to women was most insulting. Now, when I think of that high-school girl, I blush for my thoughts then, but at the time my conscience was perfectly untroubled. I, the son of honourable parents, a Christian, who had received a superior education, not naturally wicked or stupid, felt not the slightest uneasiness when I paid women *Blutgeld*, as the Germans call it, or when I followed high-school girls with insulting looks. . . . The trouble is that youth makes its demands, and our philosophy has nothing in principle against those demands, whether they are good or whether they are loathsome. One who knows that life is aimless and death inevitable is not interested in the struggle against nature or the conception of sin: whether you struggle or whether you don't, you will die and rot just the same. . . . Secondly, my friends, our philosophy instils even into very young people what is called reasonableness. The predominance of reason over the heart is simply overwhelming amongst us. Direct feeling, inspiration—everything is choked by petty analysis. Where there is reasonableness there is coldness, and cold people—it's no use to disguise it—know nothing of chastity. That virtue is only known to those who are warm, affectionate, and capable of love. Thirdly, our philosophy denies the significance of each individual personality. It's easy to see that if I deny the personality of some Natalya Stepanovna, it's absolutely nothing to me whether she is insulted or not. To-day one insults her dignity as a human being and pays her *Blutgeld*, and next day thinks no more of her.

"So I sat in the summer-house and watched the young ladies. Another woman's figure appeared in the avenue, with fair hair, her head uncovered and a white knitted shawl on her shoulders. She walked along the avenue, then came into the summer-house, and taking hold of the parapet, looked indifferently below and into the distance over the sea. As she came in she paid no attention to me, as though she did not notice me. I scrutinised her from foot to head (not from head to foot, as one scrutinises men) and found that she was young, not more than five-and-twenty, nice-looking, with a good figure, in all probability married and belonging to the class of respectable women. She was dressed as though she were at home, but fashionably and with taste, as ladies are, as a rule, in N.

" 'This one would do nicely,' I thought, looking at her handsome figure and her arms; 'she is all right. . . . She is probably the wife of some doctor or schoolmaster. . . .'

"But to make up to her—that is, to make her the heroine of one of those impromptu affairs to which tourists are so prone—was not easy and, indeed, hardly possible. I felt that as I gazed at her face. The way she looked, and the expression of her face, suggested that the sea, the smoke in the distance, and the sky had bored her long, long ago, and wearied her sight. She seemed to be tired, bored, and thinking about something dreary, and her face had not even that fussy, affectedly indifferent expression which one sees in the face of almost every woman when she is conscious of the presence of an unknown man in her vicinity.

"The fair-haired lady took a bored and passing glance at me, sat down on a seat and sank into reverie, and from her face I saw that she had no thoughts for me, and that I, with my Petersburg appearance, did not arouse in her even simple curiosity. But yet I made up my mind to speak to her, and asked: 'Madam, allow me to ask you at what time do the waggonettes go from here to the town?'

" 'At ten or eleven, I believe. . . .'

"I thanked her. She glanced at me once or twice, and suddenly there was a gleam of curiosity, then of something like wonder on her passionless face. . . . I made haste to assume an indifferent expression and to fall into a suitable attitude; she was catching on! She suddenly jumped up from the seat, as though something had bitten her, and examining me hurriedly, with a gentle smile, asked timidly:

"'Oh, aren't you Ananyev?'

"'Yes, I am Ananyev,' I answered.

"'And don't you recognise me? No?'

"I was a little confused. I looked intently at her, and—would you believe it?—I recognised her not from her face nor her figure, but from her gentle, weary smile. It was Natalya Stepanovna, or, as she was called, Kisotchka, the very girl I had been head over ears in love with seven or eight years before, when I was wearing the uniform of a high-school boy. The doings of far, vanished days, the days of long ago.... I remember this Kisotchka, a thin little high-school girl of fifteen or sixteen, when she was something just for a schoolboy's taste, created by nature especially for Platonic love. What a charming little girl she was! Pale, fragile, light—she looked as though a breath would send her flying like a feather to the skies—a gentle, perplexed face, little hands, soft long hair to her belt, a waist as thin as a wasp's—altogether something ethereal, transparent like moonlight—in fact, from the point of view of a high-school boy a peerless beauty.... Wasn't I in love with her! I did not sleep at night. I wrote verses.... Sometimes in the evenings she would sit on a seat in the park while we schoolboys crowded round her, gazing reverently; in response to our compliments, our sighing, and attitudinising, she would shrink nervously from the evening damp, screw up her eyes, and smile gently, and at such times she was awfully like a pretty little kitten. As we gazed at her every one of us had a desire to caress her and stroke her like a cat, hence her nickname of Kisotchka.

"In the course of the seven or eight years since we had met, Kisotchka had greatly changed. She had grown more robust and stouter, and had quite lost the resemblance to a soft, fluffy kitten. It was not that her features looked old or faded, but they had somehow lost their brilliance and looked sterner, her hair seemed shorter, she looked taller, and her shoulders were quite twice as broad, and what was most striking, there was already in her face the expression of motherliness and resignation commonly seen in respectable women of her age, and this, of course, I had never seen in her before. . . . In short, of the school-girlish and the Platonic her face had kept the gentle smile and nothing more. . . .

"We got into conversation. Learning that I was already an engineer, Kisotchka was immensely delighted.

" 'How good that is!' she said, looking joyfully into my face. 'Ah, how good! And how splendid you all are! Of all who left with you, not one has been a failure—they have all turned out well. One an engineer, another a doctor, a third a teacher, another, they say, is a celebrated singer in Petersburg. . . . You are all splendid, all of you. . . . Ah, how good that is!'

"Kisotchka's eyes shone with genuine goodwill and gladness. She was admiring me like an elder sister or a former governess. While I looked at her sweet face and thought, 'It wouldn't be bad to get hold of her to-day!'

" 'Do you remember, Natalya Stepanovna,' I asked her, 'how I once brought you in the park a bouquet with a note in it? You read my note, and such a look of bewilderment came into your face. . . .'

" 'No, I don't remember that,' she said, laughing. 'But I remember how you wanted to challenge Florens to a duel over me. . . .'

" 'Well, would you believe it, I don't remember that. . . .'

" 'Well, that's all over and done with . . .' sighed Kisotchka. 'At one time I was your idol, and now it is my turn to look up to all of you. . . .'

"From further conversation I learned that two years after leaving the high school, Kisotchka had been married to a resident in the town who was half Greek, half Russian, had a post either in the bank or in the insurance society, and also carried on a trade in corn. He had a strange surname, something in the style of Populaki or Skarandopulo. . . . Goodness only knows—I have forgotten. . . . As a matter of fact, Kisotchka spoke little and with reluctance about herself. The conversation was only about me. She asked me about the College of Engineering, about my comrades, about Petersburg, about my plans, and everything I said moved her to eager delight and exclamations of, 'Oh, how good that is!'

"We went down to the sea and walked over the sands; then when the night air began to blow chill and damp from the sea we climbed up

again. All the while our talk was of me and of the past. We walked
about until the reflection of the sunset had died away from the windows of the summer villas.

" 'Come in and have some tea,' Kisotchka suggested. 'The samovar
must have been on the table long ago.... I am alone at home,' she said,
as her villa came into sight through the green of the acacias. 'My husband is always in the town and only comes home at night, and not always then, and I must own that I am so dull that it's simply deadly.'

"I followed her in, admiring her back and shoulders. I was glad that
she was married. Married women are better material for temporary
love affairs than girls. I was also pleased that her husband was not at
home. At the same time I felt that the affair would not come off....

"We went into the house. The rooms were smallish and had low
ceilings, and the furniture was typical of the summer villa (Russians
like having at their summer villas uncomfortable heavy, dingy furniture which they are sorry to throw away and have nowhere to put), but
from certain details I could observe that Kisotchka and her husband
were not badly off, and must be spending five or six thousand roubles
a year. I remember that in the middle of the room which Kisotchka
called the dining-room there was a round table, supported for some
reason on six legs, and on it a samovar and cups. At the edge of the
table lay an open book, a pencil, and an exercise book. I glanced at the
book and recognised it as 'Malinin and Burenin's Arithmetical Exam-
ples.' It was open, as I now remember, at the 'Rules of Compound Interest.'

" 'To whom are you giving lessons?' I asked Kisotchka.'

" 'Nobody,' she answered. 'I am just doing some.... I have nothing
to do, and am so bored that I think of the old days and do sums.'

" 'Have you any children?'

" 'I had a baby boy, but he only lived a week.'

"We began drinking tea. Admiring me, Kisotchka said again how
good it was that I was an engineer, and how glad she was of my success.
And the more she talked and the more genuinely she smiled, the
stronger was my conviction that I should go away without having
gained my object. I was a connoisseur in love affairs in those days, and
could accurately gauge my chances of success. You can boldly reckon

on success if you are tracking down a fool or a woman as much on the look out for new experiences and sensations as yourself, or an adventuress to whom you are a stranger. If you come across a sensible and serious woman, whose face has an expression of weary submission and goodwill, who is genuinely delighted at your presence, and, above all, respects you, you may as well turn back. To succeed in that case needs longer than one day.

"And by evening light Kisotchka seemed even more charming than by day. She attracted me more and more, and apparently she liked me too, and the surroundings were most appropriate: the husband not at home, no servants visible, stillness around.... Though I had little confidence in success, I made up my mind to begin the attack anyway. First of all it was necessary to get into a familiar tone and to change Kisotchka's lyrically earnest mood into a more frivolous one.

" 'Let us change the conversation, Natalya Stepanovna,' I began. 'Let us talk of something amusing. First of all, allow me, for the sake of old times, to call you Kisotchka.'

"She allowed me.

" 'Tell me, please, Kisotchka,' I went on, 'what is the matter with all the fair sex here. What has happened to them? In old days they were all so moral and virtuous, and now, upon my word, if one asks about anyone, one is told such things that one is quite shocked at human nature.... One young lady has eloped with an officer; another has run away and carried off a high-school boy with her; another—a married woman—has run away from her husband with an actor; a fourth has left her husband and gone off with an officer, and so on and so on. It's a regular epidemic! If it goes on like this there won't be a girl or a young woman left in your town!'

"I spoke in a vulgar, playful tone. If Kisotchka had laughed in response I should have gone on in this style: 'You had better look out, Kisotchka, or some officer or actor will be carrying you off!' She would have dropped her eyes and said: 'As though anyone would care to carry me off; there are plenty younger and better looking....' And I should have said: 'Nonsense, Kisotchka—I for one should be delighted!' And so on in that style, and it would all have gone swimmingly. But

Kisotchka did not laugh in response; on the contrary, she looked grave and sighed.

" 'All you have been told is true,' she said. 'My cousin Sonya ran away from her husband with an actor. Of course, it is wrong. . . . Everyone ought to bear the lot that fate has laid on him, but I do not condemn them or blame them. . . . Circumstances are sometimes too strong for anyone!'

" 'That is so, Kisotchka, but what circumstances can produce a regular epidemic?'

" 'It's very simple and easy to understand,' replied Kisotchka, raising her eyebrows. 'There is absolutely nothing for us educated girls and women to do with ourselves. Not everyone is able to go to the University, to become a teacher, to live for ideas, in fact, as men do. They have to be married. . . . And whom would you have them marry? You boys leave the high-school and go away to the University, never to return to your native town again, and you marry in Petersburg or Moscow, while the girls remain. . . . To whom are they to be married? Why, in the absence of decent cultured men, goodness knows what sort of men they marry—stockbrokers and such people of all kinds, who can do nothing but drink and get into rows at the club. . . . A girl married like that, at random. . . . And what is her life like afterwards? You can understand: a well-educated, cultured woman is living with a stupid, boorish man; if she meets a cultivated man, an officer, an actor, or a doctor—well, she gets to love him, her life becomes unbearable to her, and she runs away from her husband. And one can't condemn her!'

" 'If that is so, Kisotchka, why get married?' I asked.

" 'Yes, of course,' said Kisotchka with a sigh, 'but you know every girl fancies that any husband is better than nothing. . . . Altogether life is horrid here, Nikolay Anastasyevitch, very horrid! Life is stifling for a girl and stifling when one is married. . . . Here they laugh at Sonya for having run away from her husband, but if they could see into her soul they would not laugh. . . . ' "

Azorka began barking outside again. He growled angrily at some one, then howled miserably and dashed with all his force against the wall of the hut. . . . Ananyev's face was puckered with pity; he broke off his story and went out. For two minutes he could be heard outside comforting his dog. "Good dog! poor dog!"

"Our Nikolay Anastasyevitch is fond of talking," said Von Schtenberg, laughing. "He is a good fellow," he added after a brief silence.

Returning to the hut, the engineer filled up our glasses and, smiling and stroking his chest, went on:

"And so my attack was unsuccessful. There was nothing for it, I put off my unclean thoughts to a more favourable occasion, resigned myself to my failure and, as the saying is, waved my hand. What is more, under the influence of Kisotchka's voice, the evening air, and the stillness, I gradually myself fell into a quiet sentimental mood. I remember I sat in an easy chair by the wide-open window and glanced at the trees and darkened sky. The outlines of the acacias and the lime trees were just the same as they had been eight years before; just as then, in the days of my childhood, somewhere far away there was the tinkling of a wretched piano, and the public had just the same habit of sauntering to and fro along the avenues, but the people were not the same. Along the avenues there walked now not my comrades and I and the object of my adoration, but schoolboys and young ladies who were strangers. And I felt melancholy. When to my inquiries about acquaintances I five times received from Kisotchka the answer, 'He is dead,' my melancholy changed into the feeling one has at the funeral service of a good man. And sitting there at the window, looking at the promenading public and listening to the tinkling piano, I saw with my own eyes for the first time in my life with what eagerness one generation hastens to replace another, and what a momentous significance even some seven or eight years may have in a man's life!

"Kisotchka put a bottle of red wine on the table. I drank it off, grew sentimental, and began telling a long story about something or other. Kisotchka listened as before, admiring me and my cleverness. And time passed. The sky was by now so dark that the outlines of the acacias and lime trees melted into one, the public was no longer walking up and down the avenues, the piano was silent and the only sound was the even murmur of the sea.

"Young people are all alike. Be friendly to a young man, make much

of him, regale him with wine, let him understand that he is attractive
and he will sit on and on, forget that it is time to go, and talk and talk
and talk. . . . His hosts cannot keep their eyes open, it's past their bedtime, and he still stays and talks. That was what I did. Once I chanced
to look at the clock; it was half-past ten. I began saying good-bye.

" 'Have another glass before your walk,' said Kisotchka.

"I took another glass, again I began talking at length, forgot it was
time to go, and sat down. Then there came the sound of men's voices,
footsteps and the clank of spurs.

" 'I think my husband has come in. . . .' said Kisotchka listening.

"The door creaked, two voices came now from the passage and I
saw two men pass the door that led into the dining-room: one a stout,
solid, dark man with a hooked nose, wearing a straw hat, and the other
a young officer in a white tunic. As they passed the door they both
glanced casually and indifferently at Kisotchka and me, and I fancied
both of them were drunk.

" 'She told you a lie then, and you believed her!' we heard a loud
voice with a marked nasal twang say a minute later. 'To begin with, it
wasn't at the big club but at the little one.'

" 'You are angry, Jupiter, so you are wrong . . ." said another voice,
obviously the officer's, laughing and coughing. 'I say, can I stay the
night? Tell me honestly, shall I be in your way?'

" 'What a question! Not only you can, but you must. What will you
have, beer or wine?'

"They were sitting two rooms away from us, talking loudly, and apparently feeling no interest in Kisotchka or her visitor. A perceptible
change came over Kisotchka on her husband's arrival. At first she
flushed red, then her face wore a timid, guilty expression; she seemed
to be troubled by some anxiety, and I began to fancy that she was
ashamed to show me her husband and wanted me to go.

"I began taking leave. Kisotchka saw me to the front door. I remember well her gentle mournful smile and kind patient eyes as she
pressed my hand and said:

" 'Most likely we shall never see each other again. Well, God give
you every blessing. Thank you!'

"Not one sigh, not one fine phrase. As she said good-bye she was holding the candle in her hand; patches of light danced over her face and neck, as though chasing her mournful smile. I pictured to myself the old Kisotchka whom one used to want to stroke like a cat, I looked intently at the present Kisotchka, and for some reason recalled her words: 'Everyone ought to bear the lot that fate has laid on him.' And I had a pang at my heart. I instinctively guessed how it was, and my conscience whispered to me that I, in my happiness and indifference, was face to face with a good, warm-hearted, loving creature, who was broken by suffering.

"I said good-bye and went to the gate. By now it was quite dark. In the south the evenings draw in early in July and it gets dark rapidly. Towards ten o'clock it is so dark that you can't see an inch before your nose. I lighted a couple of dozen matches before, almost groping, I found my way to the gate.

" 'Cab!' I shouted, going out of the gate; not a sound, not a sigh in answer.... 'Cab,' I repeated, 'hey, Cab!'

"But there was no cab of any description. The silence of the grave. I could hear nothing but the murmur of the drowsy sea and the beating of my heart from the wine. Lifting my eyes to the sky I found not a single star. It was dark and sullen. Evidently the sky was covered with clouds. For some reason I shrugged my shoulders, smiling foolishly, and once more, not quite so resolutely, shouted for a cab.

"The echo answered me. A walk of three miles across open country and in the pitch dark was not an agreeable prospect. Before making up my mind to walk, I spent a long time deliberating and shouting for a cab; then, shrugging my shoulders, I walked lazily back to the copse, with no definite object in my mind. It was dreadfully dark in the copse. Here and there between the trees the windows of the summer villas glowed a dull red. A raven, disturbed by my steps and the matches with which I lighted my way to the summer-house, flew from tree to tree and rustled among the leaves. I felt vexed and ashamed, and the raven seemed to understand this, and croaked 'krrra!' I was vexed that I had to walk, and ashamed that I had stayed on at Kisotchka's, chatting like a boy.

"I made my way to the summer-house, felt for the seat and sat down. Far below me, behind a veil of thick darkness, the sea kept up a low

angry growl. I remember that, as though I were blind, I could see neither sky nor sea, nor even the summer-house in which I was sitting.
And it seemed to me as though the whole world consisted only of the
thoughts that were straying through my head, dizzy from the wine,
and of an unseen power murmuring monotonously somewhere below.
And afterwards, as I sank into a doze, it began to seem that it was not
the sea murmuring, but my thoughts, and that the whole world consisted of nothing but me. And concentrating the whole world in myself in this way, I thought no more of cabs, of the town, and of
Kisotchka, and abandoned myself to the sensation I was so fond of:
that is, the sensation of fearful isolation when you feel that in the
whole universe, dark and formless, you alone exist. It is a proud, de-
moniac sensation, only possible to Russians whose thoughts and sensations are as large, boundless, and gloomy as their plains, their forests,
and their snow. If I had been an artist I should certainly have depicted
the expression of a Russian's face when he sits motionless and, with his
legs under him and his head clasped in his hands, abandons himself to
this sensation. . . . And together with this sensation come thoughts of
the aimlessness of life, of death, and of the darkness of the grave. . . .
The thoughts are not worth a brass farthing, but the expression of face
must be fine. . . .

"While I was sitting and dozing, unable to bring myself to get up—
I was warm and comfortable—all at once, against the even monotonous murmur of the sea, as though upon a canvas, sounds began to
grow distinct which drew my attention from myself. . . . Someone was
coming hurriedly along the avenue. Reaching the summer-house this
someone stopped, gave a sob like a little girl, and said in the voice of a
weeping child: 'My God, when will it all end! Merciful Heavens!'

"Judging from the voice and the weeping I took it to be a little girl
of ten or twelve. She walked irresolutely into the summer-house, sat
down, and began half-praying, half-complaining aloud. . . .

" 'Merciful God!' she said, crying, 'it's unbearable. It's beyond all
endurance! I suffer in silence, but I want to live too. . . . Oh, my God!
My God!'

"And so on in the same style.

"I wanted to look at the child and speak to her. So as not to frighten her I first gave a loud sigh and coughed, then cautiously struck a match. . . . There was a flash of bright light in the darkness, which lighted up the weeping figure. It was Kisotchka!"

"Marvels upon marvels!" said Von Schtenberg with a sigh. "Black night, the murmur of the sea; she in grief, he with a sensation of world-solitude. . . . It's too much of a good thing. . . . You only want Circassians with daggers to complete it."

"I am not telling you a tale, but fact."

"Well, even if it is a fact . . . it all proves nothing, and there is nothing new in it. . . ."

"Wait a little before you find fault! Let me finish," said Ananyev, waving his hand with vexation; "don't interfere, please! I am not telling you, but the doctor. . . . Well," he went on, addressing me and glancing askance at the student who bent over his books and seemed very well satisfied at having gibed at the engineer—"well, Kisotchka was not surprised or frightened at seeing me. It seemed as though she had known beforehand that she would find me in the summer-house. She was breathing in gasps and trembling all over as though in a fever, while her tear-stained face, so far as I could distinguish it as I struck match after match, was not the intelligent, submissive weary face I had seen before, but something different, which I cannot understand to this day. It did not express pain, nor anxiety, nor misery—nothing of what was expressed by her words and her tears. . . . I must own that, probably because I did not understand it, it looked to me senseless and as though she were drunk.

" 'I can't bear it,' muttered Kisotchka in the voice of a crying child. 'It's too much for me, Nikolay Anastasyitch. Forgive me, Nikolay Anastasyitch. I can't go on living like this. . . . I am going to the town to my mother's. . . . Take me there. . . . Take me there, for God's sake!'

"In the presence of tears I can neither speak nor be silent. I was flustered and muttered some nonsense, trying to comfort her.

" 'No, no; I will go to my mother's,' said Kisotchka resolutely, getting up and clutching my arm convulsively (her hands and her sleeves were wet with tears). 'Forgive me, Nikolay Anastasyitch, I am going. . . . I can bear no more. . . .'

" 'Kisotchka, but there isn't a single cab,' I said. 'How can you go?'

" 'No matter, I'll walk. . . . It's not far. I can't bear it. . . .'

"I was embarrassed, but not touched. Kisotchka's tears, her trembling, and the blank expression of her face suggested to me a trivial, French or Little Russian melodrama, in which every ounce of cheap shallow feeling is washed down with pints of tears. I didn't understand her, and knew I did not understand her; I ought to have been silent, but for some reason, most likely for fear my silence might be taken for stupidity, I thought fit to try to persuade her not to go to her mother's, but to stay at home. When people cry, they don't like their tears to be seen. And I lighted match after match and went on striking till the box was empty. What I wanted with this ungenerous illumination, I can't conceive to this day. Cold-hearted people are apt to be awkward, and even stupid.

"In the end Kisotchka took my arm and we set off. Going out of the gate, we turned to the right and sauntered slowly along the soft dusty road. It was dark. As my eyes grew gradually accustomed to the darkness, I began to distinguish the silhouettes of the old gaunt oaks and lime trees which bordered the road. The jagged, precipitous cliffs, intersected here and there by deep, narrow ravines and creeks, soon showed indistinctly, a black streak on the right. Low bushes nestled by the hollows, looking like sitting figures. It was uncanny. I looked sideways suspiciously at the cliffs, and the murmur of the sea and the stillness of the country alarmed my imagination. Kisotchka did not speak. She was still trembling, and before she had gone half a mile she was exhausted with walking and was out of breath. I too was silent.

"Three-quarters of a mile from the Quarantine Station there was a deserted building of four storeys, with a very high chimney in which there had once been a steam flour mill. It stood solitary on the cliff, and by day it could be seen for a long distance, both by sea and by land. Because it was deserted and no one lived in it, and because there was an echo in it which distinctly repeated the steps and voices of passersby, it seemed mysterious. Picture me in the dark night arm-in-arm with a woman who was running away from her husband near this tall long monster which repeated the sound of every step I took and stared at me fixedly with its hundred black windows. A normal young man would have been moved to romantic feelings in such surroundings, but

I looked at the dark windows and thought: 'All this is very impressive, but time will come when of that building and of Kisotchka and her troubles and of me with my thoughts, not one grain of dust will remain.... All is nonsense and vanity....'

"When we reached the flour mill Kisotchka suddenly stopped, took her arm out of mine, and said, no longer in a childish voice, but in her own:

" 'Nikolay Anastasvitch, I know all this seems strange to you. But I am terribly unhappy! And you cannot even imagine how unhappy! It's impossible to imagine it! I don't tell you about it because one can't talk about it.... Such a life, such a life!...'

"Kisotchka did not finish. She clenched her teeth and moaned as though she were doing her utmost not to scream with pain.

" 'Such a life!' she repeated with horror, with the cadence and the southern, rather Ukrainian accent which particularly in women gives to emotional speech the effect of singing. 'It is a life! Ah, my God, my God! what does it mean? Oh, my God, my God!'

"As though trying to solve the riddle of her fate, she shrugged her shoulders in perplexity, shook her head, and clasped her hands. She spoke as though she were singing, moved gracefully, and reminded me of a celebrated Little Russian actress.

" 'Great God, it is as though I were in a pit,' she went on. 'If one could live for one minute in happiness as other people live! Oh, my God, my God! I have come to such disgrace that before a stranger I am running away from my husband by night, like some disreputable creature! Can I expect anything good after that?'

"As I admired her movements and her voice, I began to feel annoyed that she was not on good terms with her husband. 'It would be nice to have got on into relations with her!' flitted through my mind; and this pitiless thought stayed in my brain, haunted me all the way and grew more and more alluring....

"About a mile from the flour mill we had to turn to the left by the cemetery. At the turning by the corner of the cemetery there stood a stone windmill, and by it a little hut in which the miller lived. We passed the mill and the hut, turned to the left and reached the gates of the cemetery. There Kisotchka stopped and said:

" 'I am going back, Nikolay Anastasyitch! You go home, and God bless you, but I am going back. I am not frightened.'

" 'Well, what next!' I said, disconcerted. 'If you are going, you had better go!'

" 'I have been too hasty. . . . It was all about nothing that mattered. You and your talk took me back to the past and put all sort of ideas into my head. . . . I was sad and wanted to cry, and my husband said rude things to me before that officer, and I could not bear it. . . . And what's the good of my going to the town to my mother's? Will that make me any happier? I must go back. . . . But never mind . . . let us go on,' said Kisotchka, and she laughed. 'It makes no difference!'

"I remembered that over the gate of the cemetery there was an inscription: 'The hour will come wherein all they that lie in the grave will hear the voice of the Son of God.' I knew very well that sooner of later I and Kisotchka and her husband and the officer in the white tunic would lie under the dark trees in the churchyard; I knew that an unhappy and insulted fellow-creature was walking beside me. All this I recognised distinctly, but at the same time I was troubled by an oppressive and unpleasant dread that Kisotchka would turn back, and that I should not manage to say to her what had to be said. Never at any other time in my life have thoughts of a higher order been so closely interwoven with the basest animal prose as on that night. . . . It was horrible!

"Not far from the cemetery we found a cab. When we reached the High Street, where Kisotchka's mother lived, we dismissed the cab and walked along the pavement. Kisotchka was silent all the while, while I looked at her, and I raged at myself, 'Why don't you begin? Now's the time!' About twenty paces from the hotel where I was staying, Kisotchka stopped by the lamp-post and burst into tears.

" 'Nikolay Anastasyitch!' she said, crying and laughing and looking at me with wet shining eyes, 'I shall never forget your sympathy. . . . How good you are! All of you are so splendid—all of you! Honest, great-hearted, kind, clever. . . . Ah, how good that is!'

"She saw in me a highly educated man, advanced in every sense of the word, and on her tear-stained laughing face, together with the emotion and enthusiasm aroused by my personality, there was clearly written regret that she so rarely saw such people, and that God had not vouchsafed her the bliss of being the wife of one of them. She muttered, 'Ah, how splendid it is!' The childish gladness on her face, the tears, the gentle smile, the soft hair, which had escaped from under the kerchief, and the kerchief itself thrown carelessly over her head, in the light of the street lamp reminded me of the old Kisotchka whom one had wanted to stroke like a kitten.

"I could not restrain myself, and began stroking her hair, her shoulders, and her hands. . . .

" 'Kisotchka, what do you want?' I muttered. 'I'll go to the ends of the earth with you if you like! I will take you out of this hole and give you happiness. I love you. . . . Let us go, my sweet? Yes? Will you?'

"Kisotchka's face was flooded with bewilderment. She stepped back from the street lamp and, completely overwhelmed, gazed at me with wide-open eyes. I gripped her by the arm, began showering kisses on her face, her neck, her shoulders, and went on making vows and promises. In love affairs vows and promises are almost a physiological necessity. There's no getting on without them. Sometimes you know you are lying and that promises are not necessary, but still you vow and protest. Kisotchka, utterly overwhelmed, kept staggering back and gazing at me with round eyes.

" 'Please don't! Please don't!' she muttered, holding me off with her hands.

"I clasped her tightly in my arms. All at once she broke into hysterical tears. And her face had the same senseless blank expression that I had seen in the summer-house when I lighted the matches. Without asking her consent, preventing her from speaking, I dragged her forcibly towards my hotel. She seemed almost swooning and did not walk, but I took her under the arms and almost carried her. . . . I remember, as we were going up the stairs, some man with a red band in his cap looked wonderingly at me and bowed to Kisotchka. . . ."

Ananyev flushed crimson and paused. He walked up and down near the table in silence, scratched the back of his head with an air of vexation, and several times shrugged his shoulders and twitched his shoulder-blades, while a shiver ran down his huge back. The memory was painful and made him ashamed, and he was struggling with himself. . . .

"It's horrible!" he said, draining a glass of wine and shaking his head. "I am told that in every introductory lecture on women's diseases the medical students are admonished to remember that each one of them has a mother, a sister, a fiancée, before undressing and examining a female patient. . . . That advice would be very good not only for medical students but for everyone who in one way or another has to deal with a woman's life. Now that I have a wife and a little daughter, oh, how well I understand that advice! How I understand it, my God! You may as well hear the rest, though. . . . As soon as she had become my mistress, Kisotchka's view of the position was very different from mine. First of all she felt for me a deep and passionate love. What was for me an ordinary amatory episode was for her an absolute revolution in her life. I remember, it seemed to me that she had gone out of her mind. Happy for the first time in her life, looking five years younger, with an inspired enthusiastic face, not knowing what to do with herself for happiness, she laughed and cried and never ceased dreaming aloud how next day we would set off for the Caucasus, then in the autumn to Petersburg; how we would live afterwards. . . .

" 'Don't worry yourself about my husband,' she said to reassure me. 'He is bound to give me a divorce. Everyone in the town knows that he is living with the elder Kostovitch. We will get a divorce and be married.'

"When women love they become acclimatised and at home with people very quickly, like cats. Kisotchka had only spent an hour and a half in my room when she already felt as though she were at home and was ready to treat my property as though it were her own. She packed my things in my portmanteau, scolded me for not hanging my new expensive overcoat on a peg instead of flinging it on a chair, and so on.

"I looked at her, listened, and felt weariness and vexation. I was conscious of a slight twinge of horror at the thought that a respectable, honest, and unhappy woman had so easily, after some three or four hours, succumbed to the first man she met. As a respectable man, you see, I didn't like it. Then, too, I was unpleasantly impressed by the fact that women of Kisotchka's sort, not deep or serious, are too much in love with life, and exalt what is in reality such a trifle as love for a man to the level of bliss, misery, a complete revolution in life.... Moreover, now that I was satisfied, I was vexed with myself for having been so stupid as to get entangled with a woman whom I should have to deceive. And in spite of my disorderly life I must observe that I could not bear telling lies.

"I remember that Kisotchka sat down at my feet, laid her head on my knees, and, looking at me with shining, loving eyes, asked:

" 'Kolya, do you love me? Very, very much?'

"And she laughed with happiness.... This struck me as sentimental, affected, and not clever; and meanwhile I was already inclined to look for 'depth of thought' before everything.

" 'Kisotchka, you had better go home,' I said, or else your people will be sure to miss you and will be looking for you all over the town; and it would be awkward for you to go to your mother in the morning.'

"Kisotchka agreed. At parting we arranged to meet at midday next morning in the park, and the day after to set off together to Pyatigorsk. I went into the street to see her home, and I remember that I caressed her with genuine tenderness on the way. There was a minute when I felt unbearably sorry for her, for trusting me so implicitly, and I made up my mind that I would really take her to Pyatigorsk, but remembering that I had only six hundred roubles in my portmanteau, and that it would be far more difficult to break it off with her in the autumn than now, I made haste to suppress my compassion.

"We reached the house where Kisotchka's mother lived. I pulled at the bell. When footsteps were heard at the other side of the door Kisotchka suddenly looked grave, glanced upwards to the sky, made the sign of the Cross over me several times and, clutching my hand, pressed it to her lips.

" 'Till to-morrow,' she said, and disappeared into the house.

"I crossed to the opposite pavement and from there looked at the house. At first the windows were in darkness, then in one of the windows there was the glimmer of the faint bluish flame of a newly lighted candle; the flame grew, gave more light, and I saw shadows moving about the rooms together with it.

" 'They did not expect her,' I thought.

"Returning to my hotel room I undressed, drank off a glass of red wine, ate some fresh caviare which I had bought that day in the bazaar, went to bed in a leisurely way, and slept the sound, untroubled sleep of a tourist.

"In the morning I woke up with a headache and in a bad humour. Something worried me.

" 'What's the matter?' I asked myself, trying to explain my uneasiness. 'What's upsetting me?'

"And I put down my uneasiness to the dread that Kisotchka might turn up any minute and prevent my going away, and that I should have to tell lies and act a part before her. I hurriedly dressed, packed my things, and left the hotel, giving instructions to the porter to take my luggage to the station for the seven o'clock train in the evening. I spent the whole day with a doctor friend and left the town that evening. As you see, my philosophy did not prevent me from taking to my heels in a mean and treacherous flight. . . .

"All the while that I was at my friend's, and afterwards driving to the station, I was tormented by anxiety. I fancied that I was afraid of meeting with Kisotchka and a scene. In the station I purposely remained in the toilet room till the second bell rang, and while I was making my way to my compartment, I was oppressed by a feeling as though I were covered all over with stolen things. With what impatience and terror I waited for the third bell!

"At last the third bell that brought my deliverance rang at last, the train moved; we passed the prison, the barracks, came out into the open country, and yet, to my surprise, the feeling of uneasiness still persisted, and still I felt like a thief passionately longing to escape. It was queer. To distract my mind and calm myself I looked out of the window. The train ran along the coast. The sea was smooth, and the turquoise sky, almost half covered with the tender, golden crimson light of sunset, was gaily and serenely mirrored in it. Here and there fishing boats and rafts made black patches on its surface. The town, as clean and beautiful as a toy, stood on the high cliff, and was already shrouded in the mist of evening. The golden domes of its churches, the windows and the greenery reflected the setting sun, glowing and melting like shimmering gold.... The scent of the fields mingled with the soft damp air from the sea.

"The train flew rapidly along. I heard the laughter of passengers and guards. Everyone was good-humoured and light-hearted, yet my unaccountable uneasiness grew greater and greater.... I looked at the white mist that covered the town and I imagined how a woman with a senseless blank face was hurrying up and down in that mist by the churches and the houses, looking for me and moaning, 'Oh, my God! Oh, my God!' in the voice of a little girl or the cadences of a Little Russian actress. I recalled her grave face and big anxious eyes as she made the sign of the Cross over me, as though I belonged to her, and mechanically I looked at the hand which she had kissed the day before.

" 'Surely I am not in love?' I asked myself, scratching my hand.

"Only as night came on when the passengers were asleep and I was left *tête-à-tête* with my conscience, I began to understand what I had not been able to grasp before. In the twilight of the railway carriage the image of Kisotchka rose before me, haunted me and I recognised clearly that I had committed a crime as bad as murder. My conscience tormented me. To stifle this unbearable feeling, I assured myself that everything was nonsense and vanity, that Kisotchka and I would die and decay, that her grief was nothing in comparison with death, and so on and so on ... and that if you come to that, there is no such thing as freewill, and that therefore I was not to blame. But all these arguments only irritated me and were extraordinarily quickly crowded out by other thoughts. There was a miserable feeling in the hand that Kisotchka had kissed.... I kept lying down and getting up again, drank vodka at the stations, forced myself to eat bread and butter, fell to assuring myself again that life had no meaning, but nothing was of any use. A strange and if you like absurd ferment was going on in my brain. The most incongruous ideas crowded one after another in disorder, getting more and more tangled, thwarting each other, and I, the thinker, 'with my brow bent on the earth,' could make out nothing and could not find my bearings in this mass of essential and non-essential ideas. It appeared that I, the thinker, had not mastered the technique of thinking, and that I was no more capable of managing my own brain than mending a watch. For the first time in my life I was really thinking eagerly and intensely, and that seemed to me so monstrous that I said to myself: 'I am going off my head.' A man whose brain does not work at all times, but only at painful moments, is often haunted by the thought of madness.

"I spent a day and a night in this misery, then a second night, and learning from experience how little my philosophy was to me, I came to my senses and realised at last what sort of a creature I was. I saw that my ideas were not worth a brass farthing, and that before meeting Kisotchka I had not begun to think and had not even a conception of what thinking in earnest meant; now through suffering I realised that I had neither convictions nor a definite moral standard, nor heart, nor reason; my whole intellectual and moral wealth consisted of specialist knowledge, fragments, useless memories, other people's ideas—and nothing else; and my mental processes were as lacking in complexity, as useless and as rudimentary as a Yakut's. . . . If I had disliked lying, had not stolen, had not murdered, and, in fact, made obviously gross mistakes, that was not owing to my convictions—I had none, but because I was in bondage, hand and foot, to my nurse's fairy tales and to copy-book morals, which had entered into my flesh and blood and without my noticing it guided me in life, though I looked on them as absurd. . . .

"I realised that I was not a thinker, not a philosopher, but simply a dilettante. God had given me a strong healthy Russian brain with promise of talent. And, only fancy, here was that brain at twenty-six, undisciplined, completely free from principles, not weighed down by any stores of knowledge, but only lightly sprinkled with information of a sort in the engineering line; it was young and had a physiological craving for exercise, it was on the look-out for it, when all at once quite casually the fine juicy idea of the aimlessness of life and the darkness beyond the tomb descends upon it. It greedily sucks it in, puts its whole outlook at its disposal and begins playing with it, like a cat with a mouse. There is neither learning nor system in the brain, but that does not matter. It deals with the great ideas with its own innate powers, like a self-educated man, and before a month has passed the owner of the brain can turn a potato into a hundred dainty dishes, and fancies himself a philosopher. . . .

"Our generation has carried this dilettantism, this playing with serious ideas into science, into literature, into politics, and into everything which it is not too lazy to go into, and with its dilettantism has introduced, too, its coldness, its boredom, and its one-sidedness and, as it seems to me, it has already succeeded in developing in the masses a new hitherto non-existent attitude to serious ideas.

"I realised and appreciated my abnormality and utter ignorance, thanks to a misfortune. My normal thinking, so it seems to me now, dates from the day when I began again from the A, B, C, when my conscience sent me flying back to N., when with no philosophical subleties I repented, besought Kisotchka's forgiveness like a naughty boy and wept with her...."

Ananyev briefly described his last interview with Kisotchka.

"H'm...." the student filtered through his teeth when the engineer had finished. "That's the sort of thing that happens."

His face still expressed mental inertia, and apparently Ananyev's story had not touched him in the least. Only when the engineer after a moment's pause, began expounding his view again and repeating what he had said at first, the student frowned irritably, got up from the table and walked away to his bed. He made his bed and began undressing.

"You look as though you have really convinced some one this time," he said irritably.

"Me convince anybody!" said the engineer. "My dear soul, do you suppose I claim to do that? God bless you! To convince you is impossible. You can reach conviction only by way of personal experience and suffering!"

"And then—it's queer logic!" grumbled the student as he put on his nightshirt. "The ideas which you so dislike, which are so ruinous for the young are, according to you, the normal thing for the old; it's as though it were a question of grey hairs.... Where do the old get this privilege? What is it based upon? If these ideas are poison, they are equally poisonous for all?"

"Oh, no, my dear soul, don't say so!" said the engineer with a sly wink. "Don't say so. In the first place, old men are not dilettanti. Their pessimism comes to them not casually from outside, but from the depths of their own brains, and only after they have exhaustively studied the Hegels and Kants of all sorts, have suffered, have made no end of mistakes, in fact—when they have climbed the whole ladder from bottom to top. Their pessimism has both personal experience and sound philosophic training behind it. Secondly, the pessimism of old thinkers does not take the form of idle talk, as it does with you and me, but of *Weltschmertz*, of suffering; it rests in them on a Christian foundation because it is derived from love for humanity and from thoughts about humanity, and is entirely free from the egoism which is noticeable in dilettanti. You despise life because its meaning and its object are hidden just from you, and you are only afraid of your own death, while the real thinker is unhappy because the truth is hidden from all and he is afraid for all men. For instance, there is living not far from here the Crown forester, Ivan Alexandritch. He is a nice old man. At one time he was a teacher somewhere, and used to write something; the devil only knows what he was, but anyway he is a remarkably clever fellow and in philosophy he is A1. He has read a great deal and he is continually reading now. Well, we came across him lately in the Gruzovsky district. . . . They were laying the sleepers and rails just at the time. It's not a difficult job, but Ivan Alexandritch, not being a specialist, looked at it as though it were a conjuring trick. It takes an experienced workman less than a minute to lay a sleeper and fix a rail on it. The workmen were in good form and really were working smartly and rapidly; one rascal in particular brought his hammer down with exceptional smartness on the head of the nail and drove it in at one blow, though the handle of the hammer was two yards or more in length and each nail was a foot long. Ivan Alexandritch watched the workmen a long time, was moved, and said to me with tears in his eyes:

" 'What a pity that these splendid men will die!' Such pessimism I understand."

"All that proves nothing and explains nothing," said the student, covering himself up with a sheet; "all that is simply pounding liquid in a mortar. No one knows anything and nothing can be proved by words."

He peeped out from under the sheet, lifted up his head and, frowning irritably, said quickly:

"One must be very naïve to believe in human words and logic and to ascribe any determining value to them. You can prove and disprove anything you like with words, and people will soon perfect the technique of language to such a point that they will prove with mathematical certainty that twice two is seven. I am fond of reading and listening, but as to believing, no thank you; I can't, and I don't want to. I believe only in God, but as for you, if you talk to me till the Second Coming and seduce another five hundred Kisotchkas, I shall believe in you only when I go out of my mind.... Good-night."

The student hid his head under the sheet and turned his face towards the wall, meaning by this action to let us know that he did not want to speak or listen. The argument ended at that.

Before going to bed the engineer and I went out of the hut, and I saw the lights once more.

"We have tired you out with our chatter," said Ananyev, yawning and looking at the sky. "Well, my good sir! The only pleasure we have in this dull hole is drinking and philosophising.... What an embankment, Lord have mercy on us!" he said admiringly, as we approached the embankment; "it is more like Mount Ararat than an embankment."

He paused for a little, then said: "Those lights remind the Baron of the Amalekites, but it seems to me that they are like the thoughts of man.... You know the thoughts of each individual man are scattered like that in disorder, stretch in a straight line towards some goal in the midst of the darkness, and, without shedding light on anything, without lighting up the night, they vanish somewhere far beyond old age. But enough philosophising! It's time to go bye-bye."

When we were back in the hut the engineer began begging me to take his bed.

"Oh please!" he said imploringly, pressing both hands on his heart. "I entreat you, and don't worry about me! I can sleep anywhere, and, besides, I am not going to bed just yet. Please do—it's a favour!"

I agreed, undressed, and went to bed, while he sat down to the table and set to work on the plans.

"We fellows have no time for sleep," he said in a low voice when I had got into bed and shut my eyes. "When a man has a wife and two children he can't think of sleep. One must think now of food and clothes and saving for the future. And I have two of them, a little son and a daughter.... The boy, little rascal, has a jolly little face. He's not six yet, and already he shows remarkable abilities, I assure you.... I have their photographs here, somewhere.... Ah, my children, my children!"

He rummaged among his papers, found their photographs, and began looking at them. I fell asleep.

I was awakened by the barking of Azorka and loud voices. Von Schtenberg with bare feet and ruffled hair was standing in the doorway dressed in his underclothes, talking loudly with some one ... It was getting light. A gloomy dark blue dawn was peeping in at the door, at the windows, and through the crevices in the hut walls, and casting a faint light on my bed, on the table with the papers, and on Ananyev. Stretched on the floor on a cloak, with a leather pillow under his head, the engineer lay asleep with his fleshy, hairy chest uppermost; he was snoring so loudly that I pitied the student from the bottom of my heart for having to sleep in the same room with him every night.

"Why on earth are we to take them?" shouted Von Schtenberg. "It has nothing to do with us! Go to Tchalisov! From whom do the cauldrons come?"

"From Nikitin ..." a bass voice answered gruffly.

"Well, then, take them to Tchalisov. . . . That's not in our department. What the devil are you standing there for? Drive on!"

"Your honour, we have been to Tchalisov already," said the bass voice still more gruffly. "Yesterday we were the whole day looking for him down the line, and were told at his hut that he had gone to the Dymkovsky section. Please take them, your honour! How much longer are we to go carting them about? We go carting them on and on along the line, and see no end to it."

"What is it?" Ananyev asked huskily, waking up and lifting his head quickly.

"They have brought some cauldrons from Nikitin's," said the student, "and he is begging us to take them. And what business is it of ours to take them?"

"Do be so kind, your honour, and set things right! The horses have been two days without food and the master, for sure, will be angry. Are we to take them back, or what? The railway ordered the cauldrons, so it ought to take them. . . ."

"Can't you understand, you blockhead, that it has nothing to do with us? Go on to Tchalisov!"

"What is it? Who's there?" Ananyev asked huskily again. "Damnation take them all," he said, getting up and going to the door. "What is it?"

I dressed, and two minutes later went out of the hut. Ananyev and the student, both in their underclothes and barefooted, were angrily and impatiently explaining to a peasant who was standing before them bare-headed, with his whip in his hand, apparently not understanding them. Both faces looked preoccupied with workaday cares.

"What use are your cauldrons to me," shouted Ananyev. "Am I to put them on my head, or what? If you can't find Tchalisov, find his assistant, and leave us in peace!"

Seeing me, the student probably recalled the conversation of the previous night. The workaday expression vanished from his sleepy face and a look of mental inertia came into it. He waved the peasant off and walked away absorbed in thought.

It was a cloudy morning. On the line where the lights had been gleaming the night before, the workmen, just roused from sleep, were swarming. There was a sound of voices and the squeaking of wheelbarrows. The working day was beginning. One poor little nag harnessed with cord was already plodding towards the embankment, tugging with its neck, and dragging along a cartful of sand.

I began saying good-bye. . . . A great deal had been said in the night, but I carried away with me no answer to any question, and in the morning, of the whole conversation there remained in my memory, as in a filter, only the lights and the image of Kisotchka. As I got on the horse, I looked at the student and Ananyev for the last time, at the hysterical dog with the lustreless, tipsy-looking eyes, at the workmen flitting to and fro in the morning fog, at the embankment, at the little nag straining with its neck, and thought:

"There is no making out anything in this world."

And when I lashed my horse and galloped along the line, and when a little later I saw nothing before me but the endless gloomy plain and the cold overcast sky, I recalled the questions which were discussed in the night. I pondered while the sun-scorched plain, the immense sky, the oak forest, dark on the horizon and the hazy distance, seemed saying to me:

"Yes, there's no understanding anything in this world!"

The sun began to rise. . . .

A NOTE ON THE TYPE

The principal text of this Modern Library edition
was set in a digitized version of Janson,
a typeface that dates from about 1690 and was cut by Nicholas Kis,
a Hungarian working in Amsterdam. The original matrices have
survived and are held by the Stempel foundry in Germany.
Hermann Zapf redesigned some of the weights and sizes for Stempel,
basing his revisions on the original design.